4

FICTION   Stewart, Edward, 1938-
S   Deadly rich / Edward Stewart. -- New York,
            N.Y. : Delacorte Press, 1991.

          566 p.

          ISBN 0-385-29998-2:   20.00

          I. Title.

                                        10999

                                                       19

                                      WLF00-457789
                                         MARC

DEADLY
RICH

EDWARD STEWART

DEADLY RICH

Delacorte Press

Published by
Delacorte Press
Bantam Doubleday Dell Publishing Group, Inc.
666 Fifth Avenue
New York, New York 10103

The trademark Delacorte Press® is registered in the U.S. Patent
and Trademark Office.

Library of Congress Cataloging in Publication Data

Stewart, Edward, 1938–
    Deadly rich / by Edward Stewart.
        p.   cm.
    ISBN 0-385-29998-2 : $20.00
    I. Title.
    PS3569.T46D43   1991
    813′.54—dc20   91-17638
                                                                        CIP

Manufactured in the United States of America

Published simultaneously in Canada

September 1991

10 9 8 7 6 5 4 3 2 1   DEC 1 7 1991

BVG

for Jackie Farber,
Stowe Hausner, and Steven Hollar—who made the difference

· ONE ·

SOMETHING WAS WRONG. Leigh Baker kept hearing voices. The goose-down pillows in their Porthault cases that had begun the evening under her head were now lying on top of her, like a barricade, and she had to push them aside to see.

The Levolors were angled against whatever light the sky had to offer, but her time sense told her it was night. She stared a long moment at the light that beaded the perfume bottles and silver-backed brushes on the dressing table. Her eye followed the light to its source, the TV screen.

She recognized the man who did the weather wrap-up on Fox Five. The remote was lying on the little painted papier-mâché table beside her bed, on top of *Vogue* and *Vanity Fair*. She reached for it. Her fingertips touched the highball glass. An un-thinking reflex brought the glass to her lips.

Slivered ghosts of ice cubes slid beneath her nose. The liquid had a brownish color and it smelled like Johnnie Walker and diet Pepsi. It flowed over her tongue without any flavor. To avoid spilling she drained the glass before setting it back down.

She patted her pillows into a fresh headrest behind her. She picked up the remote and pressed the Off button. The image on the TV screen collapsed into a white lozenge that sputtered and decayed into darkness.

She laid her head back and closed her eyes.

Even with the TV off she still heard those voices and she could not drop off to the state where she wanted to be, that oceanic feeling of floating nothingness.

At the sound of a latch clicking she opened her eyes again.

Light floated in from the living room, and a teenage girl

stood silhouetted and slim in the doorframe. Taking fast, shallow breaths, Leigh's daughter came into the bedroom with gingerly steps, as though she were walking on someone else's legs.

Leigh pushed herself to sitting. "What is it? Nita, what's wrong?"

The girl's face was a blank surface. She worked her throat, worked her jaw, trying to force words out. Nothing in her expression changed, but suddenly her eyes looked as if they were full of icicles and a terrible little cry came out of her. "What does it mean?"

"What does what mean, darling?"

Like a comet flicking its tail, Nita turned and tore out of the bedroom and across the darkened living room, through the French window and out onto the terrace.

Leigh touched one foot down onto the floor and then the other. She tested her standing muscles. They seemed to work, though she listed a little to the left and she knew right away that she needed another drink.

Now she tested her walking muscles. They were slow to answer her head's commands, but they took her to the bedroom door.

And then Nita's voice: "No!"

It seemed to Leigh that something flew across the terrace, low and fluttering. She blinked and it took her mind a moment to process the image. A white dress. White arms. White legs. Nita.

For a moment light and shadow alternated like flashes of a strobe. And then silence pooled. Too much silence. It was as though a magician had waved a wand and made the white rabbit disappear. There was no white dress. No white arms. No white legs. No Nita.

"Nita," Leigh whispered. "Where are you?"

A knot twisted inside her stomach. She closed her eyes, fighting back nausea. *I will not vomit,* she told herself.

When the spasm passed, she opened her eyes. Through the open French window moonlight spilled down onto the terrace in a wash of white stillness. Relief took her. There was no one there.

I was imagining it.

She moved into the living room.

I need a drink.

She turned on a light. The room was done in soft grays and deep greens—peaceful colors. Three dozen red roses with a note from her director had been placed in a tall crystal vase near the bar. She had the impression that the scene was being projected onto a 360-degree wraparound screen.

At that moment a wave of Nita's perfume floated past her.

She didn't move. She stayed exactly where she was, sniffing, listening.

"Nita?"

The silence and that faint trail of sweetness drew her toward the open French window. Her body had to fight a path through a wall of medication. Everything seemed twisted around, wrong. She stepped onto the terrace.

It took her eyes a moment to adjust to the moonlight.

Potted plants and dainty tables and chairs came into focus. She caught the trail of perfume again, and it drew her across the terrace to the low wall.

She stood there, looking out. She saw things with eerie, drugged precision. The town-house facades across the garden all glowed with the dead light of the moon.

A breeze ruffled the little boxwood bushes that the gardener had spaced along the low section of the wall. She saw that several of the branches had been freshly snapped off.

She moved a toppled chair aside. She stood a long moment staring over the waist-high wall. She slowly swung her gaze down to the garden five stories below. It was like staring down into a pool from a high diving board. The trees and the parallel dark rows of green hedge all seemed to be rippling on dark water.

A body lay directly below, splayed out across the flagstone path. White dress. White arms. White legs.

Leigh doubled forward. Disbelief physically took her. A sickening whoosh of bile and booze and half-digested diet Pepsi flooded her mouth. She could feel vomit rushing up and out of her.

Some instinctive residual sense of decorum told her to get to the john. She turned and shoved a garden chair out of the way and ran stumbling and puking back toward the living room.

A young man stood half crouched against the wall. She collided with him and stared with a hand over her mouth.

He sprang up to his full height, well over six feet, and there was something about his panicky eyes that made her think she might have to fight him.

"I didn't mean to," he whimpered.

"No, I know you didn't." Leigh kept her voice soft, nonconfrontational. She edged past him toward the open French window.

He made no move to stop her.

She darted into the living room and in the same movement swung the French window shut behind her. Her heart was banging in her chest. She fumbled her hand around the key and twisted it, and then she ran to the phone and snatched up the receiver and punched 911.

■ ■ ■

SIX WEEKS BEFORE THE TRIAL the woman who was prosecuting the case phoned Leigh and said the defense had unearthed new evidence. "Could you be in my office tomorrow morning at ten?"

Leigh wore her black-on-black Chanel. In the limo, riding to the meeting, she took twenty milligrams of prescribed Valium and twenty of unprescribed Dexedrine that her husband had left on his side of the bathroom cabinet.

At ten after ten, on the fourth floor of the State Supreme Court Building, the prosecutor introduced her to a small, stocky gray-haired woman wearing a plain black cotton dress. "Miss Baker, I'd like you to meet Xenia Delancey—the mother of the accused."

Leigh did not take the hand that Xenia Delancey offered.

"Miss Baker," Xenia Delancey said, "I'm a mother too."

"We have nothing to say to each other," Leigh said.

"On the contrary." The defense attorney placed a small leather-bound book on the conference table. He invited Leigh to read it.

The book, Leigh discovered, was a diary. She opened it. Most of the pages were blank. Where there was writing she recognized it as Nita's. The forty or so hand-written pages covered the last forty days of her daughter's life. Days of drugs and sex and recklessness.

"This is a forgery," Leigh said. "Nita never did these things."

"Miss Baker, I understand that you loved your daughter." The prosecutor spoke with an unashamed Queens Irish accent. Words sounded tough in her mouth. "I understand that the diary comes as a shock to you. But I've prosecuted six date-kill cases, and I can tell you from trial experience, young girls *are* sexual beings and they often *do* confide their sexual activities to a secret diary."

"Maybe, but this diary is a fake."

"The jury will have to decide that," the defense lawyer said.

"They're putting this forgery into *evidence*?" Leigh said. "They're allowed to do that?"

"Yes, they're allowed to do that." The prosecutor drew in a

long breath and let it out in a deeply troubled sigh. "But Mrs. Delancey has an offer to make."

"You tell the state to accept a lesser plea," Xenia Delancey said. "I'll tell my boy's lawyer not to use this diary."

"What kind of lesser plea?" Leigh said.

"Negligent manslaughter," the defense attorney said.

"At best," the prosecutor said, "the state can make a case for involuntary manslaughter."

"It was murder." Leigh heard herself speak before she'd even realized what she was going to say. It was a flat statement of fact, with no emotion in it whatsoever. "I saw him push her."

The prosecutor whirled. Her glasses flew off her nose, and her blond hair spun out like a tossed skirt. After a moment she picked her glasses up from the floor and put them back on.

The muscles in the defense attorney's jaw worked slowly. "Miss Baker didn't depose that she saw her daughter killed."

"I'm deposing it now," Leigh said.

"In other words," the defense attorney said, "you've been suppressing evidence for the better part of a year?"

"I was willing to forgive the man my daughter loved—because I believed he hadn't intended to kill her." Leigh could feel the defense attorney's gaze on her, dubious, puzzled, probing for truth and for falsity. "But that diary, that *forgery,* is an act of pure malicious calculation. I have no intention of forgiving now."

"She's lying," Xenia Delancey said.

"Mr. Lawrence," the prosecutor said, "would you and Mrs. Delancey be good enough to wait in the hallway for a moment?"

The defense attorney grumbled and stood and motioned Xenia Delancey to come with him.

Leigh and the prosecutor sat alone at the cigarette-scarred conference table. The prosecutor's glance nailed Leigh through half-tinted lenses. "What did you see *exactly*?"

I wish I'd had time to prepare this, Leigh thought. And then she remembered what Stella Adler used to say in acting class: *Who has time for sense memory? Improvise!*

For the next two minutes Leigh improvised.

"You realize," the prosecutor said, "if you change your testimony, the defense will accuse you of lying. They'll attack you, not just on the stand but in the media."

"I realize that."

"The attacks will be personal, they'll be savage, they'll reflect on your character, your habits, your morals, your marriages, your movies, your lovers, and, above all, on your use of medications, mood changers, and liquor."

Leigh understood that the prosecutor had sized her up and was strongly advising her to reconsider. But she had no intention of reconsidering. She had given her daughter very little in life, and she was determined that Nita would at least receive justice in death. "I realize all of that."

The prosecutor held up the leather-bound book. "Whether this diary is a forgery or not, the defense will use it to attack and destroy your daughter. They'll use it to create sympathy for Jim Delancey. He stands a good chance of going free. Are you willing to take that chance?"

Leigh nodded. "I'm willing. Absolutely."

The prosecutor stood motionless, staring at her. "Miss Baker, I hope you'll excuse my frankness, but in all honesty I have to tell you something."

Christ, Leigh wondered, *have I gone too far?*

"Thanks to your courage I believe we have a chance of nailing Delancey." The prosecutor shook Leigh's hand. Then she crossed swiftly to the door and flung it open and leaned triumphantly into the corridor. "Mr. Lawrence, Mrs. Delancey, would you come back, please? We're not taking the plea."

Xenia Delancey looked at Leigh with her mouth closed so tightly that her lips made a line like a fresh scar. "You're making a stupid mistake," she said. "The world is going to know what your daughter was."

"And maybe," Leigh said, "they'll learn what your son is."

▪ ▪ ▪

SIX WEEKS LATER Leigh Baker entered a packed, hushed courtroom and crossed in front of the jury to take the stand.

She had fortified herself today with thirty milligrams of Valium and thirty of Dexedrine, fifty percent more than her usual morning dose. She had washed the medicine down with a two-ounce shot glass of vodka.

She had never, despite fourteen years as a performing actress, felt less sure of the effect she was about to make. She was wearing a navy Galanos with Barbara Bush pearls. Her mouth was dry, her skin on fire, her heart thumping so hard she couldn't hear anything else, and the light in the courtroom seemed to dip in rhythm to each heartbeat that rocked her.

Dear God, she prayed soundlessly, *just get me through this and I swear I'll never break another contract, I'll never sleep with another man I'm not married to, I'll never take another drink or drug.*

"How many abortions did you procure for your daughter?" the defense attorney asked.

Leigh jumped to her feet. "That's a lie."

The judge directed her to answer the question.

Leigh sat. "Nita never had an abortion."

"Did you always give your daughter cocaine for Christmas?"

Leigh looked out at the courtroom. From the front row of the spectators' section, Xenia Delancey watched her with slit-eyed hatred.

"You're lying again," Leigh said.

The judge directed her to answer the question.

"Nita didn't take drugs."

"How many lovers did you share with your daughter?"

"You're lying and you've lied from the start of this trial."

"Objection."

"Every word you've said, every question you've asked, every glance and shrug you've directed at the jury has been an attempt to defame my daughter."

"Objection."

"Sustained. Witness will limit her response to the question."

Leigh had a panicky sense that the walls of the courtroom were slanting in on her.

"How many lovers," the court stenographer read from the trial record, "did you share with your daughter?"

There's got to be a way to answer this, she thought.

"My daughter and I loved many people in common. We never shared a lover. The only lover Nita ever had is the man who took her virginity, and he's on trial here today."

"Objection."

"Jury will disregard the witness's response."

But they didn't disregard it. Thirty-two days after the trial began, following seven hours' deliberation, the jury of seven men and five women found James Delancey guilty as charged.

"We did it, toots!" Leigh's husband sang out. They celebrated the verdict by sending the chauffeur to score eight grams of coke and four boxes of David's macadamia chocolate chip cookies.

Four days after the verdict, at three-thirty in the afternoon, California time, two bodyguards didn't exactly walk her and didn't exactly carry her but somehow managed to stand her up in front of the crisp, sober, smiling redheaded nurse at the admissions desk. Fortified with what she swore to God would be her last eight vodkas ever, Leigh Baker picked up a squirming pen and signed herself into the Betty Ford Clinic.

▪ TWO ▪

Tuesday, May 7

"*THE KING WENT into the garden the next morning, and he saw . . .*" Leigh lowered the picture book.

On the floor four feet from her the child was playing with his battery-operated toy xylophone. Each time a key lit up he pressed it, and a note sounded. The result after he had pressed enough lit-up keys was a tune. Until six months ago the xylophone had known a variety of tunes, but something had happened to the wiring and the only tune it seemed to know nowadays was "The Happy Farmer."

For the last half hour the child had shown no awareness at all of Leigh or the fairy tale, but he seemed to realize she'd stopped reading. He turned his head and at last she had his attention.

"Can you guess what the king saw?" Leigh said.

The child gazed up at her, his hair spilling out around his head like a frazzled black helmet.

"Do you think the king saw the blackbird?"

The child screwed up his face.

"Do you think the king saw the gazelle?"

The child was thoughtful.

"Then what did the king see? I bet you already know."

The child shook his head.

"Yes, you do know," Leigh said. "That's why you're smiling."

"I'm not smiling," the child said.

Leigh's heart gave a jump inside her chest. He'd said an entire sentence. He hadn't said an entire sentence for how long now—almost two weeks. "Oh, yes, you *are* smiling. I can see the smile right there." She reached out and touched the corner of his mouth.

He burst into giggles.

She opened the picture book again. *"The king went into the garden the next morning, and he saw that the snow had vanished and all the queen's—"* She peeked around the edge of the book. "And all the queen's what?"

"Roses!" the child shouted.

Leigh stretched the moment. She peered into the book with a baffled look, then back at the child with a disappointed look, then back at the book. "You're right!"

Something skimmed across the child's face, and he opened his mouth and let out a high, wild, rippling laugh.

"All the queen's roses were in bloom," Leigh read. *"And the kingdom rejoiced, for the spell of the evil wizard had at last been broken."*

Now the child was watching her closely. He had the look of a solemn deer.

He was six years old. Nothing but life had been given to him: he had had to struggle for every ounce he possessed of humanness. His name was Happy, and Leigh was as proud of her association with this child as she had been of any friendship in her life.

"The king said to the prince, 'You have vanquished the wizard, and you shall have your reward. Whatever you wish I shall grant you.' The prince said, 'I wish the hand of your daughter the princess in marriage.' "

Leigh felt morally inferior to Happy. He existed like a tree or a rock or a flower, without troubling the universe. She felt he had a great deal to teach her.

"The king blessed the royal pair, and decreed seven days of celebration. At the end of seven days the prince married the princess. And . . . ." Leigh closed the picture book. "And can you guess what happened after that?"

Happy shook his head.

"Oh, yes, you can. The prince and the princess lived . . ."

"Happily ever after!"

"You're right!"

Happy giggled and began slapping his fists on the xylophone.

The front door slammed. A moment later Happy's father strode into the living room.

"Happy and I just finished a story," Leigh said.

"Good." Ruddy-faced and military with his bristling crew cut, Luddie bent down and hugged the boy.

Happy stopped moving. Stopped laughing. Completely stopped.

Why is he always so quiet around his father? Leigh wondered. *Why does he just click off when Luddie comes into the room?*

"Coffee?" Luddie offered.

She looked at her watch. "Sure. I have a little time."

She went into the kitchen and helped Luddie load up the coffee maker.

"How's Waldo?" Luddie said.

Leigh shrugged. Waldo Carnegie was the man she'd been living with since her detox, and Luddie had an annoying habit of saying she'd exchanged one dependency for another. "Waldo's okay."

"You should leave him," Luddie said. "Really. What do you get from him?"

Leigh sighed. Every now and then Luddie got on this refrain, and she hated it.

"Money?" he said. "You're working again. You don't need money. Companionship? The only time you two even have dinner together is when he's giving himself a birthday party and inviting half the planetary media. Do you two even sleep together?"

"Come on, Waldo is a hardworking, decent human being."

"Okay, in minuscule ways, he's a mensch."

She followed Luddie back into the living room. They dropped onto the canvas-covered sofa.

"Why don't you just admit you don't like my friends?" Leigh said finally.

Luddie shrugged. "It's not that I dislike them. I'm only asking why you have to have these particular friends? For instance, why these two gals you're having lunch with tomorrow? Why if you can't stand them do you agree to meet them?"

"Because I grew up with them. They're part of me."

Happy tapped out three notes on his xylophone. The sounds hovered in the air like dust motes.

"They aren't necessary to you," Luddie said. "You've always got the option of detaching. If they live in burning houses, it doesn't mean you have to go up in flames with them."

"Why are you always tearing my world down, Luddie?"

"What do you want me to do—ask for your autograph? Get it through your head that no one's going to love you till you learn to give yourself a little unconditional love."

"What the hell *is* unconditional love?" she said.

"What do you think I give you?"

"Luddie, I'm not you. I haven't got it to give."

"Bullshit. What did you just give my son? What do you give him two times a week?"

"I play with him."

Luddie fixed her with the manic, electrifying blue of his eyes. "That is as hands-on and unconditional as love can get. You're here for him when he needs you."

"So are a lot of other people. I'm just a couple of hours a week, Tuesdays and Fridays."

Luddie shook his head and sat there for a long, silent moment appraising her. "Not only would I not lift a finger to help you when you sell yourself short like that but I wouldn't lift a leg to piss on you."

"You put it so agreeably, Luddie."

"You make choices in life every goddamned minute you breathe. Not making a choice is still choosing. It's a loser's choice, but it's a choice. Recognize it. You chose to be a drunk, and you chose to stop being a drunk. You chose to enter AA, and the latest I heard, you choose to stay in AA. You chose me to be your AA sponsor, and you can tell me to go to hell anytime you want. You chose to live with a self-important billionaire eunuch, and God knows why, you choose to keep doing it. You chose to have lunch tomorrow with a political fanatic and a drunk, and you can still pick up the phone and cancel."

"It's only twice a year—and we're friends."

"*And* you have a choice, so don't come whining to me that you're trapped. You don't have to sit there for two hours. You can take those bitches shopping."

She drew in a deep breath and pulled her voice way, way down. "There's a new boutique at Marsh and Bonner's, and I hear the designer's great. I had them pencil us in for a private showing at two-thirty. And please don't call my friends bitches."

"Cut lunch short." Luddie tossed her a lopsided, cynical grin. "Get to Marsh and Bonner's at one-thirty. Say you made a mistake."

"I thought you wanted me to be honest."

"Then get to Marsh and Bonner's at one-thirty and *don't* say you made a mistake. Just get your ass out of that restaurant before your two pals have you drinking again."

· THREE ·

Wednesday, May 8

"HI, KIDS," LEIGH SAID with her best reunion smile.

"Hi, toots," Oona said. "What's the magic word?"

Leigh bent down and exchanged the ritual lunchtime kiss with each of her schoolchums, lips barely brushing makeup. A waiter pulled out a chair for her and she sat. "Have you two said anything interesting yet?"

"Waiting for you before we bother." Tori, with her small freckle-splashed nose and dimpled cheeks, had a face that would have seemed impishly pretty if she hadn't countered the effect with enormous, rimless aviator glasses. The glasses made her look intelligent.

Leigh had never understood why Tori needed to look intelligent. Tori had been Phi Beta Kappa at Smith, and surely *being* intelligent was enough.

"Would you care for something to drink?" the waiter asked.

Leigh took the linen napkin from the wineglass and spread it on her lap. She saw that Oona was working on a split of Piper and then she saw a split already up-ended in the wine bucket and she realized this was not Oona's first.

Tori was drinking a Kir.

"Just some diet Pepsi for me." Leigh's hand went to the tiny platinum hummingbird that she had pinned to the lapel of her ecru silk jacket. She drew an instant's security from its touch. Encrusted with emerald and ruby chips no larger than grains of demerara sugar, it exactly matched the brooches that Oona and Tori were wearing.

They had made presents to one another of the three hummingbirds when they were students at Smith. They wore the brooches only when they were alone together—which had come to mean at these twice-yearly lunches, when they did their best to pretend the last fifteen years hadn't changed a thing and they loved one another just as much now as they had then.

"Ugh," Oona said. "How can you drink diet *anything*?"

Oona had been a beautiful young woman in college, in the blond way of the time, and usually Leigh saw her with the eye of memory. But today, in the noon light pouring in through the window onto the best table in Archibald's, memory didn't have a chance. Oona looked like an artifact—her face powdered white as rice paper, the makeup heavy as ink on a Chinese scroll. She was like a clumsy tracing of a beautiful picture.

"We were talking about Ronald Ballantine," Oona said.

"Never heard of Ronald Ballantine," Leigh said.

"The Wall Street lawyer." Oona nodded toward another table. "Right over there."

Leigh glanced toward the corner table. "Still haven't heard of him."

"He's on the cover of *New York* this week," Oona said.

"And he'll be the lead article in *Vanity Fair* next month," Tori said.

"I see overnight success is still a growth industry in this town," Leigh said.

"Until last night," Oona said, "Ronnie was the guy everyone wanted. Men wanted him for litigations, women wanted him for dinner parties; today no one wants him, except the SEC—for fraud. That woman he's having lunch with is Dorcas Stockelberg. She's a major stockholder in Exxon, and she's trying to leverage a takeover of Saks."

Despite herself Leigh was taken by something guileless in Oona's open love of scuttlebutt.

Tori, on the other hand, clearly was not. "That's only a rumor," she said.

"There's more than rumor to the rumor," Oona said. "Look who just joined them."

An extremely tall man in a dark blue Ralph Lauren suit and a towering brown toupee had joined the corner table. Leigh recognized Stanley Siff, the Park Avenue South–based conglomerateur whose takeover schemes had plunged three New York department stores and two national airlines into liquidation. His wife, tall and dark and stagily glamorous in a borderline anorectic way, was sitting down beside him. Under her maiden name, Gloria Spahn, she designed dresses. Leigh estimated that a dozen of them were being worn in this very room at this very moment.

"Why's Stanley involved?" Leigh said.

"The buzz is," Oona said, "Saks refused to carry Gloria's evening dresses."

"That man has destroyed retailing in this city," Tori said.

"Oh, come on," Oona said. "He happens to be damned good at what he does, and he gets a kick out of it."

"That's still no excuse for doing it," Tori said.

"I couldn't disagree more," Oona said. "We're all in a race with the Reaper, so there's no sense wasting time. You've got to pick two or three things you really like to do, and then do five of them."

Tori heaved a short sigh filled with resignation. Her eyes flicked up at Leigh.

"Waiter!" Oona snapped her fingers.

Their waiter approached the table. "Yes, ma'am?"

"This dip is rancid," Oona said.

Leigh had not seen Oona so much as taste the dip. It came in a hand-painted little Provençal terra-cotta pot and there did not appear to be even a ripple disturbing its smooth surface.

"You know we flavor it with Pernod," the waiter said.

"Young man, I've been coming to this restaurant since it opened—of course I know you flavor the dip with Pernod. The Pernod is not the problem, the rancid *crème fraîche* is the problem. Please take this dip back to the kitchen and bring us a fresh bowl."

The waiter took the pot of dip and gave a slight bow of the head.

"Really," Oona said, "this city is getting impossible."

Leigh was thinking, sadly, how alcohol could twist a person, how it had twisted her once upon a time, and how it was twisting Oona now. For almost two years something inside Oona seemed to have been losing its resilience, like a spring stretched too far: little things had begun getting on her nerves, she had begun taking them as personal affronts—and now she had begun imagining affronts as well.

"You have to fight for everything in this town," Oona was saying. "Just the other day I was at Bergdorf's and—" The flow of her words broke off. She was staring across the room. Her eyes were wide and her face had a stunned look. "I don't believe it. Oh, my God, I do *not* believe *this*!"

"What's that, darling?" Tori said.

"He's back there in the kitchen slicing endive."

"Who's back where?"

"What's his name—you remember—Jim Delancey."

Leigh felt a queasy sense of unreality. She realized her hands were cold and at the same time beginning to perspire.

The smile had dropped off Tori's face. "Oona—please."

"Don't *Oona, please* me—I'm talking about the man who killed Nita."

"We know who Jim Delancey is," Leigh said quietly.

"Well, he's in that kitchen tossing salads."

"That's not possible," Tori said.

"Just look through that door the next time it swings open. He's standing there in plain view."

Leigh turned her gaze by slow degrees. The room with its carved mahogany bar and close-packed tables seemed to narrow, pulsing with each beat of her heart. Now she could see the kitchen door.

The noise of a siren howled down the street outside.

The door swung open and their waiter stepped through. Behind him Leigh could see a Korean and a black man in chef's hats, mincing vegetables at a butcher-block counter.

She let her breath out. Of all possible delusions, she wondered, why had Oona had to imagine Nita's killer in the kitchen?

The waiter set a fresh pot of Pernod dip on their table.

"I will not eat this food." The sound of Oona's voice carried through the entire room. "Get the manager over here."

Leigh realized it was going to get worse. She lowered her eyes. She felt shrunken.

There was a silence behind her head. The other patrons in the restaurant had stopped talking. She could feel them with her skin, sitting there utterly quiet, not speaking, not clinking a fork.

A man in a dark tailored suit came rapidly across the room. "*Bonjour, mesdames,* how may I help you?"

"Are you the manager?" Oona said. "I've never seen you here before."

"The manager is not here today, ma'am. I'm the assistant manager. Could I help you?"

A tilt came into Oona's jaw and her face tightened. "Yes, you could. What is your name?"

"My name is Matthieu."

Oona foraged in her Gucci purse and pulled out an expired Percodan prescription and began writing on the back of it. "All right, Matthieu. First of all you could explain to me what a convicted murderer is doing in your kitchen slicing endive."

"I'm sorry, ma'am, but there must be some mistake."

"There sure is and I'm not the one making it."

"Oona. Please." Tori gathered up her purse. "We have to go."

"I'm not through," Oona said.

"There isn't time," Leigh said. "We have an appointment at Marsh and Bonner's."

Leigh handed Oona her jacket. "Come on, darling."

Oona waved her prescription at the assistant manager's face like a straight-edged razor. "Get rid of him," she warned, "or I will personally see to it that this restaurant is killed in the columns."

Out on the sidewalk Oona looked up at the sky. She seemed genuinely surprised to see the sun peeking through scudding clouds. She dipped a heavily braceleted arm into her bag and dragged out a pair of sunglasses. She spent much too long a moment getting them to stay on her nose. Tori hailed a cab and Leigh helped Oona into the rear seat.

"Where to, ladies?" the driver said.

"Marsh and Bonner's," Leigh said. "Fifty-seventh and Fifth."

The cab pulled into traffic.

Leigh patted Oona's hand. "You'll be calm, won't you, darling?"

■　■　■

INSIDE MARSH AND BONNER'S with its three-story atrium, the air was cool and pleasantly perfumed. Well-dressed, well-mannered customers strolled the aisles, pausing to discuss scarves or cosmetics or gloves with well-dressed, well-mannered salespeople. A subdued murmur of civilized voices flowed across the gleaming display cases.

Leigh and Tori guided Oona to the elevator.

"I swear," Oona said, "when you have murderers slicing radicchio at Archibald's, you know these are the plague years."

"Mezzanine," the elevator operator said.

"What's happening in this town?" Oona said. "Who's minding the store? The PLO? Bishop Tutu? Somebody's got to care!"

"Right." Tori glanced at Leigh.

"Second floor," the elevator operator said.

"Excuse us," Leigh said to a woman standing in the way. She and Tori shepherded Oona across the floor to the Ingrid Hansen Boutique.

It was not so much a separate store as a stage set of a sepa rate store, erected in the northwest corner of the floor. SCANDINAVIA'S LEADING DESIGN EDGE, a sign over the entrance announced.

A slender, almost fleshless blond woman sailed across the boutique toward them. Leigh recognized the boutique proprietress from her photograph.

"May I help you?"

"We have an appointment," Leigh said. "Baker and Sandberg."

The woman stood smiling with crisp formality. "I didn't realize we'd said one-thirty on the phone."

"We're a little early," Leigh said. "By the way, do you know our friend, Oona Aldrich? Oona, this is Ingrid Hansen. She designed all these terrific clothes, and she was written up in last week's *New York* magazine 'Intelligencer.' "

Ms. Hansen gave Oona a quick, appraising look. "Delighted. If Mrs. Aldrich is the friend you mentioned, I have something for her. Could you wait just a moment?"

Ms. Hansen went to the other side of the boutique and began whispering to a sales assistant.

"I can't believe it," Oona said. "I simply cannot believe it. Delancey is *everywhere.*"

Leigh had never seen Oona this out of control so early in the day. "Jim Delancey's not here." She said it calmly, easily, as though it didn't matter one way or another, as though they were idly discussing guests at a party. "Do you see him anywhere, Tori?"

"He's not here," Tori said. "Really, Oona, he's not."

"Not *him.*" Oona snapped a nod toward Ms. Hansen's sales assistant. "I'm talking about his witch of a mother."

Leigh glanced again at the stiff, stout little woman. Except for the octagonal wire-rimmed glasses, she could see a certain broad resemblance to Xenia Delancey. The saleswoman had the same sort of uptilted, thimble-sized nose. She wore her gray hair wound into the same tight sort of gray nautilus coil. She even had the same way of listening with her head cocked to the left.

What Leigh was not prepared for was the voice that came out of that thick little body, or its effect on her.

"Right away, Ms. Hansen. I'll see to it."

The voice sent an icy needle of recognition down Leigh's spine: it was unmistakably the voice of the woman whose son had murdered Nita.

Ms. Hansen returned carrying a dress and jacket ensemble.

"Usually I work in very bright colors. This is one of my first pastels." She laid the dress along a countertop. It was silk, patterned in white, black, and pale lavender swirls. The cut was extremely simple, with a slightly pulled-in waist. "And then you have the jacket, which matches."

"Where do you hire your saleswomen?" Oona said.

For just an instant Ms. Hansen looked baffled.

"Oona, please," Tori said. "Let's concentrate on the dress."

"And as a caprice," Ms. Hansen continued, "the lining is a silk screen of Warhol's Mao." She reversed the jacket to show the Warhol. "But naturally that can be changed. Some people don't like Mao—even as a joke."

"Oh, all right," Oona said. "Give it to me, I'll try it on."

"You can change right over there." Ms. Hansen pointed to a curtained doorway.

There were two crashing sounds, as though a display case had shattered.

"I don't believe this," Oona said.

Leigh turned. A Hispanic-looking young man in jogging clothes had come into the boutique. In his left hand he was carrying a two-foot long radio and a voice was booming out of it:

> Nickel-dimin' two-bit pipsqueak squirt,
> Bleedin' Thursday blood on your Tuesday shirt—

A woman had come in after him—a young black woman in a pale coffee-colored clinging lace dress. She had a strikingly aquiline profile and dark, wavy hair and she looked like a fashion model.

"Someone had better tell him to turn that racket off," Oona said.

Xenia Delancey approached the black woman. They walked over to a display rack. Xenia Delancey suggested a cream-colored blouse. The black woman held it up to her bosom. She studied her reflection in the mirror. After a moment she shook her head and handed the blouse back. Xenia Delancey began looking for another.

On the other side of the boutique, the Hispanic sauntered over to a costume-jewelry display. He set the boom box down on the counter and boosted the volume. The glass display case added a rattling vibration of its own.

Spilled a pint of plasma and you still don't hurt—

Oona's eyes had become burning slits. "This is beyond belief. Things are falling apart in this lousy city. Isn't anyone going to take a stand against that racket?"

"Oona, sweetie," Leigh said, "please don't get excited."

Oona drew in a breath, and then she was in motion. She crossed directly to the Hispanic.

"Will you kindly turn that racket off?" she said.

He turned. Sweat gleamed on the steep ridges of his cheek-bones. His dark eyes returned her gaze unflinchingly. "What?"

"I said," Oona shouted, "turn that garbage off!"

"What?"

It occurred to Leigh that the Hispanic needed a translation.

Oona walked to the boom box, snapped it open, and yanked out one of the batteries.

The music stopped.

Oona turned and picked up her dress and took the battery with her into the changing room.

The black woman burst out laughing.

"Verdict, please." Tori was holding up a green beaded bolero. "Twenty-four hundred."

"You mean for the whole dress," Leigh said.

"There isn't a whole dress. This is it."

"It seems a little expensive," Leigh said.

"I suppose." As Tori crossed back to the display rack the black woman intercepted her.

"I love that jacket on you."

"Do you really?" Tori said.

The woman nodded. "It picks up the green of your eyes. But you know, the violet might look even better." She walked to the rack and pulled out a violet bolero. *"Voilà.* Let's see it on you in the daylight." She carried the violet bolero over to the door, and Tori followed.

An alarm went off.

"Excuse me," Ms. Hansen called, raising her voice above the jangling bell. "That merchandise is tagged. It can't leave the boutique till we deactivate it."

"I'm sorry." The black woman was giggling in embarrassment.

"Will you kill that alarm!" Ms. Hansen called to Xenia Delancey.

It was a moment before silence was restored.

Leigh glanced toward the changing rooms. The curtain in the little doorway was swaying. "Did someone just come out of the changing rooms?"

"I didn't see anyone," Tori said.

■ ■ ■

OONA ALDRICH FELT TOO WOOZY to take the overhead route getting out of the one skirt and into the other. So she undid her own skirt and let it puddle around her feet. She lifted one bare foot out and with the other flipped it toward the bench. And missed.

Now she opened Ms. Ingrid Hansen's prissy little silk skirt. She held it in a hoop with both hands, lifted one leg, and tried to step into it.

Right away she saw there was going to be a balance problem. Holding the skirt open required two hands, but keeping herself upright on one foot required at least one wall and one more hand.

Oona looked around the changing room.

There's the wall, but has anyone seen a third hand?

She put her engineering smarts to work.

What about sitting down on the bench . . . ?

She sat down on the bench. Well, she'd intended to sit. It was more of a fall but no bones were broken.

And pulling the skirt up my legs . . . ?

She pulled the skirt up her legs. She stood, adjusted the hang of the pleats, fastened the belt. She looked at herself in the mirror, fore and aft.

Not bad.

She slid the jacket off the hanger and slipped her right arm into the sleeve.

Something rapped on the door.

"Just a minute!" Her left hand, halfway into the jacket, snagged the lining. She reached with her right hand and slid the door bolt back.

"How do I look?" She faced the mirror, tried to untangle her left arm, heard cloth rip. "Shit. Now I'll have to buy the damned thing. Well—what do you think?"

Funny—she liked the skirt, but the jacket struck her as sort of pukey. Well, no wonder. She was wearing it halfway on and halfway off.

"Give me a hand with this jacket, will you?"

There was a movement in the mirror behind her. For half an instant her brain recorded the image of a man standing there, two eyes staring with lids pulled back like snarling lips. At the same moment she registered two words, only one of them English.

"*Saludos,* bitch."

Before she could turn, something tugged at her hair and a sudden pressure twisted her head back. The air sparkled and silver whipped past her eyes. A hot piano-wire of pain gripped her neck and fire flicked across her throat.

She struggled to break free. The jacket held her hand like a tourniquet.

He bent her back and, with a cracking sound, she felt her spine surrender. She was on the floor, pushing up with one arm, trying to reach the bench, when a blade danced down in front of her eyes, winking right, left, up, and down.

She screamed and it was like a cartoon because she didn't hear the scream, she saw it—a red scream, liquid and hot and flying in twenty directions at once. The bubbling scream flowed back into her throat, choking off her air.

And the blade's bloody kiss went on. And on.

■ ■ ■

"THIS IS INSANE," Leigh said. "It can't take her twenty minutes to change into a simple dress."

"Take it easy," Tori said. "Oona's insecure, she's a perfectionist."

"Not on my time she isn't."

Leigh crossed the boutique to the little doorway that led to the changing rooms. She stepped past the curtain, and her glance took in a corridor with an emergency exit at the end and three doors on each side. On the right two stood half ajar.

She moved past them and stopped at the third door.

"Oona? Are you in there?" She rapped on the door. No answer. She leaned her ear against it and felt a sort of coiled stillness radiating through the wood panel.

Oh my God, she thought, *if Oona has passed out in the dressing room . . .*

Leigh tried the doorknob. It turned. She gave a push inward. The room was empty.

She went to the door directly opposite. She knocked. "Oona?"

No answer. She tried the handle. The door swung inward. The room was empty.

She went to the next door and rapped sharply. "Oona—are you in there?"

She felt the first stirrings of concern. The doorknob turned and she pushed the door open. A flash of green whooshed up in front of her face.

She recoiled.

A dress left hanging on a hook was trembling in the air current from the open door. She saw it was green linen—not the dress Oona had been trying on.

A green linen belt had been thrown across the seat of a chair, and a woman was leaning toward it.

"Excuse me," Leigh said, and when the woman refused to acknowledge her, she realized she had apologized to her own reflection.

She went to the last door.

The sounds of voices and bells floated in from the main floor —luxuriously muted as if they'd had to pass through layers of lamb's wool and silk.

"Oona!" With one rap she gripped the handle and pushed.

She stood staring at a trash basket with a botany print wrapped around it, filled with sheets of pink tissue paper. Resting in a nested indentation on the tissue were three pins with fat heads.

Damn Oona, she thought. *This can't be—there's no way out of here except the fire exit or through the boutique—*

She stepped back into the corridor. Her eye went again to the first changing room with its half-open door. She realized now that she hadn't actually looked in that room or in the one next to it —she had assumed that with their doors ajar they had to be empty.

She went to the nearest half-open door. "Oona?"

▪ ▪ ▪

"GET AN AMBULANCE."

Ms. Hansen's eyes swung up and around as though she'd been slapped. "I beg your pardon?"

Leigh seized the telephone from the counter and thrust the receiver at Ms. Hansen. She felt her voice grow teeth. "Get an ambulance this minute, or I will sue the ass off this store."

▪ FOUR ▪

"THEN YOU BOTH WERE WITH Oona Aldrich when she was killed?" Lieutenant Detective Vincent Cardozo was saying.

He was sitting in a borrowed doctor's office on the second story of Lexington Hospital, questioning two very pale, very shocked-looking women who had just lived through one of the worst experiences that New York City could offer.

Leigh Baker answered "Yes" at the exact moment that Tori Sandberg said "No."

Nervous glances flicked between the women. It seemed to Cardozo that the glances appointed Tori Sandberg spokesperson.

"All three of us went together to the boutique." Tori Sandberg held herself upright, spine straight, her back not touching the chair. "Oona took a dress into the changing room, and we were waiting for her to come out. It got to be an awfully long wait, and Leigh went to see what had happened."

Cardozo glanced toward Leigh Baker. "Then it was you who found Mrs. Aldrich after the attack."

Leigh Baker nodded.

It occurred to Cardozo that he was questioning one woman who had been a world-famous movie star, who perhaps still was, and another who as a magazine editor enjoyed national recognition and, within the bounds of New York, fame. Yet these were no enameled faces of celebrity. Fear had broken through.

"Was Mrs. Aldrich dead or alive?" Cardozo said.

"Oona was still alive," Leigh Baker said. "Barely." The sofa had two seats, but she had positioned herself at the end farthest from Cardozo, sitting forward, taking up barely half a cushion. Her wavy chestnut hair had been cut long, and a lock had fallen across her face. She pushed it aside. Her deep green eyes gazed at him. "I saw a pulse in her neck."

Cardozo, writing in his notebook, made a note of the pulse in the neck. "I'd like you both to think back carefully. At any time before or during the period that Mrs. Aldrich was changing her dress, did either of you see anyone else go into those changing rooms?"

"No," Leigh Baker said immediately.

It took Tori Sandberg longer. She was staring out the window. "No," she said finally.

"Did you see anyone come out of the dressing rooms?"

"No," Leigh Baker said.

Cardozo waited for Tori Sandberg to answer.

"No," she said.

"Who else was in the boutique?"

"There was Ms. Hansen." Tori Sandberg gave the *s* in *Ms.* a careful *z* sound: no gliding over the distinction.

"There was one salesperson," Leigh Baker said. "There were two other customers—women—white women—and there was a black woman who came in a little after we did."

"And a Hispanic man came in with her," Tori Sandberg said.

"I wouldn't say he was with her," Leigh Baker said.

"Why not?" Cardozo said.

A good deal of Leigh Baker's strength and will seemed to be concentrated on sustaining an even rate of breathing. "I couldn't say exactly. I suppose because she left alone. And they weren't really matched in any way. She had style and he—"

"He was a street lout," Tori Sandberg said. "But they were together. I'm sure of it."

Cardozo had a theory that evolution had provided one hour of grace between the experience of raw terror and the onset of shock. The purpose was to enable prehistoric hominids to slink back to the safety of their caves.

For these women the hour was running out.

"Okay," he said, anxious to cover as much as possible before they became too tired, too confused to even want to think. "There was a black woman and a male Hispanic, and they may or may not have been together. Anyone else?"

"No one else," Leigh Baker said.

"He had an enormous boom box." Tori Sandberg's teeth came down tightly on her lower lip, clenching back distaste. "He was playing rap music. Oona asked him to shut it off. He didn't understand her. At least he did a good job of pretending not to. So she took one of his batteries into the dressing room with her." Tori Sandberg had turned her head, looking directly at Cardozo with an odd intensity. "So he killed her."

"Excuse me." Cardozo's mind braked sharply. "You believe that the male Hispanic with the boom box killed Oona Aldrich *over a boom-box battery?*"

There was silence. Tori Sandberg's lids sank with a moment's weariness over her eyes.

She probably accepted that anyone could be a victim. The newspapers had taught her that. And she was probably coming to accept that anyone could be a killer. The plot of any TV movie of the week demonstrated that.

But in Cardozo's experience it was still hard for most people to believe that there were individuals in this world who could drive a nail into a grandmother's skull because she stayed on the phone too long, or force stones down a six-year-old's throat for the hell of it, or slash a woman's throat because she had challenged a guy's macho by taking the battery from his boom box.

"Yes," Tori Sandberg said quietly, firmly. "She treated him like an inferior and an idiot. She was always doing that to waiters and strangers."

An interesting vibration was coming off her: Cardozo had a sense that she was enraged at the dead woman. Some part of her felt that Oona Aldrich had provoked her own murder.

"She was out of control," Tori Sandberg said. "She made a scene at Archibald's over lunch, she made a scene outside the store, as we were going in, and she made the scene in the boutique."

Cardozo's ballpoint moved quickly, trying to keep up, leaving practically illegible tracks over the notepad. "What kind of scene did she make at lunch?"

Tori Sandberg's eyelids flicked down, paler than the color of her face. "She was drinking a lot of champagne, and who knows what pills she was on. She started arguing with the waiter about the vegetable dip. So the poor waiter got her a fresh pot and that ended that argument, so she started another. She claimed she saw someone in the kitchen who shouldn't have been there."

"And who was that?"

A moment went by. Cardozo was suddenly aware of a silence threaded through with shadow.

"A murderer," Leigh Baker said.

"She was screaming it," Tori Sandberg said. *"What is that murderer doing in your kitchen? How dare you hire a murderer!"*

"Did she have any murderer in particular in mind?"

"His name is Jim Delancey." In Leigh Baker's lap two thumbs with their clear-polished nails began probing each other. "He killed my daughter four years ago."

"And did Oona Aldrich actually see him?"

Tori Sandberg shrugged as though it should have been obvious. "She had to have been imagining it. Jim Delancey was sentenced to—what was it, Leigh—twenty-five years?"

"I could see into the kitchen from the table," Leigh Baker said. "He wasn't there."

"Oona had an instinct," Tori Sandberg said. "She zeroed in on people's dreads. I'm not saying she did it with premeditation or even consciously. But if she'd wanted to destroy our little reunion, she couldn't have picked a quicker or more effective way."

Cardozo flipped to a fresh page. "And you said Mrs. Aldrich made another scene outside the store?"

"The man with the boom box was there," Tori Sandberg said. "She insulted him."

"How did Mrs. Aldrich do that?"

"She said they shouldn't allow music like that in front of the store. She said next thing they'd be allowing it inside. He heard her and he followed us inside."

Cardozo glanced up from his notebook. "This man followed you?"

"I didn't see him," Leigh Baker said.

"Well, one moment we were outside and he was outside," Tori Sandberg said, "and the next moment we were on the second floor in the boutique and there he was."

"The same man," Cardozo said.

"Unless there were two Hispanic men with the same boom box and the same scowl wearing the same gray jogging clothes and red sweatband and red jogging pouch and white Adidas sneakers."

"I didn't think he was scowling," Leigh Baker said. "If anything, he looked easygoing."

"Killing Oona over a stupid ninety-cent battery is hardly easygoing," Tori Sandberg said.

"She wasn't killed over the battery," Leigh Baker said. "She was killed for the brooch."

"Excuse me," Cardozo said. "What brooch?"

"Oona was wearing a brooch exactly like this." Leigh Baker tapped a finger against a small platinum hummingbird pinned to her lapel.

Cardozo noticed that Tori Sandberg was wearing an identical piece of jewelry.

"We were all wearing one," Leigh Baker said, "and Oona's is gone."

"Was she wearing it when she went into the changing room?"

Leigh Baker nodded. A moment went by and then Tori Sandberg nodded.

"And when did you realize it was missing?"

"It was missing when I found her," Leigh Baker said.

Cardozo made a note. "How much is a brooch like that worth?"

"It cost about six thousand," Tori Sandberg said.

"Fifteen years ago," Leigh Baker said.

Figure forty thousand today, Cardozo calculated. "At the time Mrs. Aldrich entered the store how visible was her brooch?"

"Extremely visible," Leigh Baker said. "It was pinned to her jacket."

"It was pinned to her blouse," Tori Sandberg said. "The jacket covered it."

Cardozo reflected that if Baker was right, Aldrich's brooch had motivated the killing. But if Sandberg were right, Aldrich's *behavior* had caused the murder.

Leigh Baker's hands were in rapid motion, unpinning her brooch, practically ripping it from her blouse. She held it out to Cardozo. Her hand was shaking. "You're welcome to keep mine for reference."

Cardozo turned the brooch over in his hand. It was a beautiful little thing. The sugaring of emerald and ruby chips threw off glints of colored light.

"I'll return it as soon as we photograph it," he said.

"There's absolutely no hurry," Leigh Baker said.

It was as though she'd said, *I never want to see it again.*

"Did either of you see the man with the boom box go into the changing rooms," Cardozo said, "or come out?"

Leigh Baker shook her head immediately.

It took Tori Sandberg a moment longer. It was clear that something had convinced her of the man's guilt, and Cardozo was curious what that something was.

"When did this man leave the boutique?"

Neither answered.

"Did either of you see him leave?"

"I saw his friend leave," Tori Sandberg said. "The black woman."

"I can't believe they were friends," Leigh Baker said.

"But neither of you saw the *man* go," Cardozo said.

Neither spoke.

"Could you identify this man if you saw him again?"

"I think so," Leigh Baker said.

"I certainly could," Tori Sandberg said.

"And would you be able to describe him to a sketch artist?"

■ ■ ■

LAB REPORTS AND PHOTOGRAPHS and other people's descriptions never quite did it for Cardozo.

He was one of those cops who needed to study the crime scene with his own five senses. He needed to know how it smelled, how it felt to be there. He needed to know what the killer had seen, what the victim had seen, how it felt to move through the space they'd moved through.

So he stood in the doorway now, looking in at the changing room.

The walls and mirror and rug looked as though a defective can of raspberry soda had popped its top and exploded its full twelve ounces. The spatter could have been the work of a revved-up graffiti artist wielding a pastry gun of diluted red pigment, but the sweet, sickening smell of iron told Cardozo that this was human blood.

It was obvious that behavior in this city had crossed a new frontier.

Lou Stein from the lab was kneeling on the rug, examining the pile under a magnifying glass.

"What have you found?" Cardozo said.

Lou Stein looked up. "Hey, Vince," he said. Now that his blond hair had receded to a horseshoe fringe around the back of his head, his gold-rimmed glasses seemed to fill the upper half of his face. The trifocal lines in the lenses made his blue eyes appear to hop as they moved. "There was some stuff in the waste basket."

"Anything interesting?"

"You're the critic. Judge for yourself."

Cardozo picked up one of the evidence bags from the bench. It held two sheets of pink tissue paper, badly rumpled. Another bag held three inch-long pins with tiny spherical pink heads. The pinks in the two bags matched.

A third bag held a crumpled newspaper clipping that had been uncrumpled and laid flat. On one side a portion of an ad trumpeted a store-wide stereo equipment clearance sale. On the other side a perky blond pixie grinned out from an inch-square photo, airbrushed ageless and almost featureless in bangs. Cardozo recognized Dizey Duke, the syndicated gossip columnist of the *New York Tribune.* In bold print to her left the words "Dizey's Dish" topped today's breathless recounting of the doings of New York's glitterati.

A fourth bag held a three-inch length of burned white candle.

Cardozo frowned. "This was in the wastebasket?"

Lou Stein looked around and nodded.

"And this?" Cardozo held up the fifth bag. It contained a single Duracell type A radio battery with a gold-and-black jacket.

"That was on the floor, under the bench."

Cardozo hunkered down and ducked his head below the built-in bench. His eye ran along the crack where the baseboard met the plaster wall, then traveled the half-inch gap between the baseboard and the dark beige carpeting that hadn't quite managed to reach wall-to-wall.

He stood and stepped back into the corridor. He looked to his left, past the changing rooms and toward the emergency exit; and then to his right, where the corridor ended in an arched, curtained doorway.

He moved toward the curtain.

It was lined and hung three inches above the floor. The hooks were movable, and the rod holding them slanted upward. Cardozo opened the curtain and stepped through. Weights sewn into the bottom hem caused the hooks to slide back down the rod, and the curtain closed itself.

"Clever design, isn't it?" Ingrid Hansen was waiting for him on the other side, blond and nervous and skinny. Behind her the boutique was a softly lit space of glittering showcases and arrogantly posed free-standing mannequins and comfortable chairs.

At the moment the room was cordoned off from the rest of the store. Two uniformed cops stood guard at the entrance, fending off a horde of rubbernecking afternoon shoppers. The area bustled with crime-scene technicians measuring, dusting, photographing, searching for dust or fibers or filaments or prints that might prove relevant.

Ms. Hansen seemed to be expecting Cardozo to pronounce some sort of verdict on the curtain.

"Very clever," he said. "Self-closing. Tell me, Ms. Hansen, is the emergency exit kept locked on the stair side?"

"No. That would be against fire regulations."

"Then anyone could have used the stairs and gotten in there while Mrs. Aldrich was changing?"

She sighed. He could feel her wanting to push this entire day away, to bury this day, to exile it on a rocket.

"I saw no one."

They'd already been over it, three times. Her records showed twenty-two customers between the time the boutique opened and the time Mrs. Aldrich arrived. Nine of them had used the changing rooms, but she had seen no one go into or come out of the rooms while Mrs. Aldrich was changing.

"But if you'd like to ask my assistant—" Ms. Hansen raised her right hand, forefinger extended. The gray-haired woman sitting at the desk on the other side of the boutique immediately looked up. "Xenia, could we speak with you a moment?"

Xenia came across the boutique, short and full-bodied with apple-red cheeks and wire-rimmed spectacles. Cardozo asked if she had seen anyone go into the changing rooms or come out while Mrs. Aldrich was changing. Xenia's eyes were clear and pained, and her answer was instant and uncomplicated. "No."

"There was a man here with a portable radio. Could you describe him?"

"I can try. He was your height, your build—"

"He was younger," Ms. Hansen said. "Early twenties, I'd say. So naturally he was in better physical condition."

Thank you, Ms. Hansen, Cardozo thought, *I needed that.* In fact, he felt in damned good shape for a desk-bound cop who was never going to see forty-five again. At six feet one, thanks to diet and the occasional workout at the police gym, he still weighed the 170 he'd weighed in the army. So far nothing sagged, nothing slumped. His vision was still twenty-twenty, and he needed glasses only for prolonged reading.

"Brown eyes like the lieutenant's," Xenia said, "and the same sort of dark, curly hair, but cut short—and of course, no gray at the temples."

"Of course. And did he have a mustache like mine?"

"He was clean-shaven."

"How was he dressed?"

"He was wearing a red sweatband around his forehead and gray sweat clothes."

"Not a jogging suit?"

"You could certainly jog in them, but they were sweat clothes and they were gray."

"He had new white Adidas jogging shoes," Ms. Hansen said.

"And he was wearing a jogging pouch around his waist," Xenia said. "It was a red jogging pouch with three red plastic zippers running at a slant on the left side."

"Red," Cardozo said. It occurred to him that he'd seen plenty of black jogging pouches but never a red one.

"It matched the sweatband," Xenia said. "And there was a word stitched on the pouch in black-threaded script. *Flamenco or flamingo.*"

"You'd make a good witness."

"I try to pay attention to what's going on around me."

"What can you tell me about the woman who was with this man?"

"There was no woman with him."

"Wasn't there a black woman in the shop?"

"Yes, I waited on her and she set off the alarm."

"How did she manage to do that?"

"She was helping Miss Sandberg choose a bolero, and she stood too close to the electric eye at the door. It happens all the time."

"Where was Mrs. Aldrich when the alarm went off?"

"In the changing room."

"And could you describe this black woman?"

"She had an angular nose, very sharp features—huge eyes— longish hair—the hair seemed natural. She was wearing a pale coffee lace dress with a skin-colored slip beneath."

"Skin-colored," Cardozo said.

"The color of *her* skin." Xenia's eyes considered Ms. Hansen. "She was a little taller than Ms. Hansen. She had a lean body. Excellent physical shape. I'd say she could have been a dancer, and I'd say she was striking."

"Yes," Ms. Hansen agreed. "I'd say so too."

"Did the Hispanic and the black woman talk to each other?" Xenia answered without hesitation. "They did not."

"Which of them left first?"

"The woman."

"And when did she leave?"

"While Mrs. Aldrich was changing," Ms. Hansen said.

"How soon after her did the man leave?"

"I don't remember seeing him go. Do you remember seeing him go, Xenia?"

"I didn't see him go."

"I'm curious about something," Cardozo said. "Don't the security guards discourage radio playing in the store?"

"They certainly wouldn't discourage Mrs. Trump from play-ing one," Ms. Hansen said. "Or Mrs. Astor."

"But apparently this man wasn't Mrs. Trump or Mrs. Astor."

Ms. Hansen sighed. "Even when we see customers steal, we still have to treat them very carefully."

An erect, slender woman approached, and Cardozo ex-changed hello nods with Detective Sergeant Ellie Siegel from his precinct. She had intelligent, pale eyes that sometimes seemed hazel, but today, with the loose violet blouse she was wearing, they seemed green. They also seemed to be signaling Cardozo to step aside with her.

"I spoke to security," Ellie Siegel told him quietly. "They haven't had that many boom-box incidents. It's a gray area." Her dark brown hair was long enough to fall straight to her shoulders, but today she'd scooped it up behind in a sort of seashell whorl, exposing the clear, pale skin of her temples. "What they do have a lot of is shoplifting."

"Anything today?"

"A mother–daughter team—they boosted three thousand dollars' worth of leather goods and perfume."

Siegel and Cardozo crossed the boutique to where a haughty female mannequin in a beige dress had been sexily posed on the arm of a chair.

"Did they hit the boutique?" Cardozo asked.

"Security nabbed them before they got this far. They're in the manager's office now, if you want to talk to them. The only other incident was a man loitering in the stairwell with intent to urinate."

"When?"

"A little before two o'clock."

"That's the right time frame. Where is he?"

"The store doesn't prosecute trespass. So they threw him out." Ellie let a beat pass. "He was wearing a sweatsuit and he had a boom box."

"I want to talk to the guard who threw him out."

Cardozo went back to the changing rooms. He spent a mo-ment examining the emergency exit.

The door had a bar handle running its full width and a red sign: FIRE EXIT. EMERGENCY ONLY. ALARM WILL SOUND WHEN OPENED.

Cardozo gave a sharp push down on the bar. The steel door swung inward. First interesting discovery: No alarm sounded.

He stepped through the doorway onto a poorly lit service

stairway painted battleship gray. Looking around the landing, he made a second interesting discovery: Empty cardboard cartons and shipping material were stacked on the floor, constituting a fire hazard and a clear violation of the city safety code.

He sniffed. The air in the stairwell smelled like a cat's way of saying *This land is mine.*

The door opened behind him. Ellie Siegel was standing there with one of the security guards.

"Vince," she said, "this is Harry Danks."

Cardozo looked at him: a young man with a stomach that more than filled his gray security officer's uniform, he had a heavy square-jawed face, blond hair that badly needed barbering, blood-shot blue eyes.

Danks held out a thick-wristed hand with blunt, rough-skinned fingers. "Pleased to meet you."

"Tell me about your prowler," Cardozo said. "Where'd you find him?"

Danks shrugged, giving Cardozo a look that was hopeful and shy at the same time. Cardozo recognized that look—*Your life is happening, and mine's not.* The look made Cardozo a celebrity and the guard an autograph hunter.

"Exactly where you're standing," Danks said.

"How was he dressed?"

"Gym clothes—gray sweatshirt, gray sweatpants. Red sweat-band around his head. Red jogging pouch. White sneakers."

"What was he doing back here?"

"They usually come in to relieve themselves. Sometimes they've lifted something, want to get out fast without going through a detector. They don't realize there's a detector at the street door."

"Any idea how he got into the stairwell?"

"Could have been from any of the floors."

"How about from the street?"

"No way. The door's locked and there's a guard."

"What was in the bag?"

"Damp clothes."

"Do you mean a complete change of clothes?"

"I didn't take an inventory. None of it was our stuff. There was a sweatshirt."

"Damp with what?"

Harry Danks shrugged. "Sweat, what else."

"Could you describe this man physically?"

"He was in his twenties—your height—dark hair—could have been Spanish. And maybe a weight lifter."

"What makes you say that?"

"When I put my hand on him, it wasn't real—he was so hard." The guard slapped a hand above his hip. "Everyone's got a little extra something they'd like to lose right here, but not Mr. Boom Box. I remembering wondering, Is this guy bionic or what? But what comes to me is, he's wearing a weight-lifter's belt. Sometimes you see delivery men and moving men wearing them. Protects your back when you're lifting anything heavy. Which got me to thinking about his gloves. They didn't have fingers. Not gloves with the fingers cut off, but gloves that never had fingers to begin with."

"Weight-lifter's gloves?" Cardozo said.

The guard nodded. "And under the gloves, he was wearing throw-away surgical gloves. His fingers squeaked."

"Tell me, Harry, did you find a weapon on this guy?

"When I frisked him, he had something under his sock—a kind of splint on his shin, it felt like."

"Could this splint have been a holster for a knife?"

"I don't see why not."

"Didn't you check?"

"There wasn't time." Danks pointed to a fresh-looking three-inch black-lipped scar in the wall. "He swung the boom box at me. That was meant for my head."

The plaster had split down to the concrete underneath. "He must have pretty well wrecked the box."

"Piece of solid-state garbage. After I got him down to the street he threw it at me." Danks's forefinger tapped a small bandage on his temple.

"Where's the boom box now?"

"Probably the same place where it landed. I can't imagine anyone would want it after that bashing."

Cardozo followed Harry Danks down to street level.

Danks nodded to the guard on duty and pushed the heavy steel door open. Cardozo had not been aware that the stairwell was especially cool, but by comparison, what whooshed in from the street was a heat front from a furnace.

Above the pavement and asphalt, light rays rippled and bent like the image on a poorly tuned TV. Pedestrians and traffic moved slowly through the burning glare. Car horns blasted dissonant fanfares.

Danks stood on the sidewalk, stirring a foot with a sort of brutish daintiness through a foot-deep drift of litter.

Cardozo scanned a ten-foot radius of sidewalk. He saw news-print, flyers, junk mail, cigarette butts, gum wrappers, crumpled pizza boxes—the fallout of an average midtown workday—but nothing metal or electronic or remotely solid state. And then, through hurrying feet, his eye caught a wink of chrome from the gutter. He walked to the edge of the sidewalk and stared down.

A two-foot plastic-and-chrome radio-cassette blasting unit looked as though it had taken the full weight of a crosstown bus. He crouched for a better look, then turned and shot Danks a come-over-here nod. "Was that boom box a Sony?"

· FIVE ·

CARDOZO STEPPED FROM THE SUNLIGHT of Lexington Avenue into the soft brown-and-red interior of the restaurant that outsiders called Archibald's and Society called home.

In a place like Archibald's you waited to be seated. Cardozo waited. Now was the precocktail lull, and the only customers were two overdressed, overmade-up women at a corner table. A man in a Santa Claus–red blazer who looked like a maître d' dressed for happy hour gave him a glance and a cold shoulder, and went back to handpicking napkin lint from one of the tablecloths.

Cardozo crossed toward the kitchen.

The lint picker in the Santa jacket intercepted him. "May I help you?" He spoke with a French accent, and the offer had a broad edge of insincerity.

Cardozo showed his shield. "Do you have an employee by the name of James Delancey working here?"

The lint picker's mouth narrowed in a half smile but the expression on his face didn't at all match his eyes. "In the kitchen." He nodded toward the door.

Cardozo stepped into the kitchen.

There wasn't enough ventilation to clear the cooking smells, and the claustrophobic space seemed impossibly ill lit and hot and cluttered. A black man was stirring a cauldron on the twelve-burner stove; a Korean was rolling dough with a champagne bottle; and a Caucasian male stood behind a butcher-block counter, slicing salad vegetables.

Cardozo watched the bright, narrow blade blur up and down. It worked as fast and as expertly as a precision machine, flipping out a glint with each stroke, flicking paper-thin wafers of cucumber to the side in a neat, staggered pile.

"James Delancey?" Cardozo said.

The young white man glanced at Cardozo with a look that was curious and guarded. The click-click of the blade against the butcher block slowed. His curls were full and richly dark and the face beneath them was as tanned and unlined as a surfer's, and Cardozo wondered if they now had tanning beds along with the cable TV in the penitentiary.

Cardozo took out his shield case and flipped it open. "Wouldn't you do better using a Cuisinart on that cucumber?"

The young man's eyes flicked without visible interest to the shield. "It takes as long to clean a Cuisinart as it takes me to slice a dozen cucumbers."

"Is there somewhere we could talk?" Cardozo said.

Delancey laid his knife down on the butcher block. He wiped his hands on his apron. He was an extremely well-built boy, lean and broad-shouldered. He looked to be six feet or six one. If he weighed under 180 pounds it wasn't by much. As he stepped around the counter Cardozo saw he was wearing designer jeans and Bally loafers without socks.

Cardozo followed him out the side door onto Seventy-fourth Street. Delancey offered a cigarette and Cardozo declined.

"Have you been working here long?" Cardozo said.

"Two weeks."

"First job since you were paroled?"

"That's right."

The late spring heat held a foretaste of summer. Afternoon sun was playing shimmering riffs on upper-story windows.

"What hours do you work?"

"Mondays I work eleven A.M. to six P.M. Sundays and Wednesday through Friday I work noon to eight P.M. " Jim Delancey lit his cigarette. "I'm off Saturdays and Tuesdays."

"Then you were here during lunch hour today."

Delancey nodded.

"Are you familiar with Leigh Baker, the actress?"

Delancey sighed. "I saw a lot of her during my trial."

"Did you see Miss Baker here today with two companions?"

"I noticed her."

"And did you show yourself?"

"Look, I work in back, I don't get paid to go out in the front room and dance."

"Did you let her see you?"

Delancey stood there staring into the street at BMWs double-parked beside Porsches. "After I noticed she was here, I moved to the other end of the counter."

"Why?"

For the briefest tick of an instant Jim Delancey's eyebrows puckered and lifted. *You're playing with me, man,* his eyes said. "So she wouldn't see me when the kitchen door swung open again."

"But one of her companions did see you. And she made a scene in the restaurant."

Jim Delancey let his breath out in a sigh. "Look, I'm not a psychic. I don't know what's going through other people's heads, and I don't know why they decide to make scenes."

"Were you acquainted with Oona Aldrich?"

Delancey stared with tight lips, blank gaze. "I never met Oona Aldrich in my life."

"Do you recognize the name?"

"After today I do."

"Are you aware that after she left the restaurant today Oona Aldrich was attacked and killed?"

Cardozo waited for some reaction in the boy's face. Shock. Faked shock. Something. What he saw instead was a carefully maintained neutrality, flat and cool.

"I'm aware she was killed." He could have been saying, I'm aware the sky is blue.

"And how did you become aware of it?"

"My mother phoned me."

"And how did your mother know?"

"She works at the Ingrid Hansen Boutique at Marsh and Bonner's."

"What's your mother's name?"

"Xenia Delancey."

It struck Cardozo as a bizarre little coincidence. "Did you leave the premises anytime between one-thirty and two-thirty?"

"Maybe I came out here to smoke a cigarette."

"Maybe you came out here to smoke a cigarette, or you came out and smoked a cigarette?"

Jim Delancey drew in a deep breath that almost burst his blue button-down, open-necked shirt. "I came out here and had a smoke."

"When? For how long?"

"I don't keep a diary of this stuff. I took a five-minute break. Do you call that leaving the premises?"

"I call it leaving the premises if no one saw you."

Delancey tossed a nod toward the kitchen door. "They saw me."

Cardozo questioned the Korean and the black man. They said Delancey had been in and out of the kitchen all afternoon, but they agreed he'd never been gone for longer than a cigarette break.

The maître d' backed up their story.

Cardozo questioned the waiter. He said it had been a bitch of a lunch hour, much too hectic to allow him to notice who was in the kitchen when.

"Anyone else who might be able to tell me anything?"

"You could ask Larry—the other waiter."

"Where's Larry?"

"He went on vacation two hours ago, lucky bum—but he'll be back working the early shift next Tuesday."

"Okay. Thanks for your time." Cardozo shut his notebook and slid it back into his pocket. As he turned to go he caught Jim Delancey watching him expressionlessly from across the kitchen.

■ ■ ■

"I'M COUNTING ON YOU, VINCE." Captain Tom Reilly's gray eyes stared hopefully out of his heavy, pale face. It was late for Reilly to be at the precinct: by seven in the evening he was usually home in Queens, or out on the golf course. "There's going to be a lot of shit from this mess in Marsh and Bonner's. Stay on top of it."

"I'll do my best, sir."

They sat facing each other across a glass-topped wood desk twice the size of Cardozo's, in an air-conditioned office four times the size of his cubicle.

"Organize yourself a four-man task force," Reilly said. "Let me know in a day who you want."

"I can tell you now."

Reilly's white eyebrows shot up, surprised, as if Cardozo had to be psychic to have already been thinking of a task force.

But it was a fact of New York political life that certain corpses swung infinitely more more weight than others. The crucial factors were race and real estate. A rich white woman murdered in a Fifth Avenue store automatically got more attention from police and media than twenty poor black women murdered in grocery stores in Harlem.

"Okay, who do you want?"

"Siegel and I caught the case. We'll stay on it. And I want Monteleone, Richards, and Malloy."

Reilly lifted a pen and made a notation. "You got them."

■ ■ ■

CARDOZO SAT DRINKING a cup of coffee that had turned cold, hoping the caffeine would persuade him he was able to think. Stripes of fluorescence slanted down from the desk lamp. Light caught his fingers as they tapped a bolero on the yellowed documents of the Nita Kohler–James Delancey file.

Among the press clippings he found an interview with Delancey's lawyers. They claimed that Nita Kohler was famed among her fast-living, rich young crowd for her promiscuity, her drug-taking, her irrational violence, her addiction to kinky sex. For months she had pursued Delancey, begging him to engage with her in sodomy and intercourse. Finally, with cocaine, she had bought him.

This was not her first brush with disaster. She courted thrills. She courted death.

The file was long closed, ancient history, but still there was a movement in Cardozo's heart, a strangulation that he felt each time he ran up against one of these victim-is-guilty defenses. He knew the alibis. Society's fault. Parents' fault. The drug culture's fault. Above all, the girl's fault.

Cardozo began reading the transcript of Delancey's first interrogation. After six pages he felt his lips pull together into a thin, frustrated line. He leaned forward in his swivel chair and stared at the two arraignment photos of James Delancey the Third.

He finally chose the full-face shot with its narrow nose and full-lipped scowl and bright points of light in the eyes. The face was smooth and soft, almost without real contours, and it hadn't changed in four years.

A moment later Cardozo crossed the squad room and stepped into the little room where an Albanian stand-up comic was telling dialect jokes on the TV screen. Detective Goldberg was sitting in a chair with a coffee cup, not watching.

"Do you mind?" Cardozo slid a cassette into the VCR.

Goldberg shrugged a burly shoulder.

Cardozo started the tape. Someone had played it and not rewound it all the way, so the picture came up in the middle of Detective Carl Malloy reading the suspect his rights.

"You're entitled to a lawyer," Malloy was saying. "You have the right to remain silent."

Christ, Malloy had lost hair and put on weight since this was taken. Malloy looked *young* in this tape.

"Anything you say can and will be used against you. Do you wish to have a lawyer?"

The camera caught what the transcript hadn't, that instant where James Delancey's last remnant of bravado wordlessly slipped away. He shook his head.

It occurred to Cardozo that Delancey must have been working out with weights in prison—he was almost slim in this picture.

"Jim Delancey indicates no," Malloy said.

There was the sound of a door closing, and Ellie Siegel came onto the screen.

Ellie should give Malloy tips on not aging, Cardozo thought.

She came toward the table with a cup of coffee. Her expression was agreeable. She put the coffee down in front of the suspect. "Do you want to make a statement?" she asked gently. "Do you want to talk about it?"

Jim Delancey lowered his head and raised his eyes under his thick dark hair to look up apologetically, like a child. He brought himself up nervously erect in the metal chair. "It wasn't my fault. She attacked me."

Siegel's eyes and lips collaborated in a pleasantly skeptical half smile. "That hundred-and-two-pound girl attacked a hunk like you?"

What balls, Cardozo thought—she was flirting with the punk, and what's more, he was going for it. For ten seconds Delancey was looking at the floor, shy, and then he was looking at the detectives, half smiling, and then he leaned forward to lift his coffee cup and take a gulp from it. The light from the lamp got in his eyes and he put a hand up to shield them. It could have been some freak result of camera placement, but the hand looked huge.

"I'm not clear on this, Jim." Siegel sat looking across the table at him. "Nita Kohler attacked you tonight, on the terrace of her mother's town house?"

"She attacked me tonight and every night since we met."

"Why would anyone attack a guy like you? Especially a woman?"

"She wanted sex with me."

"She wanted sex with you," Siegel repeated with a kind of nonpressuring nonemphasis. "And how did you feel about that?"

"She didn't turn me on."

"Then why were you seeing her? Wasn't she your girlfriend?"

"She thought she was."

"If she wasn't your girlfriend, what was your relationship?"

"She was my caseworker at Renaissance House."

"That's the drug rehab up on East Ninetieth?"

Delancey nodded.

"Jim Delancey indicates yes," Malloy said.

Cardozo sensed in the image of the boy a brooding wonderment, as though somewhere along some line of coke he had lost track of how the reality outside his head was built, of what cause led to what effect.

"Are you an addict?" Siegel asked.

"I'm a recovering addict."

"Did you do drugs tonight?"

He nodded. "I did a little coke."

"Jim Delancey indicates yes," Malloy said.

"Did Nita Kohler take drugs tonight?" Siegel asked.

"She took a hit," Delancey said.

"Why don't you tell me exactly what happened tonight," Siegel suggested. "Start from the beginning. Where did you two meet?"

"We met at Achilles Foot," Delancey said. "Like always."

"That's a bar?"

He nodded.

"Jim Delancey indicates yes," Malloy said.

"She wanted to talk about where our relationship was going. She was very hurt and said we should go to her place and talk, because no one was home. So we went there, and she said how much she loved me and how could I hurt her by seeing other girls. I told her this was bullshit. Her hand came out *zap*, like that, and she scratched my face. See?"

Cardozo pressed the Pause button and froze the frame. Scabs dotted the right side of Delancey's face from his eye down to his mouth. You could connect the dots and see what had been a superficial abrasion.

Cardozo restarted the tape and when Delancey's voice came up again, he was aware of how gratingly whiny it sounded.

"I said that's it, fuck you and adios, and before I knew it she was attacking me again."

"And you defended yourself?" The way Siegel put it was halfway between question and statement. There was absolutely no tone of judgment. If anything, Siegel's voice and manner suggested it would have been the most natural thing in the world for this poor guy to defend himself against a crazed, drugged-up virago.

"I put my arms up to protect my face."

"Did you push her away?"

"I didn't touch the bitch."

Cardozo pressed the Off button. The picture on the screen froze for one split instant and then fractured into black-and-white static.

▪ ▪ ▪

ELLIE SIEGEL WAS STILL AT HER DESK, typing up the day's notes.

"Tell me about the Kohler–Delancey case," Cardozo said.

Ellie sighed. "My second homicide. All cases should be that easy."

"There's not the slightest doubt in your mind he killed her."

"More to the point, there wasn't the slightest doubt in the jury's mind. Seven hours to convict."

"The medical report mentions a straight-line bruise on the palm of Nita's left hand."

Ellie fixed softly piercing eyes on him. "You've been excavating some pretty old paper."

"Nita was right-handed."

Ellie nodded. "I know, I know, and she would have fended off a blow with her right hand and not her left. But Delancey had a knife strapped to his shin, and the hilt matched the mark in her palm."

"But it was a bruise, not a cut."

"Hilts don't cut, Vince. They're made not to cut." Her tone was flat and mild, and while it acknowledged his possible dimness it criticized nothing. "Believe me, a lot of people went over that bruise, and one thing it does not point to is one iota of innocence on the part of Jim Delancey."

"What did you think of him personally?"

"Personally he was a big, stupid, handsome, stoned schmuck. He was momma's prince, ego with no limits. Nita Kohler was obnoxious to King Me and so he pulled her life off her like wings off a fly. He knew what he was doing and, believe me, he liked doing it."

"You're speaking as a woman or a feminist or a detective?"

"I'm speaking as a human being who happens, at this point in her life, to be all of the above." Ellie switched off her electric typewriter and covered it.

"There's a lot of drugs on that first tape," Cardozo said.

"Tell me about it."

"And they were never mentioned in the trial. How come he didn't plead cocaine intoxication as a defense?"

"Beats me, because he was a heavy hitter. He was feeding his nose two-, three-hundred dollars' worth a day. Why do you think he had all that breaking and entering on his rap sheet? The week before he killed Kohler he was fencing a thousand dollars a day."

"What kind of stuff did he fence?"

"Jewelry, coins, watches, anything valuable and small he could pinch from his girlfriends' apartments."

"As I recall he had quite a few society girls interested in him."

"And it wasn't because he was interested back. It was just their bad luck that they could access the kind of cash he needed."

"He didn't like girls?"

"*Like* is not the word. He had a momma's-boy resentment of females. They owed him a living and they owed him sex and they weren't doing their job."

"Think he's twisted enough to kill Oona Aldrich?"

"If he got a chance after the grief she caused him today, absolutely."

"On his third week of parole?"

"What's parole got to do with it? It's the principle of the thing. Oona was a woman, and she bugged him. With timing and luck he could have followed her in a cab. The emergency stairway would have gotten him into the changing room and out again."

"But you're forgetting one thing: What would he tell his boss?"

"That he was stepping outside to smoke a cigarette."

Cardozo ran it through his mind. "I don't know. There's such a thing as going out to smoke a cigarette, and then there's such a thing as going out to smoke a pack."

"All I know is, Delancey had the head to kill her. Whether he had the opportunity . . ." Ellie flicked off her desk light. "Makes me tired to think about it. That's it for me. Good night."

Cardozo was suddenly aware that there was one thing he wanted to do very much, and that was go to bed. He walked with Ellie to the stairs.

"Funny," he said. "Delancey's mother working in the boutique where Oona was killed."

"What's funny? The woman ran up a quarter million in legal fees defending her golden boy. And God knows how much it cost to spring him from prison. She's got to work somewhere." Ellie shrugged. "Sometimes you just have to accept that there's such a thing as coincidence."

"But don't you sometimes have to accept that there isn't?"

"Every day."

They came to the stairway.

"Do you think Delancey could change?" Cardozo said. "Get off drugs? Hold down a job? Grow up maybe?"

Ellie tossed him a pitying glance. "People don't change, Vince. They just learn better camouflage."

"Is that your story, Ellie?"

"And yours obviously. But more to the point it's his."

Cardozo returned to his cubicle. He got out his notebook and listed reasons why Jim Delancey had to be involved. He turned the page and listed reasons why Delancey couldn't be involved.

Finally he closed the notebook and lifted the telephone and punched in a number. He leaned sideways and gave the cubicle door a push, shutting out the man-made and machine-made racket that spilled in from the squad room.

A man's voice answered on the fifth ring. "Hello?" The low-pitched, patrician drawl tortured a simple *o* into an Ivy League diphthong.

"Walter, it's Vince Cardozo."

There was an instant's lag before recognition kicked in. "Yes, Vince." Walter Vanderflood's tone was not happy—nothing that linked his world to Vince Cardozo's could ever be grounds for happiness—but it was respectful. "Is something the matter?"

"Not too much in my life and not too much in yours, I hope."

"No, I'm doing all right."

There had been a time when Walter Vanderflood had not been doing all right, when his nephew had been found murdered in a Sixtieth Street hotel, and Vince Cardozo, doing no more than his job, had helped. Walter Vanderflood had said, "If you ever need help . . ." Walter Vanderflood served on the Putnam County parole board, and three times Cardozo had taken him up on that offer.

"Jim Delancey was paroled two weeks ago."

"The young man who killed the Kohler girl?"

"The same. Somebody used a lot of influence."

"I'm not sure I can help you there. Parole proceedings are closed—there aren't even records."

"But if by any chance you happen to talk to anyone who served on that parole board . . . if you happen to talk socially, I mean."

"Of course. If by any chance I do, I'll let you know."

· SIX ·

IT WAS AFTER ELEVEN by the time Cardozo found a parking place on Broome Street. As he walked the block to his home the neighborhood felt quiet. Some kids were playing basketball over on the ball court, and somewhere a restaurant had its door open and Rosemary Clooney was singing "Baciami, Bambino" on the jukebox.

He let himself into the six-story apartment building on the corner of Sullivan and checked the mailbox to see what bills had come today. None, which meant his daughter Terri had already picked them up.

He climbed to the third floor. He'd lived in the same rent-stabilized apartment since before SoHo had become trendy, and he was still living there now that the wave of trendiness was subsiding. He let himself into the rear apartment.

The living room was dark except for a glow spilling through the windows. There was no blinking red light on the Panasonic Easa-Phone answering machine, but he crossed to the sofa and pushed the Messages button anyway, just to be sure. The machine whirred into Replay.

"Terri," a male voice said, "are you there? It's Josh."

A light went on. Cardozo turned.

Terri was standing there, straight and slender against the wall, her long, dark hair spilling over her bathrobe. She looked at him with sleepy, dark fifteen-year-old eyes.

"I already picked up that call," she said. "Why are you running through old messages?"

He pushed the button to stop the machine. "Just wanted to be sure I didn't miss anything by accident. Who's Josh?"

She was quiet, which was a very different thing from being silent, "He's a friend from school."

"You've never mentioned him."

"Dad," she said.

The tone of voice was a statement. It said he was being stuffy, unreasonable, and a little bit of a pain. Worse, the word *Dad* was a signal that she was growing up, that he was no longer Daddy. Which meant he was no longer anyone's Daddy. He felt sad at the idea: it was like being laid off, like having to say good-bye to a job he loved.

"How could I have mentioned him? We haven't had a talk in three weeks."

"Is there anything that needs to be talked about?"

She shook her head. "I'm doing fine, we don't need to worry about me."

"Because if you're seeing somebody," he said, "I'd like to know. I'd like to meet him."

"Dad—I see Josh two times a week. We're in computer-science class together. Big deal." Her tone was playful but with something really there beneath the playfulness. "He was returning my call. I phoned him because I had a question about iterative programs."

"*What* programs?"

"Yeah. That's why I needed help."

Cardozo went into the kitchen and opened the refrigerator to find something to drink.

"Your dinner's behind the lemonade," Terri called.

He moved the pitcher of fresh lemonade and found dinner for one, cold chicken and potato salad, neatly covered in Saran Wrap. "How much does he help you?" he called.

"You don't need to shout, I'm here." She was standing in the doorway. "Josh helps me a lot."

"Sounds like you're going with him."

"I'm not going with anyone."

"That wouldn't be a white lie to keep your old man from worrying?"

"Why should I worry about you worrying? You never worry."

"I'm just good at fooling you."

"Besides, there's nothing to worry about." She watched as he poured a glass of lemonade and slid the pitcher back into the refrigerator. "Aren't you going to eat your dinner?"

"Maybe later. Right now I'm just thirsty."

"You should eat. Otherwise you'll wake up in the middle of the night."

"You're not changing the subject, are you?"

"Why would I change the subject?"

"Because you might be going with someone and not telling me."

She gave him a long glance, and from across the room Cardozo opened the windowshades of all five senses, trying to catch the vibration that was suddenly coming off her.

"Don't look at me like that," he said. "It happens, you know. Sometimes kids don't tell their parents."

"I'm not a kid."

"That's why I'm asking."

"No, Dad, you're asking because you think I'm *still* a kid."

The glass of lemonade stopped halfway to his mouth. "Okay, you're not still a kid, that means I can't ask about your life anymore? Because I'll tell you something. You could be a grown woman, you could be an old woman—as long as I'm around I'm going to be interested in what's happening to you."

"I want you to be interested. I'm glad you ask."

He drained the glass in two gulps. "I'd be glad if you'd answer."

"I'm trying to answer."

"Try harder. Tell me how much you're seeing of this guy."

"Not a lot."

"Maybe I will have that chicken." He took the platter from the refrigerator to the kitchen table. He went back for a jar of mayonnaise and a jar of pickles. "Then you are seeing him. A little."

"Right." She shrugged. "A little."

"Not a lot."

"No, Dad, not a lot." She brought a place setting to the table. "We haven't reached that stage."

"I don't need the fork. I'm going to eat with my fingers."

"You're not going to eat potato salad with your fingers."

"I'm not going to eat potato salad. Then tell me, you're planning to reach that stage?"

"Planning doesn't come into it. I'm not planning, I'm not not planning."

He pulled out the chair and sat. He spread a knife-load of mayonnaise on the chicken breast. "Sounds like you wouldn't mind if you reached that stage."

"How do I know?"

"Come on, you're an intelligent kid." He ground a generous layer of pepper over the mayonnaise. "How can you not know?"

"I'm sorry, Dad. There are things I don't know till they happen. I may think about them, I may think I want them to happen, but till they do I don't know."

Are we talking about sex? he wondered. "Then you want it to happen with this kid, this Josh."

"Do I want what to happen?"

He picked up the breast in both hands and took a bite. "You want to reach that stage, is what I'm saying."

"What stage?"

He felt he was trying to ride a tricycle on a tightrope. "Have you reached that stage with anyone?"

"What stage?"

"This chicken is delicious, but why do I have the feeling this discussion is going in circles?"

"You're the one going in circles." She brought him another glass of lemonade. "I'm just trying to keep up with you."

"Sorry, kid, I'm trying to keep up with you and I guess I've had a long day, because I'm doing a lousy job of it."

"What's the matter?"

"Nothing's the matter."

"Something's the matter." She pulled out the other chair and sat across the table from him. "What happened at work?"

"What usually happens at work? Someone got killed."

"Who?"

"A woman."

"Why does that upset you?"

"Why shouldn't it upset me? Anyway, it doesn't upset me."

"You're very upset."

"I'm very upset because you're very upsetting tonight. This is very unlike you. Maybe I will have some potato salad."

"I told you you'd need the fork. Who was she?"

"I don't know her. I didn't know her. I'm not sure I'd want to know her."

"Then why does she upset you?"

He realized Terri was interrogating him. Something in their relationship, some last remnant of control, was slipping from his hands. His daughter was beginning to manage things. "She's not the one that upsets me."

"Then there is someone who does upset you."

"It's a long story."

"I like long stories."

"No, you don't. Not this one."

"Why are you in such a mood? I just want to hear about your day."

What they were doing now had started three or four years ago, he couldn't remember exactly when. It had started as a game, the little girl playing big momma to the gruff old man who played bad little boy. The game had produced tangible benefits. She ran the house for him. She cooked for him. Laundry got sent out on time, dishes got washed, beds got made. There was always soap and toothpaste and toilet paper and fresh towels. But sometime during the last year the game had become more than a game, and he realized he'd come to rely on her.

Sometimes he found himself resenting her power just a little, withholding himself just a little. Like now. "I said it's a long story."

"You said a woman got killed. Does it bother you because that's what happened to Mom?"

Suddenly he didn't want any more potato salad. "It's nothing like what happened to Mom. Stop being a psychiatrist."

"I'm just trying to understand."

"I don't think about her." He got up from the table. "That's past."

"Is it? Seven years, and you're still alone."

"Alone? Seems to me there's two people in this house."

She followed him back into the living room. "There should be three. At least."

"For a kid who says she's grown up maybe you don't know as much as you think. That was a dumb remark. About three." He flopped down on the sofa and stared at the dark TV screen. "If I wanted three people in this family, there'd be three people. I'm not an idiot."

"If you had someone, you could talk to them."

"Why should I talk to someone?" He picked up the *TV Guide* from the coffee table.

"So you wouldn't be in a mood when work gets to you."

"I can talk to you if I don't want to be in a mood." He turned to the Wednesday-night listings to see if anything was on at eleven-thirty.

"But you don't talk to me."

"This is why, because we talk like this." He didn't want *Nightline,* he'd seen enough trouble for one day. And he wasn't in the mood for *The Honeymooners;* Channel Eleven had been rerunning it for so many years that he'd seen most of the episodes two or three times.

"This is the longest we've talked in months." Terri sat on the sofa beside him. She drew her legs up under her. "We're having a good talk."

And he didn't think he could take Arsenio Hall. Not tonight. "What's good about it?"

"I like it when you tell me how you're feeling."

He glanced at her. With her serious dark eyes and her assured movements, she reminded him exactly of her dead mother.

"You know, you're just like your mother. I ask how you feel, and I wind up telling you how I feel. You're a mystery to me. I never get to find out anything about you."

"Why's it so important how I feel?"

"Because I want to know about this Josh person."

"Why?"

He closed the *TV Guide* and slapped it back on the table. "Because sometimes people get hurt. And I don't mean your mother—I'm talking about now. Sometimes young people get hurt. Sometimes they hurt one another."

"Are you talking about sex?"

He sat there, chest tight and heaving. "Okay. If you have to know, I'm talking about a girl who got thrown off a sixth-story terrace."

"Wait a minute. Something just went by me. Where did that come from?"

"It happened. And she wasn't much older than you." He realized he sounded angry, and he sounded angry because he didn't know how else to get through to her. "And she probably thought she had all the answers. Just like you do sometimes."

"When do I think I have all the answers?"

He tried to concentrate on his reflection and hers in the dark TV screen, tried to bring his reflection under control, tried to will himself into a sort of calm. "Tonight."

"Wait a minute. Are we arguing?"

Cardozo had reached that state of brain overload where all he craved was to sit still in one half of an absolute silence and know that another person was sitting still in the other half of the same silence. "I think we're arguing," he said. "No, I'm arguing."

"What about?"

"I guess what I'm arguing about is, people are losing one another all over this world, and I don't want to lose you."

"I don't want to lose you either."

He sighed. "Then why am I arguing?"

"I don't know." A smile came up on her face. "You started it."

"Josh started it. He's a troublemaker. Why do you want to run around with troublemakers?"

"Dad." She kissed him and slid off the sofa.

"Can't you tell when I'm joking?"

"No, not tonight. Are you joking?"

"Now I'm joking. I wasn't before, but I am now. See the smile?"

Something lovely and caring shaped itself in her eyes. "I'm sorry about the woman who got killed and the girl who got thrown off the terrace."

"I know you are. Don't worry. Nothing like that is going to happen to us." *It happened to your mother, but, so help me God, it will never happen to you. Not as long as Vince Cardozo is around.*

"I love you, Dad."

"And I love you too. And I'm sorry we argued."

"I'm not."

"And I want to meet Josh."

"You will." She gave him a tight, quick clasp. "Good night."

He picked up the *TV Guide* again. He heard her slippers pad into the hallway. A moment later her bedroom door shut.

"Hey," he called. "Go to bed. I'll take care of the dishes."

▪ SEVEN ▪

Thursday, May 9

"OONA ALDRICH WASN'T IMAGINING a thing," Cardozo said. "Jim Delancey was working in the kitchen, exactly where she saw him."

Sitting in the bird-print chair in a slant of lamplight, Leigh Baker looked pale, tired. "That's typical," she said. "Even drunk, Oona had better eyesight than all the rest of us put together."

They were talking, just the two of them, in the living room— a soft, generous green-walled space hung with French Impressionists. The town house belonged to Waldo Carnegie, the TV magazine publisher she was living with. Brightness billowed in through gauzy window curtains.

"When was Jim Delancey released?" she said.

"Two weeks ago."

Her hand kept going to her hair. Her fingers made a combing motion as though she were unconsciously checking the alignment of phantom loose strands. Cardozo found the movement and what it said about her present state of mind curiously touching. It was clearly unconscious, an insecure grooming movement—the female equivalent of what a cop did when he straightened his tie in front of a pretty woman.

"And who the hell wrangled a parole for him?" she said.

"Parole proceedings are secret, but we're looking into it." Cardozo laid the arraignment photo on the table between them.

She glanced at the pouting baby face and winced and pushed it away like a bad memory.

"Did you see him anywhere in the boutique? Anywhere in Marsh and Bonner's?"

"No, not that I noticed, and I would certainly have noticed."

"Did you see him in the street when you left the restaurant?"

"To me, he was a figment of Oona's second split of champagne. My mind was absolutely closed to the idea that he could be anywhere but in that prison cell where he belongs."

Cardozo took a moment to inventory the space around him. Antique secretary, silk-upholstered chairs and sofas. A concert-grand piano banked with flowers and silver-framed photographs. It was an elegant room, not at all quiet about its elegance, and it seemed to him that her surroundings suited her. "Who did you tell that you were going to Marsh and Bonner's?"

"Besides Oona and Tori, no one in particular."

"Did you mention it at the table while the waiter was there?"

"Possibly. Probably."

"When you told the cab driver where you were going, were you standing on the street? Could someone have heard you?"

"You're wondering how Delancey knew." She sat in the chair a moment, thoughtful. "I usually get into a cab first, then give directions."

She took a cigarette from an engraved crystal box. Before Cardozo could offer a light she had picked up a little silver bird from the table. She pushed its tail, the bird breathed flame, and she lit the cigarette.

"When Oona and I were young, she was one of my two best friends. We swore we'd stay best friends all our lives. And we tried to be, we really did try."

"I understand. I lost a friend like that."

Smoke floated on the still, jonquil-scented air.

"I'm sorry," she said.

"And I'm sorry you lost yours."

"I just wish—" She broke off.

Cardozo waited, giving her his cop's ear if she needed it.

"I wish I could remember her the way she used to be—fresh and funny and beautiful and brilliant. And sober. Instead of the way she died."

"Look, I know it doesn't seem to make sense—"

"No. That's the trouble. It makes too much sense. Oona lived wastefully, she died wastefully."

"Maybe her life wasn't as wasteful as you think."

She turned to look at him and her eyes were suddenly fierce. "Then, please, just tell me what the hell was she doing all her life!"

"She was living her life the best she knew how. It's not her fault that some sleaze decided to kill her."

"No, it's not her fault." Leigh Baker's eyes stayed on him, and then her pale, veined eyelids flicked down.

He could feel her mind going around, chewing on itself. "And it's not your fault either," he said.

She sighed. "But if only I'd believed her . . ."

"Believing her wouldn't have kept her out of that changing room. There was no way of predicting. These things happen. Unfortunately they happen more and more, and they happen to decent people."

"There's too much murder in this city," Leigh Baker said.

"I agree."

"And it's no good calling it random violence, as though killing were like taxes or the weather. This isn't random, this is *my life*— my family and my friends are getting killed."

He spoke gently. "It's understandable you'd feel angry. You're not alone. A lot of people are angry."

"Tell me, Lieutenant. Are you angry?"

"Yes—I'm angry."

■ ■ ■

"I'M SO UPSET FOR YOU, truly I am. I'm so sorry." Though the voice on the phone was a man's, it had the too soothing, almost fawning tone of an insecure mother. "I know exactly what you're going through—and I just want you to know, I'm here whenever you need me, day or night. *And* I make housecalls."

"Look," Leigh said, "I haven't got the strength right now to be tactful."

"Of course not, you poor thing."

"Let's be honest. You detested Oona, you fought like a dog with her, and so far as I know you never reconciled, so please, let's not make this any harder by pretending you can comfort me. I'm sorry if that sounds awful."

"It sounds tremendously human, hon, just like you. Believe me I do understand. But I wasn't phoning about Oona. Good God, I'm the first to admit I couldn't stand that broad's guts. And if you think I'm going to even *try* to pretend with you—"

She felt that old familiar rush of certainty beneath her skin. When Dick Braidy took this tone, he wanted something.

"You and I just haven't got the kind of relationship where pretending plays any role at all," he said, "and that's what I think is so great about you and me."

"Dick, if you didn't phone me about Oona, what have you been talking about for ten minutes?"

"Dizey, of course."

Hiding in her heart was a sick little fascination that Dick Braidy knew so well how to arouse. She realized that if she gave in to it, she would end up furious at herself. "What about Dizey?"

He let a moment crawl by. "Her column."

"Today?"

"You bet your sweet tush today—would I be phoning you about *yesterday's* column?"

She understood that for Dick Braidy and his hundreds of think-alikes, nothing was real or mattered till it was on TV or in the gossip columns or whispered at Park Avenue dinner parties— if you could call the level of communication at those dinners whispering. Volcanos could be blowing up in Honduras and killing three hundred people at a spurt, but for Dick Braidy the true hot poop of the hour was apt to be that a ved*dee* famous pop singer's toupee had been found in the Jacuzzi of a junk-bond mogul's mistress.

Leigh knew she should pull back, end this conversation now. But she couldn't. He'd hooked her—just as he had so many times before. "What has Dizey got in today's column?"

"You don't know? You honestly haven't seen it?"

"Of course I haven't seen it." She had to fight to control her voice now. "Would we be having this conversation if I had?"

"Then do me a favor—do us both a favor—above all do yourself a favor. Please, *please,* I'm sincerely begging you—don't, do *not* look at Dizey's column today. Promise."

"Will you please just tell me straight out what Dizey has put in her column?"

"You don't want to know."

"If you're not going to tell me," she burst out, "if all you're doing is playing one of your goddamned games with me, then . . . go to hell!"

"Now, hon, just take it easy."

"I will not take it easy."

"Now listen to me—"

"I will not listen to you. You're not helping, not one bit. You've never helped. You've always made things worse."

"Now, hon, you're understandably excited. I know you don't mean that."

"You know *shit*! I *do* mean it! Why the hell do you think I divorced you?" Leigh threw the phone receiver into the cradle.

For the next minute and a half she sat perfectly still on the edge of the bed, listening to the weightless sigh of the air conditioner as it stirred the point-lace curtains at the bedroom windows.

Then she rose and went into the hallway.

The button beside the elevator door was glowing like a ruby caught in a sunbeam, which meant the maid was still cleaning.

Leigh stared over the carved bannister down into the stairwell.

Nothing moved.

As she hurried down the two flights of carpeted stairs, she had a sense of perfumed airlessness, like the ventilation on the Concorde. Around her the town house had the quiet of a secret wrapped in cotton.

On the first floor morning sun streamed into the living room, turning beveled shelves of rare-book bindings gold. She moved quickly through the dining room, where sun touched mahogany chairs and table with streaks of rose.

Just inside the swinging pantry door, on the counter beneath the cabinets of Wedgwood and Lowestoft dinner settings, the maid had left her copy of that day's *New York Tribune.*

Leigh snatched it up.

There was an article on the killing, and Leigh was surprised to see her own photograph, captioned, FRIEND OF VICTIM. It was a publicity shot, and it struck her as glossy and false. Next to it was a photograph of Vincent Cardozo, captioned IN CHARGE. He had a dark face, made darker by serious eyes and heavy eyebrows and a mustache.

There was no photograph of Oona.

"Dizey's Dish" was located, as always, on page ten.

The loathsome preppie Jim Delancey who less than four short years ago treated the innocent body of a young girl with a brutality you would hesitate to show a wad of pizza dough, is back on the streets, and the morbidly curious and strong of stomach can catch his act—as a salad chef at Archibald's.

And how did this sickening turn of events come about?

Because under pressure from a certain highly placed and usually more responsible citizen, the parole board voted early freedom to this killer.

And to what secure facility did they entrust this menace?

Why, to his family. Which is to say, to the Marsh and Bonner's saleswoman who somehow, with or without the help of her ex-husband the railway switchman, managed to come up with the fees to pay for the defense that so slandered the memory of an angel and destroyed the marriage of Leigh Baker, one of the finest and most beloved actresses this world knows.

The paper slid from Leigh's hand to the counter. The image of her dead daughter rose up in her brain. For a moment she could not master her thoughts. They were like a knife turning in a raw wound.

Back in her bedroom she lifted the phone receiver and punched out Dizey Duke's number.

"Yeah?" Dizey's voice came on the line—bright and brash as a Texas fanfare.

"Dizey, it's Leigh."

"Just let me get rid of this jerk on the other line." There was a silence and then a click and then Dizey was back. "Did you like the plug I gave you in the column?"

"Dizey, who got Delancey out of prison?"

Dizey didn't answer.

"Come on, Dizey, the parole board didn't rise up in one body and say the Holy Ghost has commanded us to free Jim Delancey."

"I wouldn't know. I'm not on the parole board."

"Please don't give me that."

"Would you rather I say that as a journalist I don't reveal sources? Okay—I'm a journalist and I don't reveal sources."

"If that barbarian had been in prison where he belonged, I hope you realize Oona would be alive today."

"If you know that for a fact, you've got a better Ouija board than I do."

"I know it for a fact and so do you."

"Listen, Leigh, I did you a favor today, and why don't you do me one and say good-bye right now, and we'll forget this conversation ever happened."

■ ■ ■

"DIZEY DUKE IS THE *prima donna assoluta* of foul temper." Dick Braidy was all forgiveness and smiles. "All you can do when she gets that way is run for cover."

Leigh knew he didn't mean a word of it, any more than she'd really meant it when she'd blown up at him on the phone. He was only saying what he thought she needed to hear. She appreciated the kindness, but he was missing her point. "It's not the argument that upsets me."

"Of course it upsets you," Dick Braidy said. "You never hang up on me and you *never* tell me to go to hell if you're not *deeply* upset."

They were sitting in the chintz-filled living room of Dick Braidy's midtown penthouse. A milky light spilled through the glass wall that separated them from the trellised terrace.

"So please," Dick Braidy said, "please clarify for me. How did one little phone call with Dizey manage to work you into such a state? Honey, under all that glamour, you look *dreadful*."

Sometimes her ex-husband amazed her. It was as though he had no conception of what she'd been through yesterday. She lifted her glass to the light and frowned through the ripples of club soda and lime. "Looks like someone melted down an old Coke bottle."

"Someone did. His name is Jorge Sintera of Now Design, and these very tumblers are featured in the upcoming *New York Times Magazine* cover interview with Prince Frederick of Denmark."

She found herself staring at Dick Braidy with his thinning, neatly combed-back gray-blond hair. His alert, humorous eyes, blinking behind Paris-designed bifocals, reminded her of two gray-green marbles. "How do you always manage to keep up with everything?"

"It's not that hard if you're willing to devote twenty-five hours a day to it. But I believe the subject was Dizey and you."

Leigh twisted the glass between both hands and studied the miniature whirlpool she had created. "Dizey knows who got Jim Delancey out of prison, and she won't tell me."

There was a play of small muscles in Dick Braidy's forehead. "Now, just come *off* it. This is *me* you're talking to, toots. That was a half-blind item in the column today. She does it all the time— pure bluff. And besides, what good would it do you to know? What happens then? You sue the penal system?"

"This is going to sound crazy." Leigh set down her glass and wrapped her arms around herself, hugged herself close. "I could never tell anyone else—they'd think I was paranoid."

Dick Braidy guffawed. "But it's okay to tell me, because I was married to you for three years, and I *know* you're paranoid. Okay. Let the craziness commence. I'm all ears."

"Jim Delancey killed Oona."

The silence in the room changed. The muffled sound of traffic twelve stories below seemed to fade.

Dick Braidy sank into his armchair as though he'd been pushed. "And how do you know that? Did you just happen to stroll past the open door of the changing room and see it?"

"Of course not. Please don't do that to me, Dick." It hurt her to let anyone, even the closest of her ex-husbands, see what a frightened, needy, vulnerable little child she was, how aching and desperate to be reassured and, yes, believed. "I don't know it, I just feel it."

He sat with an expression of wanting intensely to understand. "Look, toots, I can state from personal experience, you're second to none in the intuition department. Now, if you're trying to put that killer back in prison where he belongs, *brava*. You can count on me to stand right beside you. But feelings are not going to do the trick in a court of law."

"I'm not the only one who feels it. The police feel it too."

He watched her with those quietly aware eyes. "And what makes you think that?"

"A long talk with the lieutenant who's heading the task force."

"So they've given poor old Oona a task force, have they? Well, it's the least she deserves."

"The *police* don't even know who got Delancey out and Dizey does and she's treating it like a gossipy little exclusive."

"After today's column don't think for a minute the police won't ask Dizey a question or two."

"She'll say freedom of the press and take her case to TV."

"Granted, Dizey has been known to possess a streak of opportunism . . ." Dick Braidy ran the tip of his finger around the rim of his glass.

"You could find out," Leigh said. "You know how to handle her."

"That I do. Dizey and I are dish buddies from way back." He sat there nodding at her. His gaze seemed laden with concern. "Do you know what you should do, hon? You should really consider joining my gym. The workouts are absolute psychotherapy, and they cost a third of what a shrink charges."

She rose from her chair. "You know, Dick, when you treat me like an idiot, it's like a telegram saying that part of me just died."

He leapt to his feet. He stood staring at her and he had an honestly bewildered look on his face. "Sweetie, I was just thinking out loud how to help you."

"I've told you how you could help. Good-bye, Dick."

He walked with her into the hallway. They reached the front door.

"That better not have been an angry good-bye."

"It wasn't." She sighed. "Even when I hate you, I can't stay angry. You're the only man in my life who makes me laugh."

"And that had better be a compliment. Kiss kiss?"

She angled her cheek, and he gave her a peck and a quick little two-finger wave. He stood in the open doorway till the elevator came and she stepped in.

What a great gal, he was thinking, *in her way.*

He closed the door and hurried to the kitchen. On the shelf above the telephone, two sixty-four-dollar bottles of olive oil were positioned with their labels and price stickers facing out.

He lifted the receiver and pushed the memory button where he had programmed Dizey Duke's unlisted number. "Dizey, toots, *c'est moi.* I've just had the most amazing talk with Leigh."

"Lucky you."

"She told me something you really ought to know about. I think our poor Betty Ford grad has flipped out. Either that or gone back to the sauce. Got a minute?"

· EIGHT ·

THE THUMB PULLED BACK HER EYELIDS one at a time. It was not a gentle thumb. "Notice we have marked hemorrhaging in the eyes," Dan Hippolito said.

The woman's face was turned toward the ceiling, and for an instant, with her eyelids open, she was looking directly at Cardozo. The eye whites were densely speckled with tiny red veins, like shrimp that needed cleaning.

Maybe Cardozo just imagined it, but he started to see things in that dead gaze—pain and fear and the certainty of death in all its undiluted brute force. He was reminded of a steer in a slaughterhouse at the instant the vacuum gun was held to its brains.

Suddenly the smell in the room came at him in a wave—formaldehyde and decayed human tissue—a stench at once acrid and sickeningly sweet.

"Strangled?" Cardozo said.

Dan Hippolito held up a finger—playing the moment like a schoolteacher. Dan Hippolito was a tough, wiry, narrow-faced man with dark, receding hair, one of the most experienced M.D.s of the city's medical examiner's office. "The pressure applied to her throat was enough to cause the *onset* of strangulation. But strangling didn't kill her. What killed her was this."

Dan Hippolito's moving finger indicated the ear-to-ear gash across the throat.

"Most probable scenario, the killer approached from the victim's rear, got a left-handed armlock around her neck. With knife clasped in his right hand, he drew the blade across her throat, from left to right—severing the windpipe and the carotid. Because of the way the head was held, sufficient blood flowed back into the throat to drown her.

"The killer then delivered a second stroke laterally across the victim's throat, right to left, intersecting the first stroke."

Dan Hippolito pointed out the second stroke—a clear gash *x*-ing across the first so that the woman appeared to be wearing a necklace of two ribbons of dull black velvet.

"These two strokes killed her. The rest is window dressing."

Dan Hippolito lifted back the sheet, and Cardozo's not-quite-believing gaze took in what Dan Hippolito called window dressing. "Now, notice the knife marks on the abdomen are roughly horizontal, four on the left side and only one, the bottom-most, on the right—five cuts in all, spaced roughly an inch apart. These are shallow cuts, but one of them—the third cut down—perforates the abdominal wall."

To Cardozo the parallel pattern of cuts seemed intentional, not random. He tried to fathom the purpose behind the pattern. After a moment his eye went to the right breastbone, to a three-inch-square area sprinkled with puncture wounds. In execution these were totally different from the horizontal cuts, as though here a crazed staple gun had attacked her.

Cardozo nodded toward the area. "What was he trying to reach?"

"The liver is all you'd find down there. But they don't penetrate. They're jabs—very fast, shallow."

"But it's as though he had a purpose."

"Absolutely. He's not just doodling. The parallel cuts are approximately even in spacing. They took time. Possibly he was marking the body."

"Why?"

"I've seen something similar in drug-cartel hits. The killer trademarks the body to prove he was the one who took her out. Or he marks her as a warning to anyone else who's thinking of crossing the cartel."

"Have you ever seen these markings on a drug-hit victim?"

"Not these exact markings. But each killer and cartel have their own trademark. It could be a newcomer."

"And what do the marks mean if it's not a drug hit?"

Dan Hippolito shook his head. "Couldn't tell you. Mind reading is your department."

Mentally Cardozo tried to resurrect the woman on the table. Alive, she would have had bright blue eyes, the desperately cheerful look of the overage all-American debutante. She would have been perky and she would have wanted to be liked.

He noticed something wrong about the cuts. All over the body the postautopsy sutures had pulled the flesh into tiny pleats. His eye went back to the throat cuts, and he noticed the same curious effect. In twenty years of seeing dead people in all possible degrees of being hacked apart and stitched back together, he had never seen a corpse with so much pursing of skin along the cuts.

"What's all the puckering where she's cut?"

There was a wedge of silence, and Dan Hippolito's deep brown eyes seemed to withdraw their gaze just a little from the world. "There's just a little more body tissue missing than the cuts can account for. Did you find any tissue at the scene?"

"There wasn't any tissue at the scene. Just blood. Plenty of that."

Dan Hippolito shrugged, and the shrug was tinged with acceptance of all things ugly and remarkable in the medical examiner's universe.

Cardozo stared at the dead woman with the missing tissue. A murmur cut into his wondering, a hissing echo that he recognized: the sound of a catheter pump draining the blood from the cadaver two tables down. He took out his notebook and began making a little sketch of the cuts on Oona Aldrich.

"I can give you photos," Dan Hippolito said. "Come on."

In the corridor they passed morgue personnel and medical examiners and med-school students wearing white cotton jackets of varying degrees of uncleanliness.

Dan Hippolito unlocked the door to his office and, motioning Cardozo inside, flipped on a ceiling fan that brought in a buzz of air from an overhead vent. "Coffee?" he offered.

"Why not."

Dan Hippolito snapped off his skintight plastic autopsy gloves. On his way to the small coffee maker that was quietly burping in the corner, he dropped the gloves into the wastebasket.

Cardozo looked around the little room. There was a reproduction of Van Gogh's sunflowers on the wall and the furniture was a mix of 1950s Scandinavian modern—showing its age—but even here the sharp odor of formaldehyde reminded you that you weren't in a living room in Queens.

"Hey, Dan, you need some fresh sunflowers. That picture looks like it's been standing in acid rain."

"In forensic medicine they don't give you a decorating budget."

"So why don't you change jobs?"

"In this field at least I'll never kill a patient."

The office was evidence of Dan Hippolito's commitment to a cheerful outlook. Against the far wall he had hung a closed curtain, as though even here, two levels below Second Avenue, there was a window and a sun so bright, it had to be kept out. In front of the curtain he had arranged a small forest of potted palms and corn plants. Gro-light played over the leaves as they stirred in the faintly rancid gusts of central air-conditioning.

Dan Hippolito came back with a tray on which he'd placed two plastic cups of black coffee, two pink packets of Sweet'n Low, a jar of generic powdered something that was meant to substitute for cream, and a tongue depressor to serve as a stir stick.

The two men settled themselves on opposite sides of the desk. Dan Hippolito slid three glossy photos across the desktop. Right, left, and center views of Oona Aldrich's abdominal cuts.

"Do I get to pick my favorite?" Cardozo asked.

"Take them all. I got plenty more." Dan Hippolito took a long swallow of coffee, then moved a blank sheet of paper to the center of the desk and began drawing lines. "To cut flesh out—as opposed to simply making a cut in flesh—you need a minimum of three cuts intersecting to form a triangle."

He had drawn a triangle, each of whose sides extended in both directions beyond the vertices. His pen began cross-hatching the area inside the triangle.

"With those three cuts, all the tissue inside the triangle is severed from the neighboring tissue—and can be extracted. But what we have in the case of Oona Aldrich is tissue that has been removed, with no indication that special cuts were made to remove it."

"So it was an accident? A by-product?"

"With what I've got now I can't figure how he did it." Dan Hippolito took another swallow of coffee. "It's not quite so hard to figure out how two pubic hairs got into the victim's mouth."

The words fell heavily into the silence.

"We also found semen in the victim's mouth. Right now the lab is examining the hairs and the semen. We should have results for you tomorrow."

Cardozo didn't move or say anything or even show he was reacting, but his mind just closed in on the implications. He began to see the killing as the ultimate kick-ass in a city where everybody was infringing on everybody else, and it got harder and harder to commit a cruelty that stood out.

"Well, Dan, which was it—did the killer force this woman to give him a blow job before he killed her? Or did he kill her and then have sex with her corpse?"

"I haven't got an answer to that."

Cardozo was swept by a marrow-deep surge of hatred for the person who had killed Oona Aldrich and for all his behavioral brothers—the people who did these things, who were out there right now doing more of them.

▪ ▪ ▪

"FROM THE BLOOD CELLS in the sperm we know he's type O." Lou Stein was standing by the window in Cardozo's cubicle, reading from his scrawled notes, because Cardozo hadn't wanted to wait for the lab report till Lou's typewriter got fixed. "And he has a very high, abnormally high, sperm count. That's about all that the fluids can tell us. However—" Lou flipped a page of his pocket-sized notebook and frowned a moment, deciphering his own hasty hieroglyphics. "The pubic hairs tell us he's technically Caucasian."

"Only technically?" Cardozo said.

"Caucasian isn't a strict category. One man's Caucasian is apt to be another man's something else."

Lou Stein had won a Purple Heart in Korea, and he still carried himself like a soldier. In the department he'd gained himself a reputation as a hard, reliable worker. He rarely talked tough or acted it, but he'd never yielded so much as a blade of grass in a turf war. Lab work was a sacred trust to him, and he'd never fudged a report, not even to save a colleague's pension. Going by the rules, doing the job, was Lou's ethic, and Cardozo could see that, in a small way, it pained him to be reading from notes instead of a completed lab form.

"This fellow is very dark-haired," Lou said. "And if you go by statistical stereotype, probably olive-skinned."

Jim Delancey is dark-haired, Cardozo thought. *On the other hand, he's fair-skinned . . .*

"You would also expect brown eyes. Of course, there can be exceptions."

Delancey has blue eyes. But he could be an exception.

"Now, here's something," Lou said, "that could give us a socio-economic fix on the perpetrator. There are trace amounts of kerosene on his pubic hair."

"I take it kerosene is some kind of kinky lubricant?"

"I doubt it very much. If you used kerosene as a lubricant, you'd feel you were washing your balls in acid. Why do you think it's such a popular torture in Central America?"

The air conditioner picked that moment to give a rattle like wheels not quite making their tracks, followed by a snap of metal hitting something it wasn't supposed to hit. Cardozo reached across the cubicle and flicked it off.

"The only reason you'd want kerosene anywhere near your pubes," Lou said, "is to kill parasites, and the only parasites that inhabit the pubes in these latitudes are crab lice. Kerosene's the traditional folk-wisdom remedy."

"What kind of folk are we talking?"

"Poor folk—very poor folk—poor whites, poor blacks, poor Hispanics. Rich people don't get crab lice—except in the armed services and prison. If and when your average middle-class Joe gets crabs, he's apt to use prescription kerosene and he probably doesn't know it's kerosene."

"Was our man using prescription kerosene?"

"Definitely not. This stuff was straight from the hardware store."

"Did it work?"

"On the hairs I saw there weren't even nits, which indicates he's pretty clean. When I lasered the hair I *did* find two green lines in the spectrograph."

"Meaning?"

A mischievous spark came into Lou's blue eyes. "Possibly the donor has been burning his food in copper-bottomed pots for—oh, the last two hundred years."

"Isn't the sperm count a little high for a two-hundred-year-old man?"

"Or he's doing cocaine."

Cardozo nodded. This would put the perpetrator solidly in the mainstream of Americans who had decided to run their lives on a daily diet of chemical enhancement. "Like eighty percent of the criminals in this town."

"Heavier. Coke like this, to show up in the spectrograph like this, our man has got major access to the stuff. We're talking five-, six-hundred-dollars-a-day street price." Lou's lids lowered a moment over his eyes. "On the other hand, the kerosene says he's not that rich. But that's your problem, not mine."

"What problem? He started poor, he got rich, but he never forgot the old folkways."

"I thought of that, but I really have trouble seeing this guy as rich."

"From one pubic hair he's not rich?"

Lou held up two fingers. "Two pubic hairs."

"So how does he get the coke?"

"Could be he's tied into the business."

Cardozo ran the idea through his mind, poking for holes. "I have trouble with that. A wacko wouldn't be working for the coke cartel."

"I have to agree he's not a good employment risk. In terms of brain function there's no question this man is diminished. Where magnesium should show in the spectrograph there's a gap, so he's washing the magnesium out of his system before it can be deposited in the hair cells."

"What does that mean in English?"

"He has a habitually high alcohol or caffeine intake, or both."

"Like ninety percent of the inhabitants of New York."

"Worse than ninety percent. You only see gaps like this in the spectrographs of Skid Row bums and members of Alcoholics Anonymous."

"No one in AA would be doing coke," Cardozo said.

"Again, that's a behavioral question. More your line than mine."

"What about the stuff in the wastebasket?"

"Unfortunately the candle is such a common item that it tells us very little. It's a Saffire-brand commercial *Shabbes* candle, available in any supermarket in New York."

"Any prints?"

"Too smudged to recover."

"How long did it burn?"

"We burned an identical candle under lab conditions, and what we came up with is nineteen, twenty seconds."

Cardozo ran the scenario through his mental movieola: The killer went into the changing room, killed Oona, lit a candle, let it burn for twenty seconds, tossed it into the wastebasket. Why?

"The pins and pink tissue paper were the wrapping on a blouse that a customer had discarded in the morning, and the stereo ad was clipped from yesterday's morning edition of the *New York Trib.*"

"The stereo ad?" Cardozo said. "You mean Dizey Duke's society column."

Lou shrugged. "The column was on the back." He clearly

couldn't conceive of anyone wanting to read, let alone clip out, any of Dizey Duke's five-times-a-week scribblings. "No prints."

"What about the boom box?" Cardozo said. "Any luck?"

"The boom box looks like a bridge fell on it. Hard to be sure, but it appears to be a Sony XX."

"Come on, Lou. I found the damned thing. There's no *appearing* about it. The trademark says Sony, loud and clear."

Lou glanced across the cubicle with just a flash of impatience. "Sorry, I wasn't being clear. It's a Sony that appears to be an XX. The model went on sale in the metropolitan area nine months ago. Two hundred and some outlets carry it."

Cardozo sighed and looked down at the scratch pad he'd been doodling on. He'd drawn five horizontal, more or less parallel lines. The bottom line lay slightly to the left of the others. "Any prints?" His hand added a sprinkle of dots in the upper left-hand corner of the design.

"There are partials all over it," Lou said. "Once we eliminate the prints of the security guards, who knows, maybe our man left a few. But what we did find is a tape. What's interesting is, he recorded it himself. Did a piss-poor job too. He took some rap music off the air or from another tape. Our sound man thinks he recorded over something else."

"Can our sound man tell us what kind of something else was recorded on this tape?"

"Maybe you should talk to him yourself. He explains it a hell of a lot better than I can."

■ ■ ■

"WHAT WE'VE GOT ON THE TAPE," Abner Love said, "are rap recordings taken from another tape—so there's hiss and accumulated signal distortion." Abner was a middle-aged skinhead with hair that would have been light brown if he'd let it grow out, but with a considerable tonsure, which maybe was why he didn't.

"Can you identify the original tapes?" Cardozo said.

"Now, you're not going to believe this—but my little kid is a fan of rap music, and he has the original tape."

They were sitting in Abner's work space on East Thirty-second Street, a loft with walls banked from floor to ceiling with high-tech sound equipment. Abner handed Cardozo a commercial tape cassette.

The front cover showed five white men who looked like younger Abners hunkered down around a floor mike on a bare stage. The album was called *Hallelujah Dirt*. The artists called themselves the Celestial Honkies and Roscoe.

Cardozo shook his head. "My kid's fifteen, she doesn't bring much of this stuff into the house anymore." He didn't bother saying, I'd murder her if she did.

"For my money they're no big deal, but *Hallelujah Dirt* went platinum six days after release."

Abner slid another cassette across the worktable. This one was commercial home-recording tape, Sony X-90, with no writing on either label on either side.

"Now, the boom-box tape," Abner said, "was recorded on a poor machine with imperfect sound-head contact. So areas on the tape retain magnetic residue from an earlier recording made on a different machine." Abner looked across the table at Cardozo. "Are you with me so far?"

"I think so."

Abner smiled. "When we play the boom-box tape, we're hearing a composite signal. But since we have the original of the rap tape, we can subtract that signal from the composite signal—and theoretically that leaves us the pure residue of the previous signal."

"The way you say *theoretically* doesn't sound too hopeful."

"Why don't I play you a little of what we've reconstructed so far?" Abner walked to the wall and flicked a switch, and three oscilloscopes lit up with amber grids laid over black backgrounds. A kind of spacious silence poured from the speakers mounted around the room.

In a moment dots like comets trailing three-inch tails made flat-line graphs across the grids. He flicked two more switches, and bright lariats of light danced across the screens.

The sound that poured from the speakers struck Cardozo as garbage made audible—screams, uh-huh's, baby-baby-baby's, clicks, bangs, drum machines, voices high, voices low, voices screeching like people getting born, people getting laid, people getting killed, people jiving, jibbering, singing English, Spanish, Korean, fading in and out—till finally a chant rose above the river of sonic chaos:

> *Nickel-dimin' two-bit pipsqueak squirt,*
> *Bleedin' Thursday blood on your Tuesday shirt—*
> *Spilled a pint of plasma and you still don't hurt,*
> *'Cause your head's in the heart of the hallelujah dirt.*

Abner strolled from wall to wall, manipulating dials and switches, and by a series of almost imperceptible shifts the sound tamped down into a structureless aural foam, and then—in some unexpected corner of that immensity of white noise, hints of another sound began to cluster.

Cardozo focused his ear on that little smidgin of sound.

Abner's finger nudged one last switch.

Now Cardozo heard it: a bright, high beep lasting maybe half a second.

Abner stopped the tape. "Recognize it?"

Was this a quiz show? Name that tune in one note? "I Left My Heart in San Francisco"? The "Hallelujah Chorus"?

Cardozo shook his head. "Sorry."

Abner smiled like the kind of guy who enjoyed having the answer that no one else did. "It's the signal an answering machine makes when a call comes in. It's a high frequency, and on a cheap machine it scars the magnetic coating. You can't record over a scar, which is why we can recover the signal. So at least we know what we're looking for."

Maybe Abner knew, but Cardozo didn't. "And what's that?"

"The in-coming messages buried under 'Hallelujah Dirt.'"

"Think you can actually pull up the messages?"

"It'll take time, but something's got to be there. At least a fragment. Possibly a range of fragments. Once we have those we put the computer to work and enhance. Same principle as your outer-space photos enhancement, except that program translates sound to light and ours translates sound to better sound. Theoretically."

· NINE ·

"VERY ROUGHLY," Ellie Siegel said, "from what I could worm out of the lawyers, if the stock market and real estate don't crash too badly in the near future, Oona Aldrich's estate is worth around seven million."

Greg Monteleone whistled.

"Who inherits?" Cardozo said.

He had gathered his task force in the spare room that the detective squad used as an extra office and storage space. The chairs they were sitting in were parochial-school surplus, wood-slatted collapsibles that had tortured generations of students; but Ellie held herself easily erect in her pale pink blouse, as though she were comfortable with her body, comfortable with the chair, comfortable even with the humidity. Though an air conditioner was clattering in the window, the air had a disturbingly unreal density.

"Oona's only immediate relative," Ellie said, "is her son by the first marriage. He gets half. A quarter goes to the Metropolitan Opera. There are cash bequests to servants, friends, local charities."

"What's the largest cash bequest?"

"The butler, the cook, and the maid get two hundred fifty thousand each. There are bequests of twenty thousand each to three friends."

"Doesn't sound as though Oona had many good friends," Sam Richards said.

"But she had great servants." With a satisfied grin Greg Monteleone pushed his hands through his curly dark hair and sat back and eyed the others. He was wearing designer chinos, Top-Siders, and an eye-curdling deep heliotrope shirt.

"What about property?" Cardozo said.

"No property bequests," Ellie said.

In the crammed, narrow room sounds seemed to hammer at the light. From the street came a gray, constant roar of cars, trucks, busses, and above them the looping wail of a siren. The precinct added its own little orchestra: through the pea-soup green walls you could hear phones jangling for attention, voices shouting, doors closing, footsteps clacking up and down the stairs, the high-pitched sigh of waterpipes.

"Where's the son?" Cardozo said.

"He's in England," Ellie said. "He's studying Classics at Oxford. I phoned him at six A.M. this morning. He and his mother were estranged. He says he's renouncing any inheritance and don't expect him at the funeral."

"Nut case," Monteleone said. "Who's going to pay the college bills?"

Ellie gave him a long, unloving glance. "The boy happens to have a father."

"So do I," said Greg, "and he never gave me a cent."

"But Greg," Ellie said, "you've always been special."

"Ellie, you'd better check that the son was in England Wednesday," Cardozo said. "Check the servants' whereabouts Wednesday. And check the previous wills—see if anyone was dropped."

"She had two ex-husbands," Ellie said, "but they're richer than she was."

"Check the exes' whereabouts yesterday. Did you find her address book?"

"It wasn't hiding—she'd left it right by the bedroom phone. I think it was her favorite bedtime reading. The bottleneck is, Aldrich never threw out a return address. She entered her Con Ed account manager into her personal phone book. Half the names aren't even alphabetical."

"Sorry to hear it. Question her friends in the New York area. And her doctor. If she had a shrink, question the shrink. If she had a personal trainer, an astrologist—anyone providing any kind of personalized service—talk to them too."

Ellie was taking it all down in her notebook. She wrote in a shorthand of her own invention that she'd once tried to explain to Cardozo, but he'd never understood how she could tell one of those squiggles from another.

"Do I get permission to sleep anytime this week?"

"I've asked Reilly to give us more detectives. Discuss it with them."

Ellie winked. "You're funny today, Vince."

Cardozo sat frowning at the blackboard that had been set up on an easel at the front of the room. The words *Oona Aldrich Homicide* had been blockprinted across the top, followed by the identifying numbers that would be used on all departmental forms referring to the case.

Beneath this Cardozo had written the forensic number assigned to the case, and below, on the left, he had listed the physical evidence so far discovered: a partial candle, a newspaper clipping, a shattered boom box, particles of dirt, a Sony answering-machine tape, seven Duracell batteries, an eighth battery listed separately because it had been found separately, the victim's clothing, and the personal effects she had carried in her purse. Beside each item he had written the property number of the voucher attached.

On the right of the board he had written the word *witnesses,* followed by the names Baker, Sandberg, Hansen, Delancey, Danks, and a question mark. There was still plenty of space in the witness column.

In the center of the board he had drawn a rough layout of the changing room and a stick figure representing the position of Aldrich's body.

Only two things on the entire board suggested there had been a rational motive for the crime: the missing brooch and, assuming they were a cartel trademark, the knife cuts on the body. Photos of Leigh Baker's brooch had gone out to all precincts and all jewelers in the city. On the chance that the killer might not be too bright, photos had gone to pawnshops as well. So far no one in Narcotics had recognized the cuts.

"Let me just throw out an idea," Cardozo said. "Dan Hippolito thinks the markings on Oona's stomach could mean it was a drug hit."

"Did she do coke?" Sam Richards said.

Ellie nodded. "Her butler says she dabbled."

"No way Oona was a drug hit," Greg Monteleone said. "The drug cartel doesn't go after its customers. It disciplines the middle men and the street retailers."

Cardozo glanced questioningly toward Ellie. "Any chance Oona was dealing?"

"Come on," Greg Monteleone groaned. "The woman was a wacko. She wouldn't have lasted ten minutes in the cartel."

Ellie sighed. "I haven't seen any evidence she was anything more than an occasional user."

Cardozo turned to Sam Richards. "Sam, how are we coming?"

Sam Richards pulled a notebook from the pocket of his blue blazer. "Jogging pouches aren't manufactured in the city."

"Nothing's manufactured in the city," Greg Monteleone said, "except crack and illegitimate babies."

Sam Richards prided himself on dressing like a gentleman, jacket and tie always, never a scuff on his shoes; and he'd mastered a cool lack of excitability to go with the dress. He gazed now at Greg Monteleone with no more involvement than the anchor on a TV news show. "Do we want to take a comedy break, or do we want to hear my report?"

"Greg will get his turn," Cardozo said.

Sam Richards continued. "Red jogging pouches with black *flamingo* stitching are made by Pedro Cardin of Taiwan, they're ripped off by Petro Cardin of Manila, they're imported into the metropolitan area by Jolly Boy Imports of East New York, and they're bootlegged by Nordic Novelty of Bushwick."

Richards had the sort of smooth African skin that seems to sweat nothing but after-shave lotion. His eyes were brown and large, and a relaxed cynicism flickered in them. As he flipped through his pages he allowed a weary smile to peep through. Every detective in the room knew that most homicide investigations were hopeless until a witness came forward or the killer gave himself up.

"Jolly Boy supplies four jobbers who wholesale to four hundred thirteen outlets. Nordic Novelty doesn't keep records."

"Under the circumstances," Cardozo said, "let's back-burner the pouches. How are we coming with sporting-goods outlets?"

"In the metropolitan area," Sam Richards said, "there are sixty-seven outlets selling those weight-lifter belts and gloves. I spoke to eighteen yesterday. Nobody recognizes the Identi-Kits or the photo."

"Fellas, we are making a fundamentally asshole assumption here." Greg Monteleone never used a word like *wrong* in front of Ellie when a word like *asshole* would do. "Why is this guy going to buy an item he could walk into any gym and rip off?"

"I was getting to gyms," Sam Richards said. "High rents have put most commercial outfits out of business. There are only about thirty left in the five boroughs. But if we're talking high school gyms and private school gyms, add a hundred twenty."

"Mr. Boom Box does not go to private school," Greg Monteleone stated flatly. "And I frankly doubt he goes to *any* school."

"Because he looks Hispanic you don't think he has an education?" Ellie challenged.

Greg Monteleone sprawled one arm over the back of his folding wooden chair. He studied Siegel with elaborate, almost theatrical disdain. "Because he acts like a jerk I know he doesn't have an education, and so do you."

"Not that I don't trust Greg's intuition," Cardozo said, "but let's still check schools."

Sam Richards sighed. "I'm only one pair of feet, Vince."

"Reilly said he can steal us two men."

"Big spender," Greg Monteleone said.

"What about me?" Ellie said.

"You get the next two." Cardozo turned in his swivel chair. "Okay, Greg. You've got the mike."

Monteleone stretched his arms overhead and yawned. "I knocked on a lot of doors in the Marsh and Bonner's area yesterday." He consulted his notepad. "Nothing useful. Two maybes on the female Identi-Kit, one on the male, nothing on Delancey. Vince, are we working to rule on this? Do you want a five on every interview?"

Regulations required a written report on every witness or potential witness interviewed. Because the number of the report form ended in a five, cops called the reports fives, and they hated them.

"I think fives are a piss-poor idea when we've got these few hands," Greg said. "Witnesses remember forty-eight hours, tops, and then their imaginations begin playing tricks. Anytime we spend now typing up notes and filling out forms is time we could be tracking down a lead before it fizzles. I spoke to forty-four people yesterday, and if I was doing a five for every interview, I wouldn't have got through ten."

"Okay," Cardozo said. "But don't anyone get eight weeks backlogged on your fives. Maybe one day a week tidy up the paper work."

"You mean Sunday," Greg Monteleone said. "Our day off."

"There's no day off," Cardozo said. "We're working overtime." Cardozo turned to Carl Malloy. "Carl, what are we finding out about Jim Delancey?"

"Enough to fill a postage stamp." Malloy took out his notepad. "At eleven fifty-five yesterday morning, Delancey showed up for work, on foot and alone. At two forty-five he took a five-minute cigarette break, alone, outside the kitchen door. At three o'clock, figuring we're more interested in what he does after work then during, I took a four-hour break."

Today everything about Carl Malloy was just a little rumpled —the trousers of his brown suit, his shirt, his half-loosened tie. His hair was still dark on top, but it was going gray at the temples and it needed a combing. He didn't exactly look bad, but he missed neatness by just enough that it was a little embarrassing to look at him. You had the feeling he was basically a nice, careful guy, but maybe he'd argued with his boss or his wife and he'd momentarily mislaid his self-respect. People would instinctively look away from a guy like that, and it was the right look if you were running a tail on a suspect.

"I was back at Archibald's at seven. At eight-twenty Delancey left, alone, and went home, on foot, to Twenty-nine Beekman Place."

"This guy's a salad chef," Greg Monteleone said, "and he lives on Beekman Place?"

"With his mother."

"What the hell do rents run over there?"

"You don't rent on Beekman Place," Malloy said. "You own."

"So what does this mother–son team own, a town house?"

"Two bedrooms on the ninth floor at number twenty-nine."

"Who paid?"

Malloy turned to beam Monteleone an acidic smile. "At the moment, Greg, I don't have that information, but if you like, I can phone Mrs. Delancey and ask."

"Did he talk to anyone on the way home?" Cardozo said. "Did he seem interested in any of the other people on the street?"

"He likes kids," Malloy said.

"Holy moly," Monteleone said, "we got us a molester."

"He smiles when he sees kids," Malloy said. "Why do I feel I'm defending this guy? Once or twice an adult went by with a child, and Delancey lit up. He didn't stop, he didn't stare, he didn't pull out a pocketful of candy. He just looked happy and kept walking. He was home at nine-oh-five. I hung around Beekman Place for two hours, and he didn't come out again. Vince, you said get a general idea what he's about and where he goes. Nobody mentioned a twenty-four-hour tail. I was getting a general idea he'd turned in for the night, and I was getting tired so I went home. I figured I'd pick him up again tonight after work and put in a full night staking him out. Unless you have other ideas?"

"No." Cardozo shook his head. "Keep going. Get a feel for what Jim Delancey is doing with his time." He turned now to Ellie Siegel. "Ellie, you're our resident expert on Judaica. If the killer lit a Jewish Sabbath candle, do you think he was Jewish?"

"It's a flaky question," she said. "But if you want a flaky answer—he wasn't Orthodox, because it's the job of the women in the house to light the candles, and the candles are lit on *Shabbes* eighteen minutes before sundown. Oona was killed on a weekday, not *Shabbes*, and she was killed in the early afternoon. I really can't see even a demented link with Jewish ritual here. But possibly the killer is Catholic. They don't sell votive candles in the supermarket so maybe he used a Jewish candle, which supermarkets in New York do carry."

"Ellie's a sly one," Greg Monteleone said. "She's going to blame it on us."

"Greg," Ellie said, "this is not an us-versus-them issue. Or do you still believe matzohs are made of Christian children's blood?"

"Which brand?"

"You're going to get me angry, Greg."

Ellie and Greg seemed to have a TV comedy act going— Greg would come on the fascist pig, and Ellie would play the outraged liberal. Cardozo had nothing against the act, but he didn't need it on company time.

"Okay." Cardozo placed both hands on the edge of the desk and stood. "Clock's ticking. Back to the hunt, guys."

Ellie did not leave with the others. "Vince, something's been bothering me."

"I don't want to hear about Greg. You two please just try to get along."

"You're not going to hear about Greg. Not from me." She laid a Xerox of a news clipping on the desk.

Cardozo's eyes went down to the heading, "Dizey's Dish" . . . He skimmed, taking in *solitaire-cut apples en salade* and *thrilled with her new Dauphine-Pléïade by Zelziac of Cologne, the ritziest bidet in the world, but you knew that.*

He recognized the column that had showed up in the wastebasket in the changing room. Now his eye came to the paragraph Ellie had highlighted in yellow.

Starting today at 10 A.M., everyone who is anyone and that includes Mrs. Charles Evremonde and Petra ("Slim") Paley, will be dropping in on the second floor at Marsh and Bonner's to see the divine little boutique that Ingrid Hansen just opened, specializing in casual, chic summer loafing clothes. If you're looking for a fair-weather silk scarf, look no farther!

"This must be the twentieth time I've read it," Cardozo said. "Still seems like a straightforward paid plug to me. What am I missing?"

"Vince, you lack what I'd call a certain fast-track sensibility." Ellie smiled. "There are those who do it, and then there are those who read about it because they can't afford to do it and wouldn't know how to, even if they struck oil. I find it a real wrong note that this item shows up in that wastebasket."

"How so?"

"Dizey Duke is a nonstop commercial masquerading as an insider society column. She syndicates her scam in eighty-some tabloids nationwide, right after the sex crimes and just before the hernia-truss ads. The people who shop at Marsh and Bonner's don't take her advice—they laugh at it."

"I thought she was sort of respected."

"Come off it, Vince. When Dizey Duke goes north, *they* stampede south. When Dizey's in Morocco noshing couscous with Malcolm Forbes, *they're* in Marietta Tree's garden nibbling blinis. If the people Dizey writes about take *any* advice besides one another's, it's *Vogue's* and *Harper's*."

"So you're telling me this clipping didn't belong to any of the customers who changed in that room."

"Not on your life."

"Then whose was it?"

"The killer's."

■ ■ ■

THEY WERE DISCUSSING DICK BRAIDY and her troublesome, contradictory feelings toward her ex-husband.

"I don't know why I got so angry at him," Leigh said.

Luddie handed her a cup of coffee. "Because he's earned your anger."

She shook her head. "No. He was really very sweet and concerned. He even tried to persuade me to exercise with his trainer."

"I take it he's still going to that jet-set gym?"

She nodded. "It must take terrific discipline. He's absolutely determined to get himself into shape."

"You mean he's absolutely determined to butter up the celebrities who go there."

She took a chair by the window of Luddie's living room and sat gazing out at the city. Beyond the glass, spires threw off sparkling points of light. "You have a truly low opinion of Dick."

Luddie gazed at her across the tips of his steepled fingers. "Does that surprise you?"

"Yes. And it hurts me. If you don't respect the people I respect, then you don't really respect me, and what's the point our even talking?"

"Leigh, this innocence of yours is wearing awfully thin. *I* know you don't even like this idiot. How come *you* don't know it?"

For a moment she felt lost. "Luddie, I resent that. I love him —I do—"

"And do you always divorce the people you love?"

"To save our friendship, yes. He's probably the best friend I ever had."

"He's a best friend like all the ten thousand other best friends in your life. Which is to say, you don't even know the guy."

She fixed disquieted eyes on Luddie. She realized he was attacking her, and she couldn't understand why. "That's a very distorted view of me and my life."

"Name me one good trait Dick Braidy possesses."

"He's generous. He's funny. He's a good listener. He's a great escort. Every woman in town swears by him."

"You mean he's a tattle-tale with the most indiscreet tongue in Manhattan."

"In all Dick Braidy's life, he has *never* spoken against a friend."

"You actually believe what you just said." Luddie's hand hesitated and it was a telling hesitation. "May I read to you from today's 'Dizey's Dish'?" He bent down to pick up that morning's *Trib* from the floor. He folded it open to a middle page.

A prominent actress-socialite, who has had no trouble convincing millions in her twenty-some starring screen roles, can't get New York State's star-chamber of a parole board or the city's disaster of police department to take her seriously. The beauty with the moss-green gaze has evidence that a certain convicted killer was prematurely paroled and at least one Manhattan figure has paid the price —with her life.

Leigh's first reaction wasn't shock, it was pure denial: she'd heard wrong. "You're kidding. You're making that up."

Luddie sat calm as a television anchorperson reporting live from the scene of someone else's catastrophe. He shook his head.

Shock slowly crystallized into understanding. "Shit. You're not kidding. She really printed that."

"And unless it was you that gave that story to Dizey, it couldn't have been anyone but your beloved ex."

"Look, he didn't mean it. She wormed it out of him."

"I don't buy it. Dick Braidy isn't a victim of some gossip columnist's cunning—he's a broker on the same exchange. He purveys rumor and hot poop to buttress his own social power, and the victim, my friend, is you." Luddie laid the newspaper down and stared at her. "And I mean that literally. A real killer has really killed, and Dick Braidy is telling the world that you're ready to finger the guy."

"What do you expect me to do about it?"

"What can you do, except your best? Don't drink, don't skip meetings, don't walk down dark alleys alone, and don't talk anymore to your ex."

■ ■ ■

LEIGH'S HEAD ACHED. She felt tired and she didn't want sunlight. She closed the curtain and switched on the bedside lamp.

The soft yellow light cast a circle of warmth that touched the edge of the quilted spread and the Tiffany traveling clock and the telephone, her own private telephone perched on its own private answering machine.

I do have real friends, she thought. *I do.*

Something clicked like the snap of a tiny mousetrap. The green light on her answering machine registered an incoming call. Before she could lift the receiver, her own recorded voice cut in. "Hello, thank you for calling."

"Oh, do shut up," she told the voice.

The beep finally came. She snatched up the receiver. "Hello, it's me, not the machine."

No one answered. From somewhere beneath her, traffic along Fifth Avenue sent a muffled vibration through the quiet cool.

"Hello, I'm on the line, who is this?"

A hang up, she thought. But the machine would have beeped if they'd hung up. *A wrong number. Someone who doesn't recognize my voice. Someone who doesn't speak English.*

She held the receiver closer. Just beyond the blanket of faint sound she sensed a disturbance, an unevenness in the flow of silence.

"Hello," she said. "Who is this? Look, if you've got the wrong number, hang up. If you don't speak English, just say so."

There was no hang up, no words in a foreign tongue. Just that same false silence.

"What are you waiting for? What do you want? *Who is this?*"

She jiggled the cradle. The connection broke. She sat for a moment listening to the hum of a dial tone, then laid the receiver again in its cradle.

Curious now, she pushed the Replay button on the answering machine.

A beep came out of the tiny speaker, and then a silence like the flow of water from a small tap, and then her own voice, like a radio signal imperfectly recovered from the past.

And then that silence.

She boosted the volume as high as it would go. The silence seemed to exhale and then inhale, exhale and inhale.

I'm imagining it, she told herself. *It's just an old tape that needed replacing long ago, and there are ghosts of old phone calls buried on it.*

She leaned forward and pressed the Erase button.

· TEN ·

CARDOZO'S EYE RAN ALONG THE WALL where a dozen different-sized and different-shaped knives dangled from a row of iron hooks. They all had a similar pale hardwood handle.

"I see your knives are a set," he said.

The Korean nodded. "Good knives. French."

Cardozo had chosen Saturday to visit Archibald's kitchen, because it was one of Jim Delancey's two days off.

It was also, obviously, brunch day. Every order the waiters shouted through the Dutch door was eggs this or eggs that. The black cook was frying up an acre of Canadian bacon on the griddle. A teenage girl stood stirring a wooden spoon through a two-gallon double-boiler of hollandaise. She had skin so clean that Cardozo couldn't believe she'd been in the city longer than an hour.

"May I?" He unhooked the strangest-looking of the knives. It had a narrow blade twisted into a spiral, with serrations on both edges. "What does this one do?"

The Korean smiled. "Apples."

Cardozo tried to visualize the blade in action. *Whatever this knife does,* he wondered, *why would you want to do it to an apple?* He replaced the knife and touched another. "This one?"

"Trout."

"Just trout?"

The Korean nodded. He reached up and ran his hand along the row. "Salmon. Chicken. Potato. Carrot. Cabbage."

"Thanks." Cardozo didn't need the entire tour. "I get the idea." He unhooked the cabbage knife and angled it to the overhead light. The manufacturer's trademark had been etched into the side of the thin tempered-steel blade. "Jobert—you said that's a French name?"

"Fine knives."

Cardozo counted the blades on the wall. "Fourteen in a set?"

The Korean nodded toward the sink. "Twenty."

All Cardozo saw was a tub of water with dish edges and pot tops poking through a Sargasso of algae'd-looking scum. "Where did you buy them?"

The Korean shook his head. "Expensive. Not for home."

"Thanks for warning me, but where did you buy them?"

The Korean smiled. "Marsh and Bonner Epicure Shop. I write it down?"

"That's okay. I know the store."

▪ ▪ ▪

CARDOZO HAILED A CAB on Lexington. He timed the ride from Archibald's to Marsh and Bonner's. Eight minutes and forty seconds.

In the Epicure Shop a dark-eyed woman asked if she could help him.

"I'm interested in Jobert knives."

"The restaurant knives? They're very popular. And very useful in the home kitchen."

She went into a back room and returned carrying a three-foot case of pale hardwood that must have weighed forty pounds. She laid it carefully on the counter.

"There are twenty in a set, right?" Cardozo said.

"No, sir, there are twenty-one." She opened the case. Twenty-one knives nested in twenty-one individually shaped hollows.

Cardozo brought out his wallet. "Do you take MasterCard?"

·ELEVEN·

"NEW YORK CITY—accept no imitations." Greg Monteleone dropped a copy of the Sunday *Tribune* on Cardozo's desk. A two-inch-thickness of tabloid, stuffed with ad supplements and color comics and coupons, thudded onto a stack of unread departmental memos.

Cardozo put down his coffee cup. Staring up at him from the center of page one was a photo of Oona Aldrich. It must have been her deb photo—she looked seventeen and her ears and neck were holding up at least three hundred thousand in diamonds.

Running across the top of the tabloid, two-inch bold caps screamed:

SAM'S BACK!

Beneath the photo was the headline:

WHY HE KILLED HER:
TRIB RECEIVES SOCIETY KILLER'S SHOCKING LETTER

Inside, a smaller photograph showed what looked like a sheet of foolscap with cut-out letters pasted to it forming the words:

HI HI SOCIETY
JUST TO INTRODUCE MY ACT
I'M SOCIETY SAM KILLER OF SOCIETY SCUM
I STORM YOUR CHARGE CARD HEAVEN
SAM SAM THANK YOU MA'AM

KILL THE GIRLS AND MAKE THEM CRUMBS
KISSES, SOCIETY SAM

The story began:

> Taplinger prize-winning New York Tribune columnist Rad
> Rheinhardt today received an anonymous letter claiming to have
> been mailed by the murderer of Manhattan socialite and philan-
> thropist Oona Mellon Aldrich.

As he read, Cardozo's mind was querying and footnoting. He
didn't know what the hell a Taplinger prize was, but he recognized the name Rad Rheinhardt—the *Trib*'s premier right-wing
gadfly columnist.

> In an eerie coincidence, the killer calls himself Society Sam, a
> name reminiscent of 1979's Son of Sam, whose serial killings
> reached a total of 12.
> In the gloating letter Society Sam states that New York Society is
> scum, and the time has come to clean it up.
> "He definitely has an agenda," says Rheinhardt.

"The *New York Trib* seems to be staking out new frontiers in
fantasy shock." Cardozo opened the tabloid, dug through a
thicket of Waldbaum and Pathmark ads, and found the editorial
page. He squinted at the phone number printed at the bottom of
the masthead, then punched the digits into his phone.

A harried-sounding woman answered and Cardozo asked if
she had any idea where he might reach Mr. Rheinhardt on a
lovely Sunday like today. There was another buzz and a male
voice growled, "Yeah?"

Cardozo was amazed how much arrogance could come
across a phone wire in one little syllable. This was the voice of a
temple flunky fed up with beating back all the faithful who
wanted thirty seconds with God. And he was talking through what
sounded like a mouthful of cream cheese.

"This is Lieutenant Vincent Cardozo of the Twenty-second
Precinct. I'm trying to locate Rad Rheinhardt."

"Hey, don't you godless bloodhounds respect anyone's Sabbath?"

Cardozo flashed that he was talking to the great man himself.
"Do Rad a favor: Tell him to get a lawyer, fast. I'm coming down
right now with a warrant for his public strangulation."

There was a pause. "Lieutenant, why don't you bring your warrant to Clancy's Bar and Grill. It's on Front Street, two blocks north of the *Trib* building."

■ ■ ■

"RAD RHEINHARDT?" Cardozo took a seat at the table where the disheveled gentleman in the mustard-stained necktie was nursing a mug of beer. "Great headline."

"Thanks." Eyes the color of slate peered out from behind Rad Rheinhardt's mildly myopic prescription lenses. "But I don't write the headlines."

"So tell me, why is a Taplinger prize-winning columnist working on a beautiful Sunday like today?"

Rheinhardt lifted his mug. "Who's working? I'm a married man and where I live it happens to be a shitty Sunday."

Cardozo turned around and signaled the bartender to bring him a draft.

The only other people in the place were two shadowy old guys bent over the bar with eight empty stools between them. Even a lobbyist for the American Distillers Association would have had trouble calling Clancy's Bar and Grill anything but what it was—a cheap dive, strictly for round-the-clock drinkers and staff from the *Tribune* next door who wished they could be round-the-clock drinkers.

"You and your paper should see some healthy circulation," Cardozo said, "with a little help from your new pen pal."

"Hard to say. He could be a one-shot."

"He? You know this guy is a guy?"

Rad Rheinhardt's eyes came up quickly. "Of course I don't know it, but Sam is a man's name."

"You never heard of anyone called Samantha?"

"Okay. You're the detective, I'm a fallible journalist."

"Why the hell did you have to run it on page one?"

The bartender brought Cardozo's draft, and without being asked, he set down a refill for Rad Rheinhardt and took back his empty mug.

"It happens to be a great story." Rad Rheinhardt took a long swig. "Great stories go on page one."

"The trouble is, page one is break-out big time. And it's a press release for every sick joker and wannabee and gonnabee killer in this city. And there are people who aren't above killing to get on page one. Because, did I mention, we *are* discussing a killing. A real woman really did die."

"The last time anyone could clear away enough blood to count the bodies, seven people a day were getting murdered in this town. Don't blame it on page one."

"I'm not blaming this killing on page one. I'm blaming the *next* killing on page one."

"You're a clairvoyant too?"

"If I were, I wouldn't need to ask how much of that letter he wrote and how much you made up."

Rad Rheinhardt's face became a little squarer, a bit ruddier, and a stubborn tilt came into the chin. "Oh, come *on*, Lieutenant."

"Call me Vince. We could wind up being friends."

"Vince. You gotta know better than to accuse me of inventing. I'm a respected columnist. I have a track record. Why do you think that letter was sent to me and not you? *Because* I'm a respected columnist. *Because* I have a track record."

Cardozo felt a tightening around the chest. The more famous these people were the less they wanted to deal with any kind of accountability for anything, anywhere, anytime. They thought their high profile and their connections to all the other high profiles in town put them above mere mortal schmucks. "Did I say you're not a respected columnist? Did I even hint you don't have a track record?"

"Frankly, yes. You as much as said it."

"All I meant is, maybe you're just highlighting part of your story—punching home the point, filling in the blanks . . . Look, I'm not criticizing. I empathize. It's not breaking a law. We've got a free country. We've got a free press. At least the guy who owns your paper has a free press."

Rad Rheinhardt held himself in an attitude somewhere between disgusted and defiant. "Lieutenant."

"Vince."

"Vince. No paper ever built circulation by lying."

"You're telling me you actually got a letter? The letter you got is the letter you printed?"

"I'm not aware that I'm telling you anything at all."

"Then why don't you change your tactic and try telling me something?"

"Why don't you change your tactic first?"

"Because I don't need to. I can put you in jail. And your publisher will let me because it'll make a great page one."

Rad Rheinhardt pulled back in his seat. His eyes were rimmed with red and his hand tightened on his beer mug. "That bluff is so old it needs a hair transplant. You expect me to believe you're dumb enough to arrest a journalist doing his job?"

"Sure. Because you're screwing up *my* job. If that letter is real, and if it's really from the guy who killed Oona Aldrich, you've withheld evidence. You've interfered in a murder investigation, which makes you an accessory after the—"

Rad Rheinhardt cut in. "The Supreme Court doesn't see it that way."

"The Supreme Court is two years from now. Appeals court could be two months from now. You want to spend two months on your tush behind bars?"

"What makes you think I wouldn't be proud to go to jail for my convictions?"

"Because you're a junkie and junk is no longer freely available in New York prisons."

Rad Rheinhardt threw his beer in Cardozo's face.

It took Cardozo a minute to be able to see again. There was only one old man left at the bar now, slumped over his can of Coors. The bartender stood behind the bar, slowly polishing a glass as if he wanted to get the shine just right.

A dribble of beer was running down Cardozo's cheek, and he caught it with a paper napkin before it could get under his collar. "You're a brave journalist to throw beer at an armed man."

"Fuck you, Cardozo."

"Fuck you, *Vince.* Please. *Amigos.*" Cardozo lifted the empty beer mug and signaled the bartender for a refill.

The refill came and Rad Rheinhardt sat mute and withdrawn, sunk so deep in whatever he was feeling that he seemed to have lost his way in it. When he finally spoke, his voice was quiet and under control.

"I've never denied that episode. My employer knows it. My wife knows it. The readers of every liberal-left rag in this town know it. And when they're old enough, my little girl, Angelica, and my little boy, Scott, will know it. Yes, six years ago I was an addict. And yes, six years ago when I was an immature idiot, I supported left-wing causes and agitated for U.S. withdrawal from Central America and the Middle East. And yes, six years ago I was busted at the Disneyland Holiday Inn when I bought a half kilo of smack from an undercover agent. I'm not proud of it. I'm not proud that I almost destroyed the only mind and body I'll ever own, I'm not proud that I advocated the destruction of the greatest country on earth—but I am proud of my recovery. And I'm proud of the example I set for others who are as needy and lost now as I was then. Because there are millions of them, and dope is the number-one problem facing this nation today, and with the grace of God and with the help of people far more understanding and forgiving than you'll ever know how to be, I fought dope and I proved dope can be licked and I'm back."

Sharks, Cardozo was reminded, had the biggest mouths and the smallest brains in the ocean. "All I can say, Rad, is welcome home, fuck dope, and God bless America."

"You're a real bastard."

"I'm glad that's clear, because remember, Rad, I'm in your league. That's why I'm confident we'll have a successful partnership."

"A *what* ship?"

"I want the letter."

"And if I don't turn it over to you?"

"More people are going to get killed."

"More people getting killed is a given of this situation."

"You have an interesting slant on this. It's a given that more people are going to get killed, but hey, in the meantime Rad Rheinhardt has a page-one running exclusive with a nut who enjoys getting his blow jobs from two-minute-old corpses."

Rad Rheinhardt jerked forward an inch into complete immobility. He wasn't even breathing, and Cardozo could feel his attention focused down to a very small, burning point, every pore in him open to receive.

"I want an exclusive on the forensic," Rad Rheinhardt said.

"Fine, so long as he doesn't share his letters with anyone but you. In exchange I want those letters physically in my possession the minute after they are physically in yours. Until I've had my look nobody else sees them, nobody else knows about them, nobody prints them. The originals stay with me. When I'm ready, you get all the copies you can eat. Till I give you your copies your lip stays zipped. I have the right to censor material that could prejudice the investigation, and you will respect this right when I invoke it."

"Deal." Rad Rheinhardt reached into his pocket and handed Cardozo a sheet of paper with bits of newsprint taped to it.

"Please, Rad, the next one—don't touch it, except at the lower left-hand corner. And put it in plastic. Is there an envelope?"

· TWELVE ·

Monday, May 13

"ZIP CODE ONE OH THREE ONE FOUR," Ellie Siegel said, "is Fairview Avenue on Staten Island. The latest the Society Sam letter could have been mailed and still made it to the *Trib* Saturday morning is three P.M. last Thursday."

Through the half-open door behind her, sounds suddenly surged in from next door: jangling phones and hunt-and-peck typing and the blare of TV newszak. Greg Monteleone got up and kicked the door shut.

"Why would anyone kill someone in Manhattan," Sam Richards said, "and go to Staten Island to mail the note?"

"No one would go to Staten Island just to mail a note," Greg Monteleone said.

"Maybe he lives on Staten Island," Carl Malloy said.

Cardozo stared at the blackboard where he had block-printed the message from Society Sam. "Delancey lives in Manhattan."

"Why does it have to be Delancey?" Monteleone folded his arms across his kiwi-green shirt. "For one thing, we know his movements last Thursday, and he wasn't day-tripping on the Staten Island ferry."

"Says who?" Malloy said. "I picked him up just before noon, at Archibald's. He could have gone out to Staten Island in the morning. He could have gone out the day before."

Cardozo sat tapping his ballpoint against the edge of the desk. "Plus—Dan Hippolito says the coring knife could have done some of the cuts on Oona."

Monteleone turned. Amazement brushed his face. "Am I hearing you right? Delancey's going to use a coring knife for *some* of the cuts? And what about the others? He takes along a grape-fruit knife? A pizza slicer?"

"Dan didn't rule out the other cuts being done with the same blade." Cardozo shrugged. "He just said there was no way of being positive."

■   ■   ■

THE NARROW STAIRWAY in the converted town house gleamed with lovingly maintained woodwork, and glowing brass rods held the carpet tight to the treads. The man who opened the door on the second-story landing had ash-colored hair and a clean-shaven face with a narrow nose and an almost generous mouth.

"Vince," he said. "Good to see you. Come on in." Dr. Martin Wilkes spoke with an educated, slightly pampered Eastern Establishment voice that went with his comfortable WASP looks. He stood aside and Cardozo stepped into the office.

It was a cozy space, with cherry-wood paneling and deep leather armchairs and an enormous wood desk with thick, solid legs.

"How have you been feeling?"

"It's not about me, Marty." Cardozo handed him the report on Oona Aldrich. "This time the Department's paying you."

Last time Marty Wilkes had treated Cardozo for depression after his wife's death, and Cardozo's insurance had paid. During the course of the therapy, Cardozo had developed a distanced but genuine friendliness with his therapist.

Wilkes gestured Cardozo to take one of the two armchairs. Cardozo chose the chair that allowed him to see the window, with its view of sky glowing down on a neatly scrubbed row of Greenwich Village town houses. Wilkes sat in the other chair and read through the report.

"Two questions," Cardozo said. "Is Oona's murder a random hit, or could Delancey have done it? And what does the letter mean?"

"Vince, I'm not a clairvoyant."

"You were damned good at reading my tea leaves. I know you have gut feelings and I want them. I know you have a few wild guesses and I want them too."

Wilkes sat tapping the sheets of the report together.

"Can we start with the letter? Whoever sent it, the killer or a prankster, whether they're sincere or deceptive, the letter still reveals the sender. And what I see in it is tremendous hatred of the rich, of rich *women*."

Wilkes took a moment to study the photographs that had been paper-clipped to the autopsy.

"I see the same rage in the defacement of the corpse. I see it in the newspaper clipping left at the scene."

"You're assuming the killer left the clipping."

"You told me to make assumptions, right? Either there's one mind behind the killing and the clipping and the letter—or we're dealing with two minds that just coincidentally share a mindset. Coincidence isn't impossible, but for the moment I'm making the simpler assumption: one and the same mind behind the killing and the letter. Which brings us to the signature he's chosen— Society Sam." Wilkes glanced at Cardozo and glumly shook his head. "He identifies with Son of Sam. Which is very bad news for us."

"Why?"

"Because Son of Sam was a serial killer, and most of your copycats are serial, and they're just as wacko as the cats they're copying. Not that we're dealing here with an exact copycat. But he obviously feels he's carrying on Sam's work. Working in Sam's tradition. It's not unusual. A certain type of sociopathic killer models himself on established, well-known serial killers. He usually has very low self-esteem."

Fuck this bastard's low self-esteem, Cardozo thought. *He's earned it.* "Does he have to be a serial killer? Couldn't this be a one-shot?"

"Sure, you get one-shot copycats—but they're usually motivated, trying to disguise a murder as the work of a wacko. In which case your job is easy. Who wanted Oona Aldrich dead? That's your killer. But to be honest, Vince, my gut feeling is—the mind that produced the killing produced the letter, and we're looking at a worst-possible-case scenario: This is the first in a series of killings."

Cardozo hoped he hadn't heard correctly. But he met Marty Wilkes's sorrowful gaze and he realized he'd heard exactly right; and it gave him just a little bit of a sick feeling.

"But there's a light at the end of our tunnel," Marty Wilkes said. "The Behavioral Sciences Unit of the FBI maintains a national register of serial killings. It lists data on every known serial killing committed in the United States in the last fifty years, and I can access it from that terminal."

Wilkes nodded toward his desk, where a PC terminal sat, its screen glowing with amber print.

Cardozo stared at the wall where Wilkes had hung a diploma,

dated nineteen years ago, from Harvard Medical School. "What about the candle? Is it his?"

"I'll make a pragmatic rather than a psychiatric inference: I can't imagine anyone else bringing a candle into a changing room. Which doesn't prove a thing. If there are more murders and more candles, we'll know for sure that the candles are his and we'll know he's sending us a message."

"And the message is—"

"The deep message, the private message, is in his own language, and he hasn't given us the dictionary yet. The surface message is that he's Catholic."

"How does a candle make him Catholic?"

"Statistical inference. There've been instances of Catholic serial killers lighting votive candles at the murder scenes. Very few Protestants. It's not surprising. Catholic liturgy and practice make much greater use of candles than Protestant denominations do."

"Couldn't he be Jewish?"

"Another statistical inference. Except for David Berkowitz/ Son of Sam, there are very few Jewish serial killers. And he was adopted."

Marty Wilkes stared across the space that separated them, and Cardozo was suddenly aware of something pale and heatless about the doctor's gaze. It seemed to him that Wilkes didn't blink.

"Tell me about the girl that may have been with him," Cardozo said.

"The black girl the witnesses reported seeing?" Wilkes shook his head. "I'd doubt she's involved. Again, the reasoning is statistical. You very rarely see women as accomplices in serial killings. Offhand, I can't think of any except Carol Fugate in Nebraska, and Myra Hindley, in Britain."

Cardozo was thinking of the utter fragility of the membrane that separates daily life from free fall. "How does the killer select his victim?"

Wilkes sighed. "We don't know yet what elements the killer is selecting out. It's almost certainly her social standing. But it could be more—some aspect of her appearance, her speech, her behavior. We need more input—more 'words in the dictionary.' "

"You mean another killing."

Wilkes nodded. "One's not enough to get a fix on these guys."

"Care to predict when he'll hit again?"

"By and large, serial killers show two classic patterns, and they tie in with the hormonal cycle. The mature male produces hormones in cycles that are roughly monthly—like the female's menstrual cycle. The cycles have a collective peak point and a collective low point. There's the max pattern, where he kills at the peak. Then there's the minimax pattern; he kills at the low point too. In some killers the act of killing seems to accelerate the hormonal cycle, and the time between peaks or nadirs shrinks."

"So if there's another killing a month after the first—"

"He's on the max cycle. And if the next killing is a half month after the first, he's on a minimax cycle. We won't know that till we see when he strikes next."

"And when might that be?"

"If I were a real pessimist, I'd give him till, oh, till next Monday."

■ ■ ■

HAPPY HOUR BEGAN, APPARENTLY, at four, and at no time since had there been fewer than three black limousines double-parked with motors idling in the street outside Archibald's.

Carl Malloy stood across the street, watching. On the sidewalk well-dressed women were quietly picketing in two separate circles. NO FREEDOM FOR KILLERS one of the signs urged. FAIR PLAY FOR ALL another sign answered.

A bored-looking cop stood between the two groups, keeping them apart.

Two gray-haired women came out of the restaurant and chatted their ambling way across the avenue. A TV newswoman and a man with a minicam came running after them. Malloy heard the newswoman ask where they stood on the controversy concerning the convict cook at Archibald's.

"I think we should learn, as a society, to forgive," one of the gray-haired women said.

"Parole hearings should be open," the other gray-haired woman said. "Victims' relatives should have the right to offer their input."

"Do you have any second thoughts about patronizing Archibald's?" the newswoman asked.

The gray-haired women looked at each other and began laughing. "Heavens no, we feel lucky to get a table!"

At ten after six the kitchen door on Seventy-fourth swung open, and Jim Delancey came out.

Malloy crossed Lexington and followed.

Delancey headed east toward Third Avenue.

The TV newswoman saw him and dashed after him. The man shouldering the minicam tried to block his way.

Malloy could see Delancey gesturing *no* over and over, refusing to be interviewed. Finally he pushed the man with the minicam to one side and strode past.

The newswoman ran after him, and the man with the minicam filmed her shouting to Jim Delancey's back. "Mr. Delancey! Sir! Mr. Delancey, sir!"

· THIRTEEN ·

Tuesday, May 14

CARDOZO SHOOK THE WAITER'S HAND. "Larry?"

"In person." Larry's sunburned, still-peeling face smiled out from under a helmet of blond-streaked hair.

Cardozo closed his shield case and slipped it back into his pocket. "I was told you waited lunch here last Wednesday."

"Did you have to remind me? I just got back from Key West, and I'd almost managed to forget."

Cardozo peeled the plaid Archibald's wrapping off a lump of sugar. He dropped the lump into his coffee and stirred. "Last Wednesday you waited on Oona Aldrich, right?"

"A pain in the ass but a great tipper, may she rest in peace. Yes, I waited on her for all of three minutes, till her friends hustled her out."

"I understand she made a scene."

"The vegetable dip was rancid. She said. The salad chef was a murderer. She said. You name it, it was giving her trouble. And Oona wasn't the only problem customer we had at lunch. She wasn't even the worst."

It was ten after eleven, well before lunch hour, and so far Cardozo was the only customer. He gestured Larry to have a seat at the table.

Larry glanced around the deserted room. He pulled out a chair and sat.

"Who was worse than Oona?" Cardozo said.

"Gloria Spahn made a scene compared to which Oona behaved like a nun at prayer."

"Gloria Spahn." Cardozo ran the name through his memory. "The dress designer?"

"She wanted romaine in her Caesar salad, and all we had was shredded Boston. Mind you, she was within her rights. Caesar salad should be made with romaine. But try telling that to a Korean chef."

■ ■ ■

"YOU RAN OUT OF ROMAINE?" Cardozo said.

The Korean withdrew the wooden spoon from the hollandaise pot, touched a forefinger to the spoon, and licked the finger. He shook his head and added salt. "No problem."

"But you did run out of romaine, and one of the customers got angry?"

"No problem. Five minutes we have six heads romaine. Jim run to Gristede's."

"You ran out of romaine, and Jim Delancey went to Gristede's and got more romaine?"

The Korean nodded. "Five minutes. No problem."

"You didn't mention this to me last week."

The Korean smiled. "Five minutes. Not important. No problem."

■ ■ ■

THE STORE MANAGER WAS in his early forties, stocky, and he radiated a sense of coiled anger. "What day was this?"

"May eighth," Cardozo said. "Last Wednesday."

He hated to make the manager search for the bill. The poor guy looked as though all he needed was one more hassle and he'd have an aneurysm.

Cardozo followed him up a flight of four steps. The office was built on a platform higher than the rest of the store. Through Plexiglas windows you could watch all the aisles and all the registers, see who was switching price tags and who was pulling a gun.

Zip-a-dee-doo music bubbled from ceiling speakers.

The manager bent over the steel-topped desk and opened a loose-leaf ledger as thick as two Manhattan phone directories. He leafed through a week's worth of carbons of phone-in charge orders. "Christ, these are a mess. Archibald's phoned in their regular Wednesday order at eight-thirty A.M."

"Any romaine on that order?"

The manager's finger went down a ten-inch column of nearly illegible carbon scrawls. "No romaine."

"They bought romaine that day."

"No, they didn't." The manager leafed deeper into the stack.

"Yes, they did. Twelve forty-five they special-ordered six heads of romaine."

"When were those picked up?"

"They went out for delivery at one-thirty."

"Are you sure they were delivered?"

"No, I'm not sure because this book is a fucking mess. But we charged for delivery." The manager leaned down and spoke into a microphone on the desk. "Paco, come to the manager's office. Paco Mendoza."

A short, skinny kid, no more than five feet two, bounded up the steps.

"You remember this order?" The manager held out the carbon.

Paco shrugged.

"The police want to know. Did you deliver it?"

"Yeah." Paco nodded.

Cardozo took the photograph of Jim Delancey from his pocket. "Have you ever seen this man?"

Paco looked at the photo. He looked at Cardozo. The boy had large, dark, expressive eyes—Cardozo wasn't sure what they were expressing, but they were good at it.

"Maybe I've seen him," the boy said. "He reminds me of that new guy in the kitchen at Archibald's."

"He says he picked up the order."

The boy shook his head firmly. "He's lying."

▪ FOURTEEN ▪

Wednesday, May 15

"CLOSE FRIENDS SAY you never went through an experience as brutal as the murder of your daughter four years ago." Dizey Duke paused to push an overhang of tinsel-colored hair back from her forehead. "When your best friend, Oona Aldrich, was murdered last week, how did that experience compare?"

The question caught Leigh like an unexpected slap to the face. She hadn't wanted to give this interview, but Dizey had promised to plug the film and the producer had pleaded with Leigh to let Dizey have five minutes.

"Come on," Leigh said. "How the hell can I answer that?"

Dizey sat there smiling, patting out the wrinkles in the thigh of her camouflage leisure suit. A green Rigaud candle burned in its silver dish on the bar, and a faint scent of cypress floated through the Winnebago.

Leigh nodded toward the snack table where Dizey had set up her thermos of iced Stoli and her tape recorder. "Do we have to have that thing running?"

"Forget the tape. It's just to help my memory."

Dizey poured herself another splash of Stoli. In years she was on the high side of fifty-something, tall and heavy-set, with a red, robust, good-humored face topped by blindingly blond bangs. On a slenderer woman without a Montana drawl the blatant dye job might have seemed a miscalculation, but on Dizey it seemed to be a screw-you declaration of fashion independence, part of her instantly recognizable image. She drained the plastic cup and set it down and wiped her lips on the back of her hand.

"Leigh Baker, here you are today, wrapping up location work on the biggest-budgeted Hollywood film of the season."

Dizey always called you by your last name when there was a tape recorder present. "Industry buzz has it that a sixty-million-dollar investment and possibly the future of the studio are riding on the kind of performance you turn in. With the responsibility of wrapping the film, with the pressure of your friend Oona Aldrich's— Is there any danger your substance-abuse problems might recur?"

A fine-grained weariness silted down on Leigh. "I hope not. I pray not. I'm a different person now. I know my weaknesses, I know how to live with them. I know where to go for help."

"A lot of people said you'd never work again after your last bout with pills and booze. Do you feel you've got the last laugh? Have you licked addiction?"

"No way. Addiction's licked me."

Made up and dressed and ready for the next take, Leigh felt uneasy, remote from herself. Through the deep amber tint of the shatter-proof windows she could see the no-parking signs and police barricades that had been set up the length of the entire block. Winnebagos and movers' trucks and klieg lights and reflectors clogged the street. A crew of at least sixty milled, drinking coffee and munching bagels from the twelve-foot streetside buffet table. The director swung into view, riding his crane-operated chair and testing the next setup through his viewfinder.

"I'm sober only so long as I don't pick up that first drink or pill."

Dizey's eyes rounded in sympathy. "Leigh Baker, you make it seem so easy—almost glamorous. What is this knack you have of getting out there and doing what has to be done and having the time of your life doing it?"

"If I had that knack, I'd be bottling it."

"People are saying you believe there's a connection between your daughter Nita's murder and your friend Oona's."

Leigh stiffened like a piece of wood, nailed to the canvas seat by the realization that Dizey was determined to trap her. "I wish you'd put this on the record, Dizey. I can't control what people say, but I never made any statement regarding Oona's murder, and outside of a courtroom, I don't intend to."

Dizey's smile flattened. "You've taken courageous and controversial stands in the past. You went public with your battle against addiction. Your compassion for the sick and dying has done a lot to change public perception of AIDS. Where do you stand on victims' rights?"

"Absolutely in favor."

"There's a lot of public disgust with the early paroling of convicted murderers. Where do you stand?"

"At the moment I don't know enough about the penal system to comment."

There was something openly dubious in Dizey's gaze. "Others have not hesitated to comment." She slipped a different cassette into the tape recorder and pressed the Play button.

A man's voice spoke thinly and nasally. "As a society we're obsessed with vengeance long after vengeance has served its purpose. Jim Delancey may have transgressed, but he's more than paid his dues and it's time we all let bygones be bygones and got on with our lives—and allowed him to get on with his."

Dizey stopped the tape player and sat staring almost slyly at Leigh.

"Who's that on the tape?" Leigh said.

Dizey sank deeper into the director's chair. The toe of one cowboy boot stretched out to nudge the leg of Leigh's chair. "Avalon Gardner."

Leigh felt as though a fist had socked her in the stomach. She'd always thought of Avalon Gardner as a friend; he'd even testified for Nita's character at the trial. "What are you going to do with that comment?"

A lazy smile touched Dizey's lips. "It's important to air all sides of the issue. I'm going to publish it."

"I wish you wouldn't."

"We all have wishes, don't we?"

The silence oozed with things unsaid.

Dizey changed cassettes and pressed the Record button. "Recently," she said, "a New York newspaper received an anonymous letter taking responsibility for the murder of Oona Aldrich. Many people believe that that letter is a smoke screen concocted to obscure the real killer's identity. What do you believe?"

"I haven't seen the letter."

"A convicted homicidal sociopath has been freed to run amok in this city, and many people are convinced the letter is a ruse to draw attention away from that fact."

"I can understand people feeling that way, but I'm just not in a position to comment."

"Anyone who could murder Nita Kohler or Oona Aldrich obviously possesses a dangerously short temper and the self-control of a trip wire. Such a young man would be perfectly willing to do the same to a half dozen other women. Have you taken any steps to protect yourself? Have you hired a bodyguard?"

"The studio provides security, and I'm insured till the completion of the film."

"In this day and age, in this city, is that enough?"

"We live in a world where there's no such thing as perfect security. But we can't fold up our lives like tents just because we're threatened."

"And how have you been threatened?"

"I didn't say that."

Dizey was gazing through half-parted lids. "Have you received threatening letters or phone calls?"

There was a knock.

"Yes?" Leigh called.

The door opened. Heat from the street eddied into the cool of the Winnebago. A curly-headed Native American man stuck his head in. "Waiting for you, Miss Baker."

"Thank you." Leigh rose quickly. "Dizey, this has been just great."

Dizey pressed the Stop button on her tape recorder and slid it back into its leather carrying case. She recapped her silver flask and dropped it into her tote bag. She stood and went to the door and then stopped and turned. "Leigh, hon, think about what I said. If you need the name of Jackie O's security people—"

"I can handle my safety, Dizey. But thanks."

Dizey gave her a hard-mouthed look, eyebrows arching. "Be careful. Love you much."

As soon as Dizey had closed the door behind her, Leigh crossed to the bar and lifted the receiver of the cellular phone. She punched in Avalon Gardner's number.

A nasal male voice answered on the third ring. "Yes?"

"Avalon, it's Leigh. Dizey just played me a tape she claims is you."

Avalon didn't answer.

"Did you go on record defending Jim Delancey?"

"I wasn't defending anyone or anything except common sense."

"It sounded as though you were excusing him."

"Let the dead bury the dead, Leigh. It's time to get on with the business of living."

"You said Jim Delancey has paid his dues?"

"And he has."

"He kills my daughter and serves *three years*? You call that payment?"

"Leigh, we have an honest difference of opinion, and I'd rather not go nuclear over it."

"I'd like you to retract that comment before Dizey prints it."

Avalon drew a deep breath. "It happens to express my considered ethical belief, and I have no intention of retracting."

"Then I never want to talk to you again."

"Suits me."

Leigh broke the connection. She dialed Tori's direct line at work.

"Tori Sandberg."

"Tori, it's Leigh."

"You sound in a foul mood."

"I am. Has Dizey tried to get you to accuse Jim Delancey on the record?"

"I'm not accusing anyone on or off the record, and I don't think you ought to talk to Dizey."

"I had to. She's promised to plug the film. Tori, she mentioned threats. Is something going on? Have you gotten any phone calls or letters?"

"Threatening phone calls or letters? No. Why, have you been getting any?"

"I can't tell."

"Now, look, you know a threat when you hear one."

"There've been hang ups on my answering machine. And a few—silences."

"Silences?"

"Someone just listens. You haven't had anything like that?"

"No, I haven't—and I think you should tell the police."

■ ■ ■

"I NEED SOMETHING to wear to Annie MacAdam's dinner," Tori Sandberg said.

"Dinner next Monday or dinner next Thursday?" Gloria Spahn said.

Tori had not heard about next Thursday's dinner. "Next Monday."

"A tad late in the day, don't you think?"

They were sitting on the white brocade sofa in Gloria's showroom, sipping iced coffee. Gloria was wearing one of her own designs, a luncheon suit of gray silk, high-skirted with a fracture in the jacket that showed a hairline of bare cleavage right down to the first rib. The suit made her look spectacularly but almost unhealthily thin. Tori had run over from the office, and she was wearing one of her work dresses, a red-and-blue Sixties-revival Pucci-style print. She realized she'd somehow gotten orange Magic Marker on the skirt.

"I honestly thought I had something to wear and"—Tori shrugged and smiled—"I don't."

"But you have that adorable salmon Saint Laurent. It's a great standby—always perfect for dinner at Annie's."

"I thought it might be nice to surprise Zack with something he hasn't seen me in."

Gloria eyed Tori for one long, appraising moment. "Since when does a literary woman believe a man even notices?"

"I may edit a magazine, but I hope I'm not a fool."

"You're not, darling. I don't let fools through that door. Okay, for Zack we'll make an effort. What did you have in mind?"

Tori had come to Gloria Spahn because Gloria was very much the right designer these days. Her reputation had been riding a thermal updraft of media exposure, and her clothes had a way of making women—even grandmothers—look rich, sexy, and confident. Tori was one of the few women in her set who had not yet married a rich husband or inherited a trust fund. Her investments had taken a clobbering on the stock market, and she felt a need for some of Gloria's image enhancement.

Tori hesitated. "What do you think Zack would like to see me in?"

Gloria stepped back a few inches. Her glance flicked over Tori thoughtfully. "You have a tall, slender body, you're toned, your tits are small but you've got the greatest ass on the Upper East Side. There's no reason to stick with the lady image. You could carry off a sexy number, and I'd love to be the designer who brought you out."

"And *I'd* love to wear something that hasn't been seen in New York."

Gloria seemed surprised. "We're talking one of a kind? For dinner at *Annie's?*"

"Why not?"

"Annie serves *Salisbury steak!*" Gloria took three steps back. "Will your hair be that color?"

"I—I hadn't planned to change it."

"I'm only asking because the dress I have in mind—actually, I've two dresses in mind and they'd both look great on you—but you might consider talking to Ron Zaporta before the party. He does coloring at the Pierre. He's booked solid, but I could get him to slip you in."

"Slip me in for what? What are we talking about?"

"Lemon microlites in your hair. The dresses would look *made* for you." Gloria clapped her hands. "Vinnie! Bring the Rothschild crepe de chine. And the Madariaga silk."

Gloria had named two of the top European countesses of the season. It was an open secret in the fashion and magazine worlds that Gloria Spahn ran a sideline: she leased premieres of her dresses to various clients to wear at various parties far distant from one another. That way, the same dress could be seen in Paris one evening, New York the next, San Francisco the third, and be considered a fashion first in each city.

An employee wheeled a dress rack into the room. He was a slim young man in tight-fitting raw-linen trousers and floppy madras shirt. Two dresses hung from the rack, cocooned in pink tissue paper.

Gloria pulled a dark raspberry crepe-de-chine dress free of its wrapping.

Her employee frowned at a small stain above the hem. "Look at this," he said. "Rothschild is a *pig*."

"Not now, Vinnie," Gloria said. "It doesn't matter."

She faced Tori toward the mirror and held the dress up in front of her.

At the sight of her reflection Tori felt herself lifted by a spurt of edgy, childlike rapture. "It's perfect."

"No, it's not," Gloria said. "Cybilla deClairville's going to that dinner, and she's wearing the same damned color."

Vinnie helped Gloria tear the tissue off the other dress, a soft apricot moiré. Vinnie inspected for stains. Gloria held the dress up to Tori. "Perfect," she announced.

Tori didn't like it nearly as well as the raspberry, but Gloria was already helping her step out of her skirt. "Let's get you pinned up."

Twelve minutes later Tori was facing the mirror again.

"Ron can see her tomorrow at five!" Vinnie called from the inner office.

Gloria circled Tori, inspecting. "We'll take in the tucks and hem it up for you this afternoon. Come back in for the final fitting Friday morning, okay?"

"I can't tell you how much I appreciate this."

"No trouble. Now, how do you want to pay?"

Tori inhaled sharply and felt a pin pop. "Pay? I'd honestly prefer to borrow the dress."

"We'd all prefer to borrow, darling, but I'm a couturiere, not an S and L."

Tori hesitated. "I thought possibly we could work out an arrangement, like two years ago."

"But you wore that dress to the Emmys, not Annie MacAdam's."

Tori sighed. "We could do an article on you in the magazine."

Gloria shook her head. "Publicity in *Matrix Magazine* isn't that valuable—my accountant says liberated women don't buy my clothes."

Tori realized she was in too deep now to back out gracefully. "All right. How much?"

"I adore Zack, so I'm going to give you a break. Twelve thousand, because this dress is going to make his evening."

Tori couldn't believe that the cost of decadence had gone that far through the roof. She did her best to fake a cool nonreaction. "Of course, it *is* used."

"And if it weren't, it would cost you twenty-four."

"Will you take a check?"

"A personal check."

Tori wondered if there'd been trouble with the magazine's checks. Gloria handed her a pen, and Tori wrote out the check at Gloria's Biedermeier desk. She ripped the check out of the book and handed it to Gloria facedown. "If I bring the dress back right away, do you think you could let me have six thousand back?"

"Come in after the party and we'll talk."

■ ■ ■

"LAST WEDNESDAY," Cardozo said, "you had lunch at Archibald's?"

"Did I?" Gloria Spahn's heavily plucked, heavily penciled eyebrows assumed a thoughtful downward pucker. "Oh, yes, I tried to. It's not easy when you have Oona Aldrich getting delusional at the next table."

"And I understand you had a problem of your own?"

"I did?"

They were alone in the showroom. The light was soft and glowing, and it gave the mirrors a friendly shimmer. The clothes on display looked to Cardozo as if they'd been designed for a cocktail party in a distant and overpriced galaxy.

"A problem with your salad," he said.

Gloria Spahn adjusted the hang of a skirt on a headless, armless mannikin. "Oh, you heard about that." She looked at him, interested now. "Archibald's serves rotten salads, don't you think?"

"I couldn't say. I've never gone there to eat."

"Then you're wiser than me."

Cardozo referred to his notebook. "You ordered a Caesar salad. The waiter brought you a salad made with shredded Boston instead of romaine. You sent the salad back."

"Did I break a law?" She had an extremely thin body, but she moved as if she had absolute confidence in it. She obviously had confidence too in the clothes she was wearing. They had an edgy quality, as if they were thinking about falling off her, but Cardozo suspected she'd designed them and knew they wouldn't.

"You didn't break any law I know of."

"Good. I try not to." She seated herself on the sofa and leaned back against the cushion. "Now, why are you interested in what I ate for lunch seven days ago?"

"Not what you ate but when you ate it."

"Sorry." She smiled. She had an enormous mouth, enormously pink. "I don't punch a time clock at lunch."

"But could you estimate—from the time you sent your salad back, to the time you got the salad you wanted—how long did that take?"

"How long did it *take*? Could I *estimate*?" Gloria Spahn's gray eyes narrowed. They seemed to flash with remembered anger. "I don't need to estimate—I know. I was there an hour before I finally got fed up and left. Those idiots never brought me the damned salad."

■ ■ ■

CARDOZO STOOD ON THE STOOP. He rapped on the kitchen screen door. "Hey, Jim."

Jim Delancey stood at the butcher-block counter, decapitating radishes four at a chop. He turned.

"Need to talk to you," Cardozo said. "Only take a minute."

Delancey sighed. He laid down his knife. "I'll be right back," he told the Korean. He came out onto the stoop. "Look, are you coming around here to bug me? Is it to get the manager pissed off at me?"

"I'm sorry, Jim. If it's inconvenient here, you can come down to the precinct."

Delancey shook his head.

"We have a chronology problem," Cardozo said. "Your chef

tells me last Wednesday, during lunch hour, he sent you out for six head of romaine?"

"I forgot. Look, I'm sorry. I've had a lot on my mind lately."

"No problem. When did you leave and when did you get back?"

"Oh, I left around quarter of one. I was back maybe fifteen minutes later."

"Gristede's has a record of that romaine going out for delivery at one-thirty."

"Gristede's is screwed up. Ask anyone in the kitchen— they're always screwing up."

"The delivery boy knows you. And he says he made the delivery."

Delancey shuffled. "Someone's screwed up."

"Maybe you?"

"I don't know."

"If you *are* mistaken—and it's a natural mistake—where did you go?"

Delancey's eyes flicked up. "I didn't go. I just told you."

"No, no, Jim. You told me you didn't pick up the romaine. But we know you left here at quarter of one. Your chef says so. You just said so."

"Look, you're confusing me. Maybe I should . . ." Delancey took a moment to wipe his hands on his apron. "Maybe I shouldn't talk to you."

"Maybe you shouldn't. That's up to you."

"Am I under suspicion? Should I get a lawyer?"

"Jim, I honestly am not the best person to advise you on that. Asking you where you went didn't strike me as asking you to incriminate yourself. But maybe it is."

"No. It's not." Delancey's eyes were evasive. "I was just ashamed of myself."

"Why? What did you do?"

Delancey took a pack of Camels from his apron pocket. He knocked one loose and put it between his lips and lit it one-handed from an Archibald's matchbook. "I was spooked after Oona Aldrich had that fit. I went and had a few drinks. It's a bad habit of mine. Just to keep calm."

"I empathize, Jim. Do you happen to remember where you had these drinks?"

▪ ▪ ▪

THE PLACE WAS CALLED TUNE'S. It was a basement on Seventy-sixth that featured poor air-conditioning and a ten ninety-nine prix fixe, and it was crowded.

Cardozo showed the waitress his shield, and then he showed her the photo of Jim Delancey. He had to shout above the roar of voices and the din of silverware attacking china. "Did you see this man here around one o'clock last Wednesday?"

She stared at him, balancing a tray of the day's special, sea scallops—four on a plate with plenty of rice. Sweat gleamed on her cheekbones. "This is a joke."

"Sorry, it's not."

"See how crowded we are right now? This is two o'clock. Postpeak. One o'clock is peak. Twice as crowded. Unless he tipped me a twenty I wouldn't remember him, and I doubt anyone else would either." She looked again at the photo. "And he didn't tip me a twenty."

■ ■ ■

CARDOZO STARED AT Lou Stein's report on the note sent by the man who signed himself Society Sam.

The lab had discovered no prints but Rad Rheinhardt's on the page. No prints on the clipped-out letters. No prints on the tape. The lab had discovered prints galore on the envelope, all useless.

Cardozo took another bite of his late-late-lunch sandwich, liverwurst and mayo on toasted rye. He chewed a moment and he could feel his appetite giving out. He'd had a craving for a carbohydrate rush, but now he was thinking it had been more of a compulsion than a craving.

He wiped the mayo off his fingertips and picked up the report again.

Most of the letters making up the message had been clipped from the April second issue of *New York* magazine, the April second issue of *Time* magazine, the April second issue of *Newsweek* magazine, the April second issue of *People,* and the April second issue of *The New Yorker.*

Sam sure likes April second, Cardozo reflected.

Sources for the letter groups TH and ET and CRU had yet to be established.

·FIFTEEN·

Thursday, May 16

XENIA DELANCEY, wearing her Sunday white hat and gloves and walking with small, hesitant steps, pushed through a glass door on the fifth floor of United Nations Tower.

The man sitting behind the kidney-shaped desk smiled without friendliness at her. "May I help you?"

Xenia told him her name. "Senator Guardella said she might be able to see me."

"Please have a seat."

Xenia took a seat on a leather sofa beside a row of potted cactuses. Through a glass wall she could see pigeons wheeling aimlessly over the East River. For thirty minutes she leafed through old magazines and senatorial newsletters. During that half hour a dozen people passed through the reception area. None of them was challenged, none of them was asked to wait.

Xenia went again to the kidney-shaped desk. "I hate to trouble the senator, but my lunch hour will be up in twelve minutes."

"Would you care to reschedule for a week from next Thursday? The senator is heavily booked today."

"No. But could you tell her I'm waiting?"

"She knows."

Forty minutes later one of the senator's aides led Xenia Delancey along a carpeted hallway. Warm yellow lights glowed. The aide knocked on a half-open door. "Senator—Xenia Delancey to see you."

The senator, tall and crisp and smiling in a gray cotton suit that matched her hair, came across the office with a hand extended. "Hello, hello, Xenia Delancey."

"I'm very sorry to be an annoyance," Xenia said.

"Not at *all*. Let's sit over here." The senator steered Xenia toward the sofa. She shifted Bergdorf's and Saks shopping bags to the floor.

"That's my store." Xenia pointed at the Marsh and Bonner's parcel in the senator's hand. "I work there—in the Ingrid Hansen Boutique."

"Really."

"Ask for me next time—I can get you a discount."

"How very kind. Sit, Xenia. Tell me what brings you here?"

Xenia sat. She began crying.

The senator came and sat beside her. "Could you use a hot cup of tea, Xenia?"

"No, thank you. I'm sorry." Xenia took a hankie from her pocketbook and dried her eyes. "We had a murder in the store last week."

"I heard about it. What a shame."

"My boy didn't do it. But he's on parole and the police are treating him like a murderer. They've questioned him at work, in front of customers. They've questioned his co-workers, they've questioned his employer. People see the police coming back again and again and they start thinking, There must be something to it, maybe Jim Delancey *did* kill Mrs. Aldrich."

The senator looked at Xenia Delancey for a long, considering moment. "Now, Xenia, let me play devil's advocate. The police have to follow every possible lead—even the remote ones."

Xenia Delancey opened her pocketbook again. She took out a plastic envelope of neatly trimmed newspaper clippings. "Have you seen the headlines and the gossip columns? They're lynching my boy."

Senator Guardella accepted the clippings. "We're dealing with human nature, which, as you know, is not always a beautiful thing. A case like the Aldrich killing is going to be played out in the media. And rightly or wrongly Jim Delancey is identified in the public mind with the death of that young girl—"

"Nita Kohler. But that was an accident. My boy didn't kill her. He didn't kill anyone."

A quick, almost startled movement brought Senator Guardella's eyes around again to Xenia Delancey. The senator seemed about to say something. And then she seemed to reconsider.

"I'm frightened," Xenia said. "Don't let them take my boy away again."

Nancy Guardella saw that Xenia Delancey was hurting. She

ached for this little gray-haired lady with her dignified posture and her spotless white gloves. She wished she could help, but she didn't have the power to twist reality around.

Or do I? she asked herself. It was as though a bell in her head was suddenly humming a high, pure note. She rose and crossed to a handsome teakwood desk covered in paperwork. She found a scratch pad, scribbled, and ripped the top sheet off.

"Here's my home phone. And here's what I'd like you to do. Keep a log. Make a note every time the police talk to your son. Note who questions him, where they question him, how long the questioning goes on. Names, dates, times, places. If it emerges that there's a pattern of harassment, maybe there's something I can do under the federal discrimination statutes."

Xenia Delancey slipped the number into her purse. Steadying herself on the arm of the sofa, she brought herself to standing. "God bless you, Senator."

Nancy Guardella watched the old woman leave, and then she poured herself a cup of herbal tea and stirred in three packets of Sweet'n Low. She emptied the cup in three gulps. She opened the door to her secretary's office. "Who do we know in the New York Police Department who owes us?"

"Would you settle for the commissioner?"

"Absolutely not. All this is, is a middle-management mix-up." Nancy Guardella was thoughtful a moment. "Who's that guy in Internal Affairs who's a real ass-kicker? The macho with the mustache that doesn't hide his harelip?"

"Lawrence Zawac."

"Captain, right? Get him on the phone for me."

The secretary spent a moment spinning through her Rolodex. She dialed a number and after a moment signaled Nancy Guardella to pick up. The senator hurried back to the blinking phone on her desk.

"Larry—it's Nancy, Nancy Guardella. How've you been?"

She stared out the window at light Ping-Ponging between forty-story glass facades. She let him go on a little bit about golf and his left wrist.

"Larry, I hate to bother you, but I can't think of anyone else who has the balls, frankly, to cut through the red tape. What's happening is, the police are harassing one of my constituents."

■ ■ ■

IT WAS A COMPLICATED SHOT: The camera had to swoop down on a crane and catch Leigh as she came out of the lamp shop, then follow her to the corner. Three dozen technicians and crew and makeup and costume people had to stay out of camera range while two dozen pedestrians had to do all those things New York extras do in New York movies.

The traffic light had to change at the exact moment that Leigh stepped into Bleecker Street, which was actually no trouble since the electrician had rewired it. And the taxi had to be approaching at just the right speed to almost run Leigh down.

The director shot and reshot all afternoon, and by the time the taxi was getting it right, Leigh was getting it wrong.

"Leigh, honey"—her director sighed—"we want to see under the surface. We want to see where the struggling, doubting, self-accusatory child lives."

"You want to see that in my *walk*?"

"You had it on the third take, where did it go?"

"I'm a little tired. I could use a cup of coffee."

"Okay. Take five, everyone."

Leigh went in search of the caterer's truck.

Normal life on the block had been totally disrupted. Traffic had been rerouted. Company men turned pedestrians away, asking them to please take another street. Lighting men angled reflectors and aimed ten-thousand-watt kliegs. Uniformed police officers stood at the edges of the crowd, looking embarrassed.

Leigh found a coffee-and-snack smorgasbord set up outside the Winnebago with the logo of the catering company, *Splendiferous Eats.* She joined the line waiting at the twenty-gallon samovar.

The woman ahead of her, one of the extras, was wearing a dress that clung to her body like a damp see-through Victorian curtain. For some reason that lace coffee-colored chemise struck Leigh as familiar.

"That's a fantastic dress," Leigh said.

The woman turned. She was a tall, striking, young, pale-skinned black. Her gaze held Leigh's an extra telltale second. "Why, thank you. Actually this dress was designed by my brother. I'm sneaking it into the movie for a free plug."

Leigh's heart gave a lurch. She realized it wasn't just the dress that she recognized: it was the woman wearing it. "You were in the Ingrid Hansen Boutique at Marsh and Bonner's. And you were wearing that same dress."

"I'm surprised you remember." The woman held out a hand. "Tamany Dillworth. It's nice to meet you, Miss Baker. You're the only star I know of, besides Vanessa, who mixes with the help. How do you like your coffee?"

"What? Oh, a little milk, thanks."

Tamany Dillworth handed her a cup and then filled one for herself.

"Have the police spoken to you?" Leigh said.

The implications of the question seemed to amuse Miss Dillworth. "The police and I have had words from time to time."

"Have they talked to you about that day in Marsh and Bonner's?"

"No, they haven't. What about it?"

"They had that killing."

Tamany Dillworth brought a hand to her mouth. "Omigod. *That* was the day that poor woman got killed?"

"Do you remember that man with the boom box?"

"Who could forget him."

"The lieutenant in charge has a theory—that maybe you knew him? And came to the boutique with him?"

Tamany Dillworth's eyes widened. "No *way.*"

For some reason Leigh felt vindicated. "You'd save the lieutenant a lot of wasted effort if you'd just explain things to him."

"I'd be glad to. What's his name?"

· SIXTEEN ·

Friday, May 17

CARDOZO LAID THE IDENTI-KIT of the male Hispanic on the desk top, angled so that Tamany Dillworth could see the face right side up.

She leaned forward in her chair, frowned, tilted her head left, then right. "That's the type, but I wouldn't say it was *him*. I mean, if I hadn't seen him, I wouldn't know that he was who *this* is supposed to be. Not to criticize your artist." Miss Dillworth had a perky way of not sitting still. Hands gestured to emphasize a point, bracelets clanked, legs crossed and uncrossed. "His eyes were sleepier. Like he wasn't interested in going to the effort of holding them open. I had a feeling he might have been on dope. I mean, you have to be a little wacked out to take a boom box into a store like Marsh and Bonner's. And you could tell he wasn't there to *shop*."

"When did he leave the boutique?"

"I don't remember seeing him leave. But I left in a hurry."

"Why was that?"

"I set off an alarm." Tamany Dillworth covered her face. "Oh, Lord, I was so *gauche*! I wanted to see how a jacket would look in the daylight, so I took it to the door—only I took it too far. When that bell went off, I thought for sure they were coming to arrest me."

Cardozo laid the photo of Jim Delancey next to the Identi-Kit. "Did you see this man in Marsh and Bonner's?"

Tamany Dillworth's lips shaped a pout. "I can't say for sure. Maybe I've just seen him in the papers or on the news. Is he famous?"

"He's had some fame."

"Nice-looking guy."

"Miss Dillworth, you're an actress?"

"That's how I ran into Miss Baker. I'm doing extra work, but we wrap in two days. I also model, I sing, I act, I have a one-woman cabaret show, I'm a stand-up comic, I do dynamite Italian catering for dinner parties, and I baby-sit. And if you're ever hiring extras for a lineup, I can look real street."

"If you'd care to leave me your phone and address, I might just take you up on that."

"My horoscope *said* this was going to be a lucky day. What can I write on?"

Cardozo slid a pad and a ballpoint across the desk.

She printed with bold, decisive strokes. "Two twenty-nine West Eighty-first. The phone's not working right now, but the address is."

■ ■ ■

FIVE MINUTES LATER Cardozo stepped into the squad room, where Carl Malloy was typing up a report on yesterday's tail.

"Hey, Carl, would you have time to confirm an address for me?"

Malloy glanced at the notepad. "No problem."

·SEVENTEEN·

Monday, May 20

"HOW MANY PLACES do I have left at your May twenty-first dinner?" Dizey Duke asked.

Annie MacAdam had to clutch the phone between her ear and shoulder while she leafed through her notebook and found the list of seventy-eight guests and the ten-table seating plan.

"You've filled your places," Annie said.

"Unless you're saving a place for Oona Aldrich's ghost, you've got room for one more."

Annie lit a cigarette and slipped into the yes role with automatic resignation. "Whatever you want, Dizey dear."

"I want you to invite Avalon Gardner."

Annie MacAdam had a hollow feeling inside. It required the strategic sense of a Soviet chess champion to put a New York dinner party together, and when Dizey Duke chose to involve herself, it was like playing with live grenades instead of chessmen.

"That could be complicated," Annie said. "Leigh and Waldo are coming, and Leigh's feuding with Avalon."

"Tell me something I don't know. That little princess needs to be taught a lesson."

Annie watched her cigarette smoke drift away, drawn into the currents hovering around the mocha velvet shade of the lamp on the Steinway grand. "I'm not going to put Leigh and Avalon at the same table."

"Did I ask for Apocalypse? O.K. Corral will do just fine."

Annie had learned to put up with Dizey's little defects—her demands, her double-dealing, her vendettas, her drunkenness. For Dizey was more than an ally, she was an essential weapon in Annie MacAdam's battle for New York social visibility.

Twelve years ago Annie had entered the game with no money, no name, no looks, no connections, no education beyond Kansas City high school. She had had two assets only: determination and a real estate broker's license.

At that time Dizey Duke's building was going co-op under an eviction plan. The conversion was sponsored by a syndicate of Kuwaiti real estate speculators and Panamanian drug barons. The plan gave Dizey and the other tenants two equally painful choices: move from their homes or cough up the quarter-million insider purchase price.

Enter Annie MacAdam.

As one of the brokers for the deal Annie had in her safe the sales contracts. It was clear that the syndicate—with the then state governor's then wife serving as director—had illegally voted tenants' shares in getting its plan passed. There was no way the state attorney general was going to question, let alone halt, any deal fronted by the governor's wife. But if the details of the conversion leaked to the papers, they could have impacted, well, negatively, on the governor's reelection prospects.

With one phone call to the governor of New York and another to Ms. Duke, Annie arranged for Dizey to keep her home at the rent-stabilized rate; and through the offices of Dizey Duke's column, Annie MacAdam became an overnight star and twelve-year survivor in the world of New York society dinners.

Every bargain has its downside. In this case there were three: Dizey had the right to fill ten percent of Annie's dinner seats with guests of her own choosing; Dizey had the right to veto any guest of Annie's choosing; and—the truly draconian clause—Annie could never, but never ever, invite any other columnist to any of her dinners.

The deal was worth the downside. On any given night during the season there were upward of a dozen A-list dinners in Manhattan. There were only four society columns—no more than a hundred twenty column–inches to cover the entire who-was-there and who-wore-what. Competition for those inches was murderous, and ambitious hostesses were willing to pay ten thousand to get mentioned, twenty to get a photo run of themselves in designer decolletage.

Thanks to Dizey's constant touting of *Annie MacAdam, New York's premier party giver,* Annie was perceived as one of the luminaries and arbiters of the New York social scene.

"All I want," Dizey said, "is to see Leigh Baker's face when she realizes she has to spend an evening in the same room with Avalon Gardner."

"I'll have to tell her that he's coming," Annie warned. "I'm not going to let her be surprised."

"Tell her." The gloat in Dizey's voice was unmistakable. "What do you bet she gets so rattled she falls off the wagon?"

Annie had noted for some time that Dizey, who rarely picked up a phone in one hand without a loaded shot glass in the other, had a voyeuristic interest in the drinking problems of famous women.

"A wise hostess never bets on her guests' sobriety," Annie said quietly.

▪ ▪ ▪

"SOMETHING HAS BEEN on my conscience, Leigh darling." Annie MacAdam's voice came over the telephone line high and flat, with a sort of florid falsity.

"And what's that?" Leigh sipped her coffee. The liquid slipped down her throat with a comfortable warmth. The maid had brought breakfast in bed—coffee, dry whole-wheat toast, a glass of freshly squeezed orange juice. To compensate for all the delicacies that were not there, a speckled blue orchid floated in a fingerbowl.

"When I sent out the dinner invitations," Annie was saying, "I had no idea that they were going to parole that unspeakable Delancey boy or that Avalon Gardner was going to defend him in Dizey's column."

There was no transition. Suddenly Leigh had crossed over the zone of gray sleepiness into full-color wakefulness. "How does Jim Delancey's parole affect dinner?"

"It affects *my* dinner, because I invited Avalon Gardner."

Leigh felt as if she had been kicked in the lungs. "Just tell me one thing. Have you invited Jim Delancey?"

"Gracious, what kind of hostess do you think I am?"

"You're up to the minute, Annie, and I have no idea what the latest chic is." Leigh hated the feeling of being one heartbeat away from a raving argument. "For all I know, it's a great social coup nowadays to have a convicted murderer at the table."

"I wouldn't consider inviting that boy. But if under the circumstances you don't care to face Avalon—"

Leigh could hear sirens coming from the back of her brain. *"Face* him? What the *hell* are you talking about?"

"Be that as it may," Annie MacAdam said, "whoever has to

face whomever, I'm calling to tell you that I will *absolutely* understand if you'd rather not see Avalon—and I wouldn't dream of holding you to your acceptance."

"Why are you dumping all this on me? Why can't you ask *him* to cancel?"

"Leigh darling, I have—and he won't. I'm sorry. You have every right to be upset, of course."

Through the quiet cool of the bedroom, traffic along Fifth Avenue sent up a faint muffled vibration.

"I'm not upset. Not in the least. And Waldo and I have no intention of changing our plans. We're coming, of course."

▪ ▪ ▪

"HERE—TASTE." Annie's daughter, Gabrielle, held out a wooden spoon dripping . . . *something.*

Annie hung up the kitchen extension phone. She turned and looked at her daughter, at the chubby pink face framed in mouse-brown ringlets; she looked at the spoon. She backed off a step. "Are you serious? It looks like a special effect in a horror movie."

"It's your party, it's your dessert." Gabrielle's face suddenly had that petulant little-girl pout it took on when she thought she was keeping her hurt feelings to herself. "I'm only trying to help."

Annie worked up her courage and tasted. The flavor was good. Far better than the caterers were capable of—and a lucky thing, since Annie had knocked their price down twenty percent and told them she'd handle her own dessert. "It's delicious. But I'm not going to put a mess like that on my guests' dessert plates. You've got to spruce it up."

Gabrielle was silent.

How the hell, Annie asked herself, *did I ever inherit a divorced, overweight live-in daughter at this stage of my life?*

"At least get it to stick together. I'll tell you what—we'll use pastry shells."

"You're not going to put my mousse in pastry shells." Gabrielle thumped the Pyrex mixing bowl down onto the counter.

There was a tiny spasm in Annie's heart. *This is my daughter,* she thought. *My own daughter, my only child. And she's hurting.* "I'm sorry if I seem tactless, but you have to grasp that there's an all-or-nothing factor attached to New York entertaining. It's an arena where you win big or lose big; and the bigger you win—and believe me, I've won very, very big—the bigger you have to *keep* winning."

Gabrielle was staring at her mother, and there was suddenly something hard and unreachable in her eyes. "You truly don't give a damn about anything going on in the world—except giving parties and going to parties and meeting people you think are extraordinary."

"And they *are* extraordinary," Annie said. "Because do you know what most people are in this life? They're extras! And do you know what you're going to turn into if you don't get a grip on yourself?"

"I've no idea. Tell me."

"If only you'd try—" Annie dropped into a kitchen chair. Suddenly she was exhausted. "You have a look that's all-American, perky, healthy. You could be spunky. You could be flirty. Add a little dignity and a little mystery and style, and people would find you very worthwhile."

"Why should I care how people I don't even know find me?"

"Because you could make something of yourself—besides a whale."

▪ ▪ ▪

THE PARTY WAS IN FULL SWING. The room glinted with the movement of evening dresses and precious stones and tuxedos, but Gabrielle felt she was alone, lost in a deep forest of black trees.

She squeezed through the crowd, looking for a wall. She found a space beside the Chippendale secretary that her mother had borrowed from Gurdon-Chappell.

"I need something amusing," she heard Gloria Spahn say, "something versatile."

Her mother and Gloria Spahn were standing on the other side of the secretary, chatting with Zack Morrow, the real estate conglomerateur and owner of the *New York Tribune*. He was good-looking, he was unmarried, and he was on the cover of *New York* magazine this week.

"But you should wear some of Fenny's designs!" Annie said. She unclipped a cameo brooch from her dress and handed it to Gloria.

"Fenny designed this?" Gloria said, turning it over in her hand. "But you know, this isn't at all bad."

Gabrielle stood there, waiting to be included. Waiting for her mother to take her hand and draw her into the circle and say to Zack Morrow, *Do you know my daughter? She's unmarried too.*

"Fenny!" Annie sang out.

Fennimore Gurdon, an overweight man with waved white hair and a humorous red face, joined the group.

"Hello, all." He gave a casual wave of his champagne glass. He was wearing antique mother-of-pearl studs in his boiled shirt and one was beginning to pop out.

"I was just telling Gloria about your brooches," Annie said.

Gabrielle stepped forward. A waiter's arm intervened, cutting her off from the group.

Gloria Spahn set her empty champagne glass on the waiter's tray and took a fresh one. "How long have you been designing such great jewelry?" she asked Fenny.

Suddenly Gabrielle felt bad about herself. She felt a sense of waste, of ugliness, of overweight. The black Gloria Spahn that her mother had lent her felt tight at the hips and bunched-up under the arms.

Don't panic, she told herself. *Concentrate. Focus on each breath. Turn the mind inward. This moment will pass. It will pass.*

"Are you okay?" Annie whispered to her, looking annoyed.

"Excuse me," Gabrielle said. "I have to go to the bathroom."

Annie watched her daughter bumble off through the crowd.

"I wish you hadn't let Gabrielle wear my dress," Gloria said. "It wasn't cut for her."

"Relax," Annie said. "You have plenty of beautiful dresses here tonight, no one's going to notice Gabrielle."

Fenny Gurdon had overheard them. "Tori's dress is stunning. That's one of yours, isn't it, Gloria?"

Annie followed the direction of Fenny's gaze across the room to where Tori Sandberg, tall and slim in one of Gloria's pale apricot sheaths, was moving through the crowd.

"You must be very proud of Tori tonight, Zack," Annie said. Zack and Tori had been living together for almost seven years.

Zack looked startled. "Why? I mean, why tonight?"

"Because she looks beautiful."

"Anyone looks beautiful," Fenny Gurdon said, "in one of Gloria's designs. Christ, *I'd* look beautiful in one."

Annie's eye took in the bustle and energy and *haute couture* eddying through the room. Her ear tuned in on all the chitchatting, the laughing, the music of life in the only lane that counted.

"Excuse me," Annie said.

The Duke and Duchess of Argyll had just come through the front door.

"Hi, your Graces!" she called out.

■ ■ ■

LEIGH TRIED HER BEST to listen. The young man was telling her about the Astor who couldn't wear pearls because her sweat was acidic and corroded them horribly. But the voices in Annie Mac-Adam's living room were all shouting in a sort of multichannel stereo, as though to make themselves heard above a roaring wind, and the volume controls in Leigh's head were set very wrong. The background was drowning out the melody.

"They have to be fed to a goose," the young man was saying.

Leigh tried to muster a shuddered outbreath of caring. An interested smile. "A goose?"

Behind her she could hear a man saying, "He's such a rotten driver he hit a *Rockefeller* while he was on antidepressants."

She didn't even have to turn to know it was Dick Braidy. After three years of marriage Dick's voice had left a scar on her brain that four years of divorce had not healed. She could come into a room full of people and her ear would tell her immediately if he was there.

"It's a riot to see him on the talk-show circuit, pushing the book about his breakdown, because the one detail he leaves out of his confession is speed—the doctors got him out of his depression with Swiss synthesized crack and now he *lives* on it."

Leigh heard a woman cackle loudly, and it was not a kindly cackle at all.

"In theory," the young man was telling Leigh, "the goose shits the pearls out clean. But Mrs. Astor's pearls *killed* Cartier's best goose. Lloyd's of London insisted on an autopsy, and what do you think they found? *Malaria*. Mrs. Astor's sweat had infected her pearls!"

"Malaria." Leigh stretched a smile over her uncertainty. She reached for some kind of comment.

Dick Braidy's voice cut in from behind her. "Lulu Rockefeller's leg was crushed. *Smithereensville.* They helicoptered her to Columbia Presbyterian because it's the closest place where they do decent microsurgery."

"Your glass is empty," the young man said. "What are you drinking?"

Leigh glanced at her empty glass. She felt the need to get much farther down the slope of uncaring than Perrier with ice and lime could ever take her. *Wouldn't it be nice,* she thought, *if I had enough courage or weakness, or whatever it takes, to ask for Johnnie Walker and diet Pepsi.* She remembered the analyst who had told her it showed low self-esteem to put Pepsi in Johnnie Walker.

"Sparkling water with a little lime." She handed the young man the glass. "Thank you."

Watching him pry his way through the crowd, she felt invisible, as if all the people around her were connected with one another by waves of insider trivia, and she was just so much spillover.

A hand touched her shoulder. She turned and saw Dizey Duke in royal blue and too much jewelry, looking like a Christmas tree that had intercepted a flying blond wig.

"Leigh hon," Dizey said. "Keep your sunny-side."

"Sorry?" Leigh said.

"Up."

Leigh met Dizey's gaze. A fine glaze of sweat had begun to highlight the soft ridges of Dizey's face. It was a round face, plump and as eerily unwrinkled as a pumped-up balloon.

"I've got to hand it to you," Dizey said. "You're a real sport."

"Because I haven't thrown my drink in Avalon Gardner's face? Hang around. The evening's young."

Dizey shrugged. "Who cares about Avalon Gardner?"

"I care about anyone who defends Jim Delancey."

"Oh, Avalon's a senile old pussy."

"Then why have you been printing his senile remarks in your column?"

"Journalists don't take sides."

"I've noticed."

"You don't seem to be taking sides either. You spent a good ten minutes being polite to Ron Zaporta. Everyone was commenting."

"Ron who?"

"The hair colorist at the Pierre. You were just talking to him."

"Is there some reason I shouldn't talk to him?"

"Well, it's up to you—but he *is* Honey Ogilvie's beard."

"Dizey, I hate it when you use this tactic. You're acting as though I know or care who Honey Ogilvie is or why she needs a beard."

"Honey Ogilvie directs New York City Outreach to the United Nations Commission on the Homeless." There was something openly probing, almost malevolent about the gaze Dizey was aiming at Leigh. "I hope I'm not telling you anything you didn't know. She's here with Waldo."

"No, Dizey. *I'm* here with Waldo."

"You're the *official* story, but—" Dizey's pale blue eyes glanced significantly toward the corner of the living room.

Across the sea of bobbing tuxedos and tanned shoulders, Leigh saw Waldo. He was seated on the piano bench, playing the right hand of "Chopsticks." A young blond woman with overexposed breasts and very fake eyelashes was seated close beside him, playing the left hand. They were both laughing.

Beneath moussed gray hair Waldo's lean but placid face had the red glow of a Santa Claus in a liquor ad. He lifted the young woman's hands from the keyboard and placed them carefully in her lap. The young woman moved them to Waldo's lap and tickled.

A wave of denial passed over Leigh like ice water. She knew Waldo had affairs, but she'd assumed he was too much a gentleman to embarrass her by appearing publicly with a playmate.

"That looks pretty *with* to me," Dizey said. "They've been having long lunch hours three times a week at the Carlyle, and it's been going on a month. Annie seated them together."

Leigh's attention flicked to the gold-and-diamond necklace around Honey Ogilvie's neck. She had seen that necklace advertised in the *New York Times Magazine* two Sundays ago. It had cost somebody fifty thousand, and she had a hunch the somebody was not Ms. Ogilvie.

"Where does Waldo get his babes from," Dizey said, "a call service?"

"Is that a rhetorical question, Dizey? Because I could ask where you get your information from, the wall of the ladies' john at '21'?"

"Come off it, Leigh. Everyone knows you don't give a damn —you and Waldo have an arrangement." Dizey was watching Leigh for a reaction, alert as a dog on the scent of shot game.

Leigh realized that Dizey didn't know for sure, and not knowing was killing her. Leigh was determined to keep at least one aspect of her private life private. She focused on Honey Ogilvie's hair—a modified Sixties-revival beehive threaded with beads and chrysanthemums and trailing dozens of tightly coiled wisps that seemed to have been dipped in oil. "And does everyone know that Honey's beard does her hair?"

▪ ▪ ▪

IN THE DINING ROOM Annie paused to admire the centerpieces of blue begonias. Then she glanced toward the kitchen and decided on a last-minute check to make sure the caterers had the first course ready to go.

Tonight's appetizer was delicate, *ancienne cuisine* portions of herbed mushrooms on toast croustade with a side garnish of miniature glazed chestnuts. Like the entire meal it was microwave warm-up food, the ultimate fail-safe cuisine.

But you never knew. Annie pushed open the pantry door.

And stopped dead in her tracks.

At first she thought a bag lady had somehow gotten into the apartment and was stealing her dinner rolls. And then she realized that the slouched figure attacking the bread basket was her own daughter.

Annie strode forward. "And just what the hell, young lady, do you think you're doing? Those rolls are for the guests, not for you to make a pig of yourself!"

Gabrielle looked up with the startled eyes of a wounded animal. A butter knife clattered to the counter. "I'm sorry," she stammered. "I was hungry."

"Hungry! You're in what could be the richest and most productive period of your life—and instead of taking advantage of it you're binging on carbo-fat! Now, get out there and mix!"

Gabrielle stood there blinking. Tears began running down her face. "I'm an outsider, Mother. I don't fit in. I don't even know what I'm supposed to be fitting into."

"Well, find out and find out fast. It's not as though you had years in front of you. Get off your butt while there's still a chance. Make your life start happening! Stop being a nobody!"

Annie whirled and strode through the pantry door back into the dining room.

The servants had announced dinner, and guests were flowing past the circular tables, searching the place cards for their names.

· EIGHTEEN ·

"FACE IT," Dick Braidy was saying between mouthfuls of Annie MacAdam's Provençal goose. "If you're talking bodyguard, you're talking law-breaker. Because the only thing that scares a criminal is a bigger criminal." The goose was marinated with calvados, mandarins, and white peppercorns, and served with grilled kiwi, and Dick Braidy carefully separated out the peppercorns with the tip of his knife. "Every one of the bodyguards in this apartment," he said, "has a rap sheet."

"There aren't bodyguards *in* the apartment!" Cybilla de-Clairville protested. She was seated on Dick Braidy's right, and she gave him a joking little jab with her elbow.

"Didn't you see those goons out there in the foyer? *And* in the hall *and* in the lobby?"

"I thought they were well-dressed delivery men."

"Well, they're not, and you'll probably be hiring one yourself as soon as you get scared enough."

"What's there to be scared of?" One of Cybilla's beautifully manicured fingers kept touching the rose quartz-and-gold dividers of her pearl necklace. "Society Sam is ninety percent publicity. The people who hire bodyguards are doing it on expense accounts to publicize themselves. Who's got the biggest and meanest bodyguard—that's all the columnists are writing about nowadays."

"You're right, of course," Dick Braidy said. "And every one of those lugs is a dope dealer on the side. As well as a user. Don't tell me they don't take coke and crack and ice to stay alert."

"A lot of servants do coke," said Gwennie Tiarks, joining the conversation from Dick Braidy's left. "I'm having to send my cook to CokEnders." Gwennie was wearing her gray hair bobbed, like a Jazz Age flapper.

"The *dream* bodyguard," Dick Braidy said, "is a certified killer who got off on a technicality. Socialites are flocking to defense lawyers and begging for their bloodiest clients. Last year the cry was victims' rights, and this year the cry is *Get me a good victimizer—with a track record.*"

"It makes sense," Gwennie Tiarks said.

"Dick, you've just given me a brainstorm," a woman across the table said. She had curly red hair and she dressed like Alice in Wonderland with too many diamonds; her name was Kristi Blackwell. "You should write an article about society bodyguards."

Kristi Blackwell edited *Fanfare Magazine,* and she wielded a power in the city second only to Dizey Duke's. She was invited by hostesses who wanted to be written up, which was just about everybody these days; and she stalked the corridors of fashion, spitting out grenades and reporting the casualties. "Who here would you say has the most expensive bodyguard?"

Dick Braidy was thoughtful for only a moment. "I'd say Nancy Guardella."

"*Senator* Nancy Guardella?" Cybilla deClairville said.

Dick Braidy nodded. "If you lean this way, you can see her. She's sitting at the table in the hallway. They say her bodyguard beat a triple-homicide rap, *and* he was guilty as hell."

"Who did he kill?" Kristi Blackwell asked.

"A family in Hicksville."

"Hicksville," Cybilla deClairville said. "How awful."

"The rumor is," Dick Braidy said, "our senator is dipping into the taxpayers' pockets to the tune of two thousand dollars a day for this man's services."

"The other rumor," Cybilla deClairville said, "is that Treasury agents are examining Senator Guardella's books. I heard she's been laundering dope money through co-op foreclosures."

"Guardella's dope link," Dick Braidy said, "is a Republican canard, and it comes out quacking every election year."

"All the same," Gwennie Tiarks said, "those are two good reasons to have a decent bodyguard."

■ ■ ■

A LITTLE DRUM of uneasiness was pulsing at the base of Leigh Baker's neck. She took a tiny nibble of her ginger mousse, separating out the candied Amazon orchids, which looked too pretty to eat. She couldn't taste the ginger.

On her left Tina Vanderbilt, doyenne of New York society, with her waved white hair and her diamond collar, was telling the table about her financial adviser at United States Trust. "He says real estate, merger stocks, and defense industries have to adjust down after the boom years. He's moved me entirely into utilities, except for one trust I set up for the Crippled Children and Burns Hospital."

"How terrific," Leigh said. "I love children too."

"I don't like children at all," Tina Vanderbilt said.

As Leigh stared at Mrs. Vanderbilt a dark current of unreality seemed to flow between them. She knew the old woman had been having strokes, and she had a premonition that some awful remark was going to pop out of her.

"One has to help somebody," Tina Vanderbilt said, "and I feel sorry for children. Especially if they're burned or crippled. Though, mind you, I've met some children who *ought* to be burned—and some who deserve a good, crippling toss from the roof."

The others at the table heard. Silence struck.

"Excuse me." Leigh rose from her chair.

A flashbulb popped in her face.

"Sorry." A heavily cologned little man with a camera was shoving a fresh multiflash into his Minolta. He wore an Yves Saint Laurent ecru dinner jacket that hung like a zoot suit from his narrow frame, and Leigh recognized Avalon Gardner, self-appointed defender of her daughter's killer and *Fanfare Magazine*'s top photographer.

"Be a darling, darling. Let me have just one more of you and Tina engrossed in chitchat."

"I'm sorry, Avalon, I have to go to the ladies' room." Leigh pushed past him.

Guests had finished their dinner and were beginning to circulate again. There were collisions, and Leigh gave appropriate little cries of pretend-recognition and said, "We must get together, do give a ring," and she forced herself to smile. All the while rage was thudding through her veins. *How could Tina have said that? Even if she's gaga, how could she have been so cruel? And Avalon—pretending we're still friends.*

Somehow Leigh found herself not in the ladies' room but in an empty pantry. An open bottle of wine sat on the counter. She poured a glass and lifted it halfway to her mouth.

She suddenly saw what she was holding. Her hand stopped. *What the hell am I doing?*

She tossed the wine down the sink and quickly rinsed the glass.

■ ■ ■

AVALON GARDNER AND TINA VANDERBILT were standing in Annie MacAdam's dressing room, just the two of them, with the door shut.

The door was mirrored, and Avalon saw that a horseshoe of gray stubble was beginning to grow back on his shaved head.

He took out his little Cartier pillbox of coke and held out a tiny rounded silver spoonful. "Just say no?" he offered.

Tina Vanderbilt shook her head. "No, thanks. I'm trying to cut down."

"For God's sake, Tina. It's a party. Fuck your diet for one night."

"Gwennie Tiark's cook has been taking me to CokEnders. I can't let her down, she's such a dear. I have three days clean."

"C'm'on, Teeny girl, this is coke classic. Uncut blow."

Tina Vanderbilt changed her mind and bent a nostril toward the spoon. Avalon Gardner reloaded the spoon and took a hit.

There was a knock on the door and a woman's voice called, "Anyone in there?"

Tina Vanderbilt clutched Avalon's arm. He opened the door.

A blond woman stood there in a gray evening dress. The small diamonds at her ears looked real, but the large diamonds around her neck did not. She was holding up a deck of slightly oversized cards, smiling brightly. "Tarot, anyone?"

"Nan Shane!" Avalon Gardner cried. "Just the woman we need!" He pulled her into the dressing room. "Tina, Nan. Nan. Tina."

Tina Vanderbilt, flying now, returned Nan Shane's hello with a merry giggle.

Avalon Gardner pointed a finger at the floor. "Nan, deal me a good one."

Nan Shane kicked her shoes off and sat down on the rug. With the agile hands of a professional gambler she began rapidly shuffling her cards. Avalon settled down comfortably beside her.

She handed him the deck. "Cut three times," she said, "and concentrate on the question you want to ask the cards."

■ ■ ■

"I SEE THAT EVEN A PARTIES have their B rooms," Gloria Spahn said, "and it looks like we're it."

She had the kind of voice that Zack Morrow had always found attractive: educated, smoldering. It went with her dark hair and huge gray eyes. Her tanned breasts were practically tumbling out of a dress of mauve silk strewn with tiny rubies. He had never been seated next to her at a dinner before, and it was like meeting someone entirely new.

"I wouldn't say this is the B room." A smile slipped across Zack's face. "We've got Dick Braidy and Kristi Blackwell at our table, you can't get more A-list than them."

"So how does the A-list wind up seated in the bedroom?"

"Would you really call this a bedroom? Isn't it more a day room?"

Gloria Spahn nodded at the space beyond her tanned, bare left shoulder. "No matter how many Provençal-chintz throw pillows you pile on, a bed is a bed is a bed. Now, there's nothing wrong with eating in the bedroom, but I can think of bedrooms a little more apropos."

Zack set down his wineglass. In the time that it took him to decipher the expression on Gloria Spahn's face, that face became the most important thing in his life. He realized that her eyes were flirting with him, and he was riveted. "How long have you and Annie been friends?"

Gloria Spahn lifted a cup of Annie MacAdam's after-dinner demitasse to her mouth. He watched her lips kiss the porcelain rim. The lips were smiling.

"What's so funny?" Zack said.

"The only thing Annie MacAdam hates worse than my guts is my husband's."

"Then why does she invite you to dinner?"

"Ten years ago Stanley and I hired a personal publicist— Robbie Danzig. Annie owed him a favor and he called it in."

"You used a publicist to meet Annie?"

"We were untouchables. We wanted in. Annie is the express to the fast track. We figured it was worth the thirty thousand. So did quite a few other people here. It's ironic. You work all your life to get out of the ghetto, and then when you reach the top you meet all the same people you wanted to leave behind. And of course they feel just the same thing about you."

"And are you from a ghetto?" Zack asked.

"Of course." Gloria Spahn raised her long eyelashes and gave him another lingering look. "Can't you sense it?"

Excitement began beating in Zack's chest. "I'm not sure what I'm sensing about you. But I like it."

"And what about you?" she said. "Are you from a ghetto?"

"Most definitely."

"Is Morrow short for Morgenstern?"

"Why would you think it's short for anything?"

A mocking little pucker came into her lips. "Come on, now. It's short for *something.*"

"Are you speaking from intuition or knowledge?"

"Doesn't all knowledge begin as intuition?"

"Does it? Give me an example."

"Two hours ago I intuited that you'd be a great way to spend dinner. So I switched place cards, and now I know you're great for dinner."

"Only great? Only for dinner?"

"Don't look now, but Tori's watching us from the table in the hallway."

"And what does your intuition say about that?"

"A woman dresses for dinner the way Tori's dressed for only one reason: She's scared her lover's playing around."

"And does your intuition say her fear is justified?"

"My intuition tells me a man who changes his name is capable of deceiving his lover. You're not sensitive about it, are you?"

"About the name?" Instinct told him that honesty would earn him massive points with this woman. "It *is* Morrow. Almost."

"Aha. Tell me about the almost."

"I added the *w.*"

"Then without the *w,* you'd be—" She stopped, as if she were trying to visualize the name in print.

"*Morro* means *Moorish* in Spanish. Like Morro castle in Havana harbor. It's a very common name in Latin countries. I'm a spick."

"But everyone thinks you're—"

He nodded.

She threw her head back with a look of good-natured ferocity and laughed. "That's *priceless.*" And then she added, "I adore Latin men."

"And I adore Jewish women."

"Tarot, anyone?" a voice cut in.

Zack looked to his right. A blond woman who had not been there for dinner was sitting in the chair that the weather girl from *A.M. New York* had vacated. He recognized Nan Shane, Annie's resident fortune-teller.

"Could you use any guidance from the cards tonight?" The pupils of Nan Shane's blue eyes were pinpricks. The concave shape of her nose suggested to Zack that she'd had at least two retreads. A kind of willed zaniness animated her.

"Why not," Gloria Spahn said.

"Would you like the Swiss spread," Nan Shane said, "the Celtic cross, or the ancient ten-card spread?"

"Which would you recommend?" Zack said.

Nan Shane looked at both of them. Her gray evening dress had a fringed neckline that reminded Zack of a beaded lampshade. She wore two tiny diamond earrings and an obviously *faux* diamond necklace. She was smiling and, despite a certain dowdy note in her appearance, she seemed to have great confidence in herself.

"I recommend Celtic cross." She reached into her oversized carpetbag purse. She produced a deck of oversized playing cards illustrated with heavy-metal comic-strip gods, goddesses, sorcerers, animals, and rock singers. She pushed away an abandoned plate of ginger mousse and cleared enough tabletop to shuffle the deck twice.

Nan Shane pushed the cards toward Gloria Spahn. "Shuffle the cards facedown. Put all thoughts and desires from your mind, except the question you wish the cards to answer."

With blinding speed Gloria Spahn separated the deck into two exactly equal parts. She riffled them together in a single snap.

"State your question," Nan Shane said.

Gloria Spahn smiled at Zack. "Is now a good time to launch a joint venture?"

■ ■ ■

ANNIE MACADAM STOOD savoring the bustle and energy and laughing that filled her eight-room rent-controlled apartment. She saw Zack Morrow in the crowd and slipped into brisk forward motion. "Zack, I'm so sorry—I had you seated next to the new Channel Four newsbreaks girl, and Gloria Spahn switched place cards. I hope it wasn't too awful."

"Annie, you always serve delicious, delicious guests. Any chance that Ms. Spahn might be interested in viewing an apartment?"

Annie had it on unimpeachable authority that Gloria Spahn was an opportunistic tramp; she'd also heard whispers that Zack Morrow's seven-year relationship with Tori Sandberg was in trouble. Annie winked. She wanted Zack to understand that she could be a good guy for the right guy. Besides, he was such a big, friendly-looking, dark-haired fellow with such gorgeous brown eyes—how could you not love him? "Real estate is my business, Zack, and I have just the apartment."

"You're a doll, Annie."

"Takes one to know one. I'll phone your office tomorrow, okay?"

Annie threw a kiss-kiss and moved on to the living room, where a little old wealth, a little old fame, a lot of new wealth and new fame had crowded together. Annie's gaze took in the dark oak paneling, the oyster-colored silk curtains on loan from Elsa Piranese Fabrics, the green marble fireplace with its brass gryphon andirons on loan from Gurdon-Chappell Interiors, the painting of a naked marquesa on loan from the Paul Redouble Gallery, the deep plush-upholstered sofas and chairs on loan from Meubles Meurice, the Steinway concert-grand piano in the sixth year of its loan from Steinway.

Annie was satisfied. The perfect, sparkling setting was in perfect, sparkling form, and the perfect, sparkling cast spilled across her stage. She knew she had hosted another hit dinner.

■ ■ ■

"ALL YOU HAVE TO DO is be photographed at Archibald's drinking Roederer Cristal champagne," Robbie Danzig said. "And mention it in the article."

Dick Braidy felt an adrenal spurt of disbelief that his own publicist could actually attempt such a hustle at a dress dinner. He stared at the bald, bespectacled little man. "I am not writing ad copy. I am not posing for endorsements. I am writing journalism and prose."

"And what the hell do people drink in your prose—water?"

Dick Braidy gave Robbie Danzig one of his famous glares. They were standing in the crook of Annie's grand piano, practically shouting and still barely hearing each other over the other voices in the room.

"Would it kill you to give the poor slobs a glass of Roederer now and then?" Robbie said. "Truman Capote was *glad* to yank every fucking Mumm from *Answered Prayers* and substitute Cristal."

"And the only reason Tru did it was because he had AIDS and he'd let his Blue Cross expire and he desperately needed the money. I happen not to be dying and I happen not to need the money, knock wood."

Gloria Spahn came and sat down on the piano bench. "I didn't know Tru died of AIDS."

"Besides which," Dick Braidy said, "I have no intention of setting foot inside Archibald's."

"That's the silliest thing I've ever heard." Avalon Gardner, camera in hand, had joined the group. "If I'm willing to take the picture, you should be willing to sit for it."

"Not so long as my daughter's killer is employed there." Leigh Baker stood beside Dick Braidy, one finger circling the rim of a tulip glass of mineral water. "And we don't think it's very nice of our friends to go there either."

Gloria Spahn had a blank look: not so much critical as completely puzzled. "But there are parolees in menial jobs all over town. If you take a stand like that, this city would have to shut down. Who'd run the service elevators?"

"There's a time to hate, and a time to forgive." Avalon Gardner fixed on Leigh Baker and Dick Braidy an earnest, unblinking gaze. "Nita is dead, God rest her soul. Nothing can bring her back. Hatred certainly won't. What the two of you have to understand is that we're all human, we all make mistakes."

"That's all it was?" Leigh said. "Killing Nita was a mistake? And I suppose killing Oona was a mistake too?"

"It's our duty to forgive," Avalon Gardner said quietly.

"It's easy for you to forgive." There was something jagged and almost hysterical in Dick Braidy's voice now, in the line of his mouth. "You've never known the agony of losing your child. And you never will!"

Avalon Gardner spun around. His cheeks stretched out as if he'd swallowed the head of a sledge hammer, and his voice was screaming. "Why don't you just take that charade and shove it! Nita Kohler wasn't your child, she wasn't your anything except the biggest break you ever got! And ever since she died you've been strip-mining her corpse for every nugget of publicity you could! Well, you're beating a very dead horse, and I suggest you stop trying to sell the result as prime cut, because by now it is rancid! Maggoty! And your public is barfing! *Barfing!*"

Stillness swept the room.

Annie MacAdam stepped quickly through the crowd. Her frown cut a space between Dick Braidy and Avalon Gardner and her body occupied it instantly. "Hey, fellas, enough's enough. Let's discuss a different subject, okay?"

"That's all right, Annie," Avalon said. "I was just about to go anyway. Thank you for a delightful evening, as always. I have only one thing more to say."

"Don't say it," Annie warned.

Avalon faced Dick Braidy. "Did it ever occur to you that despite the courtroom testimonials you two extorted from your friends, perhaps your little angel richly deserved to go out of existence?"

A gasp, part disbelief, part delight, went through the crowd.

"And so do you deserve to!" Leigh Baker shouted. "The sooner the better!"

Avalon considered Leigh with a chilly, lingering, head-to-toe examination. "You shrill, stupid, spoiled, life-destroying *lush*. I hope you've sewed up your next reservation at Betty Ford." He turned. "Good night, Annie."

■　■　■

AVALON COLLECTED HIS COAT from the caterer's hat-check man. He dropped his camera into the pocket and went to the mirror hanging just inside Annie's front door.

Tonight he was wearing something new in fashion—a summer fur. It had the look and bulk of the most luxurious, deep-pile winter fur—but, in fact, it was a fully vented featherweight Japanese synthetic.

He adjusted the coat, the lime silk scarf that matched his eyes, and finally, the broad, floppy-brimmed, prestained-at-the-factory safari hat.

He did not like what he saw: Annie's mirror turned him into a sort of Interpol mug shot, distorted unpleasantly by a kind of fishbowl lens.

He stared back at his reflection with defiance.

Mirror, he said silently, *I do not care what you or the idiots at this party say about me. My life and accomplishments beam on me from the newsstands: My town house is featured in* Architectural Digest; *my peach linen shirt in* GQ; *my avocado flan in the "Living" section of* The New York Times; *my dinner guests are listed in "Suzy." I am reported on, I am famous. I am envied. I have not only arrived, I have the keys to the castle. I am a completely fulfilled person.*

He backed away three steps, made sure there was a casual assurance in the way he stood. He allowed the maid to open the front door for him. Stepping into Annie's outer hallway was like squeezing into an off-track betting parlor in Queens.

Two dozen or more burly bodyguards had crammed into the space. They were standing, sitting, reading newspapers, drinking coffee from paper cups, dunking doughnuts, smoking. They talked in low street-wise rumbles, moved like swaggering army tanks. Hanging out there in front of their scowls, like a neon sign, was that I-dare-you readiness for violence.

By a furious convulsion of the will Avalon was able to maintain an even step, ignoring them, moving slowly among them to the elevator. Riding down to street level, Avalon was hit by a sense of elation. *Avalon, baby, you made the top exit of the evening. They'll be talking for a month.*

As he stepped onto the street a Checker cab roared down Park Avenue, ignoring his upstretched arm. Park Avenue seemed unusually deserted. He would have expected more traffic at this hour, certainly more cruising cabs. He stared south, at the sidewalk stretching out darkly between the chalk-white spills of streetlights.

What the hell. He needed the exercise.

He began walking.

Halfway down the block a movement in the darkness between two co-ops caught his eye. Something jutted for one flickering moment into the light. It came and went too quickly for Avalon to see clearly, but he had a curiously unreal impression of a smile hovering inside a steel circle.

Instinct told him to keep to the curb side of the pavement, well away from that narrow column of darkness.

Still, his photographer's mind couldn't help wondering what on earth he had seen, or imagined. And he couldn't help glancing back over his shoulder, to see if he could see it or imagine it again.

And that was how he managed to let a second Checker cab go right past him.

He realized his mind was drifting under the stress of the evening. He stopped walking and lifted an attentive gaze to the north, searching for another cab.

His eye flicked back to that dark space between the buildings. There was nothing there, of course. He could see now that the darkness was just that—darkness.

And then, floating where it could not possibly have been floating, he saw the steel circle again.

But it wasn't a circle. It was a semicircle, the band holding two Walkman earphones, and it was clasped over the head of a man who was looking across the sidewalk straight at Avalon, nodding in time to whatever music he was hearing, allowing a blade of smile to show.

Avalon's breathing became short and labored. His lungs and muscles suddenly were burning.

He saw a cab two blocks away, heading toward him.

He stepped into the street, waving.

When he glanced behind him, the dark space between the buildings was empty again.

The cab was one block away.

Avalon could feel his heart beating in his fingertips.

He kept waving as the cab approached.

Behind him, to the side, his eyes registered a dark shape, a skittering, leaping movement.

Before he could turn, a force like none he had ever felt before yanked his head back, and a light flashed before his eyes.

He saw the taxi go by.

He called out to it.

Tried to call out to it.

All that came out of his mouth was a soundless pink spray, and it dawned on him that his throat had been slashed.

• NINETEEN •

Tuesday, May 21

HE LAY ON HIS BACK on the sidewalk. A ribbon of red wound down his neck and petered out below the collar of his dress shirt. His hands were clutched over a series of deep horizontal wounds in his stomach. They were a chubby child's hands, translucent and small and white, and they had not been able to keep his stomach from spilling onto his trousers.

"Any idea who he is?" Cardozo said.

The uniformed cop was standing stone-faced, silently appalled. He handed Cardozo a billfold of leather soft enough to have been unborn kid.

Cardozo opened it and smelled sandalwood. The charge cards and driver's license said the dead man's name was Avalon Gardner, of East Sixty-third Street.

He had died four blocks from home.

A flash went off. The photographer rose from his crouch and walked around the dead man and crouched again to get a shot of the opposite angle.

Around the body each separate crack and blister in the pavement stood out like a canyon in the police floodlight. Avalon Gardner's face, with its still amazed eyes, glowed as though lit for a close-up. A man from the lab was using a tape to measure the distance from the dead man's left hand to the trash basket on the curb. A woman in blue jeans was walking around the body in a half crouch, drawing a thick outline on the sidewalk in heavy white chalk.

Day-Glo orange tape had been stretched from the trash basket to the awning poles of the nearest building, from there to the wrought-iron bars of a ground-story window, marking off a perim-

eter around the corpse. Signs the size of little greeting cards
dangled at two-foot intervals along the tape. The greeting on
them read CRIME SCENE, and a steamy breeze nudged them into a
dance.

An officer draped a slick yellow tarpaulin over Avalon
Gardner's body. A small crowd had gathered to watch. The medical examiner's men were maneuvering a stretcher through.

Traffic along Park was picking up.

Cardozo's eye scanned sightlines. On the corner diagonally
across Park Avenue, three town houses stood dark. A white-pil-
lared, Greek Revival Christian Science church took up the corner
to the south. Except for a lantern-shaped light dimly glowing
above the parish-house door, it too was dark.

"Did the doorman in this building see anything?" Cardozo
asked.

"He didn't see the killing," the cop said. "But he thinks he
may have seen the perpetrator."

The lobby door was locked. Cardozo rang the buzzer. The
doorman who let him in was a beefy, red-faced man.

"I understand you think you saw the perpetrator," Cardozo
said.

"I didn't say *perpetrator.* I said *a guy.* There's a difference."

Cardozo's eyes began to accustom themselves to the dimness. The lobby had an expensively simple look: gray walls, polished wood surfaces. Two rows of man-high corn plants stood in
Chinese vases, floodlit from beneath so that the dark green vein-
ing of each leaf stood out.

"When did you see this guy?" Cardozo said.

"About two hours ago. He was hanging out in the doorway.
We've had trouble lately. Kids come down here, graffiti the walls,
piss in the doorway, mug the residents. An old lady on the eighteenth floor was getting out of a cab. A kid tried to snatch her
purse—broke her hip, dragged her halfway down the block. I'm
sure you're aware what's happening."

Cardozo was aware. The police could no longer provide a
secure environment, and Park Avenue money knew it. "Could
you describe this guy?"

"About six feet, six one. Hundred seventy pounds. Clean-
shaven. Dark hair. He was wearing Walkman earphones. He had
on sweatpants and jogging shoes. They always wear jogging shoes,
so you don't hear them coming."

"What color sweatpants?"

"Green. And he was wearing a T-shirt that said I love Alcatraz. There's a heart where it would say *love*. I haven't seen that one before, so it stuck in my mind."

"Would you say this guy looked anything like either of these men?" Cardozo took the Identi-Kit and the photo of Jim Delancey from his pocket.

The doorman stared at them both a moment. "Maybe this one." He picked the Identi-Kit. "But the guy I saw, his eyes were a lot crazier. Like he was doing major crack."

Cardozo stepped outside again. Twenty feet away, across Sixty-seventh Street, police were setting up sawhorse barricades.

"What's happening over there?" Cardozo said.

"A film crew from You and Me Productions is in town," the cop said. "I think it's a dog-food commercial."

Cardozo watched men placing card tables in the archways of the building across the way. Lights were burning dimly behind the vaulted windows of the first story; the rest of the building was dark. Workmen were spreading tablecloths over the card tables and anchoring them with platters of bagels and oranges.

Cardozo crossed the street. The Sixty-seventh Street doors of the building had permanent brass plaques telling you this was the Dominion Club and the entrance was on Park Avenue. He went around the corner and pushed the buzzer.

A uniformed policeman with icicle eyes approached and told Cardozo he'd have to move on. "Filming is about to start. You're in the shot."

Cardozo took out his shield.

The officer blinked. He touched the brim of his cap, embarrassed, and stepped back.

In a moment, through the carved glass panels, Cardozo saw an inner door open. An ashen-faced old man shuffled down the steps, buttoning a green uniform jacket over a cotton undershirt. Cardozo held up his shield. The old man opened the front door. Cardozo saw that he was wearing slippers with his uniform trousers.

"Are you the night watchman?"

"This week."

"A man was killed about an hour ago on the southwest corner of Park and Sixty-seventh. Did you happen to see anything?"

The old man pulled at an earlobe. "Only thing I saw was a kid, hour and a half ago. He was hanging around the front door. Had to chase him away."

"Can you describe this kid?" Cardozo said.

"Dark hair, dark skin, six feet tall or so, heavy-set, could have been in his mid-twenties. He was stoned or drunk. Had head-phones."

"Did this kid seem to be any particular ethnic type? Irish? Italian? Black?"

The answer came fast. "Spanish. The music coming out of his earphones was *'ay, ay, ay, bamba, mira.'* "

Cardozo brought out the Identi-Kit drawing and the photo. "Would you say he looked like either of these men?"

The old man held the photo at arm's length, then the draw-ing. He handed back the Identi-Kit and stared a moment longer at Delancey. He nodded. "He looked like this guy. You know—His-panic."

■ ■ ■

"OKAY, CARL," Cardozo said, "where was he last night?"

Malloy sighed and pulled his notepad out of his pocket. "We're not running a twenty-four-hour surveillance, just estab-lishing his pattern. Right?"

Today two blackboards stood at the front of the room. On the right, Oona Aldrich's, with a list of possible witnesses dribbling way down the right-hand side; on the left, Avalon Gardner's, with a witness list that had gone no farther than two names: a doorman and a night watchman.

"Right," Cardozo said. "So where was he?"

Malloy puckered his lips and flipped through the pad. "All his usual places at all his usual times. Left work at eight-fifteen, that's maybe five minutes earlier than his regular check-out. Cut straight over to Third. Walked home, like he always does. Bought a Frozfruit from a deli right next to the Baronet movie theater. Reached Beekman Place at eight-fifty, went straight upstairs. I hung around till midnight."

"Till midnight." Cardozo saw what was coming. "Avalon Gardner was killed between twelve-thirty and one-thirty."

"I didn't see Delancey leave the building." Malloy's shoul-ders shaped a helpless shrug. "For thirteen days he's been a crea-ture of habit. I'm sorry, Vince. I was playing the odds. I put in my full eight hours, plus four hours overtime. I was dead tired. I went home at midnight."

During the three seconds that no one in the utility room spoke, the sounds of a traffic jam in the street seemed to be com-ing from a bank of bullhorns on the other side of the wall.

"It was a judgment call." Malloy snapped his notebook shut. "Okay, I goofed. But if you want Jim Delancey watched around the clock, you're going to have to give me two men at least, and please explain to my wife."

"Okay." Cardozo's hands made pacifying, oil-on-troubled-water movements. "It's nobody's fault but the economy's. We're way under strength. I'll try to steal a couple of detectives to help out."

Malloy sat staring at his lap, avoiding every eye in the room, looking absolutely miserable.

"Hold it." Greg Monteleone was making a face as though he'd bitten into a Tootsie Roll and found glass. "Does anyone know one good reason why Delancey would kill this guy?"

"It could be he's getting even," Ellie Siegel said. "I reviewed the newspaper reports of the trial. The defense contended that Nita Kohler was a drugged slut who deserved what she got. The state called ten character witnesses to rebut."

Cardozo waited through Ellie's dramatic little pause. "Do we get to hear the names, or do we take a lunch break first?"

"The witnesses were Leigh Baker . . . Dizey Duke . . . Benedict Braidy . . . Tori Sandberg . . . Annie MacAdam . . . Gloria Spahn . . . Sorella Chappell . . . Fennimore Gurdon—"

Cardozo stopped her. "Who are Chappell and Gurdon?"

"They run an interior decorating outfit. Avalon Gardner also testified. And so did Oona Aldrich."

"You could be right." Greg Monteleone shrugged. "But there are eight living people on that list. If Delancey's getting even, why hasn't he killed them too? He's had thirteen days."

"Does it even have to be the same guy who killed Oona?" Sam Richards said.

"The cuts looked like the same guy did them," Cardozo said. "The autopsy will clear that up. In the meantime, Ellie, will you check out Gardner's will. Check out his address book. Draw up a list of beneficiaries and friends."

Ellie Siegel's green gaze met his for just an instant of narrow-eyed silence. The ballpoint pen in her hand make a swift notation in her notebook.

Cardozo rose to his feet. "That's it, guys. Meeting adjourned, full steam ahead."

Ellie rose from her chair, but she didn't leave with the others. "I don't suppose you saw Dizey Duke's column yesterday morning?"

"Did I miss something?"

She fixed Cardozo with a look that was not quite a smile. She opened her purse and handed him a neatly scissored clipping.

Talk of *le tout* Park Avenue is the scrumptious dinner Annie
MacAdam is serving *chez elle* tonight. Annie's eight-room duplex
has been newly decorated by the hot, hot interior design firm of
Gurdon-Chappell, who (don't tell a soul) were called in last season
to rescue Prince Charles's London digs. Cahn't wait to see the blue
on that trim, said to be a dream. Bets are being taken as to dessert,
with the smart money favoring ginger crème brulée. Poor Annie
must be limp after the awesome task of whittling down the guest
list to 80 very close friends, but then she's had to do it often enough
before.

He handed back the clipping. For a moment his silence
flowed into hers.

"Twice in a row, Vince. My instinct says he's getting his
coordinates from Dizey's sneak previews."

Cardozo's phone rang. He lifted the receiver. "Cardozo."

"Vince." It was Captain Reilly's assistant. "The captain wants
to see you right now. In his office."

▪ ▪ ▪

"YOU KNOW DEPUTY COMMISSIONER Bridget Braidy," Tom Reilly
said.

"Yes indeed," Cardozo said. "We met at the PBA banquet."

Bridget Braidy rose from her chair. She wore a loosely fitted
dark blue business suit and a blouse with an enormous matching
floppy bow tie. Her broad, wide-nosed face was smiling, and the
smile showed slightly discolored, stubby teeth. "It's good to see
you again, Lieutenant."

They had to shout. A mass of radio and TV people, newspaper and wire-service reporters had jammed into Reilly's office.
Two dozen voices were screaming at once. Flashbulbs popped,
minicams fought for good angles, microphones thrust themselves
into the air.

"Commissioner Braidy has brought some terrific news," Tom
Reilly said. "We're getting fifty men."

Cardozo shook Bridget Braidy's hand, a thank-you for the
string-pulling he knew it had taken. "Believe me, they couldn't
have come at a better time." There was no such thing as extra
men in New York's permanently understaffed police force. The
mayor's new budget had slashed the carotid artery of support
services, and contrary to media hype, the latest increase in police
funding had been gobbled up by a City Hall salary-and-perks
grab.

"Okay, okay." Tom Reilly came around to the mike that had been set up in front of his desk. "A little order, please."

The sound of shouting died down to the sound of talking.

"We've got a very important announcement and we want to just make it briefly, so we can get on with our work of protecting the public and you people can get on with your work of informing the public." Tom Reilly smiled broadly at Bridget Braidy. "I don't suppose I have to introduce Assistant Deputy Commissioner Bridget Braidy to any of you."

Braidy took the mike. The talking stopped. With an almost coquettish movement her hand went up to pit-pat her hair. In the glare of photographers' lights the hair was a strange dark brown with glints of a stranger, darker brown. Tiny, barely noticeable diamond earrings made two little glints in the lobes of her ears. *I'm a woman,* they seemed to say, *but see? I don't flaunt it.*

"Ladies and gentlemen," Bridget Braidy said, "we've all been outraged, and rightly so, at the killings of Oona Aldrich and Avalon Gardner. The mayor and the commissioner have asked me to announce that an enlarged task force is being established, effective immediately, to cope with this crisis. The mayor and the commissioner are contributing twenty-five detectives each from their personal-security forces, a total of fifty men and women. Heading up the task force will be one of the Department's most experienced and distinguished officers, Lieutenant Vince Cardozo."

Bridget Braidy stepped not very far to one side, and Cardozo found himself speaking into half a mike.

"The force and I," he said, "are very grateful to the mayor and the commissioner for this assistance. It's an example of what can be done when city agencies pull together, and it's going to make a real difference."

"Any leads?" a redheaded woman called out.

"Quite a few. We're following them up right now."

"The two killings were committed by the same person?" a blond-bearded man asked.

"Very possibly."

A young guy in jeans and a Kiss-Me-I'm-Italian T-shirt jammed a mike into Cardozo's face. "Do you think a task force can compensate for the innocent lives this creep has taken?"

The young man stood there, hating, but Cardozo answered calmly, riding his own unruffled beat. "Compensation is not the issue in this or any investigation."

Bridget Braidy interposed a hand and smoothly lifted the mike. "This investigation will send an unequivocal signal that the city administration holds all human life precious and that the people of New York City will not be terrorized."

"What about the eleven people slain in New York City in the last thirty-six hours?" a young man in a New York Mets cap shouted. "Any task force for them?"

Putting together any kind of task force meant pulling cops off your everyday New York atrocities that never reached the papers, concentrating them for one splashy moment on an atrocity that had made it to page one. It meant pulling uniforms out of the high-crime neighborhoods and hoping the city's killers and robbers and muggers would not declare a two-for-one day.

"It's a horrible statistic," Bridget Braidy said, "and we cannot and will not countenance it."

"Isn't this response too little too late?" a young woman shouted. She was wearing the trademark T-shirt and red beret of the Guardian Angels.

"No," Bridget Braidy said.

"In the last ten years," the young woman shouted, "New York has seen the militarization of the entire city north of Ninety-sixth Street. There's nothing magic about the number ninety-six. The street isn't fortified. Sooner or later the killing was bound to trickle south. Isn't the question for law enforcement whether we're going to go after the causes of crime, or just throw task forces at the problem to make sure homicide stays north of Ninety-sixth?"

"Young lady," Bridget Braidy said, "we've had plenty of homicides south of Ninety-sixth, and long before Society Sam. To cite just one, my own niece—Nita Kohler—was murdered four years ago on East Seventy-eighth Street. And that tragedy has given me a very personal perspective on these homicides and a personal commitment to seeing that this perpetrator is brought to justice."

I don't believe I'm hearing this, Cardozo thought. He leaned toward Reilly. "How soon are we getting these men? I need to put a round-the-clock tail on a suspect starting today."

Reilly shook his head. "It's not going to be that soon."

"How about stealing me two detectives from the embassy watch?"

"I'll see what I can do, but don't mention anything. Keep it sweetness and light in front of these guys, okay?"

·TWENTY·

"IS SOMEONE USING AN APPLIANCE?"

The voice was female. Carl Malloy didn't recognize it. He glanced around from his desk. A young woman was standing just inside the doorway.

"What kind of appliance?" Goldberg shouted.

"Electrified marital aid?" DeVegh shouted.

Besides Goldberg and DeVegh there were four other detectives in the squad room, all men, and they broke up laughing. The girl just stood there. Malloy remembered having seen her yesterday. He'd assumed she was one more problem that had walked in off the street.

"Something's pulling the current way down." She had auburn hair, cut long and wavy.

"Way down!" DeVegh echoed.

Malloy couldn't see what was funny about that, but the detectives cracked up again. He was trying to type up a summary of last night's tail. But with all the laughing and racket he couldn't concentrate. The sound of a TV game show was spilling in from the little storage room where the detectives knocked off to have coffee; voices were shouting in the corridor and PTP radios erupted in bursts of static. Phones were ringing everywhere.

"I'm losing files," the young woman said. "Who's running a heavy-amp appliance?" She had a sweet, lost look, but she was standing her ground. Malloy found himself pulling for her.

"Check the little girls' room," Goldberg shouted. "Someone must've left a vibrator running."

Malloy could tell she was inwardly withering. One instinct said, *Leave it alone.* Another instinct said, *Go help the poor kid.*

He pushed up from the desk, put on a smile as wide as a billboard, and went to her.

"Never mind these nitwits," he said. "They're just horsing around."

She squeezed out a smile for him. "I already looked in the women's room. There's no appliance in there."

"Would you like me to check the men's room?"

Her eyes signaled gratitude.

Malloy walked into the corridor and down to the men's room. The cleaning crew used cakes of industrial-strength camphor to tamp down the stink of the urinals, and the smell of it lay heavily on the damp, unmoving air. One of the lights had blown, leaving the two toilet stalls in dimness.

Greg Monteleone was standing in front of one of the sinks, practicing his charisma in front of a mirror. In one hand he held a hair dryer and in the other a comb. He seemed to be teasing his hair into a wave while the hot breeze of the dryer strafed his receding hairline.

"You're fucking up the power," Malloy said. "Your dryer's pulling on the current, and the kid on the computer is losing her files."

Monteleone clicked off the dryer. "What do you expect me to do about it?"

"You could warn her before you turn on the dryer. You could give her enough time to save her files."

"Next time I'll give her sixty seconds' warning. Anything to save your sex life, Carl."

"Fuck you."

Back in the corridor Malloy stopped by the computer. "One of the detectives was using a hair dryer. He'll give you warning next time."

"Thanks," the young woman said. "I appreciate it."

She smiled, and Malloy could feel her looking at him, and he found himself thinking regretfully that there were more tiny lines around his eyes than when he'd been a young man, a lot more gray in his hair, and a little less hair.

"Hey, if you ever feel like taking a break," he said, "there's a really great place on the corner. They make their own ice cream."

"I didn't take a lunch hour." She looked at her watch. "I am sort of hungry."

■ ■ ■

SHE TOLD MALLOY her name was Laurie Bonasera.

They were sitting in a booth off at the side of the ice-cream shop, eating double scoops of peach ice cream with sprinkles.

"It's an Italian name," she said. "It should be spelled Bu-o-na-sera, with a *u*, but we leave the *u* out to make it more American."

Malloy was looking at her. For the first time that day all the tension had drained out of him, and his body felt relaxed. "Red hair's not usual for an Italian girl."

"That's because my father's Irish. He married an Italian."

"Marrying an Italian didn't used to be all that usual for Irish guys."

"My dad's father took a while to accept it. But when I was born with red hair, it helped bring him around."

Laurie Bonasera went on like that, telling Malloy little things about herself. Malloy nodded, liking her smile: it softened the space around her. It had a glow.

She told him she'd gone to school to be a graphic designer.

"What kind of graphic design?"

"Stationery, layouts, album covers. Nothing very important."

He had a sense of the small, decent dream of a small, decent person, and he knew it was important to her. "That's great. Graphics can make all the difference, how a thing looks."

He smiled. He was comfortable. She kept smiling and he could see she was getting comfortable too.

"So how'd you get from designing to computers?" he asked.

"There's more money in word-processing—at least there is for me. The federal government started this program to computerize local police files, and I went down to get interviewed, and they said fine. It comes at a good time. My husband's a teacher in parochial school and they just cut back his hours, so you know, I'm trying to make up the slack."

"Sorry to hear your husband got cut back." *So she's married,* he thought. *Like me.*

"It's tough on him," she said. "But it gives me a chance to get back into the world. I've been taking life as it comes for a long time now, and for a long time life's been dragging me where it wants. Till now I just had one part-time job. Now I have two, so things are looking up."

Malloy had the feeling she was telling him things were not that great at home. "So Bonasera's your married name."

She nodded. "It was Moran before."

"You have kids?"

"None yet. What about you?"

Malloy realized he'd forgotten to take his wedding ring off. "Two kids. They're grown, so it's like not having any."

She didn't answer, and he was aware of the slow trickle of time, a silence waiting to be decoded.

"You must be smart to work one of those machines," he said.

"You can be an idiot and work one."

"I can tell you're no idiot."

He felt her turning shy.

"What I'm really thinking of," she said, "is writing a book."

"What about?"

"Don't laugh. I want to write a book about cops."

"I could help you. I could tell you stuff you don't see on TV."

Before Laurie Bonasera could answer there was a sound like a motorcycle crashing into a suit of armor.

Malloy couldn't believe it. At a booth across the room a boom box sat on the table, blasting—a two-speaker state-of-the-art megadecibel doomsday machine with red lights rippling up and down the panels in time to the beat.

The owner of the boom box had sprawled back on the red vinyl seat, thrust one foot in its jogging shoe up on the table. He was defying the whole shop with the contemptuous sweep of his gaze.

The other customers went on eating their ice cream as though it weren't happening. As they lifted their little spoons to their pained little smiles, they seemed to be saying, *The man with the boom box isn't here, the boom box isn't booming, we're not getting raped by that racket.*

The proprietor, a tiny, leathery Korean woman with a shock of white hair, was trying to tell the boom-box man to please turn the boom box off.

Malloy watched the old woman's rapid, staccato gestures of pleading, and he watched the boom-box man shrug her off.

"Excuse me a minute, Laurie." Malloy pushed up from his seat. He crossed the room and stopped in front of Mr. Boom Box's table. Just stood there, letting his jacket hang open. Letting his revolver show.

Mr. Boom Box was heavyset and tanned, definitely a Latino, with *mucho* macho and a cracked-out, fuck-you glaze in his eyes. He was wearing a tight black T-shirt with shoulder pads and a yellow sweatband around his head that matched his yellow sweatpants. It took him a moment to focus on the fact that Malloy was standing there, tapping his fingers on his revolver butt.

Mr. Boom Box quickly picked up his boom box and started to leave.

"Hey," Malloy called. "Didn't you forget to pay your check?"

Mr. Boom Box slapped five dollars down at the cashier's counter and didn't wait for change.

When Malloy came back to the table, Laurie Bonasera's smile was admiring.

"It's too bad you have to go through that," she said.

"A lot of things are too bad."

In a way he was happy. The incident had given him a chance to impress her. When they left the shop, the Korean woman refused to let him pay for the ice cream.

"You have any more trouble with guys like that," Malloy said, still playing a little for Laurie's sake, "you let me know."

He gave the old woman his business card.

■ ■ ■

IT WAS CLEAR that the housekeeper was not going to sit: she regarded Cardozo as Gardner's guest, not hers. Besides, the only place to sit was a virtually floor-level gray quilted sofa. If the design wasn't Japanese, the idea had to be. Cardozo was afraid that once he got down that low, he would need help to get up again. So he stood, holding the cup of coffee she had given him.

"You were his housekeeper?" he said.

The slender, dark-haired woman nodded. She wore an old-fashioned housemaid's striped uniform. "For eight years now." She wiped at her eyes with the edge of her apron. "Mr. Gardner was a fine man and a fine employer."

Cardozo heard Irish in the voice and he saw grief in the face. He saw shock. And he saw an enormous effort at self-control.

"Do you live in the house?"

She nodded. "Mr. Gardner gave me the basement apartment. He had it completely renovated. He put in cable TV. There wasn't a kinder man in this city than Avalon Gardner."

"What can you tell me about his personal life?"

She smiled with enormous sadness. "Mr. Gardner's life was exactly like this room. He believed in keeping things simple."

The room took up an entire floor of the town house, and it seemed the kind of relentless understatement that photographed well in Sunday magazine supplements. There was a single piece of classical furniture, a Chippendale secretary, obviously placed there because it was a knockout statement in isolation.

"Did he have friends?" Cardozo said. "Family?"

"Well, like it or not, we all have family, don't we? There's a niece and a nephew. But Mr. Gardner had no time for their gadding around. Mr. Gardner worked." With a firm nod the housekeeper indicated the walls around them.

The walls were dove-colored, tightly stretched silk. Hanging over the silk were huge black-and-white Avalon Gardner photos. Where the subject of the photo was recognizable as part of a human body, it tended to be a blowup of a shoulder blade or a butt. Sex impossible to distinguish. Photos that at first glance seemed to be spotted scarves billowing in the blast of an electric fan on second glance turned out to be monstrously enlarged orchids.

"He put these up last week."

"Beautiful," Cardozo lied. "Who were his models?"

"He got them from an agency."

"Was he friendly with any of them?"

"He was friendly with everyone." The housekeeper sniffed back a sniffle. Her hand went out to touch a black marble-topped table. She seemed to draw steadiness from it. "Too friendly for this city. He drew the sharks. He had terrible experiences every time he stepped outside that front door."

"Muggings?"

"Muggings were the least of it."

"Why didn't he use a limo?"

"Mr. Gardner wasn't one to throw his money around. And he liked to walk. Besides, the party last night was practically next door. Three blocks across, three blocks up."

"Could you tell me who was giving the party?"

■ ■ ■

THEY WERE SITTING IN HER STUDY, amid bookshelves loaded with up-ended one-of-a-kind china plates.

Annie MacAdam gave Cardozo the hard data: when Avalon Gardner had arrived, who he had spoken to, where he had sat for dinner, what she'd heard him saying, what she'd heard people saying about him. She remembered he'd been wearing a new cologne. "Fortunoff is trying to get a new brand started. They've mailed half ounces to everybody on the *Vanity Fair* party list. I do think it's tacky to wear free samples at a dinner."

"Did Avalon have any enemies, any disagreements with anyone?"

"Of course he did."

"Did he have any last night?"

"He had words with Dick and Leigh—" Annie MacAdam looked at Cardozo. With her hair dyed jet-black and coiled wiglike on the side of her head, jauntily speared with a tortoiseshell pin, she resembled a Fifties musical-comedy actress working the talk-show comeback trail. "Dick Braidy and Leigh Baker. The BeeBees, we used to call them in the days when they were married."

"Avalon had words with the BeeBees—about what?"

"I don't know how the subject came up." Under high-arched eyebrows her eyes were energized, sparkling. This was a moment she was enjoying. "But their daughter was killed—I mean *her* daughter. Her name was Nita Kohler, you may have heard about it. Her boyfriend threw her off a sixth-story terrace. Jim Delancey."

Cardozo nodded.

"He's been paroled. Avalon was saying bygones are bygones and Delancey deserves a second chance. Leigh and Dick were upset with his attitude and they let him know it."

"How did they do that?"

"Leigh said she hoped Avalon would die, and the sooner the better."

A phone rang.

"Excuse me." Annie MacAdam rose from the sofa and crossed to her desk. She lifted the receiver. "Yes?" She reangled herself so that she faced away from Cardozo. "The whole world has heard." Her head turned and her eyes came around toward Cardozo. "No, I can't . . . No, of course I haven't . . . Of course I won't . . . All *right.* I promise."

She seemed rattled when she hung up the phone. She took the long way back, circling an antique globe of the earth, and sat again on the sofa. "I don't know about your business, Lieutenant, but my business brings out the absolute worst in people. They say the real estate market's soft, but you'd never know it in this part of town. Such conniving and competition every time I list a major duplex. And, of course, Avalon's town house is going to be on the market now. People will be murdering for that. Have you seen it?"

"Just this morning."

"That property is *prime.*"

"You were telling me about Avalon's disagreement with Leigh Baker and Dick Braidy."

She settled back against the cushion and sighed. "I tend to sympathize with Leigh and Dick."

"Why's that?"

"A second chance is one thing and we all deserve it. Acceptance in society is another, but it has to be earned. Jim Delancey is working as a salad chef at Archibald's, and he hasn't earned it."

"Salad chef at Archibald's is acceptance in society?"

"It's certainly visiblity, and that's nine tenths of the battle. Put a good-looking, notorious young man in that place—a man who's had as much press as Jim Delancey—and there's no telling who he'll meet—a designer, an heiress, an actress, I'm talking about people of *top* significance. There are hundreds of deserving young men who'd give their eyeteeth for a chance like that. Why waste it on a sleazy killer? Poor Avalon." She shook her head. A Lucite earring clanked. "He was always getting himself into disagreements."

"Did he ever have a disagreement with you?"

"Oh, Avalon and I had a classic feud going."

"What was that about?"

"I adored Avalon." Behind her eyes was something disdainful that she didn't bother hiding. "But he had poor judgment. It was when he and Oona—Oona *Aldrich*—were on the outs. Everyone in New York was trying to stay neutral, and Avalon tried to pull me over to his side."

"What did he and Mrs. Aldrich disagree over?"

"It was years ago. Ask Dizey Duke. She'd remember. All I recall now is, it got so bad that you couldn't invite them to the same party. You couldn't even have them to the same *funeral*."

"Did you ever invite them to the same party?"

"I haven't had them in the same room for six years."

"When was the last time?"

"Do you want to know exactly?"

"If that's possible."

"My tax records would certainly show."

Annie MacAdam rose again. She walked to the one wall of bookcases in the room that held any books at all. She bent down to a shelf of two-inch-thick black leather binders and peered along them till she found the year she wanted. She pulled out a binder, opened it, and flipped till she found the right page.

"The last time Avalon Gardner and Oona Aldrich were in this house together was dinner six years ago, the night of May sixth. Princess Margaret was guest of honor, and I served *mousse de brochet*."

■ ■ ■

WHEN CARDOZO TOLD LEIGH BAKER why he had come, she gaped at him for one wild, blank moment.

She crossed to the windows. A little gold-and-porcelain clock on the mantelpiece tinkled the quarter hour. She turned. "Do you want to hear a funny joke?" She was standing beside a vase that held a gigantic spray of tulips and amaryllis. Her head was framed in sunlight. "Avalon and I had a terrible fight last night. I told him I hoped he died, and the sooner the better. He couldn't have been more obliging, could he?"

"You had nothing to do with it," he said.

"That's very gallant of you." Her voice was tight with the determination not to be comforted. "But you're not so naive as that and neither am I. He left the party because I got into an ugly, childish, name-calling brawl with him."

"That's not a crime."

"Let's be honest. Half the real crimes on earth aren't crimes, according to law. I drove him out into the street and into the arms of that killer."

Cardozo knew what she was going through. His news had knocked her off balance and she was grabbing for steadiness at the nearest feelings she could find. What surprised him was that she'd been surprised: she hadn't seen the morning paper, and if any of her friends had seen it, they hadn't phoned her.

"There's no predicting these street-corner encounters," he said. "Even God couldn't predict them."

She came back across the Chinese carpet with its whites and faint rust tones and pale leaf-greens. They stood four feet from each other at a border of silence. They stared just an instant into each other's eyes.

"Why are we standing?" She sank into a chair. Her finger played with a seam in the upholstery. "First Oona. And now Avalon. They detested each other." Her tone was flat. There was no heat to it.

"What was their problem?"

"It had to do with photographs. Avalon had taken some pictures of her and, apparently, they weren't very flattering."

Nudies? Cardozo wondered. "Did you see them?"

"No. I didn't want to. He published them, but I didn't buy the magazine. She was horribly insecure about her appearance. Wrongly insecure, of course. And as long as we're dishing the dead, if you're curious what *my* fight with Avalon was about—"

"I know. You disagreed with him over Delancey's parole."

"As though who said what or who thought what mattered! It's who *does* what that counts. I was screaming at Avalon as though he'd opened the cell door himself."

"It's a question of fairness. Delancey gets his second chance, your daughter gets nothing. In that situation I might say a few harsh words myself."

She looked at him. He was aware of a change in her, as if she was seeing him in a way she hadn't expected to.

"And I'm sorry," he said. "A raw deal once is bad enough, but your daughter got a raw deal twice."

"Thank you. I needed to hear that somebody was on my side."

Cardozo could tell she had something more to say, but she didn't say it right away; and while he waited he could hear the muffled, distant sounds of things happening in a well-built, well-run New York town house—cooks cooking, maids vacuuming, delivery men dropping off flowers, a secretary somewhere fielding phone calls and running the printer on a PC.

"I'm getting phone calls," she said. "My machine's been getting calls."

"What kind?"

"Silences. It rings and I answer and no one's there. I find myself waiting for them. Every time the phone rings, it's hard not to think—it might be him."

"Him?" Cardozo said.

"I just assume it's—him."

"At the moment we're watching Jim Delancey."

"What does that mean, watching him?"

"It means you don't have to worry. And as for those calls, why don't you let the machine answer? Don't pick up till you know who's on the line."

· TWENTY-ONE ·

THOUGH DIZEY DUKE chronicled New York's beautiful people for eighteen million nationally syndicated readers, Cardozo was surprised to find that she lived on the Lower West Side, far from the glittering towers and the long, long limousines of midtown Manhattan.

A nonstop jam of trucks heading for the Holland Tunnel moved past her building's front door with horn blasts and loud clankings of gearshifts. It was a noisy street at this hour, and Cardozo had a feeling it was a truck route, just as noisy round the clock.

The doorman wore a uniform from the waist down, a *Quiero-Buenos-Aires* T-shirt above that. He examined Cardozo's shield, buzzed Ms. Duke's apartment, and told Cardozo to take the elevator to 12-C.

The door on the twelfth floor was opened by a short man, no more than five feet six, with no hair and extremely thick horn-rimmed glasses.

"I'm Boyd MacLean," he said. His speech was fast, clipped, nasal. "Call me Mac and come on in."

Cardozo stepped into a hallway that seemed to have been temporarily converted into an office a long, long time ago. Two scarred and dented steel desks had been pushed against one wall, and the facing wall was lined with sagging bookshelves and steel cabinets. Snowdrifts of paper overflowed every surface. A fax machine on the floor was spooling out print, and another on top of a filing cabinet was making electronic distress noises.

"She'll be right with you," Mac said. "She's on the phone."

At the far end of the corridor a tall, stocky woman in Wrangler jeans paced back and forth with a receiver pressed to her ear.

"That story is over one-hundred percent lies," Cardozo heard her saying. "They papered the house at his funeral." She took a long drag on a cigarette. "No way. Not one more free plug for Mercedes."

She made a hurry-it-up hand signal to Mac. He ripped a sheet of paper from a clattering printer before it had finished clattering. She grabbed the sheet from him. Her eyes scanned.

"Oh, yeah?" She was speaking again into the receiver. "Tough. Only the dead love everyone." She broke the connection and passed a hand over her brow. "*Oy.* Where's my Advil?" She began dialing another number.

"Dizey," Mac said, "visitor. Lieutenant Vincent Cardozo."

Dizey looked around. She dropped the receiver onto its cradle. "How do, Lieutenant. Got your message. Be right with you." She snapped the page of computer printout at Mac. "This column is cluttered. Too many nobodys."

Mac grimaced. "If you'd tell me once in a while what your lead item is going to be . . ."

"If!" Dizey returned the grimace. "If your grandpa had wings he'd be a glider on wheels! What the hell am I dealing with, the Exxon oil-spill response team? For Christ's sake, there's a catering war on Park Avenue! So is Splendiferous Eats doing the library benefit, or aren't they?" She crumpled the page into a ball and threw it at Mac. "You want coffee, Lieutenant? Mac, get us two coffees." Dizey headed for an arched doorway. She tossed Cardozo an over-the-shoulder nod. "We can talk in here."

In here was a small living room with three cats exercising squatters' rights on an ancient sectional sofa. One wall seemed to have been painted Rust-Oleum. The window commanded a view of rooftops and black and crippled antennas and beyond them a pollution-brindled sky.

Dizey dropped into an easy chair. Cardozo sat facing her on the end of the sofa where the cats weren't.

"Are we giving the killings a brand name now?" Dizey stuck a fresh cigarette in her mouth. From the embroidered breast pocket of her cowgirl shirt she pulled a green Bic lighter. "Society Sam, is it?"

"That's up to the papers."

Dizey flicked flame from the Bic and held it to the tip of her cigarette. Her eyes studied him. "Well, I'm part of the papers, and I don't like giving them a brand name. It makes them seem too

. . . established. Like, here's reality—there's nothing anyone can do about it, so love it or leave it."

"That's not a bad description of life," Cardozo said.

"You mean life in the Big Apple. This has been my adopted home for more years than I'd care to own up to, but I never saw kids strip the running shoes and Walkman off a raped woman. And now it's commonplace. And Society Sam. Why? Sex and economics have been around for a long time, and they never caused this sort of problem before."

"It could be that the city's growing a meaner type of criminal these days."

"I'd hate to think you're right, but I think you're right."

"We've been looking into links between the two victims," Cardozo said.

Dizey nodded. "There were plenty of those."

"Evidently there was some kind of problem between Oona Aldrich and Avalon Gardner—they fought at one of Annie Mac-Adam's dinners and never spoke to each other again?"

"Oh, yes, indeedy."

"Could you fill me in a little on that?"

"Tell me when to stop." Dizey exhaled twin jets of blue smoke. "It was six years ago, so this is off the top of my memory. Oona got a fish bone caught in her throat. It looked like she might choke. Avalon was at the same table, so he took her to the hospital. While she was being treated he photographed her. The photos got published in *Fanfare Magazine.* They weren't what you'd call flattering angles. Oona never forgave him."

"That's it?"

"Cross my heart, Lieutenant, that is the *ganzeh megillah.* As I've found out in my business, and as I'm sure you've found out in yours, people can be stubborn and they can be dumb."

"They can be dumb some of the time," Cardozo said.

"Beg to differ. Nowadays people are dumb all of the time. Look at the way they react to Jim Delancey. He kills a lovely girl, they give him twenty-five years. Dumb."

"Too much time?"

"You kidding? He should roast in hell for life. *Then* they give him a parole. Dumber. *Then* they give him a job in a high-status restaurant. Dumber than dumb. It's saying, What you did doesn't matter, Jimbo, we're going to eat out of your bloody hands anyway. And *then* . . . these pickets. They're well-intentioned, but it's obscene. All they're doing is giving him publicity—and he doesn't deserve it. The guy's a killer, not a cause célèbre!"

Cardozo sat nodding in silent agreement.

"Can you believe," Dizey said, "columnists are publishing his salad recipes? Archibald's can't handle the demand for reservations. The whole damned business is vile. It's a freak show and in this jaded town freak shows sell out."

"How do you suppose Delancey got the job at Archibald's?"

All of Dizey's energy suddenly went into blunt, clear-polished fingertips that slowly stroked the beveled glass edge of the coffee table. "I haven't been able to get to the bottom of that—but I'm working on it."

"I'd appreciate it if you could let me know what you find out."

"You'll find out when my readers find out, Lieutenant. I don't play favorites."

"Not even with the law?"

"Not even with the law."

"Too bad. We'd make good allies."

At that moment Mac arrived carrying a clinking plastic tray with two cups of coffee and a sugar bowl full of pink Sweet'n Low envelopes and a half-pint carton of cream. He slid the tray down onto the coffee table between them. "Cream, Lieutenant?"

"The lieutenant can handle it," Dizey said.

Mac gave her a look. "Excuse *me.*"

Dizey waved her hand. "Scram."

Mac scrammed.

Dizey helped herself to heavy cream and Sweet'n Low. "Tell me, Lieutenant, how do you think you could help me?"

"That would be up to you. But I know how you could help me."

Dizey pushed the coffee tray toward him. "I'm listening."

"The morning before Oona Aldrich was killed your column carried an item on the Hansen Boutique. Yesterday, the morning before Avalon Gardener was killed, you carried an item on Annie MacAdam's dinner."

"Are you saying there's a connection?"

"We think the killer could be getting tips from you."

"Tips?"

"As to who's going to be where."

A phone jangled in the other room. "For you," Mac hollered. "Ms. A."

Dizey picked up the phone on the coffee table.

"Yeah?" She listened a moment with drooping eyes. "Jorge Luna and Tony and Chelsea LoGrande?" Her voice had become snide and just a little nasty. "Your guest lists are getting ridiculous." She hung up. Her eyes came back to Cardozo. "You can't hold me responsible, Lieutenant. I certainly didn't mention that Oona Aldrich was expected at the boutique at one-thirty P.M. In fact, I didn't even know it."

"But you implied there would be a certain type of clientele at the boutique, and the killer has drawn two victims from that social level."

"So Oona and Avalon were killed by the same man."

"It looks like it. We'll know for sure tonight."

"Let me ask you this: Is it your eyewitness knowledge that Society Sam is choosing his hits on the basis of my column?"

"It's a strong possibility, and I have to ask you to stop previewing social events in your column."

Beneath its heavy powdering the red of Dizey Duke's face darkened. "Until you have this crazy under lock and key, I'm supposed to limit my column to past events?"

"It might save lives."

"You mean it could save the life of every other columnist in town. I don't suppose you've asked Suzy or Liz or Billy Norwich to edit coming events out of their columns?"

"If necessary we'll certainly appeal to them."

Dizey jabbed her cigarette out in her saucer. A ribbon of smoke rose twisting from the mangled stub. "Okay, I get the picture, Lieutenant. It's always easier to write prescriptions than to pay for them, right? You're looking at a gal who happens to believe the Constitution meant it when it promised freedom of the press. I'm not going to censor my column for the police or for anyone."

"No insult intended. Just asking." Cardozo smiled and took a long sip of his coffee. "Great flavor."

"Latin roast. Mac buys it down at the corner *bodega*. They grind it special." Dizey Duke turned her wrist and frowned at her Minnie Mouse watch. "Well, Lieutenant, this gal's got to get cracking. Anything else I can refuse to help you with?"

"There's one thing. How did the photos of Oona Aldrich happen to get published in a national magazine?"

"Maybe you should ask Kristi Blackwell." Dizey saw the *Who her?* look on Cardozo's face and added, "She edits *Fanfare* and she's a lot nicer than me."

▪ ▪ ▪

"WHY DID YOU PUBLISH the photos?" Cardozo said.

Kristi Blackwell gave him a slow, attentive frown. "Because they were part of the story, and the story was offbeat. It had a kick. A kind of pungency."

"But it wasn't news, was it?"

"News is what the news says is news. *Fanfare*'s beat is society. And, frankly, not much happens in society unless it's made to happen."

In some ways she had the face of a show-window mannequin —a face of no recognizable age, eerily unflawed, her skin the even white of expensive stationery. Against that skin, the red of her doll-like, tightly ringleted hair and the green of her eyes had the startling force of candied-fruit bits in a pot of *zuppa inglese.*

"There've been maybe three real social events in the last decade." She held up three fingers, and one of them wore a waterbug-sized emerald. "Brooke Astor gave a party in the public library, and a midget financier started a brawl. Malcolm Forbes couldn't get himself listed in the Social Register because a homophobe gay was blocking him, so he bought the company and listed himself. The von Bulow prosecution boomeranged, questions were asked about planted evidence and a deal had to be cut with the state to keep a half-dozen perjurors out of jail."

She spoke with an unmistakable London accent, but Cardozo's ear couldn't tell whether it was the second-best or third-best kind. It had the faint ring of supporting player in a British TV comedy.

"If *Fanfare* had published the truth about any of those stories, we would have been going up against deep pockets who could have sued us out of existence. So what can we do? We deal chitchat from the power zones—Mary-Lou's dresses and Annette's divorces and Patty's gazpacho."

She was wearing an uncomplicated lavender silk dress, and Cardozo had the impression her diet-skinny bones carried it at least as well as any of the female bodies that appeared in the ads in her magazine. The lavender matched the irises in the jade vase on her desk, and it matched the walls of her office, and he suspected the matches were not accidents.

"Gossip is our mandate. At the same time it's our problem. Nothing dates faster. Added to which, we're coming out once a month with a three-week press lag. So how are we going to keep ourselves on the cutting edge? Either we have to have an exclusive, or we have to generate the gossip."

"And which was the case with the Oona Aldrich article?"

"Both. 'Socialites in Emergency' was an exclusive, *and* we generated it. If we hadn't been in that emergency room, not only would it not have been a story—it wouldn't even have happened. What I wanted to show was, *whenever* you drop high-profile names into a low-profile environment, the whole situation *automatically* goes major."

"How did you happen to have a writer and a photographer there?"

"Purest, luckiest accident. Dick Braidy and Avalon Gardner were at the same dinner as Oona; she got a bone in her throat; they helped get her to the hospital."

"Because they saw story potential?"

"*¿Quién sabe?* Lieutenant, there are fringe benefits to every good deed. Even the Good Samaritan was playing the odds. Between you and me, nothing was wrong with Oona's windpipe that a good swift Heimlich wouldn't have cleared up in three seconds. But nobody at Annie's dinners knows anything as useful as the Heimlich, and thus are great articles born."

"I gather Aldrich and Gardner quarreled over the story."

"Oona gave us a release. Later she saw what the story did for Avalon. She got angry and, in my opinion, she got jealous."

"Jealous about what?"

"In today's society the scarce resource is media space. Oona was launching her own name-brand tofutti. *Fanfare* was going to run a story to help her out. Along came 'Socialites in Emergency,' and there was no question—it was a far stronger story. When Oona saw our July issue, and her tofutti wasn't in it—that was when the vendetta began."

"By any chance could I see the story?" Cardozo said.

"Absolutely." Kristi Blackwell picked up the receiver of her desk phone and jabbed three buttons. "Lance, would you get me the back issue with Dick Braidy's 'Socialites in Emergency' piece? I think it's July eighty-something—it has Liz and Malcolm on motorcycles on the cover."

Cardozo's eye had wandered to a painting of a vase of flowers that Kristi Blackwell, or her decorator, had hung on the wall.

"It's a Pissarro," she said.

He assumed Pissarro must be good or at least okay if she had one hanging in her office, but his face must have said something else.

"I know, I know," she said. "Not one of the leaders of the pack—but what can you do? Prices for good art are still outrageous, and my publisher wasn't about to let me hang a Cézanne there."

She was talking to him as a sort of equal, as though he too had several hundred thousand of someone else's dollars to throw away on a pretty painting. She couldn't be dumb enough to think a cop had legal access to that kind of money. It was strategy, a way of flattering him by appointing him an honorary Person Like Us.

Her young male assistant brought in the back issue. She studied the cover. "Yes, this is the one." She handed Cardozo the back issue.

Looking at the cover, with Liz Taylor and Malcolm Forbes and their bikes, he felt a rush of remember-back-when. He opened the magazine to the Benedict Braidy article: "Socialites in Emergency," a two-page spread of tilted color photographs and uncentered raggedy-edged type.

"Which photo did Oona Aldrich object to?" Cardozo said.

"All of them."

Cardozo studied the photos.

Oona's face, he thought, looked fine: a little artificially madeup, like an actress's in a Fifties film—with eyebrows where no one had eyebrows and eyeshadow where only a ballerina had eyeshadow—but pretty and striking in a jaded way. What didn't look fine against a background of hospital beds and hurrying nurses and shoot-out victims was the dress she was wearing, an extravagant construction of stiffened red silk with a high, ruffled collar that rose twelve inches in back. She looked like an Infanta hunting for an escaped dwarf.

He turned the page. A photo showed Dizey Duke wearing a long-skirted chartreuse toreador suit. "I see Dizey went too."

"Dizey wouldn't have missed it for anything."

Cardozo pointed to the photo of a dark, severely underweight woman who seemed to have attached diamonds to her wet suit. "Who's this woman?"

"That's Gloria Spahn, the dress designer. She's changed her look since then—thank God."

"May I keep this copy?"

"It's yours, Lieutenant. Compliments of the house. And if you'd like a complimentary subscription—" Kristi Blackwell smiled and tapped a finger on her phone receiver. "I'm not like the rest of you successful Yanks. I'm still in the book."

■　■　■

A SMALL MEXICAN-LOOKING WOMAN in a white smock let Cardozo into Benedict Braidy's apartment. She indicated with hand gestures that he was to take the hallway to the right. Eight strides carried him into a chintz-choked living room.

Sunlight touched the dust jackets of books filling the wall of built-in shelves. There were three entire shelves devoted to foreign-language editions of Benedict Braidy's books, and another stuffed with enormous leather-bound albums.

Through a glass-paneled door Cardozo could see into a small office. A tall, overweight gray-blond man in a flapping bathrobe stood bent over a personal computer keyboard.

"Just a sec, Lieutenant," he called. "Let me close this contraption down."

Cardozo watched Braidy jab a key and stand back, biting his lip. The faint pulsation of light on the computer screen shrank to a spot of amber and then exploded into a fading spray of little blips.

"Shit!" Benedict Braidy stomped into the living room. "Pardon my Swahili, but I have a terrible time with that PC. It's eating my files day and night."

Under the robe he was wearing a strawberry taffy–colored button-down shirt. The top two buttons were open over a gray-haired chest. He had on tan slacks and Top-Siders, no socks. Cardozo had the impression that no socks was a fashion statement.

"Dick Braidy—great to meet you." Braidy held out a hand. "What'll you have? A drink drink? Diet Pepsi? Reheated coffee?"

"Diet Pepsi will be fine, thanks."

"Juanita!" Benedict Braidy shouted. *"Dos* diet Pepsis, *por favor, inmediata!"* Benedict Braidy plopped into an armchair. "Sit, Lieutenant, please. You can't expect me to share poop with a guy who's towering over me."

Cardozo took a seat on the sofa.

"Now, tell me," Braidy said. "What's all this sudden revival of interest in 'Socialites in Emergency'?"

"That night appears to be the last time that Oona Aldrich and Avalon Gardner were on speaking terms."

"True. Up till, oh, I'd say midnight or so, when she noticed he was snapping her picture."

"She didn't notice till midnight?"

"Until the doctors got the bone out of her trachea, she had more important matters on her mind."

The Mexican servant woman brought two diet Pepsis in tall green tumblers. Benedict Braidy thanked her and dismissed her.

"You've got to bear one thing in mind about Avalon," Braidy said. "He was a sly guy. Wherever he went that camera went too —and after a while you got desensitized. You stopped noticing that it was always clicking. Always recording. You allowed him to photograph astonishing stuff. He could have had a great career in blackmail. That, by the way, is a joke."

Cardozo smiled. "Does anything stand out in your memory of the hospital that night?"

Braidy shaped his lips into a thinking man's pout. "It seemed to me it was the standard waiting-to-get-into-Emergency drama." He tapped a finger to his skull. "Six years is a long time for this poor head to retain *anything*. As I recall, the doctors were charming. The nurses were hoots and a half. We were all having a great time till Oona realized she wasn't going to die. Then, of course, she got grandiose over the photographs, and we wished she *would* die. That, by the way, is also a joke. Poor dear soul."

"You fought with Avalon Gardner," Cardozo said.

"Everyone fought with Avalon."

"Last night."

"Last night he was at his tactless, scene-making, scene-stealing worst."

"Why did he leave the party early?"

"My honest opinion? He saw a chance to make the greatest exit of the evening. He grabbed it. He was on a roll. Unfortunately he didn't know when to stop. He went into the street and he attracted one catastrophe too many." Dick Braidy smiled sadly. "But still he went out just the way he would have wanted to—like a legend, headlines and all."

Cardozo unfolded the Identi-Kit drawing from his jacket pocket. He handed it across the coffee table. "Do you recall having seen this man last night?"

Astonishment hung like a vapor in front of Dick Braidy's face. "At the *party*?"

"Anywhere at all."

Benedict Braidy stared a long moment at the Hispanic male. "Well, it's a tad hard to say—he is a rather salt-of-the-earth New York type. I honestly can't say I recall him."

"Did you see him in the Emergency Room?"

Braidy looked up, surprised. "You mean six years ago?" He took a pair of reading glasses from their case and propped the tortoiseshell wings loosely on his ears. He squinted through them as though trying to bring a memory into focus. After a moment he shook his head. "I'm sorry, I don't recall his being there. I don't recall his *not* being there. Of course he would have looked younger." Braidy slipped the glasses back into their case. "I take it this is the man with the noisy radio?"

Cardozo nodded. He handed Dick Braidy a photo. "Did you see this man last night?"

Dick Braidy frowned. "Jim Delancey? At the party? Absolutely not. Do you think he's the one?"

"We don't have enough to rule anyone in or out. We have two events linking the victims: They went from dinner to the Emergency Room six years ago—and they testified as character witnesses for Nita Kohler's character four years ago. For the last two thousand days and nights of their lives, there was no other contact between them."

Benedict Braidy's smile dropped off his face. "But they were chosen randomly, weren't they? I mean, I was at that dinner too. And I went to the Emergency Room. And I testified for Nita's character at the trial." Dick Braidy's mouth hung open. "You don't think he's going down a list."

Cardozo didn't answer.

Dick Braidy grabbed a cigarette from a cedar-lined silver box. He fumblingly lit it and then he blew smoke out. "But that note he sent didn't mention any dinner or trial." Braidy stared mournfully at the cigarette in his hand. "I haven't smoked in three years."

Cardozo nudged an ashtray toward him. "This one doesn't count."

Braidy stubbed out the cigarette and drained his diet Pepsi and set the glass down with a thunk on the male Hispanic's face.

"When I spoke to Leigh Baker this morning," Cardozo said, "she didn't know Avalon was dead. No one had told her. Didn't anyone think of picking up the phone and letting her know?"

"As a matter of fact," Dick Braidy said, "I tried. And I'm sure a lot of her friends tried. But she'd turned off her answering machine, and she'd told the servants she didn't want to be disturbed. She does that sometimes. She isolates. I think last night was very hard on her."

"I'm surprised her friend Waldo Carnegie couldn't reach her."

"Waldo's an odd person, and even though they live in the same house they have an unconventional relationship."

Cardozo took a business card from his wallet and added his home number. He laid it on the edge of the coffee table. "If you think of anything else linking Avalon Gardner and Oona Aldrich, would you let me know?"

Dick Braidy picked up the card and looked at it. "You'd better believe I'm going to be racking my brain. But I warn you: I get my best inspirations at two in the morning."

Cardozo rose from his chair. "Jot them down and hold off till dawn?"

"I'll try. No promises."

· TWENTY-TWO ·

"THEY WERE HERE the night of May sixth, nineteen eighty-five," Cardozo said, "between ten-thirty and eleven-thirty." He was explaining to the young, dark-haired woman stationed at the computer desk. "I need to know what happened in Emergency—what they saw, who they saw, who saw them."

"In *Emergency*?" The young woman shook her head. A strand of brown hair fell across her eyes, and she pushed it away. "Unless they're patients they don't get through that door. Whatever happened, happened in here in the Admitting Room."

Across the room a queue of Hispanics and blacks and Third Worlders wound past the window where the triage nurse checked who had insurance and who did not. Babes in arms were wailing. Exhausted mothers barked commands to be silent.

A babble of languages—most of them hysterical—filled the heavily disinfected air. Cardozo was able to recognize Spanish, Portuguese, and the weirdly clipped cadences of Haitian French. His ear could detect too the singsong of Korean and Vietnamese, plus a half-dozen dialects that he doubted Berlitz had ever gotten around to listing in the curriculum.

"Okay," he said, "how do I find out who was in this room?"

"Let's make sure six years ago is still on database." The young woman touched her computer keyboard like a pianist rippling out an arpeggio. A list of files began scrolling up the screen. "We're in luck. Let's check May sixth Emergency admissions." She stopped the list and touched the screen with an electronic pencil. "Sixteen between ten-thirty and eleven-thirty."

Two chairs away a Haitian woman in a green hospital smock

sat shivering, teeth chattering on a thermometer. Cardozo had seen a nurse order her out; the woman had waved the thermometer, pointing to a fever of one hundred four. The nurse had sent for Security, and Security had yet to appear.

Cardozo leaned forward in his seat to get a better look at the terminal. "Can you tell me anything about these people or their complaints?"

"If you want the admitting complaint, we're going to have to hand-comb." The young woman pushed a command key. Green-gold print began moving up the screen, like credits rolling in a movie. "Fever. Bleeding from the mouth. Laceration eye."

"How do you lacerate an eye?"

She pressed a key and stopped the print crawl. "Jennifer Molina did it by sticking a pencil in it." She pressed the key again and the crawl continued. "Fractured ankle. Obstructed trachea."

"Who was the obstructed trachea?"

"Oona Aldrich. She was sent home, so she couldn't have been dying. Not that night anyway. The next is a laceration scalp."

"What would that be, a mugging?"

"Bumped head, low-hanging beam."

"Any chance the low-hanging beam was in someone's hand?"

"Doesn't say. Usually it would say *street attack* or *assault* if the damage wasn't accidental. Fractured femoral bone."

"Fractured how?"

"Fall downstairs. And then we have a gunshot wound."

"Who got shot?" Cardozo said.

"Lopinto, Germano."

"How?"

"That would be in your files and not mine."

"Life-threatening?"

"Lobe of ear. Maybe it was intended to be life-threatening and missed. Then we have fever. Diarrhea. Fever."

"Those are three separate admissions?"

The young woman nodded. "Must've been a bug going around. Laceration torso. Looks like a stabbing. Twelve stitches. But he was sent home. Our next case is puncture wound, hand." She frowned. "Our next admission is *no complaint*."

"That's an admission?"

She nodded. "Says so here."

"Why would someone be admitted for no complaint?"

"Beats me." She studied the screen a moment and then she said, "Poison."

"*No complaint* was poison?"

"No, poison is the next admission."

"What was no complaint's name?"

"Isolda Martinez. The account was never paid."

"How much did she owe?"

"Eighty dollars."

"What would have cost eighty dollars?"

"It's a flat rate, heart surgery or a Band-Aid on a cut. If you do it through Emergency, it costs you eighty bucks."

"There's no way you can find out what she was admitted for?"

"If it's not here, it's not here."

"How could it not be there?"

"Error. Somebody forgot to enter it. Somebody also entered her out of sequence. She was admitted five minutes ahead of Jennifer Molina, eye laceration."

"How'd she get out of sequence?"

"I don't know. It happens, I guess."

"Was she admitted to the hospital from Emergency?"

"No way. She failed the wallet biopsy with a resounding thunk—no insurance, no health plan, no social-security number."

"If they can't pay, they don't get past Emergency?"

"Not here. They go to the Bronx or Harlem. It's a tough world, Lieutenant. There's a lot of competition for medical resources."

▪ ▪ ▪

BACK AT THE PRECINCT Cardozo took a cup of coffee into his cubicle and got busy on the phone. He gave Directory Assistance the names of the sixteen patients. Directory Assistance gave him 117 numbers in five boroughs.

He began by trying the nineteen I. Martinezes.

In an hour, he was able to reach half the numbers. Of the seven I. Martinezes he managed to speak to, none were Isoldas. None of the others that he reached had ever in their lives set foot in Lexington's Emergency Room.

The other half didn't answer. Cardozo put them on a keep-trying list.

▪ ▪ ▪

"THE METHOD," Dan Hippolito said, "is the same as before: Approach from the rear. Left-handed armlock around the victim's neck. Right-handed slash across the victim's throat, from left to right. A second stroke laterally across the throat in the reverse direction."

Cardozo handed back the photo of Avalon Gardner's head, throat, and shoulders.

"It's a military kill," Dan Hippolito said. "They teach it in the marines. At least in my day they did. Blood loss—even loss from a major artery like the carotid—is a slow death, whereas asphyxiation is fast. With this kill arterial blood runs back into the windpipe. You die both deaths at once—technically asphyxiation is the killer, but blood loss pulls the die-time down."

They were sitting in Dan Hippolito's office. The air-conditioning vent high up on the wall was making a low, constant hum.

"So the killer could be an ex-marine," Cardozo said.

"I'm not saying American marines have a monopoly on this method. And nothing about the rest is military." Dan Hippolito laid down another glossy on the desktop. "The abdominal cuts are roughly horizontal." The capped tip of Dan Hippolito's ballpoint followed the line of the cuts. They had a black, velvety thickness, as if they were ribbons laid on top of the dead man. "You have three on the left side. You have two on the right."

Cardozo saw that the bottom-most cut and the top-most had been made out of line with the other three, distinctly to the right of them. He asked himself, *Why?*

"Five cuts in all," Dan Hippolito said, "spaced roughly an inch apart. And then over the liver you have a sprinkling of puncture wounds."

The ballpoint made a nervous little pecking like the needle of a sewing machine.

"The liver again." Cardozo saw tiny creases where the dead flesh had pulled together along the sutures. "I see we've still got that pucker."

Dan Hippolito nodded. "Missing tissue. Not much, but definitely missing."

"Same weapon?"

"Very likely."

Cardozo lifted his coffee cup and took another swallow. His throat was dry. He needed the swallow. He didn't need the coffee. His head was throbbing from caffeine. He felt a dull fire in the arches of his feet from all the walking he'd done that day. His eyes came up from the glossy. "Oral sex again?"

Dan Hippolito nodded. "Two pubic hairs in the victim's mouth. The lab's examining them. We should have results tomorrow."

"Two again. Why two?"

"Why not? Two's a nice even number."

Cardozo couldn't think of any why not, but he couldn't think of any why either. It just struck him as odd. "Semen?"

Dan Hippolito shook his head. "This time there was no semen in the mouth."

"How do you explain that?"

"You don't have to be an astrophysicist. The killer didn't climax. But the hairs tell us he sure tried. Maybe he couldn't get hot for the guy. Maybe he's come-shy on a public thoroughfare."

▪ ▪ ▪

"YOU'RE NOT BALANCING the bar," Dick Braidy's trainer prodded.

"I'm *trying* to balance it!" Dick Braidy grunted.

"Look in the mirror. The mirror's your friend." The trainer's name was Bruce McGee. He had curly hair and a terrific build and he owned the gym. He was rumored to train Tom Cruise and Cher and Prince Wally of Yugoslavia, which was why Dick Braidy had insisted on working out with him personally.

"That mirror," Dick Braidy said, "is no friend of mine." The truth was that when he attempted the behind-the-neck military press, the mirror showed him a thickened neck with veins standing out, a vanished chin, and cheeks that had grown extra cheeks. It was that very reflection that had driven him to the gym.

He squeezed both eyes shut and, at the same moment, hands gripping the steel bar behind his head, he pushed up. It was like lifting the lid of your own coffin. Hopeless. A weight clattered loose and then gravity kicked in and the bar tipped insanely to the left.

Bruce caught the bar. "When the reps get hard is when you've got to keep a tight grip. Just like life."

Dick Braidy's eyes snapped open. "Bruce, please. No lectures on life today."

Bruce placed a hand on Dick Braidy's shoulder. "What's rattling you, fella? You're all keyed up."

"How can I not be keyed up? Horrible things are happening in this city."

"Get over it, fella. Shit's coming down all the time." Beneath the blue T-shirt stenciled with the gym's logo, Bodies-PLUS!, Bruce's chest rose and fell with slow, effortless regularity. "Use the anger. Adrenaline's your friend. Turn it into reps. We want to get you as lean as Paul Newman."

Dick Braidy braced one hand against the pec deck, catching his breath. "Speaking of Paul Newman, is it true that he—"

"Got a treat for you." Bruce smiled mysteriously. "Ten-pound lateral dumbbell raises."

The lateral raises were not a treat. Neither were the reverse-grip pull-downs or the abdominal routine that followed.

By the end of his workout Dick Braidy felt like a tin shack buckling in a Georgia heat wave. He stood on trembling knees, toweling sweat off his face, trying to catch his breath. "How many lateral raises can Paul Newman do?" he asked.

"Uh-uh, we don't discuss clients." Bruce wagged a finger. He leaned close and whispered. "Three sets of thirty." He gave Dick Braidy a slap on the bottom. "See you Thursday."

Muscles beginning to throb now, Dick Braidy retrieved his clothes from the locker and found a free changing room.

In the mirror, dimly, he could see the beginning of something: In three months at the gym he'd cut his weight from two twenty-nine to one ninety-seven, his waist from thirty-eight inches to thirty-seven.

Just the other day he'd walked up the three flights of stairs from the Fifty-second Street entrance of the Four Seasons to the Grill Room, and he hadn't even been out of breath when he reached the maître d's desk. Not bad for a sixty-year-old six-feet-two chubby who hadn't exercised in twenty years.

"Hey, you're looking good."

Dick Braidy turned at the sound of the voice with its faint foreign accent. The boy who washed towels and cleaned up around the gym stood smiling in the half-opened doorway. He was a new employee—Dick Braidy had seen him around for three weeks or so. Towel boys never lasted long at Bodies-PLUS.

The boy flexed a bicep. "Getting hard, right?"

Dick Braidy felt a glow. "Me? Come on, I'm an old wreck."

The boy shook his head. His dark eyes were grave. "No, man, you're changing, I can see it."

"Really?" Dick Braidy glanced again at his reflection, pleased. "Maybe I'm a *little* tighter."

"You're going to look great, man. People are going to think you're shooting steroids. You should enter the over-forty middle-weight triathlon."

Does he really think I'm only over forty? Dick Braidy wondered. He laughed. "Me a middleweight? When did you last have your eyes checked?"

The boy tapped a forefinger to his left temple. "I eat a dozen carrots a day. I have twenty-twenty vision and I can see in the dark."

"You're in the wrong field," Dick Braidy said. "You should be in diplomacy."

"See you," the boy said.

"See you." Dick Braidy closed the door and slid the bolt. Feeling just a little pleased with himself, he had himself a long, slow-motion shower and shampoo. He dried himself, gave his hair a quick once-over with the hairdryer provided by Bodies-PLUS, slipped back into his street clothes.

As he crossed the entrance vestibule, his journalist's eye scanned the Bodies-PLUS bulletin board. Four square feet of cork-board overflowed with ads for Bodies-PLUS vitamin supplements and unpasteurized, caffeine-free bee pollen.

Two New York Police Department flyers had been push-pinned to the bottom of the board. Both were sketches, apparently drawn by the same robot—one of a full-lipped, pouting black woman, the other of a generic male Hispanic. Both carried the same text: WANTED FOR QUESTIONING IN CONNECTION WITH HOMICIDE. With a start Dick Braidy realized that the male was the same Identi-Kit that Lieutenant Cardozo had showed him that afternoon.

Such an ordinary face, Dick Braidy thought. *You see a hundred a day of them.* Suppressing a shudder, he hurried into the hallway and pressed the elevator button.

· TWENTY-THREE ·

Wednesday, May 22

"TELL ME." Lou Stein's face was ruddy above a cotton work shirt. "Why is it the stuff you find in a Park Avenue trash basket looks exactly the same as the stuff you find in a Times Square trash basket? Same newspapers, same hot-dog wrappers, same condoms, same unidentifiable objects."

"I guess," Cardozo said, "all neighborhoods are trashy in the same way."

They were standing in Lou's lab, gloved, reviewing the contents of the trash basket from the southwest corner of Sixty-seventh and Park. Lou's gloved fingers smoothed a newspaper clipping down on the steel tabletop. He nudged his glasses lower on his nose and read aloud: *"Talk of* le tout *Park Avenue is the scrumptious dinner Annie MacAdam is serving* chez elle *tonight. Annie's eight-room duplex—"*

"Thanks, Lou, I know it by heart."

"This column was clipped," Lou said, "not torn." His tweezers tapped the faintly jagged edge of the paper. "In fact, the serrations on this column are compatible with the serrations on the first column."

"Only compatible? Don't they match?"

"Let's be grateful for what we've got. They don't *not* match. The same rinky-dink, loose-screwed, two-inch five-and-dime scissors could have cut them both out. And look what else the tooth fairy brought." Lou was holding up a three-inch length of white candle, a half inch in diameter, with a blackened wick. "This is a Saffire-brand *Shabbes*—and it's a kissing cousin of the candle we found in Oona Aldrich's changing room. Available in any New York supermarket. Not only the same brand, the same box. Saffire

Shabbes comes in cardboard packs. Whoever stacked them on the shelf dented this box. There's a groove running along the underside of candle one." Lou held up another candle. "There's a groove on the underside of candle two." He held up the two candles together. "They're the same groove. And, dollars to doughnuts, it'll be on the underside of candle three."

"I appreciate your optimism. How long did candle two burn?"

"A little under two minutes. That's lab conditions."

"Was the candle put out, or did it go out by itself?"

"Impossible to determine." Lou peeled off his gloves and moved to the desk. He picked up a lab report. "Bad news from Lifeways Lab. They haven't been able to recover usable DNA from the semen and hair in Oona Aldrich's mouth."

"How do the hair samples from Avalon Gardner's mouth match up with the Aldrich hairs?"

"Our equipment's a little behind state-of-the-art, but my microscope says they're identical."

▪ ▪ ▪

TWENTY MINUTES LATER, Cardozo stood just inside the entrance of the Dominion Club.

"A *what?*" the porter said.

"A small candle," Cardozo repeated patiently.

The porter pulled back his head and bulged his eyes. "Christ, no. People don't use candles on the street."

Two minutes later the doorman at the co-op across the street shook his head.

"No, I didn't see any candle."

▪ ▪ ▪

MARTY WILKES, the psychologist, frowned at the photographs that had been paper-clipped to Avalon Gardner's autopsy report. "Have you been able to establish the sequence of these cuts?"

"The first two cuts are to the throat," Cardozo said. "Then there's a series of horizontal slashes descending across the abdomen and then punctures over the liver." He sat clicking the push-button of his ballpoint pen. "What we're not sure of is whether he has sex first or kills them first. If he has sex first, what's to keep the victim from screaming? Or fighting him off? Or getting away?"

"Is there any sign that either victim was gagged?"

"None."

"Then he wounds them first."

"And has sex with a dying person?"

"Or a dead person. It could be a payback."

"For what?"

"I'll hazard a guess. As a child he was forced to have oral sex with an adult. And he feared for his life. Possibly this person was a woman, but the overwhelming probability is that it was a man."

Cardozo aimed a glance toward the desktop computer. "This is your database talking?"

Wilkes nodded. "According to BSU files, over eighty percent of serial killers were abused as children."

"Tell me if this is in your files." Cardozo sat forward in his chair. "Both times there's been body tissue missing."

Wilkes was silent. His arms crossed in front of his chest, erecting a tight little wall. "Are we talking body parts? Fingers? Nipples?"

"He's ripped off tissue around the cuts."

"How much tissue?"

"Just enough so you can't suture the wounds back together."

Wilkes nodded, somber. Behind him, the Levolors in the window had been angled to filter the late-afternoon sun down to a soft shimmer. "Look, it's repulsive, but it's not uncommon. The sex instinct in children is oral—you see male infants having erections at their mother's breast. For the infant, biting, chewing, even eating and devouring are sexualized. And this is the instinctual level where the serial killer is fixated."

"You're saying he's eating the tissue?"

"Maybe not on the spot, but there are instances in the database."

"And he has an orgasm while he eats it?"

"Very possibly."

Cardozo rose and moved to the window. He stood with his back to Marty Wilkes. "Let's say Delancey killed Oona in a rage. And now to cover up he's creating the appearance of a serial killing. Would he—could he go this far?"

"You're coming back to an old question. If a man kills to create the appearance of serial killing, is he a serial killer?"

Cardozo turned. "Well—is he?"

"Once he goes random he fits the definition."

"Would you say Avalon Gardner was selected randomly?"

"Random within the parameters. So far I see two critical marks in the killer's choice of victim. He's violating upper-class sanctums. And he's going for women."

Cardozo stared a moment at the face staring back at him. "Avalon Gardner was a man."

Wilkes conceded as much with a nod. "A man dressed in such a way that he could be mistaken for a woman."

"And you think the killer mistook him?"

"I believe so. Serial killing, overwhelmingly, is something men do to women."

Cardozo frowned. "I don't see Avalon as random. He's linked to Oona. They knew each other. They used to socialize."

"The killer is aiming at a small social class—the extremely conspicuous, self-publicizing people who monopolize the New York gossip columns. The link you're seeing may be one he's completely unaware of."

For a moment neither of them spoke.

"And," Wilkes said, "he may not be Jim Delancey. He could be the man with the boom box. Or someone you don't even have a lead to yet. But let's say he's the boom-box man. According to your witnesses the youngest this man could be is eighteen. So, figure that he could have been assaulted as young as six years of age— we're looking into cases at least twelve years old. And let's make a statistically based cutoff, our killer is under thirty, so we're looking no farther back than twenty-four years."

Cardozo's eye went to the Harvard Med School diploma on the wall.

"There's a sixty-percent probability that he's illegitimate. Most of these fellows never had a decent relationship with any father figure, never knew their real father, and one way or another were rejected by their mothers. What I recommend you do, Vince, is search the records. Look for an illegitimate Caucasian Catholic Hispanic who was raised by a female relative and sexually assaulted by an older male relative."

Cardozo grimaced at the thought of sifting through twelve years of uncomputerized records. "Marty, how long is he going to give us before the next killing?"

"The second was eleven days after the first, so he's on a minimax cycle. If he keeps to the statistical mainstream, no sooner than next Thursday would be a good guess."

■ ■ ■

CARDOZO DIDN'T SEE Sam Richards in the squad room.

He went to the TV room. Richards was standing by the coffee maker, waiting for the coffee to finish dripping through.

"Sam, how are you coming with the gyms and sports outlets?"

"Just about wound up. There's a gym on Staten Island I want to visit, and there are two near the Path station in Newark."

"When you get back from Newark, could you go down to Family Court on Lafayette?"

Richards looked at Cardozo with frank curiosity.

"I'd like you to look at the records from twenty-four to twelve years back," Cardozo said. "Pull any cases of Catholic Hispanic boys sexually assaulted by an older male relative."

Richards gave him a look. "Yeah. Right."

· TWENTY-FOUR ·

"WHAT ABOUT GIVING SOME SPACE to the other side of the story?" Nancy Guardella said.

"I wasn't aware," Zack Morrow said, "that we were giving space to either side."

They were coming to the end of their lunch at Le Cercle. Lunch, today, had been on Senator Guardella. She loved lunch at Le Cercle. She loved the cuisine and the pointedly snooty staff and the celebrities who fought for the right to crowd the sumptuous red plush banquettes. She loved the fact that reservations for lunch required phoning two weeks ahead, and the fact that she could get in on forty-five-minutes' notice.

"Come on," she said. "Dizey Duke is openly crusading to lynch the boy."

Zack Morrow lowered his eyes. "I have no input into Dizey's column."

A scowl slowly flattened Nancy Guardella's face. "You publish her."

"If I altered just one of her columns," Zack said, "censored just one word, she'd have the right to leave me. And I can't afford the circulation drop."

"Dizey *Duke*? She's not *that* powerful."

"If she's not that powerful," Tori Sandberg said, "why do you care what she writes?"

Nancy Guardella lifted her cappuccino and sipped. "Principle. Innocent till proven guilty. Ever hear of it?"

Tori set her lips in a thin line of impatience. "That principle binds the law. Not the press."

"And as a U.S. senator," Nancy Guardella said, "it binds me.

It binds me to stand up for you, Tori, and for you, Zack, which is easy because I love you both. And it binds me to stand up for people nobody loves, like Jim Delancey. He's getting a raw deal in the media."

Tori drew in a long breath. "He got a pretty soft deal from the justice system. Maybe he's earned a raw deal in the media."

In Nancy Guardella's eyes was a mingled expression of sadness and indignation. "Tori, don't you believe in fairness for all? Or do you just believe in fairness for some of the people?"

"I hope I believe in fairness for all."

Senator Guardella gave Tori Sandberg a slow glance. Just a glance. "If you truly believe in fairness, you'll have *Matrix Magazine* interview Xenia Delancey. She's a great subject. She's a mother, she's fighting for her kid, she's battling public opinion. Women will identify."

Tori's eyes betrayed a moment's unguarded shock. "Sorry. She's the wrong mother for me, and he's the wrong kid. I'm too good a friend of Leigh Baker's, and too many bad things have happened between her and Jim Delancey."

"That's *history*," Nancy Guardella said.

Tori shook her head. "Leigh feels they're still happening."

"Oh?"

"She thinks Delancey is making harassing phone calls."

A glaze of pure annoyance came over Nancy Guardella's face. "The kid is out of prison by the skin of his teeth. He's not going to risk his freedom just to needle Leigh Baker."

Tori smiled coolly. "Unless he's unbalanced."

Nancy Guardella's face was rigid. She gripped the armrests of her chair and was up on her feet. "Would you both excuse me a moment?"

She moved past tables of socialites and celebrities, spraying air kisses and eye contact, striding just quickly enough that waiters and table-hoppers got out of her way. She crossed the restaurant to the table where Kristi Blackwell, pale and slim in one of Gloria Spahn's raspberry sheaths, was having lunch with her husband. Today her husband looked sober.

Nancy Guardella thrust out a hand. Thirty carats flashed. Kristi looked up, quickly found a smile, and took the hand.

"One of my constituents has an interesting problem." Nancy Guardella took the unoccupied chair. "*Fanfare* might consider doing a piece."

Kristi speared a chunk of lobster, dipped it in green mayonnaise, and raised it to her mouth. "All ears."

"She's a working mother. Her son was convicted of a felony. He served his time and he's out of prison. But he's being set up by the press and the police to close an unrelated murder case."

Silence. Eye contact. Kristi Blackwell smiled.

"Nice try, Nancy, but I'm not going to touch Jim Delancey *or* the Society Sam killings. We have a three-week press lag, and we stay away from current cases. They're much too volatile."

Nancy Guardella raised her eyes toward Kristi. "You didn't stay away from the Nita Kohler killing."

"That was different. The case was going to trial and the issues were clear."

Wystan Blackwell gazed out of bloodshot eyes at Senator Guardella. His expression was slack and bored and sour. "I should think Kristi's readers have had more than enough of Jim Delancey for one lifetime."

Nancy Guardella gave Wystan Blackwell a look, and the look said, *Stay out of this.* "Doesn't anyone in this city care that the cops and the press are walking all over the boy's rights?"

"If it turns out he's guilty again," Kristi Blackwell said, "people will want to know why they didn't walk over his rights a lot harder and a lot sooner."

■ ■ ■

LEIGH CAME BACK from the half-day's shooting in a good mood. Afternoon sun reflected off the town houses across the garden, and her bedroom walls glowed like a sky full of pale pink kites. She dropped her pocketbook and her jacket on the bed. Something cooed softly, and it took her a moment to realize that the telephone was ringing.

By the time she reached the receiver, the answering machine had clicked on.

She shouted over the outgoing message. "Just a minute, let me kill this thing."

She pushed buttons and finally got her recorded voice to shut up. "Hello?" she said.

No answer.

"Hello?"

She heard something—it wasn't quite breathing and it wasn't quite knocking. It wasn't quite anything she'd ever heard on a telephone before.

"Who is this?"

The breathing-knocking went on.

"Same to you." She slammed the receiver down.

Now she was angry.

She stripped down to her underwear. She spread a towel on the rug and pushed herself through a half hour of stretching exercises. It was a punishing ritual performed for reasons that only her body knew. When she'd had enough and her nerves had calmed down, she took a twenty-minute shower.

And then she spread two bath towels on the bed and lay down and shut her eyes.

A long while later, in her dream, a man's voice was telling her that a receiver seemed to be off the hook. "Please check your extensions."

She opened her eyes and sat up. The voice didn't stop.

She looked at the phone and saw that the receiver had landed crooked. The green light on the answering machine was still lit, which meant the machine was still recording.

She replaced the receiver, correctly this time. The voice stopped. She pressed buttons and finally brought the answering machine to a halt. The tape had recorded practically to the end, and it took almost ten minutes to rewind it.

She pressed the Replay button. For the next forty-five minutes she gave the machine her undivided attention.

■ ■ ■

"HAVE YOU SEEN MY APARTMENT since I enlarged it?" Sorry Chappell said. Her name was actually Sorella, but since she was one of the giddiest people in New York, the nickname Sorry—so amusingly wrong for a rich, plump, brassy blond—had stuck.

"No, I haven't," Leigh said.

"I knocked a hole into the building next door." As one of New York's top interior designers, Sorry was famous for the holes she had knocked into Manhattan's most prestigious co-ops. "You've got to come look. Now, have you been to any good auctions lately?"

Leigh shook her head. "None."

They had met for dessert in the garden of a new French bakery on East Eighty-first. Leigh had suggested meeting, Sorry had suggested dessert.

"I've been haunting the estate sales at Sotheby's," Sorry said, "hoping some dark ruby parures will come up—*something* for late-afternoon wear."

"But you always look wonderful in late afternoon."

Sorry lifted a small amount of *sorbet de poire* to her mouth. "I've lost eight pounds and it's time to look better than wonderful.

You, by the way, look smashing. You're the only woman I know who can bring off that *dégagée* look."

"You mean I should spend more time in front of my mirror?"

"Quite the opposite. Reckless is you, darling."

Leigh supposed Sorry was referring to the crème brûlée she had ordered and already finished.

"Have you been getting strange phone calls?" Leigh said.

Sorry offered an uncertain smile. "Now, that's an interesting question. How strange is strange?"

"Hang ups, breathing . . . threats."

"None that I recall. Should I have been?"

"Have you noticed anyone following you?"

"I think IRS may have a man following me."

"Are you sure he's IRS?"

"No. I'm not even sure he's following me."

"Where have you seen him?"

"At Cartier's four times. He watches what I buy and then he whispers to the salespeople. Doesn't that sound like IRS to you?"

"What does he look like?"

"Heavy. Poor taste in clothes. He has thinning black hair and he combs it over his bald spot."

"It doesn't sound like—" Leigh was going to say *Jim Delancey,* and then she thought, *There's no sense alarming Sorry.* "Like the person I'm thinking of."

"In other words someone's phoning you, and breathing, and hanging up, and threatening you. And following you. And he's better-looking than my man in Cartier's."

"What about Fenny?" Fenny Gurdon was Sorry's partner in the interior-design firm of Gurdon-Chappell, and like Sorry, he had testified at the trial for Nita's character.

Sorry licked her spoon clean. "You know Fenny doesn't follow women."

"Is he *being* followed?"

"Not that he's mentioned to me. But he's at the shop this afternoon. He'd love to see you. Why don't you go ask him?"

■ ■ ■

LEIGH SHADED HER EYES and peered through the Madison Avenue window of Gurdon-Chappell Interiors. She saw antiques, but no Gurdon. No customers either. She pushed the buzzer.

Twenty seconds later the shop door swung open, and she stepped inside. Crystal chandeliers threw elegantly fractured light.

"Leigh—love!"

An enormous white-haired man materialized from the depth of the store, rushing toward her down the Biedermeier-cluttered aisle. They met: first their hands, then his lips and her angled cheek.

"Fennie, there's something I've got to ask you, and I hope it won't seem strange."

She caught the stillness and expectancy in his eyes. He thought she was here to buy something.

"In this business, love," he said, "no request is strange. And nine times out of ten, in this shop, the answer's yes."

Keeping her hand in his, he led her to an enormous leather-topped desk at the rear of the gallery. They sat. She picked up an embroidered velvet bell cord and began drawing it through her fingers.

He waited.

Her eye roamed a wall of marble mantelpieces, standing suits of armor, carved canopied beds. "Fennie—have you been getting phone calls?"

"I should hope so!"

"Odd phone calls. Hang ups. Silences. Breathing."

"Good Lord, love, what *are* we talking—phone sex?"

"No. I'm serious, Fennie. Something is going on. It's been going on ever since they paroled the Delancey boy."

Fennie Gurdon drew back in his chair. "I'm not exactly understanding the question, love."

"Lately have you had any feeling that someone's watching you?"

"Watching me?"

"Following you?"

"Should I have had?"

"I don't know. I'm asking you."

"I'm not exactly a household name to the broader public. As far as sex appeal goes, I'm a distinctly minority taste. Why should anyone bother with me?"

"To learn your movements. To know where you go when and what times you're apt to be alone."

The patchouli-scented face remained cool, practically dead-pan. "Sad to say, no such attention has been lavished on me, love. Don't I wish. But I'm not a celebrity like you."

"It's not a fan, Fennie."

Fennie lifted the bell cord from her fingers. "This person

seems to be making you terribly unhappy, love. Is there anything I can do?"

"Just be careful. Please." Leigh got to her feet.

Fennie rose at the same time. "I'll try, love, but you know your old Fennie—some things are easier said than done."

■ ■ ■

LEIGH BAKER STARED at the marsala-marinated strawberries heaped in a parfait cup, doused and dripping with *zabaione*. She felt an almost obscene craving for sweets; she recognized it as a transposed longing for alcohol, brought on by stress.

No, she made up her mind. *I'm not going to.*

She tore her eyes from the color photograph and closed the book of Italian desserts and replaced it on the shelf.

Most of the other customers in the shop were women. But one man standing at the biography section with his back toward her was wearing a raincoat. *Odd to be wearing a raincoat,* she thought. *It's a sunny day.*

She swung the shop door open and stepped out on Madison.

Steam pipes under the street had exploded. A Con Ed crew was working to repair the thirty-foot crater. Boys on roller skates glided through the jammed traffic, handing out restaurant flyers to stalled drivers. An ambulance was trying to get through and its siren was wailing at top decibel.

Garbage cans waiting on the curb for collection had narrowed the sidewalk to a single lane. A homeless man had picked that exact spot to spread out a bed of newspapers and fall asleep.

Leigh walked around him. He was unshaved and he'd fouled his trousers and he had open sores on his arm. She felt disgust and then she felt ashamed of her disgust and guilty that she had a home, even if it wasn't her own. She took a ten-dollar bill from her purse and bent down to slip it into his shirt pocket.

She felt like a sentimental fool. She glanced around her to see if anyone had noticed her impulsive little gesture.

Down the block a man in a raincoat was watching her. He was wearing a little cap that shaded his eyes and she couldn't see his face, but she wondered if it wasn't the man she'd seen in the bookstore.

She crossed Madison and continued north.

At Seventy-fourth she pretended to look in a window of porcelain figurines, and she half turned around. The man in the raincoat was there again, still a half block behind her.

■ ■ ■

THE ANSWERING MACHINE showed that three more calls had come in. Leigh sat down on the edge of the bed and pressed the Replay button. The first message was a neat hang up. The second was a messy hang up.

The third was a silence.

She sat forward. She focused all her power of hearing on the soft white noise hissing from the machine. She began to sense something, a presence, the held breath of another person listening, not speaking.

The even hum of a dial tone cut in.

She stopped the machine. She dialed Waldo's direct line at work. Waldo's male secretary answered.

"Horst—it's Leigh. Could I speak with Waldo for just a moment?"

"Oh, Miss Baker. I'm afraid Mr. Carnegie is in a meeting. Can he call you back?"

"I'll hold."

"I'm afraid he'll be quite some time."

■ ■ ■

SEVENTEEN MINUTES LATER Leigh was stepping out of a cab on Fifth Avenue in front of the Carnegie Building. She plunged into the lobby and took the express elevator to the penthouse. She walked rapidly down the Impressionist-lined corridor, pursued by the snapping echo of her green lizard pumps.

"Here I am," she said cheerfully, "complicating your job."

Waldo's pale-haired, pale-eyed secretary was sitting at his desk outside the inner office, and she could read nothing in his smooth, tanned face, not even a hint of surprise in the exquisite civility of his smile.

"Don't worry," she said, "I'll take *all* the blame."

"Miss Baker, I really wouldn't—"

"Honestly. I'm an old pro at it." She blew him a kiss and pushed through the door.

Waldo and three Japanese in extraordinarily beautiful Italian business suits were seated in easy chairs around the coffee table. They were drinking Bloody Marys.

Waldo's glance swung toward the door and his disbelief had an almost luminous surface. He bolted up and came toward her. "What are you doing here?" he whispered.

"I'm going to pieces. I keep getting hang ups and silences on my answering machine."

"You come busting in here because of hang ups on your machine?"

"I need you to reassure me and tell me you're not going on that business trip Thursday."

There was cold blue refusal in his eyes, and it emphasized a boundary between where they were standing and the rest of the room, with its cycloramic three-wall view of the sprawling, howling city. "Those shoes don't go with that dress," he said.

She exercised savage restraint. "Well, excuse *me.*"

Waldo continued to stare at her but with something sad creeping into his eyes now. "My office is not the ideal place for this kind of unannounced apparition."

"You know what a baby I am. Please, just hug me and give me a kiss and tell me you'll cancel your trip or take me with you—and then I'll go home like a good little girl."

He was looking her straight in the eye, the way people do when they're holding something back. "These are very important men. They haven't recognized you yet. If I kiss you, they'll know it's you and they'll know how you dress when there isn't a photographer around."

She felt an angry blush spreading from her face to her neck and shoulders. "You're not that petty. You couldn't be."

"Darling, *they're* that petty. Please?"

▪ ▪ ▪

BACK AT THE HOUSE she sat on the edge of her bed. She felt rejected, crushed. The scary thing was, she knew there was no reason for the feeling. It was like a rising tide of black water, and there was nothing she could do to stop it.

She phoned Luddie and got his answering machine. "Luddie," she pleaded, "pick up, goddammit. I've got to talk to you."

But he didn't pick up.

"Luddie, I need you. I'm falling apart and I know I'm being stupid and that's what scares me. Tell me something wise. Tell my machine something wise."

She hung up and the empty floor stretched around her in perfect, quiet dustlessness. A thought came to her that she couldn't quite explain. She wondered if anyone had bothered to disconnect Oona's machine.

She reached again for the receiver. She dialed Oona's number. The machine answered. No one had changed the message.

She sat listening to Oona's voice. "Hello, thank you for calling. You have reached—"

She felt startled and sad at the same time. This dumb, stilted recitation, read straight from the manufacturer's booklet, was all that remained of her friend, of all the years they had shared.

After the beep Leigh tried to think of a message.

"Hi, it's me. I just wanted to hear your voice. I just wanted to say I'm sorry we fought. I guess I'm beginning to understand what you were going through. I miss you terribly. I can't believe you're not there. Here. Somewhere. Oh, shit."

She broke the connection.

There was a tightness below her throat, a stinging in her eyes. She laid the receiver carefully back into the cradle.

She gazed around the bedroom—a mistress's bedroom clotted with decorator chic and spill-over doodads from houses that Waldo's designer had done for other celebrities.

She sat a moment in numbed dullness and then a message crackled along her nerve endings, too faint to be measured and yet too insistent to be ignored.

She walked into the hallway like an old woman, with small, tired steps.

One of the servants was using the elevator again, so she walked down the stairway, through latticed slashes of light and shadow.

In the living room a light like a silver tarnish fell on the eighteenth-century French secretary that Waldo's designer had converted into a bar.

The light seemed to signal a shimmering zone of safety just beyond the touch of reality.

She remembered Luddie's saying to her, long ago when he'd first become her AA sponsor, that part of self-acceptance was allowing yourself decisions, wrong decisions, mistakes even.

She opened the paneled doors of the secretary and found the silver ice bucket and the Johnnie Walker right away. She dropped two cubes into a highball glass, two long splashes of Scotch. She had to search to find the diet Pepsi. She filled the glass to the brim.

As her hands went through the old movements that she'd forgotten were there in the memory of her muscles and nerves, the old peacefulness came back that she'd forgotten was there too.

She rotated the glass and studied the little whirlpool she had created. Then she lifted the glass, and her lips touched the door to another world.

▪ TWENTY-FIVE ▪

Thursday, May 23

A LIGHT ON CARDOZO'S PHONE winked, and he punched the button and grabbed up the receiver. "Cardozo."

"Lieutenant, it's Rad Rheinhardt, down at the *Trib*. We just got another in the mail."

■ ■ ■

TWELVE MINUTES LATER Cardozo walked into Clancy's Bar and Grill and stopped by the door, giving his eyes a minute to adjust to the dimness.

The same two old-timers were sitting at the bar, but they seemed to be getting chummier. Today there were only five empty stools between them instead of eight.

The bartender stood serenely eating from a plastic salad-bar container of take-out balanced on the cash register, and he nodded at Cardozo as though, with this second appearance, he'd become a valued regular.

Rad Rheinhardt had taken a table by the window, and the sun cut him and his rumpled pale green shirt into ribbons of light and dark. He was examining his fingernails.

Cardozo glanced at the half-empty glass on the table. "Tequila Sunrise?"

Rheinhardt picked up the glass. "Tequila, hold the Sunrise." He took a long, comfortable swallow.

Cardozo pulled out a chair and sat. "Isn't it a little early in the morning for heavy metal?"

Rheinhardt spat a shaving of ice into the ashtray. "You seem to be searching for reasons to love me."

Cardozo had a sense of confronting the irreducible biology of Rad Rheinhardt. "Give me the letter and my search is over."

Rheinhardt reached down into a briefcase that he'd parked between his Top-Siders. "Coming at you live." He laid the letter on the table, wrapped in a plastic freezer bag.

Cardozo frowned. Inside the sheath, the cut-out words had been taped to a sheet of yellow foolscap.

> NO REST FOR THE WICK
> SO OUT OUT BRIEF CANDLES
> A WALKERS SHADOWS
> WHAT THIS SAGE DEMANDS.
> KISSES, SOCIETY SAM

What hooked Cardozo's gaze on the very first scan were the words *wick* and *candles.* Nothing about *Shabbes* candles had been published, so either Sam was a lucky guesser or with this letter he established his authenticity. "There's stuff in this letter that we've held back. Details of the M.O. No one knows but us and Sam. If you publish them, we risk copycats."

"Vince, when are you going to realize you and I are on the same side?"

Rheinhardt's pupils were as tiny and hard as peppercorns, and Cardozo was not reassured by the thought that Rad was doing coke or speed to balance out the booze.

"Just tell me what you want us to hold back."

"Wick," Cardozo said. *"Candle. A walkers shadows* had better go too, just to be safe."

"Doesn't leave much to work with," Rheinhardt said. "Oh, well, maybe he'll send another."

■ ■ ■

CARDOZO WATCHED ELLIE SIEGEL as she studied the letter.

She was standing beside the window in his cubicle, and she had angled the document between its two protective glassine sheets so that it caught the daylight. "Sam wants to show us he knows his way around the classics, or at least around Bartlett's *Quotations.* This letter is really kind of pathetic."

Cardozo slid the envelope toward her. "Tell you anything?"

Ellie picked the envelope up in its glassine cover. "Looks to me pretty much like the envelope the first letter came in. Except for the postmark. This one's zip-coded one-one-two-oh-one."

"And what does that mean to you?"

"It means Brooklyn, probably the Heights. It means he's mailing these from different postal zones to give us a hard time. And worst of all it means you want me to go down there and check out mail routes and pickup times."

"Only because you're the best."

Ellie Siegel's charms had their uses. Ellie knew it, Cardozo knew it. Nobody on the force looked quite like her, nobody walked or carried on a conversation quite like her. Men wanted to take her to bed, women wanted to take her shopping. The bottom line was she motivated people to cooperate with her in a way that a lot of other cops couldn't.

"Thanks, Ellie. I appreciate it."

He watched her turn and leave his cubicle and walk back across the squad room. Her stride started at the waist, purposefully. Her appearance telegraphed an unmissable message: *In this city full of filth and giving up, I, Detective Ellie Siegel, maintain my self-respect: I have fought for it, it is mine, I have a right to flaunt it, and you'd better acknowledge it, because I'll kill to keep it.*

▪ ▪ ▪

CONSIDERING THAT she said she was calling from One Police Plaza, the woman's voice on Malloy's phone was oddly soft and modulated. In Malloy's experience voices from down there had a harder edge.

She wanted to know if he could come down immediately to meet with Captain Lawrence Zawac of IAD.

Paging God, Malloy thought. If anyone from Internal Affairs wanted to talk to him, it was because he was in trouble or because they were going to ask him to help get someone else in trouble. "How soon is immediately?"

"Noon sharp," the pleasant voice said.

For a moment he sat unmoving in his chair, staring across the squad room. All kinds of terrifying thoughts came pouring into his head. "Could you tell me what this is in reference to?"

"Captain Zawac will be glad to discuss that with you personally."

Malloy told himself that it was just to discuss some routine fuck-up. Nothing serious. He looked at his watch: eleven thirty-five. Jim Delancey had been at work a little over a half hour, and he wouldn't be coming off his shift till evening.

"Sure," he said. "Tell the captain I'll be there."

■ ■ ■

"DETECTIVE MALLOY, is this yours?" With a soft snap Captain Zawac laid a small object down on his desk.

Malloy had to get up from his chair and approach the desk to see that it was a business card. He had to pick it up to see that it was one of his own. "I'd be surprised to find out it was someone else's."

Zawac's remote and uncaring eyes fixed Malloy's. "I'm not interested in what would surprise you."

Zawac was a stocky man in his late forties, with a high, smooth forehead and a pencil mustache that didn't quite succeed in covering the scar that bisected his upper lip. His face was square, with broad cheekbones and a determined tilt to the jaw.

"It says Carl Malloy." Malloy shrugged and smiled. "I don't think it's going to be much help to a guy named John Smith."

Zawac did not smile. "Are you implying that a person named John Smith is using your card?"

"I'm sorry. Bad joke." Malloy laid the card back on the desk.

"Then this is your card?"

Malloy nodded. "That's what I said."

"That's exactly what you did *not* say," the third person in the room said. These were Assistant Deputy Commissioner Bridget Braidy's first words since Malloy had been introduced to her, and it bothered him that she was involved in this. He sensed something happening that he could not quite penetrate, and until he could get a grasp on it, he intended to say as little as possible.

It was Captain Zawac who finally spoke. "Did you give this card to Dorothea Ng yesterday at four forty-five P.M.?"

"How do I know? I give my card out to a lot of people."

"Why do you give your card out to a lot of people?"

"Why does anyone? So they can phone me."

"Why do you want Dorothea Ng to phone you?"

"I don't know Dorothea Ng."

The captain and the commissioner exchanged glances.

"Why would you give one of your business cards to someone you didn't know?" Zawac asked. "Do you stand around handing them out on street corners?"

Zawac's niggling, prosecutorial tone was a bad sign. The way he'd taken back the business card, as though it were a precious relic, was another. Malloy had the feeling that he was being spectacularly set up, that the police had been ordered to offer up another sacrifice to the productivity stats of the Internal Affairs

Department. "No, I do not stand around handing my card out on street corners, and yes, I sometimes give a card to someone I don't know."

"Why do you sometimes give a card to someone you don't know?"

"Maybe I'm working on a case and I need a potential witness to phone me."

"Are you working on a case at present?"

"I'm working on a lot of cases," Malloy said. "Same as anyone else at the precinct. Matter of fact, I'm on the Society Sam task force."

"And is Dorothea Ng a witness or potential witness in the Society Sam case?" the captain asked.

"I don't know who the hell Dorothea Ng is, but I'm sure beginning to hate the name."

Malloy watched Bridget Braidy's face for a reaction: his gut told him she was the moving force behind this inquiry. Her eyes had gone soul-dead in her concrete slab of a face. They had dark circles that she had tried to hide with powder.

"Dorothea Ng runs the I Scream for Ice Cream Ice Cream Shop," Zawac said, "and she knows you."

"Then Dorothea's one-up on me, because I'm drawing a blank."

"Do you know the I Scream for Ice Cream Ice Cream Shop?"

"The name doesn't ring any bells."

"The shop is on Lexington and Sixty-sixth Street."

"I guess I've had ice cream at that location. I never noticed it was called I Scream for anything."

"You were observed having ice cream in the shop with a young lady, and you were observed giving this card to Dorothea Ng in lieu of payment."

"Are you saying I stiffed the little old lady that runs that joint?"

"You did not pay for your ice cream," Commissioner Braidy said. "You were seen accepting it as a gratuity, and you were then seen giving your card to Dorothea Ng."

Malloy sensed something hugely twisted in this discussion—they were coming down on the good guy, on Carl Malloy. "Who saw me?"

"I saw you, Sergeant Malloy," Bridget Braidy said.

It was a source of joking around the force that Bridget Braidy the cop was the sister of Benedict Braidy the society writer, but it baffled Carl Malloy that the same womb could have spit out this gorgon and that butterfly. It seemed to be proof of something twisted and contradictory in the DNA that had shaped them.

A toxic calm spread across Bridget Braidy's face. He'd seen that same calm look on the faces of nuns at parochial school the instant before they whipped your knuckles with the ruler. Iron cold locked in on his stomach. This lady was out to kick ass, and she was doing it for God.

"Did you see the guy with the boom box?" Malloy demanded. "Did you see me suggest he should take that disturbance elsewhere? Did you see how happy that old lady was to have that punk out of her place? Did you see me try to pay the old lady for the ice cream and how she fought me on it?"

"Then you're admitting you didn't pay for your ice cream," Zawac said.

Malloy's gaze went from the commissioner to the captain, and he suddenly saw them as agents in a very ancient process called career advancement. Achievement, risk-taking, effort were not required. All it took to get to the top of the police bureaucracy was ethics carved in butter and a willingness to rip up other people's careers like junk mail.

"I'm admitting these questions bother me. Maybe I should consult a lawyer."

"There's no need for a lawyer at this point." Zawac extracted a document from the folder and slid it across the desktop.

Malloy recognized the official NYPD letterhead. "What's this?"

Zawac was holding out a gold pen. "An admission that you accepted a gratuity of ice cream worth four dollars from Dorothea Ng of the I Scream for Ice Cream Ice Cream Shop."

"And what flavor was the ice cream?" Malloy couldn't resist asking. Trying to lighten things.

"It was fresh peach ice cream," the commissioner said, even more deadly serious than before. "With extra sprinkles."

Malloy wondered if these two really believed the face of crime in New York would be changed one iota by this bullshit. "I'm not signing anything without a lawyer."

"I'm glad to see Sergeant Malloy has a healthy sense of self-preservation. It must be the Irish in you, Sergeant. I have it too." The commissioner rose from her chair. "Good meeting you, Sergeant. Captain, I leave this matter in your capable hands."

Zawac threw her a salute. "It'll get handled."

Bridget Braidy shut the door behind her with a sharp snap. Glass rattled.

Zawac sat staring at Malloy, shaking his head. Thirty seconds went by. "Sergeant, Sergeant, you are in a serious pickle."

"I have nothing more to say till my lawyer's present."

"Fuck your lawyer." Zawac opened a drawer and placed two NYPD tumblers and a fifth of Jack Daniel's on the desk. "And fuck that Braidy bitch."

"Sir?"

"I hear she spent all night combing the roster, looking for the detective from the Twenty-second Precinct that had your face." Zawac filled the two tumblers to the halfway mark and held one out to Malloy. "Ice cream. Can you believe it? *Ice cream.*"

Malloy decided to trust the contempt in Zawac's eyes. He accepted the tumbler. "Why is she doing it, sir?"

Zawac sighed. "All I can figure is, she has her eye on politics. She wants it on her record that she busted corruption. To your health, fella." He tipped his head back and emptied the tumbler in two gulps.

"To your health." Malloy took a swallow. The sour mash left a burn going down his throat.

"Here's the problem, Sergeant—how are we going to save the shield and the pension of a good cop like you? Because dumb as the charge is, soliciting and accepting *any* bribe is grounds for dismissal."

"I'll get a lawyer and I'll fight the charge."

"No, you won't." Zawac picked up the confession and ripped it in half. He walked to the wastebasket and dropped the torn sheets. "There's not going to be a charge. There's not going to be a hearing."

"Sir?"

"We're going to help each other, Sergeant. I'm going to handle your problem, and you're going to handle mine."

■ ■ ■

MALLOY STEPPED OUT of One Police Plaza. Down the street he saw a blinking bar-and-grill sign.

Coming in from the daylight, he found the bar a maze of dim shadows. A jukebox was thumping:

> *Spilled a pint of plasma and you still don't hurt,*
> *'Cause your head's in the heart of the hallelujah dirt.*

He took a stool and ordered a double shot of peppermint vodka.

"You mean peppermint schnapps?" The bartender was a blond, friendly-looking fellow with huge eyes.

"Peppermint whatever." Malloy didn't care, so long as it was peppermint. He was already reeling from Zawac's bottomless tumbler of Jack Daniel's, and he didn't want his breath giving him away.

The bartender placed a double shot glass of clear liquid in front of him, and Malloy gulped it down.

Then he stared straight ahead through the reflection of the jittering neon sign, and he could see the glass-and-poured concrete facade of One P.P. raising its beehive hulk against the blue of the sky. If you were putting up a condo on the moon, that would be the architectural style.

> *Hallelujah dirt that'll do ya*
> *That'll do ya dirt hallelujah dirt.*

Pollution made a silver haze that shimmered over the street, and Malloy could feel the alcohol loosening the cords of his anxiety. For a moment he was lifted into a timeless space where there was no yesterday to regret, no tomorrow to fear, no today to hoard. For a moment he could even ignore that jukebox.

Peace was a rare thing in Carl Malloy's life, it was a rare thing in any cop's life, and once he found it he liked to float around in it and savor the weightlessness.

"Bartender," he said, and he noticed that the bartender was wearing his hair in a ponytail fastened with a single rubber band. *If I was young again,* Carl Malloy thought, *I'd wear a ponytail and a beard and an earring and let the world fuck itself.* "Hit me up again."

· TWENTY-SIX ·

GLORIA SPAHN LED ZACK MORROW into the bedroom and closed the door. They stood in silence for an instant. She smiled.

He reached for her, kissed her.

She pulled back. Still smiling, she took off her watch and placed it in a porcelain dish on the bedside table. She unbuttoned her blouse. She took it off and let it fall behind her.

She unhooked her skirt. She let it and her half slip fall.

He placed his shirt and his trousers over a chair.

She peeled her bra off her shoulders and then wriggled her panties down her hips. The panties had pearl-gray fringes of open-work lace.

He placed his underwear on the cushion.

She stepped out of the puddle of clothes at her feet.

They stared at each other. He could feel each of them liking the other's body, liking the tightness, the tans, the toned, massaged cleanliness.

Without warning she knelt down before him. She rested her forehead against the hair below his belly button, as though her eyes were so heavy that they were weighing down her entire head.

For Zack it was an instant carved out of eternity, a perfect moment of knowing exactly what was going to come next.

And of not knowing.

Because after she had taken him into the unbelievably moist, soft, warm hollow of her mouth, after he had sprung to life with a teenager's instantaneity, she rose and, holding his cock gently in one hand, led him through another door.

Light softly touched walls and floors of shrimp-pink and

mango-colored breccia perniche marble. Just above the enormous, hollowed marble bathtub and flush with the wall was a platinum door. Gloria Spahn opened it.

The minirefrigerator within was stocked with atomizers of perfumes, bottles of cologne, bath salts, body oils, liquid soaps, lubricants, condoms, glassine bags of heroin and cocaine and Ecstasy, small brown vials of crack rocks.

"You seem to know the apartment," Zack said.

Gloria Spahn smiled. "It's a well-known apartment." She eenie-meenied a moment before choosing two bags that had pink labels printed with the face of Betty Boop and below that the words THE RIGHT STUFF!

She laid the bags side by side on the rosewood vanity and then she opened the door above the fridge, and Zack saw that it was a microwave unit for sterilizing crack pipes and free-base kits and the syringes that lay in a Limoges porcelain quill dish painted with jonquils and nasturtiums.

"Who the hell installed all this stuff?" he said.

"Does it matter?" She looked at him. "Have you ever freebased Ecstasy?"

He shook his head.

"Want to try?"

He looked at her and his eyes narrowed and yesses and noes battled in his head and then he thought, *There's no point going with it if you don't go with it all the way.* He nodded slowly.

Gloria Spahn loaded a pipe with the contents of the two envelopes. She moved with great sureness. He could sense her bursting with know-how, full of living and doing and planning that didn't ask anyone's permission or dread anyone's frown.

She filled a glass bulb with water from the gold swan-shaped Hot faucet of the sink.

She connected the bulb and pipe and handed them to Zack.

As he inhaled on the pipe she played the narrow blue hissing flame of a small Cartier butane torch back and forth across the bulb. In less than ten seconds the water was bubbling, and Zack felt a *whoosh* go into him. Suddenly his head was five feet higher than his lungs.

They took turns, passing the pipe back and forth.

And then the bowl was empty.

"Lie down." She pushed him down onto the cranberry-colored pillows on the terry cloth–covered sofa. "Shut your eyes."

He shut his eyes. Something warm stroked the soles of his feet, and it took him a moment to realize it was her tongue.

Eighteen minutes later Zack Morrow and Gloria Spahn climaxed together.

My God, he was thinking. *I love this woman. I need this woman. I want this woman. I want to have sex like this every afternoon of my life.*

After a moment he heard her laugh beside him. "It's true," she said. "Rich people really do have better orgasms."

"I've got to see you again," he said.

"Next week."

"Sooner. Tomorrow."

She placed a finger across his lips. "We don't want to use a good thing up."

"Annie doesn't mind lending us the apartment."

"I don't mean Annie. I mean us. We want us to last and we won't if we overdo it. I'll phone."

■ ■ ■

"I JUST HAD A CALL from Bridget Braidy," Tom Reilly said. "She tells me there's a problem with Malloy. He's being investigated by IAD."

"What's the problem?" Cardozo said. "IAD investigates a lot of cops. That's how they goose their productivity stats."

"It doesn't look good, a man on a task force who's under suspicion."

"Suspicion of what?"

They were sitting in Reilly's office. It was one of those days when the whole precinct creaked, when the support beams of the old building made distress sounds as though they were having aneurysms in the walls.

"Corruption," Reilly said. "Soliciting a bribe."

"How large? Who from?"

"Malloy accepted ice cream from a shopkeeper without paying for it."

"One or two scoops?"

"As you're aware, Vince, it's not the quantity that counts when we're talking ethics."

"Who's the witness?"

"Bridget Braidy."

"That loudmouth isn't even IAD."

There was the beginning of a reaction on Tom Reilly's face, cut short. "Any citizen can bring a complaint."

Cardozo's hands wanted to murder. "With all due respect, sir, the assistant deputy commissioner for public relations is not *any* citizen. This looks like a setup to me, and a damned stupid one. IAD needs to prove they're keeping the force clean. Which, by the way, they're not. And I'm not handing over one of my men for a burnt offering. Malloy is a good cop, and I want him on my task force until he gets what he's entitled to—a fair hearing."

Tom Reilly wasn't there; his eyes were glassy, he was holding a cigarette with a three-inch ash about to fall. If he was seeing anything, it was a test pattern in his mind. "Bridget Braidy's a powerful woman. She's helped your task force."

"She helped herself. That was a ploy to get her face on the evening news."

"She can be a useful friend."

Cardozo breathed in slowly through his mouth. "Not after she filed that charge. The only person she could be useful to now is the neighborhood crack dealer."

Reilly sighed. "Vince, why do you have to go to the brink over a bullshit bureaucratic wrangle?"

"Because IAD and the assistant deputy commissioner for public relations are going to the brink over ice cream and *that's* the real bullshit and someone's got to say no to the bullshitters."

Reilly leaned back in his leather-upholstered swivel chair, shaking his head. "And it has to be you."

"Hell, no," Cardozo said, "it could have been you."

Reilly looked at him with undisguised hatred. The man, Cardozo realized, was retirement fodder, waiting out his last year and a half till that pension could be cashed in. Determined, in the meantime, to take no controversial stand, to offend no superior.

"Vince, I'm sure you mean well." Reilly's eyes said the exact opposite; he wasn't sure at all. "But we have to face the political realities. Braidy has power. I don't, you don't, Carl Malloy sure as hell doesn't."

"So lots were drawn and Carl Malloy won the lead role in the annual sacrifice?"

"Don't complicate this."

"I'm trying to uncomplicate this, and if you want I'll go down there and talk to that asshole myself. Is that what you want?"

"No, Vince. I want you to drop Malloy."

"It's not going to be a popular move with the Patrolmen's Benevolent Association." Which was obviously the reason Reilly wanted Cardozo to do the firing rather than handle it himself. "Is that an order?"

Reilly's bloodshot eyes locked in on his. "For the time being it's a serious request."

"Then for the time being I'll seriously consider it."

▪ ▪ ▪

"WE HAVE A PROBLEM," Cardozo said.

"I don't have a problem," Captain Lawrence Zawac said. The trimmed dark mustache that didn't quite cover the scar on his upper lip reshaped itself around a smile. "What's yours?"

"IAD is pressuring my commander to pressure me to boot Sergeant Carl Malloy off my task force."

"Not true, not true." Zawac shifted papers on his desk. "Bridget Braidy is pressuring your commander, not us." The entire wall behind him was covered with framed photos. There was no way you could look at Zawac without seeing Zawac shaking hands with George Bush, Zawac shaking hands with Liz Smith, Zawac shaking hands with Tom Cruise.

"So where do you stand?" Cardozo said.

"It's a tempest in an ice-cream dish. Not worth investigating. And it sure as hell isn't worth a good cop's shield or his pension."

Zawac was the cop, Cardozo remembered, who had gone from lunch with the Cardinal to a TV talk show and proposed the city recriminalize condoms. "I'm having a hard time believing my ears."

"Believe them," Zawac said. "Everyone knows what Bridget Braidy is. She's a publicity-hungry bitch." Zawac was smiling as though he and Cardozo both understood the differences between human nature and cop nature, but his slate-colored eyes seemed to stand back from the smile, observing his visitor. "No one takes Bridget Braidy seriously."

"I know one person who takes her seriously. Me."

"I'll handle Braidy. The corruption investigation of Carl Malloy and the ice cream is closed."

▪ ▪ ▪

"DARLING," a man's voice said.

Leigh turned and saw Waldo standing in the doorway. She picked up the remote from the coffee table, aimed it at the TV, and killed the sound.

"I have to go," he said.

"Aren't we spending the evening in?"

"Not tonight." He was carrying a suitcase. "I'm catching the eight-forty to London."

Her heart gave a sudden kick within her chest. She got up from the sofa and stared at him, looking for some sign in his face that this was a joke. "You were going to cancel that trip."

"I tried. I'll only be gone till Sunday."

Her foot felt along the floor for her shoes, couldn't find them. She crossed the library carpet barefoot. "You said you'd stay home or take me with you."

"I said you'd be taken care of. I've hired security."

She met his gaze. There was something chilled in his pale blue eyes, and furrows pulled down the corners of his mouth. She felt that she and Waldo were continents drifting apart on their own separate tectonic plates.

"You can't leave me," she said. "I'm in trouble."

"The hell you are. You've never been finer."

"I've been drinking again." She held up her glass. "Scotch in my diet Pepsi. Waldo, I'm *scared.*"

"Look," he said, "having a drink isn't the end of the world— don't buy into that AA ideology so totally that you crucify yourself for being human." He gave her arm a pat. His glance slid just a little to the side. "Leigh, this is Arnold—your guard."

She pulled back and turned.

A man of middle weight and middle years stood in the hall-way watching her. There was no expression at all on his face. His graying brown hair had been shaved practically to his scalp, and he had eyebrows as pale as the bristles on a toothbrush.

She didn't move or say anything or even show a reaction. She felt naked and small and threatened without her shoes.

"Arnie Bone, ma'am." The stranger held out a hand. Steel-colored eyes fixed on her. "Very pleased to make your acquaintance."

■ ■ ■

IT WAS ALMOST MIDNIGHT when Leigh reached forward and opened the drain. Floris-scented suds began their slow downward spiral.

She stepped out of the tub and wrapped herself in a terry-cloth robe. She toweled off a patch of mirror and brushed her teeth. After flossing she worked a Stim-U-Dent around all the crevices, gargled, and spat.

When she came back into the half-lit bedroom, the air conditioner was making a whispering sound in the curtains. She crossed to the window and stared down into the community garden. Light from the other town houses slanted across the paths and flower beds. Her mind felt sluggish.

"Will you be needing anything, ma'am?"

Leigh whirled. She instantly registered two facts: Arnie Bone was standing in her bedroom, and the door was shut.

"Don't you knock before you come into a room?"

"I did knock, ma'am." He had taken off his suit jacket. His pale, heavy-jawed face was in motion. He was chewing something. "I was wondering if you need anything."

"No." Her hand turned up the collar up the robe. "No, thank you."

"Are you turning in now, ma'am?"

"Yes." She crossed the room and opened the bedroom door. "Thank you."

"Okay." His smile was rueful. "I'll be here if you need me."

"Mr. Bone," she said.

"Arnie. The name's Arnie."

"Where will you be?"

"Just down the hall." A smile creased his lips. "Mr. Carnegie told me to take his room."

"All right. Good night."

"Good night, ma'am."

She locked the door behind him.

· TWENTY-SEVEN ·

Friday, May 24

"YOU'VE GONE BACK AGAIN," Luddie said quietly.

Leigh felt a flush mounting in her face. All she'd mentioned was Waldo deserting her for four days, and the guard Waldo had hired that she couldn't stand, and the hang ups and silences on her answering machine that were driving her crazy. She'd carefully skirted the drinking. How had he caught it? Was she talking too fast, too loud? Was there liquor on her breath?

"Don't you want to tell me about it?" he said.

Her first wild impulse was to deny it, to scream, *Three diet Pepsis with a teeny bit of Johnnie Walker is not going back. And anyway that was yesterday, I've only had one today.*

But the look on his face stopped her. She was prepared for anger, for judgment, and instead she saw sorrow and disappointment and concern. She couldn't bear the way those eyes saw into her and heaped forgiveness on her.

"Sometimes," she said, "I wish you'd shout at me."

"Next thing you'd want me to beat you. Punishment's what you're doing to yourself. I'm not here to add to it."

She gazed out the window of Luddie's living room at the summer sky and the city it glowed upon. "I wonder what you expect of me. Do I have to be a saint?"

Luddie didn't answer.

She peeled away the implications of that silence. She wanted to throw her coffee cup straight at that patient face. "Haven't things ever gotten tough for you? Haven't you ever . . . gone back?"

"Sure. When I was a state department slug, when it hurt that Happy didn't have a mother, that I didn't have a wife; when it hurt that the whole rest of the human race had wives and mothers and I had nothing."

"How did you stop hurting?"

"I quit the government and I prayed."

She sighed. "Prayer is not going to stop the hang ups and silences on my answering machine."

"How do you know? You've tried everything else."

She turned. She had a sense he was playing with her, though there was nothing in his face to show it. "You don't pray about things like phone calls."

"Why not?"

She stared at him. "God's too busy."

"But you're not."

They sat there in silence. She could hear Happy in the next room, playing with his toy xylophone.

"Do you seriously think Jim Delancey is phoning you?" Luddie said.

"I didn't say that."

"I know what you said. I'm talking about what you're thinking, because it's an extremely alcoholic thought pattern."

"Look, I have great respect for your sobriety, maybe I even envy it; but you can't blame everything rotten in this world on booze. It's not Johnnie Walker phoning me, it's a real person and I happen to believe it's Jim Delancey. And that's me talking, not Johnnie Walker."

"You're obsessed with Johnnie Walker."

"I'm weak, Luddie. And I'm frightened."

"Have you mentioned these calls to your lieutenant?"

"I have, and why do you call Vince Cardozo my lieutenant?"

"He has a crush on you, doesn't he?"

"Does he?" She felt weary and transparent and humiliated. "You seem to have a lot more confidence in my charms than I do."

"Leigh—cut it out. Stop begging. It's your worst habit. You know I love you."

She began sobbing. Everything in her collapsed. She couldn't help it. She covered her eyes. "No, I don't. How could you love me when I keep fucking myself up and letting you down?"

"I give up. If spending three years listening to you and trying to keep you sober isn't love, what the hell is? What do you want me to do—put the make on you?"

"No." She shook her head. She tried to dry her eyes. She had a claustrophobic sensation of being trapped, of having all her old reliable exits blocked. "It's too late for that. You know me."

"Leigh, that attitude is pure alcoholism. And, frankly, if you don't do some serious praying and get a grip on yourself—I think you might start drinking again."

She looked at him and blinked. "Start drinking?"

"I've seen it happen to others. Don't think you're immune."

He doesn't know, she realized. *He doesn't see.* "Luddie, what's my biggest problem? Right here and right now?"

He smiled. "Resentment. The surest road to the next drink. You've gone back to your old grievance collecting. Are you aware of it?"

■ ■ ■

LEIGH TURNED THE HANDLE. The bedroom door opened inward, coming gently to rest against the doorstop before it could connect with the bedroom wall.

Christ, she thought. *That was close.* She felt giddy and relieved, like a little girl who'd barely escaped a spanking.

A digital *two* was blinking on the answering machine. She pressed the Replay button. The first call was a hang up. The second began as silence, with noises in the background—faint electronic signals leaking in from other circuits.

A voice spoke, startling her.

"Ma'am?" Arnie Bone stood in the hallway outside her bedroom door. "Are you all right?"

"You don't have to guard me indoors," she said. "Why don't you go ask the cook to make you a snack?"

A shadow crossed his face. "If you're sure you're all right."

"I'm sure."

He raised a finger, touching the brim of a cap that wasn't there. She watched him go. He moved without noise but heavily, like a baseball player going to the plate—purposeful, centered, not about to let anything distract him from his task. She disliked his walk.

She went and closed the bedroom door. As she turned a voice began speaking on the answering machine.

"I'm watching you." It was a deep voice, rasping and hoarse. "Shut your evil trap—or you'll go to the head of the line."

There was a half tick of an instant where she realized intellectually what she'd heard, but her mind refused to believe it. She stopped the tape and played the message again.

Panic coiled in her stomach.

But this time she wasn't scared of panic. She went into the bathroom and unscrewed the Chanel Number Five cologne bottle and poured two fingers of Johnnie Walker into the toothbrush tumbler.

■ ■ ■

CARDOZO STARED at the Aldrich and Gardner glossies. He tried to put out of his mind all knowledge that these designs were carved into human flesh.

He asked himself: *What are these?* He tried to see them as drawings. What did they represent? He tried to see them as symbols. What did they embody?

A light on the phone blinked. Cardozo snapped up the receiver before it could buzz. "Vince Cardozo, how can I help you?"

"I'm sorry to bother you . . ."

The voice was hesitant, almost apologetic. He recognized Leigh Baker, and he felt an involuntary little glow in the center of his rib cage.

"That's okay. Bother me."

"I got a threatening phone call today."

He reached for his pen. He kept his voice easy and calm, not letting anything show. "What was the threat?"

"Shut your evil trap—or you'll go to the head of the line."

It was a revealing choice of words, and they set off a familiar and unpleasant resonance in his memory—part teacher talk, part abusive adult-to-child talk. The kindergarten as hell. "Did you recognize the voice?"

"No. He was disguising it. The pitch was low, soft. Almost a whisper."

"Did he have an accent?"

"No—no accent."

"Was there any kind of reverberation or delay? Could these have been long-distance or satellite calls?"

"They sounded local."

"Did you hear any background sounds—television, music, other voices, traffic?"

"No."

Cardozo ran the options through his mind. "I think we'd better install a trace."

"All right. If you think so."

"If we tap from inside the house and we have permission of the resident, we don't need a court order. The only question I'm legally required to ask you is, are you a resident?"

"I don't know how the law defines that."

"Let's go by how you define it."

"It's Waldo's house, but he's away and I suppose I'm a resident at the moment."

"Fine. I'll be over with a man after I get through here. Would six, six-thirty be okay?"

"Six or six-thirty would be fine," she said. "I haven't any plans."

That seemed odd to him: a woman like Leigh Baker spending an evening in New York, not having any plans. "Can you get the servants out of the house? It'll take a half hour, hour."

"I'll make sure they're not here."

"And till I get there it might be a good idea to let your answering machine take your calls."

■ ■ ■

WHEN LEIGH BAKER OPENED the front door, she was wearing a dress of a pale peach and her hair had a tousled and magnificent look, as though half an hour ago she'd paid a hairdresser two hundred dollars to mess it up just right.

"Miss Baker," Cardozo said, "I'd like you to meet my friend Tommy Thomas. Tommy's with Nynex."

"How do you do, ma'am," Tommy said.

Leigh Baker's eyes went right past Cardozo and raked Tommy from his face down to his shoes and then back up.

Cardozo could understand why: Tommy's sandy-brown hair was salon-cut and he wore a beautifully tailored lightweight dark gray suit. The small leather case in his left hand was made of pigskin, and it carried his initials in gold, just beneath the combination lock. When Leigh Baker took that lingering second look, Cardozo felt a tiny sting of regret that he hadn't spent a thousand dollars more grooming himself.

"Which part of the house do you need to see?" Leigh Baker asked.

"Phone lines usually come into the cellar," Tommy said.

"Then to the cellar we'll go," Leigh Baker said. The remark had an odd kind of prefabricated merriness that didn't fit Cardozo's impression of her. *Why do I suddenly hate Tommy Thomas?* he wondered.

Don't bother answering, he told himself.

Tommy Thomas was Cardozo's telephone connection.

When you needed a phone tap, the official way was to go through the law-enforcement bureaucracy. The procedure took up to three weeks, and it left a paper trail four departments wide. The unofficial way was to go through the phone company, the people who had invented the phone and the phone tap and the phone trace and who still controlled the state-of-the-art technologies of all three. This took anywhere from five minutes to an hour, and in the end, three hundred fewer people knew about it.

Leigh Baker led them through the kitchen and down a flight of stairs.

Though the chandeliers were brass instead of crystal, Waldo Carnegie's idea of a cellar could have been someone else's idea of a ballroom. Oriental rugs dotted the polished oaken parquet, and the walls and the ten-foot ceiling were paneled in molded walnut. The pipes that criss-crossed overhead were polished brass, as though someone had decided, *Hell, if we can't make them invisible, we might as well make them expensive.*

Tommy Thomas crossed the cellar and opened a small brass cabinet door, exposing a pocket of agitated dials and wheels and blinking lights. "This looks like some kind of temperature-stabilizing mechanism. What's he got down here, a wine cellar?"

"Yes, he has, and they say it's a very good one."

"Could I have a look?"

Leigh Baker unlocked a door behind the stairway.

Wine, Cardozo discovered the minute he stepped into the little windowless room, lived at a temperature ten degrees lower than people.

Leigh Baker flicked on the light.

Except where the pen-and-ink portrait of a standing Harlequin hung, the walls were x'ed with tiger-maple latticing, and the lattices were filled with bottles lying on their side, cork end out. At a quick estimate Cardozo calculated more than three thousand bottles.

Tommy lifted the Harlequin off its hook and leaned it against a low wall of white burgundies. The picture had masked a foot-square door set flush with the paneling. He jiggled it open. A nest of color-coded wires streamed through a series of tiny black boxes, looping over and under and around one another like nerve fibers in a brain.

"Bingo." Tommy snapped open the catch of his pigskin case and took out a flat, three-by-three-inch black metal box and went to work.

Leigh Baker stood quietly watching. Her face was strained and a little anxious. Cardozo could tell that the situation was giving her trouble. Till now the calls had been in the same class as nightmares: she could always tell herself she was imagining them.

With this little box that option was dead. The beast was going to leave footprints.

It took Tommy Thomas just under seven minutes to wire in the microminiaturized memory box and ring-activated cassette-recorder. "That will record the number calling in and the conversation. You'll have everything but the caller's age, weight, and social-security number."

Leigh Baker avoided looking at the tracing box. She looked at Tommy. "Could I offer you a drink, or iced tea, or whatever?

Tommy pulled back his jacket sleeve to look at his watch. "Sorry. I'd enjoy it, but I've got one more job to get to."

At that instant Cardozo loved Tommy Thomas.

■ ■ ■

"HOW ABOUT YOU, LIEUTENANT?" Leigh Baker said. "Something to drink?"

They were standing in the front hallway, just the two of them now.

"Maybe a little water," Cardozo said.

"Nothing stronger?"

"Not while I'm on duty, thanks."

"It's almost seven. Can't you go off duty?"

"If I'm off duty, I don't have a hell of lot of business being here."

Something uncertain appeared in her eyes, as though she didn't quite know which door to go through next. It was a moment before confusion reshaped itself into a smile. "In that case, you're on duty and there's water galore." She took him to the kitchen and searched through three huge, over-stocked refrigerators. "Damn. We had some Evian and some Vittel—but I can't find them."

Cardozo went to the sink and turned the tap. "This will do me fine. I'm a native."

"You need a glass." She opened a cabinet and handed him a brandy snifter. "Sorry. I haven't learned my way around Waldo's cups and saucers."

Cardozo let the water run till it was cold, and then he filled the snifter.

"You need some ice," she said.

"I'm okay."

"Let me do *something* hospitable." She took the snifter to the refrigerator and dropped three cubes of ice into it. "Do you suppose we'd be a little more comfortable in the living room?"

The living room was a high-windowed space large enough to hold a concert-grand piano and three separate groupings of tapestried sofas and chairs. Leigh Baker selected the grouping nearest the fireplace. She took one end of the sofa and Cardozo took the chair facing her.

He sat a moment, rippling the water in his glass. "Isn't your number unlisted?"

She nodded. "Yes, I have my very own secret unlisted line. Waldo insisted."

"And the calls have been coming in on that line?"

She nodded.

Cardozo looked around him. French windows sealed in the air-conditioned cool with its faint scent of potpourri that pervaded the house. It was hard to believe that, on the far side of the soundproofed outer walls, traffic was shaking the city and homeless men and women were staking out doorways for their night's sleep.

It was even harder to believe the statistics saying that somewhere in the city at this very moment seven people were getting ready to kill seven other people, five of whom would be complete strangers to their assailants.

"Who knows the number?" he said.

"A lot of people." She thought for a moment. "I've given it to my friends . . . my family . . . my agent . . . my lawyer . . . the people I worked with on my last movie—and there's always my sponsor."

Cardozo looked across at her. The soft, cone-shaped glow of the table lamp silhouetted her, touching the edge of her hair with highlights the color of fresh honey.

"What's a sponsor, some product you advertise?"

For a moment she didn't answer. He was aware of a change in her, a softening in the angle of the shield she turned to him.

"It's an AA term," she said finally. "A sponsor is someone who advises a newcomer."

"So you're an AA newcomer and you have a sponsor."

"No, I'm not a newcomer anymore, but yes, I still have a sponsor. A beautiful man. His name is Luddie Ostergate and he's gotten me through a lot. He's even getting me through this."

Cardozo let the implications of that word *beautiful* ripple through him. *This woman comes on savvy and semitough but what she really is, is lonely and a little shy and very sick of men wanting to paw her.*

"But I know it's not Luddie phoning me," she said.

"How do you know?"

"Because Luddie never phones anyone. He hasn't called me twice in the last month. I phone him when I need him." Her teeth sank down onto her lower lip. "Actually, I hardly ever phone him."

"Why not? Don't you need him anymore?"

"More than ever. But I go over to his place twice a week. We have a standing appointment."

He finished his water and set the snifter down on the table. "That was great water. Thanks." He stood and patted his legs to help the wrinkles drop off his pants.

"Do you really have to go?"

"Wish I didn't, but I really do."

She appraised him. There was something sad in her eyes now. The realization that she wanted the visit to last longer made him feel light, as though his feet were nowhere near the floor.

She yielded with a smile and walked with him back toward the hallway. They reached the front door. He could feel her delaying.

"This is for you." She opened a drawer in the hallway table and handed him a tape cassette in an unmarked plastic box.

He turned it over in his hand. "Thanks. Whose greatest hits is this?"

"The time before last—when he called—I accidentally left the machine running."

"Okay." Cardozo pocketed the tape. "I'll have the sound lab look at it." He opened the front door and then stopped. "Could I ask you a stupid question?"

"Please do."

He took out his notepad and ballpoint. "Would you give me your autograph?"

She smiled. "Of course."

"And could you make it *to Terri*—two *r*'s and an *i*?"

She wrote in looping, graceful letters. "And . . . an . . . *i*. Is Terri your wife?"

"My daughter. But my wife used to be a great fan of yours."

Leigh Baker handed the pad and pen back. "Why did your wife stop?"

"She died."

"I'm sorry."

"It was a while ago. Anyway . . ." Cardozo slid the pad back into his pocket. "You don't want to stand here with the door open. We're air-conditioning the street." Cardozo's fingers picked that moment to lose their grip. The pen dropped to the step and he bent down to retrieve it. As he straightened up again his eye caught a movement in the hallway. A man stood waiting there—a neat, frowning heavyweight in a gray summer suit.

"I'm sorry," Cardozo said. "You should have told me you had company."

"That's not company." Leigh Baker obviously knew who he was talking about without even turning. "He's guarding me till Waldo gets back."

The man was staring at Cardozo. Against the florid red of his complexion, his pale eyebrows stood out like scar tissue.

"I hope Waldo gets back soon," Cardozo said.

"So do I."

· TWENTY-EIGHT ·

Saturday, May 25

THE MINUTE FRANCOISE FORD turned off the shower she heard voices over the partition.

"You don't put weight-lifting gloves in the washing machine!" a man shouted.

She had a hunch that was Bruce, the owner of Bodies-PLUS.

"It's not the end of the goddamned world!" The second voice shouted with a slightly Central American accent. That had to be Rick, the towel boy.

"It's the end of an eight-hundred-dollar dryer if Velcro gets jammed in the heating element—and *that* will be the end of your job."

Francoise dried herself, gave her short, blond hair a quick once-over with the hairdryer provided by Bodies-PLUS, slipped back into her street clothes. She zipped her workout clothes into her gym bag and stepped out of the changing room.

The men were still shouting, only now the washing machine was making a grating noise like a rusty saw. She couldn't make out the words, only the tones. The tones told her the fight was getting meaner.

Down the hallway, past the owner's office, the door to the laundry room was open.

She tiptoed.

The smell of dirty towels grew stronger. It was a heavy, decaying body-waste odor—worse than ordinary sweat, because it combined sweat with Body-PLUS anabolic protein supplement.

She sneaked one eye around the open door, just enough to see without being seen.

"You've started showing some high negatives." Bruce was

hunched forward like a bull in search of a brawl, the veins in his face taut with hostility.

Rick held himself straight, crapped-on but tough and un-bowed, pushing out a dark stone silence.

Francoise liked that.

"I'm talking to you!" Bruce slammed a fist on the washing machine. "You could at least shave before you come to work!"

"You're paying me four-fucking-fifty an hour to wash towels and clean the shit out of toilets," Rick shouted, "not to model for your customers!"

"You have the same obligations as anyone else on the staff. Look your best! You represent Bodies-PLUS!"

"Fuck representing Bodies-PLUS!"

A glaze of pure hating came over Bruce's face. "Would you rather get paid zero dollars an hour?"

Francoise had a feeling she was seeing the downside of Bruce McGee, the side Bodies-PLUS clients never got to see. She suspected too, this was the downside of steroids, the downside of recreational coke, a lot of downsides intersecting and exploding at once.

She felt ashamed for prying where she had no business prying. She turned around and walked back through the gym.

Bodies-PLUS took up half the top story of a midtown building. Soft indirect lighting supplemented the illumination from the skylights. The floors were covered in comfortable moss-green shallow-pile carpeting, and the free weights and Polaris workout machines were placed like art works in a gallery.

The gym floor was deserted. The weights gleamed in their racks like the eyes of crocodile in a swamp.

She glanced at her watch. Six fifty-five. Bodies-PLUS closed at seven on Saturdays. She realized she was the last client to leave.

Someone had forgotten to switch off the music tapes. A stream of chin-up, cheer-up, pump-that-iron happy rock poured from the wall speakers. It struck her as eerie, like merry-go-round music when there was no merry-go-round.

She pushed the door open and had one foot in the corridor when she heard a weight crash onto the gym floor.

Rick came stumbling into the vestibule. He was holding a jockstrap to his forehead. "Don't you fucking try, man!"

I shouldn't be seeing this, Francoise thought.

Before she could get out the door Bruce stepped into the vestibule. His right hand clenched a fifteen-pound dumbbell.

Right away he saw Francoise. He gave her a look, and the look said, *Stay out of this, or I'll cut your titties off.*

"Hi," Francoise said, brightly.

Rick turned around, startled. He jerked the jockstrap away from his face. The side of his head showed a mean blue bruise.

She could feel him trying to put his dignity back together with Crazy Glue. That look on his face invaded her.

"How about dinner?" she said. "My treat."

"Who?" Rick looked shocked. "Me?"

She nodded. "You." She turned and sang out, "Good night, Bruce."

Bruce didn't answer. His gaze was fixed on her, affectless, like a dead rat's.

She held the door for Rick.

Riding down in the elevator, he looked over at her. "Did you mean that about dinner, or were you just trying to bust Bruce's chops?"

"I meant it."

A smile opened on his face. His teeth were incredibly, beautifully white.

"Do you like health food?" she said.

He nodded.

"I know a terrific restaurant," she said.

■ ■ ■

FRANCOISE'S TERRIFIC RESTAURANT was crowded and dark. The waitress gave them a table wedged in between the laser juke box and the kitchen. They both ordered tofu steak.

Rick sat there pulling apart a piece of pita bread.

"Bruce shouldn't treat you like that," Francoise said. "Why do you work for him?"

"I need the job."

"It's a lousy job—no one ever holds it more than a month. Can't you get another job?"

He shook his head. "I don't have papers."

She was jolted. She'd never before met an illegal alien. Except her stepmother. But that didn't really count.

"I'm sorry," he said. "I didn't mean to unload my life story on you."

"I want to hear it."

He seemed to make the decision right then that he trusted her. For the next ten minutes, in a gentle, sad voice, he unloaded. Francoise gradually began to get a sense of what it must be like to be driven from your own country, forced to beg for your living in a land of strangers who would prefer to see you dead.

Oddly enough it reminded her of her own life since her father's death.

"I'm fresh out of phoniness," she said. "What can I tell you that wouldn't be bullshit? I identify? I'm sorry?"

And then he reached over the table and touched her hand. The touch was sad but also sweet. "Your turn," he said.

"Complete anticlimax. I'm a rich kid. I've never had to do a day's work in my life."

"You work hard," he said. "I've seen you training."

"That's not the same. You work to stay alive. I'm trying to control a weight problem."

"Where I come from, a girl with a body like yours would be a ten."

"Maybe you should give me the address of your hometown."

"You can see my hometown over on Avenue D." In anyone else's mouth the remark would have seemed angry or self-pitying, but Rick said it in a completely matter-of-fact way. "Where would I go if I wanted to see your hometown?"

She shrugged. "Upper East Side."

"So what are you doing taking a towel boy to dinner? People like you are supposed to spend their time shopping at Bloomingdale's and partying with famous people."

She wondered if the remark was meant to sting. Because, oddly enough, it didn't. "Maybe I've tried that. Maybe I don't like it."

"I'll bet your parents want you to go to those parties and marry a rich husband."

"My parents are dead."

"Hey, we're both orphans."

There was humor floating in his gaze, humor that was utterly without malice or put-down. For a minute Francoise didn't get it. And then it dawned on her that this had to be one of the most fundamentally good-natured people she had ever met.

"How did your parents die?" Rick said.

"My mom died of cancer when I was four. My dad died last year. He had a heart attack on an airplane. What about your parents?"

"They died when the government bombed our village."

Francoise's jaw dropped. "Where was that?"

"El Salvador."

"I didn't know things like that happened in El Salvador."

"Things like that go on everywhere. So now that you're an orphan, who do you live with?"

"I live with my stepmother."

"You say *stepmother* like she's a witch."

Francoise laughed. Suddenly, telling it to Rick, it seemed funny. "She's spending my father's money, trying to make herself a big New York socialite. People think she's a joke."

"How'd your father meet her?"

"She was our cleaning lady."

"Oh, boy—so now she's going to make *you* the cleaning woman."

"Kind of. She's giving a big party on the thirteenth of June—she didn't invite me."

"Your own house, and she didn't invite you?"

"She inherited the apartment."

"Still, you should crash the party. Show that witch. Tell you what—*I'll* show her. What night is the thirteenth?"

"It's a Thursday."

"Okay. Thursday the thirteenth I'm going to come to your house with a huge bouquet for you."

"I like the way you think."

"Who would it kill her if you got flowers from?"

Francoise didn't even have to think to answer that one. "Robert de Niro. Olga's invested in his restaurant, and she'd do anything to get into one of his parties."

"Her name's *Olga*? Shit. What's your name?"

She realized she'd spent the last hour with Rick without even introducing herself. "Francoise Ford."

"I'm going to put a card with the flowers that says TO FRANCOISE FORD WITH LOVE, BOB DE NIRO. "

It was odd—sitting across a table from this complete stranger with dark brown stubble on his cheeks, Francoise felt relaxed and accepted for the first time in two years.

"You think I'm kidding," he said. "But on Thursday the thirteenth, watch out, Olga!"

▪ TWENTY-NINE ▪

Sunday, May 26

WALDO STEPPED THROUGH the front door and set his suitcase down on the floor. He picked up the mail from the silver bowl on the hall table.

"Welcome home," Leigh said.

He smiled. "You're looking well. Where's Arnie?"

"Mr. Bone is watching television in the library. Waldo, could you pay him and get rid of him—right now?"

For the briefest tick of an instant Waldo's eyes were concerned. "Any trouble with him?"

"I've had company I enjoyed better in a dentist's chair."

Five minutes later Waldo knocked on Leigh's door. "Mission accomplished."

She went to him. They embraced.

"I'm glad you're back." She sighed.

His hand patted her on the butt. "Me too."

"If you ever leave me alone again, if you ever hire me another guard, promise it won't be Arnold Bone."

"He couldn't have been all bad. He kept you alive, didn't he?"

"Promise?"

"Don't worry—I'm not planning to leave you alone for a long, long time."

· THIRTY ·

Monday, May 27

"SAME AS THE FIRST NOTE," Lou Stein said, "but more so."

"Clarify that *more so* for me," Cardozo said.

They were sitting at the worktable in Lou Stein's office, drinking coffee. Lab coffee was better than precinct coffee, and Cardozo was halfway through his second cup.

The two Society Sam notes lay side by side on the table. They were crazy quilts of typefaces, wriggling up and down the pages, but the strips of tape that held the cut-out letters had been placed exactly parallel to the top of the paper and to one another.

With an instrument that looked like a dental probe, Lou tapped the taped-on letters. "In note two, he uses the same five sources as note one, plus two still unidentified. The word that gave him the most trouble is *wick*—four separate letters. *W* is not that popular a letter in English."

"Could he be getting any of the letters from a book?"

"Since Hitler, people tend to respect books. They don't burn them, they don't cut them up."

"Paperback?"

"Possibly."

Cardozo drank his coffee quietly. "And the tape?"

"Same in both notes—Scotch Magic tape, three-quarter inch. No prints."

"DNA?"

"We'll see what we can isolate from saliva on the stamps and envelopes. If it matches the DNA in the semen, we'll know for sure we're dealing with one guy."

"Prints?"

"Only on the envelopes." Lou sighed. "Useless."

· THIRTY-ONE ·

Tuesday, May 28

TORI FINALLY FOUND A PAY PHONE that worked on the corner of Fifty-third Street. She dropped a quarter into the coin slot and dialed her office and told her assistant she was running late. "Any messages while I was out?"

"Just one from HBO. They gave you the wrong time for the screening tonight. It's eight, not eight-thirty."

HBO had invited her to another of those previews of one of their TV movies. Zack owned stock in the company, and she knew he wanted to go. She dialed his office.

"Hi, Minnie, it's me. Could I talk with Zack?"

"I'm sorry," his secretary said, "he isn't in just now. He's out looking at an apartment."

"Really?" Tori and Zack had discussed getting a larger apartment, but she hadn't realized he was already looking. "Could you tell him the screening tonight has been moved up to eight?"

"Certainly, Miss Sandberg."

Tori was about to hang up the phone. "Oh, Minnie. Whose apartment is Zack looking at?"

"He's been looking at Annie MacAdam's listings lately, but I'm not sure which one he's seeing today."

"Thanks." Tori broke the connection. In the bottom of her change purse she found two dimes and a nickel. She dialed and Annie MacAdam answered on the first ring.

"Annie, what are you doing home? I thought you were showing Zack an apartment."

There was a hesitation. "Then what are you doing phoning me?"

"I'd like to see the apartment myself."

■ ■ ■

"WITH A NEW YORK APARTMENT," Annie MacAdam said, "you usually have to choose whether you're going to have children or guests." Annie winked. "But this apartment is ideal—there's plenty of room for both."

"Yes," Tori agreed. "Ideal."

"This room, for instance, would be perfect for a child."

Tori did not go into the room. She stood at the threshold, glancing quickly at the high-molded ceiling, the three windows that looked onto East Seventy-second Street, the stripped bed.

"Zack *does* want children, doesn't he?" Annie said.

"Eventually he does."

"An apartment like this might just hurry the eventual along." Annie led Tori down a windowed gallery. Heat shimmered beyond the glass, but inside it was a cool spring day—what May should have been and never was anymore in New York.

"Zack is *mad* for the apartment," Annie said.

"Is that so? I wonder why he didn't mention it to me."

"He's looked at it twice now." Annie threw open the bedroom door and stood aside.

Tori went in.

The tan silk spread on the wide canopied bed glowed as if it were a source of light.

"This is a wonderful space," Annie said. "Of course, you'd want to do it differently. The bedroom reflects the woman. This decor is cosmopolitan, and you're down to earth."

Tori touched the bed. Her hand slid along the spread. She could feel that beneath it, the bed was ready to sleep in, made up with sheets and a light blanket.

"Wonderful silk, isn't it?" Annie said. "Sorry, nothing's for sale but the apartment."

Tori turned and saw herself in the mirror, caught in the arms of the plumply carved cherubs that formed the gilded frame. Something about her face was tired, preoccupied, wan. It was like seeing herself fifteen years from now.

"What's the bathroom like?"

"Bliss." Annie crossed to the bathroom door and flicked on the light. "This is the only bathroom that Philip Johnson ever designed for a client, and it was as a personal favor. Don't you just want to *live* in it?"

Tori's eyes did a quick scan of the sunken onyx bathtub-built-for-two, the enormous twin sinks, side by side on streamlined pedestals that seemed to grow out of the wall, the twin his-and-hers toilets with a coy chest-high screen between them, the mirrored wall with a marble counter running its length, the cabinets and laundry hamper built beneath, flush to its edge.

Why am I doing this? she asked herself, and she could only think that she was doing it because it was important for this not to be important.

"Annie, would you mind if I used the facilities?"

"Darling, help yourself—piddle in both of them."

Annie scooted out, and Tori locked the door and turned on the cold water in one of the sinks. It ran with a silky sound.

For a heavy moment she held herself motionless. She felt she was standing on a boundary that she could cross only once.

And then in one decisive step she was over it.

She yanked open the hamper. A pile of almost fresh bed linen spilled out onto the tile floor. The sheets smelled strongly of Rigaud.

She crushed each pillowcase to her nose. Beneath the Rigaud a scent of Zack's sandalwood struck her like a slap in the face.

She crouched there in silence, breathing, just breathing.

Around her sandalwood hung in the air, suspended, like a sound.

Carefully she studied the pillowcases.

Two hairs were clinging to one of them. She lifted them off—a long chestnut hair, a short darker hair.

Tori held the dark hair up to the light, then carried both to the toilet and flushed them down the drain.

She stuffed the bedclothes back into the hamper. It took three shoves to get the door to stay closed. She turned off the water and unlocked the bathroom door.

"All ready," she sang out. "Sorry to take so long."

She looked around the bedroom and was startled to realize Annie had left her alone. At almost the same instant she experienced something far more startling: a rush of memories that were not hers. She could see two bodies on the bed, floating easily, timelessly through the patterned exchanges of lovemaking.

She blinked.

The images vanished, leaving the bed darker, duller, as though the silk had turned to canvas. There was no shimmer, no vibration of light.

She flicked the switch on the bedside lamp. Nothing happened.

"Annie?" she called.

The silence in the room was suddenly flat and harsh. *The air-conditioning,* she realized. *It's stopped.*

She crossed to the window and stared down into the street. Beyond the double glazing, traffic moved with eerie soundlessness on the avenue eight stories below. *Then it couldn't be a power failure,* she realized: *the streetlights wouldn't be working.*

She crossed quickly to the bedroom door. The gallery seemed stiller, warmer than an instant ago. She sniffed. A sweet pungency hung in the air. It hadn't been there before. The smell was familiar. Guerlain.

Somehow she took a wrong turn and found herself in an enormous, empty kitchen with two double sinks and two double refrigerators.

"Annie?" she called.

The situation was laughable and at the same time just a little bit frightening. What kind of a real estate agent would take a client to view a listing and then turn off the electricity and disappear?

Certainly not Annie MacAdam.

Tori jumped at a clicking noise somewhere behind her. A door had shut.

She turned and waited, reaching out with her ears. Ten beats of silence passed. The sound repeated itself. She realized it was coming from the back stairs: someone was running the service elevator.

She stood calming her nerves, folding herself in a curtain of concentration. *It's only a New York apartment. It's not the Black Forest.*

She turned and retraced her steps.

The smell of Guerlain hung stronger in the front hall. She came to the library and stopped. Annie sat sprawled in the shadow of a leather wing-back chair. Her purse was open on her lap and her eyes were shut.

At first Tori thought she might be meditating, but Annie's hand lifted, holding an atomizer, and spritzed the air in front of her nose.

"Annie. I'm ready to go."

Annie opened her eyes and smiled. "There you are." She stood and dropped the Guerlain back into her purse. "You'll let me know quickly, won't you? It's going to be a very sought-after apartment. Dizey's putting it in her column."

■　■　■

"THEY SHOULD HAVE A DRESS CODE for these things," Dizey Duke said. "Look at Gloria Spahn. Tits the size of South *Africa* and they're falling out of her dress."

Zack Morrow looked to his right. Men's starched shirts and women's bare shoulders made bright bobbing triangles and diamonds glittered against tanned skin as two hundred fox-trotting couples spun across the floor of the Waldorf-Astoria ballroom.

"Other way," Dizey said. "She's dancing with the mayor. You'd think the chairperson of the event would set an example. She looks like a cable-TV hooker."

Zack looked to his left. The dress on Gloria Spahn was part gold bikini and part gold leotard, and she looked as lean and fit as a stripper.

Tonight's event was the fourth annual New York Ball for the Homeless. The design firm of Gurdon and Chappell had fashioned a decor out of shopping bags and cartons and crates from Cartier, Tiffany, Saks, and any other merchant who had contributed packing material. For the fourth year since PEN had fired her from its fund-raising committee, Gloria Spahn was serving as chairperson.

"Gloria *is* setting an example," Zack said. "She's wearing a quarter million, and except for ten dollars, it's all on her neck."

Something tapped Zack Morrow on the shoulder. Without releasing Dizey's left hand, he looked behind him into the eyes of Gloria Spahn's husband.

"Gotcha," Stanley Siff said. He was wearing antique emerald studs the size of the Hope diamond in his boiled shirt. "Double-cut."

"Isn't this fun," Dizey said acidly. "I haven't double-cut since Amanda Burden was a deb."

"Don't blame Stanley," Annie MacAdam said. "I put him up to it."

"*Vaya con Dios,* Dizey." Zack handed Dizey to Stanley. He took Annie's hand and spun her in time to the music. Lester Lanin's band was playing an irresistibly up-tempo arrangement of "It's Gonna Be a Great Day."

"I take it you love the apartment?" Annie said.

"What apartment is that, Annie?"

"Now, don't you get sly with me. You and Gloria looked at it twice last week. And again today."

"It's a beautiful apartment. We loved it."

"Annie MacAdam Associates aims to please. And how did Tori like the apartment?"

"You've lost me, Annie. What apartment are we talking about now?"

"We're still talking about the Vanderleeuw apartment."

"Tori hasn't seen it."

"Oh, yes, she has." Annie slowed and left Zack marking time to the music. She pulled her compact from her gold-sequinned purse and powdered a little of the shine off her nose. "I took her there not more than an hour after you and Gloria vacated."

"Why did you do that?"

"Because she phoned and asked to see it." Annie redrew her lips. "The way she examined that bathroom you'd have thought she was going to put it on the next cover of *Matrix*."

Zack stared at Annie. He didn't speak.

Annie's glance glided like smoke along his face. "I take it you're just going to let me ramble on and smile your most beguiling smile."

"I didn't know I had a beguiling smile."

Annie snapped her purse shut. Her feet took up the beat again. "You do and you use it, you handsome dog."

■ ■ ■

"WHY DID YOU LOOK at that apartment?" Zack said.

Tori glanced up. She hadn't heard him come into the bedroom. He stood in the doorway, still dressed in his dinner jacket. They'd been to separate dinners. It was one of the by-laws of their relationship that they had one night off a week from each other's friends.

She shot him a questioning expression, trying very hard to look as if she honestly couldn't imagine what he was talking about. "What apartment?"

"Annie MacAdam showed me an apartment on East Seventy-second Street. I told her I didn't like it. Tonight at the Homeless Ball she told me you'd been to see it. Why?"

Tori laid the new issue of French *Vogue* facedown on the chaise lounge. She rose. "Annie isn't being quite straight with us. She told me that you loved the apartment. If she'd told me you didn't like it, I wouldn't have bothered."

"Wait a minute. I want to get the time sequence straight. You looked at the apartment because Annie told you I loved it?"

Tori felt something constrict in her stomach. Zack rarely questioned anything she did, and he almost never questioned it in the tone of voice he was using now. "I don't remember the exact time sequence, and this really isn't worth going into. Somehow our signals got crossed. No one's to blame, and let's not make it a big deal. Please."

"I made my start in this town in real estate. I began with nothing—two tenement buildings on Avenue B that even the junkies wouldn't live in. One thing I don't need is help deciding whether or not I like an apartment. You've got terrific taste, and God knows I've relied on you for it, but I know the kind of home I want to live in. I know *exactly*."

She realized that this was the moment to confront him, to ask point-blank if he was having an affair. She realized too that she'd stepped on his macho, that he was in exactly the kind of mood where he'd say yes and tell her to get the hell out of his life.

"It was an impulse," she said. "I happened to be in Annie's neighborhood. I thought the magazine could do an article on New York apartments and how they affect life choices."

He wasn't buying it. "I don't like being checked up on."

Tori sensed a great empty space between her and Zack, more space than there was in the entire room. Something was at stake here, and it wasn't just an apartment. She knew she could buy time with a lie or an evasion, and she knew she'd hate herself if she tried. "I didn't mean to check up. I called your office and your secretary said you were looking at real estate. I was curious."

"Do I call your office and get curious when your secretary says you're out?"

"I don't know. Do you?"

Zack snapped the gold cuff links out of his shirt and dropped them into the Limoges saucer on the dresser. His shirt studs followed the cuff links with three distinctly separated pings.

Early in their relationship Tori had noticed that Zack dropped his jewelry into ashtrays and saucers. She'd given him a Vuitton stud box to break him of the habit. The stud box was right there on his dresser, and she took it as an intentional slight that tonight he was ignoring it. He was sending a message that whatever control she possessed over him was purely by his permission.

"Are you having an affair?" she said quietly.

He turned. "We agreed on a relationship with no strings and no checking up. For seven years I've kept my side of that agreement."

"For seven years I've never done anything you needed to check up on."

"That was your choice."

"It's Gloria Spahn, isn't it?"

He didn't answer. He undressed down to his Jockey shorts.

"Are you in love with her?"

"Why don't you ask me who was at the Homeless Ball?"

"Who else was at the Homeless Ball, besides Annie?"

"People. The usual."

He went into the bathroom, and a moment later the shower pattered like bullets against the curtain.

Tori sighed and got into bed. She left her light on low, a signal that if he wanted to wake her, she'd enjoy the interruption. She snuggled down under the thin cover and closed her eyes.

She could hear Zack singing in his easy, untrained baritone as he rinsed the last five hours off his body. Even angry, he enjoyed his shower. He reminded her of an animal, never letting emotion bar him from the physicality of life. Sometimes she loved that trait in him. Tonight she didn't. It meant there was a zone he could escape to that was closed to her. It meant she was alone.

She asked herself what she was doing in her life, what had she achieved and what lay ahead. She had founded *Matrix Magazine*. A modern magazine with a feminist slant, appropriate to its time and place. After seven years the magazine was in deep trouble.

She had built a relationship with Zack. A modern relationship, appropriate to its time and place. She had lived with him, loved him, hated him, battled him, gotten pregnant with his baby, aborted his baby by mutual consent, taken him for granted, allowed him to take her for granted. After seven years the relationship was in danger. She and Zack were peeling apart from each other like old weather stripping from a window.

She heard the shower stop, and then came the nightly water music of teeth being brushed and the last piss of the day being flushed away.

Finally Zack came out of the bathroom. She peeped one eye open. The extra hours with his personal trainer were paying off: new muscles ridged his back, and his waist had gotten leaner.

He climbed into bed. The springs bent under him, momentarily pulling her toward him, then recovering.

He read a book and she pretended to be asleep.

A quarter hour later his light went out. Within minutes the deep, regular breathing signaled that he was fast asleep. She lay there unable to sleep, listening to the whisper of other people's plumbing in the walls.

▪ THIRTY-TWO ▪

Wednesday, May 29

THE DESK CLERK HANDED Malloy the key. "Room 607. You know where it is."

Malloy could feel Laurie hanging back. He put an arm around her, husband-and-wife style. They crossed the lobby.

It was a typical midrange Upper East Side hotel. The red plush on the sofas and chairs had developed shining patches, but no one had tossed cigarette butts on the fake Oriental rug. The sound of a live piano spilled out from the little bar just off the lobby. There was a burst of laughter with just an edge of happy-hour drunkenness.

"They serve tea in the bar," Malloy mentioned.

"Oh, yes?" Laurie's voice was trying to be perky and interested, and Malloy could detect the trying. "That would be nice," she said. "Maybe some other time."

When they stepped into the elevator, a man in a business suit and an elderly bellboy were already waiting. The bellboy threw them a glance that was cool but humorous.

Malloy figured that this was at most a two-bellboy hotel—so the old guy had to know who was checked in and who was not, and he'd spotted them for a pair of nots.

"Floor, please," the bellboy said.

"We'll be going to six," Malloy said.

The elevator stopped on four, and the bellboy—balancing two bags—held the door for the man in the business suit.

Twenty seconds later Malloy and Laurie stepped out on six.

"Down here," Malloy said.

She followed him.

Malloy unlocked 607, flicked on the light, stood back. It was a little room with a double bed and faded print curtains and blond furniture and the big dead eye of a TV. The air smelled faintly stuffy.

Malloy crossed to the window and flicked on the air conditioner.

Laurie looked around the room. He tried to see it from her point of view. The ashtrays sparkled, the surfaces shone. The napped pattern on the bedspread had worn down a little, but the spread was clean and pulled tight and the four pillows made inviting bulges.

"Do you want the bathroom first?" She sounded nervous.

He wanted to reach out and hug her and say, *Relax, it's okay. Ten thousand women do this every day in Manhattan.*

"You go ahead," he said.

"It'll only take me a minute."

She took her purse with her. A moment later Malloy heard water running.

He took off his jacket, hung it over a chair. He laid his gun on the chair and his holster beside it.

He took his wallet out of the jacket and snapped open the catch on the change compartment. He poured three dimes and three black pills into his hand.

For Carl Malloy's money, the greatest thing, the only thing the drug culture ever did to benefit mankind was to invent sex drugs. To think a single pill could strip all the distractions from your mind, stop all the whining tapes, turn every millimeter of your skin into a receiving station.

A miracle.

He placed one of the pills on his tongue. It began to dissolve like a patch test. He tasted salt at the sides of his tongue and sour at the rear and bitter in a stripe down the middle. He swallowed.

Then he figured, *What the hell, let's celebrate,* and he popped a second pill.

He stood there listening to the air conditioner. It was making sounds like an electronic synthesizer, singing melodies that weren't quite melodies, saying words that weren't quite words.

A sudden dryness covered his mouth.

He recognized the pill kicking in. He could feel little flashes in his chest.

This is going to be good, he thought.

He unhooked the DO NOT DISTURB sign from the doorknob, opened the corridor door and hung it on the outer knob, slid the bolt.

The room seemed way too bright. He pulled the curtain across the view of the street. He shut off all the lights except the lamp by the bed, and he set that one to dim.

He pulled back the bedspread.

A patch of darning on the sheet hem leapt out at him like a fist.

He blinked, drew in a slow, deep breath and told himself, *Take it easy. They probably darn the sheets even at the Plaza.*

He sat down in the chair and undid his shoes.

Now he could recognize the song of the air conditioner. It caught at his throat, sent a trembling along his spine. "Love Me Tender," the old Elvis Presley ballad, but richer, truer than Elvis, because now it was half memory.

He had stripped down to his socks and shorts when the bathroom door opened.

A woman was standing there in her half slip, the light behind her.

"The bathroom's all yours," Laurie's voice said.

It seemed a long time ago, a forgotten moment in the very remote past that she had gone into that bathroom.

"I don't need it," he said.

He saw her hesitate, then draw her hesitation back into herself.

"Okay," she said.

He peeled off his socks, tucked them into his shoes, stood in his bare feet and shorts.

She looked at him, her head a little to one side, an odd half-questioning smile on her mouth.

His eyes took a long swig of her. The scent of her perfume floated toward him. His cock was beginning to bloat in his drawers.

God bless those pills. Should I offer her one? he wondered. No. Too early in the relationship. Might shock her.

"Hey," he said, "know something?" He moved toward her. "I missed you."

▪ ▪ ▪

AFTERWARD HE RAISED HIMSELF on one elbow and studied her.

She was lying on her back, motionless. Her head with its pale, soft face lay back on the pillow.

He put his fingertip on her wrist.

She jerked away. "Huh?"

"You were so quiet."

She gazed at him with something in her eyes. He wasn't sure what it was, what it meant. He took her hand and kissed each of the small, clear-polished nails.

"You're different now," she said.

"How am I now?"

"Gentle."

He sensed a shyness in her, a wanting. "Wasn't I gentle before?"

"You were like someone else."

"You carried me away, that's why."

"It was like you didn't know it was me."

The lovemaking was a blank in his mind. He couldn't remember what he'd done, what he'd said. Had he been too rough? Talked dirty?

There was bafflement on her face, and an awful feeling inside him that maybe he'd shocked this sweet kid.

Words for her like *shy* and *sweet* and *trusting* started coming into his mind, and words for himself like *stupid* and *selfish*.

He got out of bed and dressed.

Silently she began putting on her clothes.

▪ THIRTY-THREE ▪

Thursday, May 30

WHEN MALLOY CAME BACK to the squad room, Laurie Bonasera
was still not at her desk, and the computer screen was dark.

He glanced over to where Sergeant Goldberg was sitting at
his desk, propped on an elbow over a cup of coffee and a racing
form.

"Anyone seen Laurie?"

Goldberg looked up. "She phoned in sick."

"What's she got?"

"How the hell do I know?"

Malloy went to his desk. He dropped into the chair and let his
long legs stretch out into the aisle. He picked up the phone and
dialed Laurie's number.

She answered and he said, "Hi."

"Who's this?"

"Me."

"Oh—hi."

He had an instant recall for all her tones of voice, and this was
a new one. "You're sick?" he asked.

"Just a little temperature."

"Think you'll be well tomorrow?"

"Sure."

"Feel better," he said.

The line went dead in his hand. He let sixty seconds go by
before he dialed Laurie's number again.

"Hello?"

"Hi, it's me again. Look, I'm in the field today. Why I'm
calling is because I'll be in your neighborhood. If you're not feeling well, if you need anything . . ."

For a moment she didn't say anything, and he felt he was flying over nowhere without an engine and without a parachute.

"That's sweet of you, but you've got enough to do."

"No, no, I don't have enough to do."

"Thanks, Carl, but I really don't need anything."

He wanted to see her face. He couldn't decode her voice without the face. It was like trying to touch her through a metal wall.

"Because if you're not feeling well," he said, "it could be this summer flu that a lot of the guys in the precinct are catching. You probably picked it up here. You should rest, take it easy. I could run any errands you need."

"I really don't need anything."

His heart began going like an electric bass drum kicking out a fast dance pattern. "If you want me to just stop by . . ."

"No, that wouldn't be such a great idea."

Sweat began inching down Malloy's face. What the hell was she telling him, *My world, and get the hell out of it?*

"Carl, there's someone at the door. I gotta run."

"Okay," he said, but the phone was already dead.

He sat in a silence of his own, looking down, not believing she could actually have ended the conversation two times in a row like that, not even a good-bye.

Two minutes later Malloy was in the street, heading east under an oatmeal sky sprigged with blue.

A gray-and-white heat hovered over the pavement, and by the time he reached Bruno's Ca d'Oro Bar and Grill on Sixty-third and Second Avenue, it was a relief to find that the air-conditioning was going full blast.

He slid into a corner booth. The waitress came immediately to take his order.

"Double vodka on the rocks, please."

"Anything to eat, sir?"

"Just the vodka."

■ ■ ■

DIZEY DUKE PRESSED A FINGER, for the third time, against the doorbell of Oona Aldrich's town house.

This time, finally, Gabrielle MacAdam opened the door. She was wearing a one-size-fits-all checkered wraparound sari. She was out of breath and her face looked flushed. "Sorry. I was up-stairs. It's a big house."

"Yeah. They built it that way." Dizey had never been able to view Gabrielle as anything but an ugly duckling of thirty-something summers who hadn't inherited her mother's swan genes and who would never develop the willpower to control her weight or the know-how to take her appearance up-market.

"I think it might be better," Gabrielle said, "to put the main buffet and bar in the living room."

"Maybe." Dizey didn't remember the house all that clearly. She had agreed to help plan the cocktail-party segment of Oona's memorial, but she wanted to refresh her memory before she committed herself.

They rode in the two-person elevator up to the living room. The day had cleared, and midafternoon brightness slanted through the flowered drapes. The caterer's men were hosing down the terrace, and a breeze from the open French windows set the two chandeliers in motion. Crystal prisms jingled cheerfully and scattered rainbows.

The house had seen a lot of New York history, Dizey reflected. Six years ago it had belonged to Leigh Baker, and Jim Delancey had thrown Nita Kohler off that very terrace. Five years ago Oona Aldrich had taken possession and thrown the longest uninterrupted string of hit parties Manhattan had seen since the Eisenhower years.

And now Oona Aldrich had passed from the land of the living, and Annie MacAdam was trying to sell the old house in the worst housing market of the entire twentieth century.

"I thought the bar could go right here." Gabrielle indicated the space in front of the French windows.

"That's great, if you want to make sure no one gets to the terrace." Dizey walked slowly to the fireplace. *Bar could go here,* she thought. She walked to the opposite wall of bright photo-realist oil paintings of trees and hills. *Could go here.* She sat on the sofa that matched the curtains, on the chairs that matched the sofa, on the bench at the Baldwin grand piano. She rippled out a chorus of "The Eyes of Texas Are upon You."

"Ouch," she said. "Did you call the tuner?"

Gabrielle's face turned an even deeper shade of red. "I forgot."

Figures, Dizey figured.

"Maybe I can get a tuner from the *Village Voice* listings," Gabrielle said. "They come on short notice."

"Forget it." Dizey crossed to the wall of bookshelves. Her eye noted books in French, books in Latin. Books printed in 1592. Books printed last year. She opened a French edition of Proust and saw that the leaves had not even been cut. Who the hell had Oona Aldrich thought she was fooling?

"The bar can go here," Dizey said. "This wall."

"In front of the books?"

"No one's going to want to read. Take my word for it. Not tonight."

"But the books are so—they're so beautiful."

"So's a well-stocked bar."

"There are well-stocked bars in every town house in Manhattan," Gabrielle said. "But there isn't a collection of first editions like these."

How did Annie MacAdam conceive this moron? Dizey wondered. *She must have had help from a state trooper.* "Sweetie, people are going to be depressed as hell. Some of them may even want to get drunk. So let's put the bar where they can see it and get to it without breaking their necks or causing traffic jams."

"All right." Gabrielle took a vellum-bound book from the shelf. "But Goethe's *Faust* will go somewhere else, out of champagne-cork range."

"That's a great idea."

Gabrielle stepped through a doorway into a bedroom decorated in muted tones of brown and red. Her eyes searched for a safe place for *Faust.* There was a small canopied bed and behind it a wall full of eighteenth-century botany prints. A silk-upholstered gilt beechwood chair faced a dressing table with delicately bent legs. A triptych mirror shimmered from a painted frame of clouds and cherubs and roses.

She opened a closet door. A smell of cedar drifted out. She touched the dress bags and could feel that there was nothing in them. She stood on tiptoes and slid *Faust* onto the empty shelf.

■ ■ ■

"THIS GAL NOT ONLY *had* class *de la* class, she *was* class *de la* class." Dick Braidy, the only man in the room in evening clothes, was addressing his audience in his most just-between-thee-and-me tale-spinner's voice. "There was no occasion when Oona Mellon Aldrich did *not* shine."

Oona's friends had gathered to commemorate her in the rehearsal hall of the old Rebekkah Harkness town house on East Sixty-sixth Street. It was an odd location, but it was the *in* one this season for nonreligious memorials.

"And one story comes particularly to mind that more than

any other illustrates the *who* and the *what* and the magical *how* of Oona."

Dick Braidy played with the screw on the mike stand, lowered the mike two inches, and stepped closer. His voice dropped. "Now, those of you who don't know me may not know that my daughter was murdered four years ago and, frankly, I was going to pieces over it."

In the fifth row Dizey Duke turned to whisper to her assistant. "Did he say *stepdaughter* or *daughter*?"

"*Daughter.*"

"Cripes! One corpse at a memorial is enough. Isn't he ever going to stop yammering about that murder?"

Mac's left eyebrow shot up, saying it all. "The best publicity break he ever got."

"No class. Why's he wearing a tux?"

"Olga Ford's dinner is black tie."

"He's *not* going. He *wouldn't.*"

Olga Ford, a former charwoman and New York's newest would-be power widow, had had the gall to schedule her breakout dinner tonight, knowing it was the night of Oona's memorial. Naturally Dizey had refused. So far as Dizey knew, anyone who was anyone had refused.

So why was Dick Braidy wearing the tux?

"But Oona," he was saying, "that gem of a human being, do you know what she did? She phoned me and she said, 'Dick, I know you're blue and I know the world seems to have fallen in on you—but pull yourself together and get your ass over here, because I'm having a party to cheer you up.'"

Dick Braidy delivered the line in a dead-on imitation of Oona's hangover voice, and the audience gave him a knowing little chuckle.

"And I said, 'Oona darling, I just don't know if I could get through it.'"

Dick was the only raconteur Dizey had ever met who got it right when he imitated himself.

"And Oona said, 'Fuck it, baby'—she talked low-down and gutsy like that, in that wonderful Tallulah voice of hers—'I'll get you through it.' And do you know, when I arrived at Oona's—she was in Beekman Place in those days—I was expecting it to be *the* hardest evening of my life. I stepped through that door and Oona had rounded up every one of my chums, God knows how. Babe Paley and the Nixons and Slim Keith and George Cukor had flown in from the Coast and Liza M. and Barbara Stanwyck and Mary

Tyler M. and goddamn but Oona had even persuaded Jackie O to cancel an opera benefit—and my God, we *partied*."

Dick Braidy stepped back from the mike and looked up toward the ceiling.

"And I know that this very moment, somewhere up there in the sky, there's a great party going on and Oona is right there in the middle of it, organizing and starring in the biggest bash heaven ever saw. Good-bye, Oona. God bless—and party on!"

Dick Braidy waved good-bye.

A pianist launched into "Jesu, Joy of Man's Desiring."

Dick Braidy took the mike again. "Oona's friends have asked me to mention that food and drink are being served at Oona's. Sorry I won't be seeing you there."

"I don't believe it." Dizey gathered up her purse. "Mac, remind me to nail that bastard *and* his dead stepdaughter in my next column."

■ ■ ■

A BELL TING-A-LINGED as Rick pushed the door open and stepped into the flower shop. The air in the shop was cool and moist and heavy with sweet pungency, as though he had stepped into a tropical rain forest.

A heavy-set woman with pulled-back gray hair eyed him through thick bifocals. "Help you?"

Her face told him he was in the wrong place, Fleurs du Monde did not have his kind in mind when they put the OPEN sign in the door.

"I want something pretty," he said. "Really knockout pretty."

She sighed. "We have a minimum of twenty dollars per order."

He opened his wallet and took out four five-dollar bills and laid them on the counter.

She smiled. "Will these be a gift for a lady?"

"You'd better believe I'm not getting them for myself."

"Might I suggest some very nice Dutch tulips?"

His eye went to one of the refrigerated display cases, to a huge vase of velvety red roses caught in a sparkling slant of light. He pointed. "Those."

"The burgundy roses? They're . . . quite expensive. You'd like a half dozen?"

"Two dozen."

"That will be ninety-four dollars plus tax."

She waited till he laid down ten tens and ten singles. Her smile became pure spun sugar. She took the flowers from the case and neatly clipped each stem. She wrapped the roses in a layer of white tissue, then a layer of green, then cellophane, and finally a heavy candy-cane paper with the name of the shop embossed on it.

"Would you like to put a message with these?" She pushed a small, cream-colored card across the counter.

"I sure would." Rick wrote in large letters, in red ballpoint: *to Francoise Ford with love, Bob De Niro.*

The woman began tucking the card into an envelope and he stopped her.

"No envelope. I want it to show."

She looked at him strangely, then taped the card to the wrapping paper. "And to whom will these go?"

He nodded toward the thick black book with orange print on its spine that lay on the shelf behind her.

"Can I see your *Social Register?*"

Something suspicious flashed behind her bifocal lenses. She handed him the book.

He leafed immediately to New York, and then to the F's. He found a Mr. and Mrs. Gavin Hay Ford on East Seventy-eighth Street and saw that she was the former Olga Slimoniska. They had homes in Newport, Dark Harbor, Palm Beach, and Nassau, and there was a daughter named Francoise.

He memorized the address and closed the book.

"And where would you like these delivered?" the woman asked.

"Thanks, I'll take them myself."

▪ ▪ ▪

YOU WOULD HAVE NEEDED a traffic cop to direct the limousines arriving at Olga and Francoise Ford's building. And that was what they had. Their own traffic cop.

A stream of costumed figures swept under the awning into the lobby. The women were edged in whitecaps of diamonds and laughter splattered out of them in jagged bursts.

Rick stood on East Seventy-eighth Street, watching.

There were two black Chrysler sedans parked in the street with federal license plates. A man who looked like Secret Service stood beside the building entrance, keeping watch calmly from the outskirts.

Rick looked for an opening in the flow, and then he saw it.

One of the guests dropped her purse just outside the entrance. The Secret Service man crouched down to the sidewalk and played a flashlight across the pavement.

Rick crossed the street. He ducked around the taillights of a black Chrysler LeBaron stretch limo and cut ahead of a tall, tanned couple who were speaking Castilian Spanish.

He made it past the Secret Service man into the lobby.

A crowd of guests were waiting for the next elevator. The air swirled with perfume and laughter. Jeweled wrists and necks threw tiny explosions of color.

A uniformed employee of the building stood just outside the elevator. He caught sight of Rick and thrust out a white-gloved hand.

Rick held up the bouquet. "Flowers for Françoise Ford."

The employee nodded him through. "The service elevator's not working—take this one."

Rick squeezed into the elevator.

"What did that Rubens cost her?" a man was saying.

"Half of what Sotheby's claimed," a woman with a low voice answered.

Everybody chuckled.

A tall woman in black velvet was repositioning her diamond necklace. She pushed huge puffy sleeves against Rick's face as though he weren't there.

"You're caught in back," a man said. A hand with gold cuff links crashed through Rick's bouquet and tugged at the necklace catch.

Rick took a step backward.

A woman in green silk pulled back as though he'd tried to jab her with an AIDS-infected needle. "Do you *mind*?" she snapped. Her escort took a handkerchief from the breast pocket of his tuxedo and quickly dusted off the part of her forearm that Rick had brushed. Rick recognized the escort: Dick Braidy, from Bodies-PLUS.

Rick smiled and caught Braidy's eye. "Hi," he said.

Dick Braidy's eyebrows rose. "I beg your pardon?"

"It's me. Rick. Hi."

"Are you talking to me?" Dick Braidy said.

Rick couldn't believe Dick Braidy didn't recognize him.

"Really," the woman in green silk said.

Dick Braidy turned his head the other way.

"Don't they have a service elevator?" the woman in green said.

"The feds commandeered it," someone else said.

"Leave it to a former cleaning woman," Dick Braidy said, "to come up with the *ne plus ultra* of hired help."

Laughter exploded. The elevator stopped and the guests flowed out into a foyer papered in Chinese red. A security man stood by the doorway, checking guests' names off a list.

There were shouted greetings and kisses. A relay team of uniformed maids stood taking women's wraps. Somewhere a live orchestra was playing dance music. Rick stood close to the wall, trying to see over jeweled and dyed heads into the apartment, hoping for a glimpse of Francoise.

A stocky man wearing a dark suit, not a tuxedo, moved rapidly toward him. "May I help you?" There was nothing helpful in his challenge, and Rick could smell the government-issue revolver under his left armpit.

"Flowers for Francoise Ford."

The man practically ripped the bouquet from Rick's hands. "I'll see she gets them."

"I'd like to do the arrangement myself."

"Sorry. This is all the arranging they get."

· THIRTY-FOUR ·

IN THE LIMOUSINE Dizey unwrapped her new brooch. "Like it?"

"Divine," Mac said.

Dizey pinned the brooch to her dress. "Do I have it on straight?"

"Perfect."

Dizey gave her throat and ears fresh dabs of Guerlain. The limo stopped a half block from Oona's town house. Dizey rolled down the window to put her head out and look. The street was pure limo gridlock.

"Come on, Mac. We'll walk."

Dizey was pleased with the turnout, for Oona's sake. Inside the house she was less pleased. So many people were waiting for the elevator that she decided to take the stairs.

"Dizey baby," the bartender sang out. He had pale brown hair and a cute choir-boy nose, and Dizey liked the way his spearmint eyes were cruising her. "The usual?"

"Easy on the soda," Dizey reminded him.

This was the kid who claimed to have some very interesting love letters and Polaroids relating to Malcolm Forbes. Dizey intended to get a peek at that material.

"And a one-inch twist of"—he cocked a finger at her—"lime."

"Go to the head of the class."

He handed her the vodka and soda, and Dizey took a long sip. She stood for a moment, big-boned and proud and erect in her black Gloria Spahn pants suit, watching the crowd flow through the town house.

In the dining room, the up-and-coming catering firm of Splendiferous Eats had laid out a buffet for two hundred. Laughing *nouveaux* aristocrats explored the silver-and-flower–laden tables. They were playing New York's favorite food game: What-the-hell-is-this, or You-call-it-crêpe-fromage-but-Bubba-called-it-a-blintz.

"Oat-bran blinis," Dale Dunlop, the president of Splendiferous Eats, whispered to Dizey, "with Petrossian gray unsalted caviar."

Dale wore the beard of an El Greco saint. He had resigned a position as a Wall Street arbitrageur to plunge into New York's cutthroat catering business. Dizey didn't object to giving him a plug in her column; but she'd be damned if she'd plug Petrossian —they'd made her pay for her last meal.

Dizey nodded to her assistant. "Mac, make a note: oat-bran blinis, and see if Dale will give you the ingredients."

Dale was about to protest.

Dizey turned, smiling her biggest grin. "I didn't say the whole recipe, Dale. Just the basic *vos-iz-dos.*" She moved briskly into the crowd, with the purposefulness of a heat-seeking missile. "There'd better be some good dish here for the column."

In the living room the air was sticky, almost confining. There were too many people, too much talking at once, too many perfumes, and the caterer's hot hors d'oeuvres were giving off a sweet-sour smell, as if someone had made Chinese food and forgotten to open a window.

On the sofa, Fenny Gurdon was holding a group of listeners spellbound with the story of how he'd gone into the wrong bathroom at Stanley Siff and Gloria Spahn's thirty-eight–room Park Avenue duplex, and how he'd seen Stanley's thirty-two toupees sitting on a shelf on numbered wig stands.

"The toupees were arranged so it would look like he gets his monthly haircut on the fifteenth. But what I can't figure out"— Fenny had had a few and he was bellowing—"What's with the thirty-second toupee? What the hell day of the month is that one for? *Valentine's* Day?"

The crowd roared.

What made this story particularly fun for Dizey was that Stanley Siff and Gloria Spahn were standing by the piano, well within earshot, toughing it out.

Dizey tilted a wing and coasted near.

Gloria was trying to impress Jeanie Vanderbilt with that *ancient* story about Louis Auchincloss's wife and the sugar bowl.

"Fenny Gurdon's got a point," Dizey said in an undertone to Stanley's pink little ear. "Your rug looks like a hooker's muff."

Behind Stanley's eyes was a sudden flare-up of loathing. "You'd know all about a hooker's muff, wouldn't you, Dizey?"

Dizey felt a cold swell of outrage and no desire to control it. *Okay, Stanley,* she vowed to herself: *Death.* "Listen, if the ICC doesn't pull the plug on your next raid on the city's pension funds, my column will."

Dizey glanced across the living room toward the French windows. They led to the terrace, and the dimness beyond them was sliding toward darkness.

The beam of a soft spotlight fell across the terrace. A woman was moving through the potted trees and terrace furniture, and every now and then she passed through the shaft of light.

Dizey excused herself and opened the French window. She felt she was stepping into a furnace. How, she wondered, had Manhattanites ever managed to stay alive before air-conditioning?

"Hey," she called out, "come on back inside and circulate. This is Oona's last party!"

The silhouette held itself motionless at the terrace wall. Behind it there was only a thinning pale splash of sky over Jersey to remind you that there had ever been a day.

"I was thinking of the dead," Leigh Baker said.

Dizey crossed the terrace toward her. "What about them?"

Leigh Baker turned and stood facing Dizey.

What is it about beautiful sexy people? Dizey wondered. *Light seems to shine through them. Even in the dark.* In all her years of reporting on them, Dizey had never understood how they achieved that quality.

"So many have died," Leigh said. "Parents . . . grandparents . . . friends—you finally reach that point in your life where you know more dead people than living."

"So what?" Dizey said. "The dead may outnumber the living, but the unborn outnumber them all."

Leigh was holding a glass and she lifted it to her lips. "Why, Dizey. What a profound and spiritual thing to say."

"I'd have thought it's obvious."

Somewhere not far away a church bell was chiming the quarter hour.

Leigh lifted her eyes at Dizey. "I see your old humorous, frowning eyes looking about, and I know you're on the trail of something. And then it occurs to me; I'm your quarry, aren't I."

In the mind of any top gossip columnist is stored every impression, every sensation, every emotion and intuition she has ever experienced—ready for instant cross-reference and collating. And every bone in Dizey's body sweated with the conviction that she had seen Leigh Baker this way before, in the bad old days when Leigh had gotten plastered with daily regularity.

Dizey sat. "Your answering machine had the gall to tell me to make my message brief."

"What were you calling me about?"

"Wanted to check a rumor. How are you feeling—*really*?"

"Me? Fine."

"Honey, I know you've walked a strange and terrible road. I want to help you find your way back. You're drinking again, aren't you?"

Leigh rose and backed off a step. She was gaping at Dizey, and Dizey could feel her trying to hold herself together.

"Why is it," Leigh said, "that people like you feel alive only when you destroy things?"

"Honey, is that a line from one of your old movies, or is it just alcoholic attitude?" She rose. "There's Scotch in that glass, isn't there?"

"No."

"I want to help you find your way back."

Leigh backed off two steps more, as though Dizey were a guard dog who might at any moment break free of its leash and leap at her.

"Honey, you need me." Dizey circled nearer to that glass. "You've had your little turn on the stage of international attention and now—unless you get the right help—it's over."

"And I'm supposed to believe you're the right help?"

Leigh's nose tipped up a little, and it gave her a look of being vulnerable. Dizey could remember long, lonely years in Billings, Montana, that she'd spent wishing to hell God had given her a nose like that.

"I can't stand to see you killing yourself," Dizey said.

"That's bull. No matter what's going on you're always asking yourself, How can I get a column inch out of this?"

"There are losers and there are winners—that's life. A flip of a coin." Dizey held out her hand. "I write about the people that the coin comes up heads for. You could be one of them again. Just give me that drink."

"It's not a drink."

"Then give it to me."

"It's mine."

"And it's killing you."

"Are you really so sure of everything you're so sure of?" There was something sly about Leigh now. Gold flashed from the bracelet on her wrist. Her hand shot up, pointing. "Look out there."

Dizey's head turned just far enough to see what Leigh was pointing at. Night sky glimmered over New York.

"Somewhere in this city," Leigh said, "a man who calls himself Society Sam is watching us—and he's going to pick one of us, and he's going to rip that person apart." She turned. "And you're no different from Society Sam."

To Dizey Duke, what came next seemed to be happening to someone else.

One instant Leigh Baker was standing perfectly quietly, her head angled out toward the New York skyline; the next instant she turned toward Dizey.

Suddenly a terrible cry came out of Leigh Baker. "That's Oona's! You give that back to me, you vicious, thieving bitch! It's hers!"

The drink and the ice cubes flew out of Leigh Baker's glass and hit Dizey in the face like a stinging shower of iced needles. Dizey realized that Leigh's hand was reaching toward the brooch, toward Dizey's lovely new hummingbird brooch.

Without even thinking, Dizey hunched one shoulder up protectively and jerked backward.

Would have jerked backward.

Out of nowhere a wall took her completely by surprise, caught her just below the small of her back. Her hand clawed space and caught the back of the wrought-iron chair. The chair wasn't heavy enough to anchor her. It toppled against the wall, adding a push to the momentum already carrying her.

This isn't happening, Dizey thought.

The night sky was somersaulting over her.

This can't be happening, the voice inside her cried. *I have a column to write!*

■　■　■

THE SCREAM BROUGHT A JOLT of alertness into all Leigh's senses. Time dilated and the action in the space before her seemed to take place in slow motion, as though it had been prerecorded long, long ago.

Dizey's face of open-mouthed amazement hurtled away,

screaming. In the garden, five stories below, a shadow kissed the ground.

The scream stopped. Time reassembled itself and found its tempo.

Leigh picked up the chair from where it had fallen on the terrace floor. A damp breeze ruffled the bushes spaced along the low wall. She looked over them.

My God, she realized. *That's exactly how Nita died.* Somewhere behind her, she heard glass break. Her gaze swung toward the house. Through the French window, she could see Waldo in the living room with one arm around Honey Ogilvie's waist.

Funny, she thought, *I didn't realize Honey Ogilvie had known Oona.*

She crossed the terrace and stepped back into the air-conditioning. Music and voices rose up around her. It was eerie, walking through rooms that once upon a time she had fallen asleep drunk in, and feeling that once upon a time was happening all over again.

She smiled and, naturally, when a waiter offered her champagne, she said, "Thank you, but I don't drink."

· THIRTY-FIVE ·

Friday, May 31

ANNIE MACADAM WAS still on the telephone when her daughter Gabrielle led Vince Cardozo into the library.

She saw that the lieutenant was wearing a rumpled seer-sucker suit and a striped blue tie. *Stripes and stripes,* the part of her mind that wasn't on the phone thought. *A lawyer would never wear that.* She gestured to him to sit.

"You naughty boy," she was saying to the phone, "of course you can trust me." She saw that Lieutenant Cardozo was still standing. "I have a visitor. We'll talk later." It was a fast hang up, and then she took a seat on the sofa.

Cardozo took the matching chair that faced her.

"That was Zack Morrow on the phone," Annie said. "A friend of Dizey's and her boss to boot. You know what gets me? What really and truly gets me? He didn't even mention her."

"Maybe he didn't know," Gabrielle said.

Annie turned and saw that Gabrielle was still standing by the door. She clamped down on a surge of irritation. Since age six Gabrielle had always hung around doors, wanting to hear what the grown-ups were discussing. "Would you like some coffee, Lieutenant? Say yes, I need some."

"Sure."

"Gabrielle honey, could you bring us two cups of coffee?" Annie waited till Gabrielle was out of the room, then leaned forward and took a menthol filter-tip from the carved glass ciga-rette box on the coffee table. She lifted the table lighter and sat there puffing.

Dizey had given Annie the lighter. It was Steuben, a polar bear rearing up in milky glass that would have sold, list price, at a thousand-something. Annie didn't fool herself that Dizey had paid for the lighter, or even chosen it. Still, it had passed from Dizey's hands to hers, and Annie was thinking how strange it was that Dizey was gone, but this coolness, this hardness, remained.

"Zack Morrow knew Dizey's dead," Annie said. "It just wasn't a big deal for him."

"Sometimes people prefer to hide what they feel."

The remark, coming from a cop, surprised her and she looked over at him. "You know, that's very sweet of you. To be making someone else's excuses."

It occurred to her that his dark eyes seemed to share her sadness, and then she realized they were neutral eyes and she was reading her own feelings into his face. He had the sort of face that invited you to do that.

"How well did you know Dizey?" he said.

"How well? I'll tell you how well. Dizey and I were on that phone to each other every day, first thing, twenty minutes a day, three-hundred-sixty-five days a year, for eighteen years. And for eighteen years Dizey came to every one of my dinner parties. If she wasn't in town, I didn't give them."

"You must have been very fond of her."

Annie shrugged. "We had our ups and downs—what friendship doesn't? There are years when you love each other, years when you hate each other. There are even days when you swear to yourself you'd love to see her dead." She stubbed out her cigarette and lit another. "And then one day it happens. You have your blackest wish. She's dead. And that day isn't at all what you imagined it would be. There's no triumph, no winning. Only loss."

She glanced over at him. His eyes, deeply set in shadowed pockets, seemed to grieve with her. She couldn't escape the feeling that he was using those eyes to lure her into confiding. So what. She had to tell someone.

"Because you'd always imagined that somehow she'd be there to see you win. Everything in your life, you imagined that somehow she'd be there witnessing it —loving you for it or wishing you dead because of it—but she'd be there." Annie got up from the sofa. She gestured him to stay seated. "Don't get up—I just need to move around."

She walked to the window. Beyond the terrace splotchy sunlight was dribbling through a shadowy sky. The gray jagged horizon of the co-ops lining Madison and Fifth seemed inert and cut off, like a mountain range on a planet uninhabited by human beings.

"When you're young, you honestly believe you're going to go through your whole life making close friends—and it never works out that way. One by one they go and when they're gone, there's no one to take their place." She realized she was moaning for herself, and she felt embarrassed. She turned and saw that Lieutenant Cardozo was standing again. "But you're a cop. You've been through worse."

"There's no worse. I'm sorry you lost a friend."

Annie shrugged. "I lost a friend. I lost an enemy. I lost a part of my life. Oh, well. Look at the bright side. It saves me the trouble of killing her. Because, believe me, sometimes I wanted to. Like a million other people who knew her."

Annie returned to the sofa. She sat. She couldn't keep herself from shaking, and then to her surprise, she couldn't keep herself from crying.

Cardozo held out a handkerchief. "I need your honest opinion—as Dizey's friend."

Annie accepted the hankie. She daubed at her nose. She picked at a sleeve, adjusted her hem, neatened herself in preparation for honesty.

"Did Dizey have a drinking problem?"

"Drinking problem?" Annie smiled almost fondly. "Dizey had a drinking *fact*. The lady was a practicing, ambulatory alcoholic."

"Did she have depressions?"

"How would anyone have known? Depression didn't have a chance with all the speed her doctor prescribed."

"Is there any possibility that Dizey took her own life?"

"Dizey? Suicide?" Annie's hand slapped her bosom so hard she practically knocked herself off the sofa. *"No way.* Not while there was gossip left to gossip, or a scoop left to scoop."

Gabrielle returned with a coffee tray that should have jingled but that made a sound in her hands more like clanking. *What the hell has she got on that tray?* Annie wondered.

Annie moved the polar-bear lighter to one side, and Gabrielle set the tray on the coffee table.

"Want me to pour?" Gabrielle said.

Annie saw that Gabrielle had brought three cups. "That's okay, hon. I'll handle it. Lieutenant Cardozo and I would appreciate being alone—you don't mind."

"Oh," Gabrielle said. "Okay." She closed the door behind her.

"How do you like yours?" Annie asked.

"Milk and a little fake sugar. If you have any."

"We have fake everything in this house." Annie poured and stirred.

"Could I trouble you for another look at your guest list?" Cardozo said. "May sixth, the Princess Margaret dinner? I'd like to see the seating plan for the tables."

Annie went to the bookcase. She searched a moment through her loose-leaf binders. She brought the binder back to the coffee table. She opened it to May sixth. "Here we are. The page is practically dog-eared." Her forefinger ran halfway down the right-hand page of the binder and stopped. "This is weird."

In the silence that seemed suddenly to settle on the room, Annie could distinctly hear the ticking of the clock on the mantel.

"What's weird?" Cardozo said.

"Dizey sat at the same table as Oona and Avalon."

Cardozo came and sat beside her on the sofa. "Who else sat at that table?"

Annie sat trying to blink back moisture that was suddenly pooling in her eyes. "I never thought I'd hear myself say this, but I'm going to miss that vicious bitch." She pushed the binder toward Cardozo. "Lieutenant, can you read it? Something's wrong with my eyes, I can't see."

Cardozo angled his head. "There were eight guests."

"All my tables seat eight, it's my lucky number."

"Aldrich . . . Gardner . . . Duke . . ."

"May they rest in peace." Annie sighed.

"Spahn . . . Braidy . . ." Cardozo looked up. "Who's Chappell, S.?"

"Sorry Chappell. Sorry's short for Sorella. She's an interior designer."

"And Gurdon, F.?"

"Fenny. Short for Fennimore. Fenny and Sorry are partners."

"And van Slyke, L.?"

"Lucius." Annie sighed. "You don't have to worry about him. He died in a sailboat accident last summer in Dark Harbor." She had a hollow feeling inside. She lit herself another cigarette. "Lieutenant, do you know what I'm sitting here thinking? By the time this Society Sam bastard gets through, I won't have any friends left. And I'm too old and too tired to make any new ones." She exhaled and watched the smoke drift away. "Of course, with any luck, he'll kill me next."

"You may not be on his list," Cardozo said.

"That's encouraging," Annie said. "Care to tell me why not?"

"You testified for Nita's character, but you didn't sit at that table."

"I see. He's choosy. Then what are my chances, Lieutenant—fifty-fifty?"

"You'll be safe, Mrs. MacAdam. But I need to talk to these other people. Could you lend me your living room?"

■ ■ ■

"THE THREE PEOPLE who've died so far," Cardozo said, "are linked. All three sat at the same table at Annie MacAdam's dinner party six years ago. All three went on from that party to the Emergency Room at Lexington Hospital. Two years later, at the trial of Jim Delancey, all three testified for Nita Kohler's character."

Cardozo stood in front of the fireplace in Annie MacAdam's living room. Seven men and women had taken seats in a semicircle facing him.

"We could be dealing with coincidence," he said. "But we can't make that assumption. There's a possibility that Society Sam is killing for a reason, and one of these links could be that reason. If so, he's going to target the surviving members of one of the three groups: the dinner table, or the guests who went to the hospital, or the witnesses at the trial."

It was only eleven in the morning, but Gabrielle MacAdam, wearing an I'm-not-here face, circulated quietly with a tray of drinks.

"The dinner table gives us the largest pool: Oona Aldrich and Avalon Gardner—already killed by Society Sam. Dizey Duke, dead in what may or may not have been an accidental fall. Plus Lucius van Slyke—who died in a boating accident over a year ago."

"Lucky Lucius," Dick Braidy whispered. "At least he's out of this."

"Plus Gloria Spahn, plus Benedict Braidy, plus Sorella Chappell, plus Fennimore Gurdon—all still living, and all present."

"God be praised." Sorella Chappell, looking agitated in pink, reached out and squeezed Gloria Spahn's hand.

"The hospital gives us a smaller pool: Society Sam's three victims, plus Gloria Spahn, plus Benedict Braidy. The trial gives us the three victims, plus Benedict Braidy, Sorella Chappell, Fennimore Gurdon—and three new names: Annie MacAdam, Leigh Baker, and Tori Sandberg."

Annie MacAdam held up her highball and sent a silent long-distance clink to Tori Sandberg and another to Leigh Baker.

"Since we don't know which of these groups is the target, we have to assume they're all targeted. And that means, starting today, the police will provide round-the-clock security for each one of you."

"A cop guard?" Sorella Chappell cried.

"We're going to try to accomplish this with the least possible inconvenience or hassle to any of you. Your guards will not be in uniform."

"Do we get to pick our guard's sex?" Fennimore Gurdon said.

"No."

"Are we allowed to refuse the security?"

"I wouldn't recommend it."

"Are we expected to change our life-styles?" Annie MacAdam said.

"Realize two things and act accordingly: Your lives may be in danger, but the danger is minimal so long as you cooperate with your guard."

"What does *act accordingly* mean?" Tori Sandberg said.

"For one thing, try not to be alone on the street or in places open to the public—restaurants, movies, theaters."

"You mean when I go to the john in a restaurant," Gloria Spahn said, "take a friend?"

"That wouldn't be a bad idea. Or if you have a same-sex guard, take your guard."

"Does that mean we have to get our guards invited when we go anywhere?" Fennimore Gurdon said.

"No. Your guard isn't expecting to share your social life. But he or she has to know where you are at all times."

"But that means *I* have to know," Sorella Chappell said.

"Does that pose a problem?"

"Sometimes I like to make my day up as I go along."

"You may have to plan a little more tightly than that for a while."

"Wouldn't it be more efficient if I just took my guard with me when I go anywhere?"

"Cops can't accept services or gratuities from civilians. Your guard expects to drive himself—but he also expects to know your itinerary."

"Then wouldn't it be simpler," Dick Braidy said, "if our guards drove us too?"

"Cops are barred by statute from providing transportation to civilians. That would be embezzlement of city services."

"Wouldn't it be a lot less expensive," Leigh Baker said, "just to lock Jim Delancey up?"

"If Delancey is responsible for these killings, yes, it would, but the law doesn't allow us to make that assumption."

"Have you at least got someone watching him?" Leigh Baker said.

"We're aware of his movements. He spends most of his time at work or at home."

"And where's his home?" Leigh Baker said.

"I don't believe that information is germane," Cardozo said.

"Beekman Place," Sorella Chappell said. "Jim Delancey and his mother share an apartment in the co-op next to mine."

"Miss Chappell," Cardozo said, "that was not helpful."

Benedict Braidy whistled softly. "Beekman Place is an aw-fully snazzy address for a shop clerk and glorified busboy."

· THIRTY-SIX ·

"WHAT KILLED HER?" Cardozo said.

Dan Hippolito steepled his fingers under his nose and jittered the fingertips together. "By suffering exactly the injuries you'd expect in any seventy-eight-year-old woman who fell five stories onto hard earth."

They were sitting in Dan Hippolito's subterranean office. The preliminary bloodwork on Dizey Duke was a stack of computer pages on the desk.

"Seventy-eight?" Cardozo didn't quite manage to keep the surprise out of his voice.

"How old did she claim to be?"

"I don't know what she claimed, but I always thought late fifties."

"Dizey Duke was doubtless very young in spirit, an example to us all, but her bones had reached a very brittle old age."

Cardozo had a nagging sense that something here was wildly out of whack. "You said hard earth. She fell onto a lawn."

Dan Hippolito raised a weary hand. "This woman was in the eighth decade of life. The garden had flagstones. Vince, I know you want to tie her in with the other two, but all this woman's body is going to show is, she fell."

"No defensive wounds?"

"There's one fresh bruise." Dan Hippolito laid a glossy on the desktop. It showed the palm of Dizey Duke's left hand. A bruise ran like a faint purple stamp along the crease.

"What caused it?"

"Impact. Something struck her hard enough to rupture a vessel."

"A blade?"

"Possibly the flat of a blade."

Cardozo rotated the glossy, studying the palm from different orientations. "Could she have been fending off a blow?"

"It's possible for a right-handed person to fend off a blow with her left hand. A little unusual. Where you used to see a lot of these bruises is on young parochial-school students. Back in the days when the Sisters were allowed to use corporal punishment. The child would lay his or her left hand on the desk palm up, and Sister would thwack with a ruler. The meaner Sisters used steel rulers."

"We know Dizey wasn't in parochial school. At least not at the time of her death."

"Lucky for the school. She would have been a pretty unruly student. The alcohol level in the blood is the equivalent of eight very strong martinis."

"Eight?" Cardozo laid the glossy back on the desk. "No one mentioned she was *stinking* drunk."

"Maybe she could hold it. She was built like a workhorse. Maybe everyone else was drunk. Maybe the word *drunk* has a special meaning in Dizey Duke's set."

"Any other drugs?"

"She used a hell of a lot of cortisone—probably to control the arthritis. And a lot of codeine—I assume for arthritis pain. She was a daily amphetamine and barbiturate abuser. Probably her doctor was maintaining her. Amphetamine to get her through the day, barbiturate to get her through the night."

"Would that affect her sense of balance?"

"Absolutely. This woman would have been at risk getting out of a chair, let alone sitting in a box at the opera."

"I know it's an odd question to ask about a senior citizen, but did she have sex before she died?"

"Not that odd, Vince. But in Dizey's case there was no semen in the vagina or mouth or anus."

"Pubic hairs?"

"Only her own, where God put them." Dan Hippolito folded his arms across the front of his smock. It had a faint arc of laundered bloodstain below the neck. "All I'm giving you is preliminary conclusions, if you'll excuse the oxymoron, based on a cursory visual examination and initial bloodwork. We haven't cut yet. We haven't analyzed tissue. But she doesn't fit with your other two victims. No stab wounds. Throat untouched. The only breaks in her skin are where bones fractured through. When we go inside we'll find out a lot more about her drug habits—and her nutrition, which was piss-poor. This woman must have lived on booze and animal fats and desserts, but we're not going to find parallel lines and dots carved on her internal organs."

A kind of stillness seemed to fall from the air ducts in the ceiling.

Cardozo heaved himself to his feet. "It's weird. Because in other respects she fits. She's the kind of victim Society Sam likes."

"From what I can gather," Dan Hippolito said, "Society Sam has pretty broad tastes."

■ ■ ■

"DIZEY'S ONLY FAMILY," Ellie Siegel said, "is her mother Etiennette, who lives in a nursing home in Billings, Montana."

Cardozo sat drumming his fingers against his desktop.

"There's an ex-husband in Manila but no children or siblings." Ellie turned a page in her notepad. "Dizey named three beneficiaries: her mother, her assistant Mac, and the Gay Men's Health Crisis."

The cubicle was just large enough for Ellie to take three steps before she had to turn around. She took the third step and turned.

"The mother is one hundred seven years old, and she spent yesterday on the back porch of the nursing home. Mac was at the memorial party when Dizey died, but he was indoors and she was on the terrace. The Gay Men's Health Crisis, so far as I know, isn't killing people who name it as a beneficiary."

Cardozo still didn't speak. He pushed his lips together into a thoughtful, lopsided pout.

"Vince, you do not have the look of a happy man. Tell me what's bothering you."

"Dizey Duke wasn't Society Sam's M.O. And serial killers practically never change their method."

Ellie raised her shoulders in a what-can-you-do-about-it shrug. "To me that's statistics—and statistics are compiled from events, not vice versa. Just because Society Sam stabbed two doesn't mean he can't push the third off a roof."

"I'm not happy with it."

"No one's telling you this is cause for celebration, but why make it more of a mystery than it is? Look *who* he's killing, not how. Aldrich and Gardner were glitz-ditzes. Dizey Duke was the official media motor-mouth of the social bunny-hop." Ellie angled her head to see the files open on Cardozo's desktop.

"What do you see?" he said.

Ellie frowned at the glossies. "I see two hands. Two left

hands. An old left hand and a young left hand. I can't see the nails, since these are shots of the palm, but I'd say the hands are female."

She picked up the glossies.

"I see a bruise in the palm of each hand. The bruise runs approximately two inches along the crease of each palm. I'd guess that a similar object made the two bruises. Maybe the same object. The object has a straight, sharp edge but not necessarily a cutting edge." Ellie laid the glossies back down. "Am I close?"

"I haven't the slightest idea."

Ellie tapped her finger on the newer glossy. "This is obviously Dizey's hand. Whose hand is the other?"

"Nita Kohler's."

Ellie picked up the Kohler glossy again. "On the one hand, excuse the pun, the bruise isn't your classic Society Sam marking." She stood there knitting her eyebrows together. "On the other hand, we do know who made the bruise on Nita Kohler's palm."

■ ■ ■

"GUESS WHAT." Lou Stein allowed a suspenseful little silence to come across the phone line. "There was a wad of tissue in the left cup of Dizey's bra."

Cardozo's desk lamp dimmed and began buzzing. He slammed his fist down onto the desktop. The light blinked out and then came nervously back to normal wattage. "What was she doing, padding?"

"Doubt it. Bras have been coming prepadded for quite a few decades. Not that she needed the extra. But a lot of women use their bra as a sort of purse-away-from-the-purse. Anything can go there—money, cigarettes, drugs, phone numbers. These were used tissues."

"Used for what?"

"Come on, Vince, what do you use tissue for?"

"I know what I use them for, I want to know what she used them for."

"Blowing her nose."

"So you got snot off the tissue."

"Trace snot. She had blood in her sinuses. But also—and this is what's going to interest you—the tissue had been saturated in corn, barley, artificial caramel color, sodium, sodium saccharine, and caffeine."

"What does that add up to?"

"It adds up to a diet cola drink laced with second-rate Scotch."

"Why second-rate?"

"The Scots would never mix corn and barley malt."

"So it was a cheap knock-off Scotch."

"Let's just say domestic. Who knows how the liquor cartels price these products."

"So the party caterers were charging for Johnnie Walker and serving refunneled Laird Robbie. What did she do, dribble?"

"I said *saturated*, Vince. She must have sopped the drink up."

Cardozo tried to visualize it: Dizey Duke is schmoozing at a jet-set memorial party; she spills a drink; she reaches into her bra and pulls out a used Kleenex with sinus blood on it and sops up.

No. Maybe at home, but not in front of these people.

"I don't think she sopped up a drink. It got spilled on her."

"This had to be a hell of a spill."

"So she had a hell of a spill. It must have been just before she went over the wall, because no one at the party has mentioned seeing her with Scotch and Coke running down her front."

"You'll have it in writing tomorrow."

"Thanks, Lou."

Cardozo dialed Dizey Duke's work number. A man answered. "Duke office, MacLean speaking."

Cardozo could hear that he was hurting and depressed. "Mac, it's Vince Cardozo at the Twenty-second Precinct. Do you happen to remember what kind of liquor Ms. Duke was drinking at the memorial reception?"

A silence came over the phone like an empty ripple in space. "When Ms. Duke drank, which was infrequently, she preferred dry white wine, usually in a spritzer. When she drank hard liquor, which was *very* rarely, she stuck to vodka."

"Did she ever drink Scotch?"

"She'd sooner have drunk battery acid. She detested Scotch."

▪ ▪ ▪

A LITTLE AFTER THREE P.M. Cardozo was standing in the courtyard of the old Frick mansion on Fifth Avenue, talking with a young man by the name of Jan Bachman.

Jan had tended bar at the Aldrich memorial, and the caterers had said he'd be here working a benefit dinner. He had light hair, a turned-up nose, and cloudy blue eyes. When Cardozo asked if he could by any chance recall what Dizey Duke had been drinking, he burst out laughing.

"I sure can and it's not by chance. Vodka and soda, easy on the soda."

"Nothing but that?"

Jan nodded. He was wearing dungarees and one small cross-shaped earring, and he was carrying his waiter's tux in a suit bag. "Dizey never changed. I've been pouring booze for that lady for five years and, believe me, I knew her likes. Dizey was strictly Stoli. With a twist of lime. Not lemon, lime. She was very particular about that inch of lime peel."

"Did she really like it, or did she just drink it to give an impression?"

Cardozo and Jan Bachman formed a little island of stillness in the river of activity flowing around them. Men were setting up dining tables around the pool and arranging pink tablecloths and rose centerpieces and chintz napkins in tulip glasses. Three moving men were trying to lift a harp onto a six-inch platform.

It seemed to Cardozo it was a different century in here than it was out in the streets.

"Dizey was Billings, Montana," Jan said. "Her idea of a fun drink was probably barbecue sauce and tequila. But to get anywhere in New York you go with the flow, and Stoli and soda is definitely the flow. And insisting on a lime peel shows you have real taste—and know how to kick waiter ass."

"You never knew Dizey to lapse after a few and order something else—say, diet cola and Scotch?"

"God, no."

"Doesn't anyone drink diet cola and Scotch?"

"Not in public, not at the affairs I bartend."

"Do you remember serving diet cola and Scotch to *anyone* at the memorial party?"

Jan shook his head. "Frankly, no—and that sort of thing I'd recall, because columnists would pay good money to know."

· THIRTY-SEVEN ·

"DIZEY WAS WEARING OONA'S BROOCH," Leigh said.

"You mean, a brooch like Oona Aldrich's?" Vince Cardozo said.

They were sitting in Waldo Carnegie's library. She'd chosen the library and not the living room for this meeting, because it was a smaller space. Less could get lost in it.

"No," she said. "Van Cleef only made three of them, and the brooch Dizey had on was exactly the same as Tori's and mine. It had to be Oona's."

"Then, the day Dizey Duke died she was wearing the same brooch that Oona Aldrich wore the day *she* died?"

"I'm absolutely sure of it."

"Did you ask Dizey where she'd gotten it?"

"I accused her of stealing it . . ." She let her voice trail off, showing him that she lacked assurance, that this was difficult for her. "Dizey denied it. I called her a liar." Leigh glanced up slowly. "In fact, I'm ashamed to say, we had a fight."

She was throwing Cardozo a cue: This would have been a natural point for him to mention what the police had unearthed about Dizey's last moments, how they had reconstructed that final chronology. If anyone else had told him about a fight, now was the logical time for him to react.

But he didn't.

"Frankly," Leigh said, "I'm surprised nobody heard us."

"Where did you have this fight?"

"On the terrace." At the last moment instinct had kicked in and told Leigh not to wear black; so she faced Cardozo for the second time today with her hair freshly combed, dressed to dazzle in lilac, in carefully understated maquillage.

"Was anyone else on the terrace?"

"No—just Dizey and me."

"Who was on the terrace first?"

"I suppose I was."

"So you were alone before Dizey joined you?"

"Yes, I was."

"Why were you alone on the terrace?"

"I don't know. I suppose I wanted to be."

"Why did Dizey join you?"

"I don't think she knew I was there when she came out."

"And were you there when she fell?"

He said this so simply, so directly, that she realized he was actually a very sly man.

"When I left the terrace, she was still standing there."

"Standing there doing what?"

Leigh did not answer immediately. She lowered her eyelids just a little, as though they were an inner screen on which she had to review her memories. "Dizey had turned her back to me. She was standing there looking out over the city."

"Facing the wall?"

"Yes, looking out over the wall."

"Why did you leave the terrace?"

Keep it simple, she told herself. "Because we'd fought. I wanted to get away from her."

"How did you end your conversation with Dizey?"

"End it?" By the time she decided that the natural reaction to the question would be a rueful half smile, the rueful half smile no longer felt natural. "I don't think I exactly ended it. I suppose I said good-bye."

"Good-bye?"

She had two jobs to do at once: she had to monitor her own performance, and she had to interpret his. It really required two minds and all she had was one, and it was a not very together mind at this moment.

"Maybe not *literally* good-bye . . . Probably I said, I'm going inside; and she said, I'm staying out here; and I said, I'll see you later."

"And you didn't see her later."

"No."

"Were you the last person to see Dizey on that terrace?"

"I have no idea." *In the little parallel universe where I'm sitting,* she thought, *I'm completely innocent of wrong-doing. The only reason we're even having this chat is because you requested it, and I want to help you.*

It occurred to her that she needed a motivation for that.

I want to help you because I like you.

She let her eyes meet his.

See? My eyes say I like you.

But what were his eyes saying?

"When I came back into the house," she said, "I mixed and mingled and I honestly wasn't keeping track of who was going onto the terrace and who was coming back."

"How did Dizey seem to you during that last meeting?"

His eyes studied her, and she could feel him wondering things. What was he picking up on? Did he realize that underneath all her glib glamour, the celebrity was a vibrating wreck?

The first step was to deflect that *last-meeting* jab.

"I didn't know it was a last meeting, so I wasn't paying as much attention as I might have had I known. How did she seem? She seemed very much herself—bubbly, gossipy."

"Did it strike you as odd that she was bubbly?"

"We'd come from a memorial, and people are usually a little down after a memorial. So everybody drinks and then that kind of hysteria takes over and it seems giddy and fun, and I suppose that's how Dizey felt."

"Was she drinking?"

"Oh, yes—Dizey loved her drinking and drinks were on the house."

"Tell me, was Dizey drunk?"

"In my opinion she was very drunk."

"Do you recall what she was drinking?"

Recall, to be convincing, could not be instant. Leigh half closed her eyes as though reseeing the scene. "I think she was drinking vodka. It seems to me she only drank Stoli neat or Stoli and soda."

"Why only Stoli?"

"Maybe the Stoli people paid her."

"You say that as though you don't approve."

His eyes lingered on her face, and she could feel her face reddening. She decided the best next step would be to let a little human frailty show.

"I'm jealous of people who can drink without messing up their lives the way I did."

He had soft eyes, sad eyes, and she felt him tuning in on her in ways that had nothing to do with words.

"How long did you say you and Dizey were together on the terrace?"

She knew she hadn't said. "It could have been sixty seconds, it could have been five minutes. I'm rotten at estimating time. I was more or less sleepwalking through the memorial and the reception. And my mind was on other things."

"Could I ask what other things?"

"That house . . . used to be my house. My daughter . . . was pushed from that terrace."

She couldn't escape a nagging sense that she was saying too much, trapping herself, that he was encouraging her to get lost in her own explanations.

"I was drunk the night my daughter died. I was drunk and drugged. I was drunk and drugged a great deal in those days. And I've often thought that if I'd been sober, at least sober at that instant, she might still be alive."

"You didn't push her," he said quietly.

Leigh looked at him. She had a sense that he had decided to take her side. "Sometimes I feel I did."

"No one's going to punish you for feelings," he said. "Sometimes feelings aren't even facts."

"You're worse than my sponsor," she said.

"What's so bad about your sponsor?"

"I can't lie to him."

"Is that a bad thing?"

"It's a little something extra to remember—like brushing your teeth and putting on clean underwear and keeping your nails clean."

"And you can't lie to me?"

"I don't think it would do me any good."

He was watching her with an agreeably skeptical half smile. "By the way, were you drinking during your talk with Dizey?"

She noted that the fight had become a talk, and the question of her drinking was slipped in almost as a footnote.

"I may have had a drink in my hand."

"Do you remember what you were drinking?" The question gave the drink rock-solid reality.

"Is this a memory quiz?"

"Yes."

That threw her. Of all possible replies, she had never expected *yes.* "Well, I actually don't remember what I was drinking."

She was careful to fall in with his assumption naturally, innocently. She said *What I was drinking,* not *whether.* "So it must have been my usual."

"And what's your usual?"

"I drink diet Pepsi and—"

And she caught herself.

"And what?"

"And I don't drink alcohol."

■ ■ ■

AFTER CARDOZO LEFT Leigh stood in the living room, letting her mind curl around a thought. *I didn't play that scene at all well.*

She found herself in front of the liquor cabinet. The edge of a Chardin landscape and the blooms on a pear tree in the garden were bright splashes of color in the mirror.

Out of the corner of her eye she could see her reflection mixing a drink.

She recognized it was an old solution: When you don't know what to think or believe or feel, don't think, don't believe, don't feel.

So what.

She dropped an ice cube into the glass, stared at the bubbles rising to the top of the Johnnie Walker and diet Pepsi.

She raised the glass.

Suddenly her hand felt very weary.

She tried to remember how many times she'd told herself *just this one drink,* and wound up plastered. Because she'd been drunk she'd let one person die and she'd probably killed another.

She had a dispiriting sense that she'd worn out all her roles— the seductress, the innocent, the playgirl, the celebrity, the mistress, the drunk. She just couldn't play them anymore.

She set the glass back down on the bar.

■ ■ ■

IN THE PROPERTY ROOM Cardozo opened the plastic bag marked *Dizey M. Duke* and held it upside down. A splash of black cloth spilled to the steel-topped table, muffling the clatter of the pumps and the purse that followed.

Carefully, methodically, his eyes scanned, taking in dark mesh stockings with a silhouette motif of various bugs that had gotten caught in the mesh, a black cotton pants suit, a black silk blouse that looked pretty low cut on the table and must have looked even lower cut on a full-bodied woman, a silk scarf with an official-looking portrait of Lenin silk-screened onto it.

It all struck him as the kind of outfit that would have gone well with too much lipstick.

From the solvent odor still clinging to the clothes, it was clear that the lab had had to drench them. The rumpled cotton panties bore the heaviest smell of benzene. Cardozo took that as a sign that Dizey's sphincter, not surprisingly, had loosened during the fall.

He opened the purse, inverted it, and shook. Cosmetics, hankies, a plastic cigarette case, a plastic cigarette lighter, a small stapler, a pair of cheap-chic mirrored sunglasses tumbled out.

He studied these objects, one by one, wondering about the pack rat who had hoarded them.

What struck him about the table full of junk was that there was not a single object of beauty or value on it.

Certainly no platinum brooch shaped like a hummingbird.

He checked the inventory. No brooch had been listed.

No watch either.

No ring. No money. No credit card.

It was obvious that somebody had cleaned Dizey out, and it struck Cardozo that mugging a dead woman was a pretty foul thing to do.

■ ■ ■

AFTER THREE MINUTES the young woman returned to the window. She was short, soft-looking, with pale blond hair and a harried face. "Our records indicate that Ms. Duke's property was turned over to the police."

"That property should have been turned over to me," Cardozo said. "It wasn't. So I'd like to see who signed that receipt."

She showed him the receipt.

It was a single-page printed form headed with the shield of Lexington Hospital and the words *property of decedent.* The first thing Cardozo noticed was that the empty spaces had been filled in with loopy, barely legible red ballpoint.

The second thing he noticed was that the decedent's name had been entered as Doe, female.

"Ms. Duke's name wasn't Doe," he said.

"It was when she arrived."

"You're sure this is her form?"

The young woman pointed to the number printed in the upper left-hand corner. At first glance it looked like a social-security number combined with a nightmare zip code, but Cardozo stared at it and gradually it resolved itself into a date, the hour of day in the twenty-four-hour system, and oh-oh-eight, which Cardozo took to mean that Dizey had been the eighth arrival that particular hour.

The third thing he noticed was the familiar illegibility of Greg Monteleone's signature at the bottom of the page.

What he didn't notice, in five slow scannings of the page, was any ballpoint scratching in the space headed *jewelry*. He gave it a think. "Do you keep a record of the ambulance crews?"

"I can tell you the number of the ambulance."

She swiveled to face her computer terminal, and her two forefingers searched over the keyboard. Something finally came up on her screen. "Five," she said.

"On May eighth a woman by the name of Oona Aldrich was brought here to Emergency. What was that ambulance number?"

"Do you have her social-security number?"

"Sorry."

"What time?"

"Between two and three in the afternoon."

"Spell that name, please?"

Cardozo spelled it.

The young woman tapped more instructions into the computer. "That was ambulance one."

"Now, how do I find out who was the crew on those two ambulances?"

■ ■ ■

CARDOZO NOTICED that the thumping bass beat coming from the state-of-the-art four-speaker Sony boom box was actually making waves in the ten-gallon water-cooler tank.

The boom box was balanced on top of the cooler, and the young man in charge of the employment office was tapping his ballpoint pen in rhythm to the female rap number. Seated at his desk, turning pages in the ambulance log, he wore a vivid green sport shirt with a purple collar.

His eyes stopped for a moment halfway down one of the pages. He jotted something on a pad. Then he flipped forward through the log. His eyes darted another moment, and he made another notation. He tore the piece of paper off the pad. "Greenburg, Resch, and delMajor were staffing ambulance one. Kozloff, delMajor, and Blanco were staffing ambulance five."

Cardozo folded the paper into the breast pocket of his shirt. "Where can I find delMajor?"

"He went off duty at noon. The easiest thing would be to come back Monday and check with Dispatching. DelMajor's working the two P.M. shift."

· THIRTY-EIGHT ·

Saturday, June 1

THE SUN WAS SLANTING toward midafternoon when the taxi let Leigh off. There wasn't a breath of air in the street. She climbed the three marble steps of Waldo's Greek Revival redbrick town house. Her key wasn't where she expected it to be in her purse, and she had to forage through coins and receipts.

Behind her, brakes squealed like a skinned cat and a car horn blasted. Her eyes jerked toward the sound. Out where the street met Fifth Avenue a white superstretch limo had swerved, almost sideswiping a south-bound Checker cab.

A young man came zigzagging on foot through the traffic, setting off an orchestra of slammed brakes and blaring horns. At first she thought he was being chased by muggers, but then she realized he was calling her name. He was carrying a flopping suitbag over one shoulder, and she wondered if he might be from one of the shops with an order for her.

"Miss Baker!" He stopped, red-faced and panting, at the foot of the stoop. "I was waiting here two hours. I'd just about given up." Beneath an I-love-lithium T-shirt his chest was heaving like a sprinter's, and sweat had stickered his light brown hair to his unlined forehead.

"You almost got killed."

"I told the driver to stop, but *stop* was not an English word he understood." Still catching his breath, he shifted the suitbag from one shoulder to the other.

"Is that bag for me?" Leigh said.

His face broke into a startlingly perfect smile. She realized there was only one reason for a man that young to have his teeth capped: He had to be an actor.

He held out the bag. "It's yours," he said, "if you're looking for a three-year-old Brooks Brothers tux. But I hope you're not, because I don't have anything else to wear at the party tonight."

He stood there grinning at her, grinning *for* her, and she remembered what it was like being young and having no safety net but guts and charm and sometimes not even enough of those.

"Look," she said, "I'm sorry—and I'd be sorrier if you'd hurt yourself—but I don't give autographs."

"I know you don't. I know everything about you. I *memorize* your interviews." He pulled a wallet from his right hip pocket and flipped it open. A ladder of credit cards and plastic ID tumbled toward the sidewalk. "Just to prove I'm really me—senior server with Guy Power."

He held out an ID to her, and she saw that it said just that: *Jan Bachman, Senior Server, Guy Power.*

"You don't recognize me, do you?"

"No," she admitted, wary now of stepping into a con. She scanned the street to see if her police guard's black Plymouth was there. It was double-parked halfway down the block, with a man sitting behind the wheel. "Mr. Bachman, I'm very busy."

"I bartended the Oona Aldrich memorial."

Leigh stared at him, but there was a blank in her memory. She couldn't place the beaming blue-eyed face. "Look, let's talk inside."

"You're on. I'd love to see the inside of this place."

They went into the living room and he whistled in admiration and she asked if he'd like something to drink.

"Let me." He headed straight for the bar. "I might as well get familiar with the lay of the land, right? Maybe someday I'll be working a job here." He opened drawers and doors and seemed to find everything he needed. "Yours is Johnnie Walker and diet Pepsi, right?"

The question told her everything. "Just diet Pepsi today."

She watched him mixing drinks and it suddenly occurred to her, *Wait a minute, I don't know if this man is who he says he is.*

He brought her glass across the room to where she was sitting on the sofa. He dropped easily into the chair facing her. *"Saludos."* He lifted his glass.

Leigh lifted hers and sipped.

"Are you on the wagon again?" he said.

"Trying." *If he doesn't know me,* she thought, *he's doing an awfully good job of pushing my buttons.* "Dizey's death gave me an incentive to sober up."

He nodded. "Horrible accident. On the other hand, there wasn't a day of the year she wasn't looped by five P.M., and she was *really* looped at the memorial."

"How bad was I?" Leigh asked.

"If I hadn't been mixing your drinks, I'd have thought the strongest thing you were on was straight Pepsi." He laughed. "You asked me to mix Scotch in one of the diet Pepsi bottles and save that bottle for you and let it be our little secret."

She didn't remember doing that at the memorial, but she remembered doing it other evenings. It was one of her patented naughty tricks. "I seem to spend a lot of my life relying on the discretion of bartenders."

"Why not? We're reliable guys."

"You must be. No one's caught me yet. Or have they?"

The young man leaned forward, elbows braced on his knees. "A detective came by to question me. He asked if anyone at the party had been drinking diet cola and Scotch."

"Do you have any idea why he was asking?"

"At first he seemed to be checking out Dizey Duke. He asked me, What was she drinking? Stoli and soda, I told him, same as always. Then he said, Any chance she was drinking Scotch and diet cola? I said, No chance. Then he asked, Did I serve anyone at the party Scotch and diet cola. And I thought of you, naturally, but I said, No one who wants to survive socially drinks Scotch and diet cola in public. No offense intended, by the way."

She nodded. "So Scotch and Pepsi was what interests him. And his first thought was you'd served it to Dizey."

"I guess I wasn't as sharp as I could have been, but the way he asked, the order he put the questions, I couldn't tell where he was heading till he was there. And I didn't want to get you into trouble."

She looked at him. "Why not?"

He glanced almost shyly down toward the rug, where right-angled shadows laid a grid over smooth Chinese curves. "I couldn't do that. My mom loves you."

Cardozo's wife and this boy's mom, she thought.

"I do too."

"I'm grateful. Is there . . . any way I can help you in return?"

The smile dropped off his face. "There is—if it's not an imposition. A good friend of mine is sick. In fact, he's my best friend and the truth is he's dying."

"I'm sorry."

"What you could do, if you didn't mind . . ." The young man reached around him to open his suitbag.

The zipper squeaked like a stuck mouse, and her nerves jumped. *I'm hung over,* she realized. So hung over that she half expected to see a knife in his hand when he turned around.

He took an envelope from the inside pocket of the tux jacket. He reached across the space between them and placed the envelope in her hand. "Could you answer my friend's letter?"

She looked down at the envelope and she saw that it was addressed, simply, *Leigh Baker.* "Of course. Is that all?"

"Is that all?" He smiled. "Hell, you don't know how much it'll mean to him. He's a bigger fan than my mom." The young man rose. "You're a good woman, Miss Baker. I won't take any more of your time."

She rose quickly, holding the letter. "Mr. Bachman . . ."

"Jan."

"Jan, do you recall the detective's name?"

"Cardozo."

· THIRTY-NINE ·

Sunday, June 2

AT QUARTER TO NINE SUNDAY EVENING Carl Malloy observed Jim
Delancey come out of Twenty-nine Beekman. He observed that
Jim Delancey was not alone. The young dark-haired woman who
had gone into the building just five minutes before was now holding his arm.

The sound of their laughter carried clearly across the street
to where Malloy was waiting. They turned north on Beekman.

Malloy gave them a half-block lead.

On Fifty-second they turned west and at Second Avenue
north again. Halfway up the block they went into a deli.

Malloy got himself a sightline and watched through the window. They were standing at the cash register. The girl was trying
to pay for something, and Delancey wouldn't let her.

They came out eating ice-cream sandwiches. At the corner
they had to wait for the light.

A man and a little boy were standing at the bus stop nearby.
They seemed to interest Delancey, and he turned to watch them.

The man had a square, blocklike build, a pockmarked face,
and black hair pulled back in a ponytail. The boy had the same
coloring as the man, but he couldn't have been more than eight
years old.

The man was shouting in Spanish. The boy was doing his best
to maintain a sort of dignity in a difficult situation. He accepted
the man's shouts and instead of shouting back addressed him
quietly and respectfully. The respectful treatment only goaded
the man to louder shouts.

The light changed. Delancey's girlfriend tugged at his sleeve.
He brushed her hand away.

The boy stepped away from the man and peered up the avenue to see if the bus was coming. The man seemed to interpret the boy's movement as a lack of proper attention. He raised his hand and slapped the boy across the face. It was a hard slap, and it made a sound that carried in the street like a firecracker.

The boy looked at the man with large, hurt eyes. He turned and began walking away.

Except it wasn't a walk.

The little boy hobbled, dragging one foot behind him like a dead animal. He was a cripple.

The man strode after the boy, seized him by one arm, and spun him around. He began slapping the boy forehand, backhand.

Malloy saw that Delancey and his girlfriend were having their own troubles now. The girl was trying to hold Delancey back, but he broke loose.

He went for the man in a low, crouching run. His shoulder connected with the man's hip. The impact sheared the man away from the boy and carried him down onto the pavement.

Delancey flipped him onto his back and straddled him. His fists buffeted the man's head. The man screamed, thrashing his head left and right in a useless attempt to avoid the blows.

The little boy was staring, his mouth wide open.

Malloy realized this was going to get very bad. He stepped into the phone booth in the deli and dialed the precinct.

Through the window he could see Delancey's girlfriend trying to pull him off the man. He pushed her away. She swung her pocketbook at him.

The pocketbook didn't stop Delancey. He lifted the man's head by the ears. He spat in the man's face. He slammed the man's head down against the pavement.

At the exact moment that the man stopped screaming, the girl began.

And at the exact moment that the precinct answered, a squad car squealed to a stop at the curb. Two uniformed cops hopped out.

"Twenty-second Precinct," the voice was saying in Malloy's ear.

"Thanks anyway," he said. "It's under control."

·FORTY·

CARDOZO'S EYE DID A QUICK SCAN of the court papers. "The charges are assault and battery and resisting arrest. The judge set bail of two thousand."

Ellie Siegel, crisp and efficient-looking in her starched blouse, allowed her jaw to drop for just an instant. "Don't they know who Jim Delancey is?"

"The judges in night court," Greg Monteleone said, "know nothing." He snapped a red suspender to punctuate the remark.

"I don't get it," Sam Richards said. "Delancey's on parole. He can't afford a conviction for *littering*, let alone assault. Why did he get himself into a brawl?"

Cardozo shrugged. "He claims he was defending the kid."

"Why defend a kid he doesn't even know?"

Greg Monteleone flashed a saucer-eyed leer. "Because my name is Jim Delancey and I have a big thing for little kids. Happy Halloween!"

"Bullshit," Sam Richards said. "He has a thing for his girl-friend."

"I'll bet she paid the bail," Greg Monteleone said. "De-lancey's no dickhead—he likes them rich."

"Maybe deep down he's a little bit of a good guy," Carl Malloy said.

"Maybe deep down he's a little bit violent," Ellie said, "and maybe it's not so far deep down."

■ ■ ■

"THIRD LETTER JUST CAME IN." Rad Rheinhardt's voice had the faintest hint of a slur. "Want to hear it?"

"Not in the least." Cardozo switched the receiver to his left hand and picked up a ballpoint. "Read it to me slowly."

" *'Simple Simon meet the die man, climbing up the stair. Jack be'*—he spells that with a single capital B—*'nimble, Dick be'*—single capital B—*'quick. Your idiot quest for sex.'* Am I going too fast?"

"You're doing fine."

" *'To end all sex is there anything else in your perverted—in your perverted—'* "

"Is he repeating or are you?"

"I am."

"Your perverted what?"

"Okay. *'Worldview. Mine marks little piggies fine. Kisses, Society Sam.'* I'm sending it up by messenger—you'll have it within the hour."

"Thanks, Rad."

Cardozo laid the receiver back in the cradle. It rang again immediately. "Cardozo."

"Hi, it's Abner Love over at the sound lab. Bet you'd forgotten me."

"I haven't forgotten you, Abner."

"I've been tinkering with that other tape you gave me. There's a stretch where I've been able to pull up some background signals. They're faint, but the wave form resembles the signals on the boom-box tape. I wish you were here to see the oscilloscopes."

"How close is the resemblance?"

"Except for frequency they're a good match. Both onset with a click, both reverb at the high end of the partials, both show very little decay. If it weren't for those partials, I'd say the sound is electronically produced."

Cardozo's ears pricked up at the word *sound.* Singular, not plural. "We've got the same sound on both tapes?"

"The sequences of pitches is a little different, but it's obviously generated exactly the same way."

"Any idea what generated the sound?"

"I'd say touch-tone dial tones, except there are too many of them and the partials are wrong."

"Abner, could I have dupes of those two tapes?"

■ ■ ■

LEIGH BAKER SAT in the straight-backed metal chair, listening. A series of bright, shrill, dial-tonelike hums floated through the cubicle. And died.

Cardozo snapped the cassette out of the tape player. "And *this* was what he found on your answering-machine tape."

He slipped a second cassette into the machine and pressed the Start button. For just over twelve seconds the little speaker resonated with more of the same high-pitched hums.

"It's familiar," Leigh Baker said.

"Which one's familiar? The boom-box tape or yours?"

"They both are. But I can't quite place the sound."

"While you're thinking," Cardozo said, "how about some really rotten coffee, courtesy of the detective squad?"

"If it's not too much trouble."

"How do you take it?"

"A little fake sugar and some milk."

"Settle for fake milk?"

"Perfect."

"Don't go away."

While he was out of the cubicle she looked around the little space. It gave her the feeling that the detectives didn't clean and —what with city budget cutbacks—no one else did either. The only tidy area she could see in all the clutter was the place on the desk where a small stainless-steel framed photograph sat.

She picked it up. It showed a young girl, six years old or so, with long, straight dark hair and beautiful deep brown eyes.

"Drink at your own risk." Cardozo came back with two coffees. "The police accept no liability."

Leigh was still holding the girl's photo in her hand. "Excuse me for being snoopy." She set it back in its place of honor. "She's so pretty, I couldn't help noticing."

"My little girl," Cardozo said.

Leigh accepted a styrofoam cup from his hand. She sipped and her mouth had a sensation of thick, bitter heat, like what she imagined summer nights in Mongolia to be. "Not so bad," she said.

Cardozo dropped back into his seat. "The engineer thinks the sounds on those tapes both have the same source."

"And what's the source?"

"He doesn't know. But if the person threatening you left the sound on your machine and the same sound showed up on the boom-box tape, there's a good chance that your caller and the man with the boom box are the same person."

She shook her head firmly. "I'm sorry, but I don't believe that."

He raised an eyebrow. "And I'm sorry, but that's what the tapes say."

"Then the tapes are wrong."

A beat of silence passed. "It might interest you to know that the night Dizey Duke died, Jim Delancey never left his building."

"What does that have to do with anything? Delancey didn't—" She stopped herself. She realized what she had been about to say: *Delancey didn't push her.*

Cardozo's eyes flicked up. "Delancey didn't what?"

The air conditioner began whining. Cardozo rose and walked to the window and gave it a karate chop. The whine became a sort of muffled sobbing.

Leigh shifted in her chair, bracing herself, drawing up steadiness from the floor. "Delancey didn't leave his building? How do you know?"

Cardozo came back slowly to his desk. He gave her a look that said, *I'm going to trust you.* "We had men watching both entrances. Delancey never came out."

The cubicle suddenly seemed darker to Leigh. She couldn't tell if she was imagining it or if the current had dipped. And she couldn't tell if Vince Cardozo was saying the police no longer suspected Jim Delancey. She wanted to scream. Every instinct in her body said it was Jim Delancey. *He* was the one who was phoning her, *he* was the one who was killing her friends.

Cardozo's eyes never left her. "Are you going to be home later?"

"I can be. Why?"

"I may have some news about Oona's brooch."

■ ■ ■

A SHADOW FELL ACROSS THE DESK. Cardozo turned and saw Ellie Siegel resting a shoulder against the open door.

"What did the movie star want?"

He shrugged. "I asked her to listen to some tapes."

"And she dropped everything and came running right over?"

"I didn't time her, and I didn't ask how much she had to drop."

"Are you going Hollywood on us, Vince?"

"If all you came here for is to nag, good-bye. If something is on your mind, please get to the point."

"As a matter of fact, something *is* on my mind. It's not a big deal, but I thought you should know." Ellie stepped into the cubicle and handed him that morning's *New York Tribune,* folded open to page ten.

"What's this?"

"Benedict Braidy's society column."

"I didn't know he was writing one."

"He's replaced 'Dizey's Dish.' Now it's called 'Dick Sez.' "

Cardozo scanned. In the space where only last week an airbrushed, blond-banged Dizey had grinned, a black-banged, airbrushed Dick Braidy now solemnly frowned.

My great and good friend, Zack Morrow, publisher and owner of this newspaper, has invited me to take over the society column. Mindful of my dear friend Dizey Duke's high standards and achievement, I accepted on one condition: that I be allowed full freedom to follow in Dizey's hard-hitting footsteps.

And so, dear readers and Dizey fans, with your blessing, here goes:

What followed seemed standard Dizey fare: who went where, who wore what.

Ellie picked up the tape player and spent a moment examining it. "Is the tape secret? Is that why the door was shut?"

"Do you want to hear the tapes? Is that why you're nagging me?"

Ellie set the tape player gently down on the desk. "I didn't mean to nag, and I hope you don't feel as grumpy as you sound. I just wondered why you had your door shut."

"I was playing a tape for Leigh Baker, and I had the door shut because it's a zoo around here and you can't hear yourself fart."

"Do you *want* to hear yourself fart? Does *she* want to hear you fart?"

"The tapes happen not to be very loud. Go on. Shut the door and listen to them. Be my guest."

Ellie frowned primly. She opened a drawer of his filing cabinet and neatened the bits of paper hanging out. "I'm sure it's none of my business. I wouldn't want to intrude."

"Please, Ellie, intrude." He kicked the door shut.

"If you insist." Ellie sat and listened while Cardozo played her the two tapes. Beneath her shut eyelids her eyes moved as though she were watching butterflies in a dream.

"Very pretty," she said, when the tape finished. "Like a lonely robot humming to cheer itself up."

"Recognize it?" Cardozo said.

She shook her head. "It's familiar, but I can't place it. It'll come to me."

■ ■ ■

CARDOZO HELD UP HIS SHIELD. "Do you have an ambulance attendant here by the name of delMajor?"

"Ambrose delMajor?" In her jeans and Batman T-shirt, the dispatcher was a thick-bodied woman with a ruddy complexion and curly blond hair clipped short. "Ambrose is bringing in a coronary from Beekman Place. He should be here any minute now."

The ambulance-dispatching station of Lexington Hospital had the frightening look of a firebombed subway token booth. Reinforced movers' tape webbed out from bullet holes in the plate-glass window, and plastic garbage bagging had been taped up to cover a missing panel.

The phone rang. The dispatcher answered, listened, and then pleasantly said, "Fuck you too, ma'am," and hung up.

She smiled at Cardozo.

"There's Ambrose," she said.

A graffiti-smeared ambulance pulled out of the avenue's gridlocked traffic, wheels slipping on leaked oil, and skidded onto the indoor ramp. The rear doors burst open.

An attendant leapt down onto the ramp. Another began shoving a stretcher out.

The woman strapped to it looked dead.

"Which one's Ambrose?" Cardozo asked.

The dispatcher pointed to the second attendant.

When Cardozo stepped out of the air-conditioned booth, the heat pressed down like the lid on a simmering pan. The ramp was noisy in an insanely bad-tempered way.

"Ambrose delMajor?" Cardozo called out.

The attendant spun around and froze.

Behind him, two young-looking M.D.s were wheeling the stretcher into the Emergency Room.

Cardozo strode forward, shield extended in his left hand. "Lieutenant Vince Cardozo, Twenty-second Precinct. Could I have a word with you?"

Ambrose had a flat blue stare, expressionless as the lens of a minicam. He stood a little under six feet. He was wearing sneakers and blue jeans, and beneath his white hospital jacket one corner of the collar of his blue cotton workshirt was sticking up like a broken thumb.

"What's this about?" Ambrose spoke with a slight southern accent and a pronounced case of the sniffles.

"May eighth you were on the ambulance crew that brought Oona Aldrich to this hospital—the lady who was attacked in Marsh and Bonner's."

"Look, I bring thirty people a day to this hospital."

"And four days ago you brought Dizey Duke. That was the lady who went off the town-house terrace over on Sixty-seventh."

Cardozo sensed hesitation in Ambrose, a missed beat.

"I have no way of recalling."

"You don't need to recall anything, Ambrose, because I just got through checking the records. You were on both those crews. In fact, you were the *only* person who was on both those crews."

"Ambrose!" the dispatcher yelled.

Ambrose went over to the booth.

Cardozo could see him through the window, arguing with the dispatcher. He stalked back, sullen-faced. "Can't talk with you now. I got another call."

"I'll ride with you." Cardozo hopped up into the ambulance and offered Ambrose a hand up. A moment later the second attendant began to climb in.

"Why don't you ask your friend to ride in front?" Cardozo said.

"Fritz," Ambrose said, "ride in front."

Ambrose pulled the doors shut.

Cardozo settled himself in one of the technicians' seats.

From up front there came two shocks of the cab doors slamming. The motor ground to life. On the other side of the roof the siren cut on in midscreech.

Ambrose slipped out of his white jacket and hung it over a wall hook. He took the other seat and stuck a cigarette in his mouth and spent the next thirty seconds coaxing flame out of a green plastic Bic.

The ambulance executed a sharp left.

The door of the syringe depository swung open with a bright, startling clang. Ambrose reached a fist over and bopped the door shut. He sat there dragging on his cigarette. "I'm listening."

"I could book you on suspicion," Cardozo said. "You couldn't work for the city, Ambrose. They'd have to suspend you. Without pay. Think about it."

"Suspicion of what?"

"Suspicion of smoking on the job."

Ambrose's eyes flicked around guardedly.

Cardozo smiled. "Only joking. But that *is* oxygen in that cylinder, isn't it?"

Ambrose stretched out a foot. The tip of his blue sneaker touched the cylinder. "That's why the big letters spell *oxygen*."

"You guys sure like to live on the edge," Cardozo said.

Ambrose didn't answer. His jacket was hanging by Cardozo's left ear, and Cardozo reached a hand up into the pocket and pulled out a lady's wallet.

"Tell me, Ambrose. Do you really think blue alligator is helping the ecology?"

Ambrose stared with one instant's open astonishment. "You have no right to touch that."

"Just checking that you have a valid social-security number."

"My social-security card's not in there."

Ambrose reached for the wallet, but Cardozo leaned away. He leafed through the credit cards.

"Neither is your American Express, your Visa, your AT&T, or your Ritz limo charge—unless your name is Mitzi Lloyd Eberstadt. You don't look like a Mitzi to me, Ambrose. But that woman you guys just dropped off, now *she* looked like a Mitzi." Cardozo riffled through the bill compartment. He whistled. "Two hundred thirty, cash."

"The wallet fell out when we were moving her."

"So you're just holding on to it till you can return it to her?" Cardozo tossed the wallet to him.

Ambrose had fast reflexes. He caught it one-handed.

"Now, Ambrose, enlighten me about something. You were driving Oona Aldrich to the hospital when she lost a little platinum hummingbird brooch with ruby eyes. Three weeks later you were driving Dizey Duke to the hospital when *she* lost a little platinum hummingbird brooch."

"I wasn't driving. I never drive. I'm a trained paramedic. I stay with the patient."

"Then you were back here with these women when they lost their brooches. Maybe you saw what happened to those hummingbirds?"

Cardozo figured that, financially speaking, Ambrose had to be in a negative-asset position. He probably owed three thousand dollars to every bank that had ever been dumb enough to issue him a credit card, plus interest, plus collection charges, plus past judgments due. If he got suspended from his ambulance job, the most he could look forward to in unemployment benefits would be $175 a week. After rent that would amount to barely ten dollars a day to sustain his drinking, his drugging, and lesser needs —such as eating.

"Okay, okay. I did fence two small items. They were both cheap little hummingbird brooches. It was the only time I ever did anything like that in my life." Ambrose spoke quietly, with no physical show of emotion except for the way his sneaker ground out his cigarette on the ambulance floor. "But I didn't steal them. I saw them lying on the floor, and I have financial expenses. My mom is in Intensive Care, she's not covered by insurance—"

"Who'd you fence them to, Ambrose?"

In a toss-up between Ambrose's neck and anybody else's, Cardozo had a fair hunch whose neck Ambrose would choose.

"This fellow I know," Ambrose said. "He's a society decorator."

■ ■ ■

CARDOZO PHONED LEIGH BAKER. "Let's meet," he said, "and talk about Oona Aldrich's brooch."

■ ■ ■

"HOW WELL DO YOU KNOW Fennimore Gurdon?" Cardozo said.

"Fenny?" Leigh Baker stretched the nickname out like a piece of taffy. "I don't really know him, but I adore him."

They were sitting in a place on Madison that called itself the Fifth Avenue Tea Room. It had been Leigh Baker's suggestion.

A civilized white noise filled the room like a thin vapor— dozens of voices all modulated to the same register, silverware clacking against china, the sweetly chaotic gamelan music of leisured life. Most of the other customers were women—and they looked to Cardozo like the immaculately-maned sort who got together monthly and discussed Proust. Their clothes contrasted brightly with the honeydew-melon color of the walls and columns. Matching wooden shutters ran from floor to ceiling, shuttering windows that weren't there.

"Tell me about him," Cardozo said.

Leigh Baker took a moment collecting her thoughts. She was wearing a green blouse that brought out the color of her eyes. Little truant blips of light flashed from tiny, almost invisible diamonds in her ears. "He has terrific staying power. He's been popular with the last three generations of tastemakers. He has a home on the Vanderbilt property in Rhinebeck. If you like his style, the home's beautiful. If you don't, it's an overdecorated Victorian department store. He's considerate and charming and he's a great escort."

A waitress placed an iced cappuccino in front of Leigh Baker and a coffee in front of Cardozo. On the small table between them she set a plate of tiny, crustless sandwiches that looked as though they had been made by elves for elves.

"Your turn," Leigh Baker said. "Tell me what *you* know about Fenny."

"Oona Aldrich's brooch was fenced to him—twice."

Leigh Baker caught her breath and a hand went halfway to her mouth. "But how *could* he?" A shadow pulsed rapidly just beneath the white hollow of her throat. "*Why* would he?"

"The theory around the Fraud Bureau is, he has an expensive crack habit. He owes major back taxes to the city. So he's had to take up a few sidelines."

"Besides fencing?"

"Besides fencing. He helps people move into society. For twenty thousand a month he promises to get you into four major dinners. That's above what he charges for decorating your home."

She lifted her glass of cappuccino and sipped. "How do you know about this?"

"Some of his dissatisfied customers complained to the Better Business Bureau. There's also a possibility that he sells house-breakers the plans of the apartments he decorates. The attorney general is looking into it."

"I *never* heard that."

The remark sounded unguarded and sincere, and Cardozo took it to mean that she'd heard all the rest.

"Some of my co-workers believe he sold the Vanderbilts' security plans for the country estate—but Mrs. V. protected him from the heat."

"Why would she do that?"

"Word is, he deals dope to a few close friends who don't want to have to take deliveries personally."

"That poor old dowager is on dope?" Leigh Baker played with her cappuccino glass, turning it slowly on its paper doily.

"Here's my suggestion," Cardozo said. "I phoned and his shop will be open tomorrow between two and six. You go there and tell him you want a brooch like the one Dizey bought from him. If he produces the brooch, which he will unless he's already sold it, we have him."

She was silent. It was as though she were staring into motionless water.

"I'll be at Fenny's tomorrow," she said. "Two o'clock."

"Good. Then so will I."

■ ■ ■

THAT EVENING LEIGH LOOKED UP from her copy of French *Vogue* and saw that Waldo had laid his copy of *Forbes* down on the sofa beside him. He was staring into his highball. He seemed preoccupied, and she asked him if anything was bothering him.

"Just thinking," he said.

She'd heard on television that the Dow Jones had closed down almost two hundred points, and she wondered if that had anything to do with his mood. She crossed the room and sat beside him. She took his glass and set it on the table and took his hands in hers.

"Don't worry about business," she said. "What goes up comes down, what goes down comes back up."

"I'm not worried about business. To tell the truth, I'm worried about you."

"Don't worry about me either. I go up, I come down. I go down, I come back up."

"I promised I wouldn't leave you alone, and now I have to."

Her hands withdrew. "When?"

"I've got to go to Tokyo this Thursday. One of our companies is in trouble. I won't be able to get back till Sunday."

"And you can't take me with you?"

He shook his head. "But I've arranged for you to be taken care of."

She got to her feet. "Not that guard again—I won't have Mr. Arnold Bone following me around."

"Nothing like that. You're going to Paris for four days with Kristi and Wystan Blackwell."

She had a feeling Waldo had bribed the Blackwells to look after her, and a trip to Paris had been Kristi's price. "That's awfully sweet of you." And then she sighed. "I just wish you could come with me instead of them."

"So do I. Maybe next time."

▪ FORTY-ONE ▪

"THE ZIP CODE," Ellie Siegel said, "is one-one-eight-oh-three—Stauber Drive, Hicksville." Today she was wearing a dark blue dress with a low neck—not very low, just low enough for the heat. "Why anyone would drive thirty miles out on Long Island just to mail this note, don't ask me."

"He had an errand," Malloy said.

Sam Richards shook his head. "No one who can possibly help it has an errand in Hicksville."

Greg Monteleone yawned loudly. "He's doing it to confuse us. But we're not confused, guys, are we?"

Ellie snapped open her purse and took out her notepad. "The postmark is A.M., June first—last Saturday. Ordinarily there are two Saturday pickups from Stauber. But the regular driver was sick, and the replacement didn't make the first pickup till three P.M. Which means the letter must have been mailed Friday before three."

Siegel rose from her chair and crossed to the window and stood staring out. The view was of one of those midtown alleys where sunlight didn't fall: developers had been allowed to blot out the sky, and the only thing remotely bright on the brick wall across the way was the pigeon droppings.

"I don't often agree with Greg, but I'm coming around to his point of view. Sam's not just trying to confuse us, he's trying to wear *me* out. There's no other reason for these letters to be mailed from such crazy places."

"You're working too hard," Cardozo said.

"Tell me."

"Have to stop taking things so personally." Cardozo gave his swivel chair a push and made a quarter revolution. "Sam, how's the progress at Family Court?"

"I'm developing great respect for New York's Hispanic Catholic community." Today Sam was wearing a brass-buttoned navy-blue blazer, a regimental silk tie, and perfectly pressed gray trousers. "What impresses me is the number of boys who *haven't* been molested by older male relatives. So far we've found twenty-two hundred of them. The bad news is, we haven't found a single one who fits Wilkes's profile."

"Wilkes is a shrink," Greg Monteleone said. "Shrinks are hired guns, they'll say whatever you pay them to."

"I'm not saying his theory is wrong," Sam Richards said. "But I kept thinking about Jim Delancey telling the judge he was defending that boy against an abusive father."

Greg Monteleone snapped a blue suspender. "Delancey's saving his ass."

"I believe he's sincere," Sam Richards said.

"Why?"

"He risked his parole."

"No way." Monteleone shook his head. "The people who had the clout to get him out have the clout to keep him out."

"I feel he was taking a chance, and I feel he took it because he identified with that kid. I asked myself, What if we're looking in the wrong population? What if the kid we want is *Jim Delancey*? What if Delancey was abused and sodomized by an older male relative, what if that relative was his father, what if the case landed in Family Court?"

"A lot of what-ifs," Cardozo said.

"And here's the biggest what-if of all. What if it happened within the last eight years, and Family Court has it in the computerized records?"

"And?" Cardozo said.

"The mother's name is Xenia? The father's name is James Delancey the Second?"

"Sounds right to me."

"Eight years ago, the Child Welfare Department brought a complaint against Delancey senior."

"What was the charge?" Cardozo said.

Sam Richards turned two empty hands palm up. "The record is sealed. I'd need a court order to get into it."

"I'll get you one." Cardozo picked up his pen. "What's the number of that case?"

■ ■ ■

CARDOZO SHUT THE CUBICLE DOOR and lifted the phone and dialed. A woman's voice answered brightly. "Judge's chambers."

"Hi, Lil, it's Vince. Is himself in?"

The voice collapsed. "He hasn't been well. His prostate. Last week he had to go into University Hospital for a sonogram. The tumors were soft—nonmalignant."

"So he's in the clear?"

"I wish. Remember Bessie—his collie?"

"Sure, I remember Bessie. She liked to drink his martinis."

"She died."

Not of cirrhosis, I hope. "I'm sorry to hear that."

"So this weekend he went upstate to see the breeder. While he was parked—in Brewster, New York, this happened—his car got broken into."

"This story has a happy ending?"

"They got his reading glasses."

"The story has an ending?"

"He just came in. Act like I didn't tell you anything. Hold on a second."

Lil put him on hold, and he stared down at his desktop at the latest memo from the Puzzle Palace: a directive on blue paper ordering the precincts to crack down on parking violators. Attached to it was a yellow memo stating that the Twenty-second Precinct was expected to produce one point two million in tow charges by the end of the fiscal year.

Has law enforcement come to this? Cardozo wondered. *A last-ditch expedient to balance the city books?*

New York was crumbling, services were crippled, races were polarized, homeless flooded the streets, crack killed—and New York's finest were hunting down traffic violators.

Judge Tom Levin's voice came on the line, solid and cheerful. "I was going to call you, Vince. How about a few hands this weekend?"

Cardozo and Tom Levin had been playing poker with each other for over twenty years. "Not this weekend, Tom. I'm on a task force."

"Too bad. What can I do for you?"

"First of all, I'm sorry about Bessie."

"Thanks. But I got a great puppy—Abigail. You have to come down and meet her."

"I'd like to. Tom, I need an order unsealing a Family Court record."

"No problem. Where's my pen? Okay, what's the case number?"

■ ■ ■

SITTING IN LUDDIE'S LIVING ROOM, Leigh felt the nervousness of a cornered animal. "Why is this maniac taking blame for something he didn't do?"

"What maniac?" Luddie said.

"Sam, Society Sam, whatever his name is." Leigh handed Luddie her copy of the morning's *Trib*, folded open to the text of Sam's third letter.

Luddie read aloud. *"Simple Simon meet the die man . . ."*

"Please, Luddie. Read it to yourself."

Luddie's eyes touched her with the weightlessness of light. "Maybe in Sam's mind it's not blame he's taking. Maybe it's fame. Maybe he's addicted to headlines."

"Or maybe he's shielding me."

"And why the hell would you need shielding?"

"Because, as I just got through telling you," she said quietly, "I was drunk and killed a woman."

"You were drunk and you did not kill a woman."

"It's exactly the same as Jim Delancey and Nita—the same house, the same terrace, the same time of day, the same situation, the same result. The only difference is, Delancey went to jail for it."

"There's a second difference. Delancey pushed your daughter—and you didn't push Dizey."

Leigh was silent.

"That drunken bitch of a professional gossip fucked up her body chemistry," Luddie said. "She lost her balance and she fell. Blame her, blame God, blame John Barleycorn, but don't blame yourself."

"If I hadn't been drunk, it wouldn't have happened."

"Baloney. If *she* hadn't been drunk, it wouldn't have happened. Face it, Leigh—guilt may give you a great wallow, but much as the old bag deserved what she got, you were not the instrument God chose to deliver it. And even if you had been, how would Society Sam know? He'd have to have been there and seen the whole fight."

"I don't think it's so impossible that he was there. I don't think it's so impossible at all."

"Come *on*! What are you trying to persuade yourself of?"

"Vince Cardozo knows something happened on the terrace. He knows it wasn't an accident."

"How the hell did you get to be such an expert at reading minds? Know what I think? I think this cop is doing his job, and you resent him because he isn't giving you an obvious handle to control him. You'd love to give him a hard-on."

"Even for you, Luddie, that's a pretty crude analysis of my motives."

"Am I right?"

"Okay!" she shouted. What stopped her, what cut her short was the absolute calm of Luddie's gaze. "You're ten-percent right. He doesn't seem to want the same things from me that other men do."

"Why should he want anything from you?"

"Most men do."

"Most men that you bother with do. Look, I understand. You're used to surviving by manipulation, and you're wondering if you can manipulate this police lieutenant. Because deep down he's like every other man who ever saw one of your films—he's a fan. And the courtship dance has already started."

"Is he? Has it?"

"Don't pull that B-movie naive act on me."

"It is not an act, and I have never made a B movie."

"What the hell do you call your life?"

"Why are you trying to make me feel second-rate?"

"The only person who thinks you're second-rate is you."

"Look, I'm fresh back from a slip. I'm entitled to a little self-doubt!"

"What you're not entitled to is this poor schmo of a cop. Seducing men is spiritual and behavioral booze for you."

"You make me want to puke, you are so full of AA clichés and crap."

"Oh, yeah? Name me once, just once, when you've been up against a situation requiring even the tiniest iota of personal growth, that you've haven't run to the nearest hard dick! Which you somehow always manage to captivate!"

Through the double glazing of Luddie's windows she could hear the faint sound of traffic that never seemed to get farther or nearer. She could see trucks and cars down on Second Avenue, spitting out smoke. Men and women whose faces she couldn't see waited on corners for red to change to green. In the distance the Empire State Building reflected back a hypodermic of sunlight.

"You seem to think I'm pretty hot stuff."

"I think you're a poor little celebrity with a compulsion to reduce every man you meet to a dick because dicks don't think, and you believe if a man *could* think, he wouldn't bother with a piece of shit like you in the first place."

She turned and faced him. "You do put it gracefully, Dr. Freud."

"Sometimes grace is required. You have a twofold disease: In your case, it's not enough to put down the pills and the booze— you have to pull up your panties. Would you do your poor battered old sponsor a favor, please, Leigh? Just promise me you'll keep them up for ninety days?"

She didn't answer.

"Did you hear me, Leigh? I'm strongly advising you not to see him again."

"I can't not see him. We have a date in two hours."

"What kind of date?"

"Don't worry, it's only business. We're picking up Oona's brooch."

▪ ▪ ▪

"HELP YOU?" The red-faced, six-foot butterball of a man seemed to be one of the proprietors of Gurdon-Chappell Interiors. He wore a stoplight-red blazer with gold buttons and a huge paisley show hankie that matched his necktie. He was wearing more money in that hankie pocket than Cardozo was wearing on his whole body.

"Thanks," Cardozo said. "I'm just browsing."

Behind gold-rimmed granny glasses the eyes were cold little stars set in calculating slits. "Take your time."

Cardozo examined the fifteen-thousand-dollar price sticker clinging to the underside of a life-sized carved alabaster hand.

"That hand was carved by Bernini."

"Really," Cardozo said.

A buzzer sounded. The front door of the shop swung open, and a woman stepped briskly inside. She was wearing a suit of a pale pink like the flesh of a watermelon and a large, matching sloped hat that hid one of her eyes.

The outfit made it clear that she had a better-than-decent figure and a far better-than-decent income. What it did not make at all clear was that she was Leigh Baker. You'd have to know her, and be expecting her, to recognize her under the shadow of that hat and behind those sunglasses.

Gurdon advanced toward her. She offered her left profile to his lips. He took her hand and led her to the rear of the gallery. They sat at an enormous carved desk.

His mouth was in motion. His hands made broad, emphasizing gestures. It looked to Cardozo like a lot of hard sell.

Leigh Baker listened with a fixed expression.

Gurdon unlocked the middle drawer of the desk and took out a small, bauble-sized red felt jeweler's box.

Leigh Baker leaned forward in her seat to look.

Gurdon's hand lifted the brooch from the box. He'd attached it to a chain, and he held it dangling.

A kind of champagne-colored light blinked out from the platinum bird's tiny wings.

Leigh Baker sat quietly, looking over at him, not at it. She listened for a while and then she shook her head in a firm negative.

Gurdon leaned back and threw up his hands in a surrendering gesture.

Leigh took a checkbook out of her purse. Gurdon handed her a gold pen.

She handed him a check.

He handed her the brooch.

She rose from the chair with that same fixed look that was not quite a smile. She put her sunglasses back on.

Without so much as a glance in Cardozo's direction, she turned and left the store.

■ ■ ■

"YOU DO THAT AWFULLY WELL," Cardozo said. "Pretending to bargain."

He and Leigh Baker were sitting at a table along the dove-colored wall of what was basically a Madison Avenue upscale barroom. Green explosions of potted palms walled off their area of comfortable leather benches and small tile-top tables.

"I wasn't pretending," Leigh Baker said. "Fenny was asking way too much. Twelve thousand. I gave him eight."

Cardozo had the feeling the money wasn't real to her. "We'll see that you get it back," he said.

"I don't want it back."

He sensed in her a complicated sort of not-caring, and it made him curious. "Why not?"

"I don't want Fenny prosecuted."

Cardozo felt oddly let down that she could say that. "But he broke the law."

"And he came forward and testified for Nita at the trial. Whatever he's become, he was a friend when I needed a friend."

Their drinks came, two diet Pepsis in highball glasses with swizzle sticks. The waitress gave a little puff of indrawn breath, and Cardozo could tell she'd recognized Leigh.

They sipped their drinks. For a moment Cardozo's silence flowed into Leigh Baker's.

Suddenly she looked up at him. "Did Society Sam kill Dizey?"

"That's what his note claims."

"Is the note genuine?"

"It looks as genuine as the others."

She was silent again, and he could see something was bothering her.

" 'Sex to end all sex,' " she recited, " 'is there anything else in your perverted worldview?' "

"You've memorized it."

"Does that phrase sound familiar?"

He shrugged. "It's a familiar idea. Politicians tout war to end all war, restaurants advertise pasta to end all pasta."

"It reminds me of something else. Something in my own life."

Cardozo smiled. "Sounds interesting."

But Leigh Baker wasn't smiling. "It's something unhappy. But I must have repressed it. I can't recall what."

▪ FORTY-TWO ▪

Wednesday, June 5

"EXCUSE ME," a female voice said irritably.

Sam Richards was standing first in line in the Records Room of the Family Court Building on Lafayette Street. He turned.

A gray-suited, thick-torso'd little white woman had pushed into the line directly behind him. She was breathing heavily, as though she'd just run ten blocks.

"You have to wait your turn," the girl behind the counter said. She was a pale-skinned black girl, and her eyes were bored. Her ongoing midmorning snack was spread across the countertop: a barely begun bottle of Yoo-Hoo chocolate-flavored drink, a styrofoam cup of black coffee, half a cheese-and-cherry Danish cradled in a nest of waxed paper.

"This is an emergency." The column of the woman's neck swelled. "I have a court order. *Department of Child Welfare versus Delancey* stays sealed." She snapped open her purse and yanked out an overstuffed business envelope from the Supreme Court of the State of New York, which she threw down on the countertop.

The girl caught the Yoo-Hoo bottle before it could tip over. She pushed the envelope away. "I don't accept court papers."

"Sure, and you don't do windows either. This *is* the Department of Records, isn't it?"

The girl's dark eyes shot the woman a long, loathing glare. "Go to the Director of Services. Third floor."

"You don't have to sign it—just read it!" The woman ripped the envelope open and pulled out the order and waved it. "They did teach you to read, didn't they?"

"Why don't you teach me, bitch?"

"Excuse me, ladies." Sam Richards took out his shield case. "Could I help negotiate a truce here?"

The woman wore mildly myopic prescription lenses. Eyes the color of slate peered at the shield. "And who are you?"

"Detective Sam Richards, NYPD. How may I help you, ma'am?"

A cry broke from the woman's throat. She took a swing with the court order and batted the shield from his hand.

Sam Richards didn't move or say anything or even show he was reacting, but his mind closed in on the fact that he was dealing with a crazy. "Hold it right there, ma'am, please." Keeping his eyes fixed on hers, he crouched to retrieve his shield from the floor.

Her foot shot out and connected with his shoulder.

He almost lost his balance. His hand caught the edge of the counter. He pulled himself to standing. "I advise you never to kick an officer, ma'am. We're armed. Could I see some identification?"

An angry scarlet covered her face and neck. Sweat beaded her eyebrows. She slapped a driver's license down onto the counter and then a social-security card.

Sam Richards studied the license. She looked even meaner in the photograph, with little red dots glowing in the center of her eyeglasses. "You're Xenia Delancey?"

"I am. And I'm sorry I hit you. But this young woman's attitude enrages me."

"Would you mind showing me your court order?"

She thrust it into his hand.

He scanned the three pages of legalese. The order had been issued by Judge Anna Lubitsch of the State Supreme Court, and it restrained the Department of Records of Family Court from unsealing any documents relating to case FC-1982-124-TR-32-Z-1467, *Department of Child Welfare versus Delancey.*

"Looks like you're just in time." Sam Richards handed the order to the girl behind the counter.

She looked not at it but at him. There was a change in her expression. Nothing moved in her face, but something shifted behind her eyes.

The request form that Sam Richards had filled in still lay on the countertop. He ripped the form in two and pocketed the pieces. He took his briefcase from the counter and gave a little nod. "Good day, ladies."

He walked quickly across the room and out to the stairway.

He took the steps up to the lobby two at a leap. By the time he'd reached the street, he was sprinting.

Twelve minutes later, after executing an illegal U-turn and busting three traffic lights and double-parking in front of the precinct, Sam Richards burst into Cardozo's cubicle.

"Got it—barely." He emptied his briefcase over Cardozo's desk. Documents rained down.

Cardozo's eyes lifted to look at him. "What's wrong, Sam? You been running?"

Sam Richards stood catching his breath. "Xenia Delancey is one fearsome lady. She showed up with a restraining order. Luckily she served it on herself."

▪ ▪ ▪

WILKES FINISHED READING. He rested his forehead against the palm of his hand, as though his thoughts were weighing down his entire head. In the window behind him blinds slatted the afternoon sun.

"One hundred and four times," he said. "One hundred and four times during a four-year period, the father abused his kid. What the hell was the mother doing, keeping score?"

"Every other Thursday she worked late at the department store," Cardozo said. "One of those Thursdays she happened to come home early. She just counted up all the late Thursdays."

"That's what she says, but I don't buy it. Nine times out of ten, the nonabusive parent knows and doesn't want to face it. Was the father ever charged?"

Cardozo shook his head. "She wouldn't let the kid testify. She settled for divorce and custody."

"That's exactly what I would have figured."

"I've seen this woman in the boutique. Image matters to her."

"I've seen her too. Many, many times." Wilkes closed the file and sat drumming his fingertips on the folder. "Okay. If you want my judgment, the kid fits. Made to order."

The words fell heavily into the silence. The two men faced each other across the heavy, uncluttered wood desk.

"But if it's him," Cardozo said, "he's faking. He's a multiple murderer trying to pass as a serial killer."

"Sure. But there's only one way to fake serial killing—do it. Which makes you a serial killer. And how do you tell if the claim to be faking isn't just an unconscious rationalization?"

"I don't know how. Do you?"

"You don't. Rationality is the most common mask that compulsion wears. Look at the military. Or the police. There are compulsive killers in uniform, but we don't see them as compulsives. Neither do they. Look at drug killings. A quarter of today's drug enforcers have the drives of serial killers—and the opportunities. So what do they do? They kill—serially. But we see the slaughter as business-related. If we can find any motive at all, we prefer to deny the compulsive element. So do they."

"Would you call our man a compulsive?"

"If the drive's controlling him and not vice versa, absolutely. And there are plenty of indications that it is. So far we have three killings. After the first he waited eleven days. After the second, nine days. The interval shrank. Each time he kills he loses a little of the ability to hold off."

"So what happened to the minimax cycle?"

"In this case it's accelerating. It happens in twelve percent of the cases."

"When is he likely to kill next?"

"The last interval was nine days, so right now he's in a seven-day interval."

"Come on. The interval keeps shrinking by exactly two days?"

"If it wasn't consistent, it wouldn't be compulsion. It's too bad you don't have time to study the database." Wilkes tossed a nod toward the computer terminal. "Chances are damned good Society Sam will kill next on . . ." He leaned forward and touched a pencil tip to his desk calendar. "Two days from now. Friday, June seventh." The pencil skipped forward. "Then there'll most likely be a five-day interval before the next killing. Then three days. Then one. And then . . ."

Wilkes left the statement unfinished.

"What happens then?" Cardozo said. "The interval shrinks from five to three to one to nothing. What next?"

He saw it, the look in Wilkes's eyes, there and then quickly covered over.

"There's no way you're going to let him get that far," Wilkes said.

"But what if we don't stop him before the next killing? Or the next? Or the next? What happens?"

For a moment Wilkes sat absolutely still, and then his feet hit the floor and he was standing. "Remember what Son of Sam was planning when the cops caught him?"

"He was going to go into a Long Island disco with a sub-machine gun."

"Same principle here. Pile-up. Our man runs amok."

■ ■ ■

"THE THIRD NOTE GIVES US another source." There was a kind of glow in Lou Stein's voice. "Sam clipped letters from *US* magazine, April second."

"April second again." Cardozo shifted the receiver to his left hand and flipped back in his desk calendar. The big events of that week, according to the calendar manufacturer, were the first quarter of the moon and Palm Sunday. "What's so special to this guy about April second?"

"Maybe nothing. April second was a Monday. Weekly magazines always come out on Monday."

"You haven't found any source later than that?"

"Not so far."

"So he could have written all three notes nine weeks ago."

"Possibly. Or April second might just have been the day he decided, Hey, let's compile us an inventory of cut-out letters."

■ ■ ■

LEIGH WAS TRYING TO DECIDE which toiletries absolutely had to go with her to Paris. On the marble-topped bathroom counter, she set out the soaps, the bottles of colognes and mouthwash. She arranged them into two groups: take and leave.

At the back of the cabinet, behind the toothpaste and dental floss, she found a cache of prescription medicines she thought she'd thrown out years ago. She examined the labels and recognized her old pills for sleeping, pills for waking up, pills for anxiety, pills for depression.

Odd, she thought, *they have pills for all that and nothing for loneliness or for fear, or hurt, or guilt or anger . . .*

A calendrical card of contraceptive pills had only two of the pills popped out. She couldn't remember when her doctor had taken her off them.

"Oh, well, you're prehistory now." She dropped the card into the wastebasket.

And then she found herself staring at a barely touched tube of spermicidal gel. She had to smile. *Hope springs eternal.*

"Sorry, you're not getting a trip to Paris."

And then she thought, *But you never know . . .*

"Yes, you do," she told her reflection. "You know."

Why do I think I'm talking to a teenage girl? she wondered. She smiled at the reflection. *Don't you wish!*

Her eye went back to the tube. Her hand tightened with sudden force. It took her a moment to catch the thought that had flashed through her mind.

Sex to end all sex.

And she knew where she had seen those words before.

■ ■ ■

THE PANTRY SMELLED OF CHEMICALS. The maid, in long rubber gloves, was polishing silver.

"Mabel," Leigh said, "have you seen my policeman? He's not in front."

"He went for cigarettes." The maid set the soup ladle down on a counter covered with that morning's *Trib*. "He said he'd be right back."

Leigh glanced at her wristwatch. "If he's back before me, would you tell him I've gone to the Jefferson Storage warehouse over on West Sixty-sixth?"

■ ■ ■

A CON ED CREW WAS DRILLING a crater in the street, and traffic had jammed the intersection. Leigh asked the taxi to let her out on the corner. She walked quickly along West Sixty-sixth. Jefferson Storage, an Art Deco building with restored facade, stood a half block from the Metropolitan Opera. She pressed the buzzer and waited.

A guard in khaki work clothes finally let her in. His eyes were cold and bloodshot. She had a feeling she'd interrupted his drinking, and he resented her for it.

She showed her storage receipt and signed the register. "Nice that it's turned cooler," she said.

The guard's shoulders shaped a nowhere-to-go shrug.

"If a man asks for me, you can send him up." She took the self-service elevator up to the eighth floor. For a moment it didn't open and she thought it was going to hold her prisoner, but then the lights dipped and came up, and the steel grille heaved itself open.

She pushed the door open and hurried down a long, echoing corridor.

It took her two wrong turns to locate Room 812. She unlocked the door and switched on an overhead light. The light bulb, swinging naked from a chain, sent shadows leaping across dark, clumsy old steamer trunks and a polychrome pile-up of brand-new–looking luggage. Movers' cartons had been stacked among the suitcases, and there was hardly space to stand or move.

She sat down on a trunk, looking around her, pressing her lips together, trying to remember where she had packed what.

There was a sound of glass shattering somewhere else on the floor. It was a dead-of-night street noise, like a tossed bottle or a window breaking, and her nerves told her it had no business indoors in the middle of the day.

She tried to open the carton marked *books.* It was sealed with reinforced movers' tape, and her bare hands got more tears from the tape than they managed to inflict on it. Finally it occurred to her to take out her housekeys and use the key with the sharpest serrated edge as a saw.

After ten minutes of jabbing she managed to break into five cartons without finding what she had come for.

She peered around through dust floating in the dimness, trying to think where she could have packed it.

The shattering-glass sound came again. It seemed closer this time, and her heart gave a painful jump against her ribs.

Her eye fell on a carton with the grease-pencil–marking *china.*

She stabbed her key through the tape and pried up the lid. She peered down into the carton. A small leather-bound book had been placed as a buffer between a stack of saucers and a stack of cups.

She pulled it out.

The word *diary* was embossed in gold script on the cover.

She opened it. She skimmed through the pages, looking for those five words. She found them at the very bottom of a right-hand page.

January 11, Thursday

In counseling today I suggested to Jim we smoke a peace pipe. He was reluctant when I told him it was crack, but curiosity got the better of him and he tried it. Two tokes and we were off to the races.

He is the greatest lover I have ever had, bar none. Nothing short of sensational. It was yummy sex to end all sex . . .

Waves of icy unreality seemed to come off the lines of neatly looping handwriting. When Leigh was finally able to keep her hand from trembling, she turned the page.

Above her head the light went out.

She jumped up. Her leg struck the edge of a trunk. She groped her way to the wall. Her hand found the light switch. She jiggled it up and down.

Nothing happened.

Her hand explored and finally found the door handle. She turned it and pushed. There was no light in the hallway. In the pitch-blackness, she thought she heard someone. "Officer . . . is that you?"

No one answered.

With one hand grazing the wall, she felt her way back along the corridor. Finally she saw light: the emergency-powered red EXIT sign above the elevator.

She stood patting the wall, feeling for the call button. *This is ridiculous. There's got to be a button.* She found it and pushed.

Cables squealed and machinery hummed. She pushed again. The squealing and humming went on . . . and on . . . She kept her finger on the button.

The squealing and humming went past the floor.

"No!" she shouted. "Come back!" She pounded the door.

The humming stopped. There was a sound like a truck changing gears on a steep hill.

The humming began again and stopped again. She could hear the grille slam itself open. She gripped the handle of the elevator door and yanked it toward her.

She stood there, facing blackness.

"Hello . . . is anyone there?" It occurred to her that the right question would have been, *Hello, is there an elevator around here?*

She crouched and reached into the darkness. Her fingers touched the floor of the corridor, and then the edge of the shaftway, and beyond it—emptiness.

Her heart gave a sharp contraction. Her fingers reached farther, and her hand struck the corrugated steel of the elevator cabin.

Thank God.

She straightened and stepped into the elevator. The door closed. She patted the cabin wall till she found the button panel. She felt for the lowest button and pushed.

The grille slammed shut, almost catching her dress. She pulled herself back into the clear. The humming and squealing started, and the elevator began its crawling descent.

There was a click passing the seventh floor. A click passing the sixth. Two clicks.

"Is someone here?" she said.

No one answered.

The clicking came again.

She stretched a hand in front of her. Her hand struck something. Her fingers repeated the touch. She felt cloth. The cloth pulled away. She followed it. A jacket. Beneath the jacket, an arm.

A man's voice said, "It's me."

"Officer?" In her relief she forgot his name. "You're certainly quiet today. You frightened me."

The elevator stopped. The grille slammed itself open. He held the door for her.

She stepped out into darkness. She stood trying to find her sense of direction. To the left her eyes gradually made out a slanting shaft of gray. She went toward it.

The gray brightened. As she rounded a corner into the lobby a wall of daylight blinded her.

"Sign out, please," the guard said.

She took the pen from him and scribbled an initial in the register.

"Is your friend coming down?"

"My friend?" She saw her policeman waiting beside the lobby door. "He's right over there."

"Not him. The guy that went up looking for you."

"I don't understand." She called across to the officer. "Weren't you upstairs with me?"

He sauntered across the lobby. The name came to her. Dan. Dan with the blue eyes and the round, unlined face that looked all of eighteen years old.

"Beg pardon, ma'am?"

"Miss Baker said she was expecting someone." The guard's tone was defensive. "She said send him right up."

"You sent someone up?" the officer said.

"We were in the elevator just a minute ago," Leigh said. "I thought he was you."

Dan shook his head. "Wasn't me."

Her heart gave another sharp contraction. "Let's get out of here."

▪ ▪ ▪

LEIGH SAT ON THE EDGE OF THE BED, staring at the phone, trying to work up nerve. *I'm not imagining things.*

She lifted the receiver and dialed.

An unfriendly voice answered. "Vince Cardozo."

"I hope I'm not bothering you. It's Leigh Baker."

The voice immediately shed its gruffness. "Of course you're not."

He likes me. Even though I'm a nuisance. The thought pleased her. "I'm going to Europe tomorrow—I'll be back Sunday."

"Okay, I'll call off the guard. Have a good trip."

"You'll be getting a package from me by messenger."

"Thanks. I'll look forward to it."

"Don't. I'm afraid it's not very enjoyable. It's a diary. The diary Delancey's lawyer tried to pass off as Nita's."

He didn't answer. The quality of silence flowing across the line seemed to change. She wondered if they'd been disconnected.

"Hello?" she said.

"I'm here."

"Are your men still watching Delancey?"

"Why do you ask?" A little of that gruffness was creeping back.

I irritate him. I talk too much about Delancey. "Someone followed me today."

"That someone was a cop, I hope."

"There was someone else. Besides him."

"What time?"

"Around four."

"Delancey works noon to eight today."

"Are you sure he was at work?"

"I'll check. Would you mind telling me why you're sending the diary?"

"Look at the entry for January eleventh. I'll leave a bookmark. You'll recognize five words. I wonder if you'll think what I think."

"And what's that?"

"The person who wrote the diary wrote Society Sam's third note."

■ ■ ■

LAURIE BONASERA TOYED with objects on the counter—the sugar dispenser, the saltshaker—moving them around as if they helped her find the words she wanted to say. "This is getting complicated."

Carl Malloy touched her hand. "Hey, I've got enough pressure right now."

"I know you do." The fluorescent lighting gave her eyes a sunken-in, dark look. "But it's pressure on me too. When we're together, it always feels like an emergency. Being with each other shouldn't feel like that. It should be calm. Like it is for other people."

"Like what other people?" All he could do was smile, try to make her see there was a light side to everything. "Who's calm in this city?"

"Somebody must be."

"Do you think it's any fun for me, wanting to hold you and having to sit here and pretend I'm interested in this doughnut?"

"Is your doughnut as stale as mine?"

"Worse."

She smiled. It was only a sort-of smile. But at least her face wasn't a mystery. "They always advertise on TV that they make their own. I wouldn't be so anxious to take credit."

He couldn't think of anything to say about the doughnuts. He could feel that he and Laurie were two heartbeats away from another silence.

"Well," he said, "we're not here about a doughnut, are we?"

Her gaze flicked up. He knew she was checking to see if anyone else in the doughnut shop was noticing them.

The counter attendant was sponging off a stretch of green formica counter. He was a slender, underfed-looking man in a stained white jacket that was much too loose on him, and he moved with a sort of reggae bounce.

Halfway down the counter two old guys in New York Mets caps were arguing. At the end of the counter a bag lady had put a Saks bag on the stool beside her and was searching through it.

"I'm not good at lying," she said. "My husband isn't going to keep buying my dumb excuses for being out."

"What kind of excuses do you give him?"

"Visiting a friend in the hospital."

"That's not dumb."

"He could check the hospital."

"Is he that kind of guy? Would he check up on you?"

"He isn't yet. Carl, I don't *want* to get good at lying."

"What did you tell him for tonight?"

"I didn't. I said I'd be home."

"Home when?"

She glanced over at the clock on the wall. Just a glance. The glance said nothing, said everything. "Regular time."

Carl Malloy didn't know why his mouth was going dry with panic. He didn't know why he felt he was going to lose her, that every moment longer he could hold her was a moment snatched from annihilation. It wasn't rational, but it was what he felt.

"I know I've asked a lot of you," he said. "I know you've got a lot on your mind—but just do this one thing for me, please. Come with me now. Let's go to the hotel."

She turned her gaze on him. "I hate that hotel—I feel like a hooker."

"Just this one last time. Then I'll get a real place."

"What kind of real place?"

"I'll borrow a place."

There was a gloomy, thoughtful overtone about her. "I have to get home."

He could feel bridges burning. "Then why did you come at all?"

"To see you."

He was losing the battle to keep his nerves tucked in. He felt as though he were having a headache throughout his whole body. "This isn't seeing each other!"

She kissed him lightly and slid off the stool. "Good night, Carl."

·FORTY-THREE·

Thursday, June 6

LEIGH WATCHED THE CITY slide past the amber-tinted windows. She felt edgy, remote, in no mood for Europe.

Just beyond the LeFrak City turnoff of the Expressway, the limo hit a slowdown. A zebra-striped sawhorse blocked one of the lanes. A highway-patrol car was pulled to the divider and a highway cop stood by the sawhorse, signaling drivers to merge lanes.

"Trouble." Leigh's new private guard pushed the button that automatically rolled down the window. He leaned out and called, "Say, Officer! Officer! What's happening?"

The cop, a heavyset man with gray hair, stared in the direction of the shout. He stood for a moment with one hand on his hip holster, eyes only half visible behind their sunglasses, and then he sauntered over. "Tow truck collided with a U-Haul."

"How long's the delay?"

The cop made a helpless Italian gesture with both hands. "I hope you've got a good book or a TV in that backseat."

"Officer, I have Leigh Baker in this backseat with me. The actress. We're trying to make a plane. Any chance we could use the grass divider to get past this mess?"

The cop frowned and glanced over his shoulder at the single-lane grass divider. He gave a what-the-hell shrug. "Why not." He leaned down to the window. "Hey, Miss Baker, enjoy your trip."

■   ■   ■

AT THE CONCORDE BOARDING GATE the new man handed Leigh her ticket and passport. "Enjoy your trip, Miss Baker."

"Aren't you coming with me?"

"I wish I could." His smile took just a millisecond too long to develop. "Your guard is waiting for you on the plane. It's been a pleasure meeting you."

At the end of a blue plastic accordion-walled boarding ramp, a stewardess took Leigh's boarding pass. "How are you today, Miss Baker? You're in row six, window seat to your right."

Leigh peered into the cabin and counted rows. She recognized Kristi Blackwell in six, even though Kristi was wearing an enormous picture hat that hid one eye. In the seat beside her, Wystan Blackwell was gulping champagne as though a bartender had announced last call.

Leigh fixed her best fake smile in place and waved.

Kristi didn't see her; she was busy sniffing the perfume sample that came with the airline's overnight kit. Wystan was signaling the stewardess for another champagne.

The seat directly across the aisle from them was empty. The seat beside it was occupied by a man. He had bent sideways and was shading his eyes to peer through the window. When he took his hand down, Leigh saw that he had startling pale eyebrows. He leaned back in his seat, and she recognized Arnie Bone.

Leigh executed an about-face before he could see her.

Passengers clustered and unclustered in the aisle. She worked her way around them.

"Miss Baker, is everything all right?" the stewardess asked.

"Where's the washroom?"

"Straight ahead."

Leigh went straight ahead, but instead of turning right for the washroom she turned left and got off the plane.

▪ ▪ ▪

LEIGH TOSSED HER PURSE on the bed. Before leaving, the servants had turned the air conditioner off. In the four hours since she'd been away the bedroom had become stuffy, and she crossed to the window and pressed Low/cool. A breeze built up and gradually rippled the curtain.

In the garden below children were having a birthday party with favors and paper hats and ice cream and cake. *That's how I'd like to spend my weekend,* she thought. *Being six years old.*

She splashed water on her face and kicked off her shoes. Just as she was lying down she noticed that a phone call had come in. For an instant she had the sensation of being an inanimate object at the mercy of a malevolent box of plastic and wire.

She pressed Replay.

The message was a four-minute silence.

As she listened the silence seemed to listen back.

The machine clicked to a stop. All the emptiness of the deserted town house suddenly pressed in on her. She felt a cold buzzing like Novocain jabbed into the dead center of an ache.

I've made a dumb mistake, she realized.

She searched in the drawer of the bedside table for the card with Vince Cardozo's work number.

He answered on the fourth ring. "Cardozo."

"Hi, it's Leigh. Leigh Baker. Sorry to bother you."

"Go ahead. Bother me. Aren't you in Paris?"

"No—I'm here. And I got another one of those calls."

"Then I should come over and look at the trace."

"I wish you would."

"It may be late."

"That's okay."

■   ■   ■

CARDOZO BROKE THE CONNECTION and phoned Esther Epstein, the elderly widow who lived next door in his apartment house. "Would you mind looking in tonight to make sure that Terri's okay? I may be home late."

"How late?"

He had to smile. Mrs. Epstein was coming on like the voice of his conscience.

"Because," she said, "I have a favor to ask you. My air conditioner broke, and the man says it won't be fixed till Monday. Would you die of a heart attack if you walked in and found an old lady sleeping on the couch?"

"Esther, you're a lady, but you're not an old lady, and if I found you on my couch . . . you kidding? I'd die of joy. Sleep over, please."

■   ■   ■

CARDOZO UNLOCKED THE DOOR and stepped into Waldo Carnegie's wine cellar.

The shaded overhead light threw a pale, even glow over the walls of wine bottles. Through a mesh grille in the ceiling he could hear the faint gray pulsation of the temperature-stabilizing system.

He lifted the Harlequin drawing off its hook and swung the little door open. A digital *four* pulsed in the display window of Tommy Thomas's sound-activated cassette recorder.

It seemed odd to him that there had been only four calls. He thought of Leigh Baker as a popular person, one who'd have celebrities on her private line all hours of the day and night.

He pushed the Rewind button and then Play. There was a moment's transistorized silence, then three buzzes, a click.

In the trace window area code 212 flashed.

An answering machine came on, speaking with Leigh Baker's voice. "Hello, you have reached . . ." She gave just the number, no name, no promise to call back, no assurance of anything.

A 929 appeared next to the area code. Cardozo recognized a lower Manhattan exchange.

Beep. Obviously a hang up. Too fast for the tracing mechanism to capture the rest of the caller's number. The trace window went blank.

Another span of silence. Another three buzzes. A click. In the window, area code 212 flashed a second time.

The answering machine cut in. Beside the area code flashed 555.

There was a beep and then a man's voice, with a kind of upper-class East Coast arrogance encoded in its nasality. "Leigh, are you there? It's Waldo. Are you there, honey?"

The trace window said Waldo was calling from 555-1923.

I don't need to listen to this, Cardozo thought. Before he could press the Fast Forward button, her voice came on the line.

"Hi, darling. Where are you?"

He realized he'd been hearing that voice since he'd been a boy. It was as familiar to him as his own mother's or his daughter's or his dead wife's. Maybe, in a way, more familiar. It pervaded entire areas of his memory, and so unobtrusively that he hadn't been aware, till this moment, how much it was part of his recall. A hundred masks in his mind spoke with it: the rich girl, the spoiled college-sorority girl, the small-town sweetheart, the hooker, the wartime nurse, the nun . . .

"I'm still at work," Waldo's voice said. "Look, I'd like to get in a little squash at the Racquet Club. Do you mind if I'm late?"

"Not at all—I haven't got anything planned."

Funny, Cardozo thought. *I'd have thought that's when she'd mind most.* He fast-forwarded.

The next call was Tori Sandberg phoning from a midtown exchange. Lunch plans.

He fast-forwarded to the final call.

Three buzzes, a click. The call was coming from area code 212.

The answering machine picked up.

Now the exchange appeared: 617.

The answering machine beeped.

Then came the silence. It had a hollow, pulsating quality, like the sound you get when you hold a seashell up to your ear. Now and then electronic blips sounded faintly, as though the phone company's sensors had detected an empty circuit and were trying to reroute traffic through it.

The silence was coming from 617-4336.

Cardozo copied the number on his notepad.

■ ■ ■

"WHEN DO YOUR SERVANTS get back?" Cardozo said.

They were in the living room. Leigh Baker was sitting at one end of a sofa, and Cardozo sat in the chair facing her. She pulled a needlepoint cushion in front of her and wrapped her arms around it, like a little girl rocking a doll. "I expected to be in Europe. I gave them till Sunday night."

He fixed her with a disbelieving stare. "You're going to spend three days and nights alone?"

"I'm not alone. You're here."

"I'm here now, but—"

"But what?"

He shrugged. "Now's now."

"Luckily." She tossed the pillow onto the sofa beside her. "How are you coming with your killer?" she asked.

He shrugged. "All you can do is do everything you can do."

A soft flow of lacquered light spilled across Oriental rugs and carved mahogany tables. Ornately framed French Impressionists glowed from pale walls, and alabaster busts of fellows who could have been Roman emperors stood guard at either end of the mantel of the hooded marble fireplace.

"It was luck that broke Son of Sam," he said. "A parking ticket. They had a three-hundred-man task force, but without that parking ticket three hundred pairs of hands would have been as useful as three hundred pairs of tweezers."

Her head with its beautifully messy hair rested back on satin cushions. "But Son of Sam was crazy. Isn't it always harder when you're looking for a madman?"

"Society Sam's probably crazy too. At least that's what the psychological profile says."

"Do you believe it?"

He rippled the water in his glass studiously. "Not as much as the psychologists do, but some of it rings true. For example, I buy very much that it's a class thing."

"Class?" she said.

Without gawking too openly, Cardozo glanced around him, at Chinese vases of fresh-cut chrysanthemums, crystal bookends enclosing single silk-bound volumes, gold table clocks and porcelain figurines and marble goose eggs upended on intricate ebony stands. They were objects that spoke of wealth in the most straightforward voice imaginable. There was nothing coded about them.

"Look at the locations Society Sam chooses," he said. "Marsh and Bonner's, Park Avenue and Sixty-eighth Street, an Upper East Side town house—he's hitting in the Golden Ghetto. It's an envy thing, a rage thing. And the victims: they're wearing jewelry, fine clothes—emblems of money. And they're fashionable . . . they have long hair . . . they're tall—"

"Avalon wasn't tall."

"For a woman he was tall."

"The killer mistook Avalon for a woman?"

"We're guessing."

"So if I pin my hair up and wear a cotton coat and low heels and slouch and stay away from expensive shops and this area—"

"Then you'll be a lot safer. Unless . . . you see, here's where my expert and I disagree."

"Your expert?"

"You really want to hear me grouse about work?" he said.

"Absolutely."

"I have a friend who's a clinical psychologist. He thinks the victims are chosen at random—the killer's psycho-biological clock alarm goes off, the killer goes into his gotta-kill cycle, prowls till he sees a candidate. He stalks that candidate and when the opportunity presents itself, he hits. The only connection between the killer and the victim is that the victim is the first candidate to cross the killer's path after the cycle starts. In a technical sense the killer and victim are strangers."

"Why only in a technical sense? It seems to me they *are* strangers."

"My friend calls it 'an unsymmetrical relationship.' The victim doesn't know who the killer is—but the killer knows who the victim is."

He was aware of a change in her, in the quality of her attention.

"You don't mean the killer personally knows who he's killing," she said.

"He doesn't know in your sense and mine. He knows in the sense that, from his point of view, the victim is wearing a flag or a label. The killer can read that flag. The killer knows the most likely place to find a victim with that label, the most likely time to find one. But when the victim looks at the killer, there's no flag, no label—no warning—until that last instant when the knife comes out."

"Do you agree with any of this?"

"Not completely. I don't think the killings are random."

She shifted slightly. "That's interesting. Why not?"

"Look at the original Son of Sam killings. None of those victims knew one another. There wasn't a single link. They didn't eat at the same restaurants, they didn't share employers, they didn't ride the same busses or live on the same streets. That's random. But Society Sam's victims know each other."

She gave a half nod of assent. "Are the police sure the victims were all killed by one person?"

"It's the simplest theory."

"But is the simplest always right? What if those Society Sam letters are fakes?"

"We're sure the first two are the same killer."

"But you're not sure who killed Dizey?"

"Completely different MO. No cuts."

"If it isn't the same killer, is there anyone you suspect?"

"A lot of people had access to Dizey that night. A lot of them had been stung at one time or another by that column of hers."

"You think it was someone she'd blasted in the column?"

"It's the sort of possibility we have to consider. But don't forget the ones who never got mentioned—because they might have had a grudge against her too."

"In other words, you're considering practically everyone at that memorial."

"We have to."

"Tell me, just for example, would you consider me?"

Cardozo found himself enjoying this woman. She had something unpredictable about her. He liked not knowing exactly how she would react, because he didn't know exactly how he'd respond, and that made him interesting to himself again. "Would I consider you as Society Sam? No, you're a woman."

"What about just killing Dizey?"

"I'd consider it."

"How could you prove it?"

"You have to understand—most homicide investigations are closed one way: a witness talks."

"What if there's no witness?"

"There's always one witness, and that's the one that usually talks."

Her hands rested on her lap, locked. "The killer confesses?"

"Or gives himself away."

"How?"

"Surprisingly dumb ways. A lot of killers can't resist cozying up to the cops."

"Why's that?"

"I have a theory it's fear. Some part of them is afraid that punishment is inevitable. They want to speed things up a little, end the waiting. A lot of killers actually try to help the cops. For example, if you were the killer, you'd be making a big mistake now—asking me about the investigation."

"Then let's change the subject before I get myself sentenced to life. Are you hungry?"

"Cops are always hungry."

"Let's eat in. Do you mind?"

"Who, me?"

He followed her into the kitchen. She opened an armoire-sized refrigerator and stood rattling the ice cubes in her empty glass. The freezer compartment exhaled white mist around her face.

"How would you feel about tomato and fennel soup, rack of lamb, vanilla ice cream with lingonberries that were fresh once upon a time?"

"*What*-berries?"

"They grow in Sweden. They're supposed to be a delicacy."

"How are you going to make all that?"

"Waldo's chef froze some leftovers. I'll just heat them up." She pulled three quart-sized plastic bags from the freezer and thunked them down on the counter. They looked like petrified swamp. She slit knife holes in the bags and arranged them on plates and slid them into the microwave. She set dials with a matter-of-factness that made him think she'd mastered basic microwave cookery.

She went and pulled another bag from the freezer. This one looked like a red woolen cap that had frozen in a snow drift. She set it in a mixing bowl.

She arranged two place settings on a butcher-block table in a corner of the kitchen. Two dozen gleaming copper pans hung from a rack directly overhead.

"Could I ask a rude question?" Cardozo pointed a thumb upward. "Does anyone ever cook in those things?"

She smiled. "I don't pry into the servants' lives, and they don't tattle on me to the magazines."

She went down to the cellar and returned with a bottle of wine. A heavy coat of whitish dust lay on the neck of the bottle, and he could see a 1969 on the label.

"Mouton-Rothschild." She spoke the French syllables as though they were the name of a never-to-be-forgotten lover. "It was the only wine that ever did all those things to my mouth that connoisseurs say a great wine should."

The name rang a distant, five-hundred-dollar-a-bottle bell in his mind. He remembered reading about it in *The New York Times*.

"Hey," he said. "I'm not that much of a wine drinker."

"You are tonight." She got the cork out with three twists of something that looked like obstetrics forceps for midgets. "To hell with letting it breathe. It can breathe in the glass." She poured two glasses.

"Are you drinking?" he said.

"One glass looks lonely. I like two on the table, don't you? When you finish yours, we'll switch."

When the bell on the microwave went off, she got up and took out their thawed dinners and brought the soup bowls and plates back to the table.

During dinner she turned giddy, talkative, as though she were the one who was drinking the wine. She told him about having a French mademoiselle and an English nanny when she was a child and going to the Brearley school over on East End Avenue when she was twelve, and sitting next to Rockefellers and Vanderbilts in class.

"That's where I met Oona and Tori. We were instant chums for life. When we were seventeen we all made our debut together at the Infirmary Ball at the Plaza. Lester Lanin conducted the orchestra, and do you know who I danced my first dance with? Truman Capote."

"Why not your father?"

"Dad had died."

"What about your mother?"

"Mom didn't."

The silence told him that Leigh Baker's mother was not her favorite person.

"By the time Tori and Oona and I were twenty-one, we were all engaged. And by twenty-two Oona and I were married."

"How many times have you been married?"

"Four. But Charley was the one I loved. Charley Kohler."

"The producer? Tell me about him."

She drew in a breath and sat with her hands flat on the table, thinking. "I've always thought happiness is not even knowing you're happy till you look back and you say, Wow, that was it. After he died I looked back at those years and I realized that was it."

"What did you like most about him?"

There was something in her eyes that was deeper than loss. They were deep-set eyes and of such a dark green that they appeared almost brown around the pupils. "I loved his laughter. I loved the way he laughed. I loved the times he chose to laugh. I loved the reasons he laughed."

"No one since?"

"Not like him. It would be what researchers call a statistical fluke."

"Flukes happen."

"All the time. But I've had mine. Mustn't be greedy."

He was feeling a glow throughout his body, a flush over every inch of his skin, and he felt free to ask her questions he might not have if he hadn't had that second glass of Mouton-Rothschild.

"What about Dick Braidy? I have trouble seeing you married to him."

"He was Charley's personal assistant and after Charley died he was there when I needed him, and most of the time he was sweet. It counts for something, when a person's sweet to you."

"Doesn't sound like many people have been sweet to you."

"Maybe I have exaggerated expectations."

"What about you and Waldo?"

Her fork stopped halfway to her mouth and went back to her plate. "It's not the same at all. We're not married."

"I know, but . . ." He shrugged. "You live here."

"He's lonely." She said it as though it was the reason they were together.

"And are you lonely?"

"I thought I was."

"Why don't you marry him?"

"We're not in love. He wants a friend, he wants a hostess, he wants some glitz—I'm it."

"And what do you want?"

"I'm not sure."

He sat there in the stillness of that moment. *What am I doing?* he wondered. *Hoping for a twenty-ton truck to run my life over?*

She got up from the table. She went to the counter where she'd left the ice cream to thaw.

Cardozo watched the way she walked. It was fluid, easy, with no wasted movement.

She squeezed the ice-cream bag and made a pouting face. "It's going to be another hour before it's soft."

It occurred to Cardozo that she could have thawed it in two minutes in the microwave. Obviously she was in no hurry. That suited him.

"Let's watch a movie," he said. "Let's watch one of yours."

"You're either a sadist or a masochist. Which one?"

"How about the last one you made for TV? I missed that one."

"I hate my TV movies." Her eyes came around to his, thoughtfully. "Which of my movies did your wife like best?"

"The one she loved was where you were the plain Jane married to the actor with the drinking problem."

"*Cassandra*—that was fifteen years ago."

"So we've all added a little mileage."

"Did you like it too?"

"Well, at the time . . ."

"You didn't."

"I thought it was good, but . . ." He sighed. "I've worked with people like the husband you had in that movie. I still do. For me it was like two hours overtime."

"Without pay?"

He smiled.

"I was a mess in that movie. Glasses and floppy sweaters."

"My wife loved it that you weren't glamorous. She thought you *were* that woman."

"A lot of people did. Funny, I was a roaring drunk. And my costar, who was playing a drunk, wasn't. In fact, he was the one who persuaded me to go to AA. The first time."

"Could we see it?" Cardozo said. "I think I'll like it better this time."

They went to the library on the second floor. He sat on the sofa. She loaded the tape into the VCR. She turned off all the lights except for one dim little lamp above the TV, and she came to the sofa and kicked off her shoes and sat beside him.

"Lights, camera, oops!" She aimed the remote and pushed a button, and there was a fanfare and the studio logo came up on the TV screen.

Now and then during the movie he had the feeling she was watching him, and he turned several times to check, but she was sitting forward with her chin resting on one fist, watching the screen. And then she seemed to know he was going to turn, and her eyes met his with a look that hovered between amused and uneasy, as though she hoped they were sharing something, but she wasn't a hundred percent sure.

The light and shadow moving across the screen threw an easy shimmer out into the room, and Cardozo felt his body floating away from him. She slid over on the sofa, closing the space between them, and her bare arm lay so near to his skin where he had rolled up his shirtsleeve that he could feel warmth coming off her.

When her head dropped toward his shoulder, it was the most automatic, natural thing in the world to let his arm go around her. The part of his brain that cared about survival was telling him, *Get up, get out of here,* and the rest of him had no desire to go anywhere.

It was the rest of him that won.

He pulled her deeper into the warm place she had made on his shoulder. He turned her head and began to kiss her, easily at first, nibbling her lips softly, then biting gently, then moving deeper.

"Let's go somewhere else," she said.

▪ ▪ ▪

AFTERWARD, CARDOZO SAT UP and dropped his feet over the edge of the bed. He was having trouble recognizing himself.

"Jesus," he said. "I don't believe I did that."

She raised her eyes toward him. He sensed a kind of gentle acceptance in them.

"We *both* did it," she said, "and it was damned nice."

"I guess I'm not used to damned nice."

"You should get used to it. You deserve a little."

"How do you know what I deserve?"

"Everybody deserves a little."

He stood and began gathering up his underwear.

"What are you doing?"

"I'll take my things and sleep down the hall."

"Oh, come on, we've done the deed. At least you could stay and cuddle. Cuddling's the nicest part."

He looked at her and something in the way she was looking back at him made him realize that she and Waldo had not been lovers in a long time. "Why, you're just a big, sentimental broad."

"You better believe it."

■ ■ ■

A CLICKING SOUND reached down into Cardozo's dream. For a transitional moment he was still floating through a turquoise Caribbean sea. And then he was not.

He opened one eye. A soft flutter of shadows filled the unfamiliar bedroom.

He raised his head. The window curtains were stirring in the air-conditioning. Just beyond the rise-and-fall of Leigh Baker's sleeping body, the fluorescent hands on the bedside clock pointed to three-twenty. Beneath them the answering machine was flashing a green light.

The machine beeped. "Miss Baker." It was a man's voice. "This is your security service."

"Oh, shut up," she moaned.

"You seem to have been separated from your guard. Could you give us a call as soon as you get this message? We're at area code 212 . . ."

Her hand went to the machine and killed the sound.

"What did you do?" Cardozo said. "Run away from your guard?"

"It's a long story. I can't stand him." Her arm came back to bed and went around him. "Let's go back to sleep."

· FORTY-FOUR ·

Friday, June 7

ZACK CAME BACK TO REALITY with a sense of exhilaration and release.

The curtains were drawn and the bedroom was half light, half dark. The bathroom door was open a generous crack and the light had been left on, and it threw a soft spill into the space beyond the canopied bed.

Beside him Gloria Spahn was lying on her side, breathing deeply and peacefully.

He allowed his body time to take back its boundaries, then gently pulled away. He rose by swinging his legs out off the bed and putting both feet on the floor. He felt weightless. Colors seemed sharper and sounds brighter. He sensed that the world wanted to sparkle and sing if only he'd let it.

Making love is great, he thought. *I've been making love since I was fourteen and it's still great. There's something about making love that catches me up no matter what kind of mood I'm in—it gets me out of myself, out of whatever paper bag I've sealed myself into.*

"Boo!" she cried.

He jumped.

She bounded up and into the bathroom and began running the bath water and filling the tub with scents and soaps and oils and salts.

"You know what the greatest feeling in the world is?" She was kneeling on the rim of the sunken tub, her hand testing the temperature of the water beneath the foam. "A hot tub after hot sex. Nothing beats it." She motioned him. "Come on—I'll scrub your back."

In the tub he said, "We could be great together."

Gloria Spahn kissed her fingers and pressed them over Zack's lips. "Don't spoil it."

He felt sudden uncertainty, and its presence was like a cold shadow. He could read no hint of her thoughts in the blank, self-satisfied beauty of her face.

The drug high was still carrying him, and his sense of her was sketchy, unfinished, as though nothing he could imagine would ever quite enclose her or confine her.

"Look," he said.

She looked at him.

"Let's keep the keys," he said. "Let's let this be our place."

"Let me think about it," she said.

■ ■ ■

FOR THE SAKE OF APPEARANCE Zack left the apartment first. Coming down alone in the mirrored self-service elevator, he checked his reflection, patting a dark lock of still-damp hair into place.

The elevator deposited him smoothly on the ground floor. The doorman held the front door. "Beautiful day, sir," he said.

"You're telling me." Whistling, Zack stepped onto the sidewalk.

■ ■ ■

AT TEN MINUTES BEFORE MIDNIGHT Detective John Ferrara sat behind the wheel of his Toyota. He had parked on East Fifty-second Street, but he was keeping his eye on the entrance to the residential high-rise at Twenty-three Beekman Place.

He was indulging in his worst nocturnal habit, a thick bologna sandwich on white bread, with lettuce, tomato, and double mayo. He had spread waxed paper on his lap. This was a necessary precaution when eating one of these deli monsters. The juice from the tomato had thinned the extra mayo into a liquid that began dripping as soon as he pressed the sandwich thin enough to wedge the corner of it into his mouth.

At three minutes before midnight an unforeseen problem began to develop, and it was twofold: The waxed paper started sliding off Detective Ferrara's lap, and the tomato slice began to slip sideways, off the bologna. Detective Ferrara's hands could feel the sandwich beginning to destabilize, like a drunk tightwire walker a half second before the plunge.

Thirty seconds later a man stepped out of the service entrance of Twenty-three Beekman. He was short, he was whistling, and where he wasn't bald he was dark-haired. Detective Ferrara recognized the afternoon doorman.

The doorman's shift was over, and he had changed from uniform to street clothes—a Hawaiian shirt and dark slacks. He stood a moment on the sidewalk. He looked up at the full moon hanging over Beekman Place. He jingled the change in his pockets and sauntered west on Fifty-first.

Meanwhile the edge of the tomato slice was peeking out from between the bread, and Detective Ferrara could feel it getting ready to make the jump. A glance downward told him that the waxed paper was seriously overleveraged, with no more than an inch to go before it fluttered down to the gas pedal.

A bicyclist rode east on Fifty-second, passing Detective Ferrara's car. The cyclist turned onto Beekman Place, cycled past Twenty-nine, and stopped at Twenty-three. Detective Ferrara recognized the Korean delivery boy from the deli where he'd bought his sandwich.

Without quite stepping off his cycle, the boy touched one foot down to the pavement and handed the doorman a large paper bag. The doorman counted out a handful of singles. The boy waved and turned his bike around and came back past Detective Ferrara.

By now Detective Ferrara had a dilemma. It required two hands to hold a bologna with double mayo, though in an emergency, such as the one developing, one hand could do the job for a second or so. The choice was this: Would it be better to use the free hand and the one second to catch the waxed paper or the tomato?

If he caught the waxed paper, he would save his trousers but guarantee himself a sandwich fallen apart in his lap.

If he tried to catch the tomato, he might lose everything and wind up with mayo on his trousers. On the other hand, he might hit the jackpot, come out with trousers clean and sandwich intact.

What it came down to was, was he a gambler or not?

He never got to answer the question.

A white flare exploded on his left side, practically blinding him. A woman's voice screamed: "Leave us alone!"

Detective Ferrara's head jerked around toward the screams, and the white-out in his field of vision traveled with him. All he could see was the silhouette of a human being, a black lump like a monster animated cartoon, jumping and waving what looked like a rock.

"What did he ever do to you?" the voice screamed.

The rock flashed again, and Detective Ferrara realized she had a camera, and she was photographing the stakeout.

"Leave us alone! Damn you!"

Something thumped, and a vibration traveled through the car. She was kicking the door. Another flash went off, and now neither of Detective Ferrara's eyes could see. "Lady, just calm it, will you?"

"We've never hurt you!" the voice screamed.

Gradually he began seeing her. She wore steel-rimmed glasses, like the meanest grade-school teacher you ever saw, and she had white hair that was thrashing behind her like a two-foot tail on a berserk pony. Every line in her face, and there were many, had bunched into a single snarl. She had eyes of distilled red hatred. "We've never hurt anyone! Can't you just let us live our lives?"

There was a cracking sound. She'd broken his window.

"Lady, shut the fuck up." As Detective Ferrara opened the car door and put a foot out on the pavement, the waxed paper, and with it his entire sandwich, slid to the street.

■   ■   ■

FROM THE BEDSIDE TABLE Cardozo's beeper was issuing a direct, unapologetic summons. He opened one eye. His fist swung down.

The beeping didn't stop. He realized he'd missed. He turned on the bedside light. This time his fist connected with the target.

"Turn it off," Leigh Baker moaned.

He turned the light off. Four seconds later he was sitting up on the edge of the bed, talking to the precinct.

"I'll patch you through," the operator said.

John Ferrara came on the line. Bursts of static alternated with bursts of apology. "She was photographing the stakeouts with a flash camera—blinding us."

Cardozo felt himself drop through slow layers of understanding. "Did her son get past?"

"She distracted me a good ten, fifteen seconds. I didn't see him, but there's a possibility."

It seemed to Cardozo that the words hung like a bad smell in the air. "Okay," he said. "Where's Xenia Delancey now?"

"Back inside. She says she's calling the police."

"Keep watching. If she comes out again, be charming." Cardozo set the receiver back in the cradle. His hands pushed him up from the bed, and the next thing he realized he was up on his feet, trying very hard to get his right foot into his right trouser leg in the dark.

The light went on again and Leigh Baker sat up from her pillow. "Vince? Why are you dressing?"

"I have to go to the precinct."

"What's happened?" She combed her hair with her hand away from her face, blinking in the soft cone of dimmed light.

How does any human being look that beautiful, Cardozo wondered, *when she's just opened her eyes?* "According to the formula, this is Society Sam's night."

"He's killed someone else?"

"Not yet, not that we know of. But Xenia Delancey spotted one of the cops on the stakeout. She went at him with a flashbulb. It may have been a diversion. Delancey could have slipped past him."

"Poor Vince. Just when you thought you'd get a little rest."

Cardozo tucked his shirt into his trousers. He hated putting on a shirt he'd worn the day before. "You know, we canceled your guard till you're due back from Paris."

"And I never went. Is that a problem?"

"Do you mind if I make another call?" He dialed Sam Richards's number. "Sam, I know it's a rotten time to call, but I need you."

"What's happening?" Sam Richards's voice said.

"Could you keep an eye on a friend of mine?"

"Now?" A little curl of disbelief to the tone.

"It's an emergency."

▪ ▪ ▪

LEIGH LOST TRACK OF TIME. She had no idea how long she'd been sitting there on the edge of the bed.

Downstairs the front doorbell chimed.

She crossed to the front of the house. She moved aside a curtain and peered down into the darkened street.

She didn't see a police car.

The doorbell chimed again.

She took the elevator down. She spoke to the front door. "Vince, is that you?"

No one answered.

She drew the belt of her robe more tightly around her. She put her face to the window and looked out. There was no one on the front stoop, no one on the sidewalk. A lone cab passed in the street with its off-duty light on.

In a moment she heard a buzz in another part of the house. The kitchen door, she realized.

She crossed the darkened dining room. She didn't turn on the lights. Lights would have been visible from the street.

She pushed through the swinging door to the pantry. There was no window, and it was pitch-black here. She turned on the light.

The sudden brightness stung her eyes. She stood blinking.

The buzz came again—nearer and sharp this time, impatient, like a message in Morse code.

The door between the kitchen and the pantry was open. She approached the darkness beyond it. She stood a moment at the threshold. She listened and watched.

Copper pots made silhouettes overhead like giant dangling leaves. At the far end of the room streetlight fell in a pale yellow slant through panes of frosted glass.

Outside, something passed through the slant. Now it blacked out the glass panel in the door. Something scratched at the doorway.

She felt along the counter. Her hand found a drawer. She pulled it open and felt inside. Her fingers fumbled through eggbeaters and whisks.

She opened the next drawer and found a poultry knife. The drawer crashed to the floor. Cutlery clattered.

The scratching stopped. After a moment it began again.

There was a click, and the kitchen door opened.

Leigh stepped backward toward the pantry. Her slipper struck a knife and sent it spinning across the tiling. She ducked into the pantry and clicked off the light.

She heard three footsteps. They had a man's weight. The street door made a firm, solid sound closing.

"Miss Baker?" The kitchen light went on. "Is anyone home?"

He must have known she was there. As he came around the corner he caught her knife hand in midmovement.

"You shouldn't have gotten off the plane without telling me." Arnie Bone lifted the poultry knife from her fist and laid it on the counter. "Do you have any idea of the trouble you've caused?"

The front doorbell chimed. She spun around and ran.

A man's arm was holding something up to the window. A shield winked gold. She threw the door open.

"Sam Richards, ma'am." His dark face was expressionless behind his gunfighter mustache. "Lieutenant Cardozo asked me to keep an eye on you."

She stood aside and gestured him to come in.

"Are you all right, ma'am?"

"No. I'm not."

She looked behind her. Arnie Bone stood at the end of the hallway, watching her.

"This man broke into the house."

"Officer, that's not exactly correct." Arnie Bone came forward.

"Could you please ask him to go?" Leigh said.

Arnie Bone handed his wallet to Sam Richards.

Sam Richards studied the color photograph on the driver's license. He flipped a thick cellophane page and studied the color photo on the guard's license. He handed the wallet back. He turned to Leigh. "This man is a licensed private guard."

"I know that," she said. "But I didn't hire a private guard, and I don't want this one."

"Waldo Carnegie hired me," Arnie Bone said. "This house is his—not hers."

Sam Richards looked from the man to the woman and back again to the man. "Did Mr. Carnegie hire you to guard the house?"

"Mr. Carnegie hired me to guard Miss Baker."

"I don't wish to be guarded," Leigh said. "Not by this man. He broke into the house. It's the second time he's almost frightened me to death."

"I didn't intend to frighten Miss Baker," Arnie Bone said. "I apologize. Mr. Carnegie gave me the keys to the back door. I rang at the front door and no one answered. I let myself in."

"Please ask him to go," Leigh said.

"Mr. Bone, your services aren't required."

Arnie Bone's eyes gave Leigh permission to drop dead. He walked to the front door.

"Just one thing," Sam Richards said. "Could I see those keys?"

Arnie Bone took a key ring from his pocket. Two bright new keys jingled.

Sam Richards lifted the key ring from Arnie Bone's hand and placed it in Leigh Baker's hand. He opened the front door. "Thank you, Mr. Bone."

Leigh watched Arnie Bone go. There was anger and stony nonacceptance in his face.

His fingers touched the brim of a nonexistent hat. "Good-bye for now, folks."

▪ FORTY-FIVE ▪

Saturday, June 8

NAN SHANE LAID THE FINAL CARD faceup on the table. "Six of cups, reversed. You have opportunities ahead. New vistas."

The waiter shook his head. "New vistas? *Again?* Send those cards back to the factory for a tune-up."

Nan cupped a hand around a yawn. "I don't think these jerks are ever going to show up." She lifted her drink, a Tequila Sunrise in a stem glass, and drained the last diluted dregs. "Do me a favor, J.J.—see if you can get me a refill?"

The thin-hipped, redheaded waiter carried Nan's glass across the softly lit interior of Tiffany lamps and red-checked tablecloths. There was practically nobody in the place.

The bartender—a young, overweight guy in shirtsleeves—wore a jowl-to-jowl frown as he polished the gleaming maple bar with slow swipes of a chamois. Nan could see him refuse to make her another drink. Hostility came off him in waves.

She gathered up her cards and shuffled them into a neat stack.

The waiter returned. "Sorry."

"Doesn't matter." Nan slipped the cards back into their box and dropped the box into her tote bag. She gave the waiter's hand a pat. "But thanks for trying."

In the corner of the bar a four-year-old with blond pigtails stood on tiptoe playing with the buttons on an old-fashioned rainbow-colored jukebox. Nan Shane snapped a finger. "Come on, Dodie. Hit the road to dreamland."

The little girl turned. She had huge eyes and pouting lips.

"No," Nan said. "Don't even ask. You've played that song enough."

Dodie didn't move.

"I said come here."

Dodie began crying.

Nan Shane had to cross the bar and take Dodie by the hand and pull her to the door. The child whined and held on to chairs and table legs. Nan kicked the door open, and Dodie's wail hit the night air like shattering glass.

"Shut up," Nan said.

Dodie didn't shut up.

There was really no decision to be made. Nan let Dodie have it across the face, outer edge of the backhand.

"And that," Nan said, "is just a warning."

Dodie was quiet now. Nan could hear the city again. Overhead, the bar's sign gave a squeak in the steamy breeze. Nan loved that sign. The owner had promised she could have it if he ever closed the bar. It was varnished driftwood, with rustic carved letters, and the letters spelled ACHILLES FOOT.

"Lady," a voice said.

Nan Shane blinked. Out of nowhere a man was coming toward her. She realized he'd been standing just beyond the circle of light that fell from the window, but standing so still that she'd mistaken him for a shadow.

"Lady, why did you hit that child?"

Why was it, Nan Shane asked herself, that everyone in New York City knew how to run a single mother's life better than she did herself? "This is my child. Thank you for your concern, but this is mother–daughter business. Please keep out of it. Come on, Dodie. Homeward-bound."

Dodie began crying again.

"Don't you know children belong to God?"

He said it so quietly, with a look of such gentleness on his face, that at first Nan registered nothing but his tone. It was the tone for saying, *What a lovely child.*

"I beg your pardon?" Nan said.

"You mustn't slap that child. God hates people who beat children."

Her head felt like a TV set that was picking up video from one channel and audio from another. What she was hearing and what she was seeing didn't go together. He was dressed in clean jogging clothes, like a stockbroker out for a late-night run, and he had a smile you'd say yes to in a minute if you met him in a bar. But what he was saying was crazy. God and hate and beating children—what kind of a conversation was that to start with a stranger at two A.M. on a New York sidewalk?

Nan Shane sensed a creepie vibe coming off this guy.

"Come on, Dodie. Beddie-bye." She reached for her daughter's hand.

But Dodie didn't move. She just stood there and stared at the man. Ever since Nan had split from Dodie's father, the girl had stared at men.

"Come *on.*" Nan gave Dodie's hand a yank. "We're going home. *Now.*"

Dodie began screaming. Nan gripped the child's hand hard and didn't let go and took off at a fast walk. She'd drunk a little more than she ought to have, and Dodie decided it would be cute to act like a deadweight, and between the booze and the brat Nan had a difficult time walking straight.

The child stumbled and fell. Wouldn't you know it, the screams got even louder. Any minute now people would be sticking their heads out the windows to see who was getting murdered.

"Will you stop play-acting?" Nan gave the girl a good hard pull to stand her up straight. "You're embarrassing me!"

"You're abusing that little girl," the man said.

Nan didn't believe it. The man was walking right alongside them, grinning, happy with himself, sure as hell happy with something. You'd have thought she'd invited him to walk her home and stop up for a drink.

"Will you do me a favor and get lost?" she said.

He was not one to take a hint.

Nan glanced up and down the street. A taxi with its off-duty light on had passed them and was waiting at a red light two blocks north. Except for parked cars and that one taxi, Third Avenue was empty.

"You don't deserve a child," the man said.

"What I don't deserve at two o'clock in the morning is *you,* you goddamn creep. So fuck off before I call a cop."

"You don't deserve anyone."

"You want me to scream? Because my kid gets it from me. I taught her how." Speaking of which, Nan brought the flat of her hand down sharp on Dodie's skull. "Shut up, the both of you!"

"You're a monster, and I'm not going to let you abuse that little girl anymore."

Nan stopped and whirled to face him, so angry now that she could see her own spittle fly. "You want to adopt a kid, go to Family Services. This one's mine—so butt out, asshole!"

That did it. There was a startle reflex in his eyes. He fell back a step.

Nan Shane grabbed Dodie's hand tight. "Come on, kid, move it. He's a weirdo."

Nan began running.

But suddenly it felt all wrong.

Her feet were running in a dream, getting nowhere. Something was holding her from behind. A mirror flashed in front of her eyes, left to right. A burn went across her throat. The mirror flashed again, going the other way, and then she felt a hot stinging dampness burst under her chin.

Pink was spraying in front of her, and Dodie was looking up at her, wide-eyed. The child's face was nothing but a baby-toothed shrieking hole, and blood was flying, like the time Nan's Aunt Mattie put a finger in the blender to unstick the Bloody Mary mix.

Then gravity kicked in, and Nan hit the sidewalk in a tangle of arms and shawl and necklace and legs and skirt.

And then the pain in her stomach began.

▪ FORTY-SIX ▪

AT THREE-EIGHTEEN THAT MORNING the phone in Cardozo's office finally rang.

"Vince Cardozo."

"Looks like we got another," the night operator said. "Officer reports a dead woman on Third and Seventy-seventh, southwest corner."

▪ ▪ ▪

SHE STARED AT CARDOZO with wide-open, startled eyes. Her legs were drawn up to the side and halfway under her. Her head lay back, touching the pavement. The position drew her neck out taut and separated the lips of the two dark slashes that *x*'ed her throat.

Cardozo stood a long, considering moment, returning her stare.

"Any ID?" he asked the sergeant who had been the first officer on the scene.

"Full purse," the sergeant said. "Driver's license, charge cards, housekeys, seventy-three cents."

"Seventy-three cents? That's all?"

The sergeant nodded.

"What's her name?" Cardozo asked.

"Nan Shane. She lived on Seventy-seventh."

"So he hit her three blocks from home." Cardozo crouched down beside Nan Shane.

Beneath the heavy makeup, her face was bloated and pale. The skin around her startlingly blue eyes was puffed up and purplish as if she'd had some kind of allergy. Her long blond hair had roots going gray at the temples.

The only distinguishing marks on Nan Shane had been put there by her killer.

Cardozo rose, stepping out of her gaze, and moved to the curb. He glanced at the trash basket, full to overflowing with newspapers, food wrappers, soda cans. The cans were a good sign. They meant that the five-cent-deposit scavengers had not yet been through the basket.

A crime-scene technician was fencing off the murder perimeter with strips of orange tape. Cardozo called to him. "Bag the contents of this trash can, will you?"

Cardozo stepped into the street. He stood with his back to the corpse. Overhead, the sky was beginning to lighten, but down here the last of night was clinging to the streets. His gaze panned from left to right, trying to see what she had seen, what she hadn't seen, and noticing the windows from which someone else might have seen her.

"Any witnesses?" Cardozo asked the sergeant.

The sergeant shook his head.

"Who called the cops?"

"Jonathan Feuerstein." The sergeant nodded. Ten feet away, under a boutique-and-card-shop awning, a gangly skinhead in a sleeveless denim jacket stood nervously smoking a cigarette. A little girl in toddler's jeans and a striped blue shirt stood clutching the skinhead's leg. She wore her blond hair in braids, and she couldn't have been more than four years old.

Cardozo went over and introduced himself. "Hi, Jonathan. Can I call you Jonathan?"

"Why not? That's my name."

"Hi, sweetie." Cardozo bent down to tickle the little girl under her chin. She rewarded him with a silent, freckled frown. Cardozo asked Jonathan how he'd happened to find the dead woman.

"I came around the corner, she was lying there." Jonathan spoke with the almost toneless rasp of a two-pack-a-day man. He had wary eyes the color of soapstone, and a small vampire's-bite tattoo on his throat, and tension lines played permanent tic-tac-toe across his forehead. "I went over, I spoke to her, she didn't answer, I gave her shoulder a push—"

"A push with your foot?"

Jonathan looked shocked. "I bent down. I pushed with my hand. You don't push a lady with your foot."

"I'm glad to hear it."

"I lifted her hand to feel for a pulse, and there wasn't any."

"Are you a doctor?"

"No. Do I have to be a doctor to lift a woman's hand who's bleeding in the street and needs help?"

Christ, Cardozo thought, *why am I trying to argue with this guy? Because I was beeped out of a bed I was sharing with the most beautiful woman I've ever known?* "Absolutely not."

"I saw she was dead, and I went to that pay phone." Jonathan nodded toward the pay phone halfway up the block. "I called nine-one-one and they told me to wait and in a couple of hours you guys finally got here."

"What were you doing out at this hour, Jonathan?"

"What am I, trying to be helpful and that makes me a suspect?"

"We just need the details. Details help fill in the picture."

An ambulance sped up Third Avenue, siren screaming.

"I work nights at the Carnation Deli down on Second. I always buy an early-edition *Post* from the newsstand three blocks up. Ask them, they know me."

"Coming up from Second, which street did you take?"

"Seventy-fourth. I always take Seventy-fourth."

"Why?"

"It's the cleanest block. Why walk through shit?"

"Who did you pass tonight coming from work?"

"No one. The sidewalk was dead. Like it is now."

"How was the traffic?"

"Very light. Maybe one cruising taxi."

"Were these parked cars all here?"

Jonathan nodded.

"Any parked cars gone now that were here then?"

Jonathan shook his head.

"Did you see anyone who might have been a witness? Anyone in a car, in a window, anyone passing or loitering or just standing or taking a piss against a wall?"

"Well, I wouldn't be surprised if the kid saw it."

"The kid."

Jonathan pointed a finger straight down. *"This* kid."

"She isn't yours?"

Jonathan shook his head, an emphatic *no.* "She was standing right over there."

He nodded toward the building. There was an ornamental but otherwise useless hollow in the wall, as though a door had been bricked up, and there was an ornamental but otherwise useless step leading up to it.

"Alone?" Cardozo said.

Jonathan nodded.

"Does she talk?"

"Not to me she doesn't."

Cardozo crouched down again. He touched the girl's cheek. "Hi, honey. My name's Vince. What's yours?"

She wouldn't look at him.

Cardozo smoothed a wisp of blond hair away from the child's eyes. "What kind of candy do you like, honey? You like chocolate? You want a Hershey's?"

Without looking at him, the little girl nodded.

Cardozo shouted to the officer. "Hey, Sarge, can you get a Hershey bar from the newsstand? Get a dozen. Candy for everyone." He lifted the child's chin. "Did you see what happened? Can you tell me what happened to the lady?"

The girl didn't answer. She put a thumb in her mouth.

"Do you know that lady? Can you tell me who she is?"

The girl began sniffling.

"Is that lady your mommy? Is that your mommy over there? Is that who she is? Mommy?"

The girl nodded. Her eyes glistened and silent tears began rolling down her freckled cheeks. And then the freckles began rolling down her cheeks.

Cardozo touched one of the freckles. It came off on his finger. He studied the fingertip. He took a second look at the little girl's face and hair and arms and shirt.

Poor kid. She must have seen it all. She was covered in her mom's blood.

▪ ▪ ▪

THE WALLS WERE PAINTED flat landlord-white. There were kick marks on the baseboard, most of them near the bathroom door. Faint partial prints of small hands ran around the walls up to a height of four feet.

The furnishings struck Cardozo as pathetic: a futon mattress on the floor, a twenty-inch Sony Trinitron with remote, a six-foot avocado tree growing out of a copper tub on the floor that Nan Shane had probably nursed to maturity from the leftover pit of a salad avocado.

Greg Monteleone was standing in the kitchen alcove in front of the open refrigerator, searching through half-empty jars of

Hellmann's Real Mayonnaise. Nan Shane had amassed over twenty.

"Nan never finished eating anything," Monteleone said.

"New York career women live on the run," Cardozo said.

"Want to take a guess what Nan Shane did for a career?" Monteleone was examining a half-empty carton of La Yogurt raspberry yogurt. "She read society Tarots."

"So? Tarot readers live on the run." Cardozo studied the bamboo étagère that stood against an empty wall. Several of the open shelves held bric-a-brac, and the others served as a bookcase. He could see no order to Nan Shane's books—biographies of Marie of Rumania were crammed between thrillers and studies of parapsychology.

Holding up one end of the row of books was an Aleister Crowley Tarot set. The Tarot box opened like a videocassette case. Inside a hollowed-out plastic nest Cardozo found a how-to paperback, with Nan Shane's own color-coded underlinings, and a deck of cards with illustrations of heavy-metal sorcerers, warrior women, and dragons.

Cardozo dropped the Tarot how-to book into an evidence bag.

On the floor beside the étagère was a wicker hamper, the kind a family of four might have taken on a picnic in the country in 1903. Cardozo lifted the lid. The hamper contained children's toys—dolls, animals, coloring books—most of them torn and battered. There was a color-coded miniature xylophone with soft mallets and a one-octave range.

"You haven't seen her phone book anywhere, have you?"

"Over there." Monteleone nodded to where the avocado-green touch-tone phone sat on the floor on a stack of Nynex directories.

Cardozo glanced through Nan Shane's Manhattan directory to see if she'd written any most-called numbers in the margins or on the most-called page. "What about Shane's address book?"

"Haven't seen it. Try the closet—I haven't been in there yet."

The clothes closet was the sort of walk-in you couldn't walk into anymore. Shelves and drawers took up half the space; dresses, skirts, and jackets, all on hangers and stored in their plastic dry-cleaner's bags, were jammed into the other half. A raincoat hung from a red plastic hook that had been epoxied to the inside of the door.

Cardozo went through the drawers: the top seven were

women's things: beads and belts and imitation jewelry in the uppermost; designer scarves in the next; sweaters and underclothes in the rest. There was no address book, but under a pile of lace-fringed panties he found Nan Shane's passport.

He flipped it open. The passport had been issued two years ago. Ms. Shane grinned out at him from a color photo in a blouse cut so low that none of it showed in the picture, and she looked like a topless waitress nearing mandatory retirement.

He flipped to the visas and counted ten pages of entries into and exits from El Salvador. "Hey, Greg—what do you think of a society Tarot reader who takes thirty-one trips to El Salvador in twenty-three months for an average stay of two days each?"

Greg Monteleone's eyebrows went up. "She either loves the place or she has business down there."

"Tell me honestly, who have you ever heard of that loved El Salvador?" Cardozo dropped the passport into an evidence bag.

He returned to the closet and searched the four bottom drawers. They held clothes for a four-year-old girl. He searched the pockets of the clothes on hangers; he found eight restaurant matchbooks and bagged them.

He wondered if maybe she had an extension in the bathroom and kept her address book in there. He opened the bathroom door and flicked on the light switch.

Plenty of shelves but no phone.

Rubber Donald Duck decals had been glued to the floor of the tub, and extra shelves had been hung from the walls of the stall for soaps and bath toys. Cardozo sniffed the containers of liquid soap and body moisturizer and stuck his ballpoint pen down through the gook in each, probing to see if she'd hidden anything. She hadn't.

The sink was clean. No drips under the soap dish and no drips under the toothbrush holder with its two toothbrushes, one adult-sized and one child-sized.

The medicine cabinet seemed standard: three brands of toothpaste, prescription tranquilizers, children's aspirin, over-the-counter sleeping pills, feminine-hygiene basics, first-aid stuff.

Cardozo lifted the toilet seat. The toilet bowl was clean, the water an inky blue from some kind of thousand-flush bowl cleaner.

The built-in hamper was filled to the halfway point with towels, underwear, children's clothes.

There was something underneath the pink bathmat, rippling it. Cardozo crouched and turned the mat over and found a dog's leash coiled on the tiles. One end was fastened with a slip-choke around the sink stand. The other was a padded halter with a label from a shop called Togs-4-Tots.

Without unhooking it, Cardozo walked the halter back into the main room. It allowed a radius of five feet of maneuverability: enough to reach the toy chest, the futon, the TV—but not the window or the phone or the stove. "I take it Ms. Shane was a single mother?"

"No one ever heard of a Mr. Shane."

"How did she treat her daughter?"

Greg Monteleone shrugged. "No one heard the kid scream."

"Did anyone ever hear her laugh?"

"Vince, this building has very thick walls."

Cardozo waved the halter. "Nan Shane's day care. She used it on the kid."

"Get out of here." Monteleone had found an eight-ounce can of GNC protein-supplement powder in the freezer. He popped the plastic lid off. "Oh boy oh boy, what some people won't do for fast energy." He held out the can.

Cardozo looked. The can was a quarter full of loosely packed white powder. He licked the tip of his forefinger, touched it to the powder, tasted. He whistled.

"Those trips to El Salvador were definitely tax-deductible," Greg said.

"Or she had a nasty habit. Or both." Greg slid out the shelf beneath the freezer compartment. "Vince. This what you're looking for?"

A small leather booklet lay between the frozen peas and the loose ice cubes. The cover was initialed N.S., and it had deep fray marks along the edges.

Greg Monteleone popped the booklet loose and handed it to Cardozo. The pages were interlarded with chits of paper that poked out like two dozen place markers.

"What do you bet she was dealing too?" Greg said.

Cardozo shook his head. "If she lived like this place looks, she must have been the worst-paid dealer in the city."

"The doorman says she hung out at a Third Avenue bar."

"Dealing?"

"He didn't exactly say dealing. But he didn't exactly say not dealing. She did Tarot readings for the customers."

"What's the name of this bar?"

▪ FORTY-SEVEN ▪

CARDOZO WALKED OVER to the end of the bar where the lone woman customer wasn't and pulled out a stool. While he waited for the bartender he looked around at the almost empty table area and saw three customers sitting alone with their morning drinks at separate tables.

A mirrored wall gave the impression of doubling the space and the population. In the reflection the gold saloon-style lettering in the window that spelled *Achilles Foot* came out unreversed.

The bartender rang up a sale. The mirrored cash register tinkled and zinged and threw a splash of light across his dazzling electric-blue silk shirt. As he came toward Cardozo a gold chain twinkled in the chest hairs of his open collar. His smile telegraphed a synthetic good mood. "Hi, what'll it be?"

"How about a diet cola?"

The bartender was a thick-featured, fat guy in his late twenties. "Coming up."

He brought the drink, and Cardozo laid his shield on the bar.

"Who was tending bar when you closed this morning?"

"Me." The bartender held out a hand. "Yip Guardella. Good to meet you."

"I'd like to ask you some questions about Nan Shane."

Yip Guardella shook his head, sending a wave through his expensively layer-cut dark hair. "This city is going to hell."

"How long did Shane spend here yesterday?"

"On my shift? Oh, she showed up around midnight and stayed till around two, two-thirty this morning."

"Why so long?"

"She was doing good business."

"And what kind of business was that?"

"She did Tarot readings for the customers. She was sort of a tradition here—going back six or seven years."

"How well did you know her?"

"Me?"

The corners of Yip Guardella's mouth began to sneak up into a grin, slowly disclosing well-tended white teeth. He had a dimple smack in the center of his chin, and Cardozo had a hunch that that dimple made him feel he was the sexiest devil this side of Chippendale's.

"I knew her to say hello to, shoot the breeze, you know, nothing deep, nothing special."

"Did she ever talk to you about her personal life?"

"Not to me."

Cardozo let his eyebrows say it: *What do you mean, a slick stud like you?*

Yip Guardella got the message and shot back a crinkled grin. "We made it once or twice, you know, but it wasn't a talk relationship."

Cardozo nodded. "Did she ever mention other boyfriends, business associates, social acquaintances?"

"Not to me."

"Would you know of anyone who might have had a reason to hurt her?"

"Absolutely no way. Nan was the sweetest bar nun."

It took Cardozo a moment to realize that Yip had said that Nan was the sweetest, bar none.

The woman customer stretched her Where-is-Josef-Stalin-now-that-we-need-him T-shirt tight across heavy, braless breasts. "I'm out of quarters, Yip—could you beam me a cut?"

Guardella zinged the cash register open and scrounged in the change drawer. He found what looked like the remote control of a TV set and aimed it at the jukebox. "You're on, Mandy."

"You're a *vraie poupée.*" The woman pushed back her shoulders and crossed to the jukebox and jabbed three buttons. A spinning compact disc threw off fractured rainbows and a synthesized machine-drum–backed rap number began pounding from the speaker:

Nickel-dimin' two-bit pipsqueak squirt,
Bleedin' Thursday blood on your Tuesday shirt—

Cardozo glanced toward the jukebox. "Is that song popular?"

"Number three this week," Yip Guardella said.

Cardozo suppressed a shudder. He laid a photograph and an Identi-Kit drawing side by side on the bar top. "Did you happen to see either of these guys last night?"

"At the bar?" Yip Guardella studied the photo. He studied the drawing.

A change came over him. Cardozo could see his eyes stop and skip back and stop again.

Yip pursed his lips till they resembled a guppy's. "No, not last night."

> *Spilled a pint of plasma and you still don't hurt,*
> *'Cause your head's in the heart of the hallelujah dirt*

"Have you ever seen them?"

"This one, no." Yip Guardella pushed the Identi-Kit back toward Cardozo. "This one . . ." His fingers drummed a nervous rhythm on Jim Delancey's head. "He was in the papers a lot, four years ago."

"He's been in the papers a lot lately too. You recognize him?"

"Jim Delancey. He killed that movie actress's daughter, right?"

"Right."

> *Hallelujah dirt that'll do ya*
> *That'll do ya dirt hallelujah dirt.*

"Wasn't there a kid with Nan?" Cardozo said.

Yip's face whitened. "A kid?"

"Her four-year-old daughter?"

"You kidding?" Yip Guardella's reaction was mostly in the eyebrows. "If we let kids that young in here, we'd lose our license. They have to at least look within striking distance of twenty-one."

"Was anyone besides you here when Nan Shane left this morning?"

Yip Guardella folded heavy arms across his chest. "The crowd had pretty well thinned out—in fact, now that I think of it, they'd all gone home. She was the last customer."

The door to Third Avenue swung open and a thin, red-haired young man wearing designer janitor's overalls sauntered in. "Hi, Yip." He gave a wave and crossed to the men's room.

Yip waved back.

"Who's that?" Cardozo said.

"That's J.J." A fine line of sweat was trickling down from Yip's hairline across his forehead. "He waits tables."

■ ■ ■

CARDOZO SWUNG THE MEN'S ROOM DOOR OPEN and stepped into heavily camphorated air. "Hey, J.J. I need to talk to you."

The young man stood bent over a cold-water-only sink, rinsing his hands. He looked over his shoulder at Cardozo's shield.

"When did you see Nan Shane last?"

J.J. straightened. He turned. He left the water running. "Around two, two-thirty this morning." He dried his hands on a filthy-looking continuous roll of cotton towel. "What's happened?"

"Bad news. Nan was killed on her way home."

J.J.'s jaw dropped. He stared at Cardozo from under a cliff of curly red hair that badly needed a trim.

"I take it you two were friends?" Cardozo said.

J.J. stood there pushing out shock. "Not good friends, but I liked her."

"I'm sorry." Cardozo handed J.J. the Identi-Kit. "Did you happen to see this man last night?"

"No."

"Ever see him?"

"No."

Cardozo handed J.J. the photo of Delancey. "Him?"

"Not last night."

"Ever see him?"

"Sure."

"Know him?"

"Not personally—and I wouldn't want to."

"Why not?"

"He's noisy. Makes too much of a fuss."

"Know who he is?"

"Not by name. He's a friend of Yip's."

"You've seen him with Yip?"

"Sure."

"When was this?"

"Oh, the last time was . . . about four weeks ago."

"Happen to remember the day?"

"It was a Wednesday. Lunch hour."

■ ■ ■

"VINCE CARDOZO?"

Cardozo stopped to see who on the crowded Third Avenue sidewalk had called to him.

A woman was prying her way through the jostling crowd, and the jeweled forearm she was using as a crowbar remained outstretched, offering a handshake. "Nancy Guardella, U.S. Senate."

It took Cardozo an instant to recognize her, chiefly because her jaw was far stronger than in her photos. She had gray hair that had been dyed somebody's idea of blue, and her makeup looked as though it was designed to show up on TV and to hell with how it looked in real life.

"You were in the bar talking to my son Yip, am I right? I'm sure he talked your ear off—but could you give me a minute so I can put in my two bits?"

Now this is interesting, Cardozo was thinking. "Senator Guardella, how do you know my name?"

"How do I know your name? You're running the Society Sam task force—you're a media presence."

"Were you, by any chance, waiting for me just now?"

"I sure was." Facing him in heels that exactly matched her pink-and-beige suit, she stood an extremely heavy five eight, and something in the way she held her weight at the ready suggested a particularly grumpy chow chow. "Let me give you a lift. Which way are you going?"

"Seventy-first and Park."

She steered him toward the curb. A white stretch limo with diplomat's plates was idling in the space reserved for express busses. Cardozo half expected a liveried chauffeur to dash around the gleaming hood and open the passenger door, but Senator Guardella opened it herself. She motioned Cardozo to hop in and slid in behind him.

The backseat came equipped with TV and a bar heavily stocked with up-market labels. The cooled air was saturated in musk potpourri.

"Leo," Mrs. Guardella said to the back of the driver's head, "Seventy-first and Park and take your time." She turned. "Okay, Vince. Cards on the table. You may not know that I'm chairman of the oversight committee of the DEA. Not that it's a secret."

Cardozo nodded. The DEA—Drug Enforcement Agency— was one of the fastest-growing federal agencies; a lot of taxpayer dollars were flowing their way, and it made sense that they'd need an oversight committee.

"The reason I'm here is, I saw the Shane thing on TV. I knew Yip would be questioned. Now, there's something you have to know, and this *is* secret." Nancy Guardella pressed a button on a remote control. A tinted glass partition rose between the seats. She sat back and smiled at Cardozo. The limo eased into traffic. "Achilles Foot is ours," she said.

Cardozo turned. *"Ours?"*

"It's a front. A sting operation."

Cardozo sat letting his mind comb through the implications.

"Unfortunately," Nancy Guardella said, "the agency is fighting other agencies for a slice of a shrinking budgetary pie. Agencies are not above sabotaging one another. You may remember a big to-do five years ago—my son Yip was accused of dealing coke at Princeton?"

"I do remember."

"Okay, Yip is a normal guy with normal curiosity. Yes, he experimented with drugs, like ninety percent of his Princeton classmates. But because his name was Guardella, the New Jersey cops set him up and busted him."

Cardozo remembered the incident, though not with quite the entrapment spin Nancy Guardella was putting on it.

"A lot of people would like to embarrass the agency and embarrass me. They'd like to see our bust-and-conviction rate brought down. Not to sound my own trumpet, Vince, but we make the other agencies look worse than sick. They look terminal."

"Are you telling me your son's an agent?"

"He's not listed on any roster, if that's what you're asking. But sure—he works for us."

"And Nan Shane?"

"One of our best. She'll be missed. I understand you have to investigate her death the same as any other homicide, but you also have a right to know the background. And to know it off the bat, without any futzing about clearance."

"I appreciate your help," Cardozo said.

Nancy Guardella handed him a business card from her purse. There were five extensions listed. "Call me if I can help with anything."

The driver pulled over to the curb. When the limo stopped, Nancy Guardella looked out the window. "Say, this is the building where Annie MacAdam lives. You know Annie?"

Cardozo set one foot outside the limo. "I've met her."

"If you see her, tell her hello for me. And let's do this again soon."

■ ■ ■

THEY WERE SITTING ON FACING SOFAS in Annie MacAdam's living room. Awnings on the terrace had been pulled to shade the French windows, and a cool, trembling green-washed light filtered indoors.

"Her name was Nan Shane," Cardozo said. "Your name is in her address book."

"Christ. Poor Nan." There were thought lines around Annie MacAdam's eyes. She was wearing a Coca-Cola–logo white satin blouse with silver sequin embroidery and over it a big-shouldered, gold-brocade jacket. She adjusted a sleeve.

"Any chance Nan Shane was here at your Princess Margaret dinner?"

"You have my word that Nan Shane was never a dinner guest in this house."

"Let's just double-check and look at the guest list for that night."

They went to the library. Annie MacAdam handed Cardozo the loose-leaf binder for April, May, June of 1985.

Cardozo found the ten-table seating plan for May sixth and the list of seventy-nine guests. The name *Shane* did not appear on either.

"We really weren't at all the same world," Annie MacAdam said. "In fact, I'm just a little bit ashamed of my relationship with her. At the time we met I needed information. We struck a deal." She lit a cigarette and blew smoke toward the ceiling. "I know this sounds venal as hell—but Nan Shane gave me insider intelligence when her building was going co-op. She did Tarot readings for a living, and in exchange, I let her bring her cards to my parties— after dinner, with coffee. People turned to her when their buildings went co-op. They wanted readings to tell them whether or not to buy. In time she came to know a great deal about a great many buildings."

"It sounds as though you and Nan Shane became fairly useful to each other."

Annie MacAdam seemed to blush beneath her powder. "I didn't have the heart to turn her away. She was having a hard time these last two years."

"In what way?"

"She kept wearing the same four gowns—a rose Givenchy

knockoff, a kelly-green Scaasi, a Mary MacFadden cocktail thing—
black silk, a little too basic—and a divine blue de la Renta that
looked genuine, though even in a thrift shop it would have cost six
thousand. I don't think Ms. Shane had a head for money."

"Do you know for a fact she was having money problems?"

"I really know nothing about her. As I said, we were very
different worlds."

"Could she have been here at your party six years ago—
reading Tarots?"

"It's very possible."

"Some of the guests might remember," Cardozo said.

"I'm sure some of the men would remember very clearly."

·FORTY-EIGHT·

"OH, NO!" Shock hung in the air three feet in front of Dick Braidy's face. "That poor woman. That poor, *poor* woman."

"How well did you know her?" Cardozo said.

"I didn't know her at all well. I saw her more as a type than as an individual. To me, Nan Shane was a New York tragedy long before she was murdered."

"Why do you say that?"

"It was the old story: She wanted a great deal, she could afford very little. This town does that to so many young men and women. And so many not-so-young."

In the living room windows behind Dick Braidy, curtains moved softly in the air-conditioned breeze.

On the end table beside the sofa, a scented blue candle burned in a small silver dish. Incandescent particles whirled upward through the tiny halo of light.

"You'd see her at parties. Always wearing that same de la Renta cocktail number. Poor thing, she was caught between two worlds. Too useful to invite as a guest—and too useless to hire as a servant. She generally appeared as designated fortune-teller, just around the time the after-dinner liqueurs came out. She'd smile and spread her cards and predict sweet generalities—and ask for a twenty-five-dollar tip."

"That's how she made her living?"

"There was a rumor that she had a sideline. I hate to speak ill of the dead. But you heard it so much, you had to wonder. Why were people *always* whispering that Nan Shane was a dope courier?"

"Maybe because she was."

"I have no idea. Personally, I never required her services—for anything."

"The night of May sixth, nineteen eighty-five—the night you described in 'Socialites in Emergency'—do you recall if Nan Shane joined your table at dinner?"

A moment went by and then Dick Braidy nodded.

"I seem to recall she did. Sorella Chappell was feeling insecure about some job or other for the British royal family, and Nan swore it would come through. Nan's forecasts tended to be the kiss of death, so needless to say, it did *not.*"

"And afterward—did she go to the hospital with you?"

"Nan *Shane*? Leave before she'd worked every room in the apartment? No *way.*"

■　■　■

"WHAT WE'RE LOOKING AT," Dan Hippolito said, "is a physical impossibility."

He dealt the glossies out one by one on his desktop, turned so Cardozo could see them headup. They lay there like a gruesome, oversized hand of solitaire: Oona, Avalon, and Nan.

"Missing tissue," Dan said, "is very, very rare in stab wounds. With bullets, with bombs, with speeding cars, yes—it's in the nature of high-velocity impacts that flesh gets severed from the victim and scatters. Even with a rotary saw you see a little scatter, a little loss. But with a knife?"

Cardozo's eyes slowly scanned the photos, comparing. In the preautopsy shots, the victims had been stripped and washed. No dried blood obscured the killer's artwork. Each abdomen showed deep-lipped horizontal slashes and rat-a-tat punctures. In places the killer's blade had opened the intestine.

In the postautopsy shots, the wounds puckered like the drawn purse strings of a miser's moneybag.

"I reviewed over two hundred lethal stabbings in the last quarter," Dan said. "Not one single instance of tissue missing. So I had to wonder. Why this particular tissue? It didn't seem to be especially meaningful tissue. We're talking microscopic bits of abdominal skin and fat and muscle. Who would want them? No one. Why would he take them? No reason. So why are they missing?"

Viewed chronologically, from Oona to Nan, the photos showed a progression. Cardozo could clearly see the killer's hand becoming surer, the horizontal slashes becoming more nearly parallel, more nearly aligned and equal. The photos could have been sketches of a corporate logo struggling to find that final, instantly recognizable image.

"I gave this a lot of thought," Dan said. "It took me till yesterday to find the answer. In fact, you might say the answer found me."

He took a small copper watering can from his desk and leaned in his swivel chair to tip water at a thirsty-looking philodendron.

"My wife and I were having dinner at a friend's home, and the lady of the house is a terrific cook. Last night we had tournedos—you ever had tournedos?"

Cardozo shook his head. "Haute cuisine isn't my thing, Dan. Offhand I couldn't say."

"It's a filet of beef. The usual way to fix it is tournedos Rossini, dark sauce and marrow. Now, the marrow that my friend's wife put in the center of each tournedos was shaped like an ace of spades. Sitting right there on the beef, this little ace of spades. How did she do that? I wondered. So I asked. So she told me. A cookie cutter."

Dan Hippolito gave Cardozo a careful, level look.

"That's when it hit me. It wasn't Sam *trying* to take these microscopic bits of flesh, it was his weapon that couldn't *help* taking them. He was using the equivalent of a cookie cutter to slash his victims." Dan Hippolito leaned forward. "It's called a Darby blade. Invented, strangely enough, by a man called Darby. Which is all I know about Mr. Darby. The interesting thing about the Darby is, the blade starts with a point, but as you travel down to the hilt, the cross section becomes triangular. Why triangular, you ask."

Dan Hippolito took a piece of scratch paper.

"Here's your traditional cut with a two-edged blade."

He drew an up-and-down line on the paper.

"Withdraw the knife and the flesh readheres to itself, because this side of the cut"—the tip of his pen tapped both sides of the line—"comes back into contact with this side of the cut. This process is called healing. But with the Darby there can't be any healing."

Dan Hippolito drew a small triangle, a quarter inch on each side.

"Withdraw the knife and the flesh can't readhere to itself, because this side of the wound"—the pen tapped the three sides of the triangle—"doesn't touch this side or this side. As a result the wound never closes, it never heals. Now, who would want such a weapon? An army fighting a guerrilla war. Which army? The U.S. army."

"This thing *exists*?"

"It used to exist. We used it in Vietnam."

"Then there are still some of them around."

Dan Hippolito rotated his swivel chair and reached for the coffeepot. He refilled Cardozo's cup and then his own. "We know for a fact there's at least one Darby still around—and Society Sam's got it."

Cardozo sat tapping his fingers on his knee.

"Vince, I was a medic in that war. I had to ship boys to Japan who had cut themselves with their own Darbys. There was no way you could stitch a Darby wound in the field. The only reason we can stitch *these* people is, they're dead. I could not be more positive. What we are seeing here is Darby work."

"Okay, if you're positive, then I am. The killer used a Darby blade on the three victims. Now what about the rest of the MO? Was there semen in Nan Shane's mouth?"

"Didn't I say classic MO?"

"Pubic hairs in the mouth?"

"This time three. The lab's taking a look. You should have the results tomorrow."

■ ■ ■

CARDOZO CALLED Sam Richards into his cubicle.

"Sam, you fought in Vietnam."

There was a flick of wariness in Sam Richards's eyes, like that reflexive drawing back when a hand slaps you in the face. "I saw a little of it."

"Did you ever run into a Darby blade?" Cardozo said.

Richards gave him a sideways look, as though he had to be crazy. "If I'd ever run into a Darby, I wouldn't be standing here."

"Then I take it you saw what a Darby could do."

"I saw one or two cases."

Cardozo laid three glossies out on his desk. *Oona. Avalon. Nan.* Preautopsy but tidied up. "We think these might be Darbys."

Richards blinked. "I never saw a Darby do this."

"So what did it?"

"Don't get me wrong, Vince. A Darby could do this, easily. But over there Darbys were used in guerrilla combat, hand-to-hand. They were for fast, serious killing, not for drawing pictures."

"You think Society Sam is drawing pictures?"

"I don't know what he's doing, but I can tell you what he's *not* doing. He's not improvising. He's not making it up as he goes along. These cuts aren't random, they're not accidental. The similarities are too strong—the parallel horizontal lines, the dots. They're intentional."

"What do they mean to you?"

"To me they mean these were three very unlucky people." Richards's forefinger tapped Oona's puncture wounds. "Now, this is the kind of work the Darby was made for. Jab it in, pull it out. It really wasn't designed for these long cuts or slicing. I'm surprised it's Society Sam's weapon of choice."

"How old would he have to be to have used it in Vietnam?"

"My age. Or older. And appearances to the contrary, I'm no kid."

Cardozo frowned. "Was the Darby standard issue over there?"

"The elite units had them. The marines, the Green Berets."

"How many of them are still in circulation?"

"I haven't seen any since the war. They don't turn up on the street. But they must exist somewhere. They have a rarity value, like gold dollars."

"Let's find out who's making them, who's dealing them, who's buying them."

"I can check into it. I'll have to go through the Pentagon. It could take a while."

"Okay, take a while—but find out by tomorrow."

Sam Richards gave him a friendly finger.

■ ■ ■

THERE WAS A KNOCK and the cubicle door opened. Noise floated in from the squad room, followed by Ellie Siegel. She looked cool and unharried in a dress that had the color of the glow on a twilight beach.

Slanting back in his swivel chair, legs stretched out, and one foot crossed cowboy-fashion over the other, Cardozo set his lips in a thin line of annoyance.

Ellie picked up a photo, frowned at it, tossed it back onto the desk. "So . . . Sam did Shane too. Don't tell me it's a surprise."

"Nothing's a surprise."

"So what's bothering you?"

"I've been sitting here trying to figure out, when you're talking to the wall, do you call it Mr. or Mrs. Wall?"

"Don't talk to a wall you haven't been introduced to. Talk to me instead."

"You wouldn't be interested."

"Neither would the wall. Come on."

Cardozo sighed and sat there, two fingers tapping paradiddles on the edge of the desk. "How long have we been watching Delancey?"

"Over four weeks now."

"How many man-hours, how many dollars have we spent?"

"I don't know. Enough to retire on."

"And every time Sam hits, something screws up the tail. Four weeks of watching the guy and it's useless—we still don't know where the hell he is when the killing goes down."

"So? Accidents happen. Nobody's perfect. The best-laid plans. We'll clean up our act."

"Excuse me. I wasn't quite accurate. Wednesday, May eighth, Jim Delancey disappears from work for over an hour. During that hour Oona Aldrich is killed. Where's Delancey? Today a witness turns up, says he saw Delancey at Achilles Foot up on Third Avenue."

"During that same hour?"

"During that very same hour."

"So Delancey has an alibi."

"He didn't *use* the alibi. He did just the opposite—he hid it from us." Cardozo got up and paced to the window. He punched a button on the air conditioner. The compressor labored to life, pulling down the wattage in the desk lamp, kicking out a cycle of gasps and clanks. "I thought I had a handle on this case—but it's falling apart."

"Vince, you're a big baby." Ellie neatened a stack of papers on the desk. "Nothing's falling apart except your housekeeping."

"Nan Shane didn't testify for Nita Kohler. She didn't eat at table eight at Annie MacAdam's. She didn't go to the Emergency Room. She wasn't even part of a social group. She was a hanger-on. Why's she dead?"

"She's dead because Society Sam drew crisscrosses all over her with a pointed instrument."

"There was no *reason* for him to pick her."

"Vince. If there was a reason for the others, there was a reason for Nan. Count on it." Ellie adjusted the hang of her dress. "I've been wondering about Nan myself. Matter of fact, I checked to see if she had an arrest sheet."

"And?"

Ellie beckoned. "This way, please."

Cardozo followed her into the squad room.

At the moment the squad's one computer was unattended. Ellie seated herself at the terminal and booted the computer. Something inside it made a sound like teeth coming down on a spoonful of chipped ice. Her fingers clicked rapidly over the keyboard, typing the word *finest.*

"Where did you learn to work one of these things?"

"Four nights at the New School. Essential Computer Literacy. The department paid. You could have learned too, Vince."

A message appeared on the screen: WELCOME TO FINEST.

"Do these machines always say welcome?"

"If they've got any manners." Now the computer offered a menu of choices. Ellie selected *criminal records.*

The computer asked for her ID. She typed in *Reilly.*

"You're not Reilly," Cardozo said.

"Don't tell the computer."

A river of amber print flowed across the screen. Ellie pushed two keys, and the river widened into a screen-filling ocean.

Cardozo hunched down and squinted.

"Can you read it?" Ellie said. *"Arrest March twenty-seven. Possession one-half-ounce cocaine. Attempted sale to undercover agent. Arresting officer: Det. Robert Q. O'Rourke, Narcotics South. Arraigned March twenty-seven. Bail five thousand. Hearing set June twenty-five."*

Cardozo did not speak. He just stared at the screen.

"Is one of you Vincent Cardozo?" A young man in need of a shave stood in the corridor. His T-shirt bore the sweat-soaked logo All Day–All Night Messengers.

"That's right," Cardozo said, "and no prize for guessing which one."

The messenger handed him a package the size of a VCR cassette. Cardozo glanced at the return address and saw that the sender's name was Baker.

"You guys really live up to the all-day-all-night name. This was supposed to be here yesterday."

The messenger shrugged. He held out a clipboard and a pen. "Sign at the *X*, please."

Cardozo signed and gave the kid a dollar tip.

Ellie Siegel lifted the package. "Wrong weight for a letter bomb. May I?"

Cardozo was frowning at the screen. "Go ahead."

She opened the bubble-wrapped envelope and pulled out a leather-bound book. She studied the cover. "This is downright interesting. The twelve-karat gold lettering says *diary,* but it doesn't say whose. I won't open it. It may be personal."

"It's Nita Kohler's."

Ellie handed it to him. "The infamous sex diary?"

He nodded. "That's the one."

■ ■ ■

January 1, Monday

New Year's resolution: must brighten up my image. Must get away from black. Must dress in upbeat colors—purples, mustards, pumpkin-oranges.

January 2, Tuesday

Counseled D.V. She is a crack-addicted, child-abusing mother of three and comes for counseling only because the court ordered it. In three months I have still not gotten through to her. I am pretty sure she is still using. I may have to confront her.

Dinner at Domi's. It was another world from that of Renaissance House.

Christina Onassis was there, designer Perry Ellis, Nobel prizewinning writer Samuel Beckett. Greta Garbo dropped by for dessert—her dress was by Adrian. How does she eat all those sweets and stay so thin?

Why is Nita Kohler writing this? Cardozo asked himself.

The tone was wrong. There was a name-dropping gushing, as though the reader was meant to feel informed and at the same time goaded into envy.

But Nita hadn't intended any reader to see these pages. So who was she trying to impress? Her diary? Herself?

I was seated next to Dooney Heinz, who is the dunderhead of the Western world but, they say, great sex. So I decided to give it a try. Maybe it was one of his off nights, or bad coke, but I'd rate him, on a scale of ten, a three.

January 3, Wednesday

Hung over from Domi's and romping too hard with Dooney. Up at ten for policy meeting of the emergency drug-intervention unit at Renaissance. *Quel* drag to be talking drugs when all I craved was to pop another codeine or Darvon.

January 5, Friday

Didn't know how to get through to D.V. I confronted her on her using. She at first denied but finally admitted. Something weird happened.

D.V. told me I was too white, too Anglo, and too scared to smoke crack, and so long as I did not understand the crack experience from the inside, I would remain a typical white applause-and-publicity junkie, slumming on the problems of the poor.

So I did it with D.V.—smoked my first crack. The rush was immediate, intense. I think D.V. now trusts me and this can only push our therapeutic relationship forward.

Then on to dinner at Roxanne Ricci's.

Philanthropist Lily Firestone, playwright Tom Waring, who is doing the script of You-and-Me Productions' film "Ain't No Time," Sammy Davis, Jr., who is costarring, Lady Keith—why do they call her Slim? She is as pudgy as Elaine of Elaine's.

Cardozo felt a sort of disappointment. You read a person's diary, you expect it to be like a lamp lighting a door to an unexplored part of them. But this was an all-too-familiar story.

Okay, he told himself. *So no one on crack is original.*

I went home with Tom Waring—he is great sex. Very old-fashioned in his choice of accoutrements—Thai sticks, Quaaludes—he must have a medicine chest left over from the sixties!

I think to give great head you've got to have a great head. Tom has and does.

January 7, Sunday

Service at St. John the Divine. My coreader was a guy called Jim Delancey, and he is astonishing. I could hardly read the gospel —everything was shaking; my voice, my knees, my hands.

Afterward at the movie brunch we talked. And talked. I have never felt so attracted to another human being in my life. Jim is new in Renaissance House, and I am going to arrange to be his counselor.

January 8, Monday

I coached Jim in how best to appeal to Marci so as to be transferred to my caseload. It worked! Now we will be seeing each other for at least one hour a day, five days a week—more if I can manage it.

January 9, Tuesday

I suggested to Jim that for him to truly trust me as his caseworker we must make love.

Jim said he would have to think about this.

January 10, Wednesday

Jim said he does not think we should make love.

In session with D.V. I broke down. D.V. was extremely sisterly and solicitous and listened. Funny how our situation reversed. She was counseling me.

Smoke crack with Jim, she said. This will do it.

I bought enough crack from her to last the week.

January 11, Thursday

In counseling today I suggested to Jim that we smoke a peace pipe. He was reluctant when I told him it was crack, but curiosity got the better of him and he tried it. Two tokes and we were off to the races.

He is the greatest lover I have ever had, bar none, nothing short of sensational. It was yummy sex to end all sex—

It was there that Leigh Baker had placed the bookmark. Cardozo closed the diary.

On the other side of the library Leigh Baker sat with a magazine on her lap. She was turning pages, not reading. She looked over at Cardozo. A little line of wariness ran from her eye down to the corner of her mouth. "Do you recognize the phrase?"

"Sure. The same five words in exactly the same order."

"Nita was intelligent. She was educated. She was sane . . . And she was a woman. No woman would write those five words, not in a diary, not in a letter, not in a soft-core novel. It's a man's wish-fulfillment of how a horny woman thinks."

She took her glass in both hands. It was a brandy snifter of diet Pepsi. She sat staring into it.

"The diary's a forgery," she said.

There was extraordinary calm in the way she made that statement. He wondered at the ferocity of that calm.

"As I recollect," he said, "it must have been an awfully good forgery. Didn't experts say the handwriting was your daughter's? Wasn't there information only your daughter could have known?"

Leigh tapped a finger on the edge of the snifter. "It was well researched. It was skillful. But it was a fake."

"All right, say it was a fake. Still, *sex to end all sex*—those are five very ordinary words. A very common figure of speech. I think it's a coincidence. And I think you're hanging way too much hope on way too little fact."

She blinked hard, as though her eyes were stinging. "You're determined not to believe me, aren't you?"

Ten seconds passed.

She dried her eyes on the back of her hand.

"Come on." Cardozo crossed to the sofa and sat beside her. "Don't cry. Come on. Please."

"What makes you think I'm crying?"

"Your face is wet. Come here."

She buried her face in his chest.

"You could be wrong, you know." His arms went around her and hugged her softly. "All of us are wrong some of the time. Delancey has an alibi for Oona's killing. We don't have witnesses to link him to any of the others."

She held on to him, and he could feel her body breathing. "Are you going to stop watching him?"

"We may have to cut back a little."

She pulled away. Her eyes met his without blinking. "Don't."

He stared at her. "You couldn't save Nita from Delancey then, so you're going to move heaven and earth to save her from him now. Why?"

"I owe it to her."

"Who says?"

She looked at him, trying to make a smile for him. She brought her leg out from under her and touched her bare foot to the carpeted floor. She stood. "Is anyone around here getting hungry? Let's see what else the chef left on ice."

· FORTY-NINE ·

Sunday, June 9

CARDOZO WAS CURIOUS about this man that Leigh Baker said she depended on.

"You're in Nan Shane's address book," he said.

"I'm not surprised," Luddie Ostergate said. "She used to be in mine. How's she doing?"

"She's dead."

"Nan? Nan *Shane*?" Luddie Ostergate held himself absolutely still in the chair. "How did it happen?"

Cardozo told him how Nan Shane had died.

They were sitting in Ostergate's living room, a minimally furnished loft space with two walls of windows and a knockout view of the Chrysler Building.

Ostergate listened, his face unmoving, but when Cardozo described the knife cuts, he flinched.

"Jesus. She may have done some dumb things in her life, but she didn't deserve to go like that."

"How well did you two know each other?"

"Not well. She came into AA about three years ago. She was a cross-addicted alcoholic and cokehead, and she picked me to be her sponsor."

"How did she happen to pick you?" Cardozo asked.

"Strictly potluck. She drew my name out of a box."

Ostergate had insisted on Cardozo's having a cup of coffee. Now that he had the cup in his hand Cardozo was glad he'd insisted. It turned out to be a thick brew, edged in the charcoal overroastedness that Cardozo associated with waking up in the morning.

"I've been in the program over five years," Ostergate said.

"That qualifies me as an old-timer. We old guys put our names in the sponsor box and theoretically every newcomer picks a sponsor, and that's how we keep an eye on the beginners. Sometimes the relationship takes and lasts twenty years. Sometimes it doesn't and it lasts twenty minutes."

"You were crossed out of Nan Shane's address book."

"I'm not surprised. Nan didn't stay in the program long."

"How long?" Cardozo asked.

"Three, four months. When we lost touch, I assumed she was out coking and boozing."

"You didn't go after her?"

"It's not that kind of a program, and I'm not that kind of a guy." Ostergate's voice seemed to give in to a bone-deep tiredness. "I nagged her about her coke habit. She lied about it, and by lying she made it clear she wasn't ready for AA."

"Tell me about her coke habit."

"Her per-diem habit would have cost . . ." Ostergate's fingers seemed to be tapping out abacus movements on his knee. "Three hundred dollars. But Nan got it wholesale. She had connections in the industry."

"What can you tell me about her connections?"

"I didn't ask, I didn't want to know. Far as I was concerned that was between her, God, and the cops. I told her she had to get out of the coke business—told her she'd never beat her addiction if she was peddling it to other people."

Ostergate was silent for one shadowed moment, and the air seemed to vibrate with his dislike of what this woman had come to represent in his life.

"But she had a whole head trip about her East Side apartment and her life-style, and being a single mother and owing the kid a decent life. To Nan, decency was a private kindergarten and designer playclothes. She had a lot of expenses and she had no skills and she didn't want to learn any. So she stayed in the dope-peddling business. She tried to kick coke, but naturally, dealing it all the time, she couldn't."

For a moment Ostergate's gaze touched Cardozo, as though they both knew all eighty-nine flavors of human weakness.

"She must have had a hundred coke slips in a hundred days. After the hundred first, I told her to change professions or get her ass out of my life. This was maybe a year ago. I never saw her again —never heard her name again—till you phoned."

"Did you ever meet her kid?"

"Never."

"Ever see her apartment?"

"She'd visit me here or meet me in a coffee house, but as you can see, I'm a pretty casual dresser—I don't think she wanted to take the chance that anyone who counted might see a slob like me going into her apartment."

Luddie Ostergate's dress didn't look all that casual to Cardozo: a sport shirt that had been machine washed often enough to have softened to pale designer blue, gray cotton trousers that were supposed to have the wrinkled look and did, athletic socks, unadorned brown loafers that matched the brown leather belt. Cardozo would have called the look careful casual. It would have set you back a lot at Barney's, not so much at the Gap.

"Was Nan actually in with any society types?"

Ostergate smiled. "She wanted to think she was. She applied herself to it. She was a real networker. As in *tireless.* Nan was the kind of woman who went to funerals of prominent people she'd never even met, and shook every hand in the church. And I think she actually got a few invitations out of it. I remember once she was scheduled to speak at a meeting, and she canceled at the last moment because some social star had invited her to coffee."

"Coffee?" Cardozo said.

"That's right. Not dinner. Coffee *after* dinner. A lot of times. Coffee after dinner."

"Think she was dealing coke at these dinners?"

Ostergate sat a moment in cool, smiling cynicism. "In all the months I knew her, Nan was never *not* dealing coke. Meetings she had the decency not to deal at. But there was always some deal going down in Beekman Place or Sutton Place or some club where your ancestors had to have sailed A deck on the *Mayflower.*"

"I don't suppose you take notes when someone you're sponsoring talks to you."

"No, nothing like that. Usually it's just shit they need to ventilate—the sooner it's out and forgotten, the better."

Ostergate seemed to live simply: no art treasures hung on his walls, his furnishings made no designer statement. The most expensive object in the room was probably the computer set up on a worktable: it looked to Cardozo like a twin of the computer in Dr. Wilkes's office.

"Have you sponsored many people?" Cardozo said.

"In all, I'd say ten. I'm not trying to set a record. I sponsor as many as I'm comfortable with, two or three at a time. At the moment I sponsor only two."

"We have a friend in common."

"Who's that?"

"Leigh Baker."

Luddie Ostergate blinked as if for an instant something had almost thrown him off balance. "Sorry, I live in so many different worlds, I sometimes get thrown for a loop when a name crosses over."

"She says you help her get through what she's going through."

"And she's going through a lot. To tell the truth, I'm surprised I'm any help to anyone at the moment. Work's keeping me busy. Too busy."

"Could I ask what kind of work you do?"

"I run a chain of thrift shops." There was a touch of self-disparagement in Luddie Ostergate's shrug. "They're staffed with men and women from AA. By the way, if the NYPD is ever looking for first-rate part-time help, you can't do better than hire someone from AA."

"I'll remember that." Cardozo set down his cup. He rose and strolled to the bookcase, making no secret of his curiosity. On the top two shelves Ostergate had arranged history books and biographies alphabetically by author. A third shelf held foreign-language manuals and a fourth, books on economics and foreign policy.

Cardozo examined the computer. It was an NEC Powermate 2—exactly the same as Wilkes's. "You use this in your work?"

"I'd be dead without it."

Cardozo leaned down to read the print on the screen: *Condor 90397 ROM BIOS PLUS Version 5. 10 Copyright © 1989–1991.* "What's 'Condor'?"

"My computer program gives you the option to name it." Luddie Ostergate rose from his chair and came across the room. "I named it Condor." He pushed a control button on the keyboard. His knuckles were reddened, swollen, his nails unevenly trimmed. The screen went blank. "Ever seen one?"

"A condor? No."

"Fantastic birds."

"You must have spent time in South America."

"A little."

A coaxial line had been attached to the computer housing. Cardozo's eye followed it to the phone jack on the baseboard. "What kind of program do you use?"

"Standard small corporate bookkeeping—tracks inventory and expenses and payroll. Do you use a computer?"

Cardozo shook his head. "Me? No way. But I have a friend who talks to Washington on one of these. From his desk in Manhattan he can read files in a subbasement in Virginia."

"These machines are the greatest communicators on earth today."

"Where's your mainframe?"

"Beg your pardon?"

"That phone line—isn't it your link to the mainframe?"

Luddie Ostergate's face seemed to hesitate before breaking into a grin. "No, that's the stores' link to me. I'm the mainframe." He placed a hand on the computer casing. "This little eighty-meg baby is the brains of the whole operation."

■ ■ ■

DICK BRAIDY TURNED A PAGE.

He had wrapped himself in a rumpled bathrobe and a day's worth of whiskers stubbled his cheeks gray. His eyes were bloodshot and the skin beneath them looked puffy and tender.

He sat there in the armchair, staring at the diary. He hardly breathed, hardly moved. Finally he floated a glance toward Leigh.

"Everyone else says I'm exaggerating," she said. "Am I?"

"No." The word was hardly more than a breath.

"So it's more than a five-word coincidence?"

"Much more." He handed back the diary. "You didn't turn the page. Nine words are the same. In his note Society Sam said *Sex to end all sex, is there anything else in your perverted worldview?*'"

She turned the page. She saw that he was right. The line began *sex to end all sex* at the bottom of the right-hand page, and it continued on the next page: *is there anything else?*

"I wish I'd seen that." She slapped the covers shut. "The police would have *had* to believe me. Well, they'll believe me now."

"Don't tell them yet." Dick looked up at her almost beseechingly, the way a little boy might. "If you let me keep the diary, I can prove that Nita didn't write any of it."

"How can you prove that?"

"Trust me?"

She laid the diary down on the coffee table. She laid it down gently, because the table was a three-thousand-dollar antique, King George papier-mâché. It had been featured in the "Living" section of the *Times,* and she knew her ex-husband was very proud of it. "Keep it for as long as you need."

"Only a day or two."

Dick Braidy's apartment was quiet. Rain nattered softly against the window panes. Beyond the glass the evening sky was a dull, sharkskin gray.

"I guess you could use a drink," Dick said. "Meaning, I could."

He walked into the kitchen and came back with two tumblers of ice cubes and a can of diet Pepsi. He prised off the flip top and half filled a tumbler and handed it to her.

He went to the secretary and poured himself a straight Chivas. "Have you heard that Jim Delancey has a girlfriend now?"

"No, I hadn't heard."

"Apparently she's an Egyptian."

"Do you know her?"

Dick came back to his armchair. "Never met her. Some people were talking about her at Betty Bacall's the other night."

They sat gazing at each other. Something like death seemed to look at Leigh through Dick Braidy's eyes.

He leaned toward the sofa and touched her arm. "Mustn't worry about it though. I'm going to take care of everything."

■   ■   ■

WALDO WAS ALREADY HOME when Leigh returned. "And how was the City of Light?" he asked.

"I didn't go to Paris."

Waldo's highball stopped halfway to his mouth. "Did something go wrong?"

"Yes, something went wrong. You hired that guard again. Arnold Bone."

"Darling—I'm sorry." Waldo set down his drink and came across the room and put his hands on her shoulders. "The security people misunderstood me. I told them *not* to give you Arnie."

"It doesn't matter. It really doesn't. I stayed home by myself and got a rest."

· FIFTY ·

Monday, June 10

ZACK SAT DOWN at his office desk, opened the *Trib* and read as far as the third item in "Dick Sez."

> A certain real-estate-and-media mogul is taking very long lunch hours looking at posh pied-à-terres or, pardonnez my French, do I mean pieds-à-terre? Accompanying him on these urban field trips is a certain designing lady who, according to those who've been there, has a lot more to offer the eye and the bankbook than his current live-in.

The blood raced along Zack's face and scalp. The fingers of his right hand clumped into a fist, and his left hand grabbed the phone. He told his secretary to ring Dick Braidy.

"What the hell are you trying to do to me? I gave you Dizey's column as a favor! I thought you were a *friend*, for Christ's sake!"

"I'm a journalist, Zack, and if you don't like the way I run the column, just say the word and the *Post* will be glad to buy out my contract."

"Who gave you that item?"

"You're not hearing me, Zack. I'm a journalist—not a stool pigeon."

There was a click and then the desolate hum of a dial tone. Zack told his secretary to ring Annie MacAdam's unlisted number.

"You vicious bitch. You gave that item to Dick Braidy."

"I did not," Annie MacAdam said.

"You're the only one who knows."

"You own the goddamn paper, can't you control your own

columnists? Can't you read what you print before you print it? Or at least remember to tip the doorman?"

"What are you talking about?"

"How long have you lived in this town, Zack? You met with a woman three times in an apartment that wasn't yours. The doorman saw it, you never once gave him a tip."

"Oh, Christ." A button on Zack's phone was flashing. "Excuse me, Annie, there's another call I have to take."

The other call was Gloria Spahn. "This has gone too far." There was no anger in her voice, just a cool matter-of-factness. "I can't afford this kind of publicity."

"It won't happen again. Just meet me and I'll explain."

"Zack, you're fun to play with and we're great together, but I can't afford to be perceived as *anybody's* main squeeze. I'm a married woman and my company stock is publicly traded."

"That blind item was a one-in-a-million fluke and I *promise,* never again. Just let me see you."

"This is a rotten week for me. I don't have any free time."

"You must have free time *some*time."

"All I have is maybe from five to six P.M. Thursday."

"Save that hour. Please, Gloria."

"Maybe. We'll talk. Good-bye, Zack."

■ ■ ■

GLORIA BROKE THE CONNECTION. Lines one and three on her phone were blinking. She was about to push *three* when she realized her husband was staring at her.

"Are you crazy?" Three buttons on Stanley's phone were blinking at once and he was ignoring them all.

"No," Gloria said. "I'm not crazy."

Something was clearly bothering Stanley. And he clearly wanted to bother her with it. His eyebrows had crawled so high up his forehead that they were almost touching the hem of his toupee. "You *can't* see him at five P.M. on Thursday. We're taking the helicopter up to Groton."

"Relax. I'm just getting him off my back." Both one and three had stopped blinking. The service must have picked up. Gloria lifted the silver coffeepot and poured herself a fresh half cup. "He's in love with me."

"Whether he's in love with you or not, you shouldn't have to be evasive with him." Stanley had finished skimming his financial updates. He slapped the reports down on his place mat. "You should tell him straight out, my sons are graduating and the rector's giving us dinner."

Stanley's twin sons by his first marriage were graduating from prep school Friday. Stanley had given Groton a new gym, and the rector had invited him and Gloria to dinner Thursday. To Stanley, the dinner signified a new level of social acceptance. He had gone so far as to tell Gloria she had to wear a high-neck dress.

"Zack Morrow isn't interested in your sons," Gloria said. And neither was she. She hated the idea of breaking off work to go to Groton. She hated the idea that Stanley had been previously married, that he had two kids.

Stanley poured skim milk on his high-fibre oat-'n'-almond breakfast flakes. He had dressed for breakfast in a burgundy silk bathrobe with a matching velvet collar and a pink silk show hankie in the pocket. "Have you decided yet what you're going to wear?"

Gloria sat a moment, feeling guilty that he was counting on her. She had no intention of going to Groton with him, but two days ahead of time was a little early to start the argument. "I'm going to wear a high, white-lace collar. The rector won't even know I have tits."

"And?" Stanley leaned forward as if to pull words out of her. *"And?"*

"And what?"

"What are you wearing for the ceremony? The graduation's outdoors, it's okay to show a little skin."

Gloria shrugged. "I'm going to wear a WASPy little country-club number. Pale blue linen."

"How are you going to accessorize?"

Stanley always needed to hear the details. Every time she went to bed with another man, he wanted to know how big the dick was. The only rule Stanley had about Gloria's other men was, they had to be at least six feet tall.

"I'll wear last year's Bulgari pearls."

"Only one strand."

"Of course only one strand."

"And not the earrings."

Gloria had a sudden sense of the pettiness of the male power drive. "Of course not the earrings. Believe me, they won't know me from a *Social Register* volunteer ticket taker at a Junior League buffet."

Stanley pushed back his chair and stood. He strolled to the window and stood staring out at the view across Central Park. He clasped his hands behind him. He turned and gazed at the view he was proudest of, the Titian "Vespers of Cosima de' Medici" that occupied the entire west wall of the breakfast room.

"Know something?" he said. "It's going to be the greatest day of my life."

▪ ▪ ▪

"BINGO." It was Lou Stein on the line, calling from the lab. "We found a candle in the trash basket. It was sticking to a page of the *National Enquirer,* which also had some five-day-old doggie-doo sticking to it."

"Five-day-old?" Cardozo said.

"As nearly as we can approximate these things."

Cardozo had checked with the Department of Sanitation. The trash basket on the corner of Seventy-fourth and Third was scheduled to be emptied three times a week—Monday, Wednesday, and Friday between five and six A.M. But the truck had missed Friday because of street repairs, so anything found in the trash could theoretically date back to Wednesday.

"Okay, so the dog shit was from Thursday," Cardozo said, "but that doesn't mean the candle can't be from early Saturday morning. He might have just shoved it down a layer or two. How does it match up to the others?"

"Same type—Saffire *Shabbes.* And it's from the same six-pack."

"Any idea how long it burned?"

"Allowing the usual margin for error—at least twenty-five seconds."

Cardozo shook his head. "Where the hell does this guy get the *time?*"

"Excuse me?"

"Just thinking out loud. Any newspaper clippings?"

"You're right on the money today, Vince. Benedict Braidy's May thirty-first column was sticking to the candle that was sticking to the *Enquirer.*"

"Torn or clipped?"

"Clipped. Probably with the same scissors that clipped Dizey's columns."

"Do the serrations match any on the letters in the notes?"

"If they do, my microscope can't see it. I'm not ruling it out, but I just can't rule it in."

"Okay, Lou. Thanks."

When Cardozo looked up, Ellie Siegel was standing in the doorway.

"I did some reading last night." She thunked an oversized, falling-apart, dog-eared paperback on the desk, angled so he could read the title: *Your Congress—Newly Updated Edition.* "Nancy Guardella serves on eight committees and subcommittees, but her power base is the chair of the DEA-oversight committee. They watch the black budget."

"What the hell is a black budget?"

"Off-the-books expenditures." Ellie was wearing a cotton print dress, and though it was barely ten in the morning, her hair was already curling around her face from the humidity. "The stuff that's so secret you can't keep a cost-accounting, because then the Russians would know."

"The Russians aren't a problem anymore."

Ellie shrugged. "Okay, the drug lords would know. The Americans would know. Someone would know."

She waited while he adjusted the temperature control on the air conditioner. Adjusting the control in no way adjusted the temperature, but it sometimes lowered the noise and it made him feel that at least he tried to be a considerate host.

"Now and then Guardella makes a stink in Congress, and something slips into the record that shouldn't."

"Like what?" Cardozo said.

"She raised a huge ruckus last year to get dentistry and psychiatry fully reimbursed."

"Reimbursed for who?"

"For agents who can't be put on the roster, because it would blow their cover and endanger their lives."

"Thoughtful of Nancy. Did she get her way?"

"The resolution passed. Vince, we should have someone like that fighting for *our* dentistry reimbursements. On my last crown I had to pay a three-hundred-dollar deductible."

Cardozo riffled the pages of *Your Congress.*

"I also did some digging into Nan Shane's will," Ellie said. "Nan Shane left two surviving relatives, her daughter Dodie and her mother Olivia. The mother lives in Mattoon, Illinois. She has no idea where Nan's husband is, but she thinks they were divorced two years ago by Salvadorean decree."

"Who inherits?" The phone rang. Cardozo lifted the receiver. "Cardozo."

"Vince, it's Tommy at Nynex. That 617 number you wanted is a pay phone."

Another button on Cardozo's phone began blinking. "Shit." He put his hand over the mouthpiece. "Ellie, could you pick up on two and see who's calling?" He uncovered the receiver. "Sorry, Tommy. Where's that pay phone?"

"You're not going to believe this."

"Try me."

"This is the guy that's making nuisance calls to Leigh Baker, right? He's phoning from the pay phone right in front of the precinct. Go out your front door, look left. Maybe he's there right now."

"You're probably right, and it's probably one of my own men. Thanks, Tommy."

Ellie knocked on the open door. "To answer your last question, Nan died intestate."

"And who was that on the phone?"

"Rad Rheinhardt. He just got a fourth letter from Society Sam. I don't know whether it's my shorthand or Sam's train of thought, but this one doesn't make much sense." She consulted a sheet of scratch paper covered with squiggles and phone numbers. "Sam says, quote, *'ta ra ta ra ta ra ta roo.'* "

" *'Ta roo?'* What the hell is *'ta ra ta roo'* ?"

Ellie shrugged. "I may not have the right number of *ta ra's*, but Rheinhardt's sending the letter up. *'Me ow and the poody tat, ow can you see, Humpty's dumpty got the bumpty. Kisses, Society Sam.'* "

▪ ▪ ▪

"I SUGGEST, Let's go party at my place."

Cardozo and Narcotics Detective Bob O'Rourke were sitting at a table in a half-deserted Chelsea diner that called itself Mama's Greasy Spoon. The table was gleaming, not greasy. O'Rourke was dipping his chocolate eclair into his espresso, and in between mouthfuls he was telling Cardozo how he'd busted Nan Shane.

"She says, Fine. So we jump into a cab outside Achilles Foot. I get her to sell me some coke in the backseat, and I bust her. The rest is mystery."

"Tell me about the mystery," Cardozo said.

"I have Shane booked and arraigned. The court date's set. And then a federal narc stops me on the courthouse steps, and *he* busts me for using and dealing."

"*Were* you using and dealing?"

"Hell, no. I was sent into Achilles Foot under cover, to buy."

Cardozo could see why the city narcs had sent O'Rourke

under cover into a teen drug scene. The guy was a not-yet-aging thirty-two who'd kept his baby face.

"Why Achilles Foot?" Cardozo said. "It's a federal sting operation."

O'Rourke gave him a Where-have-you-been-hiding-for-the-last-quarter-century? look. "Somehow the feds forgot to tell New York that the place was theirs. As far as New York could tell, Achilles Foot was your normal, everyday, obnoxious dope scene, no different from your average Times Square movie theater. Same product. Same activity. The only difference I could see was, the clientele's whiter, the prices are higher. You have exactly the same dealing in the front room, exactly the same using in the men's room. Which is also the women's room. Which is also the sex room."

"What do you mean, the sex room?"

"I mean, when you find used rubbers lying on the floor, fresh, that's the sex room."

Something slimy crawled through Cardozo's stomach. "So the feds bust you on the courthouse steps, and you show them your shield."

"I show them my shield, and they say bullshit. They show me a video of me dealing—instead of just buying like I was sent into Achilles Foot to do." O'Rourke stared out the window at traffic rumbling north on Eighth Avenue. "And I have to say, this video was awesome."

Cardozo felt a subtle increase of atmospheric weight. "They caught you dealing."

For a moment O'Rourke didn't answer and he didn't exactly react, but his eyes fixed Cardozo with a flat green stare. "No way. Would I be telling you this if they caught me dealing? I may be a little slow, but I'm not crooked. They faked it. What they had was a camera in the wall. Shane was doing this thing with cards. She was telling my fortune, my future, the usual."

"Tarot."

"On the tape they changed the audio. The way the video came out, I was quoting coke prices and Shane was ordering."

"How did they fake that?"

"Shane wasn't facing the camera. They dubbed her voice. How they did mine . . . obviously these people possess a high-tech forgery capability. It sounded like me, so it had to be some kind of voice sampler. It didn't come out quite in sync, and I was facing the camera, but you had to watch real close to know."

O'Rourke threw Cardozo a baleful glance under hooded lids. "And that was when they told me Nan Shane was a federal agent."

"Who told you?"

"Senator Nancy Guardella."

Cardozo played with a ballpoint pen, clicking the point in and out. "Did Guardella show you any proof?"

"The only proof I got was, Guardella offered me health insurance if I'd keep my mouth shut."

"Health insurance?"

"It's a scam. They funnel money to you as medical reimbursements, and it's untaxed. I assume the money's unlaundered dope funds."

"Why do you think Guardella made the offer?"

"Because Nan Shane may have been an agent, but she was also dealing for real. And so was Guardella's son. And they both had major habits to support."

"Does Senator Guardella know?"

O'Rourke tossed Cardozo a look that was laden with cold reverberation. "She's a mother. Mothers know what they want to know."

"Can you prove that Yip Guardella's dealing?"

"Not anymore, but I could have proved it when Shane was alive. She was ready to take the stand." O'Rourke gave a little smile that wasn't a smile at all. "But a funny thing happened on the way to the hearing. A psycho slasher got Shane."

For a moment Cardozo sat unmoving in his chair, staring across the diner. He was seized with a sudden pessimism about the universe. "I take it you don't buy that explanation."

"If you ask me, the people running Achilles Foot work in mysterious ways." O'Rourke shrugged. "So I don't get my big case. Or the big promotion that would have come with it. But look at the bright side. I'm doing better than Shane. I'm alive."

"I don't suppose you owe your life to any of that health insurance you mentioned."

For ten seconds O'Rourke was looking out the window and then he was looking at Cardozo and then he spoke. "No, Lieutenant. That big a fool I'm not. But I was offered a two-year New York State grant to study drug enforcement in Melbourne, and I grabbed it."

"When do you leave?"

"You found me just in time. My wife and I leave tomorrow."

▪ FIFTY-ONE ▪

Tuesday, June 11

"YOU'RE GOING TO KILL ME. Or spank me. Or stop sponsoring me when I tell you what I've done."

"Tell me what you've done, so I can decide whether it's murder or a spanking."

They were sitting in Luddie's living room. Happy's exercises were finished, and the child was resting now in his bed, and they were drinking Luddie's home-ground coffee.

"I spent the weekend with Vince Cardozo," Leigh said.

Luddie's face held itself—all stern bone, capped by a bristling crop of gray hair—but something impatient and disapproving skittered behind his flat blue gaze.

"You're playing your old games," he said. "You're trying to neutralize this man."

"I have to survive."

"He's not going to harm you."

"I had to know that for sure." She ignored the look of skepticism playing across Luddie's face. "He doesn't think I'm involved in Dizey's death. Except as a witness."

"You know, Leigh, I don't think you're involved either—except as a witness. Did it ever occur to you, you're going to enormous lengths to cover up a fiction?"

"Possibly."

"Are you going to see him again?" Luddie asked.

She looked around at the view through the windows, at the city caught by the oncoming storm. Dark, massed arches of cloud hung pink-bellied in the sky.

She met Luddie's gaze with bold, unresigned eyes. "Of course I'm going to see him again."

"What'll you do if he falls in love with you?"

She smiled. "I'll be nice to him."

"And what will you do if you fall in love with him?"

"I'll try to be nice to myself."

Luddie's large eyes were heavy with silent knowing. "Leigh, how long have I known you?"

"Four years, give or take three months."

"How many times have you been in love during that time?"

"Does it matter?"

"With you, love is a very public business. You're going to feel a great need to go public with this cop. And as I understand your relationship with Waldo, he'll put up with a lot, but he won't put up with sexual humiliation."

"I'm tired of being someone else's image. I want a little something of my own."

"And you really think a homicide detective is going to turn out to be a little something just for Leigh?"

"Well, why not? Is it all that ridiculous?"

She looked over at Luddie, but the fight she had expected wasn't there in his face. Anger seemed to have faded, and in its place she read a sort of stony and sad acceptance.

"Can't you ever think of anyone's well-being besides your own?"

"I care about Vince. I do."

"Haven't you ever felt *disinterested* concern for another human being?"

"I care about Jasmin Hakim."

"Jasmin *who*?"

"Dick says she's dating Jim Delancey."

"I don't think you should be putting stock in what your ex-husband says. He's a professional gossip. Why do you bother with him?"

"Because I need information about Delancey's girlfriend."

"Why?"

"I have to warn her. She's in danger."

"Is she? And is it your responsibility?"

"I think it is. You obviously think it's not."

"I think you're pushing yourself very hard, Leigh. What are you planning to do?"

"Tonight I'm going to follow Jim Delancey from work."

"What's the point of that?"

"The police are following me, so they'll be following him; and if he's meeting with her, he won't be able to hurt her."

"Don't do that," Luddie said. "Please don't."

"I can't just sit and let it happen all over again."

■ ■ ■

IN THE COFFEE SHOP across the street from Archibald's, she waited at a table in the rear. She made no attempt to disguise who she was or what she was doing: she was Leigh Baker, and she was watching Archibald's two doors through the window.

Outside the front entrance women wearing diamonds clutched escorts' arms and picked their way through parked limousines. A line of taxis stretched up Lexington.

Outside the kitchen door nothing moved.

Leigh ripped open a pink envelope of Sweet'n Low. A cloud of powder misted down into her cup. She stirred, sipped the coffee, found it horrible, and told herself she wasn't going to drink it. She picked up her doughnut and bit into the oiliest, most sugar-sodden lump of dough she had ever tasted. She told herself she wasn't going to eat it.

Across the street the kitchen door opened, and a Korean in a chef's hat lugged a garbage can out and set it on the sidewalk. A moment later the door opened again, and Jim Delancey stepped out wearing an apron. He lit a cigarette and looked in her direction.

Maybe he saw her, maybe he didn't. She couldn't tell. Nothing happened on his face.

The Korean said something. Delancey gave him a cigarette, and the two men stood on the stoop smoking, not talking. Delancey finished his cigarette and tossed the butt into the gutter. He went back inside.

Leigh looked around her. The coffee shop was almost deserted. In the booth by the front door a uniformed cop sat alone, hunched over a piece of pie. His fingers tapped the edge of his plate in time to a Tony Bennett song playing softly on the radio. A wedding band glinted.

The counterman was passing a damp cloth over the counter. The movement was aimless: it wasn't cleaning anything, because there was nothing to clean. Maybe it was just a way of passing the dead hours of evening.

Leigh looked again at her watch. Five to nine.

The kitchen door of Archibald's opened and Delancey stepped out. He wasn't wearing his apron.

Leigh signaled the counterman. "Could I have my check, please?"

The counterman brought her a check for a dollar eighty. She was horrified to see that she had drunk the coffee and finished the doughnut. She opened her purse and put down three dollars.

Outside, a summer wind gusted hotly along the pavement, swirling sheets of newspaper.

Delancey turned south on Lexington. People were moving at a leisured pace from storefront to storefront, slowing to glance at the latest in designer rumple wear, at the thirty-nine flavors listed in the window of David's Cone.

She followed Delancey at a half-block's distance.

He turned east on Seventy-second.

Traffic thinned. Headlights reflected off the minuscule glass particles that formed part of the glistening asphalt.

She followed Delancey to the five-hundred block, where Seventy-second Street dead-ended at the East River. It was a preserve of solidly built co-ops, with the odd brownstone sprinkled in. A glass-and-marble condo towered over a vest-pocket park.

Delancey went into the condo lobby. The uniformed doorman smiled and went to a bank of buzzers and pushed the top buzzer in the last row. After a moment he turned and nodded Delancey through.

They know him here, she thought. *They trust him.* Something skittered in her stomach.

She waited sixty seconds, then approached the lobby.

"Help you, ma'am?" The doorman gave her that glance she always got from strangers, the one that said, *Do you know who you look exactly like? But you couldn't be . . .*

She nodded and answered with the glance that said, *Right. I just look like her.*

"Verna Higgins to see Charlotte Mayes. I'm expected."

"I'm sorry, there's no Mayes in the building."

"Are you sure? She used to live in Apartment—" Leigh approached the bank of buzzers and memorized the name at the top buzzer in the last row. Bailey, C. Apartment 4-A. Jasmin Hakim lived either in a sublet or under an assumed name. "She used to live up on the eighth floor. In apartment 8-A, I think. Isn't the A line the apartments right over there?" She pointed west.

"No, ma'am, A line are the apartments with the small terrace on the river. You must have been here some time ago."

"I guess she moved. Thanks anyway."

Leigh crossed the street. The far side of Seventy-second gave her a better sightline on the small fourth-story terrace. The terrace was dark, but there was a light on inside the apartment.

A group of people came out of the condo lobby. They were obviously a party on their way to dinner, laughing and happily tipsy. Their voices receded.

A girl came out onto the fourth-story terrace. She wore blue jeans and a loose shirt. She went to the railing and looked out over the river. Her slim body glowed in the light from indoors.

Jim Delancey joined her. Leigh could see him going straight into his rap. His expression was warm and humorous and friendly. His gestures were graceful and flowing—courtship gestures. His hand smoothed the hair that fell over the girl's face, hair that was dark and perfect and straight.

The girl laughed.

They kissed.

Jim Delancey lit a cigarette, and they spent five minutes passing it back and forth. The girl stood swaying on legs that seemed gradually to lose their steadiness. Jim Delancey's hand played with a loose strand of her hair and then her face broke into a smile and she gave a shrug.

He kissed her again, a serious kiss this time. He backed her against the railing.

A tide of recollection rushed in on Leigh. She felt a pang, a sense of helplessness in the face of inevitability.

The whisper of distant traffic came softly. In the street around her there was now only stillness—parked cars, deserted doorways spilling light, a phone booth.

She walked quickly to the phone booth. She dialed 411. "Operator, do you have a number listed for C as in Carol Bailey, Five ninety-one East Seventy-second Street?"

The operator gave her the number. She dropped a quarter into the slot and dialed. The phone rang once. Twice.

On the terrace the girl pulled away from Delancey. She stood with her back to him. She turned and said something.

Delancey crossed to her, almost knocking over a porch chair. He was not managing things with any sort of grace, and there was something in his manner that seemed to enjoy not managing, almost a defiant child's strut.

He followed her inside.

On the fifth ring the girl answered. "Hello?"

Leigh swallowed. "Jasmin Hakim?"

There was a millisecond's wariness. "Yes?"

"The man you're with is a murderer."

"Who is this?"

"This is—someone who's seen what James Delancey is capable of."

"If this is a joke, it's one of the sickest I've ever heard." The girl spoke perfect British English. Even her indignation was British.

"This is not a joke. For your own safety, please don't go back onto the terrace with him."

There was a silence, as though a message had to blip back from a satellite, and then the in-taken breath of recognition. "I know who you are. You have gall. You have nerve, phoning me."

"Get Jim Delancey out of your apartment, or get yourself out. Don't let him trap you alone."

"You're a meddling, psychotic, injustice collector!"

"For God's sake, just get out of there!"

Something struck the phone booth. It had the weight of a hurled motorcycle, bursting up and out in one explosive, metal-crumpling movement.

Leigh whirled halfway around.

Someone grabbed her from behind. A hand clamped over her mouth. A forearm locked over her throat.

"Don't scream," a man's voice warned.

The smell of sweat on a leather watchband flooded her nostrils. She couldn't pull air into her lungs. She looked down and saw metal glint in his hand.

"Don't make this any harder than it has to be."

Her knees snapped. Gripping tightly, pulling her out onto the pavement, her attacker slowly bent her backward.

∎ ∎ ∎

AT TEN TWENTY-TWO, on Seventy-second Street near the East River, Patrolman Dan Rivera of the Twenty-second Precinct noticed a phone booth with a smashed glass panel that had not been smashed twenty minutes earlier.

He slowed his blue-and-white cruiser.

A phone receiver twirled at the end of a cord. The pavement around the booth was covered with shards of broken glass, as though a mad philanthropist had scattered a bucket of oversized diamonds.

Patrolman Rivera pulled up to the curb, idled the motor, and stepped out of his cruiser.

He crouched down by the pavement. He played the beam of his flashlight over the glass, looking for blood.

Two feet away, in the gutter, he found a woman's shoe.

■ ■ ■

"HELLO. WALDO CARNEGIE SPEAKING." Waldo Carnegie apparently was one of those men who were so rich that they could afford to answer their own phone.

"Mr. Carnegie, I'm sorry to disturb you." Cardozo's heart was thumping double-time in his chest, and his palms were sweating so hard that he had to grip the phone with both hands. *I'll kill Society Sam,* he was thinking. *I will personally hunt that bastard down and execute him on the spot if he touched her.* "This is Lieutenant Vince Cardozo at the Twenty-second Precinct. I don't want to alarm you, but there may have been . . . an unfortunate incident. Would you happen to know what kind of shoes Miss Baker was wearing tonight?"

"Shoes?"

"By any chance, were they pale gray alligator pumps?" *Let them be green,* he was thinking. *Please, God, let them be moccasins. Running shoes. Anything but gray alligator pumps.*

"Hold on. Leigh darling, were you wearing pale gray alligator pumps tonight?" In the distance a woman's voice said something. Carnegie came back on the line. "Yes, she was, but she lost one of them."

It was as though a hand squeezing Cardozo's heart had suddenly let go and he could draw breath again. But instead of relief, he felt rage sweeping in like a black tide. "You mean she's there?"

"Yes. She's right here."

■ ■ ■

TWELVE MINUTES LATER, in the third-floor drawing room of the Carnegie town house, Cardozo listened to Leigh Baker describe the attack.

"I must have passed out for a minute." She spoke quietly, in a voice bled of all expression. Sitting there on the sofa, she seemed small and touching and scared, undeserving of his or anyone's anger.

"And he let you go," Cardozo said. It was part statement, part wondering.

"When I came to, he wasn't there."

"How did you get home?"

"I only had one shoe, so I took the first cab I could find."

"The attacker left you your money?"

She nodded.

"Why didn't you phone the police?"

She bit her lip. "I'm sorry. I wasn't thinking."

On his sofa across the room Waldo Carnegie laid down the new issue of *Forbes* and looked up. "No. *I'm* sorry," he said. "*I wasn't thinking.*"

Leigh Baker and Waldo Carnegie glanced at each other across the ten-foot gap between sofas. There was gratitude in Leigh Baker's eyes and for one irrational moment Cardozo was jealous.

Be grateful to me, he wanted to shout, *not to him. I'm the one who worries about you. I'm the one who almost had the heart attack. He's the one who sits around in patent leather slippers and a smoking jacket, feeling smug and hiring guards to do his worrying.*

"The important thing," Waldo Carnegie said, "is that Leigh is safe and sound."

Cardozo found himself gazing at her. He could feel her avoiding his eyes. She looked disheveled, maybe a little mauled, but nothing you'd go to the Emergency Room about. There were no visible bruises or cuts, and that struck Cardozo as curious.

He ran it through his mind. *The attacker had her, and he let her go.* Why would he have done that? Had she fought him off? Had someone else come along and surprised him?

"Did you get a look at him?" Cardozo said.

She shook her head. "It was too sudden."

"Did you hear his voice?"

She took a swallow of her diet Pepsi and put her snifter down on the coffee table. She was thoughtful. "He told me not to scream."

"Did he have a Hispanic accent?"

"Not remotely."

"Did you notice anything distinctive about the voice?"

"Yes—I've heard it before."

"Do you remember where?"

"A week ago. In the elevator at Jefferson Storage."

"Lieutenant," Waldo Carnegie said, "it's obvious that this man has been stalking Leigh."

"We've been keeping a guard on Miss Baker," Cardozo said, "and we haven't seen him."

"You weren't guarding her tonight," Waldo Carnegie said.

"The cop had car trouble," Cardozo said. In fact, there was a possibility that the car had been sabotaged. While Leigh Baker had been nursing a coffee in the shop across the street from Archibald's, her guard had gone for a cup of coffee himself and had left the car unguarded. But Cardozo wasn't going to mention that. "He lost her."

"The police are underpaid and overworked," Waldo Carnegie said. "Maybe we should consider hiring a private guard again."

"That's your right," Cardozo said. "It might not be a bad idea, especially if Miss Baker intends to keep striking out on her own."

"I beg your pardon?" Waldo Carnegie said.

"Miss Baker was following Jim Delancey tonight—weren't you, Miss Baker?"

Waldo Carnegie rose from his sofa. He crossed to the sofa where Leigh Baker was sitting and took her hand. "Is that true, dear?"

Leigh Baker looked down at her lap. "I wanted to warn his girlfriend."

"We *are* aware of Jim Delancey's movements," Cardozo said.

"Not aware enough," Leigh Baker said.

"Darling," Waldo Carnegie said, "I understand your concern, and I'm sure Lieutenant Cardozo does too, but you mustn't complicate the work of the police. You don't want to become a contributory factor to the problem, do you?"

"I don't want Jim Delancey to kill again."

Waldo Carnegie bent and kissed the top of her head. When he turned to Cardozo, the smile on his face was that of a proud possessor. "What are we going to do with our little girl, Lieutenant—hold her in protective custody?"

"I'm sure that won't be necessary." Cardozo rose. "Good night."

Leigh Baker's eyes met his. He saw panic in them that she didn't even know was there. It would hit her in an hour, he reflected. She'd sleep with the light on tonight. He wanted to reach out and hold her and protect her. He tried to tell her all that with his eyes.

"I'm glad you're safe, Miss Baker."

■ ■ ■

"DID DELANCEY COME OUT of the building anytime tonight?" Cardozo was sitting at his desk. The switchboard had patched his phone through to the radio car.

"I haven't seen him so far." Carl Malloy had to shout over radio interference. His voice could have been coming by satellite from a Middle East war zone. "Not since he went into the girl's apartment at nine-thirty."

"Is there a service entrance?"

"Yes, there's a service entrance."

"Can you see it?"

"From where I'm parked now? No."

"Can you see the phone booth?"

"From where I'm parked now there's a truck in the way."

"So he could have come out the service entrance?"

"It's possible, but to get from the service entrance to that phone booth, he'd have had to cross Seventy-second, and I would have seen him."

· FIFTY-TWO ·

"THIS IS WHAT KILLED OONA and Avalon and Nan Shane." Sam Richards reached one hand into a Brooks Brothers shopping bag and brought out what looked like a thin mirror with a long handle.

Since ventilation in task-force headquarters was nonexistent, the door had to be kept half open. Sounds and cigarette smoke drifted in from the squad room. Cardozo waved a hand to shoo away a nebula layering the air in front of his face.

As Richards held the thing up, Cardozo could see it wasn't a mirror at all: It was a ten-inch knife.

"It's called a Darby knife," Sam Richards said. "The patented feature is the three-sided blade. It makes a triangular incision. When you're cut by a Darby, you stay cut. Salmaggi Blades of Worcester, Mass, manufactured about thirty thousand till the army stopped ordering them in 1979. The Darwin Darby estate controls the patent, and they've granted no license since." He leaned forward and handed the knife to Cardozo, rubber handle first.

Cardozo frowned. At the base where the blade joined the handle, it had three edges and three sides. They tapered out to a deadly-looking point. "I've never seen anything like it."

"It's weighted, so watch it. It has a will of its own."

Cardozo held the knife out horizontally above the floor. He could feel it, almost a living thing, a thinking thing, wanting not just to drop but to tip.

He released it.

The blade tipped forward and down, plunging in an arc like an Olympic high-diver. It hit linoleum point-first with the sound of a thump on a bass drum. It also hit with what must have been a thirty-pound-per-square-inch force.

A shock rippled up through the room. A wave rocked the coffee in Cardozo's cup. Sunk a half inch deep into the floor, the knife vibrated, sending out a tone like a plucked harp string.

It took Cardozo both hands and three grunts to work the blade loose. "Sharp little baby." He laid the knife down carefully on his desktop.

"I'm offended," Ellie said. "There's enough sadism and torture in the world without the American government jumping into the act."

"Write to your congressman," Greg Monteleone said.

▪ ▪ ▪

DICK BRAIDY STARED at the lunch menu. "What are you having, hon?"

"Sole *véronique,* " Leigh Baker said.

"I suppose I'll have the same." Dick Braidy sighed.

"And for vegetable, *madame?*" the waiter said.

"Whatever." Leigh Baker closed her menu and handed the gold-tooled Florentine leather binder back into the waiter's outstretched palm.

"Et pour m'sieur?"

"Well . . ." Dick Braidy prolonged the syllable, taking his time scanning the veggies *du jour. "Pommes vapeur."* He snapped the menu shut. *"And* a wastebasket."

"A *wastebasket, m'sieur?"*

"With the appetizer."

The wastebasket arrived before the appetizer. A busboy carried it across the crowded restaurant and set it on the floor beside the table. It was molded cedar, with a Stubbs horse print découpaged around it. It had come from the maître d's little peachwood standing desk by the front door.

"I know I promised to give back the diary today," Dick Braidy said. "But I'd like to keep it a little longer."

"Keep it as long as you need," Leigh said.

A manila envelope from *Fanfare Magazine* lay midway between Dick Braidy's champagne glass and Leigh Baker's glass of diet Pepsi. He pulled a smaller envelope out of it. He opened the smaller envelope and frowned for a microinstant at a printed invitation. He ripped the invitation into halves and tossed the halves into the wastebasket.

"This is the first time I've really had a chance to look at the diary," he said. "The only parts I'd ever read before are the pages the newspapers published."

"And now that you've seen it complete, what do you make of it?"

"I'm revolted. Disgusted. Outraged."

The tables and banquettes around them were crowded with designer-dressed society women and designer-dressed wannabee society women and their Lauren- and Armani-suited walkers. The air was feverish with clinking silver and tinkling wineglasses and a hundred simultaneous caffeine-rushed conversations.

"I want to stand up on a roof," Dick Braidy said, "and shout *fraud . . . fake . . . forgery!*"

"I did that and no one believed me."

He pulled a postcard from the *Fanfare* envelope, glanced at the photo of the Pope, and tossed it into the wastebasket. "But darling—you didn't have a roof to stand on."

"And do you have one?"

He pulled out yet another invitation, sighed, and sailed it into the wastebasket. "Absolutely. If the evidence warrants it."

"What evidence is that?"

"Now, you've got to promise. What I'm about to tell you, you'll keep under your hat. The forgers left tracks in the diary. They stole. I've never in my life seen such a brazen, undisguised act of appropriation."

"What did they steal?"

"Practically every word."

"Who from?"

"From me."

"You're joking."

Dick Braidy ripped up his last rejected invitation of the day's mail. By now the wastebasket was full of postcards, letters, solicitations, announcements, all ripped neatly in half. His foot pushed it toward the busboy.

"You can take this away," Dick Braidy told the busboy. He leaned closer to Leigh and spoke in a lowered voice. "I wish I *were* joking. But I've been over the pages, and it couldn't be clearer."

"It may be clear to you, but you're not making it very clear to me."

"In time, my darling. Let me just get my proof organized and in order, and you'll understand—and so will the world."

The waiter brought Dick Braidy's endive and Leigh Baker's asparagus, each appetizer with its own little silver bowl of vinaigrette.

"But what did you have," Leigh Baker said, "that they could possibly have wanted to steal?"

"The information that made the diary persuasive. The information that could have won Jim Delancey's acquittal."

"But he wasn't acquitted."

"Thanks to you, love. And he's not going to get away this time either. Just give me a few days to organize my facts."

"Tell the police now."

"No. It's premature."

"It's not premature. He attacked me last night."

Dick Braidy laid his fork down with a leaf of endive still clinging to the tines. "Jim Delancey attacked you?"

"I tried to warn his girlfriend . . . Oh, Dick, when I saw her —she so reminded me of Nita."

"Yes, Nita's type does seem to appeal to him."

"They were standing together on her balcony. She looked so trusting, so in love, I had to do *something.*"

"So what *did* you do?"

"I phoned her. Just to get her away from that railing. And while I was standing in the phone booth, he grabbed me from behind." She lowered her collar.

Dick Braidy gawked at the bruise. "He did *that*?"

■ ■ ■

AFTER DESSERT AND COFFEE Dick Braidy walked Leigh Baker to the door of Le Cercle. "I'll handle it, hon. The important thing is, *don't you worry.*"

She kissed him fondly. "Thanks for lunch. And everything else. I always feel better after we talk."

He waved good-bye. "Lots more talk where that came from."

He watched her cross the sidewalk and step into a cab. A moment later a black Plymouth double-parked at the curb pulled into traffic behind her, and he recognized it as the unmarked police car keeping watch on her movements. He turned and began making his way back across the restaurant. It was table-hopping time, and the narrow room was bright with the colors of *haute couture* and ringing with antiphonies of chattering voices and clattering silver.

Dick Braidy was wearing lightweight mocha silk slacks by Ernanno of Milan. He was wearing hand-dyed goatskin loafers by Horst of Lyons. He was not wearing socks. He was the only man in Le Cercle at that instant not wearing socks, and his bare ankles were East Hampton–tan, and proud.

He was setting a trend, and he knew it. Sockless lunch at Le Cercle.

Social collisions were hectic and free-spinning, and he negotiated them smoothly, dodging busboys at just the right moment, aiming the right smile at the right face, landing the right kiss on the right cheek. One right move after another brought him, finally, to Gloria Spahn's table.

Gloria was sitting at her usual corner table with Annie Mac-Adam. They made a high-contrast couple—Annie with her hennaed hair, looking like a chubby woman yearning to be anorectic, and Gloria overbejeweled and bizarrely made up in a way that you knew would be chic two months from now.

"Hi, gals." Dick Braidy helped himself to a chair. "Mucho poop."

A cigarette dangled from Gloria's make-this-quick-and-make-it-good scowl. Dick Braidy gave her a light.

"I advise you to get a good look at Kristi Blackwell over there," he said.

Gloria and Annie turned to look. Kristi was sitting with the Assistant Secretary of State for Latin American Affairs at table four, by the north pillar. Four was the President's table, Jackie's table, Liz's table.

"You're not going to see our little Kristi at the star table much longer," Dick Braidy said. "She's about to be a dead woman."

"Promises, promises," Gloria said without interest.

"Kid you not," Dick Braidy said. "A big exposé is in the works."

"Who's exposing her?" Annie said.

Dick Braidy pointed a thumb at himself. *"Moi.* How's that for hot?"

▪ FIFTY-THREE ▪

Thursday, June 13

ZACK'S SECRETARY, Minnie Simpson, buzzed on the intercom. "Annie MacAdam Associates is still busy, sir."

"*All* the numbers?" Zack said. It had been forty-eight hours since Annie had promised him that key. It seemed like an aching century since he'd last seen Gloria Spahn.

"All of them, sir."

"That's not possible, not even with her mouth. Check with the operator. Maybe there's trouble on the line."

Minnie buzzed him again. "The three lines are out of order, sir."

"Christ—this town's infrastructure is rotting."

Zack went to his desk and picked up tomorrow's editorial page. *To Restore Free Enterprise and Civic Self-Respect—Repeal the City Income Tax.* His eye skimmed the cooked figures from the mayor's office that Rad Rheinhardt had mixed in with Ayn Rand outtakes.

An image took shape on the retina of his mind. It was Gloria Spahn's breasts, floating weightlessly above the low, cupping bodice of her evening dress.

The intercom buzzed.

He laid the page down. "Yes?"

"Annie MacAdam to see you, sir."

All the tension drained out of Zack, and he took his first real breath of the day. "Send her in."

The door opened.

The woman who glided into his office was not Annie Mac-Adam.

Considering that she couldn't have been taller than five feet one and she must have weighed close to two hundred pounds, she moved with astonishing speed and lightness. She had pinned her dark hair back from her forehead, and she had made her eyes up with heavy accents of green and purple and blue. She wore an East Indian silk paisley shawl, and a brightly patterned maxiskirt swirled around her red calf walking boots.

She was smiling at him, and the energy of that smile took over the office immediately.

"Mr. Morrow? I'm Annie MacAdam's daughter, Gabrielle. Mother apologizes, but really Con Ed should do the apologizing, because they blew up our phone lines."

Zack blinked. It was the right size to be Annie's daughter, it was the right shape, but it was the wrong style. That little fatty had been a sick dog, but this little puppy had bounce.

"Mother asked me to bring you a key."

Zack came around the desk and thrust out a handshake. "Please call me Zack."

"If you'll call me Gaby."

"Hi, Gaby." *Cute nickname,* he thought.

"You know, Zack, we've met many, many times at Mother's dinners, but we've never had a chance to say a real hello. So— hello at last."

She took his hand. A key ring pressed with a cool little shock into his palm, and he felt inexplicably charmed.

"I wish I could stay and chat and get to know you," she said, "but I have another viewing. The address is on the key tag. It's Oona Aldrich's old town house."

"I know the place."

"Then do you think you could manage by yourself? Mother will be through showing it after four, so the place will be all yours from then on."

"I could manage." Zack returned her smile, thinking how sweet she was to have come all this way just to give him a key. "Sure. I think I could manage that."

■　■　■

IN THE BACKSEAT OF THE LIMO, the car phone rang.

Gloria Spahn felt a spasm in her intestine. It had to be Stanley calling from the heliport to ask why she was late. She still hadn't told him she didn't want to come to his boys' graduation. Usually she had no trouble telling Stanley no. But this time it had been bothering her, and for two days she hadn't been able to say the four simple words *I am not going.*

She lifted the receiver. "Hello?"

"Gloria, that you? Dick Braidy."

"I'm kind of in a rush, Dick."

"If you're rushing to the rector's dinner at Groton, I'm glad I caught you, because do you know who else is going to that dinner?"

Gloria wondered how the hell Dick found out about these things. "Stanley may have told me. I forget."

"Ruthie Sears is going." Ruthie was Stanley's ex-wife, the boys' mother. In the Eighties Ruthie and her third husband had served as coambassadors to Trinidad and Tobago. "She's guest speaker at the commencement exercises tomorrow."

"Christ. Does Stanley know?"

"Does the Pope speak Polish? The information is printed on the commencement program I am holding in my hand even as we speak."

"That bastard." Gloria made her fist tight around the receiver and willed the rage in her mind to slow. "Thanks, Dick. I owe you one."

The buildings along Lower Broadway glided past with a machine-tooled smoothness. The drone of traffic came through the smoked glass like waves of a faraway ocean. As the age-blackened tombstones of Trinity Church graveyard came into view, the limo swung east.

Gloria felt her nerves fraying and snapping one by one. Since seven o'clock last night she'd been caught in a scheduling logjam. She hadn't stayed for dinner—she didn't trust Splendiferous Eats's catering—but she couldn't be rude to Helen Hayes and she'd stayed much too long at Jackie O's fundraiser for the Metropolitan Museum costume collection. Then that crazed dash across town to River House for Lady Churchill's dinner in honor of Princess Di. The pheasant had been undercooked, but supposedly the prince had shot it and supposedly Ted Turner had flown it over in his corporate jet, so Gloria had had to smile at Lord Weidenfeld as she swallowed every detestable pink mouthful.

God, she thought, *I hate raconteurs.*

Even though the Peruvian ambassador lived just around the corner from River House at Sutton Place, it had still been a rush to get there in time for dessert. In the confusion she'd somehow managed to lose her only gold shawl. She loved that shawl—it had been a gift from Franco's widow. She was certain she'd left it in the Aga Khan's limousine, but this morning Karim's secretary had said the chauffeur swore she had not.

I never trusted that chauffeur of Karim's.

Then at lunch today, in the Grill Room at the Four Seasons, Donald Trump's new mistress had walked in wearing Gloria's shawl, not a similar shawl, but the very same shawl, with a Bulgari diamond brooch as big as a *fist* stuck right through it, and Gloria had turned to Philip Johnson and said, "That's it—there goes the city."

She'd been in a bad mood all afternoon, hadn't been able to concentrate on the horse show, hadn't thought Jeanie Vanderbilt's box was all that great for viewing the jumps, had barely managed to hold up her end of conversation with the First Lady.

As she thought back on it she realized these last twenty-four hours had left her drained, and she was in no mood to cap them off with cheddar cheese and stale crackers in a New England rectory.

Let Stanley try to give me an argument, she thought. *Let him just try.*

The limo came to a stop at the heliport. The uniformed driver stepped smartly around the limo, touched a finger to the brim of his cap, and held the passenger door. Gloria took her dark glasses from her pocketbook and slipped them on.

Stanley came striding toward her across the tarmac. "You're late. Where's your bag? Why aren't you dressed?"

"I'm not going to Groton."

Stanley's face held like a struck mirror determined not to break apart. "When the hell did you decide this?"

"When the hell did you learn Ruthie was going to be there? No way I'm going to sit and watch that bitch in a pink Scaasi cozy up to the rector."

"Do you object to the color pink or to Scaasi?"

"She always wears Scaasi when we're anywhere near each other, she does it to humiliate me."

At the end of the pier a helicopter engine roared to life. The rotors picked up spin, throwing off stroboscopic glints of fractured sunlight.

"Do you expect her to wear one of your designs?" Stanley shouted.

"I married *you*," Gloria shouted, "not your kids or your ex-wife! And I resent your using me like a red flag to wave in her face!"

"And I resent your not being by my side at this event!" Stanley clamped a hand on his head to steady the toupee. "And I resent your canceling forty-five minutes before we're expected at cocktails!"

"You and Ruthie can go have sherry with those Episcopalians! I'd rather do something important! Like work!" She turned on her heel and stepped back into her limo. *"Bon voyage,* big boy!" She only called him *big boy* when she was deeply annoyed with him.

Stanley gave her the finger. She gave him two fingers back, one with each hand.

The driver shut the door.

A moment later, peering through the window, Gloria saw Stanley's Sifcor helicopter rise from the end of the pier without her.

■ ■ ■

ZACK MORROW LOOKED AT HIS WATCH. Six o'clock. She was an hour late.

He opened the French window and stepped out into the silent, empty heat of the terrace. He crossed to the wall. He looked down five stories into a community garden. Boxwood hedges and inlaid paths of little flagstones outlined a neat mandala pattern. Through a wrought-iron fence, he could see the street.

His eye went to a grouping of wrought-iron garden furniture on the other side of the terrace. Chairs with circular pillows covered in waterproof blue canvas had been set around a square glass-topped table.

He pulled one of the chairs over to the wall. He sat, watching street traffic move past the garden fence.

■ ■ ■

AT NINE-FIFTEEN ZACK MORROW TOOK a little burgundy velvet jeweler's box from his pocket. He raised the little hinged lid. He lifted the cabochon-cut ruby-and-diamond ring from its velvet nest and held it up to the night sky, seeing it against the dense sprawl of the city.

After four hours he was still waiting, still alone.

He put the ring back in the box.

At nine-sixteen he saw movement down in the street. A white stretch limousine slowed to a stop at the curb. *It's her,* he thought.

The driver sprinted nimbly around and opened the passenger door. A woman got out.

Zack's stomach clenched when he saw she was not Gloria Spahn. She gave quick glances right and left, as though to be sure no serial killer was lurking. She hurried into the building next door.

In the hour since sunset all Zack's hopes and plans had dissolved in a kind of slow motion and now, suddenly, they weren't part of him anymore. It was obvious that Gloria Spahn was not going to keep their date.

When he lifted his gaze to the silver-gray skyline, he saw a city that was no longer worth owning.

He lifted a half-empty bottle of Stolichnaya from the terrace floor.

We could have been enjoying this Stoli.

He took a long, stinging belt of vodka from the bottle. He rose unsteadily from the chair and crossed the terrace. Inside the house he stepped into a bedroom decorated in muted tones of brown and red. He stared at the canopied bed.

We could have been enjoying that bed.

In the little bathroom, silver-backed brushes and mirrors and combs had been laid out on the little counter by the sink.

From his pocket he brought out the jeweler's box. He set it on the sink. He felt his pockets again and brought out a pillbox of uncut Bolivian flake.

We could have been enjoying this coke.

He dipped a coke spoon into the white powder. He fed one nostril, dipped the spoon again and fed the other. While his head orbited, he braced himself against the tiled wall and took a long, messy piss.

A dish of lemon-shaped soaps sat on top of the commode, scenting the air. He took one of the soaps and washed his hands. As he put the soap back he accidentally knocked the jeweler's box. It clattered to the floor.

Zack stood swaying, thinking about bending over and picking the box up. As he ran all the steps through his mind, he felt an exhaustion greater than any he had ever known.

No, he decided. He wouldn't bend. He wouldn't stoop. Leave it there. He'd done enough for her.

■ ■ ■

AT QUARTER PAST ELEVEN, the question Gloria Spahn was trying to resolve was this: Can the same eighteen-thousand-dollar cocktail dress attend a *thé dansant* in Cleveland at four-thirty in the afternoon, enjoy a presymphony lunch in Chicago at twelve-thirty the next day, and reach San Francisco in time for eight o'clock dinner at the Bohemian Club?

The answer, if the girl fielding phone calls for United Airlines weren't such a bimbo, would have been and should have been *yes.*

"I'm still entitled to forty-four-hundred miles on my frequent-flyer discount," Gloria told the girl.

"I understand, ma'am." The girl had a strong Texas accent that almost *smelled* of barbecue. "But that's a personal frequent-flyer account you're quoting."

"It's a company frequent-flyer account. I never fly *anywhere* personally."

"I'm sorry, but unless you yourself are flying we cannot prepay this booking on that account."

Gloria was speaking into the cellular phone. It allowed her to go from room to room, shutting off lights. "I'm not getting off this phone till you give me a confirmation number for this reservation."

"Then you're going to have to give me the number and expiration date of a valid major credit card *and* the name of the person who will be flying."

"I don't *know* who'll be flying." Gloria repinned a linen jacket sleeve on a tailor's dummy. "It'll be someone from my office."

"FAA regulations do not permit us to reserve seats on flights without the passenger's name."

Gloria had ordered in a *timbale de légumes,* a cold half of applewood-smoked chicken and a split of Piper. She rewrapped the uneaten portion of the chicken and slipped it into the refrigerator. "They've allowed it for the eight years that I've been flying my messengers United."

"Would you care to open a messenger account with us?"

Gloria rinsed the empty Piper bottle and put it in the rack beside the sink to drain. "I would care to speak with your supervisor."

A Texas sigh came across the line. The phone began serenading her with Muzak.

While Gloria waited she neatened her desk. The employees had gone home at six, and she was the last to leave today. She often worked best in the evening, when she could work uninterrupted.

A voice cut into "Begin the Beguine." "May I help you?"

Thank God—a man. "I know you could and I wish you would. This is Gloria Spahn, of Gloria Spahn Designs, Ltd.? I'd like a confirmation number on a reservation."

One minute and eighteen seconds later Gloria laid the phone in the recharging unit on her desk. She had her confirmation number, and the dress was set to fly Monday with a frequent-flyer discount.

She took one last look around the office to make sure she hadn't left anything running that shouldn't be. She crossed the showroom, tapped her code into the burglar alarm, turned off the lights, and let herself out.

In the hallway she pushed the elevator button. There were two elevators, and neither of them came. She pushed again, leaning hard on the button this time. Elevators were like people: It didn't pay to treat them subtly. Somewhere down the shaft she heard a buzz.

Two other businesses—Saul MacGuire Skin Care and Marianna Cosmetics—shared the floor with Gloria Spahn Designs, Ltd. There were no lights under either of their doors. Gloria checked her watch. The little platinum watch hands formed a tilted right angle that spelled eleven-twenty.

Gloria felt proud of herself. She hadn't wasted a thought on Groton, or Stanley, or the ex-Mrs. Siff, for more than four hours.

She leaned an ear against the door of the north elevator. The machinery could have died and gone to heaven. Not even a hum.

She listened at the door of the south elevator. The loudest sound was her own heartbeat.

She pushed the button and waited, waited and pushed the button.

What the shit is wrong with these elevators? With the service fees we pay the contractor, they can't both have crapped out at once. . . .

But obviously they had done exactly that.

Gloria considered her options. No one was going to come to her rescue at this hour. She was the last person on the floor, possibly the last person in the building. From the ninth floor to street level was a walk down eight flights of stairs.

"Fuck."

She went around the bend in the corridor to the service stairwell. A sign on the door warned:

EMERGENCY EXIT ONLY. WARNING. ALARM WILL SOUND. NO REEN-
TRY FROM STAIRWELL—ALL DOORS ARE LOCKED EXCEPT GROUND
STORY.

She pushed through the door. The alarm activated. It made a deafening sound, like the gargling of an electronic mouth.

With one hand holding the door open, she peered over the iron bannister down the well.

The lights were out on one of the floors below.

Do I really want to do this? she wondered.

She thought about having the bed to herself all night.

I really want to do this.

She let the edge of the door slide off her fingers. It shut with a soft, air-braked slam. The alarm stopped. Silence fell like the drop of a blade.

Muggy, foul-smelling air stagnated around her.

She began walking. Her shoes clicked on each steel step, sending out a little tap that triggered an avalanche of echoing taps.

Halfway down the flight she wobbled. Two-inch heels, she realized, were not the best equipment for this hike. She attached a hand to the railing.

She passed the eighth-story landing.

Then the seventh. The sixth.

As she approached the fifth she saw that it was here that the lights were out. She looked over the bannister and saw that there was no light below her.

That struck her as wrong. When she had looked down a moment ago, hadn't the lights been out on only one floor?

With slow, echoing taps she passed from light into twilight. She gripped the bannister tighter. As her steps took her deeper into darkness, she had more and more trouble seeing her feet and estimating how far down *down* was.

Her left foot completely missed the next step, swinging out into emptiness. The rest of her followed in a sickening lurch. She grabbed for the handrail.

She landed hard on her left assbone. A pain shot through her butt that was like a flash of blue in front of her eyes.

She tried to pull herself up. First problem: Where was the rest of her? A throb in her right ankle told her that her leg was somewhere in front of her, twisted very, very wrong.

Using the bannister as a crutch, she pulled herself to half standing.

As she put weight on her ankle she saw red flashes. The pain was so much worse than anything she'd expected that she wanted to scream.

Shit. Double shit.

She realized she actually had screamed.

Shit . . . shit . . . shit . . . The syllable bounced like a pebble ricocheting off the walls of the dark well, pursued by *Double shit . . . double shit . . . double shit . . .*

She lowered herself to the step. Both hands explored slowly down the leg. When they reached the ankle they found a hard, stinging edge of cartilage where she had never felt a hard, stinging edge of anything before.

She sighed.

"All right, God, you made your point. I should have gone to Groton."

After a few minutes she levered herself forward, bracing with the left leg. When she was far enough out, she lowered her butt to the next step. She sat catching her breath. Her mouth was parched and her heart was pounding.

She levered herself out again, down to the next step.

This, she realized, *is going to take all fucking night.*

Somewhere in the darkness above her an air brake exhaled.

She looked around. A door thudded softly.

"Who's there? Is someone there?"

The word *there . . . there . . . there . . .* echoed around her.

Nothing moved.

She lowered herself another step. She thought she heard the tap of a footstep.

"Hello," she sang out. "Is there a Good Samaritan somewhere around here?"

New dimensions in wishful thinking, she reflected.

She lowered herself two more steps. And another two. And then she rested, trying to catch her breath.

Something slid into her mind, just beneath the threshold of awareness. She tried to bring it up into consciousness.

Her eyes circled the darkness.

What? she wondered. *What's wrong?*

Her instincts were flashing her a warning.

What am I hearing?

She turned her head and squinted. The darkness seemed to be waiting for her, holding its breath. . . .

The breathing, she realized. *That's not me. I'm holding my breath.*

Someone else was breathing.

Her ears strained to localize the sound. It seemed to be coming from no more than six feet away, up the stairs behind her.

The breathing stopped.

The seconds ticked by, crawling like cockroaches over her skin.

She heard three distinct taps. Three distinct footsteps. Each one closer, each one setting off a cascade of fading echoes.

"Please," she said. "Don't hurt me."

Two more taps.

Now he was standing on the step directly above her. She could feel his body pushing out a heat that was different from the heat of the stairwell.

"I have money," she said. "I'll pay you. Let me go."

A man's voice said two words. "Stupid bitch."

Something stranglingly powerful went around her and jerked her upward, up to her feet and then up higher. A *whoosh* came through the air, stinging hotly across her throat, and then a second *whoosh,* another sting.

Out of nowhere hot water gushed down the front of her dress.

That's impossible, she thought, her mind flailing in denial. *This isn't happening. There's no hot water here.*

But each *whoosh* cut deeper, and with each unbearable sting she realized that it truly was happening, and *she* was the hot water.

▪ FIFTY-FOUR ▪

"BUT WHEN YOU TAKE A LOOK AROUND," Tori said, "you have to know the city is in trouble."

"But darling," Kristi Blackwell said, "that's only part of the story. Why not get people's minds off all the mess?"

Tori shook her head. "That's like putting Scotch tape over the cracks in a crumbling building."

They had come, finally, to the end of an all-right meal at what struck Tori as a barely all-right new TriBeCa restaurant. She was on automatic pilot, trying to keep conversation going and at the same time swiveling in her seat and trying to signal the waiter for the check. All evening long she had felt Zack's unexplained absence like a nagging ache.

"New York may be crumbling," Kristi Blackwell said. "But this restaurant certainly is not. It's thriving. And everyone here tonight is thriving. Look around you. I see the two top decorators in Manhattan sitting three tables away. The Eastern Seaboard's most important philanthropist is entertaining eleven over there. Three top couturiers are here tonight, Bunny Dexter is over there with Claus von Bulow—and isn't that Julia and Marty? Have they reconciled? This is, to put it bluntly, *the* hot spot. And it's just as real and just as important as any slum or abortion clinic or crackhouse in this city."

"But it's not," Tori said. "The slums and the crackhouses in this city could wind up destroying us."

"And if I saw the prices on that menu correctly," Kristi Blackwell said, "so could this restaurant!"

Kristi's husband Wystan burst out laughing. "Touché, Kristi—touché!"

The waiter finally brought the check, snugly hidden inside a handsome Florentine leather folder. He set it on the table at Tori's right hand.

The protocols of cool forbade Tori's opening the folder and seeing how much was to be paid. In this age, in this social set, you simply slapped a charge card down and signed whatever came back. Anything else suggested that you doubted the restaurant's addition or your own credit.

But she had expected Zack to be here to pay for tonight's meal, and she tried to recall which of her cards left her the greatest leeway. American Express had no limit—on the other hand, that was the magazine's card, and the magazine was three months behind on its accounts payable.

She decided MasterCard was her best bet—she couldn't recall having used it lately.

With a small, courtly bow the waiter took the card.

"Why the hell," Kristi Blackwell was saying, "should I dress down, just because bag ladies have no style sense?"

"Overdressing might be an incitement," Tori said.

"An incitement to whom?" Wystan Blackwell said.

"To people who can't even afford rags."

"People who can't afford rags in this city," he said, "in this day and age, don't exist." Three weeks ago he had been installed as East Coast vice president of the country's largest talent agency. His vice-presidential qualifications, so far as Tori could see, were two: a booming British public-school accent, and a gray goatee. He had begun taking himself very seriously. "The homeless," he said, "are largely a creation of *The Village Voice.*"

"And just because they look horrible," Kristi Blackwell said, "why must the rest of us? My friends get a kick out of my clothes. My husband gets a kick out of my clothes—don't you, darling. Christ, my *doorman* gets a kick out of my clothes. My clothes make this city a better environment, and so do the clothes of every New York woman who has the taste and dedication to buy couture originals. We're not just dressing ourselves—we're dressing the city. And I'm damned tired of being accused of selfishness."

The maître d' brought Tori's charge card back to the table. "I'm sorry, madam, but the bank has declined your card."

"How annoying." Tori engineered the stress of a smile over her cheekbones. "Oh, well, that happens—it looks like a case of corporate overstretch."

He did not join in her smile. He did not even make the attempt.

"Did they say how close to the credit limit I was charged?"

"Madam, they simply said *declined.*"

"Okay, let's have a look at where we are." Tori waved a merry hand to the others. "Just a little mix-up. Everybody, please have some more coffee or order a liqueur."

"I'd like a double Courvoisier," Wystan said. "With a dash of bitters."

Tori pushed her glasses down as far as they would go without falling off her nose. She examined the bill with its scrawl of illegible detail.

What was not illegible was the total: one thousand four hundred sixty-four dollars.

That couldn't be right, she thought. They'd all had that consommé of white truffle in stock of unborn veal and then some pheasant, some duck, some salmon, and somewhere during the evening, in some salad or on some vegetable or other, she remembered alphabet pieces of fresh Dutch yellow and red peppers.

And dessert, of course, and wine . . .

The wine, she realized. The two bottles of Château Margaux '85 and the two of Clos de Vougeot '83. Nine hundred dollars for four bottles.

"Okay," Tori said in her brightest, most can-do voice, "you'll have to divide the bill." She opened her purse and took out her Discover card, her Visa, her American Express. "Between them they'll cover it. Just keep juggling."

The maître d's face became a blank wall of refusal. "I cannot do that, madam."

"Darling," Kristi Blackwell called over from her side of the table, "are we still having trouble?"

"It's all under control," Tori said.

Kristi Blackwell opened her purse. She took out her American Express card.

"No, Kristi," Tori said. "Please. You're a guest."

"Next time." Kristi handed the card to the maître d'. "These mix-ups can take forever. I've really got to get home. I hate being out late with that killer on the loose."

"Thank you, madam." The maître d' bowed to Kristi Blackwell and took the card away.

■   ■   ■

TORI WAS TRYING TO READ the new issue of *Fanfare* when she heard the front door slam. Her ear followed Zack's steps up the stairs.

When she looked across the bedroom, he was standing there with his jacket slung over his shoulder and his shirt unbuttoned. She slapped down the magazine. "You and I had a dinner date tonight."

Zack's face expressed apology only in that it expressed nothing. "I'm sorry. I got sidetracked."

"You were inexcusably rude not only to me but to two of your friends." She stood, tightening the sash of her nightgown. "*Your* friends, not mine."

He gave a vague shrug. "They'll handle it."

"I was stuck for fifteen hundred dollars, plus tip, and the restaurant turned down my charge card."

He swayed a little. "You look like you handled it."

"Maybe it's macho to be casual out there in your world of deals and bullshit, but not in our relationship."

"Look," he said, "today has not exactly been my day at the beach. Whatever argument you've got your heart set on, I'm not up for it. So could you please minimize this hyper thing you do?"

"The hell I'll minimize! I waited five hours for you to show up, wondering if you'd been hit by a truck, wondering if some tenant activist had sent you a letter bomb. Wondering if Society Sam had decided to carve you up. You could have phoned."

"I said I'm sorry."

"A relationship has *rules.*"

"Rules are for games. I don't play games."

"I was raised with the old-fashioned notion that we keep the commitments we make."

"Why the hell can't you just accept that you're pissed off and give me the silent treatment?"

"Because I am not a bimbo who's going to resort to bimbo tactics."

"Bimbo tactics might work a little better than yours."

"What the hell is that supposed to mean?"

"It means the wee hours of the morning are turning into the wee-wee hours, so excuse me."

He didn't use their bathroom. He stumbled into the hall and she heard the toilet flush in the guest bathroom. When he stumbled back, he was in his undershirt, with a beer in one hand and a cigarette in the other.

"I thought you'd stopped smoking," Tori said. "We promised each other."

"That was three years ago. Three years is long enough to keep a promise."

She stared at him. His eyes were red, his face puffy. "You're drunk, and you've been doing coke."

"Can I level with you? I'm drunk, I've been doing coke."

She watched him stumble over a footstool and fall. The can of beer sent a foaming arc across the Oriental rug. *Christ,* she thought. *This is the man I want to marry?*

She rose and moved to the window. She stood staring out at night silhouettes of the beautifully maintained co-ops of Park Avenue.

"I've accepted a lot about our relationship," she said. "I accept that we don't agree politically. Within limits I accept your womanizing. But I cannot accept your publicly humiliating me in front of people I have to work with."

He sat on the floor blinking his eyes. "My head is killing me."

"How serious are you about Gloria Spahn?"

"This discussion is killing me."

She turned. "If you don't give me a straight answer, Zack, I swear, I'm going to—"

"You're going to what?"

For a moment she stood perfectly still, staring at the man in front of her. She had a complicated sense that they were both playing roles, and they both knew it. "I'm going to leave you."

"Okay."

She couldn't believe he'd said it. She saw something goofy in his face. *It's the booze talking,* she told herself. *It's the coke.*

But she could see in his eyes that whether he meant it or not, he wasn't going to back down.

For that instant she was flailing in her mind, trying to persuade herself that she wasn't choking to death. She realized that if ever there was a time that called for faith in herself, it was this instant, right now.

"You've got it," she said. It took her two minutes to throw on a dress and another five to toss some things into a suitcase.

All the while he sat there, swaying a little on the edge of the bed, watching her with that slightly daffy look.

"I'll send for the rest," she said.

■ ■ ■

ZACK HEARD THE FRONT DOOR CLOSE. Just a closing, not even a slam. As though, even at the end, she had it all under control, didn't care.

A silence slipped by and sank in.

Zack pulled himself to the bed. He turned off the light. He listened as though, if he listened hard enough, the dark could tell him a secret.

And then he pulled a pillow to his body and curled around it and began crying.

▪ FIFTY-FIVE ▪

Friday, June 14

CARDOZO SHOWED HIS SHIELD.

"In the stairwell." The super breathed out a plume of gray smoke. "Fourth floor. You can take the elevator."

"Thanks," Cardozo said. "I'll walk." After all, the dead woman obviously hadn't taken the elevator.

The air in the stairwell was damp and uncomfortably warm. As he climbed it got warmer, and a smell like unwashed towels grew stronger.

He stopped to wipe the sweat away from his eyes. Only six-thirty in the morning, and he felt himself perspiring, his undershirt already beginning to stick to his skin.

Overhead on each landing, a naked hundred-watt bulb glowed like a tired moon. Behind the wall he could hear something whirring and dropping inside the elevator shaft.

As he climbed up the half flight to the fourth-story landing, a flashbulb went off. The police photographer rose from a crouch. There was a whirring as film automatically rolled forward to the next exposure. The photographer found a smile for Cardozo. "Starting work early today, hey, Lieutenant?"

"No earlier than you," Cardozo said.

A light had been set up on a tripod, as if this were a movie. A thousand watts beamed down on the dead woman. She lay on her back, sprawled diagonally across the landing. Her legs were splayed out, and one of her shoes was missing.

"Why'd she take the stairs?" Cardozo said.

"The super found two *New York Posts* jammed in the elevator doors," Lou Stein said. He had hung the jacket of his summer-weight suit over the bannister. From a crouched position he was playing the beam of his high-intensity flashlight over the ridges and valleys of the landing and the steps below.

Cardozo studied Gloria Spahn's face, and she seemed to study his. She had a baffled look, and it occurred to him that she was trying her damnedest to bring him into focus.

"Did she wear contacts?"

The assistant M.E. had assumed a half-lotus position beside the dead woman. She was working with tweezers and her upper-body movements were easy and unrushed. She nodded. She had a low-pitched, extremely cultivated voice. "And she lost one of them."

"It's over here." Lou Stein flicked the beam of his flashlight toward the wall. The missing lens sparkled like a drop of glycer-ine.

"Be sure to bag that," Cardozo reminded the redheaded man from the crime-scene truck. The redheaded man was busy tag-ging items from the dead woman's spilled purse, and he gave a barely perceptible nod.

Cardozo's gaze went back to Gloria. Spattered blood had mottled her blouse like a rotten pear. His eye traced the punc-tures where the blade had entered, the rips where it had pulled.

"Yeah," the M.E. said, noticing his attention. "Beautiful ma-terial, isn't it?"

The skirt was no longer exactly clothing, and it wasn't yet exactly garbage. It was an assemblage of scrap and beads and blood-soaked fiber, and it had the frightening look of something that had been shoved through a threshing machine.

Cardozo sniffed. His nostrils took in the metallic residue of blood and the petroleum residue of the chemicals that had been used to lift the stains from the floor. He also smelled decay and a faint odor of fecal matter.

"That's her," the assistant M.E. said. "She shit her panties."

"Hey, Vince." Lou Stein was shining his light along one of the steps. There were gray rings where a track shoe had left an im-print in a spill of white. "Candle wax."

"What about the clipping?" Cardozo said. "Anyone find a newspaper clipping anywhere?"

■ ■ ■

ONE BY ONE Cardozo angled the Polaroids of Gloria Spahn under the cone of fluorescence that flickered from his desk lamp. His left hand rapped a ballpoint pen against the lamp. He took a swallow of coffee. The taste was supermarket generic, but his nerves craved the kick.

The phone rang. He snatched up the receiver before a second ring could jangle his nerves. "Vince Cardozo."

"Vince, it's Walter Vanderflood here. Wanted you to know I haven't forgotten our little chat. Am I calling too early?"

"Hell, no. I've been up since quarter of six."

"What the hell were you doing at that hour, jogging?"

"Nothing so healthy, I'm afraid. Just doing my job."

"Sounds like an awful job."

"It can be."

"I had dinner at the Union Club last night."

Good for you, Walter. Cardozo sat tapping his pen, waiting for the punch line. *How was the filet mignon?*

"I ran into Charley Benziger. Do you know him? Big, athletic fellow, affiliated with Morgan Stanley. He also serves on the Dutchess County parole board, which is why I'm calling. He wasn't at the meeting where they considered Jim Delancey's application. He was down in the Bahamas, taking a little time off to recover from surgery—poor guy had triple by-pass."

"Poor guy." *And why are you telling me about him?*

"But he did get briefed on how the board voted in his absence, and one of the board members told him the most extraordinary thing. Apparently Senator Nancy Guardella brought ungodly pressure to make sure Delancey got parole."

"Senator *Guardella?*" Cardozo reached behind him and swung the cubicle door closed, shutting out a little of the clanging, banging world. "Is Guardella a member of the parole board?"

"Christ, no. The woman's not a member of anything except those clubs in Congress. But she's on the House Energy Committee, and two directors of Dutchess Light and Power do happen to serve on the parole board. Now, please don't quote me, but she agreed not to block an energy excise-tax rollback, *provided* Delancey got parole. You know, everything I hear about that woman convinces me I was right to vote against her in the last election."

"I appreciate your help, Walter."

"Anytime, Vince."

■ ■ ■

"THERE WAS ONLY one party preview in the society column in yesterday's *Trib.*" Seated at the desk in task-force headquarters, Cardozo read from the crime-scene photo of the clipping that had been found under Gloria Spahn's body. "*Princess Hedwig von und zu Aschenbach is not running out of pizazz. Tonight the red-hot center of* le tout *New York will be the two Park Avenue apartments that ever-resourceful Hedi, with a little help from everybody's friend, designer hyphen decorator Fennimore Gurdon, has converted into one simply nifty Park Avenue duplex. La Divina Hedi will be treating ninety-two of her intimates to a dinner of pheasant carpaccio"*—and so on and so forth.

"Don't stop." Greg Monteleone guffawed, clasping his arms around his chest. Today he was wearing a chocolate-colored shirt and bright green suspenders. "I'm coming!"

"Gloria wasn't killed anywhere near that party," Sam Richards said. "She was killed on a back stairway two miles away."

"So why did the killer leave the column?" Cardozo said.

"Because he's goofing," Greg Monteleone said.

"I disagree," Ellie Siegel said. "The *Trib* society columns are somehow pointing the killer to his victims."

"It's a free country." Greg Monteleone gave one of his suspenders a snap. "You're entitled to your opinion."

I've got enough problems in my life, Cardozo decided, *without having to listen to the Greg and Ellie Show.* "Okay, guys. I want everyone to think back four years. Did Nancy Guardella's name ever come up in the Delancey case?"

"Not that I recall," Ellie said.

"Then why's Guardella interested in him?" Cardozo said.

"Who says she's interested?" Sam Richards said.

"She traded his parole for her vote on the energy committee."

"That bitch doesn't do anything for anyone," Greg Monteleone said, "unless there's a wheelbarrow of unmarked bills under the table."

"What can a punk like Delancey offer a U.S. Senator?" Sam Richards said.

Monteleone arched an eyebrow. "Salad."

"Maybe he's connected," Ellie said.

"Sure he's connected," Monteleone said. "His mom sells summer scarves at a boutique in a Fifth Avenue department store."

"Carl," Cardozo said, "where was Jim Delancey last night?"

"Delancey left work a little later than usual." Carl Malloy hadn't shaved this morning. His eyes were bloodshot and he took a moment to refer to his notepad. "Eight-fifty. He took his usual slow walk down to Beekman Place. He reached Twenty-nine Beekman at nine thirty-five and went upstairs."

I've also got enough problems, Cardozo realized, *without this coffee.* He set the styrofoam cup down on the desk and pushed it far enough away that he couldn't unthinkingly pick it up again.

"Over the next twelve hours," Carl Malloy said, "two detectives watched the front entrance, two detectives watched the back entrance. Jim Delancey didn't leave the building till eight-thirty this morning, when he walked to the corner and bought a newspaper."

Sam Richards sat pulling at his right ear. "That shoots Delancey out of the running."

"You never seriously believed Delancey did *that*," Greg Monteleone said. With a sweeping movement of his hand he indicated the five blackboards now standing at the front of the room. Each had its own sad little stick figure: Oona, Avalon, Dizey, Nan, and—today's newcomer—Gloria.

"Tell me, Greg," Ellie Siegel said, "why couldn't Delancey have done that?"

"Because he's chickenshit."

"And was he chickenshit when he threw Nita Kohler off the terrace?"

"I must be in the wrong room. I thought this was a task-force meeting, not the Feminist Day of Rage."

"Maybe you are in the wrong room," Ellie said. "Or maybe I am." She rose and marched out of the room.

Greg Monteleone leaned back in his chair and smiled, folded in a curtain of smugness.

"Ellie," Cardozo said. "For God's sake, come back." He went into the squad room after her.

She was standing at her desk, leafing through a manila folder full of clippings.

"Greg was goofing," Cardozo said. "Don't let it get to you like that."

"Nothing that adolescent does could get to me." She handed Cardozo a clipping. "Have a look at the column Dick Braidy published Tuesday."

Cardozo saw that she had highlighted one of the paragraphs.

A certain real-estate-and-media mogul is taking very long lunch hours looking at posh pied-à-terres or, pardonnez my French, do I mean pieds-à-terre? Accompanying him on these urban field trips is a certain designing lady who, according to those who've been there, has a lot more to offer the eye and the bankbook than his current live-in.

Cardozo's eyes met Ellie's.

"Does that designing woman remind you of anyone?" she said.

▪ ▪ ▪

THE MEXICAN SERVANT WOMAN led Cardozo into Dick Braidy's living room.

"I'm sorry," Cardozo said. "Did I wake you up?"

"Yes, Lieutenant," Dick Braidy said, "and that's my excuse for wearing a bathrobe at nine-thirty in the morning. How can I help you?"

Cardozo handed him the clipping. "You can tell me if the woman in that item is Gloria Spahn. And if it is, who's the man?"

Dick Braidy was silent. His lips thinned, and Cardozo could feel him running scenarios through his mind.

"Why do you ask?"

"Because Gloria Spahn was murdered early this morning."

"Oh, my God." Dick Braidy sank onto the sofa. "I hate to name names. I don't even know if the story was true." Something very much like panic was creeping into his eyes. "I got it from a doorman."

"What was the story?"

"He said Gloria was having assignations with Zack Morrow in an apartment Annie MacAdam was trying to sell."

▪ ▪ ▪

"ACCORDING TO ANNIE MACADAM'S RECORDS," Cardozo said, "you looked at two properties—an apartment and a town house."

Zack Morrow nodded grimly. "That's right."

They were sitting in Zack Morrow's office on the top floor of the *Tribune* building. It was a corner office, with mostly Mission furniture and a picture postcard view of the South Street Seaport.

"According to Mrs. MacAdam's records, Gloria Spahn looked at the same two properties at the same time."

Zack Morrow thought for a moment. He spun around slowly in his swivel chair. It was a high-tech design, with chrome rods and white leather padding and tiny radial wheels, and it looked as though it ought to be able to lie down like the front seat in a BMW. "Annie's records aren't quite right. Gloria never came to the town house."

"But you and Miss Spahn did look at the apartment at One twelve East Seventy-second together?"

"Yes, we did. Three times."

"Why was that? Were you two thinking of buying a property together?"

"No, not quite." Morrow's white dress shirt was open at the collar. His finger went up to trace out the faintly contrasting off-white monogram on the pocket. "Not exactly. Gloria was a married woman, and at the moment I . . ." Morrow's lips pulled together into a thin, unhappy line. "I'm in a relationship . . . and we had no place to meet."

"You and Miss Spahn were having an affair?"

Zack Morrow's eyes met Cardozo's carefully. Cardozo detected hesitation.

"I would have liked for it to be an affair. I don't know whether she felt the same."

"Apparently she felt enough the same to meet you in properties that Annie MacAdam was offering for sale."

"We met three times in the apartment on Seventy-second. I asked Gloria to meet me a fourth time, five o'clock yesterday, in the Aldrich town house. I waited for her till midnight, but she never showed up."

"You waited till midnight?"

Zack Morrow nodded. "Yes. Till midnight."

"Do you have any idea why she didn't keep the date?"

"She was angry at me."

"Why was she angry?"

"Dick Braidy published a blind item. It hinted that Gloria and I were seeing each other. She told me she wouldn't see me if it was going to involve her in publicity."

"Could she have decided to break with you over that item?"

"Look," Zack Morrow said, "I don't know what the hell Gloria was thinking. To be absolutely frank, I don't even know what the hell *I* was thinking. She never said she'd come to the town house. I just made the appointment—and hoped."

■ ■ ■

"ONE THING MATRIX MAGAZINE does not need," Tori Sandberg said, "is another ghostwritten profile in bullshit. She conned you. She cons everyone." Tori read from one of the pages of the proposed article: *"Are we as a nation comfortable with sex-selection abortions?"*

Beneath schoolgirlish blond bangs, Anita Flynn's pale green eyes stared out pleasantly. "Well, are we?" Anita's position at *Matrix Magazine* was, nominally, editorial assistant. It was part of the outdated feminism around the office that no one was a secre-

414 ■ EDWARD STEWART

tary—they were editorial assistants instead. Which meant that, in addition to answering phones, Anita wrote occasional filler and took home a secretary's salary and lived in hope of one day seeing her by-line in print.

"The question's a trap," Tori said. "You shouldn't have given her the opening. The issue isn't sex-selection abortions or incest abortions or any *kind* of abortions, it's choice *period.* Choice is a woman's right. You don't protect rights by subdividing them like a condo and selling them off to interest groups. Bridget Braidy is a publicist for the policies of the most feudal archdiocese in the nation, and I'm not happy giving her space in the magazine."

Anita's smile caved in. She pointed a thumb to the wall. "Commissioner Braidy can hear you. She's right outside that door waiting for her appointment."

"Appointment?" Tori glanced down at the date book. Anita had scribbled something in the ten-thirty space, and it just conceivably could have been the word *commissioner.*

The phone on Tori's desk chose that moment to ring.

"Christ," Tori said, "I don't even want to know who that is."

The problem with having an editorial assistant was that there were times when you could really have used a secretary.

"Anita, would you please?"

Anita picked up the receiver. "Ms. Sandberg's line. Oh, Mr. Morrow, she's stepped away from her desk."

"I'll take it." Tori reached a hand. "Zack, I'm running late for an appointment, and I have to catch a 'copter to the Hamptons at five."

"Don't leave me. You're the only decent thing in my life."

"I'm in a rotten mood, so if you're trying to persuade me to come back, don't try today."

"You're part of me, Tori. I can't go through another night without you. When my arms reach out and you're not next to me, I feel like dying. I'm nothing without you."

"Give it a rest, Zack." Didn't he have any idea how cornball he sounded when he drank? He must have had a night of insomnia and TV movies. *Poor guy.* Tori flipped the weekend pages of her date book. "I'll be back Monday morning. How about lunch? I have a cancellation. But do me a favor and be sober."

"Tori, I'm in trouble. Gloria Spahn's been murdered."

"Come off it, Zack." Channel Eleven must have been showing a Forties' *film noir.* "That's not funny. Not with what's been going on. Not funny at all."

"I didn't touch her. I didn't even *see* her. You're the one I want. Not her. Marry me, Tori."

"Zack, what have you been taking?"

"Marry me today. Now. Right away."

"I can't talk with you when you're like this, and anyway I can't talk now. Just don't drink and whatever you've been doing—don't do it anymore. And don't forget Monday." Tori broke the connection. She tried to force her face into a semibelievable smile. "Anita, would you ask Commissioner Braidy to step in?"

■ ■ ■

GABRIELLE USED THE KEY with the Annie MacAdam Associates tag to let herself in. The entrance hall of Oona Aldrich's town house smelled of old furniture polish and emptiness. Gabrielle closed the front door behind her and took the elevator up to the living room floor.

One of the French windows that led to the terrace had been left open.

"Honestly." Gabrielle glanced out onto the terrace and saw that a chair had been dragged to the wall. *Let it be,* she decided. She saw an empty bottle sitting beside the chair. *No,* she decided. *That will never do.*

She went and got the bottle and brought it into the house. She closed the French window and twisted the key in the lock.

She stepped into the brown-and-red bedroom that had been Oona Aldrich's. She set her oversized Annie MacAdam Associates briefcase down on the gilt beechwood chair and snapped it open. She lifted out two fresh sheets and two fresh pillowcases and made space for them on the table beside the small, canopied bed.

She folded back the silk bedspread. What she saw startled her. The pillows were undented. Unslept-on.

She pulled the spread farther back. The sheets were unwrinkled.

Nobody used the bed, she realized.

She frowned.

But somebody was here. Somebody drank the vodka and left the bottle on the terrace and forgot to close the French window.

The MacAdam Associates log had listed two five o'clock viewers yesterday for the Aldrich town house: Zack Morrow and Gloria Spahn. Which was why Annie had sent Gabrielle yesterday to put fresh sheets on the bed. Which was why Gabrielle had returned today with a fresh set of fresh sheets.

Something must have happened, Gabrielle realized; and

then, looking at the two sets of fresh sheets, *Something must not have happened.*

Gabrielle was just as glad. She was tired of changing sheets for her mother. She was tired of being a combination cook-chambermaid.

As she returned to the living room her eye caught the gap in the bookshelf and she remembered the vellum-bound copy of *Faust* that she had hidden. She opened the bedroom closet and stood on tiptoe. The smell of cedar engulfed her. Her hands explored the upper shelf and finally found the book. She put it back in its place in the living room bookcase.

Now, she saw with irritation, there was dust on her hands. She went into the bathroom and washed. Once her hands were clean she rinsed the lemon-shaped ball of tea-rose glycerine soap till it too was clean. She set it back in its little marble tray.

The soap, still damp, rolled off the tray onto the floor.

"Shit." Gabrielle got down on all fours and chased the soap under the sink. It bounced off the wall and struck something.

The something, Gabrielle saw with surprise, was a small burgundy-velvet jeweler's box that, for some reason, was sitting beside the drainpipe.

Gabrielle picked up the jeweler's box. She shook it. Whatever was inside made a velvety sort of rattle. She placed the box carefully on the edge of the sink.

She picked up the soap. She washed her hands again. She washed the soap again and placed it firmly in its tray. She dried her hands on one of Oona Aldrich's monogrammed towels, and then she arranged the towel on the rack so the monogram showed and the dampness didn't.

Finally she opened the jeweler's box.

A cabochon-cut ruby-and-diamond ring winked at her.

▪ ▪ ▪

THE FRONT DOORBELL WAS JANGLING in the rhythm of a Sousa march. Zack realized it was Tori, she'd forgotten her key, she was ready to make up. He pulled on his Jockey shorts and stumbled through his dizziness down the stairs and opened the front door.

A short, fat woman in a gold lamé shawl was standing in the outer vestibule. He had the impression that she was already talking to somebody.

"I was on Sixty-fifth Street," she was saying. "I saw a light on. Did I wake you up?"

He hadn't the faintest idea who she could be or what she

could be doing there at that hour. The extraordinary greens and purples and blues of her eye shadow reminded him of a ballerina's stage makeup, but she couldn't be a ballerina—not with two hundred pounds on a five-foot-one frame.

"Who are you?" he said. "Who let you up here?"

"I'm Gaby—Annie MacAdam's daughter, remember? I've shown apartments in this building. The doormen know me."

"It's two o'clock in the morning."

"It's *three* o'clock in the morning." She reached into an enormous straw beach bag and took out a small burgundy-velvet jeweler's box. "And do *you* know where your ruby-and-diamond ring is?"

"Oh, Christ. The ring." He didn't take the box from her. "Keep it."

"What?"

"Keep it. It's yours."

"What's the matter? I mean, seriously, what's the matter with you?"

"A crazy man just gave you a forty-two-thousand-dollar ring. If you had any brains, you'd be out of here and halfway across town by now."

"Maybe I don't have that kind of brains. And maybe I don't want to." As though she'd been invited in, she walked past him into the apartment. She plunked the jeweler's box down on the hall table. She glanced at the Brancusi, the Arp, the Bracque pen-and-ink hanging on the wall, and then her eyes came back to him. "Now, tell me what's bothering you."

"I want to sleep. That's what's bothering me."

"You're not going to sleep unless you tell someone." She lowered her shawl to her shoulders. Her dark hair was pinned back from her forehead with carved ivory combs. She closed the front door. "I'm someone. I'm here. Tell. Why are you giving away the ring? It's a beautiful ring."

"Because the woman I bought it for broke our date."

"She broke a date, so you're giving her ring to a stranger?" She had an odd way of snapping questions right out, as though she had a right to the answers.

"She's dead. Does that satisfy you? I don't want the damned ring. It reminds me of her. So take it and get out."

"I'm not going to take a present you give me when you're not yourself."

"Trust me—I'm myself."

"When did you last eat?"

"How do I know when I last ate?"

A smile opened on her face. "You don't have any idea what makes you feel the way you feel. You don't know what makes you sad, what makes you happy. I don't think you even have any idea what really turns you on."

"On that subject, little girl, I am the expert."

"I could turn your life around right now—without forty-two-thousand-dollar rings, without women, with nothing more than you've already got in the house."

"Only one thing could turn my life around—and they've both walked out on me."

"Want to bet?" She held out her right hand. She had strangely slender fingers, so pale and soft that a pink light seemed to shine through them. "Come on. What have you got to lose?"

Her mouth was smiling, but something serious peeped through her brown eyes.

Why not? he thought. *I can't feel worse than I do now.*

"Okay," he said. "Bet."

She looked straight at him, firm-jawed, and gave his hand a single, brisk shake. He felt something energizing shoot through him.

"What have you got in that kitchen?" she said.

"I don't know. What do you need?"

"Butter, flour, sugar, eggs, vanilla, cocoa, cinnamon, a dash of salt, and forty-two minutes."

"What the hell are you going to do with all that at this hour?"

"I'm going to make you the best chocolate pudding you've had since you were three years old."

He wasn't sure which of them was hallucinating. "Are you serious?"

"Where in the law books does it say it's wrong or illegal or impossible to have a simple solution to a complicated problem? Look—I may not know much, but one thing I do know is desserts. I studied in Paris. My chocolate pudding could save the world. But I'll settle for pulling you out of your funk. In forty-two minutes you're going to be the happiest man in New York City—and then if you still want to give me that ring, I'll take it."

▪ FIFTY-SIX ▪

Saturday, June 15

CARDOZO LIFTED THE PHONE on the second ring. "Cardozo."

No one answered, and at first he thought he was the recipient of some electronic mistake, and then he thought, *I'll be damned, I've got a breather.* And then a woman's voice said, "Vince, it's Leigh. Do you have a minute?"

His heart took a little running jump in his throat, and that jump gave him a scare. *Do I have a minute?* he thought. *I've had a minute all week.* He realized he'd been waiting for this call, hoping for it. "Sure. I've got a minute. Just a sec." He reached out and closed the cubicle door. "How are you?"

"I'm fine."

"Is Waldo away?" Right away he regretted asking that. It sounded too eager. Pushy, almost.

"No," she said. "I'm not calling about that."

He tried to ignore the falling sensation in his stomach. He tried not to let his disappointment show in his voice. "Then . . . is something the matter?"

"Annie MacAdam had lunch at Archibald's. She says Jim Delancey is still working there."

"Why's that a problem?"

"You know why."

"No. I don't know why."

She didn't answer.

Cardozo realized he was playing dumb, getting back at her. It was petty, but he felt just a little bit rejected that she hadn't phoned before now and he couldn't help it.

"Jim Delancey should be behind bars," she said.

"Look," he said, "it might interest you to know that the night

Gloria Spahn was killed, Jim Delancey was home and he didn't leave the building."

"How do you know he didn't?"

"We had men watching both entrances. Delancey never came out."

"You mean your men never saw him come out."

"That's right. They never saw him." Cardozo realized he was arguing with her, and it bothered him because it meant he'd lost control. "They're good men with twelve years on the force, and they weren't sleeping on the job."

"You're angry with me."

"No, not angry. Just busy."

"I'm sorry to bother you. Good-bye, Vince."

She clicked off, and Cardozo sat there holding the dead receiver, thinking, *Vince Cardozo, you're an idiot.*

■ ■ ■

TORI DIDN'T SEE THE *TIMES* till late Saturday afternoon, sitting on the beach. Gloria Spahn's death had three inches on an inside page of Section Two.

"My God."

She tried to reach Zack from the pay phone at the yacht club. The answering machine picked up.

"Zack, it's Tori—I just saw about Gloria in the *Times.* How horrible! You can reach me at Sorry Chappell's." She gave him the number. "I'll try again later."

She phoned again when she got back to Sorry's, and again the machine answered.

"Hi. It's me again. I'll be spending tonight and tomorrow night here unless I hear from you. Call me if you need me."

■ ■ ■

LEIGH PAID THE CABBIE and got out on Fifty-first. She waited till she saw her guard's black Plymouth pull to a stop, and then she walked north on Beekman Place, past beautifully maintained town houses. It was after eight, and a soft evening light suffused the street, giving it the quality of a stage set. Stone and glass and brass glowed with cleanliness.

Two high-rises had been built at the end of the block. Number Twenty-three, where Jim Delancey lived, was an eighteen-story building immaculately surfaced in brown granite. Its brick neighbor, number Twenty-nine, was twenty stories, with contrasting white marble window ledges.

Twenty-nine occupied the corner lot, and though it had a Beekman Place address, Leigh realized as she approached that it had no entrance on Beekman Place.

She reached Fifty-second Street and turned east. A third of the way up the block she came to the entrance of Twenty-nine. A uniformed doorman sat on a stool just inside the glass-paned door, reading a newspaper.

Leigh turned and retraced her steps. She wanted to see if there was any way that one person could watch the two entrances.

On Fifty-second, west of the Beekman intersection, there was a twenty-foot stretch where both doors were visible.

But Beekman was a different story. If you positioned yourself anywhere besides the corner, there was no way you could see the entrance to Twenty-nine. And even from the corner you didn't see the door itself, only the awning over the sidewalk. If someone came out of Twenty-nine and turned east, away from Beekman, it would be impossible to get a good look at them.

Leigh returned to Twenty-nine. The doorman laid down his paper and held the door for her. "May I help you, ma'am?"

"Sorella Chappell said she might be getting back from the Hamptons today. Is she in?"

▪ ▪ ▪

AFTER FORTY MINUTES OF CHITCHAT and iced tea and Sorry Chappell asking what on earth was making Tori so nervous these days ("She was so antsy she drove me out of my own house!"), Leigh brought the conversation back once more to how beautifully Sorry had designed and decorated her apartment. "Didn't you say you'd added a room on?"

"Why, yes," Sorry said, "I did add on last year. A little studio next door came on the market. They were asking much too much, but it was a chance at last to have a decent library. And you know how I love books."

"You had to take down a wall?"

Sorry nodded. "A wall into the building next door. And you wouldn't believe the construction permits it required. And the bribes that had to be paid. Three hundred thousand to the owners for a room no larger than a maid's, and one hundred eighty thousand to commissioners in outright graft. And not a penny tax deductible. Would you like to see?"

"I'd love to."

Sorry took her through the living room.

"Here's where we go next door." Sorry opened a sliding

glass-paneled door with an arched lintel. "There's a three-inch drop between buildings, so we decided to raise the floor. Fenny found the most beautiful parquet in a pre–Civil War mansion in Newark."

Leigh glanced down at the parquetry—L-shaped pieces of dark oak and paler maple laid in an interlocking grid. Sorry had hidden most of it under a tan-and-jade Persian rug.

"At the last minute," Sorry said, "an awful little man from the Landmarks Commission stepped in and tried to stop everything. Twenty-nine Beekman is Sullivan and Sons, and Twenty-three is Sanford White. You'd have thought I'd asked an Orthodox Jew to mix milk and meatballs. But I gave a party for the mayor—and contributed to his campaign—and it all worked out. What do you think of it?"

Against the north wall, on a Biedermeier rosewood-and-green-marble table, an enormous Tiffany vase held an arrangement of blue iris and anemones. Their airy scent filled the room. At the west wall the faint last light of day fell through French windows. On the south wall light from beaded shades softly touched shelves of rare bindings.

On the east wall, between two Sargent portraits of the Duchess of Marlborough, a mahogany door with a peephole and two Fichet locks stood unobstructed.

"And that door—" Leigh said.

"They wouldn't let me block it up. Fire laws."

That's how he did it, Leigh realized. *He used this apartment to cross from one building to the other.*

She nodded. "You've done an absolutely lovely job. I can't imagine a more perfect spot for reading."

The compliment seemed to strike a glow in Sorry. "One does want one's home to be just right, doesn't one?"

"One wants it, but so few of us have your knack."

"Well, as they say at dinner parties—I *am* in the book."

Leigh looked at her watch. "I've taken up much too much of your time. Can I get out this way?"

"You don't want to do that—use the front door."

"I'd like to see the building next door."

"Suit yourself." Sorry unlocked two bolts, opened the door and stood aside. "Heaven to see you."

They touched cheeks.

"Oh, Leigh, by the way"—Sorry lowered her voice—"are you getting along with your police guard?"

"It's a perfect marriage," Leigh said. "I hardly know he's there."

"I never see mine," Sorry said. "I wonder if he still exists."

"He's probably sitting downstairs in an unmarked car right now."

"I've seen a man down there in an unmarked car, but I don't think he's mine." Sorry raised an eyebrow. "I'll say no more about unpleasant subjects. Let's get together soon. Lunch?"

"Lunch."

They touched cheeks one last time. Leigh stepped into the corridor and pressed the elevator button. Behind her she heard Sorry's two locks snap back into place.

In the shaftway gears hummed.

Leigh studied the corridor. There were only four doors: the elevator, the stairs, Sorry's studio, and another apartment with ten days' worth of *New York Times* piled up on the doormat.

The elevator came. She stepped in and pushed the button for the ground floor.

The door closed. The elevator dropped smoothly. On fourteen it stopped again.

A young man stepped on. He was flawlessly dressed, like a male model, in a double-breasted navy-blue blazer, pale pink shirt, regimental tie. He glanced automatically at Leigh, didn't seem to see her.

Her heart contracted. It was Jim Delancey.

He faced the front of the car and pressed the button for *one.* The door closed and the elevator began dropping again. He didn't turn around. There was no more than three feet of space between them.

The elevator stopped on eleven. A blond woman in designer jeans and a batik blouse got on. She glanced at her fellow passengers. It was an automatic checking-out-the-danger New York glance: *Are you muggers, or can I safely ignore you?*

The woman pressed the button for *six* and stepped back to let the door close. After a moment she turned her head and looked over at Leigh.

Leigh read embarrassment and indecision on the woman's face.

On six the elevator door opened. The sounds of a party in progress rolled down the corridor: voices and laughter and Bobby Short singing Cole Porter.

The woman held the door. She looked again at Leigh, this

time with a kind of guileless amiability, like a child. "Excuse me, aren't you Leigh Baker?"

"Why, no." Leigh's voice felt tight and too high in her throat. From the edge of her vision she watched Delancey. He showed no reaction. "People ask me all the time—but my eyes aren't her color."

"I could have sworn," the woman said. She got off and let the door close.

Leigh stepped to the side of the elevator, as far from Delancey as the cabin allowed. He turned his head slightly, showing her a half profile. He was smiling.

She tried to push down her terror, tried to concentrate on the panel where blinking lights counted out the descending floors. *Five . . . four . . .*

Delancey let his blazer drop open. Metal glinted.

Leigh felt the strength sliding out of her knees. *Dear God, no.*

It took her a moment to realize the glinting thing was only the clip on his suspender. He was wearing regimental-striped suspenders that matched his tie. He snapped the right suspender.

She gave an involuntary start.

Delancey's expression stayed cool and indifferent. His thumb hooked the suspender again, pulled it out till it was as taut as a bowstring. Then released it.

Even though she knew the snap was coming she gave a start. She couldn't control her reaction.

He snapped the suspender again. And again.

She wanted to scream.

The elevator slowed to a stop at street level. The door opened. Delancey was nearer the door, but he made no move to get out. Nor did he make any move to let her pass.

She pulled in a deep breath. "Excuse me."

For just an instant they were facing each other. The tiny black pupils of his eyes jabbed like needle points. *Lady,* the look said, *I am going to get you.*

She pushed past him into the lobby.

Jasmin Hakim was waiting on one of the sofas. Her long dark hair and pale, ivory-skinned face could have been taken from a Victorian cameo. *She looks so much like Nita,* Leigh thought.

The girl looked at Leigh as she passed.

"Jimmy," Leigh heard her say. "I missed you."

"Me too," she heard Delancey say.

A knot twisted in Leigh's stomach. She hurried into the street.

▪ FIFTY-SEVEN ▪

Sunday, June 16

LEIGH KNOCKED ON THE OPEN DOOR. "Am I interrupting?"

Vince Cardozo was sitting in his shirtsleeves, frowning at a photograph. He looked up and turned the photograph over. "Please," he said, rising, "come in and interrupt."

He moved a stack of documents from a chair to the floor.

She sat. "I'm sorry I bothered you yesterday."

"You didn't bother me. I'm sorry I was grumpy."

"You weren't grumpy."

"I guess that establishes that we both have perfect manners." He was watching her with an odd sort of half smile, and she couldn't tell if he was glad to see her or not. "Coffee?" he offered.

"I can only stay a minute."

"Fake sugar and fake milk, right?"

While he was out of the cubicle she turned over the photograph he had been studying. She recognized Gloria Spahn's corpse. She winced and laid the photo back on the desk, facedown.

Cardozo came back. He closed the door. She accepted a styrofoam cup. She sipped. "Not bad," she said. "Better than last time."

"But you didn't come here for our famous coffee." Cardozo dropped back into his seat.

"I saw Jim Delancey yesterday."

Vince Cardozo's face seemed to crumple. "Yesterday."

She nodded. "I was standing closer to him than you and I are now. The expression on his face told me everything." Her voice began edging up. "Vince, it's him. He's the one."

For a moment Vince Cardozo didn't speak or react in any way. "Where did this happen?"

"In the elevator in his building."

"What were you doing there?"

"You said he was home the night Gloria was killed. I was afraid . . . you weren't going to watch him anymore."

"So you decided to help me out and keep an eye on him?"

Even with the door shut noise poured in from the squad room. The consensus in there seemed to be, Why talk when you can yell. Telephones were jangling. Someone was slamming through metal cabinet drawers, and each slam was like thunder.

"Delancey has a breaking-and-entering record." Leigh sat forward in the metal chair. "He's broken into dozens of girls' apartments. He's stolen valuables and pawned them. You must know that—it all came out in the trial."

Cardozo's eyes flicked up. "Excuse me. We seem to be talking different time frames. I'm discussing now, not four years ago."

"So am I. Sorella Chappell has a studio in Jim Delancey's building. It connects to the building next door. She wasn't home Thursday night. He could have broken into her apartment and gone out through the other building."

Cardozo watched her levelly. He sighed.

"That's how he did it! Why can't you believe me? I'm not crazy and I'm not lying to you!"

"But you do hate Jim Delancey."

She didn't bother to deny it. "You don't have to take my word for it—go look at the apartment."

Cardozo picked up his pen. "What's the apartment number?"

"Sixteen. Sorella Chappell. You have a man guarding her right now. At least you say you do."

▪ ▪ ▪

TWO MINUTES AFTER LEIGH BAKER had gone there was another knock on Cardozo's door. He turned.

Ellie Siegel stood in the doorway. She had a smile like a twirling lariat. "And how's Miss Silver Screen?"

"Ellie, I'm sorry. I'm going to have to take back two of the men I gave you."

"Indian-giver. Why?"

"Looks like Delancey's in the running again. We may have to put back the round-the-clock tail."

▪ FIFTY-EIGHT ▪

Monday, June 17

TORI STEPPED OUT OF THE CAB. The shadow that hovered behind the glass-paneled door leapt forward. The door swung inward.

"Good morning, Chuck." She zipped past the doorman into the air-conditioned lobby.

"G'morning, Miss Sandberg," he called out behind her. "Are you back?"

Not breaking stride, she pondered the implications of that particular greeting. Had Zack told the staff she'd moved out? "That's right, Chuck. I'm back."

Her forefinger, riding through space two feet ahead of her, connected with the elevator button. The door opened. Inside the mahogany-paneled cabin the air smelled sweet, for fresh anemones had been placed in the decorative wall brackets. She pressed the button for *eighteen*.

As the elevator rose she gave herself a last-minute look-over in the little mirror. She saw dark circles under her eyes and a smile that did not disguise a thing. Not the best face for greeting your sexist-capitalist lunk of a lover and telling him, *Surprise, darling, I've thought it over and I'm back.*

She opened her compact and did a quick cover-up.

The elevator door opened. She stepped into the little foyer outside the apartment.

She was gripped by an upsurge of affection for the Regency table and the Jasper Johns signed litho hanging above it, for the peach-upholstered banquette that matched the stripes in the hand-blocked wallpaper.

She took the door key out of her purse.

Until eleven forty-eight that morning everything in her life was solid and brick-simple. But something funny happened on the way to eleven forty-nine.

The lock gave a click of refusal. The key wouldn't turn clockwise. It wouldn't turn counterclockwise.

She couldn't believe that her fingers and wrist had forgotten how to turn *this* key in *this* lock. Something here felt like the essence of totally off.

She examined the other four keys on her chain. She tried each of them in turn. None of them would so much as slide into the lock.

It came to her that she could die of old age trying to get one of these keys to do what obviously none of them were going to. Zack had changed the lock. She had to smile. *What a petulant little boy!*

She leaned an ear against the door. A phone was ringing inside the apartment. She heard the fast slaps of the Guatemalan maid's sandals, one side of a muffled conversation.

She pushed the doorbell. She fixed an agreeable, relaxed expression securely in place.

The door opened and the maid, with one fist raised to her mouth, was staring at Tori in white-knuckled disbelief.

"I'm not a ghost, Josefina." Tori entered the apartment. She let its familiarity flow around her. "Did Mr. Morrow change the lock?"

Josefina nodded.

"Wait till I talk to that idiot. Where is he?"

Josefina just stood there, twisting a dust rag in both hands. "They went to TriBeCa."

"*They,* Josefina? Who's *they*?"

The maid burst into tears. She pointed to the copy of that morning's *Trib* that lay on the hall table. "Society page," she said, sobbing.

Tori opened the paper. A photo leapt up at her. She felt as though a revolver had been fired inside her brain. The picture showed a grinning Zack with both arms around a grinning Gabrielle MacAdam.

Beneath the picture, Dick Braidy's gossip column burbled:

The ultraprivate ceremony takes place this morning at ten sharp at Robert De Niro's ultra-in and ultra-now TriBeCa Grill. It is all very hush-hush and very spur-of-the-moment, but the buzz is Hizzoner the Mayor and the Assistant Secretary of State for Latin American Affairs will serve as witnesses. The newlyweds will host a little reception Friday for 200 close friends at the Jeu de Paume at Le Cercle.

But all is not unalloyed merriment in Gotham's fair city. For, as Gilbert and Sullivan so presciently remarked a century ago . . .

■ ■ ■

WHEN CARDOZO OPENED the door, the air in his cubicle was the temperature of a car that had been parked all day in the sun with the windows up.

He punched a button on the air conditioner, and the compressor labored to life, pulling down the wattage in the desk lamp, kicking out a cycle of gasps and clanks.

He sat at his desk and looked through his phone messages. Three were from relatives of homicide victims whose cases were still, technically, on-going, and these would be calls for hand-holding and reassurance.

The fourth was a Chinese restaurant flyer with an order-out number; on the back, in Monteleone's handwriting, were the words:

11:20 A.M. Cassandra called, says Hi.

Cardozo frowned. He didn't know any Cassandra. The message had obviously come to the wrong extension. He crumpled it and tossed it into the wastebasket.

He let his eye roam across the paper that had piled up on his desk: white and pink and yellow color-coded flash reports, interim orders, multiple orders.

He reached for the freshest-looking mound. Most of it was interdepartmental b.s.—clearance needed on an order to print flyers, notice of triplicate missing on a form, mayor's office for films wanting a lieutenant to vet a script.

Ellie Siegel knocked on the door. "Have you read Benedict Braidy's column?"

"Not today. Am I missing something?"

"Very definitely." She handed him that morning's *Trib,* folded open to "Dick Sez." "Enjoy."

"Thanks, Ellie." Cardozo leaned back in his swivel chair and read the paragraphs that Ellie had circled in red:

But all is not unalloyed merriment in Gotham's fair city. For, as Gilbert and Sullivan so presciently remarked a century ago, things are seldom what they seem. Case in point:

Kristi Blackwell, editor of *Fanfare Magazine,* has long presented herself as a crusader. But in fact she is a hired gun, peddling slick disinformation. Query: in whose employ is our fair lady of the terrible swift red pencil?

To cite only the most flagrant abuses, Blackwell has published:

(1) an article falsely attributing the paternity of Jean Seberg's still-born child to a leader of the Black Panthers. The article, printed as a favor to the FBI, triggered Miss Seberg's suicide.

(2) an article alleging that socialite-suicide Anne Woodward was already married at the time of her marriage to William Woodward. The charge was false, as Truman Capote, who had first launched it, confessed on his deathbed. Kristi Blackwell detested the Woodwards for blackballing her from the co-op at 820 Fifth Avenue.

(3) an article maintaining the existence of a second syringe in the 1987 Thoroughbred-doping scandal that cost Rex Imperator his Triple Crown.

(4) an article detailing Princess Caroline of Monaco's alleged inhumane treatment of palace animals; a leak from the office of an ambitious Monégasque prosecutor (and financial partner of Ms. Blackwell), the article was intended to bolster his political career and was never substantiated.

(5) For reasons known only to her baroque brain, Blackwell heavily cut my article "Socialites in Emergency," suppressing all mention of a lawsuit against Lexington Hospital.

(6) Most painful of all to me personally, Blackwell published an article that served as the basis for forged evidence in the trial of my daughter's murderer. I will discuss this case in detail in tomorrow's column.

A chain reaction of thoughts went off in Cardozo's head: *So Nita Kohler has been promoted to daughter—or has Dick Braidy promoted himself to father? I wonder what Leigh Baker would have to say about that?*

The thought of Leigh Baker reminded him of the movie they had watched on the VCR. She'd played a character named Cassandra.

Which, he realized, was the name on the phone message.

He retrieved the restaurant flyer from the wastebasket. He was carefully flattening it out when the phone rang. "Cardozo."

"Hi, Vince, Rad Rheinhardt. Surprise, surprise."

"Read it to me."

" '*Sam's one itch is your big breeches.*' "

Cardozo wrote quickly. "Go on."

" '*Rags to riches take three stitches fit for bitches.*' And he signs himself '*Kisses, Society Sam.*' He misspells *breeches*—

b-r-i-t-c-h-e-s. It's hard to tell if Sam's being ignorant or clever. He spells *to* with a *w* and *for* with a *u*—like numbers. I guess that could be clever. It gives you *one, two, three, four*. I'm sending it up."

"Thanks, Rad." Cardozo hung up and stared a moment at his scribbling, then *x*'ed out *to* and *for* and wrote in *two* and *four*. He pondered *'rags two riches'* and *'fit four bitches'* and then he decided he'd rather ponder Leigh Baker's little message on the back of the Chinese-restaurant flyer.

Cassandra called, says Hi.

He smiled for ten seconds or so, feeling an odd delight, feeling odd that there was anything left on earth he could still feel odd delight about.

Then he neatly ripped away the parts of the menu that were not message. He folded the rest and slipped it into his wallet.

■ ■ ■

"TELL ME EXACTLY WHAT YOU WANT," Zack Morrow said.

"Tell Dick Braidy to retract today's column," Kristi Blackwell said. "Kill any follow-up column that accuses me of journalistic wrongdoing. He can go after my wardrobe or my love life with a machete, for all I care—but I won't have my work slandered."

Zack shook his head. "That's prior restraint, and we don't do it in this country. This isn't Great Britain."

They were sitting at table four at Le Cercle, Kristi's regular table. Noise filled the room like a hissing vapor—dozens of voices all trying to be heard at once, silverware clacking against china.

"Hold it, hold it." The third person at the table raised two hands, gesturing for calm. His name was Langford Jennings, Lang for short, and he had blond Establishment good looks and an educated drawl that—to many people's way of thinking—more than qualified him to be a lawyer. Kristi Blackwell suspected that Lang Jennings was the kind of man who put on a three-piece business suit to take the garbage out.

"Are we determined to go the legal route?" At that moment Lang had the smiling, secret look of a man listening to the waves of his own private lake lap against his own private shore. "Why not settle this here, at this table?"

"I want a retraction," Kristi said.

"Unless a court finds against Braidy," Zack said, "I can't compel him to retract. My contract with him is the same as Dizey's, and it's specific on that point."

"Then *you* retract," Kristi said.

"Me? I didn't write it."

"You published it. And what about the next column? He says I forged evidence."

"He doesn't say that," Zack said. "Read what he wrote. He says *maybe* he's going to say it."

Lang took another forkful of Linzer torte. "Kristi, you're a public figure. So the issue becomes not malice, which for all I know Dick Braidy is full of, but falsehood."

The mouthful of espresso that Kristi had been about to swallow went down in a gulp instead.

"Tell me, Kristi," Zack said. "Would Dick Braidy be lying if he came right out and said you forged evidence? Do you think a jury would find for him or for you?"

Kristi sat twisting her wedding ring. She felt something end there, with her silence.

"I suggest a compromise," Lang said, "a gentleman's agreement. Kristi will forgo the retraction, and Zack will print no further statements impugning her journalistic ethics."

"It's going to get me in trouble with Dick." Zack shrugged. "But I'll do my best." He extended a hand across the table.

Kristi didn't move.

"Come on, Kristi. Zack just got married. He left his bride to meet with you. The least you can do is shake his hand. As a wedding present."

After a moment Kristi reached across the table and took Zack's hand.

"Caught in the act, I see." Dick Braidy stood in the aisle, holding his head abnormally high under a doughnut-shaped helmet of gray-blond hair. "Do I spy a nonaggression pact between my two publishers?"

"Hello, Dick," Zack said. "Have a good lunch?"

"Excellent, thank you. And congratulations." Dick Braidy leaned forward and planted a kiss embarrassingly near Zack's mouth. "I've known Gaby forever and I just love, love, love her, and I wish you both all the happiness in the world."

The speech struck Kristi as perfunctory and more than a little insincere. It struck her too that Dick Braidy's appearance had radically changed. He'd had his hair rinsed a sort of yellowy blond, like a see-through varnish. But the change went deeper. There was sadness in him now, and—especially when he looked at her— a sort of disgust.

"I don't believe we've met." Lang rose from his chair. "I'm Langford Jennings, Ms. Blackwell's attorney."

"Dick Braidy. It's a pleasure." Dick Braidy took the hand that Lang offered him. "I have a feeling we're going to be seeing a good deal of each other." He slid a glance toward Kristi.

"Won't you join us?" Lang said.

Dick Braidy thrust a wrist out of his sleeve and frowned at his watch. "Sorry—I've got a date with my trainer."

■ ■ ■

"LET'S TRY A LIGHT SET to warm up." Bruce McGee, the owner and top trainer of Bodies-PLUS, placed a barbell in Dick Braidy's hands.

Dick Braidy couldn't concentrate. The barbell crashed immediately to the floor. He felt like a fool. "I'm sorry. I don't know what's wrong."

But he knew, all right. What was wrong was Zack Morrow not inviting him to the wedding. What was wrong was Zack Morrow lunching and schmoozing with that back-stabbing bitch Kristi Blackwell in full view of three dozen of the fastest and most important mouths in Manhattan. "I just can't seem to grip it."

His trainer was watching him curiously. "That's okay. Your hands are slippery. We'll find you some weight-lifting gloves."

Dick Braidy followed Bruce to the wall rack where the gloves were supposed to be kept.

No gloves.

"Tell you what," Bruce said. "I'll set up the next set. Why don't you look in the changing rooms and see if someone left a pair of gloves."

■ ■ ■

DICK BRAIDY OBSERVED HIMSELF in the changing-room mirror. He drew himself up to full standing height, squared his shoulders, sucked in his gut.

He defied his reflection: "This is me, the only me I have. I am going to make something of this mess! I have proved I am capable of achievement, and I will achieve this too."

A space opened somewhere behind him. A warm, damp breeze drifted across from the shower next door. He turned.

He had company.

The towel boy had entered his cubicle without knocking. The boy was leaning sideways against the wall, the wide chest of his Bodies-PLUS T-shirt split by a vertical stripe of sweat.

A finger of embarrassment tapped Dick Braidy's heart. He had forgotten to lock the door, and the boy must have seen him talking to his reflection.

The boy's eyes were staring, bold as a fox's, and his mouth seemed to be holding back a smile.

"Excuse me," Dick Braidy said, "but I'm not through with this room. I'll only be a minute."

The boy eased the door shut with his foot. The latch gave a click as it caught. He slid the bolt shut.

Dick Braidy drew in a shallow breath, quickly. He searched the boy's eyes for some statement of purpose, but all he could see was a flat, affectless gaze.

Dick Braidy moved to the left. The boy blocked him. He tried a move to the right and was blocked again.

"What is it you want?"

The boy gave him a quiet smile—a dangerous smile.

"You're not angry because of the other night, are you? Look, I honestly didn't recognize you. I'm used to seeing you here, and when I saw you out of context—"

The boy made a quick movement.

Dick Braidy's gaze flicked to the boy's hand. It was holding a straight ten-inch blade.

Dick Braidy's hands, now in a panic, patted his pockets, but he'd left his wallet outside in his locker. He held out his empty palms. "My money is outside." He pointed to the door. "*Dinero* out there. I have charge cards. American Express. Diners Club. *Bueno. Muy bueno.* I'll give you anyth—"

The boy lunged. The blade hissed through the air.

Dick Braidy couldn't believe this was really happening. His body and mind slipped into dream mode. The moment enveloped him in a paralyzing gelatin.

The force of the first slash spun Dick Braidy around. An arm caught his throat from behind. His breath choked off.

The blade opened the side of his throat, flicked out a flap of flesh. Metal drove stinging through his windpipe, digging through flesh and cartilage and artery and tendon. A bright gop of red flipped out of him onto the mirror.

"Holy Mother of God!"

Dick Braidy stumbled, collapsed to his knees, blinked through geysering blood and gristle. The razor scored a bull's-eye in the bulge of his gut.

And another.

And another.

Blood whooshed out of Dick Braidy with the hot stench of rust. An overpoweringly stale smell like the inside of an old car filled his nostrils.

A million red-hot perforations went through him at once.

"Why?" he moaned. "Why?"

Beyond the stinging, sinking horizon of his awareness, the blade arced up and down through warm, quiet air.

▪ ▪ ▪

CARDOZO CAUGHT HIS PHONE on the second ring. "Cardozo."

"Lieutenant, it's John Ferrara."

"Yes, Sergeant."

"Benedict Braidy's been killed."

▪ ▪ ▪

THE FLOOR OF THE CHANGING ROOM looked as if someone had spilled a two-gallon tureen of Manhattan clam chowder.

Dick Braidy lay on his back in the middle of the spill, his legs spread. One sneakered foot rested almost casually on the built-in wooden bench. His arms were clutched to his chest, folding the shower curtain to wounds that had gashed through his once-green Lacoste shirt and his still-blue nylon jogging shorts.

His head rested on the step of the shower stall. His eyes were still open, still huge. Standing in the doorway of the changing room, Cardozo met their silent surprise with his own wondering gaze.

"The way we put it together," Detective John Ferrara was saying, "Braidy left the gym floor in the middle of his workout and came back here."

Cardozo sniffed. The air held a sweetly brackish smell of sweat, heavily overlaid with floral room deodorizer. "Why? What did he come back here for?"

"He was looking for weight-lifting gloves."

"Why didn't you come with him?"

"He didn't tell me he was leaving the floor." It had been Ferrara's assignment to guard Dick Braidy from eight till four today. His pale brown eyes betrayed shock and guilt, as though his own negligence had thrust Dick Braidy into the path of the killer's blade. "I was out front watching the main door. For just that little stretch of time I didn't have him in my sight."

It had been Braidy's responsibility to tell his guard where he was going; it had been his guard's responsibility not to need to be told.

A police photographer was taking pictures, and Cardozo stepped back to give him room. A shower was running in a far cubicle with the soft, melancholy sound of rain.

"Who found Braidy?"

"I did."

Cardozo turned. At first glance he thought the young woman had had a bad hockey accident, but then he saw that it was just white rubber wraps hugging her kneecaps.

"Bobo Bidwell," she said pleasantly. She had straight black hair cut long, like a schoolgirl's, and her nose ended in a perky little upturn.

"How'd you happen to find him?"

"I'd finished my workout and I needed to shower and change. I was waiting here for a room, and Rick came whipping out of changing room five, so I assumed it was empty."

"Who's Rick?" Cardozo said.

"Rick Martinez," Detective Ferrara said. "The kid that does janitorial work."

"Where is he now?"

"Martinez was through the front door before I even heard Miss Bidwell holler. By the time I secured the crime scene and backup arrived, he was long gone."

Cardozo stepped aside as two orderlies from the medical examiner's office maneuvered their narrow stretcher past him. Inside the changing room, a brisk, redheaded young man was raking a flashlight beam beneath the bench.

Cardozo watched the slow dance of exploring light.

The young man pulled a small wastebasket from under the bench that appeared to have rolled or been kicked there. He shook the basket empty over a sheet of clear plastic. Soap wrappings and tissue paper floated down. A newspaper clipping hovered for an instant, like a paper glider. A three-inch cylinder of white wax plopped to the floor.

Cardozo felt a cold hand grip his intestine. "Who runs this place?"

Detective Ferrara led him down a corridor past the gym floor and rapped on the half-open door of a softly lit office.

A curly-haired young man was sitting behind the desk, looking worried. He was wearing a T-shirt with the message Sexy and Dangerous, and he had the mashed face of a former boxer.

Detective Ferrara made introductions. "Lieutenant Vince Cardozo, Bruce McGee."

Bruce rose to shake Cardozo's hand.

"Tell me about Martinez," Cardozo said.

"I don't know a hell of a lot." Bruce seemed to be suffering an overload of nervous energy that had nowhere to go except into fingertips nattering on the edge of his desk. "He's been working here six weeks. Quiet guy. Never talked much, never bothered anyone, never seem to get bothered."

"You must have interviewed him when you hired him."

"It was basically a handshake interview for a menial position."

"What exactly was Rick's job?"

Bruce shrugged. "Keeping the gym clean, seeing that the soap and towels were stocked."

"How long has he worked here?"

"Since April thirtieth."

"What's his home address?"

"Haven't got it."

"Where did you send his paychecks?"

"I paid him in cash."

"Do you have a home phone for him?"

"Rick doesn't have a phone. It's the standard undocumented-alien hard-luck story. He just arrived here from Salvador."

"How'd you and Rick happen to find each other?"

"I advertised in a body-building magazine." Bruce pulled a magazine out of a rack.

The magazine was called *Bodybuilding for You.* On the cover it showed an overmuscled, overtanned man and woman posing in workout unitards. Inside were ads for vitamin supplements and workout machines, articles touting the supplements and machines, and personal ads broken down by city.

"Can you describe Rick for me?"

"Settle for a photograph?"

Bruce handed Cardozo a folded, four-page newsletter—*Bodies-PLUS Gazette.* Page one featured a group photo captioned "Your Staff."

Bruce's forefinger pointed to a smiling, dark-haired, dark-eyed young man holding a stack of clean towels.

"That answers one question," Cardozo said. "Why nobody recognized him from the Identi-Kit. I wouldn't have recognized him either."

"That thing out on the bulletin board?" Bruce said. "That's meant to be Rick?"

"That was the intention." Cardozo sighed. "Did anyone here know Rick personally?"

Bruce scratched the scalp just above his right ear. "Rick didn't talk too much to the staff or the clients. The guy he seemed friendliest with was Dick Braidy. That's not going to help you much."

"No one else?"

"I did see one of the clients talking to him once. A young girl. Francoise Ford."

■ ■ ■

"I CAN'T BELIEVE we're talking about the same Rick." Francoise Ford couldn't have been more than eighteen years old. She had short blond hair and flawless skin and pale blue eyes that, at the moment, expressed shock and disbelief. "He seemed so gentle. Almost vulnerable."

"How well did you know him?"

They were sitting in a small study in the Ford apartment. Young Miss Ford reached a hand out and gave the globe of the world an absentminded spin.

"We got used to seeing each other around the gym, and we'd say hi. Then one night the owner was picking on him, and I felt sorry for him. I invited him to dinner. We talked."

"Did he tell you anything about himself?"

"He said he was from El Salvador. He said his parents had been killed by government soldiers. He said he was here illegally."

"Did he tell you where he lived?"

She shook her head. "We didn't exchange addresses or phone numbers. He did say if I wanted to see his hometown, all I had to do was go to Avenue D. I don't know if he meant he lived there."

"You only saw him outside the gym that one time?"

"That's the only time." She was thoughtful. "He came here once though. My stepmother was giving a party. He brought me some flowers. I didn't even get to see him. But I still have the note."

She left the room and returned with a small florist's card. The message had been written in large ballpoint letters: *Love, Bob De Niro.*

"Why *Love, Bob De Niro*?"

"It was a joke on my stepmother."

"I'd like to keep this."

For just an instant she seemed sad. "Okay. You can keep it."

"What night was the party?"

"Last Thursday."

▪ FIFTY-NINE ▪

"The article's called 'Socialites in Emergency,'" Cardozo said. "We're looking for any drafts he may have hiding in there."

Neat and darkly pretty and silent, Laurie Bonasera was seated in front of Benedict Braidy's computer, punching commands into the keyboard. She had spent a quarter hour at the same C prompt on the terminal, digging for some combination of keys that would snap the data free of the hard disk and bring it up on the screen.

"I'm not getting any files named *socialite* or *social* anything," she said. "You don't happen to know if Braidy had some system for naming his files?"

"All I know is, he handled that computer the way a Jersey driver handles a car in Manhattan. He told me he was always losing files."

Laurie shook her head. "He was obviously doing a lot wrong. Either he didn't know how or he didn't want to bother to create directories. All his files are in the root directory."

"That doesn't mean anything to me—I'm not computer-literate."

"It's as though he were putting all the numbers in his phone book under the letter *A*. He's got a thousand files in the root directory on an eighty-meg hard disk, and that's way beyond what the disk-operating system can cope with. Added to which . . ."

Laurie's shoulders moved forward beneath her blue cotton print blouse. She squinted a moment at the information on the screen.

"Let's run check-disk and just see."

Her hands moved like a pianist's, fingers tapping a command into the keyboard. "I have a hunch he forgot to save files."

"What does that mean?"

"After he wrote something he left it on the screen and turned the power off. Anything on the screen when you close down is lost. What he should have done was press the Save key."

"So how did he save things?"

"He didn't always save them on the disk. He printed them out. He was way underutilizing his system."

Judging by the sounds the computer had started making, something was snapping and bursting inside. Then there was silence, and a series of amber characters floated up from the bottom of the screen.

"He's got over three hundred lost files," Laurie said. "Plus a quarter of his disk space is broken chains."

"What's a broken chain?"

"The program writes on the nearest available space, which may be anywhere on the disk. Files wind up hopping all over the place. The program can't track them. What started happening was, each new file went into the space of the last file he lost, but if the new file was shorter than the lost file, a little of the old file was left on the disk. So there's a little bit of everything he ever wrote still on the disk."

"Then maybe we can find some of 'Socialites in Emergency.' "

"I asked the computer very politely if it had any kind of socialites in its directory. It doesn't."

The computer made a sound like seeds jumping inside a maraca.

"Hey, wait a minute," Laurie said. "This is strange. He's got one subdirectory."

"Why's that strange?"

"If he could make one, he could have made a dozen and saved his files—and his sanity."

A river of amber print flowed across the screen.

Laurie pushed two keys and the river widened into a screen-filling ocean.

She did not speak. She sat frowning at the screen. A strand of wavy dark hair fell over her forehead, and she let it lie there. She kept pushing the key with the downward-pointing arrow, and each time the glowing amber print edged upward a line at a time.

"He couldn't have made this directory himself. It's got to be a default command."

"What's that?"

"It's something the computer's programmed to do unless you specifically tell it not to. This directory is too neat to be his. Whoever installed the computer put this command in. What I think it is—and this would make sense with the kind of computer operator he was—it's a backup command. It automatically saves the files before he can lose them. But it saves them under a different name, because you can't have two files with the same name."

"What name does it use?"

"That's what I'm trying to find out . . ."

The fingers began moving again, at first doubtfully and then picking up confidence till they were jumping over the keys.

And then three columns of print froze on the screen.

"Joseph, Mary, and Mickey Mouse."

"What's the trouble?"

There was a strained look on her face. "The name of the backup is the date and hour and minute the file was created."

"The file we're looking for would have been written six years ago, shortly after May sixth."

She sent information with rapid, clicking fingers into the keyboard. A moment later a new directory of files came up on the screen.

"Hey! It's going to work!" She pushed a button and the printer clattered to life.

Cardozo strolled into the living room. He felt he was standing on the carefully constructed stage set of someone else's life.

Silver-framed photographs artfully scattered on tabletops pictured Benedict Braidy and various members in good standing of the international jet set. The lowest shelf of the bookcase held a set of untitled leather-bound albums.

Cardozo crouched down and opened one. He turned through page after page of photos of society and entertainment and finance celebrities. Celebrities walking, dancing, eating. Celebrities swimming, goofing for the camera, kissing. Twelve volumes of celebrities of the last thirty years.

There was a nagging wrongness about the photos. The makeup was too heavy, the expressions exaggerated, every mood was stretched to a grimace and held for the camera. He didn't see in these people's faces what he saw in the faces of his co-workers or most of the people in the streets of New York—the simple daily pleasure in living.

And he didn't see Benedict Braidy. Except in one photo—taken in the apartment, where Judy Garland was offering a poorly rolled joint to Ava Gardner, and there, half of him dimly visible in the mirror, Benedict Braidy was holding a camera.

And it dawned on Cardozo. Braidy wasn't in the pictures, because he'd taken them all. Here was a man who had never been present for his own life, who had always stood behind a lens, clicking away like a tourist, never quite believing any of it was real, needing photographic proof that he had been part of it, that he had lived Technicolor friendships with the celebrities of his time.

Cardozo came to the photographs of Leigh Baker.

There she was, carefully centered on the page, standing with melancholy elegance in hunting clothes outside a French château. There she was, dashing in a low-cut, jeweled evening dress across a mobbed sidewalk into the Academy Awards, a valiant smile making tiny lines in her face. There she was, curtseying to the Queen of England and looking as if she wished she had something to grip for support; and there in the front of the crowd, holding a miniature camera, was Dick Braidy.

Cardozo looked for some sign that Braidy had loved Baker or that she had loved him, that their marriage had been anything more than the fleeting intersection of two publicity campaigns. He didn't see it.

The thirteenth and last album held an almost helter-skelter collection of faded, crumbling snapshots and clippings. Many had come loose from their white corner moorings.

Cardozo considered a barefoot six-year-old girl with pigtails and smudged cheeks, fists clenching the skirt of her checkered dress. She stood beside a ramshackle porch, staring with tomboy-ish defiance into the camera.

Good God, Cardozo realized. It was a childhood snapshot of Assistant Deputy Commissioner Bridget Braidy.

And here was a boy of eight or so, in patched knickers, hugging a Labrador. Cardozo recognized Dick Braidy—superstar gossip-to-be.

A snapshot of Bridget's first communion. She was standing outside the church, wearing a clean white dress, and her face was scrubbed.

Dick's first communion—same church. A white jacket, dark trousers, dark necktie, shined shoes.

On and on the collection went: prayer cards, Mass cards, funeral announcements, obituaries of Braidys clipped from small-town newspapers, the yellowed title page of a Baltimore Catechism, ripped from its binding, that bore the successive inscriptions John Patrick Braidy, Phillip Michael Braidy, Benedict O'Houlihan Braidy.

Page after page of the same four grim faces—mother and father and the two kids—gathered around picnic tables, dining tables, Christmas trees, Model-T's, wood shacks in the country, brick-and-concrete shacks in the city.

As Cardozo turned the pages he felt Braidy's wistfulness and a yearning almost too deep to give voice to: It was as though the people in these photos spoke to him in tones low, flat, and weary: *Get rich! Get famous! Above all, get out!*

In the next room the printer finally stopped clattering.

Laurie stood in the doorway, holding a twenty-eight-page accordion-fold list of dates and times. "The nearest he's got to May sixth six years ago is May seventh, ten-forty A.M."

"Let's give it a try," Cardozo said.

Laurie sat down at the terminal, cleared the screen, and punched in an instruction. The message *One Moment Please* flashed, and ten seconds later a page of amber print scrolled up the screen.

"He's got a title on this," she said, leaning forward in the seat. " 'Society Goes to Emergency.' "

"That's it."

"Want to print it?"

"Please."

Four minutes later Cardozo sat on Dick Braidy's bird-chintz sofa, comparing the printout of "Socialites" with the version published in *Fanfare Magazine*. With a red Magic Marker he drew wavy lines alongside passages that had been cut from the magazine version. He found four.

At the nurse's window—which is made, ominously, of steel-mesh–reinforced safety glass—Dizey exchanges a few to-the-point words with the triage nurse, whose grim face would have been at home on Madame Defarge in *A Tale of Two Cities*.

"My name is Dizey Duke. My friends and I are with Oona Aldrich, who is an annual benefactor of this hospital. Mrs. Aldrich is choking and requires immediate attention."

Madame Defarge snaps to. She makes one phone call, and seconds later the duty doctor opens a door and invites our party into Emergency.

Three pages later:

In the most crowded corridor of the Emergency Room, a frail, malnourished-looking dusky-skinned young woman lies feverish on a gurney. Sweat has matted her thin cotton dress to her body, and the sheet wrapped around her stomach and legs is becoming blood-soaked.

And on the next-to-last page:

Chairs are in short supply, but miraculously three are conjured up for our group. A cheerful young nurse who has the face of a fashion model offers us coffee.

"You'd better watch those pearls," the nurse advises Dizey, referring to her two-strand necklace. "Security isn't what it should be in here—we're having a lot of thefts." The nurse adds, "None of us feel safe wearing any jewelry here anymore."

In fact, I subsequently learned from a lawyer for Lexington Hospital that the free-wheeling chaos around the Emergency Room this very night was later to result in a law suit against the hospital.

Both drafts ended jauntily:

Thirty-five minutes later the doctor pronounces Oona able to breathe again without assistance.

"That's news to me," quips Oona. "If I'm breathing so well, why is my face still green?"

"Blue, darling," interjects Avalon, "your face is blue."

"I hope that's a step up from green," says Oona.

"You'll be pink in no time," the doctor promises.

But Braidy's original continued with a sort of postscript:

Oona, who learned Spanish as a frequent child visitor to Ernest Hemingway's home outside Havana, the legendary Finca Vigia, pauses and chats with Señorita in the gurney as though the two of them were oldest of chums.

Oona turns to the doctor. "I hope you realize that this young lady is having a baby," she informs him.

"Omigod," cries the doctor, blushing a shade that can only be called redder-than-red, "is that what *embarazada* means?"

Cardozo laid the sheets down on the sofa beside him. He stood, stretched, and tried to put his impressions together.

The way the magazine had edited the piece, no one but Oona ever got inside Emergency; everything in the article took place in the waiting room *outside*.

But in Braidy's draft everything after the triage nurse took place *inside* the Emergency Room. Visitors' chairs were set up in a crowded corridor. A woman lay on a gurney bleeding while the doctor who should have been tending her chatted up the celebrities, and nurses brought coffee and stopped by to get autographs.

And—most interesting of all—someone had sued the hospital because of conditions in the Emergency Room that night.

"It's getting pretty late," Laurie said. "Do you need me for anything else?"

Cardozo started. He had forgotten she was there. "No, thanks. I think I've got it all."

She stood shifting weight self-consciously, playing with her wedding ring. "My husband's expecting me to cook dinner."

"Better not keep him waiting. Thanks for your help. I appreciate it."

"Good night."

"Good night." Cardozo crouched down to open a cabinet beneath one of the bookcases. Inside, he found a large cardboard box with a delivery ticket from d'Agostino's.

Down the hallway he heard Laurie close the front door behind her.

He opened the box. Overpacked papers sprang out like a Jack-in-the-box. The top-most layers were social notes, mostly thank-you's penned on crested folds of pastel stationery. There was a press kit from a firm of publicists—Robbie Danzig and Associates—that contained a glossy, smiling photo of Braidy, impeccable in a blazer and regimental tie. An accompanying biography—*for immediate release!*—suggested by omission that he'd been born in Hollywood.

There were dozens of letters from Danzig—*Dick, here is list of names and brand-names to mention favorably in your writing.* And another: *Dick, I can get you on the* Today Show, *but you must have hard, fresh, inside dish on Nita's murder.*

Cardozo kept digging.

He found pages recording dinner-party politics: who sat where, who switched place cards. There were profiles of outer-circuit celebrities: the caterer of the moment, the society whore of the moment, the insider-novelist of the moment.

Then there were what seemed to be proposals for magazine articles:

Does New York really need two Jeanie Vanderbilts?

The enduring glamour of Madonna—she's cheap, she's trashy, she's divine.

Dinner with Oscar and Annette de la Renta is a peak experience.

Cardozo had to smile when he came across a page that stated, *Annie MacAdam's parties are tax deductions, full of people that gossip columnists like to call glittery and swank. Annie has claimed successfully in tax court that the only way to sell an eight-million-dollar apartment is to get eighty "marvelous people" drunk at a "perfect dinner."*

A page that began *Ronald ditched Geraldine, called her a lousy lay at the dinner Mitzi Astor gave for Raquel Welch's book* carried the red-inked notation: *Who let that story out of the cage?* On another page the red ink remarked, *The market in glamour would crash if this got published,* and Cardozo concluded that the red felt-tip belonged to Braidy's editor, Kristi Blackwell.

He came to a wad of word-processed sheets that had been paper-clipped together with a headline and subheading torn from a slick-papered magazine: *"Pavane pour une Infante Défunte":* Fanfare Magazine *takes you inside the gritty, glittering world of a murdered girl.*

Intrigued by the quantity of red *X*'s and cross-outs on the pages, Cardozo leafed through them. On the third page the red pen had underlined: *Among her friends Nita numbered dozens of society and show-business celebrities that you and I only dream about.* It had written in the margin, *Enlarge on this, s.v.p.*

It dawned on Cardozo that this was Braidy's article on the murder of his ex-wife's daughter.

His eye slowed at red brackets around a quote: *"I think somebody ought to be doing what I'm doing, caring for these people,"* Nita was fond of saying. *"So I'm doing it."*

In the margin came the bold red query: *Do our readers honestly need to know the day-by-day boreena details of a socialite spending her summer vacation playing Lady Bountiful at a coke 'n' crack detox? We just had a piece on Covenant House, and nobody believes these joints are legit anymore.* Huge red *X*'s crossed out enormous chunks of the next dozen pages.

Cardozo felt a stab of empathy for Braidy: he had obviously believed in this piece and tried to give it some depth, but his editor had cut everything but the glitz.

On the final page the marginal exclamation *FAB!* caught Cardozo's eye. Red arrows pointed to red brackets around three lines of text: *Hours after Nita's death hit the wires, calls were pouring in, along with notes, flowers, and condolences from the likes of Andy Warhol, Joan Bennett, and Bette Davis.*

The pen wanted to know, *Can we get reprint rights to Davis or Warhol condolences?*

There was a click. In the zone of emptiness behind Cardozo something moved. He turned. Beyond the windows twilight was rapidly fading to the deep purple of a Manhattan summer night. The apartment had grown dark.

"Laurie?" he called. "Forget something?"

A woman's voice spoke from the shadow. "No . . . it's me. The doorman let me in."

He switched on a lamp.

Leigh Baker pulled back, blinking in the sudden light. "Do you mind my being here?" She took an unsteady step into the room. "I wanted to see the place one last time—and say good-bye."

She looked the way a woman looks when she's stopped giving a damn: hair disheveled, face furrowed, mascara clotted. The clothes could have been something that had fallen on her when she'd opened a closet and walked in with her eyes shut.

"What's happened to you?" he said.

"I guess I'm hysterical."

He could smell Scotch hanging like a vapor in the air in front of her.

"Come on." He took her gently by the elbow. "Let's get you home."

She pulled away. "No. I have to show you something."

He followed her into the bedroom. The bed was still unmade, and Cardozo was surprised to see that Dick Braidy had slept in a hospital bed with buttons and cranks for raising and lowering it in sections, and bird-and-flower-print covers for disguising the steel-barred head- and footboard.

Over the chest of drawers a mirror with an elaborately carved frame loomed like something from a stage set, more for self-congratulation, he sensed, than simple self-acceptance. Two dozen invitations, most of them engraved, had been stuffed into the frame.

Leigh Baker went to the bookcase. Starting at the top shelf, she ran her finger along the bindings. She was searching for something, and the search seemed to be giving her trouble.

There was a thump. She hadn't quite lowered herself and she hadn't quite collapsed, but somehow she had ended up sitting on the floor. She squinted at the bottom shelf, pulled out two books and punched them back, and finally held out a small leather-bound volume.

He helped her back to her feet.

Her hands were now in rapid motion, sifting through pages. "Here."

She handed him the book. He recognized Nita Kohler's diary and the page that ended *sex to end all sex.*

"I've already seen this."

"No, you haven't. Dick was the only one who saw it. Turn the page."

Cardozo turned the page. *Is there anything else that really matters in this life?*

For Cardozo, the moment had a glassy, slowed-down quality.

"You see?" she said. "We were both wrong. It's not a five-word coincidence—it's a nine-word coincidence."

He turned back and counted the words: *sex to end all sex is there anything else.*

"You're right." A stop light flashed in his mind. You could make a coincidence out of five words, but you'd have a hard time doing it with nine.

"That poor, lonely, harmless, sweet, silly guy." She was playing with a vase of dried flowers that stood neatly centered on an inlaid mahogany chess table. "He was so proud when *Architectural Digest* photographed this place. They had to use a wide-angle lens to make it look larger." She turned suddenly. "Do I sound hysterical to you?"

"Not especially."

"Funny. I sound hysterical to me."

He held out his hand. "Say good-bye and let's go."

Riding down in the elevator, she studied her reflection in the mirror. She shook her head sorrowfully. "Not looking good."

Cardozo held the elevator door on the ground floor. He offered his arm.

The doorman opened the street door for them and touched a finger to the brim of his cap. A chorus of shouts rose and a mob of reporters came at them in a wave.

"Hey, Leigh, how are you taking it?"

"Did you see the body?"

Dusk disintegrated into retina-ripping explosions of flash-bulbs. A reporter's microphone slammed Leigh on the shoulder. "Do you have a statement?"

"Cut it out!" Cardozo shouted. "Leave the lady alone!" Brandishing his police shield at them, he pulled her through the crowd to his parked Honda.

Inside the car Leigh drew in a shuddering breath and seemed to forget to let it out. "I guess I'm news again. Sorry."

Cardozo steered the car into west-bound traffic. "Where to? Waldo's place?"

"No."

"Have you got a place of your own?"

"I can't go there, it's sublet."

"Do you want to go to a hotel?"

"Vince—can I talk to you about something that's bothering me?"

"Sure."

"I've spent the whole day drunk. I don't want to be alone, and I don't want to be with Waldo. If I don't have some kind of a private, gentle moment, I have a scary premonition that this bender's going to last a long, long time. Would it be asking too much for you to take me to your place?"

"You wouldn't have much chance for a private moment at my place. I'm a family man. A single parent. I live with my teen-age daughter."

She looked at him. He could have sworn her gaze was suddenly sober.

"Do you and Terri have a sofa?"

He was surprised she remembered his daughter's name. "Doesn't everybody have a sofa?"

"Okay, I'm sorry." She pulled a Kleenex from her purse and bunched it to her nose and sniffled. "It was a dumb, pushy idea. Drop me off at any hotel that takes American Express."

The choice was to keep heading west and drop her at a hotel, or turn south on Lexington and take her to his place. There was no exact instant when he was aware of making up his mind. Lexington was coming up, and then it was there in front of him, and then he signaled a left-hand turn.

"I don't know," he said. "Maybe it's not such a dumb idea."

· SIXTY ·

CARDOZO SWUNG THE APARTMENT DOOR open. "Anyone home?"

"Me," Terri called from the living room.

"We have a houseguest."

"You're joking." Terri came into the hallway. She saw Leigh and the smile fell off her face.

Cardozo made introductions.

"Sorry to bust in on you," Leigh said. "Your dad's being a Good Samaritan."

"And rescuing you from those cruddy reporters." Terri made a face.

"More from myself, I'm afraid."

"How did you know about the reporters?" Cardozo said.

"They had a news break on TV just a minute ago. You both looked great." Terri's glance went curiously from Cardozo to Leigh and then, shrewd now, back to her father. "Anyone need anything to drink?"

"How about two gallons of black coffee?" Leigh said.

"Settle for one?"

"I'd settle for a cup."

"I'll make the coffee," Cardozo said. "You two get acquainted, and when I come back, I hope one of you will explain the other to me."

Terri put a hand on her hip and stared at him. "Ha ha."

"Seriously," he said.

Two minutes later Terri joined him in the kitchen. "Hold the coffee. She fell asleep on the sofa."

"Just like that?"

"Just like that." Terri came and hugged him. "I wish I'd taped you on TV."

"Come on, give me a break. All I did was walk a famous lady through a hostile crowd so she could have her breakdown in private."

"I'm not talking about you and the movie star in there. I'm talking about you, period."

"What about me, period?"

"You looked so happy."

Cardozo felt his face flush. "Go on. Me, happy?"

■ ■ ■

A BUZZER SOUNDED. It seemed to clang through the little apartment like a racing fire truck. Cardozo hurried to the hallway and opened the front door.

"Guess what?" Ellie Siegel took two breathless steps into the apartment. "The *New York Trib* has killed tomorrow's Braidy column." She grabbed Cardozo's hand. "Just balance me for a second —one of us has to go, this shoe or me."

Cardozo held Ellie's hand.

Balancing on one high-heeled foot, she lifted a knee and reached with her free hand for her foot. After ten seconds of failing to connect she managed to wrench the shoe off. She shook it. Nothing came out. She thumped it with her fist. With a clunk heavy enough to be a five-dollar gold piece, a black pebble dropped to the floor.

She stooped, with dainty disgust picked up the pebble between thumb and forefinger, and dropped it into her pocket. "I wonder what volcano coughed that up." She stepped back into the shoe and, testing her walk, advanced cautiously toward the living room.

"Maybe you'd better not go in there," Cardozo said.

Ellie stopped at the threshold and for one long, craning moment squinted into the dimness. "Aha. Company."

"She's sleeping. We can talk in here." Cardozo led the way down the hall and switched on the kitchen light. "Why did the *Trib* kill the column?"

Ellie dropped her purse on the kitchen table. "You should see what Braidy wrote. You'd have killed it too."

"You managed to see it?"

"Better than that. I was charming to one of the *Trib*'s com-

puterized press jockeys, and he let me take a printer's proof."
Ellie snapped open her purse and pulled out something that
looked like a neatly folded four-foot square of Third World toilet
paper. She unfolded it. The toilet paper had printing on one side.
"Shall I read?"

"Please."

" 'Dick Sez,' by Benedict Braidy. Two months—" Ellie
cleared her throat. "Excuse me. Summer cold coming on. *Two
months after the death of my daughter Nita Kohler, the editor of*
Fanfare Magazine, *Kristi Blackwell, commissioned me to—*"

"Daughter?" Cardozo wheeled. "He's calling Nita Kohler his
daughter? Again?"

"He's not calling Greta Garbo his daughter."

"But that's a lie."

"Be charitable, Vince. It's an understandable exaggeration.
But if you want to quibble, quibble with him, not me." Ellie thrust
the press proof into Cardozo's hand.

He dropped into a chair.

Two months after the death of my daughter Nita Kohler, the
editor of *Fanfare Magazine,* Kristi Blackwell, asked me to write an
article dealing with the last forty days of Nita's life. I interviewed
friends, family, co-workers, and four weeks later produced a detailed day-by-day account. Ms. Blackwell found the result "too mor-
bid" for *Fanfare* readers and cut it by eighty percent.

"Would I be disturbing the household if I got myself something to drink?" Ellie said.

"Sorry." Cardozo nodded over his shoulder toward the refrigerator. "Help yourself."

Five months later, at the disclosure stage in the trial of Nita's
accused murderer, lawyers for James Delancey produced a diary,
certified by handwriting experts and criminal investigators to be
Nita's. Neither I nor my wife, actress Leigh Baker, had ever known
Nita to keep a diary. Shocking passages of this diary, detailing Nita's
alleged drug use and sex life, were put into evidence.

I did not see the unpublished passages of the diary until Sunday,
June 9 of this year. They were, word for word, the passages that
Kristi Blackwell cut from my article. Quite clearly the diary had
been forged, and Ms. Blackwell used me as an unwitting Deep
Throat to dilute blatant fabrications with persuasively "authentic"
material.

Ellie returned to the table with a glass of sparkling water. She sat on the chair facing Cardozo. She raised the glass in a silent toast and took a long, thirsty swallow.

This was not the only time—merely the most egregious—that Ms. Blackwell, after having lashed me on to exhaustively detailed work, removed and sequestered chunks of my material.

From "Gotham's Grandest Dame," she cut Mrs. Astor's bitterly fought divorce, reducing a hard-hitting exposé into yet another oafish fan letter.

From "The Prince They Now Call Sir," she cut human-rights abuses, animal sacrifice, slavery, and drug-running, reducing meaningful journalism to an inane puff piece for Cayman Islands tourism.

From "Socialites in Emergency," she cut the wrongful-death lawsuit resulting from conditions in Lexington Hospital's Emergency Room.

A clear pattern of abuse emerges. Ms. Blackwell has consistently commissioned, and then withheld from publication, material threatening America's vested interests. Is she really the public-spirited crusader she presents herself as? Or is she, like the late J. Edgar Hoover, abusing her position in order to amass private files—and with them to wield private power over the mighty of the land? It is a question whose time has come.

Cardozo tipped his chair back against the kitchen wall. "It's a question whose time has come, and it's sitting on the shelf right behind you."

Ellie twisted around in the chair and frowned at the row of bottles and books. "Garlic salt. Garlic pepper. What are you talking about? Macrobiotic cooking for two. Who cooks macrobiotic?"

"Not those," Cardozo said. "Nita Kohler's diary."

"This?" Ellie picked up the leather-bound volume.

"Turn to the entry for January eleventh."

Ellie sat reading. After a moment she looked at Cardozo.

"Turn the page," he said.

She turned the page. After a moment she beckoned for the press proof. He slid it to her across the table. She spent another silent moment rereading. She looked up.

"I've read Braidy's first draft," Cardozo said. "He's telling the truth. Three quarters of that diary is lifted from him. But not those nine words."

With a moment's perplexity Ellie's eyelids sank over her eyes. "The nine words are fake. They showed up in the diary four years ago, and they showed up in Sam's third note a week ago. Okay, it's a small world but not that small, right? So the third note is fake. And if the third note's a fake, why not all the notes?"

"You said it, Ellie, not me."

She sat slowly shaking her head. "But why would anyone copy this diary to fake a Society Sam note?"

"It may not have happened that way. The diary and the note could both have been copied from a third source."

"What third source? Why bother? Why not make it up from scratch?"

"Tell me the truth, Ellie. Have you ever met a killer as bright as you?"

"Plenty. But this guy isn't one of them."

Their gazes met.

"Before I forget." Ellie reached again into her purse and pulled out her notepad. "Sam's moving up. Zip code one-oh-seven-oh-three is Douglas Avenue, Yonkers. The best neighborhood he's yet mailed a note from. The postmaster says it was mailed no later than eleven fifty-five A.M. yesterday, which was a Sunday. And mailed no earlier than eleven fifty-five A.M. last Friday—which happens to have been a Friday. Vince—I made a joke."

"I'll laugh in a minute."

Ellie slipped the notepad back into the purse. "Doesn't it seem odd—killing a guy in a place where you work and everybody knows you?"

"There could be a reason. Sam alias Rick Martinez may not be planning to return to work."

"Then you think Sam alias Rick is the kind of guy who plans."

"Possibly." Cardozo rose from the chair and went to the refrigerator. "And it could be he's reached the end of his list."

"What leads you to that optimistic conclusion?"

"He's let us know who he is." Cardozo bent down to see if there was any lemonade left.

"Has he? Then how come we haven't found him?"

"Miracles take time. Thirty-eight men are out looking for him right now." Cardozo found the lemonade hiding behind the milk. "On the other hand . . ." He brought the pitcher and two glasses back to the table. "Wilkes thinks Sam could be building up to an explosion."

"What kind of explosion?"

"A mass killing."

· SIXTY-ONE ·

Tuesday, June 18

THE PHONE RANG.

With shaving cream still covering half his face, Cardozo ran to lift the receiver before the third ring could rouse the answering machine. "Vince Cardozo," he said quietly.

"Where is she?" The rasping, cigarette-ravaged voice had to belong to Tom Reilly, and the clinking sound suggested he'd put ice and maybe something else in his morning orange juice.

"She's on the sofa."

"Send her home."

"She says she doesn't have a home."

"Send her anyway."

From the hallway Cardozo could see into the darkened living room, where a dark-haired woman in stocking feet lay on the sofa, curled around a pillow that she was hugging like a doll. That she should be there at all struck him as an illogical extension of a daydream he had barely known he was dreaming.

"I can't. She's asleep."

"She's a public personality. A police lieutenant heading up a highly visible investigation cannot have this kind of public personality sleeping on his sofa."

"Where does it say that in the statutes?"

"I'm talking image. Word has traveled fast. Some very important people are having coronaries over this."

Which, Cardozo understood, was Tom Reilly's way of saying that he was being nagged by the borough commander, who was being nudged by the chief of detectives, who'd been queried by the chief of police, who'd had a call from the mayor, who'd gotten a threat from Waldo Carnegie that he was going to move his publishing empire to New Jersey.

"Tell these important people they're welcome to try to wake her up, but I doubt they'll have any more luck than I did."

"Waldo Carnegie is not taking this personally. He is not angry. He does not believe the rumors. He is willing to send a limousine."

"Waldo Carnegie has already sent a limousine." Shifting the window curtain an inch to the side, Cardozo looked down into the street. The long, black BMW limousine was still double-parked in front of the building. "It's been here since ten last night."

"What are you trying to do? What do you expect people to *think* you're trying to do?"

"Right now I'm trying to make my breakfast, and the toast's burning. Can we talk this over later?"

Terri came into the kitchen, rubbing her eyes. She sniffed and went to the oven. "Toast's burning." She speared two chunks of smoking carbon with a carving fork and carried them to the garbage pail.

Right away the room felt a lot nicer, just because her face was in it.

"I'm sorry," Cardozo said. "I was on the phone."

She opened the refrigerator. Containers clattered. "Would you consider eating a decent breakfast?"

"Depends on the decent breakfast."

He watched her break eggs into a mixing bowl. She added a little milk, paprika, salt, and pepper. She tipped the mixture into a hot frying pan, and the pan hissed.

"Know what I hate?" he said. "I hate it when, first thing in the morning, you tolerate me."

She smiled. "Get over it." She brought two plates of scrambled eggs to the table. "*Dad,*" she groaned. "I borrowed this issue. What have you done to it?" She was holding *People* magazine open to a page that he'd been doodling on.

"Sorry."

She sat and frowned at his drawing and she looked like a little girl trying to play a grandmother in a school drama-society production. "You're drawing this all the time. You're drawing it on napkins and newspapers and envelopes."

"Am I?"

"Why are you so hung up on the flag all of a sudden?"

He sat motionless, hearing the words; and then he turned his head and looked at her eyes—brown, luminous, veiled with dark lashes. "What did you just say?"

"I said why does the flag interest you so much?"

"The American flag, right?" A wave of certainty shot through him. "Stripes and little stars over in the upper left-hand corner?" He sprang up and grabbed the telephone and dialed Marty Wilkes's home number. "Marty, it's Vince. We have to talk. Right away. Sam's logo is an American flag."

"I'll meet you in my office in fifteen minutes."

Maybe Cardozo was just imagining it, but when he hung up his daughter seemed to be looking at him as though he were a seriously bad comedian. "I hate to ask you to be late for school," he said. "But I'd rather Leigh didn't wake up . . . you know . . ."

"You don't want her to wake up alone. In a strange place."

He nodded. "Do you think you could hang around till she leaves?"

"Sure." Terri smiled. "I'll be glad to."

■ ■ ■

"YOU ASKED ME if I'd ever run across a serial killer who carved flags on his victim's bodies." Marty Wilkes leaned back in his chair. The facades of Greenwich Village town houses glowed in the window behind him. "I ran a quick computer search. Does it matter if it's not a national flag?"

"Hell, no," Cardozo said. "A flag is a flag."

"If you don't mind the flag of the Commonwealth of Puerto Rico—the so-called *bonita bandera*—then La Rue Newton is your boy. Between June 1942 and September 1944 he murdered eight residents of the South Jersey shore and carved the *bonita bandera* on their bodies with a poultry knife."

He swiveled to face his computer terminal. His fingers drifted over the keyboard, touching keys, making no more sound than a rain of talcum powder.

From his chair Cardozo could see the blinking amber cursor dart beneath the glass screen, leaving a four-line spill of words and numbers too fleeting and too faraway to read.

Wilkes touched the Enter button. The screen emptied. There was a silent space in time, and then the microcircuitry kicked in with a soft clatter as the printer activated. He leaned sideways to detach a sheet of printout from the printer. He handed it to Cardozo. "Read all about it."

Cardozo scanned La Rue Newton's curriculum vitae: a list of eight murder victims, the address of the federal facility for the criminally insane to which he'd been remanded, and vital stats that ended with the date of his death three years ago. "Seems weird. Newton was carving flags on people's stomachs forty years ago, and Society Sam is doing the same thing now."

"There are copycat killings all the time."

"But usually the cat who gets copied is in the headlines."

"La Rue Newton got headlines. In his day."

"According to witnesses' descriptions, Society Sam wasn't born till fifteen, twenty years after Newton was put away. Why would Society Sam copy a cat that no one remembers?"

"Vince, at the moment I can't answer that. Serial killers have been known to base their careers on *famous* serial killers of the past—look at all the Jack-the-Ripper rip-offs—but why Sam likes La Rue is something you may have to ask him personally when you get around to meeting him."

"I'd also like to ask him why he likes society columns. He left one at the scene of every kill but Dizey's."

"Other killers have left newspaper clippings at the scene."

"It's always the column printed in the *Trib* the morning before the kill. At Oona's the column mentioned the boutique. At Avalon's the column mentioned the dinner party. But at Gloria's the column described a dinner she hadn't even gone to. There was no connection."

"It could be the message he's sending is the date, not the content."

"But two days earlier Dizey ran a blind item about Gloria. Sam passed it up. I can't figure it out. He's telling us these columns are important, and at the same time he's telling us he doesn't bother reading them."

Wilkes was thoughtful for a moment. "I'm going to dig a little deeper into the literature this weekend. I'll check killers who left society columns at the scene. And that *'sex to end all sex'* line in the third letter . . ."

Cardozo's glance flicked up. "What about it?"

Wilkes shrugged. "It reminds me of something. I've seen it somewhere else."

"We've all seen it somewhere else."

"You recognize it?"

Cardozo nodded. "But I'm not going to spoil it for you."

He could see the remark bothered Wilkes.

"Vince, this isn't a game. If you know something—tell me."

"The same five words showed up in Nita Kohler's diary. In

fact the same nine words. *'Sex to end all sex, is there anything else?'* "

Wilkes shook his head. "No, I'm not familiar with that diary. I've seen the words somewhere else."

Cardozo sighed. "Marty, is it possible we've gone off on a tangent? Is it possible Martinez is doing all this to get even?"

"It's not just possible, it's certain. Serial killing is *about* getting even."

"I mean, striking back at specific people that he has a specific grudge against? Could he be doing that and dressing it up as serial killing?"

Wilkes nodded. "There are examples of that in the literature. At least four of them. I'll dig them up for you."

■   ■   ■

THE DOOR MARKED LEGAL RECORDS was ajar. Cardozo gave two staccato raps on the glass and walked in.

A young woman seated at a computer terminal glanced up at him. He held out his shield.

She pushed back her chair and rose. "Shamma Dailey. Records." She was tall, slim, with blue-gray eyes, crisply waving brown hair. "How can I help you?"

Behind Ms. Dailey, half-lowered shades jittered in the current of the air conditioners.

Cardozo's eye traveled from the two desks, each with its own computer terminal, to the wall that was gunmetal gray filing cabinets from floor to ten-foot ceiling.

"You had a problem in your Emergency Room, the night of May sixth, nineteen eighty-five. There was a lawsuit."

"It would be right here. Off-database." She moved to the files at the extreme right of the wall. She spent a moment peering at dates on the drawers, then pulled out the next-to-bottom drawer. "Who sued?"

"That's what I want to find out."

"Oh, boy." She did some thinking. "In that case, here's what has to be done. These files are arranged by year, alphabetized under the plaintiff's name. Assuming your suit was filed within a year of the alleged damage, it'll be in this drawer. Someone has to go through this whole drawer from here back. It can't be me because I have work to do, and it shouldn't be you because you're not on the staff . . . but seeing as you're a cop and this is need-to-know—right?"

Cardozo crouched on the floor, and when he realized that

the crouch would kill his thighs during the hour or more this search could very likely require, he sat cross-legged and let his lower back do the suffering.

He worked his way through the files slowly. He carefully examined the covering page of each lawsuit, not wanting to miss a single May sixth that might be hiding in the boldfaced legalese. At the end of an hour and a half he found a suit brought by Richard Martinez for recovery in the wrongful death of Isolda Martinez.

Cardozo took the file to Ms. Dailey. "Sorry to bother you again, but could you tell me what the hell this last paragraph means in English?"

Ms. Dailey's gaze moved quietly over the page. "Isolda Martinez died in Emergency the night of May sixth, nineteen eighty-five. She had no proof of insurance, and the hospital refused to treat her."

"That much I got."

"Isolda was covered on Richard Martinez's insurance, and he claimed the hospital should have known. He also accused the hospital of letting *Fanfare Magazine* create a noxious condition in Emergency that contributed to Isolda's death."

"I got that too."

"The jury awarded two million dollars to Martinez. The judge set the award aside."

"Why?"

"Okay. Here's the hard part. A cash award would have initiated the hospital's collateral suit against the insurer. And that would have raised the employer's premiums."

"But why does that mean Martinez can't collect his damages?"

She floated him a disheartened look. "Because the employer was a federal agency. The federal government can be sued only if it consents. The government refused to pay increased premiums, and it refused to be sued for them. Therefore the premiums couldn't be raised. Therefore the hospital couldn't collect from the insurer. Therefore Martinez couldn't collect from the hospital. All the contract-law dominos fell backward and Martinez got crushed."

Cardozo felt a pang for Martinez, a sense of raw helplessness in the face of the majestic riffing and doo-wopping of the law. "Tell me if I'm understanding this. The insurer didn't tell the hospital this woman was insured, so the hospital didn't treat her, so she died—and everyone admits to this —and her husband still couldn't collect a dollar?"

Ms. Dailey's smile flattened and she continued with a different tone, hesitant, maybe just a little bit apologetic. "It was unfair. But it *was* legal. The crux of the matter is the insurance contract. I'd talk with the insurer."

"And who's the insurer?"

"Blue Cross Blue Shield—they're down on Forty-first Street. I'm sure they'd be more than prepared to give you an expert runaround."

■ ■ ■

CARDOZO STEPPED OFF THE ELEVATOR on the fourteenth floor of the Blue Cross building into a warren of corridors bounded by flatwhite, head-high partitions. He explored and finally found the opening marked 1412. He rapped on the wall. "Is Monte Horlick around?"

A young man with red suspenders sat at a modular desk, staring at figures scrolling up the screen of a computer terminal. A two-foot-high paper dandelion stood in a Perrier bottle on the desk beside the terminal. The face drawn in the center of the dandelion was smiling with berserk good cheer.

The young man turned in his chair. "Horlick is right here. What's up?"

Cardozo showed his shield. "They told me downstairs you could run down the records on a policy."

"Shoot me the stats." Horlick pressed buttons on his keyboard and cleared the computer screen. "Policy number?"

Cardozo read the number from his notebook.

Horlick entered the digits and letters. Lines of type began scrolling up the screen. Horlick gazed at the screen through halfparted lids. "What we have here is a gentleman by the name of Richard no middle name no initial Martinez. It's a terrific policy: wraparound benefits plus psychiatric plus dentistry. Mr. Martinez's most recent reimbursement was for dental work performed April eighteenth."

For Cardozo it happened in a split millisecond—the realization that something had dropped into his lap. "April eighteenth *this* year? Do you mean this policy is current?"

"Current and kicking."

"Where did you mail that reimbursement?"

■ ■ ■

CARDOZO FINALLY FOUND A PAY PHONE in the street that worked. He called Carl Malloy at the precinct.

"Carl, I need you to stake out a mailing address. Box 108-E, Four twelve West Fortieth Street. It's an outfit called Mailsafe. The box is rented in the name of Richard Martinez."

"Jesus Christ, is that Rick Martinez?"

"It's him."

▪ SIXTY-TWO ▪

"TELL ME ABOUT DICK BRAIDY," Cardozo said.

"Dick?" Kristi Blackwell gazed thoughtfully across her desk with its computer terminal and its vase of bloodred roses. "He was always charming, often honest, and he was very, very driven."

"Driven by what?"

Kristi Blackwell was wearing a high-fashion dark business suit, but she radiated an easy, at-home sort of power.

"Dick was leading a life where everyone he ever heard of was a millionaire—except him. In his heart he was a runty little Irish kid from north Boston, and he never got over it." She turned up her eyes and smiled. "Shall I tell you his most painful memory?"

Cardozo could feel her bursting to tell him. "Please."

"He rarely discussed this, though I pleaded with him to put it in an article—his most painful memory was having been invited, as a teenager, to a debutante cotillion at the Brookline Country Club. They were serving beef Wellington at the sit-down dinner but it was Friday night, and of course in those days Catholics couldn't eat meat on Fridays. So the old Irish biddy who was waiting on Dick's table brought him a plate of scrambled eggs and she whispered in his ear, in brogue if you please, 'I know you're a nice Irish boy, so I made these for you myself.'"

Kristi Blackwell delivered the line in a little brogue of her own. Her eyes were on Cardozo and there was a how'm-I-doin' look in them.

This was an odd way, Cardozo couldn't help but think, to be talking about a friend who was both dear and dead.

"Well," Kristi Blackwell said, "one of the Cabot girls was

sitting at poor Dick's table and she just took one look at those *sad* eggs and she burst out laughing."

"Laughing because he was Catholic?"

"Laughing because he was *ignorant* Catholic. What poor Dick didn't realize was that Cardinal Cushing had given social Catholics permission to cool that no-meat rule. Dick told me he never forgot that girl's laughter—and he never knew how the serving woman had spotted him."

"How had she spotted him?"

"The place card—Braidy."

"He never figured that out?"

"Dick was a puzzling man. For all his shrewdness he had more blind sides than an accordion."

"Such as?"

"He yearned to be a major player, but he never truly understood what the game was about. He had no sense of what was stylish or awful. For example—the major boo-boo of his career: when he got his first big check from the magazine, he realized he'd never be taken seriously if he didn't move out of that seedy little hotel where he'd been living. So he went out and bought a rundown co-op in a dingy little building that didn't allow Jews. He honestly thought it was more chic if *somebody* wasn't allowed in. Of course, in New York, that kind of anti-Semitism is provincial."

Cardozo got the impression from the way she said it that perhaps there were other kinds of anti-Semitism that weren't provincial.

"Dick never truly understood the basics. To an extent he could fake it. He watched other people and imitated their behavior, but he overdid it. He filibustered every dinner party he could get into. He thought that made him a good seat. In the last decade of the twentieth century he was still sending to Turnbull and Asser in London for his shirts. He thought *that* was chic. He sincerely believed that gossip was the prime energizer of the universe. So he told that *stupid* story about Barbara Walter's bidet much too often and he infuriated Louis Auchincloss with that canard about Lily and the sugar bowl. In fact, that ridiculous sugar bowl got him blackballed from the Union Club *and* the Century."

"I don't know either of those stories."

"And you don't want to. The point is, Dick did himself huge damage with that hara-kiri mouth of his. If Louis doesn't like you, Brooke is not going to have you in the house—and that's exactly what happened. And then on top of having no judgment about gossip, he told all sorts of needless lies—no one ever knew why."

"Could you give me an example?"

"Silly things. Who-cares kinds of things. He said Harrison Ford had painted his house before he became a star."

"Not true?"

"Not true. Harrison Ford painted his *sister's* house. Dick tried to imply that he and Leigh had never divorced, and when that didn't fly he tried to imply they had secretly remarried."

"Why did he want to imply that?"

"He was star struck. And he didn't want to be called gay."

"Was he?"

"Gay? How could anyone tell? He was so scared after Leigh divorced him that he never had sex with anyone."

She was trying to seem easy and hard-boiled about this, but it was giving her trouble. Cardozo sensed something unresolved in this woman's feelings about her dead author.

"But," she said, "with all his denial and all his limitations, he was one hell of a writer. Nothing escaped him. He could spot the gonnabee alumni of Betty Ford at a glance, and he knew who'd changed what place card at whose dinner—because to Dick Braidy everything in New York society happened during prime time and he was thrilled, just thrilled, to be a part of it. He adored the old rich and famous and he was fascinated by the *nouveaux* rich and famous. He believed they walked, talked, dreamed, and excuse me, farted Technicolor. And he communicated his excitement to his readers."

Cardozo understood what Kristi Blackwell was telling him: Guys like Dick Braidy were about power worship. Over at the precinct they would have called it ass-kissing.

He understood too that guys like Kristi Blackwell—for all their airs of being above mere money-grubbing—were about keeping their own breadbaskets full, which in this case meant turning Dick Braidy's worship of the wealthy into a commercial cult and peddling it to all the other Dick Braidy think-alikes in the world.

What he didn't understand was how deep her dislike for the man really ran. Was this just mean-spirited kidding, or was it something more?

"It's a sad fact," Kristi Blackwell said, "that today most Americans are outside the economy looking in. Dick grasped that, because he was an outsider himself. He may have gone to Bobo Vanderbilt's in twelve-hundred-dollar patent-leather pumps, but he was still that hungry little mick from the ghetto, scared that he was going to be the only kid at the table eating scrambled eggs."

Her eyes were on Cardozo now. One eyebrow lifted, sly and more than a little manipulative. It was a distinctly italicized moment. That eyebrow was saying, *We understand these things— you and I.*

"Society sensed that outsider thing about him and—frankly —society laughed. But readers sensed it about him too and they loved it, because it made Dick Braidy exactly the same as them. Our readers are going to miss him. The magazine is truly going to miss him. And God knows, so am I."

"If he was that great for the magazine," Cardozo said, "why did you make so many cuts in his articles?"

"I never cut Dick's articles. Not without his consent."

"He says you did."

"He *says?*" This time both of Kristi Blackwell's eyebrows lifted. The upper sockets of her eyes had been painted deep blue, like a ballet dancer's. She leaned forward on her elbows. Two dozen bracelets clanked. "I doubt that at this moment Dick Braidy is saying anything on that or any other subject."

Cardozo handed her the proof of the unpublished column.

Kristi Blackwell brought her eyeglasses down out of her curls and balanced them on the tip of her nose. As she read the column her lips narrowed into a thin pink gash.

"Dick Braidy was a child." She snapped the proof onto the desk. "Like a child he had great pride in his work—often justified —and very little understanding of how the real world works. It never occurred to him that there were valid reasons for toning down his articles—oh, no, only a conspiracy could explain why a single comma was moved."

"Would you happen to remember any of these valid reasons?"

Kristi Blackwell shrugged. "Sometimes he was puncturing somebody's aura, and the somebody owned a store that advertised. Or he violated a taboo. *Nobody* discusses Mrs. Astor's first marriage. *Nobody.* Sometimes his eye was a little too sharp. I mean, we *all* agree that Gayfryd's party for Saul's fiftieth was *tawdry,* it was a stewardess's idea of chic, but that's no reason to come out and say it. You have to leave the reader *something* to believe in."

"Why did you cut 'Socialites in Emergency'?"

"I honestly don't remember what cuts I made or why. We *are* a monthly, and if I do say so, a very thick one."

"I realize that." Cardozo had brought Dick Braidy's first-draft pages in an NYPD manila envelope. He reached across the desk and handed them to her. "I've marked your cuts in red."

"Is that what all these pretty lines are." It took her a little under a minute to scan Dick Braidy's twelve pages. She tapped the sheets neatly together and pushed her glasses back up into her hair. She gazed across the desk. "What's your point, Lieutenant?"

"All of Society Sam's victims, except one, play starring roles in that article."

Kristi Blackwell's chin rose. "You find that a meaningful coincidence?"

"Possibly. But in Dick Braidy's draft the socialites are *inside* the Emergency Room. Dizey is chatting up the nurses and Gloria is flirting with the doctors and Avalon is posing Oona for photographs—and Dick Braidy is busily getting it all down on paper. But your cuts move them back into the Admitting Room."

"You think that was the purpose of my cuts?"

"Wasn't it?"

"Why would I or anyone care whether they're in this room or that room?"

"Somebody cared enough to sue."

"Who?"

"Richard a.k.a. Rick Martinez. His wife Isolda died in Emergency. Braidy mentions the suit. You've cut every reference to it."

"It wasn't germane."

"Then you remember it."

"Not at all."

"*Fanfare Magazine* was named in the suit."

"I've never heard of the lawsuit or him or her."

"How do you answer Dick Braidy's charges about the Nita Kohler diary?"

"Lieutenant, it was my understanding that you wished to discuss the Society Sam killings. And within reasonable limits I'm willing to help. But isn't Nita Kohler a little far afield?"

"Possibly not. How do you answer the allegations?"

"Why should I answer them? Why should I even draw attention to them? They're paranoid and he's dead."

"What did you do with the material you cut from 'Pavane'?"

"Do?" Kristi Blackwell bent sideways and swung a wastebasket up from beneath the desk. For an instant Cardozo thought she intended to hurl it at him. Instead she thumped it down onto the desktop. "Whatever was cut from that article went right there, Lieutenant. Where it belonged."

"And where did it go from there? How did it wind up where it *didn't* belong?"

"It didn't wind up anywhere, Lieutenant. Dick Braidy's chronology is way off. He didn't even *write* the article till after Delancey's lawyer discovered that diary. If anyone plagiarized, it was Dick lifting from the diary and not vice versa."

Cardozo raised a doubting eyebrow.

"He was a highly unoriginal writer," Kristi Blackwell said. "He lifted half his stuff from Marietta Tree's butler and he never credited *anyone*." She consulted the thin gold lozenge of her wristwatch.

"Ms. Blackwell, are you aware that in the United States we have a penalty for falsifying evidence?"

Kristi Blackwell pushed the proof sheet toward Cardozo's side of the desk. "And for libel too, which is all this ridiculous column of his is. I intend to have a talk with my lawyer."

"Make that a long talk. And make it within the next forty-eight hours."

"And what happens after forty-eight hours?"

"You tell me who you gave that material to—or I tell the District Attorney we have a problem."

■ ■ ■

"WE RECOVERED SEMEN and pubic hairs from Braidy's mouth," Lou Stein said.

"What's the blood type?" Cardozo said.

"Type O—same as the others."

"Do the hairs match?"

"Same donor."

"Any surprises?" Cardozo said.

"One. At least it's a surprise to me. Sam's still dousing his pubes in kerosene."

"Maybe his lice reinfested."

"Then why aren't there nits on these latest hairs?"

"I'm not the man to ask about pubic lice, Lou. It's outside my competence."

"After five weeks of this home remedy Sam's got to have a very raw groin. I'd frankly expect him to be too sensitive to allow himself to be fellated."

"Who knows. Maybe he's got nerves of steel."

"I'm surprised whole blood isn't showing up in the victims' saliva. But what the hell, tomorrow is always another day."

Cardozo's stomach felt hollow at the thought. "Please, Lou, don't remind me."

"Oh, Vince. He started on a new box of Saffire *Shabbes* candles."

Cardozo broke the connection and dialed Dan Hippolito's number.

"Make it official for me, Dan—did Sam kill Braidy?"

"Same knife, same pattern of cuts. It's Sam, all right."

■ ■ ■

CARDOZO WENT TO THE LITTLE PANTRY off the squad room to get himself some coffee. The pot was almost empty, which meant someone in the squad had been shirking: it was the responsibility of the detective who took the last cup to start another pot.

There were no fresh filters in the cabinet, so Cardozo opened the Mr. Coffee and lifted out the used filter and emptied the wet grounds into the wastepaper basket.

He reinserted the filter, careful not to rip it, and searched the cabinet till he found the can of ground coffee. He tapped a flow into the used filter and then took the pot to the men's room to get water.

The air smelled of overkill levels of camphor and ammonia. A uniformed black cop had planted himself beside the urinals. He was staring hard at the ceiling, whistling atonally, and his right hand was swinging a nightstick from its leather thong. His left hand was cuffed to a small, Middle Eastern–looking man in a sweat-stained khaki nylon shirt who was taking a leak.

Carl Malloy was sitting on the ledge by the raised window, smoking a cigarette and staring moodily at the cinderblock wall across the alley. "Heard you were doing computer work over at Dick Braidy's apartment," he said.

Cardozo crossed to the sink and turned on the hot water so it ran hard into the pot. "Laurie Bonasera did the work. I did the watching."

Malloy slid down from the ledge and came over to the sink. He stared at himself in the mirror and adjusted a graying forelock. "So how is she with a computer?"

Cardozo managed to blast the inside of the pot free of most of this year's cooked-on residue, but he wasn't sure about last year's. "Bonasera's a miracle worker with a computer."

"Yeah. She's great." Malloy gave a laugh and froze a smile. "So what did you two talk about for two hours?"

Cardozo decided the pot was as clean as it was going to get.

He filled it with water from the cold faucet. "Files and directories and default commands." He sensed that something alien and odd was passing through the space between him and Malloy. "How's Delia?"

Delia, for the last twenty-one years, had been Mrs. Carl Malloy. In that time she had borne him a son and a daughter.

The answer came in a manic blast. "Great, great. Delia's just great."

"Glad to hear it." Cardozo snapped a paper towel down from the holder and carefully wiped the bottom of the coffeepot dry. "Be sure to tell her and the kids hello for me, will you?"

■ ■ ■

IT WAS A SETTING Leigh had expected to live the rest of her life in, to die in.

She saw the tall glass in her right hand; she saw her arms, with their gold-and-diamond bracelets, lying on the armrests of the overstuffed chair in Waldo's library. She saw the skirt of her silk dress, and she saw that it exactly matched her gray suede pumps, resting on the cozy little needlepoint footrest.

She saw Waldo on the sofa facing her.

After tonight, she thought, *I'll never be part of this picture again.*

"There's something we've got to discuss," she said.

"Oh, yes?" he said in his best interested voice. He turned a page of *The New Yorker.*

"I don't know how to say this."

Waldo sat there like a tree, earnest. Wanting to make it clear he was willing to listen for the next thirty seconds to whatever she had to say.

"I don't know how to say this, but I'm going to say it anyway." She smiled. *This smile for hire,* she thought. "And I hope you'll understand I'm saying it with love and friendship and respect."

Waldo laid down his magazine. He struck that attitude of listening that passed for caring.

"I have to leave you, Waldo."

The silence in the room was suddenly flat and harsh. He stared at her, and he had an honestly bewildered look on his face.

"Could I ask you one question?" His voice sounded drawn back and clogged, as though he had to clear his throat. "Just tell me why."

"Because I can't do it anymore. I can't keep going through the motions."

He sat with an expression of wanting intensely to understand. "Is that all it is to you?"

"That's all it is to either of us."

"No. What we've got is worth something to me. It's worth a great deal to me."

"I'm grateful you feel that way, Waldo. And I'm sorry that I don't. And I'm still leaving you."

"Is it because you feel I've neglected you?"

"Neglect isn't the problem. We've neglected each other from the beginning."

"Is it because I've had affairs? You know those women have never meant anything to me."

She thought of all the time she and Waldo had been together, and all the waste they'd made of it, all the memories they would never have—the evening walks they'd never taken, the meals they'd never cooked for each other, the confidences they'd never shared. "I'm not jealous, Waldo. I've been annoyed but never jealous."

"Is it because you're in love with your detective?"

"I'm not in love with anyone. Not yet."

"Then you don't need to leave."

"But I do and I'm going to."

"I'm sorry. I can't permit it."

There was that half tick of an instant where she realized intellectually what she'd heard, but her mind refused to believe it. "I beg your pardon?"

"You're not going to leave me."

He said it with an offhand sort of coolness that enraged her. "And just how do you propose to prevent me?"

"You don't seem to realize how very much I care for you. How very much concern I feel for you. I've had you guarded since the first Society Sam note."

"That was very considerate of you."

"The guard, naturally, told me when you had tea with your detective. He told me when you spent the night with your detective."

It was Leigh's turn to be surprised. "Don't tell me you're jealous."

"Jealous? No more than you. Concerned? How could I not be concerned when the guard told me what you did at Oona's memorial."

She stared a moment at the face staring back at her. It was like being pinned in the headlights of an oncoming vehicle.

"Do I need to refresh your memory?" Waldo said. "You had a little contretemps with Dizey. And if you try to leave me, if you even think of subjecting me to that humiliation, I'll see to it that Cardozo learns what really happened on the terrace that evening."

A spike of panic ran up her spine. She stared at this gray-haired, WASPy, aging gentleman in his elegantly cut gray suit, with the look in his eyes she was not certain she had ever really decoded. "You selfish bastard," she said. "All you've ever wanted me for is to look famous and keep you company."

"And you're very good at it."

"We're not even lovers anymore."

He shrugged. "The public likes to think we are."

"You mean *you* like the public to think we are. Well, what the hell is so sacred about your public image that it gives you the right to violate my life?"

"My dear, I have exactly the same right to violate another person's life as you do."

"I didn't lay a hand on Dizey."

"I'm sure your lieutenant will want to draw his own conclusions."

Something shifted in the perspective around her. She rose to her feet, and suddenly she was standing in a zone of strangeness. "Then so be it."

"He won't be happy when he finds out. Whatever else he is, he is a cop. And an honest one, they tell me."

"I'll just have to take that chance."

■ ■ ■

"ANYONE HOME?" Cardozo called out.

"Me." Terri was sprawled on the living room rug, reading a book by the light of the MTV music video exploding across the TV screen. She reached up a hand and waved.

"Aren't you going to kill your eyes that way?"

"Leigh phoned," she said.

Cardozo crossed to the TV and turned down the volume. "What did she say?"

Terri turned a page. "She said thanks and she has some hard thinking to do and she won't be coming back."

Cardozo felt a sudden deflation. "What does that mean, thanks and she has some hard thinking to do and she won't be coming back?"

Terri turned and saw the look on his face. She got to her feet and came to him. "Dad, if the two of you aren't going to sleep in your bedroom, it *is* kind of a small apartment."

Cardozo dropped heavily onto the sofa.

"It's not the end of the world," Terri said.

He didn't answer.

She sat beside him and looked at him. "Or is it?"

He felt embarrassed and he tried to concentrate on the music video, on kids in bright-colored clothes diving off cliffs.

"Wow," Terri said. "That's great."

"What's great?"

She was grinning at him happily. "You're in love."

▪ SIXTY-THREE ▪

Wednesday, June 19

MALLOY STOPPED in front of the column of mailboxes numbered 108. They ran floor to ceiling. He had to relax his knees just a little, and stoop before he could see into the boxes in the E row.

The window of 108-E showed him three envelopes still undisturbed, still lying diagonally across the box.

It had been boring enough tailing Delancey, he thought, but at least Delancey had *moved*. Tailing a mailbox was the pits.

He straightened up and turned.

Two girls in jeans and *Yo-quiero-la-Habana* T-shirts were standing at the counter, giggling in Spanish, not noticing him.

He pushed open the glass door and stepped again into the steambath of West Forty-eighth Street. He stepped around a mumbling knot of crackheads. They'd been there all afternoon, never moving from that spot, handing dirty dollar bills and crack vials back and forth, about as inconspicuous as a lighthouse.

He watched them laughing and grinning and swaying and moving as if it were all a dance, as if all of life were just a question of feeling the beat and putting your foot in the right place at the right time.

A Cuban-Chinese *bodega*-deli across the street caught his eye. He went in. The little old lady at the counter wore a peasant-style scarf and with her bright eyes distinct as new blooms on a tough old trunk, she looked like a 350-year-old bonsai.

He pointed to the pot gurgling on the coffee machine.

The old woman placed a styrofoam cup of coffee on the counter. She slid a sugar dispenser and a pint carton of milk toward him.

He put a dollar bill on the counter.

The old woman shook her head and pushed it back.

He flashed that she didn't want to take money from a cop. Which meant, among other things, that he must be pretty obvious.

I'm not going to go through this again. He left the money on the counter and ambled toward the window. He studied the hand that was holding the coffee. The hand was trembling badly. Either his blood sugar had dipped or vodka wasn't the greatest lunch for a working cop.

His free hand took a little plastic prescription bottle out of his pocket. His fingers worked the top off and a rainbow of pills spilled into his palm. He jiggled his hand till two black pills separated from the others.

The two black pills went into his mouth. He chased them with a slug of coffee. The lady narc who had sold him the pills swore they didn't show up in urine tests, but you had to drink coffee—lots of it.

He glanced toward the window. Traffic was crawling around Con Ed–generated potholes and the firebombed carcass of a green Honda Accord. Even with the door of the *bodega* shut and the air conditioner rattling in the transom, he could hear horns blaring at the pushcarts that sold paper cups of shaved ice and syrup.

Pedestrians were jaywalking as though they were exercising a constitutional right. Wherever Malloy looked he saw people breaking one law or another: peddling stolen goods, making drug deals, getting high, dancing to the beat and yowl of Latino boom boxes, dozing, cruising for sex—and none of it seemed to be a big deal to anyone.

It made Carl Malloy wonder if his existence made any difference at all, if he had any power to influence the movement of the smallest molecule in the universe. Sometimes he felt too old, too hot, too tired for this kind of work. Sometimes he wished he could just walk away from it.

At that instant he registered something out there in the street. A woman heading down the sidewalk had caught his eye. Maybe twenty-four years old. Five feet ten. Black, with the body of an anorectic, swiveling through the crowd. She was wearing a man's black shirt and black slacks and a wide black belt studded with colored stones that marked the exact moment in each step when her weight shifted from one hip to the other. She had long, slightly waved hair and she was wearing huge dark glasses.

She slowed at a newsstand and bought a paper.

Now she was walking past the maildrop. Two storefronts beyond Mailsafe she stopped. She turned, doubled back, caught the door of Mailsafe just as the two giggling Spanish girls were coming out, and walked right in.

Malloy could see her through the window. She was standing by the counter, and she was going through her newspaper, pulling out unwanted pages and dropping them into the wastebasket.

Now she was crossing to the mailboxes. Little glints of metal and glass sparkled off the wall of locks. She went toward the 108 column. Her body blocked Malloy's view.

Her hand stretched out. He could see her wrist twisting, engaging the whole arm, and then the hand reappeared, and it was holding three envelopes.

Malloy gulped his coffee and was out the door in two strides, halfway across the street in the next three, and then he was at the door to Mailsafe.

She was coming toward him. She made eye contact and smiled. He realized he was holding the door. She glided into the street.

He scooted over to 108-E. He ducked down just far enough to see up the tunnel.

The box was empty.

He spun around. At first he thought he'd lost her, and then he saw her, at the edge of the window—heading west.

■ ■ ■

THE PHONE RANG.

Cardozo lifted the receiver and even before it reached his ear he could hear music and screaming. The music was a heavy-metal derivative of mariachi. The screaming was Carl Malloy.

"I staked the box out, a woman came. She looked kind of like the Identi-Kit drawing of Tamany Dillworth."

"What do you mean, kind of?"

"Vince, those are lousy drawings. I followed her to Four-fifty-seven West Forty-ninth. I checked the mailboxes and there's a Martinez in 3-F. I'm calling from a pay phone right across from the building. She's upstairs now."

"I'll be right down."

■ ■ ■

A HOT BREEZE WAS GUSTING IN from the Hudson as Cardozo hurried west on Forty-ninth Street.

Malloy was waiting on the corner of the five hundred block.

He was the only man within five square blocks wearing a jacket, and Cardozo realized they must both be pathetically easy to tag as cops.

"End of the block," Malloy said.

"Has she come out yet?"

"Not yet."

The building was a standard, decomposing 1890s six-story tenement. They climbed the stoop. The outer door was held open by a little eye-and-hook latch in the baseboard.

Cardozo glanced at the mailboxes. The name *Martinez* had been penciled on a piece of brown paper and shoved into the slot of Box 3-F. A flyer from a Japanese restaurant had been folded and wedged through one of the decorative perforations.

Malloy shaded his eyes and peered through the glass-paneled door into the empty vestibule. He gave the door a little push. Like the outer door it was unlocked. No slumlord in this neighborhood would lock a front door unless he wanted to replace it every time housebreakers knocked it down.

Cooking fumes and oil-saturated smoke ripened the air of the hallway.

They started up the stairs, Malloy first. The steps tilted and several were beginning to come loose. The fluorescent tube in the ceiling flickered, creating the optical illusion that the steps were rising and falling.

On the third floor landing a cat came out of the shadow. It pressed against Cardozo's leg. He petted the animal and felt ribs. The cat arched its back and let out a good shrill street meow.

"Hey, kitty," Cardozo whispered, "where does Martinez live?"

The cat went straight to the door of 3-F.

Malloy leaned an ear against the door. He beckoned Cardozo. Dead silence pressed on the other side of the panel.

Overhead there was a sudden clatter of sandals slapping against steps. Cardozo and Malloy pressed themselves into the shadow. The sandals were heading rapidly up the stairs, not down. At the top of the stairwell a roof door slid open and thumped shut.

Malloy gave the door handle of 3-F a try. He took out his wallet and removed his Visa card. He slid the card into the crack between the door and the jamb. He jimmied it back and forth till there was a soft click. The door swung inward.

Cardozo drew his gun and edged around Malloy and flattened himself against the inner wall of the apartment. It took a moment to blink the darkness out of his eyes. The air was sweltering, sticky—worse than the hallway, with a thick stench of fried food.

His eyes began adjusting, and impressions started to form. He could make out a lattice of light and shade falling across the surfaces of a stove, a sink, a refrigerator.

A hallway stretched to the right, toward the street, and at the end of it light flecks leapt fitfully. In another moment Cardozo saw that a tiny current of air was stirring one of the blackout shades that had been drawn in the windows.

Cardozo nodded Malloy into the apartment. He motioned Malloy to check the back room.

Cardozo crept soundlessly to the front room. He saw that it was small, sparsely furnished, and deserted. He flicked the kitchen light switch.

In the sudden light of the naked sixty-watt bulb, the world of Rick Martinez and Society Sam began disclosing itself. A poster of Rambo shouldering an automatic rifle had been taped to the side of the refrigerator. A pack of Saffire-brand *Shabbes* candles sat on the drainboard. A half-dozen plates and pans had been stacked unscraped in the sink. Cockroaches had free run of the place. The floor had been overlaid with black-and-white linoleum tiles, and in places open chancres of wood showed through.

In the front room foam-rubber stuffing was leaking out of a foldout sofa-bed. Dumbbells and barbells had been parked against the window wall, with weight-lifting plates stacked beside them. Between the windows, in the space where another homemaker might have placed a picture or maybe a crucifix, Martinez had hung a brown leather weight-lifting belt. Sweat had mottled it darkly.

A bookcase held three books and a potted plant that looked like a seriously endangered species. A scruffy little stuffed bear sat on top of a new-looking Sony tape deck. The bear wore a cheap rosary around its neck and a wool cap with stitching that spelled *Rick's Christmas Bear.* Cassette tapes had been piled chaotically on the bottom shelf. Cardozo crouched down to read the titles: there were albums by the Grateful Dead and Iron Maiden and Kiss and Devil Dolls, and there was one called *Charles Manson's Greatest Hits.*

Malloy reappeared. "She's not in back."

"She's not up here." Cardozo studied two pieces of unopened mail lying on the air conditioner. A hand-written aerogram from Colombia was addressed to Mr. Ricardo Martinez, c/o Malsaf, Box 108-E, 412 West 48th Street. A stapled, mimeographed flyer from a Pentecostal church in Brooklyn was addressed to Rick Martinez, Box 108-E, 412 West 48th Street. "You said there was a third piece of mail."

"There was," Malloy said. "But I don't see it."

Cardozo held the aerogram up to the light. He could make out two layers of tiny, spidery handwriting, and the signature, *tu mama.*

"You have to look what he's got in back," Malloy said. "You're not going to believe it."

"Says who?"

In the back room a box spring and mattress had been stacked on the bare floor. Beyond the mattress a cork bulletin board had been fastened to an artist's easel. Eleven front pages of the *New York Tribune* were displayed: one for each of Society Sam's killings, except Dizey Duke, and one for each of his letters.

In the center of the bulletin board Martinez had placed the Identi-Kit drawing of the male Hispanic. In red Magic Marker he had drawn a five-pointed king's crown on the head.

Cardozo walked to the bathroom. There was no light switch. He moved a hand through the dark and connected with a cord. He pulled and a naked light bulb went on over the sink. Forty watts' worth of ash-gray light spilled over the grungy tiles and stained plumbing.

On the sink a plastic oral syringe had been placed plunger end–up in an unwashed tumbler. Beside it a shot glass held what looked like a dozen beard hairs.

Cardozo opened the medicine cabinet. A capless bottle of pink-ribbed amphetamine tablets tipped. He caught it before it could clatter into the sink. Dozens of bottles of Squibb and Geigy and Sandoz pharmaceuticals, all labeled in Spanish, clogged the shelves. There was enough stockpiled to macerate the brains of a regiment of Rick Martinezes.

A phone and answering machine sat on the floor beside the toilet. No light blinked on the machine. Apparently no messages had come in since Martinez had last replayed them. Cardozo crouched and pressed Rewind, and then Play.

There was a beep, a hang up, another beep, another hang up, a third beep, and a man's voice.

"Hi, Rick, how are you doing? I'm phoning Tuesday, June eighteenth. Thanks for completing the pickup yesterday. You have one more pickup scheduled, the timing and the merchandise are up to you. Have fun. I'll meet you Thursday, June twentieth, two P.M., on the path at West Seventy-first, just inside the park. Look for me on the bench. See you then."

Malloy stood in the bathroom doorway. "I hope *one more pickup* doesn't mean what it sounds like."

▪ ▪ ▪

THE FIRST THING that Cardozo noticed about 229 West Eighty-first Street was that the front door and the windows in all six stories had been covered over with steel plates. The second thing was that smoke had streaked most of the brick facade pitch-black.

A man was spraying down the sidewalk in front of the twelve-story white-brick apartment building next door. He averted his hose so that Cardozo could walk by.

Cardozo didn't walk by.

"Can I help you?" the man asked. The tone of voice was more a challenge than an offer.

"I'm looking for a young woman by the name of Tamany Dillworth." Cardozo double-checked the address she had given him. She could not have printed the numbers more clearly or decisively. "She said she lived at 229."

"Maybe two weeks ago," the man said. "Before the crack factory in the basement exploded and burned the building down."

▪ SIXTY-FOUR ▪

As Cardozo let himself into his apartment, he saw Leigh Baker rising from the sofa and his heart skipped a half-dozen beats in a row.

"Terri let me in," she said. "I hope you don't mind. I need to talk to you."

"Of course I don't mind." He dropped his keys into the bowl on the hall table. "Where's Terri?"

"She said she was going to a movie. I think she really just wanted to leave us alone."

He came into the living room. He crossed to her. "Terri likes you. So do I."

They kissed and she drew back.

"Can I get you anything?" he offered.

"I'm okay, thanks."

"Just give me a minute." He went into the bathroom and splashed water on his face, thought seriously about shaving, decided he was crazy, and went to his bedroom to put on a clean shirt. He went into the kitchen and got the ice tray from the refrigerator and banged it against the sink.

"Hey," he called. "Would you have any way of getting hold of Tamany Dillworth's address?"

"Possibly. Why?"

"Her old address burned down." He dropped three cubes into a glass and filled it with ginger ale. "And she's picking up mail for Rick Martinez."

"Should I know who Rick Martinez is?"

He came back into the living room. "You met him in Marsh and Bonner's."

She was seated on the old flowered sofa. The standing lamp threw a circle of light around her. "The man with the boom box?"

Cardozo nodded. "He was married to a woman called Isolda Martinez. She died in the Emergency Room the night those socialites went partying. Rick Martinez blamed them. And it looks like he killed them."

Leigh Baker was silent for a moment, thinking. "I was so certain it was Jim Delancey. How could I have been so certain and so *wrong*?"

"It's happened to me more than once." Cardozo sat on the sofa close to her. "Where did you go? I missed you."

"I'm sorry. I missed you too. But I had to be by myself. I had to make some decisions."

He could feel her trying to hold a smile and not coming anywhere near managing.

A dry swallow rode down her throat. "They say you can't get clean and sober without getting honest. They say you're as sick as your secrets. If you hold back even a single lie, that lie will keep pulling you back down into drugs and liquor."

"Who's this *they*?"

"I don't know." She shrugged. "Experts."

"There are too many experts in this world."

"And too many lies in my life. I keep getting twisted around and winding up at the same wall. So maybe I should tell the truth, for a change."

"Are you asking for my advice or my ears?"

"Your ears. Maybe your shoulder in a while."

"My shoulder's not planning to go anywhere."

Her eyes were anxious, tired. "The letter that was sent to the newspaper after Dizey died—it was a lie."

He released her hand. "*Lie* is a strange word."

"It's the right word."

"To lie, you have to say something. That letter was gibberish. It didn't say anything."

"Yes, it did. It said he killed her. And he didn't."

He set his glass down on the side table. "How do you know?"

"I'm still doing it." She shook her head. "I'm still lying. I don't know how to stop. The reason I'm here isn't to be honest or stay sober—it's because Waldo knows and he's about to blast it to you and the world." She gazed over at him. "Unless he's told you already."

Cardozo shook his head.

She pulled in a slow breath and let it out in a sigh. "I was on the terrace when Dizey went over the wall."

Suddenly Cardozo's stomach felt like eight miles of dead intestine. "Did you push her?"

"Everything but. I called her a thief and I threw my drink in her face. She accused me of drinking again."

"*Were* you drinking?"

"I was very drunk and paranoiacally defensive."

"Paranoiacally defensive about what?"

"I was afraid she'd publish an item saying I'd fallen off the wagon."

"Had she done anything like that before?"

"Every damned time."

"Okay, so maybe you wanted to kill her. But you didn't. Wanting isn't criminal. What you did wasn't planned. It wasn't malicious. It wasn't intentional. Keeping silent wasn't breaking the law." *Why am I talking so fast?* he wondered. *Who am I trying to convince?* "You weren't withholding evidence of a crime. It wasn't as though by keeping silent you implicated an innocent person."

"Maybe not this time." She stared down at her hands. "But there's something else. When I saw Dizey fall, when I saw how easily a person could go over that wall—I realized Nita could have died the same way." She swallowed. "And Delancey could have been innocent."

"Jim Delancey got his rights, which was more than he gave your daughter. Granted, he wasn't judged by a wolfpack of his peers, but at least it was a jury. Besides, you saw him push her."

"No." She shook her head. "I *didn't* see him push her."

"But you testified under oath—"

"I lied." She stood. She wheeled around. "I *would* have told the truth. I was ready to, I was going to—but they produced that diary—and people were *believing* it."

"But why did *you* have to lie? Why *you*?"

"I honestly thought I was doing the right thing. That diary was such an obvious forgery—he *had* to be guilty. Why would an innocent man forge proof?"

"How do you know he forged it?"

"I don't know how I knew anything. I was drunk, I was drugged, I was convinced I had to take some kind of action." She spoke in a bitter, bottomed-out voice. "I give great performances drunk. My movies didn't get lousy till I sobered up."

"I don't want to believe this." He couldn't think over the

clatter of dominos falling in his head. He stared at her. He felt remote from her and could not overcome the feeling. *Either this is the most naive person I've ever met,* he thought, *or the most cunning.*

"Vince," she said quietly, "I made a choice, it was the wrong choice. I've been living with the consequences, and it hasn't been the most entertaining company."

He felt strong in the wrong way and weak in the wrong way. "Unfortunately someone else had to live with the consequences too."

Her gaze fastened on him, grim and pleading. "I didn't realize it was a cop's job to judge people. I thought that was why we have juries."

He stood. He wasn't sure what he was doing or why. "This cop judges people. That's how he stays alive."

"You mean you're disappointed that I don't fit into your glamorous little picture of me."

"It wasn't even your life at stake." His voice felt tight in his throat.

"But I had to make Nita's life mean *something.*"

"Even God couldn't have done that. Her life was over. The returns were in."

"You're sober and you think like a sober person, and I'm an alcoholic and I was thinking like one."

"Three cheers for AA, three cheers for the disease model of alcoholism. But I don't buy the disease model of irresponsibility. It's a cop-out." He moved toward the window. Once he got there he just stared out over the roofs. "You didn't even lie to me straight out, like an honest liar. You let me lie to myself."

"I did what I thought I had to."

"Everything you said, everything you didn't say, everything you let me believe—it was all because you were scared of me. Am I right?"

"Yes." She said it in a voice that was barely audible.

"You could have told me straight out about Dizey. It was a natural New York death. Drunks fall off terraces all the time in this city."

"I was afraid."

Sunset lit the water towers and church spires like a pinball machine. This was one of the last areas in Manhattan where the steeples were still higher than the apartment buildings.

"You couldn't even take the chance of trusting me?"

"I wasn't sure."

Cardozo shook his head. "You can go to bed with someone and not be sure if you *trust* them? What were you doing, faking? Giving another great performance?"

"I'm trying to be honest. Help me."

He just stood there, hurting, waiting for something inside his head to happen and point him to the next moment. He heard her say his name.

"Vince. For the part that was fake—I'm sorry. But it wasn't all fake."

He turned around and she was standing there.

"I'm sorry too," he said. "The idea that you could want me was just so . . . it made me feel so terrific. Like a kid. Like the first time I went to the movies. All your men felt that way, didn't they? Proves I'm a star-struck nitwit like the whole rest of the world."

She looked at him. He had the feeling she was searching for something in his eyes, and it wasn't there anymore.

"I won't stay," she said.

He watched her go. A moment later he heard the front door shut.

■ ■ ■

"LEIGH BAKER SAYS she made a mistake," Cardozo said. "She didn't see you push Nita."

Jim Delancey, neat and trim in his baggy linen trousers and red Reeboks, didn't answer.

"That gives you grounds for a retrial," Cardozo said. "Without her testimony the state has no case."

They were standing just outside the kitchen door of Archibald's. East Seventy-fourth Street was dark.

"I'm not going to discuss it," Jim Delancey said.

"If you didn't kill Nita Kohler, what the hell can't you discuss?"

Jim Delancey drew in a breath and his I-love-Archibald's T-shirt swelled beneath his I-love-Archibald's apron. "There's a trial record. Read it. I've said everything I have to say."

"Jim, look at me. I'm not wearing a wire." Cardozo opened his jacket, pulled up his shirt, showed that the only thing attached to his skin was skin. "There's no court stenographer here. You're not going on the record."

Delancey stood there tight-lipped, leaning against the hood of a burgundy-colored Rolls.

"Weren't you high the night Nita died?" Cardozo said.

"I'm not going to discuss it."

"Wasn't Nita high?"

"I'm not going to discuss it."

"Why didn't you plead drug intoxication as a defense?"

Down the block, lobbies spilled light under numbered awnings. A breeze rocked the saplings that had been newly planted along the pavement. Reflections of streetlights glinted off the hoods of slow-passing taxis and limos.

"Where did Nita's diary come from?" Cardozo said.

Delancey's fingertips chattered on his knee.

"Who forged it?"

Delancey's heavy shoulders rose and fell in a sigh.

"Who paid for your defense?"

Delancey exhaled, setting his fingers into a steeple. A twilight flow of resignation rippled out from him, and Cardozo was baffled by it.

"Why didn't you tell us where you were when Oona Aldrich was killed?"

A muscle jumped just above Delancey's jaw. "I did tell you."

"Why didn't you tell us the truth? You had a witness on your side. Why didn't you use him?"

The screen door slammed open, and a Korean in a New York Mets cap leaned out to dump a thirty-gallon trash bag of kitchen scraps into a garbage can.

"Are you charging me?" Jim Delancey said.

Cardozo waited for the Korean to go back inside. "There doesn't seem to be much left to charge you with."

"Then I don't have to answer."

▪ ▪ ▪

RICK SAUNTERED WEST on Forty-eighth.

At first he didn't pay any particular attention to the '87 green Celica parked outside Ming Lee's all-night Chinese restaurant. But as he walked past, a taxi happened to be turning and its headlights swept the Celica. Rick glanced sideways and he saw a man sitting in the front seat. A heavy-set man gnawing on a hero sandwich.

I wouldn't mind eating a hero right now, Rick thought. *Genoa salami and provolone and red peppers—*

The thought stopped right there, bumped by a second thought: You couldn't buy a hero at Ming Lee's. You couldn't buy a hero within five blocks of Ming Lee's. *So how come that guy's*

*eating a sandwich that he had to have brought from at least five
blocks away?*

Rick slowed at the window of a darkened *bodega.* He pretended to be studying the *cerveza* posters, but he placed himself
so he could see the reflection of the Celica. A U-Haul van made a
turn and the headlights caught the windshield of the Celica.

The guy in the car held his head angled sideways. Except for
the chewing the head didn't move. *Who the hell,* Rick asked
himself, *eats with his head turned sideways?*

It came to Rick that the hungry man in the Celica was just
possibly a stakeout, and just possibly he was watching the doorway
of 457 West Forty-ninth Street.

Rick was careful to keep walking naturally, like your typical
no-harm-intended nighttime stroller. He strolled right past his
doorway, didn't even slow, didn't even glance at it. *See, man? No
way I live in that building.* He turned north on Tenth Avenue,
and when he was sure the cop in the Celica couldn't see him, he
broke into a run.

■ ■ ■

THE GIRL STOOD bathed in the jittering light of the pizza-parlor
window.

Rick drifted to the next storefront, an all-night head shop. He
stopped, looked across at the girl, gauging her openness. He
judged her to be fourteen, trying hard to look nineteen. She had
pale, small features and she'd rewritten them in heavy makeup
and framed them in ringlets of reddish-blond hair.

She was wearing jeans and a blue-and-gold toreador jacket
over bare tits, with the sequined collar turned up. She had obviously been dressed by her pimp.

Rick felt a complex flutter in his stomach. She was attractive
to him in a way he couldn't quite explain to himself. He smiled his
broadest smile, inviting hers.

Her glance floated slowly across the sidewalk. The pavement
was full of people, every one of them alone. She let her gaze slide
over Rick.

He saw that her blue eyes were scared, blinking behind spi-
ders' legs of fake lashes.

*Baby, you think you're scared now, just wait till you see what
Rick's got for you.*

He took three steps toward her and simply stood there, pre-
senting himself, solid, unmoving, a fact of the universe. "Hi," he
said. "I'm a statistic."

"I can see that." She had a midwestern accent.

"I wanna fuck you," he blurted.

"No problem. I live over there." She nodded at a blinking hotel sign across the street.

He followed her through stalled, honking traffic.

The hotel lobby smelled of ammonia and hot spices. A hand-lettered sign said ABSOLUTELY NO VISITORS. A fat Chinese man at the desk gave her half a glance and handed her a key.

The girl stepped into the elevator and Rick stepped in behind her. She pushed the button for *five*. Rattling rhythmically, the elevator clunked upward.

Rick brought his face close to the girl's. He could smell the sweet residue of cinnamon-flavored chewing gum on her breath. He looked into her eyes and she looked straight back into his, not smiling. Slowly he reached over and wrapped a hand around her shoulder. He slid his other hand up between the legs of her jeans.

The elevator stopped. She pulled away. He followed her down a corridor with most of its forty-watt light bulbs blown out.

She put a key into a lock but did not turn it. "What's in the pouch?"

"Crack, ice, and money."

She swung the door open. It was a small, bare room, and Rick could see her housekeeping was even worse than his. A bath towel had been stuck across the window with screwdrivers. An ancient Tina Turner poster had been taped to the wall.

Rick laughed. "What the well-dressed wall is wearing, hey?"

The girl sat on the unmade bed, one leg tucked under her. She looked at him. "I wish I was as weird as you. That crack must be pretty good."

Rick gave the door a push shut. The latch clicked and they were alone. "Know what I want to do?"

"No, surprise me."

"I want to get high with you and spend the night." He took out his crack pipe, dropped a rock into the bowl, lit it with his Bic. He took a deep drag and passed the pipe to the girl.

She took a hit and handed the pipe back. "My man doesn't like me to have sleepovers."

"So, how many customers do you usually have between now and noon?"

"On a slow night, enough to make three hundred."

"Bullshit." He took out his wallet and handed her seven fifties.

She fanned the money out, waving it slowly back and forth in front of her. "I didn't say yes."

His lips shaped a coaxing smile. He tapped a finger against his jogging pouch. "Come on. It's two in the morning and I'm beat and I'm horny and there's nowhere else I can go."

"Boo-hoo. What are you, a poor little orphan?"

"Yeah, that's what I am tonight. An orphan."

She reached for a jam jar sitting on the windowsill. She unscrewed the top and dropped the money in. "I'm strictly safe sex. My man's the only man I go down on without protection." She took a rubber from the jar. "Sit down."

He sat down on the bed beside her. She unzipped his fly and began slipping the rubber around his cock.

He touched the side of her throat. "You're so soft."

She smiled. "You're not."

· SIXTY-FIVE ·

Thursday, June 20

"AS WE ALL KNOW, my brother was not always pious." Bridget Braidy was leaning just a little too close into the mike. "But he was devout in the way that counted: in his actions."

She was standing at the lectern of Saint Anne's Roman Catholic church, dressed in the same navy-blue suit Cardozo had seen her in at the last Police Academy graduation. She wore three strands of pearls, and her white Peter Pan collar had half snagged in the uppermost.

"And one story," she said, "comes particularly to mind, illustrating that side of him. Now, some of you may know that Dick's death is not the first time our family has been devastated by murder. Four years ago my beloved niece Nita Kohler was murdered."

A woman in the pew ahead of Cardozo whispered loudly to the woman next to her, "Nita Kohler was her *niece?*"

"Her niece by marriage, you might say," Cardozo heard the second woman say, and he realized she was Kristi Blackwell wearing a red Orphan Annie wig, and then he realized that the wig was her real hair.

The first woman took out her compact, studied her reflection, and touched up her powder. "Are you going to the Jeu de Paume tomorrow?"

"How could I miss Zack's wedding party?"

"I can't believe he's marrying that fat nobody."

"She must know how to do something Tori Sandberg doesn't."

"Or something Tori Sandberg *won't* do."

"Let me tell you what my big brother did," Bridget Braidy

was saying. "Benedict O'Houlihan Braidy was a grand guy—anyone who reads the columns knows that. But he wasn't just grand. He was warm too, and human, and he could scale himself down. When my niece was murdered, he phoned me and he said, 'Sis, I know how you're feeling, because I'm feeling exactly the same. So let's do something about it. I'll be by in ten minutes to pick you up . . .'"

Cardozo was waiting for a murderer—a young male Hispanic murderer of athletic build with short-cropped dark hair. He and the murderer had no formal date to meet, but an astonishing number of killers showed up for their victims' funerals—so why not the man who had murdered Benedict Braidy?

His nose took in that smell peculiar to houses of worship—the mixture of incense and altar flowers, but with a moneyed accent here, the spice of women wearing expensive perfumes. His eye circled the nave with its high-arched shadows, and the stained-glass windows with their rich hue of Tiffany lamps, and the spectacular carved ivory altarpiece.

He saw no agony of Christ pictured here, only a serene crucifixion and can-do–looking saints with golden spears. The memorial plaques on the wall amounted to a century's worth of New York movers and shakers. The communion rail shone like a piece of yacht's brass, and he could imagine the city's country-club set tinkling delicately against each other as they knelt for noonday wafers.

Dick Braidy's funeral had drawn a respectable turnout, filling the front twenty pews. Most of the women wore diamonds. Many were bare-shouldered. Most had their hair done in airy, expensive-looking arrangements. Their men wore tailored dark suits. There was a lot of looking around in the pews to see who else was there; kisses were blown, hand signals exchanged, fingers waved.

A sound behind him drew Cardozo's eyes toward the nave.

A young man with dark, cropped hair, heavy-set and tanned, had darted into the church. The right age. The right build. Eyes sunken in, lazy-lidded, dark-looking. Possibly Hispanic.

He was dressed carefully, but the clothes were not expensive: a gray tweed jacket that was the wrong weight for today's heat wave, and so large on him that it had to be second-hand; gray cotton trousers that looked pressed for the occasion; no boom box.

He hung back a moment at the rear of the nave. Hesitation flickered over him. He came noiselessly down the side aisle. He passed within a foot of where Cardozo was sitting. He was wearing white Adidas jogging shoes. His affable, slightly sad smile sloped down at the corners.

Cardozo smelled something streetwise, almost a put-on.

The young man genuflected, crossed himself with simple Catholic gravity, and stepped into an empty pew.

Cardozo leaned down toward the little Japanese mike fastened like a tie clip to his necktie. "Can you hear me, Ellie?"

Her voice came out of the tiny transistor plugged into his left ear. "I'm hearing you."

She was seated across the church, eight aisles back, and he could see her pale key-lime suit motionless through all the shifting, glittering socialites and celebrities.

"You see the guy alone in the front pew, my section?"

"I see him."

". . . I panicked," Commissioner Braidy's amplified voice was saying, *p*'s exploding in the vaulted space like cherry bombs. "Because when my brother said, *Let's do something*, he usually meant dancing the hustle with Jackie O or hunting down New York's best pizza with Greta Garbo. I said, 'Dick, I'm not dressed, I'm not in any condition to do anything.' And my big brother said, 'That's when you've got to be good to yourself. You'll hear me honk three times—just come as you are.' "

"He's got to come down my aisle," Cardozo said, "or the center, or yours."

"Okay," Ellie's voice answered in his ear. "I'll cover this aisle."

"Greg," Cardozo said, "do you see him?"

"I see him," Monteleone's voice said.

"Cover the center aisle, okay?"

"The horn honked three times," Commissioner Braidy was saying. "I threw on a windbreaker and went downstairs—and there was the biggest, whitest, stretchiest limo you ever did see, with a uniformed chauffeur, and inside was my big brother, in blue jeans and a parka, with his arms spread and tears running down his big Irish mug—and I just fell into those arms, and we had the cry of our lives. And then Dick said to the driver, 'Driver, take us to the nearest David's Cookies.' "

Bridget Braidy looked out over the congregation.

"Now *that* is style. *That* is class. And I'll tell you one thing: When my big brother and I left that David's cookie shop three hours later, there was not a single macadamia chocolate chip remaining on the premises."

Commissioner Braidy paused. She mugged cookie munching. There was laughter. A few hands applauded. The sound of the traffic on Park Avenue seemed remote, not just in space but in time, like remembered thunder.

"And I'll tell you something else," Bridget Braidy said. "This city has seen too much crime. This city has seen too many of its decent citizens terrorized and murdered. As God and this gathering are my witnesses, I make this vow to my murdered brother: Your death and Nita Kohler's, and the deaths of the thousands of New Yorkers sacrificed this and every year to the tide of random violence—your deaths shall not have been in vain. If I have to turn in my commissioner's badge and run for mayor myself, I will fight, to the last fiber and breath of my body, the evil that has stolen you from us. So help me God."

She blew a kiss over the heads of the congregation.

"Good-bye, Dick. Earth was better for your being here, and heaven's better now that you're there where you belong. We love you. We miss you. God bless you—put in a good word for us with You Know Who. And how about saving us just a drop of—what do you call that stuff they drink up there?—Roederer Cristal!"

Twenty minutes later the priest blessed the departed and blessed the congregation. The pallbearers wheeled the coffin back down the aisle. Two doors slammed like cannon shots and the organ broke into a roof-ripping postlude —Cole Porter's "From This Moment On."

The congregation rose and spilled into the aisles. Expensive pumps clicked on marble floors like tap-dancing castanets. Voices broke into an almost deafening chatter. The center aisle jammed with little kiss-kiss groups.

The young man stayed seated in the front pew. He looked around at the congregation. It seemed to Cardozo that there was a curl of disdain to his smile, as though he had a secret inside him that he was not allowing to slip out.

When the young man rose, Cardozo rose.

"If ever you needed proof that Dick Braidy was a somebody," Cardozo heard Kristi Blackwell say, "look at the turnout."

"The Nixons are here," her companion said. "And Madonna. And *Jackie.* Is Jackie going to Jeu de Paume?"

The young man walked forward to the front pew. He crossed in front of the communion rail. He started up the middle aisle and immediately met a traffic jam of glitterati.

For the next three minutes Cardozo thought he'd lost the young man, and then Ellie's voice hissed in his left ear, "By the baptismal font."

"Where the hell's the baptismal font?" Cardozo growled into his tie clip.

"Southeast corner of church."

Cardozo peered over an ocean of bobbing coiffed heads, of couture dresses and dark suits. He saw the carved marble font, and he saw Siegel and Monteleone and the young man in the tweed jacket standing between them. They hadn't exactly put him under restraint, but his shocked and disbelieving face said he didn't feel exactly free to go either.

"Stay right there," Cardozo told the mike. "Stay visible."

He had to squeeze around a woman in slinky gray who was saying to a man in a blue blazer, "I don't know if Jeu de Paume's going to be worth it. Are you bothering to go?"

Three feet away Leigh Baker stood talking with her friend Tori Sandberg. They were the only women in the church who were wearing black. Cardozo reached out and touched Leigh's shoulder. She looked over at him. He saw surprise in her face, and something else, quickly controlled and covered over.

"Ladies, I'm sorry to interrupt," he said. "But can you see the baptismal font? The young man in a gray tweed jacket?"

Leigh Baker turned toward the font. "The oversized gray herringbone tweed jacket with elbow patches?"

"Is that the male Hispanic you saw in the boutique at Marsh and Bonner's?"

For an instant she seemed utterly baffled, and then she shook her head. "That's Juanito. He was Dick's gardener. He took care of the terrace plants. He wasn't the man in Marsh and Bonner's."

"Absolutely not," Tori Sandberg said.

"Sorry to bother you." Cardozo spoke to the mike. "Wrong man. Let him go."

■   ■   ■

"ONE NEW LETTER SOURCE in note five," Lou Stein was saying. *"U.S. News and World Report."*

"Which issue?"

Lou's sigh traveled across the line. "April second, what else."

"I wish I could figure out why he loves magazines that went on sale April second."

"You got it wrong, Vince. They're *dated* April second. They went on sale March twenty-sixth. April second was the day the April ninth issues came out."

Cardozo frowned. He flipped his calendar to the week of March twenty-sixth. The only event of interest listed by the publisher was the new moon, a black circle in the blank space for Monday. He tapped his ballpoint against the calendar's spiral binding. Something nagged at him. It was like hearing a name that almost rang a bell but not quite. "Why does March twenty-sixth seem more interesting to me than April second?"

"It's farther from April Fool's. And it's something new to think about."

"Thanks, Lou."

The instant Cardozo laid the receiver down the phone rang. What was it about his telephone? he wondered. For years it had been content to ring with a low-key obnoxious buzz. But today there was a distinctly new ugliness in the ring—an ear-flaying overtone that he could swear he'd never detected before.

He caught the phone before it could inflict a second jangle on his nerves. "Cardozo."

"Lieutenant, it's Rad Rheinhardt at the *Trib*. We've got another letter from Society Sam. I'm sending it up by messenger."

▪ ▪ ▪

DRIZZLE WAS DROPPING from a sullen, leaden sky. The wet pavement shimmered, and the drizzle turned everything to distance. Cardozo and Malloy were sitting in the Honda, illegally parked south of the West Seventy-second Street entrance to Central Park. They were watching the bench on the pedestrian path just inside the park wall.

A solitary figure sat on the bench: a woman, wearing a big-shouldered green jacket, her long blond hair done up in a fat blond bun. She was holding a pink Mylar umbrella. One silver high-heeled boot tapped restlessly against the paved path.

Rick Martinez was seven minutes late for his two o'clock date.

Malloy stared through the spattered windshield up the avenue, at art-deco condos layered like birthday cakes. He raised a paper cup of deli coffee to his mouth. He had dark crescents under his eyes like a linebacker's glare smudges. "Where the hell is this fucker? Can't he even keep an appointment?"

It was ninety seconds later that Cardozo saw a young man in a red T-shirt step out of the Seventy-second Street subway exit, across the avenue. He stood a moment in the drizzle, waiting for the traffic light. He crossed the avenue and turned south. He passed within ten feet of the Honda, close enough for Cardozo to recognize the face in the Bodies-PLUS photo.

"It's Martinez." Malloy crunched the empty coffee cup and stuffed it halfway into the ashtray.

"With his head shaved." Cardozo lifted the radio mike. "Attention all units, suspect Martinez wearing red T-shirt, approaching pedestrian path."

Martinez reached the path and turned. He walked past the bench, slowed, turned around. He stared at the woman sitting there in the green jacket.

"Think the woman's his contact?" Malloy said.

Cardozo frowned. "The man on the phone said meet *me,* not *her.*"

Martinez doubled back to the bench. He sat half a bench-length from the woman. She glanced at him and reangled her Mylar umbrella to ward off eye contact.

Cardozo spoke into the mike. "Martinez is seated on bench."

"Either these two are playing it supercool," Malloy said, "or they really don't know each other."

"I get the feeling she doesn't intend to know him," Cardozo said.

After a moment Martinez glanced again at the woman.

"He's wondering if she's the contact," Malloy said.

Martinez looked at his watch. He leaned toward the woman and said something. The umbrella shifted and the woman gave him a you've-got-to-be-kidding sneer.

"And now he knows she's not," Cardozo said.

"His contact's almost fifteen minutes late."

"Give him another five minutes."

Three minutes passed and Martinez rose from the bench. He stood a moment in indecision, and then he began ambling down the path into the park.

Cardozo grabbed the radio mike. "Martinez is heading east on pedestrian path toward Sheep Meadow."

Malloy slid out of the car and started after Martinez. At the sound of the car door slamming, Martinez glanced back. He saw Malloy and broke into a run.

Cardozo shoved the mike back into its dashboard bracket. His feet slammed the floor, and he was up and out of the car in one thrust.

Both Martinez and Malloy had vanished. He sprinted up the path. It branched two ways.

He checked right, checked left. His eye caught Martinez's red T-shirt flashing through the foliage to the right.

The next sixty seconds seemed to happen on the other side of a plate-glass wall.

A rising hill brought Cardozo to an open meadow.

Martinez was forty yards ahead, running.

Parallel to the path, in the bushes, something was moving and it was Malloy, leaping out and punching the air. Compacted steel flashed in his hand.

It was as though Malloy had lost control of his body, as though it had become something that was not an overweight middle-aged cop's body.

In a crackle of raw acceleration Martinez became a smudge of speed cutting through misty drizzle.

It amazed Cardozo that Malloy had the swiftness. He was actually closing the gap between himself and the red T-shirt.

And then Cardozo heard the gunshot and the warning: "Stop! Police!"

No, that wasn't right. My mind reversed it, Cardozo thought. *First the warning. Then the gunshot.*

Cardozo broke into a run.

Time became a liquid rush, and Malloy and Martinez became two particles caught in the whirlpool. Martinez was darting in and around the bushes, but there was a drag on his movements. Swerving around a tree, he went into a skid and then he was down, kneecaps kissing mud.

Malloy approached, taut and ready, service revolver drawn. "Police!" Cardozo could hear him shouting. "Police! Surrender your weapon! Give yourself up!"

Something flashed between them, and Cardozo heard the second shot.

Martinez was on the ground, writhing, kicking, and then he was still.

When Cardozo reached them, Malloy was still shouting at Martinez to drop his gun. Cardozo raised a hand, palm out, signaling Malloy to holster the gun, back off.

Martinez was lying in a fetal curl on his side. His arms were locked tight around the part of his chest that was coming to pieces. He was gasping, pulling in air through a gaping mouth. He had eyes the color of wind, and he had that look that meant nerves and brain cells were going off-line fast.

Cardozo crouched down on one knee. He spoke gently: "Martinez—can you hear me?"

Martinez's sweat had activated his cologne. A dense sweetness like church incense rose from his body.

"Me entiendes?" Cardozo said.

For one brief instant Martinez's eyes looked directly into Cardozo's. His throat was going like a scared pigeon's, pushing out air.

Cardozo leaned his ear down. He could make out whispered, disconnected syllables.

"Maria . . . mother . . . *Dios . . . ruega . . . sotros . . .*"

Either Martinez was trying to squeeze in a quick Hail Mary before he slipped across, or he was sinking into bilingual delirium.

Across the meadow an ambulance careened down the jogging path. Even at this distance Cardozo could hear the siren blipping get-out-of-my-way screeches.

Cop cars were cutting across the turf.

Martinez was very quiet now. His eyes had a dreamily surrendering gaze. Cardozo sensed he was in bad shape, getting rapidly worse.

Two cop cars arrived and then the ambulance. Three paramedics lifted Martinez onto a stretcher.

"Whose gun?"

A cop was standing there holding a ballpoint pen through the trigger guard of a small black revolver.

"Where'd you find that?" Cardozo said.

The cop kicked dead leaves. "Right here."

Malloy's face was shocked, pale. He nodded toward the ambulance. "It was his."

■　■　■

RICK MARTINEZ DIED at three-ten that afternoon in the Emergency Room of Saint Agnes Hospital.

A half hour later, when Cardozo returned to the precinct, there was hardly any activity in the detective squad room. Malloy sat at one of the old-junk typewriters, hunting for the keys to fill in a departmental report. He looked exhausted.

Captain Lawrence Zawac from Internal Affairs was standing beside him, reading over his shoulder.

"What's happening?" Cardozo said.

"Sergeant Malloy is telling me about the shooting," Zawac said.

Cardozo noticed that the typing on the form already ran down half the page.

"What are you telling him, Carl?"

"Just how it happened." Malloy had the face of a man saying hello to mortality a few decades earlier than he'd ever expected.

Cardozo glanced at Zawac. "Is this official?"

Zawac had a smug, secret look. "Call it friendly."

"Maybe you should talk to a lawyer," Cardozo told Malloy.

"We've discussed that option," Zawac said, "and Sergeant Malloy has decided to go another route."

The scar that cut Zawac's upper lip in two seemed far redder than Cardozo remembered. It showed clearly through his dark mustache. His eyes were gloating.

"Another route?" Cardozo said. "Well, whatever you're doing, make it fast. We have to get down to Martinez's apartment."

"Vince," Malloy said, "I have to—" He stopped and made a new start. "I'm going to turn over my gun till the hearing."

"Okay, you'll turn over your gun." Cardozo was sure Zawac had fed Malloy some kind of IAD hype, and Malloy had bought into it. But he shrugged as though it didn't matter. His object now was simply to get Malloy alone. "Where does the rule book say you need a gun to search an apartment anyway?"

Zawac shifted weight. The change of position had the effect of placing him between Cardozo and Malloy.

"Sergeant Malloy will be staying at the precinct," Zawac said.

Cardozo sensed something dangerous now: Malloy was smiling, but the smile was crazed and wrong. Cardozo read panic in the eyes, the kind where the panicky person was literally blocking out the signals reality was sending him.

"Sorry," Cardozo said, "Malloy doesn't sit at the precinct on my task force's time."

"Sergeant Malloy is off the task force."

"I take orders from the top—not from left field." Cardozo held out a hand. "Show me the paper on this."

"If you want to see paper, Lieutenant, I guarantee I can arrange for you to see paper."

"Show me the order, or Malloy's walking out this door with me."

Silence, eye contact.

"Carl, come on," Cardozo said.

Malloy just sat there. There was something missing in him. He looked hurt, beaten, not quite understanding what life was suddenly about or where the next blow was going to fall from.

Malloy said, "Vince—let it go."

"Look, Carl, even if IAD has persuaded you to give up your rights, they haven't persuaded me to give up mine. I'm ordering you back to work."

"I'm resigning from the task force."

"What the hell are you doing, Carl? If you play scapegoat now, the hyenas are going to go for you. They're already smelling dead meat."

"I've thought it over and this is the way I have to handle it, Vince. I'm sorry."

■ ■ ■

"SOMETHING THE MATTER with the ice cream?" Malloy asked.

Laurie Bonasera shook her head.

They were at a table by the back wall of the ice-cream shop. She was eating peach, and just for a change, he was trying boysenberry. He could feel that something was off between them.

"What's the matter, then?" he said.

She shrugged. "I guess I just don't feel comfortable being watched."

"Who's watching you?"

She was wearing a yellow-and-white–striped cotton dress, and her hair was curling around her face. "It's you they've got their eye on."

"Who's they?"

"Everyone."

"Well, everyone's not here. You're oversensitive."

"I have to trust my instincts. They're all I've got."

"Did your instincts tell you not to talk to me? Because you haven't spoken to me in two days. You haven't even looked at me."

"I'm looking at you now."

"Like you wish I wasn't here."

"Like I wish *I* wasn't here."

He lost a heartbeat. "What are you telling me? You don't want to be with me?"

She picked at her peach ice cream as though she'd lost an earring in it. "How do you expect me to feel? Carl, you *killed* a man."

A moment slipped mutely by. He felt slack and empty. "I killed a killer in the line of duty, and unless you're working for Internal Affairs, don't you think that subject can maybe wait?"

"It happens to be on my mind."

"He killed six people, and now he's not going to kill another six. It's done and I did it and I'm not sorry. What's the matter, you *want* me to be sorry?"

She was watching him with firm-jawed thoughtfulness. "No, that's not what I want."

"Because I'm a decent guy. I *am.*"

"I know you're a decent guy."

Carl Malloy had always had the belief that someday he would meet someone who would make his life okay. When he met his wife, he'd thought it was going to happen, but his life had never become okay with Delia. Since then he'd believed that one day he'd meet someone else who'd make his life okay.

He stared at Laurie Bonasera and he had a flash, a running sensation his last chance was slipping away from him. "Then when can I see you again?"

It was as though breathing was an effort for her. "We have to be careful till you're cleared."

He felt his dreams getting snipped smaller and smaller. "Cleared—what am I, some kind of criminal?"

"You're married," she said. "I'm married."

"We're working for the New York Police Department, not the archdiocese."

"They're still going to look into every detail of your life. We don't need to make the situation worse."

He could feel a darkness settling over him like a layer of ash from a nuclear accident. "Fuck situations. I'm not a marriage license, I'm not a gold shield—I'm a person and I need to know that I exist, that I still matter to someone."

She took a long, careful look at him. "You are a master manipulator."

"Where did that come from? What do I say to that, thank you?"

"The less said the better. This conversation is running downhill." She got up from the table. "Let's get out of here."

He reached out and took her wrist. She looked down at his hand and he let go.

"I'm sorry." He felt horribly apart from her. "I love you." He waited for something magical. He waited for her to say she loved him too.

After a moment she sighed. "I know."

He followed her to the front of the shop. He didn't know how long he could go on feeling this sense of waste about what was happening in his life.

The old Korean woman who owned the business was standing guard behind the cash register. She recognized Malloy, and when he put down a five-dollar bill, she smiled, shook her head emphatically, and pushed the money back to him.

Malloy thanked her and tucked the five back into his wallet.

Laurie's jaw dropped. "Are you crazy?"

"It's just ice cream," Malloy said.

"Just ice cream is what practically got you busted from the force. You can't afford to cut corners anymore."

Everything that had built up inside him chose that moment to explode. "Get off my ass!" he cried.

He could see she had to clamp down to keep from shouting right back at him.

"I don't believe this," she said. "I don't believe you. I don't believe me."

She slapped down five singles for the ice cream.

She turned to face him, and he could feel her hating him.

"My fucking treat, okay, Malloy? Okay, just this once? The bimbo pays?"

She pushed through the door and turned north on Lexington, and she was gone.

· SIXTY-SIX ·

Friday, June 21

THERE WAS A KNOCK and Cardozo looked up.

"Zip code eleven-four-two-one is Ninety-seventh Street, Jamaica, Queens." One tanned arm outstretched, Ellie Siegel was leaning against the doorframe.

He lobbed a smile up at her. "Tell me more."

She came in and sat down in the empty chair. "The worst neighborhood Sam ever picked to mail a letter from. If you're not packing heat, you're underdressed."

"Then you were dressed right."

"Barely. All I had was a dinky service revolver. The natives are carrying Uzis."

She laid the Xerox of Society Sam's sixth note down on the desk. Jumbled typefaces formed seven more or less horizontal, more or less parallel lines across the page.

> CAN THE CUT JUDGE THE CUTTER
> PAPER THE SCISSORS
> I WILL NOT JOIN YOUR MAKE BELIEVE
> WEEP NO TEARS FOR CUT UP CUT OUTS
> WHEN WILL DOLLS LEARN
> PAPER YOU WERE TO PAPER YOU RETURN
> KISSES, SOCIETY SAM

"When did he mail it?" Cardozo said.

"With a P.M. 18 June postmark the latest it could have been mailed was noon Tuesday—but the postmaster says pickups have been running late. Gangs have been shooting the trucks with rock salt."

"Rock salt?"

Ellie nodded. "He says it could have been mailed before the weekend."

Cardozo handed her a Xerox of the note Society Sam had sent after Dizey's death. "Does it seem to you Dizey's note got reversed with Dick Braidy's?"

"Because Dizey's says *Dick be quick* and Braidy's talks about paper and paper dolls?" Ellie's expression said she wasn't buying it. "Braidy was a journalist too, *paper* could refer to him."

"But Dizey's name wasn't Dick." Cardozo held a pencil chopstick-fashion between two fingers and rat-a-tatted on the edge of the desk. "Sam's pattern was to leave a society column published the morning before a killing. There was no clipping when Dizey went off the roof."

"No candle either," Ellie reminded him.

He nodded. "But this was the column Dizey published that morning." He handed her a newspaper clipping. The photograph showed an ex-cleaning woman and now-socialite by the name of Olga Ford. Her hair had been clipped like a hedge imitating an animal. A silver net kept it from running away. Her Slovenian eyes seemed to gloat, *I am the ladder to greatness.*

Ellie read aloud, her voice carefully suspending all judgment. *"Tonight Mrs. Gavin Hay (Olga to you, kid) Ford, the newest power widow around town, is hostessing an event at her East 78th Street duplex. Friends of Oona Aldrich, whose memorial is being held tonight, are understandably in no mood to go. Mrs. F. has warned those who accepted the ill-timed invite to be prepared for a mystery guest. The event is sure to shake up society's notion of acceptable chic, because megabucks like Olga's spell megaswank, and Olga is not about to let anyone forget it."*

"According to his engagement calendar," Cardozo said, "Dick Braidy went to that dinner. According to last Friday's *New York Post*, the First Lady was also there."

"Got it," Ellie said. "The mystery guest. How much do you suppose Olga had to contribute to the President's reelection committee?"

"Only her accountant and the IRS have the answer to that." Cardozo took a half rotation in his swivel chair. "According to Mrs. Ford's stepdaughter, Rick Martinez, a.k.a. Society Sam, delivered a bunch of flowers to that party with this note." Cardozo laid the little note on the desk.

Ellie scowled. *"Love, Bob De Niro?"*

"The girl says it was meant to be a goof on the stepmother.

But I wonder if it wasn't Rick's way of getting into the party. Because here's what I'm thinking: Rick, alias Sam, was aiming for Braidy the night Dizey died. But Braidy was at a dinner party where the surprise guest turned out to be the First Lady. Surprise guest meant surprise security. Sam's bouquet got through the security, but Sam couldn't. He missed his hit."

"If Sam was at Olga's, who killed Dizey?"

"No one. Dizey was on the still-to-be-hit list, but she died ahead of time—and accidentally."

"Then why did Sam mail the wrong note?"

Cardozo sat listening to the faint chug-a-lug of the air conditioner. "You know something, Ellie? I haven't got the answer to that one."

■ ■ ■

"THE BLUE CROSS and the Medicaid card," Lou Stein said, "are genuine. The driver's license is a fake, but it's an excellent fake."

Documents and personal possessions had been spread out across Lou's worktable. Except for the Darby knife, Cardozo had recovered them all from Rick Martinez's apartment yesterday after the shooting. An Emergency Room nurse had found the Darby strapped to the left shin of Rick Martinez's corpse.

"The passports are genuine," Lou Stein said.

Cardozo opened the United States passport. "Has the printing on the bearer page been tampered with?"

"No. The bearer page is genuine. So once upon a time there was a real Richard Martinez, American citizen, born March 8, 1951, in New York. And this was his passport, issued April 18, 1986, in New York."

"But the Richard Martinez in that photo," Cardozo said, "looks ten, fifteen years younger than anyone born in 1951."

"The very point I was about to make." Lou Stein took the passport and turned to the bearer's photo. "This page has been subjected to at least four laminations. This isn't the original photo."

"Is the bearer signature the original?"

"The signature hasn't been tampered with—but the signature *page* is younger than the passport." Lou Stein flipped through seventeen pages of U.S. and Salvadorean immigration stamps. "My guess is, every time a new Richard Martinez was created, they took out the old signature page and stitched in a fresh one."

Cardozo picked up the Colombian passport and opened it to

the bearer page. The passport had been issued three years ago in Medellín to Manuel Gomez Ybarra. The photo of Gomez Ybarra in the Colombian passport was the same as the photo of Richard Martinez in the American—*exactly* the same: same young face, same young smile showing the same crooked incisor, same shirt with the same jauntily unbuttoned collar.

According to the information in the passport, Manuel had been born in Medellín in 1970. Cardozo had telephoned the Medellín police yesterday, and they had telexed the rap sheet that Cardozo now held in his left hand. Manuel had a record of juvenile theft and had spent his fourteenth year in reformatory; since then a charge of pimping had been brought and dropped. At present he was wanted for questioning in connection with three drug-related shootings and one suspected *muerte de prueba.*

Lou Stein squinted at the rap sheet. "What the hell's a *muerte de prueba*?"

"It's a service the free-lance killers offer in Medellín. Before a client signs them on for a hit they kill any stranger the client points out."

For an instant Lou Stein seemed to have to work to keep his mouth from falling open. "Why?"

"To prove they have the right stuff. Medellín drug barons want to be sure they hire the very best." Cardozo flipped the passport back onto the table. His eye went now to the typewriter, a lightweight, forty-year-old Olivetti Lettera 22. The black-plastic spacer key was chipped, and the tan paint was peeling off the steel body. "And you're sure that's the Olivetti he used to type the envelopes?"

"Sure, we're sure. Same way we're sure that the Darby knife strapped to his leg was the murder weapon. The signatures match."

A sheet of departmental letterhead had been rolled into the typewriter carriage, and Lou had typed Rad Rheinhardt's address at the *New York Trib.* He pulled the sheet out and handed Cardozo a magnifying glass. "See the way the letter *h* loses a little of the lower left there? And the *k* in *New York*?"

Cardozo handed back the magnifying glass. "I believe you, Lou. Just tell me if you found any fingerprints, any particles?"

"None. He wore surgical gloves when he handled the machine—prepowdered. Some of the powder fell between the keys and inside the machine."

Cardozo's gaze traveled to the cardboard carton. Issues of *Time* and *Newsweek* and *People* and God only knew what other mass-circulation national weeklies had been crammed into it so tightly that the seams had begun to pull apart. "Any prints on the magazines?"

"No clear fingerprints, but we've got plenty of exact matches in the typefonts and in the scissoring. For instance, in the second letter, *idiot quest*—the whole phrase comes from this copy of *Foreign Affairs.*" Lou pulled a sober-looking gray magazine out of the carton. There was nothing on its cover but print.

Cardozo frowned. He had a sense that the magazine didn't go with the others. "Can I look at that?" He opened the copy, flipped through it. Nothing was missing until page fifty-seven, where Lou had stuck a bookmark. A hole had been cut through the heavy paper, leaving a blank in the thicket of words:

> the longstanding perception that 19th-century style imperialism is an   to which the vaster majority cannot acquiesce

"Who said *idiot quest?*" Cardozo asked.

"Henry Kissinger."

"What was he talking about?"

"Hegemony."

"Hard to imagine Rick Martinez or Manuel Gomez Ybarra bothering with articles about hegemony."

"What can I tell you? People are funny. Our Creator made us that way."

"I'll tell you what's even funnier. I was in Rick Martinez's apartment twenty-two hours before we got him, and this typewriter and these magazines weren't there. I was back in that apartment less than two hours after he died, and this typewriter and those magazines were sitting on the floor in the bedroom."

Lou's eyes were a pale clear blue like water under ice. "Maybe he took them out of the closet in between your visits. Did you search the closet the first time you went in?"

"Lou, we staked the apartment out. After I went in, Rick Martinez never came home."

"Well, you got a mystery."

Lou Stein's finger went to the side of his nose and pushed his glasses higher. Possibly his glasses needed the push. But to Cardozo it seemed out of character—a guilty movement, a stalling movement, as though Lou was unhappy with what he was about to have to say.

"Here's another mystery." Lou tapped the magnifying glass

against the glass of hairs that Cardozo had found on the bathroom sink. "These are pubic hairs. They matched the hairs we found in the victims' mouths. But they aren't Martinez's."

"Hold on." A black hole had suddenly opened in Cardozo's universe. "What the hell are you telling me?"

"The semen in every instance was his. The pubic hair in every instance was not."

"Whose was it?"

"Donor X's."

"Help me, Lou. I'm having trouble putting this together."

"It's my fault, Vince. I was sloppy. From the very first victim on, I should have checked that the pubic hair and the semen came from the same donor. Frankly it never occurred to me they wouldn't."

"*Different* donors. How would that work?"

"It would be very hard for a donor to ejaculate semen in another person's mouth without leaving some pubic hair. The fact that the perpetrator did *not* deposit pubic hair in his earlier victims indicates he didn't deposit semen there either."

"But we have his semen in all the victims and we know it's his."

"I'm using the word *deposit* in a technical sense. The semen and the pubic hairs both got into the mouth the same way—he put them there."

"How?"

"Oral syringe and tweezers."

Cardozo reached for an explanation. "Why?"

"Why is your province."

▪ SIXTY-SEVEN ▪

FROM TWO BLOCKS AWAY, Cardozo heard the honking chorus of automobile horns and the voice shouting in Spanish and English: *"Qué queremos? Guerra!* What do we want? War!"

As he turned onto Sixty-sixth he saw that the street had been blocked off by an *Eyewitness News* TV truck. Picketers waved signs lettered as neatly as cigarette advertisements:

> NYPD IS RACIST!
> NYPD MURDERERS!
> MALLOY ES VERDUGO!
> MALLOY IS AN EXECUTIONER!
> ANGLO COPS KILL HISPANICS!

Cardozo caught the drift.

In front of the precinct hundreds of protesters had formed a roiling, jitterbugging mass, overturning police barricades, going at the windshields of parked cars with baseball bats and bottles and bricks.

Up on the roof of the TV truck three cameramen were trying to catch it all with their minicams.

One of the picketers, seeing his TV opportunity, grabbed a trash can, shouldered it, made a run toward the window of the I Scream for Ice Cream Ice Cream Shop.

The trash can went sailing through the plate glass.

A single-voiced roar of approval went up, and a wave of protesters became a wave of looters.

Cardozo stood there behind the TV truck, in the space where nothing was happening, because no camera was watching.

When the cameramen climbed back down into the truck, he sensed a slacking-off of crowd spirit. He lowered his head, shielded his eyes with his forearm, and ran forward. A bottle whizzed past his ear to crash against the precinct door.

A sergeant let him inside.

The vestibule was mobbed with cops in riot gear.

"What's happening?" Cardozo said. "Why's everyone in here and not out on the street?"

"Mayor's orders." The sergeant shrugged. "He doesn't want anything ugly while the TV truck's here."

Cardozo grimaced. "And I suppose what's out there now is pretty?"

■ ■ ■

THE BLACK-AND-WHITE GLOSSIES showed Rick Martinez's apartment as it had been two hours after Martinez had been shot. The police photographer had used a flash and fast film, and the pictures had the stark, high-contrast look of photos in a true-crime paperback.

Cardozo reviewed them one by one. The poster of Rambo taped to the refrigerator. The filthy plates in the sink and the *Shabbes* candles on the drainboard. The bookcase with the little stuffed bear sitting on the tape deck. The bulletin board displaying the press record of Society Sam's achievements.

And then the joker: the Olivetti Lettera 22 typewriter on the bedroom floor next to the answering machine and the carton of magazines.

Ellie Siegel stepped into the cubicle.

"There's no table in Martinez's apartment," Cardozo said.

"So?" She handed him the stakeout log.

"Where did Rick type?"

"On his knees."

"Come on."

"Come on yourself. It's possible."

"Then where did he cut and paste the letters?"

"On the floor."

"That floor's filthy. That whole place is filthy. The letters were clean. They were put together somewhere else. The typewriter and magazines were brought to the apartment later."

"When?"

"Let's see when." Cardozo opened the log to Wednesday, June nineteenth. "Malloy staked it out till four P.M. and I was there at four, and there was no typewriter or magazines. So they had to have come in later."

He turned the page. Ellie took a step forward to read over his shoulder.

The log showed that Detective Goldberg had run the stakeout from four P.M. to midnight. He reported plenty of human traffic in and out of the building. A lot of paper bags had gone in, a lot had come out.

But no typewriter had gone in. No cartons had gone in.

Cardozo turned to the next sheet.

Detective Ferrara had handled the stakeout from midnight to eight A.M. Thursday. Same story. No typewriter, no cartons.

Carl Malloy had taken over at eight A.M. and worked till noon. No typewriter, no cartons.

Goldberg had been scheduled to run the stakeout from noon to eight P.M. He'd ended early, when the crime scene crew arrived at four.

"Three thirty-five." Ellie's finger pointed to the entry in the log. *"Black female took packages into building. Two separate trips. Woman wore kerchief on hair but resembled Identi-Kit of T. Dillworth."*

Cardozo took the log to Sergeant Goldberg's desk. "Sergeant —how come you didn't mention you'd seen Dillworth going into the Martinez building?"

Goldberg shot him an impatient glance. "I mentioned it— right there in the log, where I was supposed to."

"How come you didn't mention it to me?"

"Because, in the first place, I forgot and because, in the second place, I assumed you'd read the log, because you're the lieutenant on the case and that's what the log's for, right?"

"Why didn't you follow her?"

"Those weren't my orders."

Goldberg had a point.

"It was my goof," Cardozo said.

He went to get himself a coffee. In the little service room off the squad room, the detectives had crowded around the TV. He could see the image on the screen: a dozen hands, in close-up, shredding an American flag.

The detectives booed.

"Hey, Greg." Cardozo jabbed Monteleone gently. "What's going on? Where's that happening?"

"Right out in front of the precinct. Live."

"I didn't see any flag-trashing out there."

"You're seeing it now."

On the screen the camera pulled back to a longer view. A man with a shaved head was dousing the torn flag with a jet of clear liquid from a gallon can. When he tossed a match, the flag seemed to explode. So did a half-dozen hands. Rioters ran from the flames, streaming into a blur on the sidewalk.

A cheer went up from the detectives. Hearing his own men applaud like that, Cardozo had a nightmare vision that the whole city was coming unglued.

On the TV screen, behind the mob, you could see the precinct steps and the grilles on the precinct windows. Cops were looking out from behind the grilles. A solitary man stood on the edge of the crowd, motionless in a world of movement. His half-zipped Mets warmup jacket outlined a gut pushing out over an unbuckled belt.

Cardozo didn't know why he was noticing that motionless figure in the background, except that he had a feeling the guy didn't belong in this scene: the guy was trouble—he was going to toss a grenade or drop his pants and exhibit himself right there on live TV. He had that kind of face—crazed, spaced-out.

"Christ," Cardozo said.

It was Carl Malloy's face and it needed a shave.

▪ ▪ ▪

BY THE TIME CARDOZO REACHED the vestibule two sergeants had pulled Malloy inside. He was rocking on his heels, stinking of vodka.

Cardozo steered him upstairs and into the squad room.

As they passed Laurie Bonasera's desk Malloy stopped. "Aren't you even going to say hi?" His speech was all drunken stresses and slurred plosives.

Laurie Bonasera turned in her chair, startled. "Good morning, Officer Malloy."

Malloy stared across the squad room, frowning. "Where is everyone?"

Cardozo steered him toward his desk. "Watching you on TV."

Malloy pulled the chair out and slumped down into it.

"Could I give you some advice, Carl? Pull yourself together and then go home."

"Fuck you, Vince. I work here."

"Not today you don't. Take a sick day."

"So what am I supposed to do? Stay home and read the *New York Tribune* in my sunny bay window?"

Malloy tried to get up, lost his balance, fell back into the chair. "I feel a little twisted, Vince."

"Right now you're looking at the absolute worst life has to offer. This is it. It's not going to get any worse. And you're doing fine, you're getting through it."

Malloy laid his head down on the desktop.

"Carl, this is just a suggestion, but maybe you'd be more comfortable resting in the men's room."

Malloy raised his head, interested in the idea. A smile shone thinly over his uncertainty. He tried to stand up again and this time he managed.

Cardozo watched him walk an almost straight line to the door.

A blare of newszak spilled in from the TV room.

Cardozo headed toward his cubicle. Behind him he heard Laurie Bonasera's voice, in a high, almost startled key. "Officer Malloy, I'm working."

Cardozo turned.

Malloy was standing accusingly beside Laurie's desk. "Don't 'Officer Malloy' me."

Laurie rose, protecting her space with one outstretched arm.

Cardozo approached. "Carl, what's going on?"

Malloy glared over at him. "What am I, tried and convicted already? Don't I have rights? I can't even talk to somebody?"

"You're off duty, Laurie's on duty."

"This is a private conversation," Malloy said.

"Private conversations can be held after work hours." Cardozo put a guiding hand on Malloy's elbow. "Carl, come here."

Back in his cubicle Cardozo shut the door.

"What the hell is going on between you and her?"

Malloy's face clenched and Cardozo could feel him seething with rage and hurt.

"Carl, you're in deep shit enough. Don't complicate it. If Laurie Bonasera doesn't want to see you, don't try to see her. And don't drink in public. Not like this. You're out of control."

"I have rights, Vince."

"Yes, you have rights and if you have any sense, you want to keep those rights. Right now you have IAD gunning for your shield and your pension and you have two hundred people out there in that street gunning for your life. Why the hell do you have to make it easy for them?"

"Vince . . . I can't help it. I love her."

How does this happen? Cardozo wondered. *How do cops get this twisted around, why do they divorce their own common sense?* "Fine. Why don't you just love yourself a little. Because not everyone on the other side of that door is your pal. Chances are, somebody out there is IAD. And they're hearing you."

"Why won't she talk to me? Why can't she just talk to me?"

"Maybe because she's a married woman. Maybe because you're a married man. Maybe because you're going on paid suspension and you're coming up on a hearing. Maybe because she's a friend and she doesn't want to complicate things for you. Maybe she cares what happens to you. The same as Ellie and Greg and Sam and I do."

Malloy started sobbing.

■ ■ ■

CARDOZO RETURNED to the squad room. "Laurie," he said.

She turned in her chair to look at him, but her fingers kept dancing over the keyboard of her computer.

"I'm not going to mention anything about Carl," he said, "and I hope you won't either."

Her eyes flicked back to the screen. The silence rising from her had the smell of acute embarrassment. The computer suddenly let out a single, chicken-pitched squawk, and she jumped.

A message flashed at the top of the screen: *Name your file immediately and press Save or you will lose your data.* Below the message the word *file* appeared, followed by a colon and a blank space.

For Cardozo it was as though the light in the squad room had changed, as though the surrounding area had dimmed out and a white spot had focused on that screen.

Laurie sat silent, unreacting, staring at the message. It was a moment before she tapped a message into the keys. On the screen, in the space beside the word *file,* the word *file* appeared a second time. Laurie pressed the Save button and the screen cleared.

"What did you just do?" Cardozo said.

"I forgot to name the file. The computer won't store unnamed files longer than three thousand bytes, and I was about to lose it, so I named it *file.*"

At that instant a doorway swung open in Cardozo's mind and

he reached back through it with his memory. "You said Dick Braidy's computer automatically named his files."

She nodded. "The backups are named with the date and time he created them."

"Then if we could locate the backup of one of his articles, the name would tell us when he wrote the article."

She was staring at him with a puzzled look. It took an instant before she found a smile for him. "That's right."

A knot of excitement was forming inside Cardozo's stomach. "Could you come with me right now?"

Her voice took on an edge of wariness. "Where to?"

"Dick Braidy's apartment."

■ ■ ■

CARDOZO CROSSED TO THE WINDOW of Dick Braidy's workroom and flicked a switch. A soft purr rose from the air conditioner.

Laurie Bonasersa was hanging back at the door.

"It's okay." Cardozo lifted the dust cover from Dick Braidy's PC. "We're not breaking any law."

She dropped her purse on a chair. "What are we looking for?"

"The backup of an article called 'Pavane pour une Infante Défunte.' "

She came around the desk and switched the computer on. Her hands hardly seemed to touch the keyboard. Page after page of data scrolled past. Frowning, squinting, she watched the shifting, glittering maze of eye-killingly tiny print.

Cardozo waited with a sort of willed calm. Forty-five minutes passed.

Laurie suddenly sat forward in the chair. "I've got something called 'Pavane for Nita Kohler,' dated June ninth, eight forty-two A.M."

"That's it."

"Want me to print it?"

"Please."

■ ■ ■

IT WAS ALMOST TWO in the afternoon when Cardozo and Laurie Bonasera returned to the no-parking stretch on East Seventy-sixth Street where he'd left his car. The sun pressed down like the lid on a baking pan, and the air had the choking thickness of a fire in a pizza shop.

Cardozo unlocked the passenger door. He was broadsided by

a stench of cooked leatherette riding a wave of stale heat. "Better let it cool a minute before you get in," he told Laurie.

He went around and unlocked the driver's door. As he swung it open the side-view mirror caught a reflection of Carl Malloy sauntering across the street.

"Hi, Vince," Malloy said. His cheekbones were ridged in sweat and the hollows of his eyes were tunnels. He walked around the front of the car. "Hi, Laurie."

Laurie Bonasera folded her arms in front of her. For just an instant she closed her eyes and Cardozo could sense there was a squall in the space behind them.

"Sick and tired of me popping up all over the place?" Malloy grinned.

Laurie stood there, constructing a weary half smile. "Carl, this isn't a good time."

"You're always saying it's not a good time."

"I really can't talk now. I'm working."

They stared at each other. The space between them vibrated with a skittering energy.

Cardozo had a feeling that in four weeks these two had developed a lifetime's history of not getting along.

Carl Malloy turned. "How is she, Vince—as good the second time around as the first?"

"Laurie knows her way around a computer." Cardozo slid into the driver's seat and started the engine. "Can we give you a lift anywhere, Carl?"

For a moment Carl Malloy didn't move or say anything. And then he looked at Laurie, and he very slowly arched one eyebrow. His breath came out in a long sigh. His hand dropped toward his right hip.

The bullet hit her like a fist, whipping her head around to the left, taking the eye. She spun and staggered backward into the hood of the Toyota. Her body lost its balance and crumpled down onto the sidewalk.

Malloy strolled over to where she lay, taking his time, as though nothing from the outside world was going to hurry him or bother him ever again.

Cardozo leapt out of the car. He drew his revolver. "Drop your gun, Carl. Drop it."

It was as though Carl Malloy hadn't heard, as though Cardozo hadn't even spoken.

Carl Malloy seemed to be looking away, listening to the traffic-and-boom-box music of New York that was floating down the street.

Then he raised his revolver a second time and fired a bullet into his mouth.

▪ SIXTY-EIGHT ▪

ELECTRONIC CHIMES DING-DONGED the opening notes of "Home Sweet Home," and Cardozo wished he were anywhere but here. The door opened.

"Hi, Vince." Delia Malloy was smiling, but she didn't look good. She still had the bright green eyes and dark wavy hair he remembered from Christmas two years ago, but they didn't add up to the same woman. She'd put on weight. Her cheeks had lost their color. "You should've phoned before you came all this way. Carl's not home yet."

There was a beat where Cardozo should have answered, and he missed it. She looked at his face and frowned, reading something there.

"Carl's hurt?" she said.

Cardozo didn't answer.

Delia Malloy took a stumbling step backward from the doorway. "Oh, Christ." Her teeth bit down hard on her lip.

Cardozo felt a tightening in his throat and chest. "Delia, I'm sorry."

She flung herself against him, and he could feel her fingers digging through his jacket into his back. Her brown hair was soft in his face, with faint streaks of gray, and a just-shampooed sweetness hovered around it. He could feel a spasm in her breathing, as if she was barely managing to hold back tears. "Maybe you should sit down," he said after a moment.

"Come in, Vince, come in." Delia's wedding ring glinted as she pushed hair back from her face. "Maybe we should both sit down."

Lace curtains in the Malloys' living room softened the light to a pale glow, and in the window you could see the sun blinking off the windows of the two-family houses across the street.

"I appreciate your coming," Delia said. "I'm glad it was you that told me." Delia sighed. "I'm going to have a drink. You feel like a drink?"

"Sure," Cardozo said.

There was a built-in bar and Delia searched the cabinet.

She was wearing a plain brown house dress now, and Cardozo remembered how great she had looked dressed up for the commissioner's retirement dinner two years ago.

"You're not going to believe this," Delia said. "I forgot to go to the liquor store. We're out of everything but rye. How about a shot of rye?"

Cardozo didn't think she'd forgotten anything. He had a hunch her husband had finished off every other bottle.

"I don't drink single shots," Cardozo said.

Delia tonged ice into two highball glasses and filled them and came across the room and handed Cardozo his glass. The glass had an NYPD shield etched into it.

Delia sat on the edge of the chair facing him. "So tell me."

"You really want it now?"

"I want it now. While I'm still in shock."

He told her. There wasn't any way he could soften it or leave the Bonasera girl out of it. Delia didn't flinch during the telling. She didn't strike him as all that surprised either.

"I don't want you to take what I'm about to say as an insult, Vince. Promise you won't."

"Of course I won't."

"Carl never really wanted to be a cop." She looked up apologetically. "It was just his luck to come from a cop family. His father was a cop, his grandfather was a cop, his great-grandfather was a cop. So there was no question what Carl was going to do with his life. And he was a good cop, wouldn't you say? Until . . . lately?"

"He was good. That's why I picked him for my team."

"I'm glad you did that. He valued your opinion, Vince." She broke off and shook her head slowly. "He'd have been happier if he'd bucked his old man. You know what he wanted in his heart to be? What he could have been professionally? He could have made furniture professionally."

She tapped her finger on the mahogany coffee table with hinged oval borders that separated their two chairs.

"Look at this table. He made it himself."

"He made it?" Cardozo found it hard to believe that a man

who kept as messy a desk as Carl Malloy could have shaped a piece of wood so perfectly. His hand went out and touched the cool, faultless glow of the finish. "It's beautiful."

"Doesn't seem like Carl, hey? He loved beautiful things. He loved to make them down in his workshop in the cellar."

"I didn't know he had a workshop in the cellar."

"Oh, sure, it was his mania. Design, inlays, carving, finishing —he could make wood sit up and dance." A sigh came out of her. "He could have had his own furniture business. He could have supported a family. People on Park Avenue pay fifteen hundred for a coffee table this good. But Carl just didn't want to let his old man down."

"Was he depressed?" Cardozo said.

"You mean why did he do it?" There was just a hint of hesitation before Delia's next breath. "Some people can kill another person and walk away from it. Carl wasn't that kind of guy. Taking a life was serious to him. Even killing that serial killer—he was miserable over it. Once he pulled the trigger on the girl, it was foregone. He had to kill himself."

"Did you know her?"

"No."

"Know about her?"

"I was getting a feeling. He was staying out late at work—a lot. Bringing me presents for no reason. Only there's always a reason, right? When two plus two starts coming out six, I can generally figure out what the x in the equation is. And this last month, things were coming out six most of the time. But Vince—I don't understand why he killed that girl."

"Maybe he thought he loved her. Maybe he thought he couldn't have her and maybe it made him desperate."

Delia's gaze didn't move away. "Do you think he loved her?"

"I think one day he looked around him and saw he was farther along the road than he'd realized. Time was running out and he was trapped. If that's love, then he loved her."

"Did he feel trapped?"

"Same job every day."

"You mean same wife every day."

"I don't mean that, Delia. It was between him and himself. It was the way he chose to see things."

Delia nodded. "I saw he was exploring. Trying new ways of dressing, new ways of cutting his hair, going to the gym, dieting— when he wasn't looking, he was getting ready to look. It was bound to happen that he'd meet somebody. And you know, for a long time . . . we weren't lovers the way we used to be. There always seemed to be something in the way. His hours. My headaches. His headaches."

"But there must have been something there. You two must have wanted to stay together."

A silence hovered.

Delia finally answered with a shrug. "My point of view? I loved him. His point of view? I guess he didn't want to let me down. He hated letting people down. That's the one thing he could not do and be at peace with himself. He was decent to the core. Saying he was a bad man is absolutely untrue."

"No one is saying Carl was a bad man."

Her eyes stayed on Cardozo, tough now, almost accusing. "They've been saying it, Vince, and you've heard them saying it. But if any of you knew how hard he tried, how long he held on, long after anyone else would have cracked . . . If you knew the half of it, you'd give him a medal."

Nothing moved in the room except the sunlight glinting off the edge of the coffee table.

"Okay," Delia said, "he did a lot of things I don't know about, and he probably did a lot of things even you don't know about. He had women, he played around, he went to the races, he drank too much. And when he turned on the TV he watched too much. Big deal."

She was sinking into her feelings now, and the silence was heavy with all the things she needed to say.

"In the end, it's funny, but once he got all that out of his system I think he would have stayed home. He would have kept tinkering around in the cellar. He was a homebody, deep down. Because for Carl the bottom line was to live life with a little decency and dignity. And IAD took that away from him. Over a plate of ice cream."

Delia's voice was glacial with controlled fury.

"Carl's problem was, he wasn't a big enough crook. Be a big enough crook and no one can touch you. Look at all the mayor's appointees. Look at the senators and congressmen and state reps. They shove public money into their pockets and drive to the bank in a stretch limo that's paid for by taxes. They take millions and Carl took two dollars' worth of dessert. Even Jack the Ripper gets a second chance nowadays. But not a cop. Not Carl Malloy. Toward the end he had to fight for everything—even for the chance to fight."

Delia got up and brought the bottle from the bar.

"I could kill that Braidy bitch. And as for IAD, don't even talk to me about IAD."

"But Delia," Cardozo said, "IAD dropped the charge."

"Sure, they dropped it and made him wear a wire."

Cardozo brought his eyes up slowly. "Carl was wearing a wire?"

Delia Malloy didn't answer. It was as if for once in the life of this cop's wife there was an instant of power she could savor. And then she nodded. "Carl was going crazy, he felt he was Judas sitting there in task-force meetings with that wire. Why the hell did IAD need a recording? It wasn't as though you guys were talking about skimming a shipment of coke."

"Who in IAD wired him?"

"Zawac. He gave Carl a choice: get busted for corruption, lose his job, his pension because of two plates of ice cream—or wear the wire."

"Why the hell would Zawac want a wire in Society Sam task-force meetings?"

"Who asks why when it's IAD? They had Carl cold. Bridget Braidy saw him accept the free ice cream. Zawac wanted a wire in the Society Sam task force and Carl fell into his lap and Zawac got his wire."

■ ■ ■

CARDOZO STEPPED INTO THE CUBICLE. He closed the door. He searched his desktop and found last July's police-department roster. He looked up Internal Affairs Division, ISB in the index, and he found Captain Lawrence Zawac on page four. He punched the number into his phone. A flunky answered. Cardozo had no trouble mustering his nastiest voice, and his nastiest voice did the trick. The flunky put him through.

"I've just been talking to the widow of a friend of yours," Cardozo said. "Delia Malloy."

A silence came across the line. Then Zawac said, "I hope you told her how very sorry I was to learn about her husband."

"I couldn't vouch for how sorry you felt," Cardozo said. "Delia tells me you had Carl wear a wire into my task force."

Zawac didn't deny it.

"Mrs. Malloy is willing to testify in an independent probe of IAD tactics. Unless you'd care to tell me why you wired Carl. Who you were giving the information to?"

"Lieutenant, we're discussing extremely sensitive issues. This is not a secure phone. I'm not about to comment."

"Then let me ask you this. How did Xenia Delancey know we were unsealing a Family Court file?"

"I can't comment."

"In that case, Captain, I hope you have good health coverage, because your ass is in the frying pan."

■ ■ ■

CARDOZO CAME DOWN THE PRECINCT STEPS. The light in Sixty-sixth Street had softened. On the rooftops and in the windows of upper stories the sun cast a late-afternoon glow.

He was heading east when a woman's voice called to him. "Vince—could I ask you a favor?"

He turned. A white stretch limo had slowed at the curb, and Senator Nancy Guardella was leaning out of the open passenger door. He didn't answer, but his face must have said it for him.

"I know you hate my guts," Nancy Guardella said. "And I don't blame you, but just do me one favor: Ride with me—give me a chance to tell my side of the story."

Cardozo slid into the coolness of the backseat.

"Leo," Senator Guardella told the back of her driver's head, "drive around a little."

The limo eased into the east-bound traffic. Nancy Guardella pressed the remote and raised the glass partition between the seats. "I just had a talk with Larry Zawac."

"I'm not surprised."

"Vince, these things happen. I chair a complex agency that handles complex problems that there are no magic, simple solutions for. I wish to hell there were. I wish I could snap my fingers, wave a magic wand, and solve the drug crisis without bending a single law."

The limo stopped for the Lexington Avenue light. Sunlight reflected off an Absolut vodka bottle sitting on the fully stocked bar.

"We both know that's wishful thinking," Nancy Guardella said. "To get the goods on the drug cartel, to get a charge that holds up in an American court, we have to allow the drug cartel to operate. It's called entrapment. It's a dirty word, and it's a dirty way of solving a dirty problem. But if you know a clean way, Vince, I wish you'd let me know."

Cardozo brought his eyes up slowly. There was a beat where he could have answered, and he let it go by.

Nancy Guardella's teeth came down on her lower lip. "Nan

Shane had infiltrated the Salvador drug cartel. For three years she was handing us terrific intelligence."

Cardozo said nothing. He just sat, counting the karats on the fingers and arms and ears and neck of the junior senator from New York.

After a moment Nancy Guardella's gaze flicked away from his. She sighed. "Last March twenty-seventh, we had a screw-up. A New York City undercover drug cop busted Nan Shane for possession with intent to sell. Robert Q. O'Rourke. A sweet kid, but not the brightest man ever born."

Cardozo's mind played with two dates: On March twenty-sixth, the magazines went on sale from which Society Sam clipped his words and partial words and single letters. They stayed on sale seven days. On March twenty-seventh, Nan Shane was busted and became a liability to her masters in the drug trade.

"He was new to the job," Nancy Guardella said. "He was new to the Upper East Side beat. And someone forgot to clue him in that Nan was one of ours." Her voice took on an edge like a chisel digging into blackboard. "And I wish I knew who that someone was so I could gut his pension."

Nancy Guardella leaned toward the bar and tonged ice into two highball glasses.

"From what our intelligence arm has been able to put together, an order came down from the directorate of the Salvador cartel: Nan Shane is a liability, she's been busted, eliminate her."

Nancy Guardella filled the glasses with mineral water.

"The cartel sent a hit man to take out Shane. His name was Rick Martinez, and he turned out to be a psycho." She added a wedge of lime to each glass. "That part of the story you already know. Not only did Rick Martinez kill Nan Shane, on his own he took the lives of five innocent men and women." She handed Cardozo a glass. The glass had a United States Senate shield etched into it.

"Why did you want a wire in my task force?" he said.

"We couldn't risk your investigation blowing the Achilles Foot sting. I'm sorry, Vince. What it comes down to, is federal versus local. We had to protect ourselves. You may not be in agreement, but that's the way it is."

"When did you know Society Sam was the cartel's hit man?"

"When he killed our operative."

"But Nan Shane was killed three weeks *after* you sent the wire in."

"I'm sorry. I thought you meant when did I have *personal* knowledge. Our intelligence arm knew earlier."

"May I see the intelligence reports?"

She smiled at Cardozo, shaking her head. "Vince, if I showed you those reports, I could be sent to a federal penitentiary for revealing government secrets. You're going to have to take my word for it, and take my word that we have the situation under control."

"Would you mind telling me why you backed Jim Delancey for early parole? Or is that a classified federal secret too?"

Her eyes flicked up. She pulled in a deep breath. "Complicated problem, Vince. Xenia Delancey commands a lot of sympathy—and press. She's the biological mother of a son gone bad and she's pleading for a second chance for her boy—and she's one of my constituents. I studied the record and I was struck by the strides Jim Delancey had made. I felt it was in the interests of justice, and rehabilitation, and freeing up valuable jail space to parole him. Does that answer your question?"

"You tell me."

Nancy Guardella smiled as though he'd said, *Yes, thank you.*

"You can stop the car," Cardozo said. "I'll get out here."

■   ■   ■

THE JEU DE PAUME AT LE CERCLE sparkled with the movement of cocktail dresses and Italian suits. Two hundred of the most important mouths in Manhattan feasted on a buffet that included grilled gulf shrimp with pumpkin-ginger chutney, roast partridge mousse with onion marmalade, and Roederer Cristal champagne.

In the southwest corner of the room Zack Morrow kissed Gabrielle MacAdam Morrow, and then Gabrielle kissed Zack. They were the worst-matched couple Kristi Blackwell had ever seen.

"Is the angle okay?" Zack shouted.

The photographer kept snapping away, darting lithely around them, stooping and dipping down on one knee and crouching and stretching with his Minolta pressed to one eye. "You're perfect!" he called. "Keep going, don't worry about me!"

He had a light Austrian accent. His name was Wolfgang Neuhaus and he had a dueling scar and in America he photographed exclusively for *Fanfare.*

"You heard the gentleman," Kristi heard Gabrielle whisper. A sickeningly arch, *faux*-baby whisper. "Keep going."

Zack stood there smiling at his fat bride, looking very much the man in love, impeccably groomed in his tailored summer-weight Armani. The subtle pinstripes in the deep charcoal harmonized perfectly with the gray beginning to glint in his dark, softly waved hair.

Gabrielle, on the other hand, was wearing wide-wale burgundy corduroy trousers and a tie-dyed linen jacket and big, hippie-looking flea-market jewelry. She'd made no attempt to hide her weight or her age, no attempt to pass as glamorous.

Kristi wondered if that look and that attitude was the wave of the future. She shuddered to think of the impact on advertising revenue.

"Gabrielle," she sang out, "what a great idea to have your reception in the midafternoon—just when working people really need a lift."

"It's exactly what the working world needs," Zack said. "Some good food, some good chitchat, some good drink—and we'll all be ourselves again."

"I don't want to be myself again *ever!*" Kristi said. "I want to live like this for the rest of my life!"

At that instant the part of Kristi Blackwell that always stood guard registered something. In all the bustle and movement she was aware of someone standing motionless against one of the decorative columns just to her right.

She turned her head, just a little. She recognized Lieutenant Vincent Cardozo, wearing chinos and a sport jacket, watching her.

She made a quick gesture of suddenly remembering something. "Would you guys excuse me for just a minute? A certain friend of mine will *murder* me if I don't tell her you're serving wild-mushroom-and-baby-leek millefeuille. Who's got a quarter?"

"You do, honeychile." Zack dropped a coin into her hand.

Kristi pried her way through socialites throwing attitude and rich would-be's posing big. She smiled at a few, frowned at more than a few, and for the most part affected her trademark tunnel vision.

Tunnel vision got her as far as the door. Arriving guests formed a glittering traffic jam. She pushed through them.

The door of the Jeu de Paume at Le Cercle did not lead to Le Cercle itself. It led to the lobby of an old remodeled hotel. Le Cercle stood on the far side of the lobby, and the Jeu de Paume was attached to it in no way except by name and by Kristi's publicizing. Her magazine had plugged the windowless, renovated utility room so relentlessly that it was now *the* spot for private parties away from home.

The lobby housed three phone booths, and they were the old-fashioned wooden kind with accordion-fold doors.

Kristi attempted to make her phone call.

The phone in the first booth had no dial tone.

The second had no dial.

The third took her quarter, and her call went through with more crackles and squeaks than a shortwave radio in peak sunspot season.

"Maslow and Maslow," a woman's harried voice answered.

"Langford Jennings, please."

"I'm sorry, Mr. Jennings is in conference."

"Put me through. This is Kristi Blackwell and it's an emergency."

Kristi's lawyer picked up with a clatter. "This had better be important. And brief."

"The police want to know who I gave the 'Pavane' outtakes to."

"Why do they want to know?"

"Because the outtakes were used to forge the Nita Kohler diary."

Whoever had last used the phone booth had doused himself in nose-boggling quantities of Chanel's Pour Monsieur. Kristi eased the door open a generous crack, hoping to get a little ventilation going.

"Did you give evidence in the trial of Kohler's murderer?" her lawyer said.

"No."

"Did you depose as to the authenticity of the diary?"

"I never—" Kristi's voice suddenly broke off. She could see the revolving street door from the booth, and three people had just walked into the lobby.

Kristi had nothing against blacks and Hispanics, but *these* blacks and Hispanics were clearly street people. The woman was carrying at least five rag-stuffed D'Agostino bags under each arm. The man was carrying a television set. The leopard-skirted drag queen was stuffing coke rocks into a crack pipe.

"Then you're in the clear," her lawyer said.

"But what do I tell the police?"

"The truth."

"The *truth*?"

"Forging of evidence is a felony. Dissociate yourself from the forger."

"Dissociate?" Kristi tried to focus her mind on the conversation, but she could not believe what she was seeing.

The lone guard in the lobby, a gray, crunched husk of a man, sat in a folding chair, eyes half shut beneath a chauffeur-style cap with *Le Cercle* stitched in gold script across its brim. He held a styrofoam cup of coffee in his lap, and he gazed at it, never once lifting it to his lips. His manner was one of jittery resignation, and he was scrupulously not noticing anything going on around him.

The bag woman had pulled a brand-new–looking ghetto-blaster from one of her bags. The drag queen passed her the crack pipe.

"Kristi, what the hell is that noise?"

The bag woman had found a rap station.

"I don't believe what's happening," Kristi said, "I don't *believe* it!" She didn't believe it either when the man with the TV stepped into the booth next to hers and began urinating. "Excuse me," she cried, "I've got to get out of here."

She slammed down the receiver and practically jumped from the booth. She hit the lobby floor skidding, barely managed to regain her balance. When she saw the squish of dog shit coating her right Ferragamo green lizard half heel, she heard her own voice break into a sob. "I don't believe this!"

And then she remembered that dogs don't shit in phone booths.

She found a statueless niche in the wall where she could rest her derriere. She took a small packet of Kleenex from her purse, took off her shoe, and began cleaning the sole.

Lieutenant Cardozo sauntered into the lobby. "Well, well, a lady in distress."

"I see you're as good as your word, Lieutenant. You said forty-eight hours, and here you are." She smiled as if she had been looking for him all over the party, as though they had been friends for years and it was delightful having this chance to chat with him privately. "I take it you've spoken with the district attorney about me?"

Cardozo smiled. "I take it you've spoken with your lawyer about the 'Pavane' outtakes?"

"My lawyer says I've committed no crime."

"Dick Braidy's computer dated his backup files. The date on 'Pavane' is June eleventh—five months *before* the Kohler diary was introduced as evidence. Which means Braidy couldn't have stolen from the diary. The diary writer stole Braidy's outtakes. So the question is—who gave the diary writer the outtakes, and who wrote the diary?"

Kristi wished that the woman with the boom box would turn that rap music down. "Lieutenant, when I arrived in this country from England, I had no working papers. The government gave me a green card with the understanding that from time to time I'd help them. They asked me to cut 'Pavane' and give them the outtakes. There was nothing more to it than that, so please don't treat me as though I'd sold atom bomb plans to the Soviet Union."

"Who built the diary out of those outtakes?"

Kristi slipped her foot back into the shoe and took two testing steps. "I had nothing to do with reshaping the outtakes."

Cardozo just stood there. In a casually understated manner he was blocking her way.

"I honestly *don't* know who wrote the diary," she said. "Not for sure."

His lack of expression, his lack of movement made it clear he was willing to wait there, blocking her, for the next ten seconds or the next ten days, however long it took.

And meanwhile that rap music was rapping.

Kristi opened her hand and let the soiled Kleenex drop into a standing bronze ashtray. "I messengered the pages to Nancy Guardella's office in U.N. Tower. If you want to know who forged the diary, ask her."

"One last question." Cardozo was still blocking her way. "Did you rewrite 'Socialites in Emergency' at Nancy Guardella's request?"

"She asked me to drop any mention of the lawsuit."

"Why was that?"

"Because the lawsuit was brought by one of her operatives and it could have exposed an on-going sting."

Cardozo frowned as though something was not computing. "You're sure she said one of *her* operatives?"

"Lieutenant, my lawyer told me to tell you the truth. His advice is much too expensive to disregard. And yes, I'm sure."

·SIXTY-NINE·

Saturday, June 22

"THERE ARE TWO LETTERS IN THE BOX." The background noise behind Greg Monteleone's voice on the phone was a mix of indoor-outdoor: screeching salsa and screeching traffic. "But no one's come for them. Know what? I think Martinez's mailbox is as dead as he is."

"Blue Cross sends checks to that box," Cardozo said. "The checks are negotiable. Somebody's going to pick them up."

"Vince, this work is very boring. And I hate this music. And it never stops."

"Buy some earplugs. Watch the box till Mailsafe closes shop. If no one comes today, go back Monday."

Without waiting for Monteleone's protest, Cardozo broke the connection and hung up the phone. He picked up Lou Stein's report on Society Sam's fifth letter. He speed-read the inventory of letter sources. *This doesn't tell me anything I don't already know,* he thought.

The phone rang. Cardozo braced himself for an angry Monteleone. "Cardozo."

"You are fucking not going to believe this," a male voice rasped.

"Who is this?"

"What's the matter, are we strangers today? This is Rad, Rad Rheinhardt, who do you think?"

Cardozo drew a deep, ragged breath. "Hello, Rad, what's happening?"

"What do you think's happening? We got another Society Son of Sam letter. It just came in the mail. Postmarked yesterday."

"Yesterday." Cardozo's chest felt hollow. "Messenger it to me right away, will you?"

■ ■ ■

THERE WAS A KNOCK ON THE DOOR. "Come in," Cardozo called.

A gray-haired man well past old age stood in the doorway breathing heavily. He wore a *New York Trib* T-shirt and what had begun as half-moons of sweat under his arms had become full moons that collided over his ribs.

"What have you got for me?"

The old man handed Cardozo a chit of paper to sign and then handed over a reinforced bubble envelope.

"Just a minute." Cardozo gave him five dollars, and the old man thanked him with a crooked smile.

Cardozo began carefully tearing the outer envelope open along the line marked *tear here.* Ellie came and watched over his shoulder.

He studied the envelope inside the cellophane. The address was typed and the capital *R*'s in the *Rad* and the *Rheinhardt* looked out of whack in the same way as the *R*'s on the others. There was no return address, and the zip code in the postmark was a brand-new one.

"Oh-oh-five." Ellie Siegel was frowning at the postmark. "Wall Street."

Cardozo pulled open a desk drawer, took out a pair of throw-away evidence gloves, and slipped them on. He reached inside the cellophane and inside the envelope and drew out Society Sam's latest.

Breathing slowly, he laid the letter flat on the desk, centered in the milky gray light of the failing fluorescent desklamp. As before, single letters and parts of words and sometimes entire words had been clipped from an astonishing variety of print sources, producing a dismaying babel of fonts and typefaces.

> HOW CAN SAM SINK WITHOUT SEX
> SET WITHOUT TWEET
> SHE SPENT HER LAST
> SHES THRIFTY NOW
> FINDER KEEPER WEEPER
> KISSES SOCIETY SAM

"Ellie, I hate to ask—but could you get down to oh-oh-five? Check the mailboxes? Check the pickup times?"

Ellie gave him a long gaze, just seeming to weigh the proposal. "Vince, how important is this?"

"It'll be pretty damned important if it turns out he killed someone else before he died."

The touch of her attention was skeptical. "Isn't it standard operating procedure in these days of manpower shortage to wait for the corpse to come to us?" She glanced down at the files and diagrams spread across his desk. A look crossed her face. "Vince, what is this workaholic's compulsion you have to torture yourself about something that's just been officially declared a nothing?"

"It's not nothing," Cardozo said, "and I'm not torturing myself."

"I'll rephrase that. Why are you torturing *me* with a closed case?"

The phone rang. "Cardozo."

"Vince, it's Marty Wilkes." He sounded in a panic.

"Yes, Marty."

"I've got to talk to you right away."

■　■　■

"LET'S START WITH THE LINE from the third letter," Marty Wilkes said. *"Sex to end all sex, is there anything else in your perverted world view."*

Wilkes sat at his computer terminal and tapped an instruction into the keyboard. A line split the display screen. The quote from Society Sam appeared in the space above it. A moment later, below the line, a longer document unscrolled.

"Can you read it?" Wilkes asked.

Cardozo leaned toward the screen and squinted.

The West fixates on the search for the wealth to end all wealth, the power to end all power; for the high to end all highs, the sex to end all sex: is there anything else that can more quickly pervert the worldview of the spirit than the ceaseless recourse to material measures of transcendence?

"Who wrote that?"

"Believe it or not," Wilkes said, "it's a letter Rumford Haynes wrote to the Rahway, New Jersey, police in April 1964. Rumford Haynes was a handyman who read a lot. Between January 1964 and August 1965 he raped one hundred twenty-three women and murdered twelve."

"Where did you access the letter?"

"The BSU keeps a file of letters from serial killers. They also keep a concordance to the letters."

"Concordance," Cardozo said. The idea struck him as bizarre. "Like in the Bible?"

"Exactly. Ask the concordance for the word *worldview,* and you learn it's occurred only this once in BSU history."

"Okay. Whoever wrote the Society Sam notes dipped into the database for his raw material. But why did that *sex to end all sex* phrase show up four years earlier in the forged Kohler diary?"

"The same passage is cross-referenced on the database under *obsessive personality disorder.* Maybe the diary was meant to prove Kohler was a sexual compulsive." Wilkes cleared the screen. A quote from the first note appeared above the split:

> SAM SAM THANK YOU MAAM
> KILL THE GIRLS AND MAKE THEM CRUMB
> BYE BYE SOCIETY SCUM

Below the split a new document unscrolled:

> *Slam bang thank you ma'am*
> *kiss the girls and make them cum*
> *bye bye human scum*

"The author's name," Wilkes said, "was Nelson MacIntyre. San Diego, November 1972. Eight victims."

Another Sam quote, this time from letter four:

> ME OW AND THE POODY TAT
> OW CAN YOU SEE
> HUMPTY DUMPTY GOT THE BUMPTY

And below the split:

> *The owl and the pussy cat want to see Humpty Dumpty get the bumpty.*

"Carla Fugazy and Charles Strickland—Billings, Montana, May 1981. A team effort. One of the few instances of a female serial killer. They called themselves the owl and the pussy cat. Carla was the owl and Charles was the pussy. They scored seven victims that we know of."

A quote from letter six:

WEEP NO TEARS FOR CUT UP CUT OUTS

Below the split:

cut in, cut up, cut out

"Lance Mitchelmore, Seattle, Washington, February 1984. He killed eight women with his mother's pinking shears. Always sent the same note."
From the seventh note:

HOW CAN SAM SINK WITHOUT SEX
SET WITHOUT TWEET

Below the split:

pas de cinq sans six
pas de sept sans huit

"Hidalgo Beausoleil, Bangor, Maine, October 1979. Killed seven prostitutes. He wrote his letters in French, always *un-deux-trois* stuff." Marty Wilkes shook his head with a ruefulness that seemed to say all human suffering was a single self-inflicted hurt. "I doubt there's a single phrase in Society Sam's letters that we couldn't dig up in the concordance. And that thought made me question an assumption I'd made. I'd assumed that Society Sam was a person."

There must have been something amusing in the idea, because Wilkes smiled, and Cardozo had the impression that his own universe and the world of clinical psychology rotated around distinctly different axes.

"Look at the dates of Society Sam's hits." Wilkes tapped an instruction into the keyboard. "See anything odd?"

Seven familiar dates scrolled up the screen.

"The oddity," Wilkes said, "is that there's no oddity. They're spaced at exactly descending time intervals—eleven days, nine days, seven, five, three, one. Most serial killers' hits approximate a time formula—but Sam's hits don't approximate a formula, they *are* a formula."

"I told you they were too good to be true."

"The killings seem to have been scheduled to fit the database."

"So whoever scheduled them was able to access the BSU files?"

Wilkes nodded. "Now in the database there's no concordance to serial killings. But there is an index. For example, the markings on the bodies resembled flags. So we search the index for every occurrence of *flags.*"

Wilkes typed an instruction. A list of twenty-seven names came up on the screen.

"And you'll notice," Wilkes said, "La Rue Newton heads the list. Let's consider another aspect of the killings. Location. Obviously *street* and *stairway* are going to turn up a lot of examples. So let's look at something more unusual—*boutique.*"

Wilkes typed in the word *boutique.*

"Three," Cardozo observed.

"Let's look at instance number one. The unsolved murder of Minnie Wells in the Marcella Lambiani Boutique, San Francisco, May 1983." As Wilkes spoke, the data scrolled up the screen. "The victim was murdered in a changing room. The suspected assailant carried a boom box, and he played a rap music tape. Is the tune familiar? Okay, let's ask the index about clippings."

Wilkes typed the word *clippings* on the keyboard. The computer flashed the message *One Moment Please,* and ten seconds later an endless page of amber print scrolled up the screen. "There've been over two hundred documented instances of newspaper clippings left at the murder scene."

"How many were society columns?"

"Four. Now here's the big one. Candles." Wilkes typed the word and pressed the Enter key. A river of print began climbing up the screen—and up, and up. "We're dealing with close to a thousand instances of candles."

"Semen," Cardozo said.

"With semen you hit the jackpot. Practically ninety percent of serial killings involve the transfer of semen."

"Ever had a killer who syringed his own semen into his victims' mouths? Or dropped in pubic hair from a collection that wasn't even his?"

"Not till Society Sam," Wilkes said, "and believe me, he'll be a fresh entry in the database: the first serial killer totally synthesized from the literature."

Cardozo had a sudden, almost drugged awareness of another reality co-existing within the one he was sworn to uphold and protect—and totally opposed to it. "Could a United States senator access this material?"

Wilkes looked over at Cardozo and his mouth shaped a grim smile. "Anyone in a government office would be able to. A cleaning woman could do it. None of this stuff is classified."

▪ SEVENTY ▪

Sunday, June 23

TERRI STOOD BY THE STOVE, breaking eggs into a mixing bowl. "Did you know the city has a museum of old fire trucks?"

Cardozo shook his head. He'd spent the night tossing, too restless to sleep, and now he felt too unrested to wake up. "I think I read about it."

"Does it interest you? Because Josh is a fire-truck nut and we're going this afternoon. He thought you might like to come along."

"*He* thought?"

She looked over at him. "Something wrong?"

"It seems funny *you* didn't think I might like to come along."

Her face crinkled. "I just thought you might like to meet Josh. Or have you lost interest?"

"Not if you haven't."

"I don't know." She beat the eggs with a fork. As she tipped them into the frying pan they made a hiss. "Josh gets excited about a lot of so-what things. Like old fire trucks."

Cardozo took a long swallow of coffee and waited for it to pry his senses open. "Maybe we could skip the fire trucks and Josh could come over for lunch."

"Today?"

"Why not? I'm home."

"I'll ask him."

Across the kitchen, the telephone made a purring sound.

Why can't my phone at work sound like that? Cardozo thought.

"Maybe that's him." Terri lifted the receiver off the wall. She listened for a moment and turned. "For you, Dad." She handed the receiver across the table.

"Cardozo."

It was the call he'd been dreading—the precinct, saying a seventh Society Sam victim had been found.

■　■　■

"HOW DID SHE DIE?" Cardozo said.

The assistant M.E. was kneeling over the body. She had long cinnamon hair, and she worked with an expression of cool, unhurried detachment. "Bled to death."

Cardozo frowned. "Are you sure? The others died of asphyxiation. The stomach cuts were postmortem."

The assistant M.E. glanced at him through huge, untinted fashion glasses. "Just look at this floor. If these cuts were postmortem, that was a nosebleed."

Cardozo looked at the floor. Blood had pooled in a three-foot-diameter oval and caked deep rust-brown. Toward the edge of the pool it was beginning to flake.

He gazed down at the dead girl. She lay faceup, long blond hair splayed out on the warped, scuffed floor-boarding of the narrow hotel room. She couldn't have been more than fourteen years old.

Younger than Terri.

At one time she must have had a pretty, rather doll-like face. Now it was puffy and startlingly white. Her abdomen had been slashed in the same flag design as the others—except this time the killer had pulled her clothing out of the way and cut directly into the skin. The pattern seemed extraordinarily clear and exact.

The killer had left her breasts exposed. They were the small prematernal breasts of puberty.

The room had no wastebasket. The victim had used a Woolworth's shopping bag instead. A young male detective was bagging the contents in separately labeled evidence Baggies: an empty yogurt carton, a give-away sample of hair-conditioner, an empty carton of Maxx larger-shape lubricated condoms, and Robbie Danzig's new gossip column "Robbie's Rumors," neatly clipped from the June nineteenth edition of the *New York Tribune.*

There was a hard white flash of light as the police photographer snapped a picture of coins and cosmetics and bits of paper that littered the dressing table.

"She's in pretty good shape. Most of these kindergarten cases are." Using steel tweezers, the assistant M.E. was lifting particles from the mouth area that Cardozo couldn't even see. She transferred them one by one to a plastic evidence Baggie. "Not that they take any care of themselves at all. They're just too young for anything to have started falling apart."

This living woman, Cardozo thought, *resents this dead woman.* "How long's she been dead?"

"From what I can see, around four days."

That figured. It was usually around day four that a dead body began stinking badly enough to annoy the neighbors, and Lorna Webster was stinking so strongly the lab men had scattered ammonia crystals to counteract the smell.

Classical music was playing softly from a small portable radio on the windowsill. "What's the music?" Cardozo said.

"Mozart's twenty-fifth piano concerto." Lou Stein was crouched at the edge of a pink bath mat that had been pressed into duty as a scatter carpet. He was examining a dark area on the fringe that could have been the dirty heel print of a jogging sneaker.

He was smoking a cigar, and the dark lump of ash winked red. On crime scenes where there was a rotting body, nonuniformed male personnel sometimes smoked cigars to cover the stink. To Cardozo's nose, Lou's cigar didn't cover anything—it just added a stink of its own.

"Wait a minute." Lou Stein's flash beam rippled along the edge of the mat and stopped. "What the hell's that?"

His gloved finger folded back a corner of the mat. The beam of light played over a two-inch area of pale white seepage in a crack between floorboards.

"That looks to me," Cardozo said, "like what's left when a candle burns down."

· SEVENTY-ONE ·

Monday, June 24

"THE CHAIR ON OONA ALDRICH'S TERRACE," Dan Hippolito said, "is wrought iron. If Dizey Duke had gripped the back hard enough, it could have caused the bruise on her left hand."

"If she was in fear for her life," Cardozo said, "if she was trying to anchor herself to keep from going over the wall?"

"That would do it."

"And the bruise on Nita Kohler's left hand?"

"Going by the photos, I'd say it could have been caused the same way—gripping the back of the same chair or a similar chair in the same or similar circumstances."

"Thanks, Dan. You've cleared up a lot. I appreciate it." Cardozo hung up the phone, not at all happy.

In the squad room a detective was screaming, "We got a squeal. Who's up?"

Ellie Siegel stepped through the door. "Any surprises in the reports?"

Cardozo shook his head. "The seventh note was assembled from the same materials as the other six. The little hooker was killed with the same knife, same MO as the others. The blood cells in the semen are type O—same as Rick Martinez's. No surprises. Except this time the pubic hair is his too."

"That's a switch."

"He had time, this time, for real sex. Syringeless." Cardozo stretched and pushed himself an arm's length from the desk. "What did you find out from the Wall Street post office?"

Ellie helped herself to a chair. "You're not going to love me, Vince."

"Love was never an issue between us."

"The note was postmarked P.M. Friday. The earliest, the *very* earliest it could have been mailed is Friday morning."

"But Martinez died Thursday afternoon." Cardozo sighed. "Okay. Dead men don't mail letters, right?"

"In an imperfect world like ours, they do not."

"Then someone else mailed it. Someone who didn't know Martinez was dead till they heard it on the Friday afternoon news." Cardozo sat there letting the implications drift through his mind. "Look at Society Sam's notes—they're written in idiomatic, quirky English. People who spoke with Martinez don't remember him having that kind of command of the language. And there's no way he could have gotten to those mailboxes all over hell and back. He had a regular job and he was there six days a week. An accomplice had to have written and mailed *all* the notes."

Ellie smoothed out her skirt. "Could I ask a rude question? Who's the accomplice?"

"I can't give you the name." Cardozo opened his desk drawer. "But this is the voice." He brought out the Sony cassette player and placed it on the desktop. He pressed the play-back button. After three beeps and two hang ups a man's voice spoke.

"Hi Rick, how are you doing? I'm phoning Tuesday, June eighteenth. Thanks for completing the pickup yesterday. You have one more pickup scheduled, the timing and the merchandise are up to you. Have fun. I'll meet you Thursday, June twentieth, two P.M., on the path at West Seventy-first, just inside the park. Look for me on the bench. See you then."

There was the clicking sound of a phone hang up. Cardozo stopped the tape.

"That's not an accomplice," Ellie said, "that's an employer. Martinez was his hit man."

Cardozo nodded. "A Medellín hit man. Import the very best."

"Vince, you're a mess." Ellie rose and walked to the filing cabinet. "I tidy this up for you every day, and every day it looks like a dog was digging for a bone." She opened the drawer and tucked dangling papers back into their proper folders.

"I wish you wouldn't do that. You're spoiling my filing system."

Ellie turned. "Why was Martinez working at the gym? He didn't need the second paycheck."

"I can think of reasons. It made him less of an unexplained presence in the city—and so long as Braidy was scheduled last, it simplified one of the hits."

Ellie closed the drawer. "Do you recognize the voice on that tape?"

"No. Do you?"

She shook her head. "Did he show up in the park?"

"Didn't see him."

"So you have no idea who he could be."

"Except for one thing: Either he knew Carl or he knew me, or he knew us both. Because he was there. And he saw us first."

There was a distinct wryness in Ellie's smile. "That narrows it down to half the New York phone directory."

Cardozo frowned. He made a complete 360-degree turn in his swivel chair.

"Wait a minute," Ellie said. "He has some kind of connection with Bodies-PLUS. He knew they had an opening for a towel boy. And he knew Dick Braidy worked out there."

Suddenly something inside Cardozo's chest took a flying jump. "Hold it. I think I know—in fact, I know I know where this guy gets his medical insurance."

▪ ▪ ▪

"I NEED A FAVOR." Cardozo was leaning against the head-high partition that separated Monte Horlick's cubicle from the rest of the fourteenth floor of the Blue Cross building. "Was Richard Martinez covered on a group policy?"

Monte Horlick's fingers danced over his computer keyboard. Amber print crawled up the screen. "SACBA. They're a Federal subagency. Substance Abuse Control Budget Administration."

"Could you give me a list of all the policy holders?"

Horlick brushed the low-hanging blond bangs out of his left eye and tapped an instruction into the keys. The printer beside his desk clattered to life.

Eight minutes later, Cardozo was squinting at eleven accordion-fold sheets of single-spaced dot-matrix print. Here and there a familiar name leapt out at him: Kristi Blackwell, the Delanceys, the Guardellas, mother and son, Rad Rheinhardt of the *New York Trib*, Lawrence Zawac of Internal Affairs. Most of them were followed by the suffix *cow*. "What does *cow* mean?"

"Cooperative wraparound. The holder has his primary wraparound with another employer. The SACBA contract picks up the slack."

"What does this capital *T* after Nan Shane's policy number mean?"

"Terminated."

■ ■ ■

"ARE WE STILL ON FOR LUNCH?" Tori said. "One sharp at Archibald's?"

"Does it have to be Archibald's?" Leigh said.

"My, my, are we still boycotting Archibald's?"

"No. Of course not. I just . . . I don't know if I'm ready to face that place."

"Of course you're ready. And if you're not, all the more reason to go. It'll be therapy. And I'll be with you." There was a click on Tori's end of the line. "Sorry. Let me see who's phoning." In a moment she was back. "I have to take this call. Can I call you right back?"

"I'll be here."

Leigh spent the next three minutes in front of her mirror, trying to decide whether to wear her hummingbird brooch on her blouse or on her jacket. She'd pinned it to her blouse, for the second time, when the phone gave a soft buzz.

"Tori?" Leigh arranged a pillow against the headboard and pulled her feet up onto the bed. "I was being silly. Archibald's will be fine."

Tori didn't answer.

"Tori? Do you hear me?"

Still no answer.

Leigh sat up. "Are you there?"

The silence flowing over the line had a familiar, disturbing resonance. It was as though someone had boosted the volume on a radio receiver that was tuned to no station at all.

And then she heard breathing. Exactly the same breathing as before. A spike of panic ran up her spine.

"Don't think anything's changed." It was the same voice as before, softly rasping, forced down to an abnormally low register. It didn't have the slightest trace of a Hispanic accent. "Don't think you're safe. I'm watching you. I'll get you very soon."

■ ■ ■

XENIA DELANCEY OPENED the bedroom door. At the end of the corridor she could see Jimmy sitting on the living room sofa. He seemed to have forgotten that the phone was still resting in his lap.

"Aren't you working today?" she said.

He gave a start—that child-caught-out look. "You're home early, Mom."

"Yes, I felt poorly."

Jimmy's glance did not stay on her. She could tell he was hiding something.

"Me too," he said.

"Are you phoning someone?"

"No, just sitting here." He placed the phone back on the end table. It seemed to her a guilty movement.

"I made these for you." She handed him a milk-pint–sized package neatly wrapped in tinfoil, with a red ribbon tied in a perfect bow.

He unwrapped the package. "Wow. Chocolate chip cookies. Thanks, Mom. These are great." He just sat there staring at them.

"Would you like some milk to go with them? Or a nice cup of cocoa?"

"No, thanks." His voice was oddly low and without expression. He still wouldn't look at her. "I'm going out. There's something I have to do."

■ ■ ■

ON THE BEDSIDE TABLE the phone purred softly. Even though Leigh had been waiting for the sound, the mouse gnawing at her nerves gave a leap forward.

The purr came again. Beneath the telephone the answering machine clicked into life. One eye winked green.

"Hi, it's Tori again. Sorry to take so long. You haven't left, have you?"

Leigh lifted the receiver. "No, I'm here."

"Has something happened? You sound awful."

"The man who attacked me wasn't Rick Martinez. The man who rode in the warehouse elevator with me wasn't Rick Martinez. And the man who just phoned threatening my life wasn't Rick Martinez."

"Wait a minute. You just had a threatening call?"

"Two minutes ago. It was the same voice as before—and the same threat. The police *didn't* get him. He's still out there."

"Phone Vince Cardozo. I'm not kidding. *Right away.*"

Leigh dialed Vince Cardozo's direct line. After six rings a woman answered. "Vince Cardozo's line. Ellie Siegel speaking."

Some instinct made Leigh hesitate. "Detective Siegel, it's Leigh Baker."

"Yes, Miss Baker. How can we help you?"

Leigh noted the *we.* "Could you ask Vince—could you ask Lieutenant Cardozo to phone me? It's an emergency."

"Is it anything I can help you with?"

"I've had another threatening phone call."

"And are you still at Mr. Carnegie's?"

"Yes. At Waldo's."

"Vince should be back in ten minutes. Let your machine take calls and don't answer till you know who's calling."

"I'll do that. Thank you."

Pacing her bedroom, Leigh felt trapped, walled in. *Feelings are not facts,* a voice in her mind prodded. It was Luddie's voice. She heard all the AA slogans in Luddie's voice.

She dialed Luddie's number. The line was busy. Her finger broke the connection. There was too much fight-or-flight energy jittering through her now to allow her to sit still. She paced to the window.

The sun was stroking the slate rooftops of the town houses across the garden. In the sky a lemon crescent of moon hung steady through pale, drifting clouds.

She crossed back to the phone and called Waldo's number at work.

"He's not in," the male secretary apologized. "Can I take a message?"

"No, thank you." She dialed Luddie again. The line was still busy. "Luddie, damn you, stop yakking. I've got to talk to you!"

The answering machine gave a click.

Her nerves jumped at the sound.

Nothing more happened. The machine sat there mute and still. Something shivered through her like the buzzing of a fly against a window screen. And then the green light went on, and she heard her voice recite its message, and the beep beeped.

She waited.

No one spoke.

Silence flowed across the line.

Instinct was shouting at her: *He knows you're here! Don't let him trap you! Get out! Get to safety!*

A kerchief, she decided; dark glasses.

Hide as much of myself as possible. Mustn't let him recognize me.

She pulled open the top right-hand bureau drawer and chose the plainest of her Hermès silk scarves. She knotted it like a hood around her hair.

In the left-hand top drawer she found an enormous pair of polarized Ray-Bans. She put them on and studied herself in the mirror. Very little of Leigh Baker showed, and the room looked pink.

She left the house through the kitchen door. A taxi was passing in the street. She hailed it.

Twelve minutes later, outside the door of Luddie's building, she stood pressing his buzzer.

A buzz replied and the door swung open.

▪ ▪ ▪

WITH A LURCH AND A JERK the elevator finally deposited Leigh on the eleventh floor. Luddie's door was already open, and a thin, beautiful black woman stood there looking surprised.

Leigh took off the dark glasses and the kerchief.

"Leigh Baker," the woman said. "Has the world gotten smaller, or are we running into each other all over the place?"

Even without her clinging coffee lace dress, Leigh recognized Tamany Dillworth. "I didn't know you knew Luddie."

"Luddie and I go way back."

I sincerely doubt it, Leigh thought. "I've been trying to reach him for half an hour and the line's been busy."

"Believe it or not, it was not me tying up the line. A Con Ed crew cut through something in the street they shouldn't have."

Behind Leigh the elevator door closed, and she heard the elevator begin its redescent. "Is he home?"

"He should be back any minute now." Tamany stood aside to let Leigh past her into the apartment. "I've been keeping Happy company."

Leigh's heart sank. *This woman was running errands for Society Sam and somehow she's wormed her way into Luddie's trust.* "Are you one of Happy's regulars?"

Tamany nodded. "Twice weekly—Mondays and Thursdays. You too?"

"Tuesdays and Fridays." Leigh walked to the living room. Bright girders of sunlight slanted through the windows. Happy sat on the floor, dressed in a sailor suit, gazing at the keys of his toy piano.

She bent and kissed him. He looked up at her and then punched the first four notes of "The Happy Farmer."

"You seem to bring out the composer in that child." Tamany flicked a smile at Leigh as if they'd become old friends. "Say—as long as you're here, how would you like to save my ass? I have an audition at two, and I want to be cool and collected and glamorous *and* on time. Luddie's already twenty minutes late. Would you mind sitting with Happy till he gets back?"

"I wouldn't mind at all," Leigh said with all the phony good cheer she could muster. "What role are you up for?"

"The first black bitch on a national-network daytime soap." Tamany burst into laughter. "They're casting *heavily* against type."

Leigh walked with her into the hallway. The elevator was waiting, the door already open. "By the way, my producer's looking for featured bit players, but I couldn't find you at the address you gave Lieutenant Cardozo."

Tamany snapped her fingers. "I moved. I forgot to tell him. But you can always reach me through Luddie." She stepped into the elevator. "Before I forget. Shows you what a scatterbrain poor Tam is today." She opened her purse and took out two letters. "Could you give these to Luddie?"

"I'll be glad to."

As the elevator door closed Tamany waved and blew a kiss.

Leigh turned and crossed the hallway. A small pewter vase sat on the drop-leaf table beside Luddie's door. She laid the letters beside the vase. Behind her the chains in the elevator shaft clunked like medieval clockwork. A sense of incompleteness, of something left undone, nagged at her.

She turned and looked again at the elevator door.

The elevator went back down after I arrived. But it was waiting on this floor just a moment ago. Which means somebody took it back up. But Luddie's is the only apartment on the floor. So where did they go?

Her eye traveled from the elevator to the emergency stairway. The doors matched: both were steel, painted dark green. The only difference between them was that the stairway door had been left open an inch and a half, and a narrow ribbon of darkness fluttered at its edge.

There, she realized, *behind that door.*

She picked up the letters from the table. She tried to look natural, as if she hadn't the least idea that she was being watched. She stepped back into Luddie's apartment, closed the door quickly behind her, and bolted it.

▪ SEVENTY-TWO ▪

"DON'T THINK ANYTHING'S CHANGED." Jim Delancey forced his voice down into a toneless, rasping register. *"Don't think you're safe. I'm watching you. I'll get you very soon."*

"Those were her words?" Cardozo said.

"Her exact words and her exact voice. Deep. Growling. Like laryngitis."

They were sitting in Cardozo's cubicle. The door to the squad room was shut. In the window the air conditioner was laboring like a stressed-out life-support system.

"How do you know your mother was calling Leigh Baker?"

"When I picked up the phone, a woman's voice was saying, *Is that you? Lunch is okay*—something like that. It was Leigh Baker's voice, exactly the same as in her movies."

"How did your mother get the number? It's unlisted."

"Baker has a charge account at Marsh and Bonner's. The credit department has the number." Delancey released a breath slowly and his broad shoulders sagged. "How much trouble is my mother going to be in?"

"Threatening a person's life is against the law."

"But it's my fault. She was doing it to help me."

Cardozo gave a half nod of assent. "And she's not the only woman who's bent the law trying to help you. Tell me something, Jim. Why did Nancy Guardella go to bat for you on the parole?"

The answer was silence.

Cardozo held his gaze on the well-built, pale young man—trying to read the meaning of that silence. He knew Delancey wasn't stonewalling. The boy had come to the precinct of his own free will. He was here to protect his mother, here to deal.

Delancey took a pack of Camels from his shirt pocket. "I had a record of drug busts and burglaries." He tapped a cigarette loose. It took him three matches to light it. "I'd beaten up two girlfriends and tried to kill a third." He exhaled a long, fluttering feather of smoke. "And then Nita went over that wall. Who in his right mind was going to believe I was innocent?"

"Somebody might have believed it. Who knows, maybe I would have. You should at least have given the truth a try."

Jim Delancey's head came up and his eyes seemed to say, *Lieutenant, you've got to be an even bigger fool than me.*

"Yip Guardella was my coke dealer. He sold me drugs the night Nita died." There was a frightening coldness in the way Delancey was speaking of the past and of himself, as if he were discussing someone he had once known but hoped to God he'd never run into again. "Nancy Guardella freaked when she found out. Achilles Foot was a government sting operation. She didn't want it coming out in the trial that her son was dealing when he should have been stinging. So we made a deal: She'd get me off, but I could never mention drugs, or her son's dealing, or who was paying for my defense. And I could never say where that diary had come from."

"Nancy Guardella had the diary faked to get you off?"

"Which it didn't do."

"So then she got you early parole?"

"And she's taking care of my mom."

"She must be taking very good care of your mom."

"She is."

"I assume that's why you didn't use Yip as an alibi when Oona was killed?"

Delancey nodded. "I couldn't involve him."

"Then why go to Achilles Foot at all?"

"I wanted him to know Aldrich was making trouble. I had to make him understand there was no way I was going back to prison, no way I'd let them take that parole away from me."

That's why Guardella wanted the wire in my task force, Cardozo realized. *She had to be ready. For all she knew, Delancey was killing the socialites. If the task force turned up evidence of his guilt, Xenia would have tried to leverage a second defense the same way as the first: by threatening to expose Yip and Achilles Foot and Guardella's whole sick setup.*

The phone on Cardozo's desk rang. "Excuse me." He lifted the receiver. "Cardozo."

"Today there was mail," Greg Monteleone said. "And guess

who picked it up. Tamany Dillworth. She took it to Five twenty-three East Fifty-ninth, eleventh floor."

"Who lives on the eleventh floor?"

"Ostergate, Ludwig. She spent a little over an hour. Then another woman went up and Dillworth came back down."

"Who was the other woman that went up?"

"Never saw her before. Kind of dowdy, with a kerchief. Might have been a cleaning woman."

"Where did Dillworth go?"

"Right now she's across the street from this pay phone—Four seventy-eight East Eightieth. The buzzer's got her name taped over it."

▪ ▪ ▪

LEIGH FELT A PRESENCE like a cold shadow. She'd felt it for almost a half hour now.

Nothing moved in the room but the squares of reflected sunlight trembling on the wall. Happy had stopped playing with his piano; he'd gone to his room. There was no sound now but the soft electric hum of the refrigerator in the kitchen.

From time to time she rose from her chair. Sometimes it was to get up and look at the clock in the kitchen. Sometimes it was to go to the front door. Through the peephole she could see the entrance to the stairway. The inch and a half between the door and the jamb never changed, never shrank, never grew.

She crossed to the living room window and stared down into the street. Cars and pedestrians battled for possession of the intersection. Con Ed men climbed in and out of a ten-foot trench in the asphalt. Maybe they'd repaired the phone line.

She went to Luddie's desk. Only two of the five buttons on the push-button phone had been labeled with numbers. As she lifted the receiver the first labeled button lit.

She held the receiver to her ear and listened. The line was dead.

The second button lit as she pushed it, and the light went out behind the first. Again she listened, and again the line was dead.

She laid the receiver back in the cradle. The second button stayed lit. *How could that be?* she thought.

She was about to lift the receiver again when the light went out.

Luddie had an extension in his bedroom, she remembered. Someone must have lifted it while she was checking the line.

She realized it had to be Happy, playing with the phone. She went to the corridor. Both bedroom doors were open. "Happy?" she called.

No one answered.

Happy's was the first door. She looked into the bedroom.

Happy sat quietly on the floor arranging alphabet blocks. He turned around and smiled at her. She went to him and kissed her fingers and pressed them over his lips.

But if it wasn't Happy playing with the phone, then who . . .

Her heart dropped three stories inside her chest.

He's in the apartment, she realized. *He slipped in while the front door was open, while I was at the elevator talking to Tamany.*

There was a scratching sound behind her.

She went softly, quickly to the bedroom door.

The scratching came again. And then the door buzzer.

"Luddie!" She ran to the front door. "He got in! He's in here!" She grabbed the bolt and pushed it back.

Tried to push it back. She couldn't get it to slide far enough.

"Take it easy," a man's voice said behind her.

She froze.

There was an instant when the only sound was the scratching of Luddie's key in the lock.

She turned.

Arnie Bone, the hired guard, stood ten feet from her, face expressionless, legs spread in a soldier's stance. He began walking toward her, taking all the time in the world. "You just love making my work difficult, don't you."

"What the hell are you doing here?"

"Keeping an eye on you. It's not an easy job, with you running wild all over the city. Dashing into old warehouses. Harassing Delancey. Harassing his girlfriend."

"Then it was you in the elevator. It was you who attacked me at the phone booth."

"Just trying to discourage you from chasing trouble." He brushed against her and took the knob of the doorbolt between his thumb and forefinger.

"Luddie!" she screamed. "Watch out!"

"Lady, you watch too many cop shows." Arnie Bone slid the bolt back. He opened the door. He made a disgusted sound, like spitting into his own throat, then turned and fixed her with his flat steel-colored stare. "Too many cop shows are bad for the imagination."

She thought he smiled, but it might have been nothing more than a shadow on his face.

"What the hell am I going to do with you?"

He was making a strange sort of eye contact. It felt like a sexual come-on, or at least a sexual game.

"Any suggestions?" He let the door swing itself halfway shut.

Behind him the pewter vase from the hallway table flashed through the air and crashed into his skull. There was a pop like wood snapping. Arnie Bone's knees both folded at the same time. He collapsed gracefully into a kneeling position, and then the rest of him fell facedown onto the floor.

Luddie stepped into the apartment. He gazed regretfully at a dent in the vase, then set it down on the floor. He took Arnie Bone by both arms and dragged him into the living room. "Friend of yours?"

"He was one of my guards," Leigh said. "I asked Waldo to fire him. He's been following me."

"Then Waldo didn't fire him. These guys don't work for free." Luddie went into the kitchen and came back testing the strength of an extension cord. He straddled Arnie and felt in the jacket and pulled out a wallet. He flipped to the ID. "Kensington Security. Licensed to carry a gun. Well, where there's smoke . . ."

He frisked Arnie and pulled a revolver from the belt and laid it on the rug. He rolled Arnie onto his stomach and tied his hands behind his back, then hog-tied his hands to his ankles.

"Where's Tamany?" he said.

"She said she had to go to an audition."

Luddie looked at her curiously. "What are you doing here?"

"Your phone was out of order. I needed to talk to you, so I came over."

Luddie dusted his hands off and got to his feet. "Sorry I wasn't home."

"Luddie, how well do you know Tamany?"

"I don't like to talk about my sponsees."

"She's a sponsee?"

"What's so startling about that?"

Leigh tried to choose her words diplomatically. "I realize you like to be everybody's Good Samaritan, but did you know the police are looking for her?"

"Really? She told me she'd cleaned up her act."

"Luddie—what *is* her act? Do you know exactly what she does?"

"She's an actress. And she baby-sits Happy and she runs errands for me. Any other questions?" Luddie looked around the living room. "Did she leave any mail for me?"

■ ■ ■

THE STAIRWELL WAS DIM with the grayness of perpetual evening. Just as Cardozo reached the landing a door opened, and the head of a young black woman popped out.

"Was that you?" she asked.

"It was me."

"Were you ringing for me?"

"If you're Tamany Dillworth." And he could see that she was. He held out his shield case. "Vince Cardozo again. Can we talk?"

She held her head back, staring at him from wide-open eyes. "Of course. How are you? Look, I'm running late for an audition. Could we possibly postpone this?"

"I'll only take a minute of your time."

He followed her into the studio apartment.

The room was furnished modestly: a plain gray three-seater sofa that hid a bed but didn't quite hide a trailing corner of pink-striped bed sheet, two matching plain gray chairs, a table stacked with theatrical publications and health-watch newsletters.

"Did I break a law?" She sat on the edge of one of the chairs.

Cardozo took the other chair. "Last Thursday, a little after two-thirty in the afternoon, our surveillance officer saw you take two cartons into Four fifty-seven West Forty-ninth Street."

He could feel her lining up the alternatives in her mind. Deny it, admit it—she was weighing the respective costs and benefits.

"That was an errand for my AA sponsor."

"And who's your AA sponsor?"

For a moment she didn't answer. Her finger tapped against one of the Lucite pyramids dangling from her necklace. "His name is Luddie Ostergate."

"What was in those cartons?"

She shrugged. "I don't know. One was heavy and rattled, one was heavy and didn't rattle."

"Which apartment did you take them to?"

She twisted a strand of hair in her fingers. "Look, couldn't this please wait? I'm missing an audition."

"I'm sorry, it can't wait."

"Rick Martinez's apartment."

"You've been taking mail to that apartment too. Why? What does Rick Martinez have to do with Luddie Ostergate?"

"Luddie rents a mailbox on West Forty-ninth. He pays me ten dollars a week to take care of it. Blue Cross goes to Luddie's place. Junk mail and letters for Rick Martinez go to the apartment on West Forty-ninth. That's all I know."

"Did you personally know Rick Martinez?"

"Which one? Everyone who ever lived in that apartment was called Rick Martinez."

"The most recent Rick."

"I met him two or three times when I was dropping off mail."

"Only when you were dropping off mail?"

"I ran into him once in a department store."

"Which store?"

"Marsh and Bonner's."

"You ran into him or you were sent to run into him?"

"Luddie sent me."

"Why?"

"He told me to go there and shop."

"Shop for what?"

"It didn't matter. He wanted me to set off the burglar alarm."

"Why?"

"I don't know. Luddie saved my life and I don't ask why when he tells me to do things."

Cardozo found Tamany Dillworth's I-was-just-following-orders explanation a little hard to swallow. He couldn't believe she saw no connection between that alarm and Oona Aldrich's murder.

"You just spent over an hour in Luddie's apartment. What were you doing there?"

"I was minding his kid for him till he got back."

"Our surveillance officer says he didn't get back."

"A friend showed up and I left the boy with her."

That had to be the dowdy woman with the kerchief. "Who was the friend?"

"Leigh Baker."

Cardozo jumped up. "You left Leigh Baker in that apartment?"

• SEVENTY-THREE •

LEIGH CROSSED TO THE TABLE where she had left the two letters. For the first time she looked at the address. Her heart gave a sickening, lopsided lurch in her chest.

She turned and watched Luddie take off his jacket and drape it over the back of a chair. "Could I ask you something, Luddie? Why are you getting mail for Rick Martinez?"

The question hung a moment in the air, unanswered. Luddie seemed dissatisfied with the hang of his jacket. He rearranged it on the chair. The sound of Happy's toy piano floated in from the bedroom.

Luddie smiled. "There are more Rick Martinezes in this city than the one that's been so famous lately. The Rick Martinez you've got in your hand is me. It's the name I used in my old soldier-of-fortune days."

She gave him a long glance. The top letter had been post-marked two days ago. "Why do you use the name now?"

"My old employer still provides my health insurance."

"I thought you'd severed all ties to them. At meetings you always call them your ex-employers—the bad guys from the bad old days."

He sighed. "Not quite."

The first two notes of "The Happy Farmer" repeated them-selves, over and over, bell-like on the toy piano.

"Why does Tamany deliver your mail?"

Luddie shrugged. "It's sent to my old address. She lives in the neighborhood."

Leigh stood staring at Luddie. For the first time in her four years of start-and-stop sobriety, she didn't believe her sponsor.

She looked at the second envelope. "And Al Nino Martinez? Who's he?"

"It means *to the Martinez child*. Happy's covered on my policy."

"Why in Spanish?"

"My wife didn't speak English. The hospital didn't speak Spanish. They misunderstood her the night that Happy was born."

She handed Luddie the letters. "What was your wife's name?"

"Isolda."

"She died the night Happy was born," Leigh said.

Luddie nodded.

The sound of the toy piano came to her like a delayed echo, setting up a resonance in her memory. "And that's the sound on my answering machine—Happy's toy piano. You phoned me and left a message and Happy was playing his toy piano in the background and that's how that sound got on my phone tape. You phoned Martinez and left a message and Happy was playing his toy piano and that's how the sound got on Martinez's phone tape. And Martinez used his phone tape in the boom box and that's why the same sound showed up on my answering machine tape and the boom-box tape."

The moment seemed to stretch out in space. A wave of silence and distance rushed in.

"You lied to me, Luddie. You told me resentment was poison. You told me to give up my resentments, the way you had. But you've never given yours up."

She waited for him to deny it, to say the words that would make her life right again. But he didn't speak. His face had a stunned look, as if she had thrown him completely off balance.

"You *still* work for the bad old company." Understanding imploded on her. "You never stopped. The thrift shops are a front. Martinez was your agent. He was carrying out *your* revenge, not his. You sent him to kill six innocent people."

Something metallic glinted in Luddie's eyes, in the line of their narrowing. "They weren't innocent."

"Weren't they? Who appointed you God—the CIA?"

"If they hadn't been partying in that Emergency Room, Happy would have a mother today. I'd have a wife. Those selfish idiots took my family from me."

"If all you got sober for was to kill people, you should have stayed drunk! You're a clean and sober asshole!"

Luddie crouched down to pick up the revolver from the rug. His eyes never left her. "Leigh—just this once, shut your movie-star mouth."

"Fuck you, Ostergate!"

He aimed the gun at her.

"I believed in you!" she shouted. "I was honest with you! You never believed in me, you never once were straight with me!"

Luddie drew in a deep breath. He clicked the safety off. His mouth shaped a half smile, and it left a sting as it flicked across her. "Because beneath that desperate veneer of occasional sobriety you're the same as all your friends. So selfish you can't even see the destruction you cause."

"Don't count on it." She dove at him, hands flailing.

The barrel of the gun come down like a karate chop across her shoulder. She took a staggering step backward. The wall caught her and propped her up.

The barrel came down again and just as the shot ripped out, something pushed Luddie from behind and threw him off balance. Suddenly he was down on all fours, and Happy was running toward Leigh. She grabbed the child up into her arms. She lunged for the front door, twisted locks and slid bolts and couldn't open it, twisted again, still couldn't open it.

Behind her she heard Luddie trying to pull himself to his feet and pulling a bookcase down instead.

She twisted the lock the other way, and this time the door flew open.

The blood was thudding so hard through her veins that the image of the hallway trembled before her eyes. Pulling Happy with her, she ran to the elevator. She pressed the button. Ancient chains and counterweights clanked into motion. Too slow, she realized.

She pushed opened the door to the stairway. The clattering echo of her own footsteps pursued her. There was no light. There wasn't time to find the switch. Her heart was pounding at her ribs, and a battle was going on in her lungs. She had to help Happy down the steps one at a time. They reached the first half landing.

Above them the door slammed open.

"Bring him back," Luddie shouted. "You're not taking my son."

▪ ▪ ▪

THE ELEVATOR STOPPED. Cardozo stepped out onto the eleventh floor. He crossed to the door of Luddie Ostergate's apartment.

He placed his ear against the wood, and that tiny pressure was enough to set the door in motion. It swung inward.

In front of him was a dark, narrow hallway opening into a wider, brighter room. The floor inside was littered with books, and halfway down the dimness he could see the humped shape of a bookcase lying on its side.

He stood listening, sniffing the silence. The faint, muffled vibration of a refrigerator came to him through the air.

He drew his gun.

He flattened himself against the wall and moved slowly forward. As he reached the end of the hallway he took a slow, deep breath, readying himself. He raised the gun in both hands.

He sprang forward, up and out and around the corner in one single, wall-hugging movement. His eye scanned the living room.

A man hog-tied with an extension cord lay unconscious on the floor.

▪ ▪ ▪

IN THE DARK Leigh bent down toward the child, gripping him near, holding tight to his shoulders, feeling his terror and his heart beating against her.

On the landing twelve steps above, Luddie stood in a half crouch, his silhouette backlit by smoke-colored light washing in from the hallway. He held himself motionless. He had turned his head and angled it upward toward the next landing. She could feel him sniffing the darkness above him, reaching out for her with all his senses. The walls seemed to slant.

Now his head came slowly around and angled downward, toward her and the boy. As his head moved, the gun swept out a slow arc in front of him.

The door swung shut behind him, and darkness erased his shape.

Leigh's eyes began playing tricks on her. The darkness seemed to sparkle with points of light. She had a drowning sense of standing on the edge of something about to happen, knowing she had to make her move now.

Her fingers went to the hummingbird brooch that she had pinned to her blouse. They found the catch, fumbled with it, snapped it open.

A little *ping* vibrated through the darkness.

She unpinned the brooch. She fixed her eyes on an imaginary point on the stairway above Luddie. She let her hand drop back. She pulled in a deep breath and swung the hand up. At the top of the swing she opened it. The hummingbird flew up into the vibrating blackness.

Time dilated. From the far side of a long silence the hummingbird clattered brightly on one of the steps near Luddie.

She sensed him shift position in the darkness. She heard him exhale, and the exhalation was directed away from her, toward the hummingbird. There was a metallic ricochet as the brooch bounced down a step, then another bright, clattering drop to the step below, then another and another.

And then absolute stillness, absolute blackness.

She heard the rustling movement of cloth against cloth.

Luddie yanked the door open. Light exploded, dousing her and the child in a bright silver spill.

For one instant Luddie's eyes were searching the empty stairwell above him. The next instant he whirled and saw Leigh and the boy.

He took three steps down the stairway. He gestured with the gun. "Let the boy go."

Leigh lifted her hand from Happy's shoulder.

"Happy," Luddie said. "Come here."

The child did not move.

"Come here!" Luddie barked.

A figure stepped onto the landing behind him. "Luddie. Drop the gun." The voice was Vince Cardozo's.

Luddie's gun hand came down slowly and hung at his side.

"Drop it," Cardozo repeated.

Luddie's arms whipped up into firing position, and in one seamless movement, he turned toward Cardozo and dropped into a crouch.

As his knee struck the step he howled in sudden pain. He lurched up and backward. The gun fired. It was a wild, uncontrolled shot. There was a white flash and the bullet pinged into the wall.

Luddie was half standing now, both hands waving, trying to grab some balance from the empty air. He took a stumbling step backward. He was kicking crazily, as though an animal had sunk teeth into his left leg and wouldn't let go.

He fired again. The recoil slammed him against the steel bannister. His weight was centered high. The bannister held him like a fulcrum. Momentum levered him over and flipped him out into the well.

He seemed to fall in slow motion, as though he were an image on a prerecorded tape dropping down the stairwell toward some final moment that had already, ineradicably happened.

When the police found Luddie's body ten stories below, the pin of Leigh's hummingbird brooch was stuck two inches deep into the flesh of his leg.

▪ SEVENTY-FOUR ▪

Monday, July 1

"DELANCEY DOESN'T WANT TO REOPEN the case," Cardozo said.

Leigh lifted her gaze. "Neither does my agent."

"Does that mean you're working on another movie?"

A smile crept into her voice. "There's nothing like a headline or two to stir up studio interest."

They were sitting at the corner table at Archibald's. Needle-hipped waiters barely managed to slide between crowded, jammed-together tables.

"Why did you pick this place for lunch?" Cardozo said. "I thought you were boycotting the salads here."

"I'm not angry at Jim Delancey anymore. He's the one who should be angry at me. So . . . here's his chance."

Cardozo caught something in her voice, in her eyes, that had not been there a month ago. "Sounds like you've decided to take some risks."

"Let's just say I'm shaking the lead out of my ass. I'm getting my own place." She spent a moment aligning a little spoon with a big spoon. "I'm leaving Waldo."

Cardozo was aware of the faint, sweet perfume that rippled out from her.

"Care to comment?" she said.

"Definitely a right decision."

"And I'm adopting Happy."

He looked at her. He couldn't believe he'd heard her right.

"Luddie's child," she said.

"I know who Happy is."

"Then why do you have that baffled look?"

"Not baffled. Just impressed. I'm seeing a new side of you."

"I love Happy. I want a child. I want a home. And a career. And a tan." She said it with a tone of lighthearted adventure, and then there was a split-second hesitation. "And I want the right man."

Cardozo noted things about her: the dark pupils; the smooth, faintly glowing texture of her skin; the deep shining brown of her hair.

"I'd like the right man to be you." She tipped her head a little to the side, studying him for a reaction. "But I know that's not going to happen."

"Who says?"

"Stop being gallant."

"It's not gallantry. The truth is, I had a crush on you."

"Did you?" For a single unguarded moment she looked eager and almost childishly happy.

"Actually, that's not the truth. I was in love with you."

"Were you? Honestly?" She smiled as though he'd paid her the most captivating compliment she'd ever had. "And what went wrong? Reality reared its ugly head and you got to know me?"

"Not quite." He shook his head. "I got to know myself."

There was a lemon wedge perched on the rim of her tulip glass. She studied it, then lifted it and gave it a careful squeeze directly into her diet Pepsi.

"Vince, something's been bothering me. I keep thinking of Luddie's wife—alone, in labor, dying in a New York City Emergency Room. Why wasn't he with her?"

"From the information I've been able to dig up, he was in El Salvador on assignment machine-gunning nuns."

She gave the lemon another squeeze. And another. The movement seemed like a stalling action in a play. "I loved Luddie. I trusted him. He saved my life. How could he have been a killer? Explain him to me, Vince. I want to understand."

"He never stopped resenting the five people he held responsible for his wife's death."

"But he always warned me that resentment was a killer."

"Because he knew. He was the expert resenter. I'll bet he never threw away a resentment in his life. And when the order came to hit Shane, he padded the hit list with his five pet hates. Plus one random hit to confuse the scent."

"What kind of a man could do that?"

"A methodical man. Someone who likes to live in separate compartments. One hand does the dirty work that pays the bills, the other hand saves souls to make up for the dirty work."

Leigh was somber, disbelieving. "How could his superiors have let him do it?"

"The war against drugs is a legal twilight zone. There's no centralized supervision. Too much money can be made by looking the other way. Some of the drug warriors bend the law pretty far. The others don't want to know, because if they knew, they'd be indictable."

Leigh's hand went to the platinum hummingbird that glinted on her dove gray lapel. Her finger rested a moment, touching the jeweled wing as though drawing assurance from it. "Who ordered Nan Shane killed?"

"I have a feeling Senator Guardella has classified that information secret. And for a very good reason."

"And what's going to happen to the little girl?"

"Shane's mother is taking her in."

"I'd like to contribute something. Could you help me arrange it anonymously?"

"To hell with anonymity. Take credit when you do a good deed. I'll give you the address."

Her hand went again to the hummingbird and made that same gesture of grounding herself.

"Why are you wearing your brooch?" he said. "I thought it came out only for class reunions."

"Tori's joining us. I know this was supposed to be our good-bye lunch, but I'm not leaving for two weeks. And didn't you say you had something for me to give her?"

"I left it with the coat check."

"Well, as long as we're exchanging parcels . . ." Leigh opened her purse and took out a small package. "I know cops can't accept gifts—so I'd like Terri to have this."

Cardozo stared at the red velvet jeweler's box tied with a thin gold-colored chain. "What is it?"

She moved the package across the table toward him. "It's Oona's hummingbird."

He didn't take it. "I can't let you do that."

"Come on, Vince—it's worthless in a vault and it's meaningless on the wrong person. I want Terri to have it."

Tori Sandberg picked that moment to come at a brisk, swivel-hipped walk through the narrow aisle.

"Hi, all. Sorry to be late." She exchanged cheek-to-cheeks with Leigh and held out a hand to Cardozo. He stood and pulled back a chair for her.

"Tori, have champagne," Leigh said. "They'll never make any money off us if someone doesn't."

Tori Sandberg settled herself in her chair. She took off her silk scarf. She had pinned her hummingbird to the bodice of her écru blouse. She smiled at Cardozo. Her eyes were luminous and her face had the glow of a girl's. "Something tells me I'm butting in."

"Not at all," Cardozo said. "Good to see you."

"It *is* good to see you," Leigh said. "You're looking terrific. Like you've just had a Swiss rest cure. What have you done to yourself?"

"I owe it all to my changed living situation."

"Is there someone new?"

Tori Sandberg laughed. "Don't I wish. No, there's no one new. But I haven't had a knock-down drag-out domestic brawl in two weeks."

Leigh placed a hand on Tori's. "Enjoy it while it lasts. And how's the magazine?"

"Problems." Tori shrugged. "*Fanfare*'s beating us in ad pages for the fifth straight month."

Cardozo took his coat-check tag from his breast pocket. "This is for you." He laid the tag on the pink tablecloth. "I think it might help."

Tori Sandberg stared at the number, thirty-two, on the plastic tag and then at him. "This is the way Nelson Rockefeller used to give his secretaries minks, but it's the wrong season for mink."

"Don't worry, it's just some reading matter. Unpublished drafts of magazine articles, an unpublished 'Dick Sez' column, a list of subscribers to the SACBA employee health plan."

"SACBA?" Tori looked perplexed.

"If you've ever heard of them, they're not doing their job. The health-plan subscribers are quite a collection. A magazine publisher, a newspaper columnist, New York state's junior senator, a bartender with a drug-dealing record who happens to be her son, a Society Sam victim who happens to have been a coke mule, a captain in the NYPD Internal Affairs Division . . . and a few hundred others."

"Sounds yummy," Tori Sandberg said.

"You might be interested in the size of the medical reimbursements. Your friend Kristi Blackwell's heart surgery brought her close to eighty thousand. Untaxed."

Something puzzled was creeping into Tori's eyes. "But Kristi has never had—"

Cardozo nodded. "Call it cash transfers in consideration of services Ms. Blackwell rendered on the QT. And Blackwell's a relatively small fry as this list goes. I think there's the making of a magazine article."

"Why, Vince," Leigh said, "are you going into the literary business?"

"Frankly, Senator Guardella burns me up. I want to stick it to her and as many of her hirelings as I can."

"I'll drink to that," Tori Sandberg said. "How about some champagne, Lieutenant? On the magazine. You've just given us a cover story."

"I'm on the job," Cardozo said.

"Quit your job for an hour," Leigh said.

"Waiter!" Tori Sandberg signaled. "We'll have some Moët *brut*—and another diet Pepsi." Her pinkie came down on the coat-check tag. She drew it toward her across the tablecloth, detouring around the red velvet jewel box. "And whose pretty little package is that?"

"Ask Vince," Leigh said.

Tori Sandberg was looking at him curiously. "Lieutenant?"

Leigh was watching him too, and he realized he was smiling. He realized he felt happy and just a little irresponsible.

"It belongs to my daughter." He reached out and took the box. "It's Terri's."